A PLACELESS SUN

TOWARD OUR CONFIGURED DESTINY

DIMITRI TISHLER

Editor
ANN PHILPOTT

Editor
ELIZABETH THORLTON

The Ninth Bird Press

Published by The Ninth Bird Press 2023

ISBN: 978-0-646-86806-6 (PB)
ISBN: 978-0-646-87931-4 (HB)

This book comes in two forms: in digital form as a free eBook and in printed form. The price of the printed version only covers the cost of printing. Individuals, companies, or organizations may distribute or host the eBook version on their websites but should not sell on or charge for its use in any way. The only exception to this rule is if a website has a "minimum charge," in which case royalties should be paid to the author.

Disclaimer: This book is in no way an official representation or interpretation of the Bahá'í Faith and its beliefs. In many instances the concepts highlighted or presented are purely those of the author, which is his personal understanding of Bahá'í beliefs. The characters' beliefs or actions are not necessarily representative of the author's views or actions. However, the quoted Bahá'í writings themselves are authoritative, and all source material can be found in the notes and bibliography. For all authoritative material and interpretations of the Bahá'í Faith please visit www.bahai.org.

Icon for The Ninth Bird Press sourced for free from www.icon-library.com. Attribution link: https://icon-library.com/icon/bird-icon-vector-25.html.html>Bird Icon Vector # 170406.

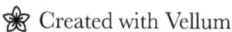

This book is dedicated to Bahíyyih Khánum.

PREFACE

As you read the quotes at the beginning of each chapter from *The Seven Valleys* and the *Gems of Divine Mysteries*, you will notice that their meaning does not relate directly to each chapter. If I had made the narrative conform to this structure, the story would have become too inflexible. I have tried to keep the basic linear order of the quotes relative to *The Seven Valleys*, which expresses the logical and gradual progression of the soul through the hierarchical levels of consciousness. And it is my hope that if you find any of these quotations beautiful or inspiring, you will read *The Seven Valleys* in its entirety.

You may find the quotes a little hard to penetrate at first, but don't worry, as this is normal. The style of *The Seven Valleys* is poetic and mystical, so it requires a little effort and contemplation; it took me many years to even come close to a cursory understanding of its themes. In fact, *The Seven Valleys* was one of the first Bahá'í books I ever read, and I remember clearly now putting it down and wondering what it was about; at the time I understood close to nothing about it, but I felt that there was something about it that was deep and enduring. So I guess my advice is to persist with it.

Also, a quick overview of spiritual principles of the Bahá'í Faith will help you read this book, as many of its beliefs, several of its teachings, and some of its history are explored in this novel. Please see Appendix

1: Brief Overview of Spiritual Principles and Teachings of the Bahá'í
Faith. You will also find a large and comprehensive body of material
related to the principles of the Bahá'í Faith on the internet. Start with
www.bahai.org.

I would now like to talk about my weaknesses as a writer and my
literary journey. This novel represents my first attempt at fiction. During
the time that I have been writing it, roughly nineteen years, I thought
several times that I might have overstretched myself as I was tackling
many difficult and complex subjects and themes; many times, I couldn't
even face writing it. It seemed far beyond my abilities. And even with all
the research in the world, a writer makes mistakes with either content or
artistic treatment, and my limited knowledge of the Bahá'í Faith was
another obstacle; it can take an entire lifetime to come to grips with its
teachings, and in many cases a lifetime may not be enough, let alone the
entire panorama of philosophy, religion, and history. And because of
this I felt alone at many stages in the development of the work, and I
asked myself if what I was saying was true, real, or even relevant. Was
there an audience for this book, I wondered.

So this book is an imperfect attempt on my part to write an idealized
work of art and to try not to distort the subjects I have been grappling
with, and I hope the reader will paper over the cracks with any ideas
that don't ring true or seem poorly expressed. This book is more of an
open-ended journey rather than a definitive destination. Even my own
characters are better people than I am, and I hope that the art will transcend the imperfections of the artist.

Future writers will come closer to realizing the spiritual foundations
of the Bahá'í Faith and will be able to reflect more faithfully on its principles. The world as it is today is a distorted lens through which to
perceive humanity's true spiritual potentialities, either now or in the
future: a lens that I cannot escape from, but through which, on the one
hand, I have tried to correct or understand any distortions I have seen,
but paradoxically, on the other hand, through which I have perceived
alluring fragments of an ideal future society that fills me with hope for
humanity's ultimate destiny—its symmetrical and configured destiny.

Anyway, ultimately, I hope the reader enjoys something here in these
pages and that this book does find a place in the world. I wanted to
leave behind, in this ephemeral world, an object that represents my

worship of God and his staggering beauty through all the endless worlds in eternity—a house of words.

Lastly, the quote below is a reflection of the entire seven valleys, and my entire novel revolves around this one pivot.

I'll see you all on the other side.

Praise be to God Who hath made being to come forth from nothingness; graven upon the tablet of man a measure of the mysteries of His eternity; taught him from the storehouse of divine utterance that which he knew not; made him a perspicuous book unto such as have believed and surrendered their souls; given him to behold, in this dark and ruinous age, a new creation within all things; and caused him to speak forth, from the midmost heart of eternity, and in a new and wondrous voice, embodied in the most excellent Temple.◊ *And all to this end: that every man may testify, in himself and by himself, before the Seat of the revelation of his Lord, that there is none other God but Him; and that all may reach that summit of realities where none shall contemplate anything but that he shall perceive God therein.*[1]

—Bahá'u'lláh, *The Seven Valleys*

◊ The Manifestation of God / a Prophet

A WORD ON SYMMETRY

*. . . in each realm, to every letter a meaning is allotted which pertaineth to that
realm. Indeed, the wayfarer findeth a secret in every name and a mystery in every
letter.* [1]

—Bahá'u'lláh, *The Seven Valleys*

This book introduces the reader to the idea of symmetry and
asymmetry in letters, names, actions, and visual phenomena as we see it
in nature, like flowers, Romanesco (spiral) broccoli, Nautilus shells,
human faces, and even our own Milky Way galaxy. We actually
encounter symmetry and asymmetry every day but overlook its mystery
purely through overfamiliarity; the mystery of all reality is in plain sight.

*How strange that the Beloved is as visible as the sun and yet the heedless still hunt
after tinsel and base metal. Yea, the intensity of His revelation hath veiled Him,
and the fullness of His shining forth hath hidden Him.* [2]

—Bahá'u'lláh, *The Seven Valleys*

I would like the reader to be aware of this idea as they read the
book. Be aware that the repetition of character names and the names of

ix

objects or places is intentional and not intended to confuse the reader but rather to show how we are all interconnected through the symmetries and asymmetries in language and names in particular. Just let the names wash over you as you read and avoid trying to work out if you have met this character before. A more detailed analysis of the symmetry and asymmetry of names can be found in the appendix. Please see Appendix 4: Symmetry of Names and Letters.

CONTENTS

1

COMING TO AMERICA

By My life, O friend! Wert thou to taste the fruits of these verdant trees that spring from the soil of true understanding, once the effulgent light of His Essence hath been reflected in the Mirrors of His names and attributes, yearning would seize the reins of patience and restraint from out thy hand and stir thy spirit into commotion with the splendours of His light. It would draw thee from this abode of dust unto thy true and heavenly habitation in the midmost heart of mystic knowledge, and raise thee to a station wherein thou wilt soar in the air even as thou treadest upon the earth, and wilt walk upon the water even as thou movest over the land.[1]

— BAHÁ'U'LLÁH, *THE SEVEN VALLEYS*

The plane passed over Manhattan. The city's buildings were lit by the warm colors that came with the beginning of the evening light. It overshot the city and turned over Upper Bay's dark water. Allison stared at the texture of the water for a moment before looking up at the sun.

She held an origami bird up to the light to observe the translucent shapes in the paper; it was a powerful symbol for the contours of humanity's collective destiny. She imagined that the edges of the folds and the shapes between folds represented nations, and as each fold crossed another fold, intersections in people's lives in the past, present, and future became inextricably bound, and the bird then stood for the entirety of the planet. The ubiquitous phenomenon associated with the symbol of the bird was flight; it denoted freedom in the mind and imagination, where the intellect and heart could fly on the horizon of life, beyond any physical limitation.

The knowledge of flight had come down the tree of history with birds, until its secrets were molded into airplanes—metal birds. This had led to the migration of people around the planet and the gradual fusing of cultural diversity. The emergence of the consciousness of the oneness of humanity had arisen from this integration.

Her thoughts turned to her own migration. She knew that the subtle differences in American culture would highlight the limits surrounding her identity and allow her to remold herself. This had also been the case when she had lived in Paris and London. But it was the cancer that had invaded her body six years before, and more recently, that had really transformed her. Her ongoing illness had forced her to reprioritize her life. Consequently, the inconsequential aspects of her life had fallen away. In 1992 Allison had her right breast removed, but the doctors had said there was no guarantee that all the cancer had been removed, and at the time they could not give her a definitive long-term prognosis. In the previous two months, a small secondary tumor had appeared in her left breast, which the doctors had also removed.

The plane turned again and lined up with the runway. She placed the paper bird in her top pocket. After a few minutes, her body dropped with the plane as its wheels touched down on a snow-covered runway.

The plane made its way through the traffic of other planes. It pulled into gate nine. She stared into patches of snow surrounding the airport buildings. The snow was pure and luminescent in the warm light.

People shuffled in their seats. A domino of buckles clicked at random around her as people undid their seat belts. She watched other passengers search for magazines, books, and other paraphernalia to pack into their carry-on bags. She took a large notepad, which she had used to make her origami bird, from the flap in front of her. On the top page she had been practicing versions of her signature. The woman who had sat next to her on the flight left her seat. Allison followed her and moved into the aisle. She took her backpack down from the overhead compartment. She checked for all her travel documents and then put the notepad into the backpack. Rummaging further through her bag, she found feta cheese, olives, and Lebanese bread. Her brother, Paul, had bought it so she could avoid plane food. The feta had broken through its packaging. Some of it had crumbled onto her 1970s Soviet-era camera. She picked it up and wiped the metal casing clean with her sleeve. She also had a mid-eighties Leica, which she used to take most of her higher-quality photographs. As she put the camera back into her bag, the sweet smell of tobacco and ashes rose up and permeated the cabin around her. Deeper in her bag she saw the old pipe and a pouch of tobacco that she had bought at Melbourne's Queen Victoria Market two days before her flight.

The aircraft door opened, and more passengers milled into the aisle. In the first-class section, the cabin crew assembled near the exit door. They were preparing for pleasant and superficial departing smiles. She wondered about their motivations, and what life would be like if we were never paid to be accommodating—if our smiles were underpinned by pure motives rather than the inspiration of trying to make the monthly rent. And what would remain if human motive could be stripped away? Peeled back one lie at a time, until a selfless instinct at the core of the psyche was found undamaged behind changing masks.

Allison focused on one of the flight attendants, whose teeth were over-white. Her lipstick flashed with the color and lushness of a tropical flower, but Allison thought she was insincere—hiding behind a plastic smile. Allison saw two worlds: the world of her face, with its changing landscape, and its subterranean counterpart, the world of feeling, where truth, in all its beauty and ugly terror, was held tightly within her. She passed the flight attendant and walked toward the door.

As she stepped off the plane, her thoughts narrowed quickly to the shock of cold that enveloped her body. She had no solid memory of this kind of temperature in Australia. Even Paris had never seemed this cold in winter.

She walked into the main building. Her feet were especially cold; she had worn her white Birkenstock sandals. She looked around and absorbed the minutiae of the terminal and the people spread around her; she knew already that New York would be an immersive experience. In the plane American accents, with their New York nasal pitch, had rung out, and as she chatted to the customs officer checking her passport, the din of difference grew. Her Australian accent felt clearer and more defined as it contrasted with the American voices that surrounded her.

The airport wore a skin older and shabbier than she had expected: the walls were drearily colored, the green linoleum on the floors was shoe scuffed, and the faded orange plastic furniture was something out of the seventies. Even the models in the advertisements appeared slightly dated. The models were definitely nineties but with a thin overlay of the fifties. The past seemed closer to the present here.

Her own appearance felt shabbier too. It had been dulled by the flight. After customs, she went into a bathroom. She saw her disheveled hair as she looked into a mirror above a washbasin. She surveyed the effects of summer. Her skin was tanned and covered with a thin, greasy film. She refreshed her face with water and wiped the oil off with a paper towel. She smiled and slapped her cheeks. Her smile was sincere and real. As it should be, she mused.

———

Light streamed down into a small courtyard in the back of one of Paul and Allison's restaurants. They were sitting alone at a table near the back fence. After the death of their father, they were jointly left the two restaurants. Paul managed the restaurants. Allison helped out when she wasn't studying or volunteering at Friends of the Earth.

Both restaurants were located on Lygon Street in Carlton, an inner-city suburb, and known as the Little Italy of Melbourne. Allison was nineteen then, and even in those early years Paul always had the impression that his sister was an odd person; he had followed her development from childhood. But the strangeness in her personality was not always immediately obvious to a casual observer—inconsistencies only emerged over time, and only those close to her saw her subtle but odd nature. Her friends knew her to be a cross between an intellectual and a hippie, though there were even stranger dimensions of Allison's nature that made her more divergent relative to mainstream society.

An example of her divergence had come in the previous week when

Paul was hosting one of his dinner parties. Paul had listened uncomfortably as she summed up what he knew was her view of the widespread mediocrity and materialism in mainstream Western society. The room went predictably silent after she had slipped her opinion into the conversation. "Humans never like to talk about subjects with no easy or immediate answer. For that reason, most conversations between people are highly prefabricated and fall into circular patterns of cliché: like the cliché of the security in having an investment property or an investment portfolio."

Only friends who were close to her could cope with her intense, shifting, and polarized personality and her penchant for killing, with utter precision, any congenial suburban mood.

Paul aired his concerns as she was looking at the sky above the courtyard.

"You know, some of our friends find you difficult to understand. They think you need to chill out and settle on one thing for a while." Under this facade Paul hid his real thoughts: that she should try to be more conventional. He was about to return to a conversation that they had had many times before.

"I'm not mixed up, you know. I just like to be in other people's skins. I want to be objective and empathetic. It's my way. My way to understand myself."

Paul did not respond. He was still considering her words. So she added something to strengthen her point. "Or at least find the human archetypes in me."

Frustration washed over him. "But you can't be anybody but yourself. We're all limited, Allison. Each person is a piece in a puzzle. We're limited, but we fit with each other. It's not bad to be fixed in one kind of way. You don't need to immerse yourself in others in the way that you do."

Allison was silent for a moment, then said, "You're right in a way. Because I can't absorb everyone's feelings or perceptions. I have to pull myself out before I drown in them."

"This is what I mean, Allison! People don't drown in others. Not to mention that you're a walking fashion freak half the time. You swing from tie-dye skirts to builder's overalls. I wish you would stop dressing like the next random stranger that you meet." He regretted this comment immediately, and despite this feeling added, "People don't know who you are. You're always shifting around."

Tears ran down her face. He got up from his chair and bent down to embrace her.

"But this is who I am," she said.

He could not ignore the sadness in her face, and he knew his words were a revelation to her. His real intentions were partially revealed now. The trust that had always existed between them lessened after this conversation.

"I suppose, in the end, it doesn't matter what you wear or say. I will always love you. You're my little sister. That will never change. It's only when other people say . . . you're . . ."

"Odd," she offered.

"No . . . no, just . . . interesting, I would say." But this was a lie. "Odd" was definitely a more appropriate word to describe her behavior. He felt her body slump slightly in his arms as she whimpered. Paul knew that some of the instability in her life had come from the death of their father when she was sixteen. Their parents had been in a car crash. Their mother, who was also in the crash, had been in a coma for the last three years. Allison visited her nearly every week, and Paul came when he could, but he had always felt Allison's deep love for their parents.

———

Paul had driven Allison to Melbourne Airport to catch her flight to New York. He looked over at her in the passenger seat and remembered that conversation vividly. It was now 1998. Six years had passed, yet it felt like only a year or two. He was amazed how the years had smeared over each other and contracted. He knew now that he had been superficial in his assessments of her character, but recently old fears about her mental stability had resurfaced. Some of Allison's colleagues at Friends of the Earth, where she worked as a volunteer on occasion, had expressed this to Paul. On the surface their remarks seemed straightforward enough. They joked about her strange comments and behavior, but their words were veiled intimations that her mental stability might be in question.

A few months before she left for New York, a few specific words resonated in his memory. Allison had brought one of the volunteers from Friends of the Earth into the restaurant. The guy looked like he was straight out of a hippie commune, but one thing he said, when Allison was out the back, did strike him.

"Your sister, she's a real head-trip, man." Even he could see what Paul did. Those were the resonating words. She was a head-trip.

———

While waiting with fellow travelers at the baggage carousel, she observed what she assumed were New York locals, who wore big puffer jackets and snow boots, and although her retro leather jacket kept her relatively warm, she felt the cold air penetrate her feet and legs.

She remembered seeing vast stretches of snow several hours before landing, and she wondered why she had not considered the possibility of the cold. The plane had flown over broken ice sheets floating on the Great Lakes. It had glided over what must be either Chicago or Detroit; she could not remember which was which. At the time the flat whiteness was expansive and dead yet in the same instant compelling. The snow had been no more than a curiosity and a picture with no other context than her detached imagination. The comfort and protective envelope of the plane's interior had masked the difference in temperature.

"You look a little cold." An older voice vibrated behind her.

She turned around. "Yes, I'm afraid I underestimated the weather."

A lady in her sixties smiled and stared at her feet. Allison recognized the lady from the plane. She had sat next to her on the flight from the Los Angeles leg of the journey.

"Yes! I know . . . I don't know why I wore these sandals. They are totally impractical in this weather, although I can get away with it in Australian winters."

"It's twenty-seven degrees Fahrenheit windchill factor out there, dear. You had better put something else on."

Staring longer than needed, Allison presumed the woman was curious about the missing toe on her right foot.

"Are you from New York?" Allison asked.

"No, dear! My son and his wife live here. I visit twice a year to catch up with my grandchild. You know how it is—Christmas get-togethers and all that."

Allison nodded but was not sure what "you know how it is" meant exactly.

The woman looked at Allison's wrist. "Nice watch, dear."

"Yes, it's vintage. A bit tatty, but I like it. I've had it for years."

In the periphery of her vision, Allison saw bags spilling onto the carousel. She turned back to see them pass by her and searched for her own baggage. The woman did not take the conversation any further. Allison saw her worn red hiking pack come onto the carousel. She slipped it over her shoulder as she turned around again. She now took the woman's aging face more firmly into her memory. The woman's iridescent green eyes reminded her of the old man who had sold her the pipe at Queen Victoria Market. The shade of green in both their eyes was similar. Allison felt around in her top pocket. She grasped the paper bird.

"Okay then. Nice to meet you . . . and I hope you have a nice stay with your son and family . . . this particular year." She wanted to be truthful and sincere. She raised her hand with her fingers clasped around the bird. "Can I give you this?"

"Yes, dear. What is it?"

"A paper bird." She opened her hand to reveal the bird.

"Why?"

"I don't know exactly. I just feel compelled to give it to you. There's a poem inside the bird. If you unfold the paper, you'll find it."

The woman took the bird, looked at it for a few moments, and placed it in her handbag. "And you have a nice time here in the Big Apple. And don't forget to put some cold-weather shoes on." The old woman stared at her feet again.

"Yes . . . yes, I will, thanks . . . bye." Allison waved.

Turning, she walked toward the arrivals exit. She felt vaguely connected to this stranger even in this transitory slice of time, which seemed like another addition to the anonymous and disconnected chunks of her life: the comings and goings of strangers and those wearing plastic smiles.

People were spread around the arrival area as she walked through. If she had told Nava about coming here, she would have a friendly face to look for in the crowd and a warm car to zip away in, but she had not wanted to impose on Nava.

She had kept in regular contact with Nava until a year ago; then the emails had stopped, and Nava gave up contacting her. She supposed that if she did call her, Nava would be glad to see her, but she pushed that thought away.

Arriving at the main exit, she paused to think. What next? The automatic doors opened and closed periodically as people left for destinations unknown to her. Air carrying heavy snow wafted through the automatic doors whenever they opened. She asked herself again whether she should call Nava. The other option was to catch a taxi and find a hotel. As these thoughts went through her mind, a yellow taxi pulled up almost in front of the doors. Her eyes moved between the people leaving the taxi and the slow drift of heavy flakes floating into the foreground of spotlights. The beginning of night, and the snowfall, had come when she was in the airport building. She stared in wonder at the snowflakes and the way their weight made some of the flakes almost hover in midair, much like a bumblebee, before continuing their descent to the ground. Her mind took a snapshot of this curious vista.

The driver gave change to his passengers and stepped onto the side-walk. He panned around the entrance area. He then looked straight through the doors and met Allison's stare. She smiled and waved.

"You want a ride?" he shouted through the closing doors, but she did not answer. She waved again.

He came through the doors, brushing the snow off his jacket as he walked. "Did you want a taxi, or are you just saying hello?"

"Do you know of any cheap accommodations near Columbia University?"

"I think so . . . yes. I'm not sure of the exact prices, but I've been told about a hotel on the Upper West Side recently . . . it's close enough to Columbia."

"Great! Let's go."

They walked back to the taxi.

"Can I help you with your hiking pack?" he asked as they walked.

"Thanks. I'm okay, but you can take my backpack if you want."

He took the backpack.

He opened the back door, and she threw her hiking pack onto the seat. She then turned around and slipped out of her sandals. She began to trace a small circle in the snow collected on the sidewalk. "It's so soft and powdery. Wow . . . it really feels nice against my skin." She smiled at him.

Looking at the circle and her bare feet, he commented, "If you continue like this for much longer, you won't feel anything." Grinning, he added, "You obviously don't get to see much snow."

"I'm glad that you are amused by my little adventure here," she said.

He passed her the backpack, and she slipped back into her sandals and got into the taxi. The warm air in the taxi enveloped her body. In her hiking pack she found protection from the cold. She put socks on and pushed her feet into a pair of well-worn brown builder's boots. The taxi pulled away from the terminal and began to ascend a steep ramp. It lifted imperceptibly into flight at the crest, and from that higher vantage point a white and organic-looking modernist building came into sight. Terminal 5 glowed in the night like an otherworldly pod. She suppressed an urge to stop and look at the interior of the terminal; she remembered the interior from an architectural book she had seen when she had studied photography years before.

The taxi left the airport and turned onto a highway. She looked down at the white sidelines twisting and curving on a glistening wet backdrop. Dim orange streetlamps highlighted continuous patches of snowbound New York suburbia.

"Are we near Manhattan yet?" she asked after some time had passed.

"Soon . . . yes. We are getting close to the Queensboro Bridge."

The warmth in the taxi and the hum of the engine soothed her. Tilting her head so that it rested on the frosty glass, she watched snowflakes melding with water droplets before they slipped down the glass. She drew shapes mindlessly where her breath left its mark. Gradually the snow fell heavier and thicker until it built a slushy crust at the base of the taxi window.

The sensations inside the taxi evoked memories of childhood vacations during long Australian summers. From the back seat of her parents' car, she had stared for hours at all the twisting variations in the sideline, which flowed in a blur beside her. She had felt the wind and the sun and her hair rhythmically whipping her face as she stuck her head out the window into the stream of air. She had tried to make out muted conversations between her parents, which competed with the music playing on the car stereo.

The song "Forever and Ever" by Demis Roussos played incessantly in the car then. At the time Allison had hated the music because of the continual repetition, but she enjoyed the memory of it now because of the memories connected with it: her parents and the long trips that the family made up the east Australian coast over the years. She missed having them in her life all these years after their deaths. The song played away in her mind for a while. Its sentimentality took deeper root before fading into the sound of the taxi engine. In another memory she saw an image of her face in the side mirror of her parents' car; the air pressure forced streaming tears out of her eyes. Those tears distorted the sunlit world before her. In the present she mimicked that earlier time by squinting her eyes at the orange streetlights flowing by rhythmically in the dark sky.

"You're from Australia, right?" the taxi driver said.

"You recognize my accent."

He smiled and looked at her in the mirror. "I have some Australian friends here, so I know the accent . . . I'm Paul, by the way."

"Oh, my brother's name is Paul."

"Oh really?"

After a short silence, she asked, "Do you like driving taxis? Does it make you happy?"

"Happy . . . I suppose that is one way to describe it, but it's just a job to me . . . Midtown Manhattan is coming up on the left."

"Oh right, thanks," she exclaimed with a touch of exuberance.

The taxi turned onto the bridge and merged into the end of rush-hour traffic.

The traffic slowed. They stared through the steel supports on the bridge that slid by slowly as they passed.

"This is a great view of the skyline." She closed her eyes for a few moments.

When she opened them, she tried to perceive the panorama of the city, through the gauze of snow, as just a collection of disconnected abstract colors and shapes with no reference to either the past or future, an escape from clichéd observations of the city that she had remembered seeing in various books over the years before.

"The city looks familiar and unknown at the same time, and almost alien," she said almost to herself. But she could not see it without the past or the future, without memory, and her mind asserted an order on what she saw.

She opened the window just enough for a breath of cool air. The city and its lights exuded an intangible allure, and the temptation to give in to it was real and visceral. The haze of snow fell into the taxi's interior through the gap in the window. The snow melted on her warm face.

"You don't mind if I roll the window down farther?" she asked.

"No, go ahead."

She rolled it fully open. Resting her head on her folded arms, she leaned on the windowsill. The snow hit her face with more intent now. She imagined the snow forming in continuous layers on her skin, and inside the oblivion of time, she would be cocooned forever.

The traffic began to move again.

"I've seen this view so much that I don't see it anymore. I'm blind to it now," he said.

"Maybe you need to forget it, so you can remember it again and see it new."

"Maybe, yeah."

"Are there really people out there? It seems like an empty city from here, in a way. I can't tell which light and which room has a person in it." Were they all just empty rooms with the lights on? So she added, "They are all boxes of light, filled with people who live out an existence in a bliss of clichés." She was thinking of the stewardess on the plane as an empty room with a smile that was represented as a light. This gave the impression that someone was home when in fact the room was deserted. And so much of life fell within the influence of certain empty social expectations.

"What do you mean by a bliss of clichés?" he asked.

"Oh, nothing much. I was just thinking how all our lives, our actions, fall into predictable and circular patterns, which sometimes bear no real connection to who we are potentially. We never move beyond the obvious surface of our life. We exist in the marginal aspects, content with superficial appearance. It is, I suppose, a kind of social veneer that we all take part in. What I think we need is a form of truthfulness and a purity of motive that transcends all our empty smiles."

———

"This girl . . . she was wearing clothes stranger than hell for this weather. Strange for any weather now that I think about it." Rose, the lady who had sat next to Allison on the airplane, was speaking, and Paul Nightingale was listening; he was listening patiently to his mother, who was sitting diagonally behind him in the back seat of his car. Mapping the time from her door in Los Angeles to his in New York, he knew she would give him a rundown of the world's misdemeanors. She had fallen into this groove over many years, and she would start talking from the airport until they got home. He would listen until she ran out of things to say, and then they would talk about his world.

"Stranger than hell. I haven't heard you use that phrase before. Where did you get it from?" he said.

"Huh. What? It doesn't matter. She was wearing sandals. In this weather, if you can believe it! She was sweet . . . but strange. Definitely. She had nine toes. There was something else about her . . . about her manner. And I only said a few words to her, and then she gives me this." Rose leaned forward, and her son took the paper bird from her hand.

He turned it over. "What sort of bird is it, I wonder? Maybe a white swan. Or some other bird."

"I don't really care for it. I just wanted to be polite, so I took it."

"I'll give it to Alison, then." Paul thought of his adopted daughter.

His mother went quiet. He guessed she was ruminating on the girl and the ongoing theme of a world that represented a future of decadence and maladaptation. He smiled and thought about his mother's fixed nature.

"Mother."

"Yes, what is it?"

"I'm going away for a few days. To Europe. I'm attending a law conference . . . I'll be leaving soon. Will you be okay without me around? I mean with Sophie and Alison."

"Okay? I'll be fine. I'll be teaching your daughter some manners."

"Go easy, Mother. Alison is only a child. She's afraid of you."

"She's soft. Way too soft. Thanks mainly to you, of course."

"Try to include Sophie, please."

Paul's wife and his mother had a distant regard for each other, and he would try to pull the two personalities closer, but his mother was hardened against sentimentality. His kind of love—a soft and yielding kind, as she had repeated over the years—was a commodity for the weak-minded.

"She's soft too. They both are." She paused for a moment. "That girl. I can't get her out of my head. There's something irregular about her."

"What do you mean by irregular?"

"I don't know. I can't define it. Work it out for yourself."

Paul negotiated the Manhattan traffic silently for several minutes. His mother continued as he parked in front of his Upper West Side house. "That's it! I knew I'd seen that before." His mother raised her voice. "Her watch. It was male and vintage. Your father had one for a few years before he died. It was a gold watch. The gold leaf on hers, it was wearing away . . . and I remember the pattern on the front. It was a diamond lattice weave. And the face had a greenish tint to it."

"Yes, that's interesting."

He closed the driver's door and walked around the car to open the passenger door. He took her hand and helped her step onto the sidewalk. "When I get back to Los Angeles, I think I'll start wearing your father's watch. Like her. Like the girl," she said.

————

Allison had drifted through high school, not making any lasting friendships. She was intelligent and so she was able to maintain good grades, but nothing interested her. All her subjects seemed empty or bland. In fact, her whole life up to recent times had seemed like a haze of background noise; she was just passing through it like a detached observer in an alternate and alien culture—an anthropologist. She felt compassion and empathy for people and their different lives, but no one seemed to be able to see her as a viable friend, so she just moved on, contented within herself, knowing that she would find a place in the world eventually if she just kept moving on as she always had.

Even enrolling in a photography course was an impulse decision, and she didn't expect to become a photographer as such. She couldn't see herself as anything, and the whole idea of a career seemed slightly shallow. She had always wanted to be defined by her own humanity and not by what she did for a job. Oddly, the only person remotely interested in her as a friend was Nava, which made no sense to her since Nava was quite mainstream. She only really found friends in the photography course and a few more friends at Friends of the Earth, who were a more community-minded and a largely alternative crowd.

She realized in the end that she needed to seek out people that were interesting to her but who were not going to be friends, and she would live through these people in a melded empathy.

Toward the end of November 1992, Allison's Certificate IV in Photography and Photo Imaging course was winding up. Three weeks later RMIT University held an exhibition of the students' artwork on December 18, which almost coincided with her twentieth birthday on the 19th.

At the exhibition Allison was dressed in her usual "odd" style that seemed to match her "odd" behavior, an observation that her brother, Paul, had made to her five months earlier as they chatted in the court-yard garden of one of their restaurants. She was friendly with her fellow students but felt a growing distance between herself and people. She had felt it quite intensely as she walked around the gallery. The people in the room seemed empty: there, but not in reality, or her reality at least; people were almost cardboard cutouts. This feeling of emptiness was accentuated by the death of her mother on the ninth.

The only people she was glad to see at the exhibition were Jasper, a lecturer in philosophy at the University of Melbourne, and Nava. A friend of Jasper's taught the History of Art and Design class that had been part of her degree, and it was where she had met Nava. Allison had met Jasper at a student party at the beginning of the year, and they had hung out regularly most of that year. He had encouraged her to come back to university after her road trip and complete a BA with a philosophy major and maybe French as the other major, a double major.

Jasper and Nava were standing in front of her photographic trip-tych. She had borrowed a medium-format Hasselblad from the university store and taken shots of homeless people in St. Kilda and the Central Business District.

She walked up behind Jasper.

"What do you think?" she said.

He turned around. "Fabulous, darling," he said, putting on a camp voice.

She put her arm around both Jasper's and Nava's waists.

"Hello, babe," Allison said to Nava.

"I love these photos," Nava said.

"So, don't forget to stop at my shack when you get to Queensland," he said.

"I won't forget. Thank you."

"It's not far past Fraser Island."

She had bought an old Holden a few days before the exhibition and had packed the car, ready for a long journey, the road trip around Australia that she had planned to make for many years. Finally, she could travel alone and leave humanity and those too-familiar relationships behind her. As much as she loved Paul, she wanted some emotional distance from him. After that conversation in the restaurant, she realized that he loved her but did not understand her. Jasper had given her a collection of books on philosophy, particularly the existentialists and postmodernists. She planned to read them during her trip. And in the previous month, she had bought a secondhand 35mm Leica M6 camera, built in the mid-eighties, which she planned to use to document her travels, like a visual diary.

She had left her Fitzroy house a few days before. She had found someone to take over her room, someone that her fellow roommates were happy with. She had packed most of her belongings into Paul's garage in St. Kilda.

On the day after the exhibition, the day of her birthday, Paul and Nava were standing next to her car in front of his house. She hugged him and Nava and then removed a pair of bricks from the front tires before getting into the driver's seat.

"What are the bricks for?" Paul said.

"The handbrake is broken."

"Is that safe?"

"Probably not. I'll call you in a few weeks," she said.

"I love you, babe," he said.

"I love you too, babe," Allison said.

"So, I'll see you in Perth next Christmas," Nava said.

"Where are you going to stay tonight?" Paul asked.

"In the desert in Northern Victoria. I'm going to return to Hattah-Kulkyne National Park."

"Yes. Okay, cool. Be careful on the road."

"Where will you go after Hattah-Kulkyne?"

"I'm going to spend New Year's Eve at ConFest." She knew he was worried about the cancer returning, but he had not said anything in the last few months. She wondered if he would say anything now since she had said she wouldn't be following up with any doctors until she got back to Melbourne in a year. But he did not say anything. "I'll have a checkup when I get to Adelaide," she said.

"Oh, babe, that would be great."

She reached over and took one of the nine mixtapes that she had made for the trip.

He leaned through the car window and kissed her on the cheek.

She smiled and waved to them both. She drove away, but after only nineteen feet, she stopped and leaned out of the window, looking back at Paul and Nava.

"Visit Mum and Dad while I am away."

"I will, babe. I'll look after their graves. Please don't worry."

The first song on the tape was Tracy Chapman's "Fast Car."

She put her left turn signal on and merged into rush-hour traffic on Barkley Street. As she drove past Acland Street, she took one last look at St. Kilda's main shopping area, knowing that she would not see it again for at least a year.

2

THE GIRL WITH THE YELLOW DRESS

The true seeker hunteth naught but the object of his quest, and the sincere lover hath no desire save reunion with his beloved. Nor shall the seeker reach his goal unless he sacrifice all things. That is, whatever he hath seen, and heard, and understood—all he must set at naught with "no God is there", that he may enter into the realm of the spirit, which is the city of "but God"[1]. Labour is needed, if we are to seek Him; ardour is needed, if we are to drink the nectar of reunion with Him; and if we taste of this cup, we shall cast away the world.[2]

— BAHÁ'U'LLÁH, *THE SEVEN VALLEYS*

The city's windows presented Hooman with an array of altered mirrors. He contemplated the buildings surrounding his corner office. He thought of Alice and the book *Through the Looking-Glass*. In each reflection he saw a slightly changed world and thousands of worlds in parallel.

Hooman's laptop dinged. There was a task he needed to complete, and he looked at the screen. His diary said, "Monday, December 14, 1998, 4:15 p.m. Complete paper for law conference."

He looked at the Hudson River in the distance. The thick, polluted air textured the sun and obscured the outline of buildings beyond the river in New Jersey.

He glanced in the other direction toward the East River. Through the glass walls that separated all the other offices on his floor, a flash of sunlight from a reflection cut into his eyes as he looked at another building in the distance.

Beginning to feel tired, he supported his head in his hands and closed his eyes for a while. His mind vanished into brief moments of unconscious time, and as his head lolled, his cell phone rang. It hammered his ears as it vibrated on the desk.

"Hello . . . this is . . ." He tried to remember his name, but nothing came.

A metallic laugh rattled down the line.

"You're so cute when you're disorientated. Are you sure you know who you are?" she said in a low, even voice. "Anyway, what are we doing for dinner tonight?"

"Oh . . . yeah, some of the girls in the office have invited us to dinner in the Village. I'm going to leave work early today. Do you want to go?"

"Sure, why not. So anyway, text me the address, and I'll see you there. But I'll be a bit late, as I have to see a client—just half an hour or so. Okay, so text me," Nava said.

"There's no need for a text. It's at the Seven Stars Café. Do you remember it? We were there a few months back."

"It's on West 8th Street, right? Near 6th Avenue?"

"Yes, that's it . . . so I'll see you there then . . . bye."

"Bye, sleepy head."

He attempted to respond and was contemplating one of his standard verbal parries when she hung up. He flipped the phone shut and placed it in his shirt pocket.

Taking the laptop from the desk, he tried to relax on the couch near the window. He followed this pattern at the end of every day to extract a few extra words from his tired and unwilling brain. He started to reread the document he had been working on over the last week; he tried to fall into the flow of it. The paper explored trends in globalization and the need for world citizenship. He was scheduled to present it at a law conference in Europe. Though on this evening, he felt like a toy that was overwound. Continual late nights were beginning to accumulate.

After a few minutes of writing, where nothing of significance came into his mind, he stared over the screen and focused on the world outside. He did not have the concentration to continue writing, so he closed the laptop. He got up and walked over to the intersection of glass in the corner of his office. He looked down at Bryant Park. People were walking through the snow, and as he glanced at another building, he saw people through office windows. He saw the worlds beyond the mirrors and a plethora of human activity. He looked back at the main office space on his floor, and he saw yet more people: his colleagues and office staff. They look happy, for the most part, he thought. He was content with what he saw.

Daylight was fading as he gazed out over the city. In concurrence, artificial lights slowly appeared. The reds and oranges of sunset gradually gave way to blue-white illumination. New York would soon take on its nightly transformation, a rhythm that was worn into his daily life, and he noted that his own reflection in the window had appeared now as the light outside continued receding. He stared at his face for a few moments, then went back to the couch and lay down. He closed his eyes for what he thought would be only a few minutes. He intended to rest and then head out to the café. He glided steadily into the horizon of sleep. The borders between waking and dreaming seamlessly folded into each other.

In a dream he found himself lying on the couch. He opened his eyes and stared at the ceiling for a moment. He thought that he was still awake, so standing up and walking over to the window, he looked down at Bryant Park and then at 42nd Street.

A girl in an intense yellow dress was walking through a large crowd of people, and she cut through them effortlessly. The shade of yellow in her dress struck like a bell against muted tones in the dusk-lit snow.

Leaving the sidewalk behind her, she crossed the street near one side of the New York Public Library and the beginning of Bryant Park. She walked in a perfect line and fell in flawlessly with the crisscross of the traffic. She did not deviate for them or they for her. Each passed by unhindered in a harmony of color and movement.

Entering the park, she walked along a sidewalk that ran parallel with 42nd Street. The stark, denuded trees and their entangled branches obscured her figure. He realized that she would eventually disappear behind buildings on the far side of the park, and he felt a strong need to run after her. If he lost her now, he may never find her again. He sprinted from the office to the elevator and soon found himself in the park, crunching the snow beneath his shoes as he followed her. At a distance ahead, near the end of the park, was a fountain. She passed by it, then crossed a street and disappeared into 41st Street. He increased his pace to try to catch her, but she moved farther away: she was moving quickly through the streets without the need to run and seemed to be skipping through time in fast-forward.

By the time he ran from 41st Street into Broadway, the beginning of night had come. He continued to run toward the center of Times Square. He caught sight of her in the distance for a moment, but she was soon lost in a blur of people. He stopped and leaned on his knees to catch his breath. As he looked around, he saw that the square was filled with knee-high grass and a light layer of snow. The streets and sidewalks were replaced by a large meadow. The advertising lights and glass structures rising up from the meadow were more than alien in this context. The grass was suffused with subtle, muted colors coming from the lights in the square.

At the center of the square, he walked on into the meadow. Tears ran down his face. He stopped again and slumped to the ground. The soft grass pushed against his knees, and, in that instance, he felt someone's arms supporting his body from behind.

"I know who you are," a female voice uttered in delight.

She laughed as if she had just solved a playful riddle, and her voice was overlaid with harmonic resonance and echo.

And arising from her words, his feelings changed from depressed to exuberant. He felt an absolute radiance penetrate deep into his body. It imparted a drug-like ecstasy that was both beautiful and personal. He then rose to his feet and in the periphery of his vision saw the yellow fabric in her dress. As he was about to act on the impulse to turn around and face this unknown person, he heard a voice. Initially it was in the tone of the woman behind him, but then it morphed into another voice.

"Hooman . . . Hooman. Hey, Hooman! I'm sorry to wake you, but the others are gone."

In a daze he sat up. He looked up at Elliot. "Sorry, I don't understand. Who is gone?"

"They went to the café. I had a few things to do, so I stayed back."

"Oh . . . the café."

"Are you sure you still want to come? You look tired."

"No, I'm fine . . . and besides, my sister is meeting us there later."

"Shall we go together, then?"

Still in a daze he looked straight ahead. Fragments of the dream were still replaying in his mind, and he could still feel a faint resonance of ecstasy in his body.

She went to the corner of the office and took his herringbone suit jacket and scarf from the coat stand. She came back and said, "Here's your jacket. I'll wait next to the elevator." She smiled, placed his jacket and scarf in his lap, and then left the office. After a minute, he got up and left.

In silence they took the elevator to the first floor.

Walking through the lobby, their footsteps echoed on the black granite floors and reverberated off the gray and white marble walls.

Hooman looked over at her. "It's great to have you as part of our team. And I'm sorry I haven't said hello earlier, but work has been hectic recently."

"That's all right. The girls in the office said you would say hello eventually."

As they stepped through the rotating doors and out onto the street, a flurry of snow fell over the park.

Putting his hand out, he commented in a whimsical tone, "Look, a new season. Winter is on its way."

"Apparently it's going to come down heavy soon."

"Oh good. I like the snow at this time of year. It's decorative but without the full intensity of winter. But strangely today has been quite cold for this time of year. It's twenty-nine degrees Fahrenheit, and with the windchill factor that makes it twenty-seven, and I didn't bring my overcoat today. I didn't think it would be this cold. I guess we should find a taxi, or we could take the subway, I suppose."

They crossed 42nd Street. As Hooman stepped off the road, he realized they were standing near the sidewalk that the girl in his dream had walked along. He stopped for a moment and stared at the sidewalk.

After a while, he realized he was staring into space. "Sorry, I just zoned out there," he said.

They walked on toward the other end of the park, where they crossed 6th Avenue and found themselves near one of his favorite bookshops.

"Hey, can we stop at that bookshop?" he asked. He pointed at it down 42nd Street.

The bookshop was old. It had overtones of a neglected warehouse. The books were stacked into teetering piles, and the space was generally chaotic in appearance, although books stocked here were of a higher quality than the surroundings suggested. Hooman had bought many obscure titles here that were not available in more mainstream bookshops.

Squeezing their way toward the back of the store through the narrowing aisles, they slowed in the middle of the long room.

"Are you looking for something in particular?" Elliot said.

"Huh . . . oh, no, I just had a feeling . . . I mean over the last couple of days . . . that I should go look for a book. Any book, really. I don't know which one in particular. I'm guessing that may sound a bit random."

"No, not at all. I sometimes get an urge for chocolate that I can't explain either."

He laughed. "You're funny."

Hooman continued to push toward the back of the bookshop. They stopped at tables stocking architecture books. He flicked through a few titles. "I was sure I would find something here . . . well, maybe I'll try somewhere else. None of these books look very interesting." He was quiet for a while, then turned to her. "You know, I had an odd but compelling dream when you came into the office."

"Really . . . I hope I didn't cut it short."

"No, well, actually, I think you woke me at a pertinent time in the dream."

"What do you mean?"

"I am not sure exactly why . . . but, anyway, I saw this girl. And she was wearing an intense yellow dress. She was walking through Bryant Park . . . it's hard for me to describe the way she was beautiful."

"Was she beautiful like a model is beautiful? I would have thought it was easy to describe a beautiful woman."

"You think so? I didn't see her face . . . it's like you know things in some dreams. You don't know how you know, you just know . . . intuitively. This was more like . . ."—he hesitated—"a personal beauty."

"A personal beauty? I think I know what you mean. Her personality was compelling."

"Sort of . . . but it seemed broader than just personality. She seemed transcendent. I can't capture it in my mind. She had a certain uniqueness . . . indefinable, really. And when I woke, I had a certain ecstasy in my body that I have never felt before."

"Sorry to change the subject, but are you into things of a philosophical bent?"

"Actually, probably more . . . metaphysical or religious, but, yes, for the most part philosophical. Can you tell?"

"I have to be honest. I heard from colleagues at the office that you are not to be asked about philosophy or religion. I was just curious because someone said . . . well, you seem like an interesting person. From what I've heard. But I find it strange that people have a need for spirituality . . . or metaphysics these days. A need for philosophy is understandable, stripped of religion. And I heard you follow some kind of Eastern religion."

"Yes, I'm a Bahá'í."

"Oh, yes . . . I've heard of that religion, vaguely. I think it developed in what used to be the Ottoman and Persian Empires in the 1800s. But these days it's more global . . . right?"

"Yes, that's right."

"It is obscure, isn't it? I read an article about it a long time ago. Something about all religions being one and all humanity united as one. I think the article revolved around the idea that there is only one God for every religion. But it doesn't mean much to me personally. I'm not a believer in anything much . . . least of all metaphysics or religion. Are your parents Bahá'í as well?"

"No, they're Jewish. I became a Bahá'í in my early twenties. My parents knew Bahá'ís in Iran and hooked up with them in Australia after they emigrated. That's where I learned about it. But I didn't become a Bahá'í officially until I came to New York to study law. There was a Bahá'í Society at New York University."

"Yes, I heard you're from Iran. But your accent? It's very international. I couldn't fully tell where you were from when I first heard you in the office. You have a bit of an Australian and American accent . . . it's always moving around, between the two."

"Like I said, my parents immigrated to Perth when I was a kid. That's where I got the Australian accent from. My father's brother had a business in Perth, so the family moved to Australia to help him with the business, but many Jews were repatriated to Israel after the formation of the state in 1948. Since then, there has been a steady flow out of Iran. And a lot left after the Iranian and Cultural Revolutions in Iran too."

"I can't say I know much about Iranian politics, other than snippets in the news."

"Well, it has always been difficult for minorities in Iran in recent history. I mean I never had anything but good memories of Iran, mostly. But as some of my friends point out, I never lived through either of the revolutions. When you are a child, your parents tend to shield you from certain negative aspects of life, so I was oblivious to the hardships back then. I wasn't very aware of the difficulties in Iran, politically or religiously. My innocence and ignorance of life was only broken in my teens."

"And your sister, is she Jewish too?"

"Nominally, let's say. She does believe in God but has never elaborated on her belief much. Which is fine. But what about you?"

"Oh, me? Well, my parents are loosely Russian Orthodox Christians. My grandparents were stricter, but I don't subscribe to their faith. I don't believe in God really and can't see the point. I think it's just a kind of mass . . . well, a sad delusion, like fairy tales or something. I mean, I suppose a belief in God is based on ancient myths, before science could actually explain existence in real terms, you know, scientifically and rationally."

"I see," he said, smiling.

"Oh . . . I'm sorry. I realize that sounds like I think believing in a God is childlike or something."

"No, that's fine. Being childlike has its advantages." He smiled and continued. "Do you mind working with a person who is irrational and unscientific?"

"That doesn't mean that I think your beliefs are silly. I am just speaking from my own perspective . . . about religion in general.

Growing up as I did, religion seemed like another type of Santa Claus story, a fairy tale or something, like I said before. Like God being an old man who lives in the sky and who enjoys punishing us for our sins. Do you know what I'm trying to say?" she said.

"Well, yes, I do, but I think religion is a little more complex than Santa Claus and the old man in the sky. But, hey, don't worry. It's great that you have thought about it that much. You're very honest and I like that. Most people in the office ignore me when I start talking about subjects with even the faintest religious aspect. It makes me feel like a child who has an imaginary friend." They laughed, and he continued. "I don't mind you saying God is like a child's fairy tale. Life itself is a fairy tale and full of its own particular illusions. Every person has their own subjective expression of the strange, unexplainable beauty of it all."

"Yes, it is like that sometimes, I guess," she responded.

"Religion is just a collective way to organize the fairy tale. And it is possible for religion and science to find some middle ground when it comes to explaining the mysteries of existence. Well, that's how it is in my world."

She laughed at that last comment.

Hooman noticed that Elliot's hand was unconsciously resting on a book titled *Modernist Architecture in America*. The cover was an interior photograph of Terminal 5 at JFK Airport.

"This looks nice." She picked it up and turned the pages over in a measured way. "The print quality is quite special. Nice thick pages too," she said and rubbed a page between her thumb and forefinger.

He looked at it with more intent. "Oh, yes. It might make a good coffee-table book." She passed the book to him, and he opened it and buried his face in its pages. His muffled voice escaped. "I love the smell of books, the ink and paper. It's the perfume of meaning." He withdrew his face from the pages. "Shall I get it? What do you think?" he asked.

"I would buy it," she exclaimed with restrained enthusiasm.

A line of people stood at the counter in the front of the shop. He glanced at his watch. "Actually, we better go . . . we're already late. Maybe I'll get it another time."

"Don't worry, Hooman, I think it's a fairly loose arrangement tonight at the café. Let's go line up at the counter."

Hooman stepped out of the bookshop and onto the sidewalk. He noticed that the snow had dissipated. Instead of taking the subway, they hailed a taxi and headed toward Greenwich Village. Hooman leafed through the pages of his new book with an absent mind; he strained his eyes in the low and dappled light that filled the taxi.

Elliot stared out of the window. He looked over at her and noted her pale skin and high cheekbones contrasting against the multicolored blur of the street passing by outside; the colored lights passed through the foggy glass and painted her skin in soft, subtle hues. Her life played out against the backdrop of many others. She was an interesting person: initially shy but direct and honest. He liked her. The snow began to fall heavily as their taxi found a way through the streets in Greenwich Village.

As they arrived, two of their colleagues were visible from the street. They were huddled around a rickety wooden table. The café, darkly lit, exuded a retro air. Liberal helpings of secondhand, mismatched furniture crowded the space, and every table had its own 1950s lampshade.

Hooman and Elliot came through the door, and a bell rang out. He moved toward his colleagues and sat beside a lampshade near the table.

After sitting down, Elliot tapped the cover of Hooman's new book. It now lay in the light of the lamp. She tried to attract his gaze.

Picking it up, he reciprocated. "Yes, this is an interesting book. There are some great black-and-white shots."

He was looking at Paula now, who was about to reply, but he peered over her shoulder at the door. The bell had rung, and Nava came through the doorway with an unfamiliar figure behind her.

"I thought you were coming later?" he asked.

"I was. But I was diverted. A pleasant diversion, I might add."

The shape of Allison's face emerged from the half-light. As she came closer to the table, everyone swiveled to greet her and Nava.

"Hi . . . I'm Allison . . . from Melbourne, Australia."

"This is Hooman," Nava said, pointing at her brother.

"Hi, Hooman, it's nice to meet you." Allison leaned over the table and shook his hand.

He returned her gaze. Something about her voice seemed familiar to him, but he could not quite place the tone in her voice; he thought he could hear a faint version of the harmonic resonance in the voice of the woman in his dream. This soon faded, and he did not take the impression any further.

Nava introduced Allison to the others. "This is Paula, Rachel, and, sorry, I don't know your name."

"I'm Elliot."

"These are Hooman's law colleagues, from the firm."

Allison walked around the table and took a big leather armchair from another table. She dragged it between Elliot and Hooman. Everyone slipped back into the groove of previous talk, which was mostly legal. Allison slumped into the seat, and, after a while, Hooman observed her listening quietly to the various conversations around the table. She maintained a pseudo interest in Nava's conversation. Nava animatedly recounted the events of the day so far and ended with her surprise at Allison's out-of-the-blue phone call. Allison seemed to exude a certain indefinable detachment.

Nava giggled, turning to Allison. "It's going to be such fun, showing you around the city. It's a much better place than boring old Melbourne! I can't understand you. Were you really thinking not to call me straight away? You crazy girl!" Allison smiled.

Allison was out of place amongst the crisp-suited gathering but perfectly in keeping with the establishment. Allison's tired leather jacket and her male vintage watch blended with the faded armchair. Hooman hoped she felt comfortable with the group, and after several minutes of seeming to ignore her, he turned to Allison. "You look worn out. I hope Nava didn't drag you out against your will?" he asked.

"Well, yes, I am a bit tired from the flight over. I didn't sleep much, but that's okay. I would have been bored in the hotel staring at the ceiling and attempting to sleep." She glanced at her watch and tapped it. "My watch is still set to Australian time. It's nine in the morning, but I feel relatively bright considering the time difference. Waking up tomorrow and staying awake, that's going to be interesting. Hopefully the jet lag will wear off soon."

"Nava has told me a lot about what you two got up to . . . studying together at RMIT Uni," Hooman said.

"Yes, we were in different degrees but shared a crossover class: the History of Art and Design. At the time I was studying photography."

"But didn't you study something else? I can't remember what it was now."

"Yes. After RMIT, I went to the University of Melbourne, where I did a bachelor of arts with two majors in philosophy and French. When I think back, we had some great times together," she said, smiling.

"Are you visiting for a while?"

"I am, yes. I'll continue my studies here: a master's in philosophy at Columbia University. It's been two years since I finished that University of Melbourne course."

"Don't mention philosophy, Allison," Nava interrupted. "He'll start talking about religion." She rolled her head back, closed her eyes, and pretended to snore.

The others laughed.

Allison put her hand on Hooman's arm. "It's a guess on my part, but Hooman seems intelligent enough not to be fanatical," she said.

"Oh noooo . . . not you too. Are you on Hooman's side now?" Nava asked.

Allison laughed, looking at Hooman. He turned to Nava with a faint smile. He wanted to laugh but held himself back.

"I know being part of a religion these days can be considered *abnormal* by some. But just think of all the wars humanity would be missing out on. There's nothing like a religious war to divert the great unwashed from their suburban slavery. I'm grateful to religion for that. Aren't you?" Allison asked in mock seriousness.

She looked around the table for a response and finally to Hooman. He smirked.

"Don't start, Allison! You're getting too serious. No serious talk please. Weirdo alert!" Nava bleated out *blip* sounds, which increased when she directed her hand, with her pretend weirdo meter, toward Allison.

"Blip . . . blip . . . blip . . . blip, blip, blip, blip, blip."

"Hey, hey! Don't be mean, Nava. That's enough," Hooman inserted.

Nava ignored him. "I'm so very sorry, Allison, but it appears you have some worthy competition in the running for the weirdo awards." She now pointed her pretend meter at her brother, but this time with no blipping sound.

"It's not working," he said, raising his eyebrows.

"It broke . . . it couldn't handle the strain," Nava said.

He smiled and shook his head.

Nava then leaped into his lap, nearly toppling the chair he was sitting on and bumping the table. "Oh, I'm sorry. Do you forgive me?" She wrapped her arms around his neck.

"Of course, I forgive you. It goes without saying, but you spilled Rachel's coffee." Rachel began to soak up the spill with napkins.

"Sorry, Rachel," Hooman said and smiled.

"That's okay. I'm enjoying the spectacle," Rachel replied.

"Gee, thanks for the support." He stretched his neck and peered over Nava's shoulder at Allison. "Do you want to have a hug, too, from my wonderful sister?" he asked Allison.

"No, thanks. I'm fine over here. She's all yours. Besides, she looks comfortable with you."

"Hey! That's a great idea." Nava swapped laps and wrapped her arms around Allison. "You little devil! Here you are, after no word for a year, and, of course, I forgive you for ignoring me. You're always depressed—you can't help it."

"Yes, yes . . . I'm always depressed and I can't help it," Allison said in a monotone, robotic voice. They laughed.

Nava turned to Hooman and began telling him about Allison's road trip around Australia. Hooman tried to talk further with Allison about her travels, but Nava, still sitting in Allison's lap, was painfully hyperactive and kept sidelining the flow of their conversation until Elliot engaged Nava. Asking the standard questions, Elliot started with what Nava did for a living. Once distracted by Elliot's questions, Nava took a seat next to her, and they began talking about the latest developments in the world of interior design.

"Hey, I'm sorry about that. Nava can be a bit over the top sometimes, but you may already know that," Hooman remarked sympathetically.

Allison nodded once and slowly said, "That's what I love about her. Nava is playful, but what comes with that is a certain openness. And I like her exuberance and radiance. It gives me energy."

"That's true. You're right. I guess I might take that for granted sometimes. When we were growing up, she was always the same."

For some time Hooman was attentive, with his usual politeness.

Dinner came and disappeared, but eventually—with a mixture of his week's accumulated fatigue and the warmth coming from the café kitchen—he found his mind drifting sideways. Allison's mouth opened and closed silently. He saw the words come out but did not hear them.

Following the lines and forms of her face, his vision arrived at her eyes. In an instance of languid, still time, he saw clear white, then blue rims enclosing a black sea of circular space. He noted his own face and the dark reflection of the café interior sitting on the curve of her eye. After a few moments of staring, and with the faintest embarrassment, he felt that he had stared too long at her and somehow saw through to her more private self.

Overwhelmed with sleep, his eyelids closed involuntarily for a moment. Then with no idea of the line of conversation, he asked, "Sorry, what was that?"

"I was saying, I loved the view of Manhattan when I came over the bridge tonight. Isn't it great? I can't help liking it. Do you get sick of people like me, tourists, asking you about New York?"

"No, of course not. No, you're excited. You've never been here before, so that's only natural. I haven't tired of New York yet. The view from our apartment is good too. Come over and have a look whenever you want. Where are you staying?"

He took his jacket off and sipped more coffee as he tried to re-enter the waking world.

"In a hotel on the Upper West Side, but I hope to find something more permanent near the university."

"I imagine you will find something soon. There is plenty of student accommodations up near Columbia. And I am sure Nava has already asked you to stay with us."

"Yes, on the way over here. That's kind of you both, but I'll be fine."

"Why don't you come for dinner tomorrow? I'll make some Persian rice and kebab and . . . and something else, when I think of it."

"That's all arranged."

"Oh! It is? Of course, I should have guessed Nava would ask you."

He pushed the corner of the book unconsciously and then rhythmically tapped his fingers on its cover.

He watched Allison stare at the cover image, which was an interior shot of Terminal 5. She picked the book up. "That's such a lovely building. What's your opinion? I passed it tonight on the way out of the airport. I saw photos of the interior years ago," she said.

"Yes, it is an interesting building—though I've never been inside."

"Really! How long have you been here in New York?"

"I haven't seen the Statue of Liberty either. Not up close, anyway."

"Oh, well, that's forgivable, but not seeing an Eero Saarinen building in the flesh, that is bad," she said and smiled.

"Well, yes, I've been busy. You like the building that much?"

"Yes, of course. I like a few key pieces of modernist architecture. Not everything . . . just some of it, and that is really a beautiful example. It's the interior that I am really fond of. I mean, it's an instance where the circular form has been used in modernist architecture instead of the dreaded utilitarian square. And did you know Saarinen used two curved triangles back-to-back, to make it look like an abstract bird with its wings outstretched?"

"No, I didn't, but I get it. It makes sense now that you point it out," said Hooman.

"And, well, I like anything connected to the image or likeness of a bird."

"Really, why?" asked Hooman.

"My surname is Bird."

"Oh . . . okay." Hooman nodded.

She put the book back on the table, and he then picked it up and slowly flipped through its pages. The book cover of the interior of the terminal had intimated something to him: a connection to Allison, the girl whose voice was like the voice of the girl in the yellow dress in his dream who had said to him, "I know who you are." The building's forms tugged at him. He resisted the urge to read more into this; however, the fragments of the day had an underlying power and floated up into his consciousness. They shuffled into a compelling order. He found it hard to shake the prescience of this meeting, which had become clear in retrospect. It seemed that he had already met her in the past and knew the exact moment that he would find her again in the future.

"You seem distracted," she said.

"Oh, no. Just tired. I'm sorry. I haven't been entirely present with you tonight, but I am now."

3

THE LION AND THE SUN

On this journey the wayfarer dwelleth in every abode, however humble, and resideth in every land. In every face he seeketh the beauty of the Friend; in every region he searcheth after the Beloved. He joineth every company and seeketh fellowship with every soul, that haply in some heart he may discern the secret of the Beloved, or in some face behold the beauty of the Adored One. [1]

— BAHÁ'U'LLÁH, *THE SEVEN VALLEYS*

Late in the morning on the following day, Allison stood in line for coffee at a Starbucks café on Times Square. Although it was not snowing, the air was still frigid. Before leaving the Seven Stars Café on the previous night, Nava had loaned Allison her thickly lined winter jacket, a scarf, and a beanie. Allison felt insulated from the weather now.

Her body swayed slightly, and she fought to keep her eyes open; the effects of jet lag had set in now. She ordered two small coffees: a mocha and a latte.

She found a table under an intense halogen light near the front window. The glass front of the café was a border between two worlds: the warm, bright interior and the blue, overcast light in Times Square. Rummaging around her backpack, she felt her camera and then her *Rough Guide to New York*. She took the guide out, opened it, and scanned the contents page. But her lack of sleep and the general din of surrounding chatter coalesced and broke her concentration. She gave up reading and began to observe people in Times Square walking past the café window.

On the previous day, the plane had picked up more American passengers on the Los Angeles to New York leg of the flight. At the time she had noted that the hum in the cabin had increased. American voices were slightly louder than other nationalities. Beyond voices there were other signs of cultural inflation: the size of food servings was one thing she noticed immediately. She recalled the size of her diner breakfast early that morning on Amsterdam Avenue. She had felt thoroughly bloated afterward and did not understand her compulsion to eat it all; it seemed like a waste to just leave it unfinished. She took a sip of her mocha, and her thoughts returned to the night before. As she was about to get into the taxi, she remembered seeing cars picking people up at the entrance to the terminal. The cars were gargantuan even by Australian standards. Everything was big, and people swelled to accommodate it as they gulped it all down either literally or figuratively. Everything hummed and vibrated as if it were a large furnace-like god (a Deva) unconsciously consuming and burning energy. Now she could throw her meager sacrificial offerings into its mouth.

Attempting to read again, she looked down at the guide. Once more, the volume of everyone's conversations drew her attention into other peoples' lives. It was hard to resist becoming an invisible symbiotic organism, and she had to concentrate to block out the conversations around her. Opening the book at random, and with her latte in hand, she began to read. The information in the guide was the customary fare one would have expected: summaries of watered-down facts about the many neighborhoods in Manhattan. But only one area on the island seemed interesting to her: Harlem. She flicked through the book until she found it.

The neighborhood was referred to in the first paragraph as an area in which early Dutch settlers tended farms in the early to mid-1600s. Roughly three hundred years after this, the Harlem Renaissance movement flourished, and she highlighted one sentence in her mind: "Jazz musicians and writers who emerged from Harlem at that time increased the credibility of the artistic contributions of all African Americans to the life of America, and because of this, they have left an indelible mark on history generally, above and beyond American history."

Although Harlem's famous historical figures were interesting to her, what really interested her were the many secret histories of ordinary people: the average person's contribution to Harlem may be just as significant as that of its public figures. One unseen act of selflessness by someone whose life seems ordinary might create a ripple in time and positively affect the course of history.

But the lives of average people were always shrouded in historical darkness and obscurity. Their lives were never recorded tangibly beyond a few artifacts, photographs, or home movies. Their memories—the keepers of all their secret histories, with all their uncertainty and fuzzy subjectivity—died with them. And this was how history faded out after successive generations, with no way to tell what a person's contribution to this life had been or would be if it were carried over into the future. As Allison was a newcomer to America, and more specifically Manhattan and Harlem, it would be hard for her to penetrate the historical undercurrents flowing beneath these places.

Her solution to reveal the hidden mask of history was to construct a thought experiment: to follow the life of every individual in Manhattan in an imagined omnipresence. To make it workable for her imagination, she narrowed the proportions of the idea down to everyone she could observe milling past the café or through Times Square generally. For each person she imagined fresh pages written on the fly and stored, at the end of each day, in a massive life-story depository—an infinite version of the New York Public Library. In each life-book Allison could examine personal attributes, loves, hates, goals, predicted fates, or any other conceivable type of information from droll facts to sublime aspirations.

As she took another sip from her latte, she thought about the man who served it. She had read his name tag and pondered the name, Frank Paul. What was his secret history? What action, reaction, or memory of his had silently entered into the slipstream of life and indelibly changed the course of the future for everyone? Then she thought about the power of names to underpin our lives because names were the fundamental tags that ordered the conceptual hierarchy of people who had influenced the course of history. She wondered what the power of his name was. She thought about the symmetry of Frank's name. "Frank" and "Paul" were two first names, so his name had first-name symmetry instead of first and last name asymmetry; when she had read his name tag, he felt like two people instead of one. She then realized that if she switched his name around, it would come out as Paul Frank, the clothing designer.

In her mind she began to construct sentences to add to Frank's life-book:

> *Frank Paul, a man with first-name symmetry, serves Allison Bird, the one person, two different coffees. He worries about his impending exams in French. God, ever the unhelpful narrator, would continue with, "If Frank had known that Allison had taken the same major in her undergraduate degree, she could help him review the mock exam papers. Coincidentally, Allison was on her road trip, and Frank was on vacation. On January 4, 1993, with only 130 feet separating them, they stood with their hands on the railing of Sydney Harbour Bridge. Looking out at blue-green, sun-saturated views, Frank saw the Opera House. From her own vantage point, Allison gazed out at the bay. She watched all the intense white sails tilting on the water and boats cutting white wounds into the bay's rich blue flesh." Allison took over the narration again. Frank then worries he has put too much froth on Allison's latte.*

This kind of knowledge would be useful, she thought. Because if she had known that in her future she would meet Frank, she could have walked the 130 feet that had separated them and introduce herself. "Hello. You don't know me, but we are going to meet again in roughly six years, in a café in Manhattan, and you are going to serve me a mocha and a latte coffee. And even though you're not interested in it now, you will study French. But don't worry, you will like it, and I will be able to help you . . . in five years and eleven months." But her thought experiment was no more than a whimsical attempt to deny reality its many masks and find the counterpoint between our desires to achieve great things in the future and the vagaries of history that bring us low and prove the powerlessness of our dreams.

And beyond the individual contributions in history were the collective contributions, made up of crisscrossing individual journeys. She could see in this the possibility of rich personal intersections in lives, which if consciously pursued, rather than left to chance, could lift every person a little higher in their understanding of our collective and configured destiny. A configured destiny is a destiny by design, a destiny that each person can, by the choices they make, shape and form themselves into a desired arrangement or configuration of intersecting pathways that move them toward their individual and collective destiny in this life and beyond.

And even though it might seem trivial that a person could lift another higher in the evolution of humankind by serving the other coffee, when thinking about Frank Paul again, Allison's latte tasted fractionally better. Her coffee was not just a crass, mass commercial latte pumped out by an impersonal, global coffee grinder. Frank Paul's latte had been made especially for Allison Bird, with all his care and attention, and that was a useful intersection in the lives of two people, a small act of selflessness that made the experience of being human a little better. As she finished her latte, Allison had thought up a new name for her own fantastical organically grown and ethical coffee company: The Selfless Latte Company.

By now her mocha coffee was lukewarm, and she gulped most of it down before it became cold. She looked around cautiously before letting out a burp and laughed at her own impertinence. As she dumped the cup onto the side table, it tipped over, and a small amount of coffee spilled out; it formed a random shape. Its attractive form impelled her to think about the possibility that her imaginary life-story depository could store books on more than just people, but objects also, and perhaps concepts, places, and any other conceivable entity, be the entity concretely tangible or not. Objects could have meaningful intersections too, and these could become symbiotically fused with human existence and become an extension of the mind.

Allison now added the possibility of a book of *Numbers* and books of *Coffee Spills*, *Impertinent Burps*, and *Red-Sock-Wearing People*—the last book was inspired by a girl passing the café with a pair of red socks so vivid that they burnt a faint echoing impression into her retinas.

But these books in isolation would not necessarily be significant, because each book would only be a catalog of names, dates, times, or lists of attributes with a certain linear logic that might be interesting but not remarkable. The crisscrossing intersections, the invisible hyperlink-like connections, across each book were what really interested her. She arranged a sequence of superficially disconnected events in her imagination: these were herself burping and spilling the coffee, the spill forming a shape, everyone in Manhattan wearing red socks on that day, and a mathematician in Columbia University's School of Mathematics who would be working away on an algorithm.

As the mathematician wrote the final answer to his algorithm and penned the final digit, the last stroke of his pen would coincide with her burping. At the time of the burp, all the red-sock wearers would align into the exact shape of her coffee spill. Unconsciously the algorithm was pushed from the mathematician's mind into a larger algorithm that controlled the movement of the people wearing red socks. There must be many hidden algorithms supporting the delicate interplay and dance of the universe; thus the mathematical complexity of the universe must be large and incomprehensible.

Even to a person flying over Manhattan at that exact moment, this shape would seem random unless they knew that this was the exact shape of Allison's coffee spill, and only then might it seem oddly coincidental. All this might be recorded in a book entitled *Totally Ridiculous Symmetrical Conjunctions of Happenings*, and this was how it was—the strange, wonderful, and surreal wonderland of her mind.

In reality no one could ever really know these connections, because people commonly existed in a finite bubble of awareness and did not see the connections in life beyond the limits of their senses. Nor did they look past what they classed as rational. People usually looked for symmetrical relationships in nature and humanity, which were obvious and easy to see; this ruled out a large chunk of the hidden asymmetric universe. People did not see the synergy in their everyday life, the web of causation that came down the line of history, and the remarkable beauty of the unremarkable that they took for granted with every breath. Every seemingly disparate thing in the universe was held together with a web of gossamer threads. Allison desperately wanted to see the web of creation shimmer in the light of her mind in a unity of unshakable connections.

———

After several minutes of staring out the café window, she drifted back to reality. She flicked to the section in the guide on Soho and Tribeca. She had wanted to visit some of the galleries in that area, so flipping to the map of the Times Square area, she worked out a possible route to the nearest subway entrance, which was not far from the café.

Near the entrance to 42nd Street Station, she stopped in front of a subway map. Her finger traced along the A train line until her finger stopped at Canal Street Station near Chinatown. She then descended into the subway tunnels, which were dusty and tortuous, and the platforms, with their connecting gangways, felt like an Escher drawing. She waited, and after a few minutes, a train came into the platform.

At Canal Street she got off and walked out of the subway via the stairway. Chinatown was a visual feast. There was a mass of gaudy trinkets, cheap computer books, strange herbs, and empty crates with rotting vegetables sporadically strewn about; Melbourne's Chinatown seemed small and clinical by comparison. She walked past several side streets before stopping in front of a fish market. Her hands felt the shock of cold as she took her hands out of her pockets to find her guidebook in her backpack. The pungent smell of dried fish was something she had not experienced before, and it was on par with the shock of the cold. She looked at the map in her book and decided to walk up Broadway. Walking along the sidewalk for a few more minutes, she passed several side streets, then turned left onto Broadway. After nine minutes, she heard a train rumble beneath her as she passed over a grilled air vent. On a street corner she noticed a thick ice sheet on a large puddle. She cracked the ice's surface with her foot and felt the pleasant vibration rise through the sole of her boot.

As she neared the heart of Soho, the shop fronts became smarter. Outside a Prada store she peered through large windows. She eventually turned around and saw a gallery on the other side of the street. She crossed over and walked up to the gallery. Its polished brass window trim framed a stark, white, halogen-lit interior; the searing whiteness of it pulled her into the gallery.

After she walked by the large color-saturated, abstract canvases at the front of the gallery, she saw a curious exhibit toward the back. She walked up to a series of small white cubes that sat atop waist-high white plinths. At first glance they appeared quite plain, but as she walked closer, she could see that a glass lens sat on the top of each cube. The lenses were roughly the size of her hand. Beneath the lens of the first cube, she peered at a small sculpture of a green-bronze lion swallowing a yellow sun. The surface of the lion had a certain rough texture to it, and on its side were seven yellow stars. Each lens gave the illusion that the lion was sitting on the top of the white cube rather than being trapped inside. As her hand reached out and touched where she expected the sculpture to be, her skin felt only the cool curved glass of the lens.

"It's fun, isn't it?" came a voice from behind her.

Startled, she jumped back. She turned to find a well-dressed man in his early fifties.

"I'm sorry . . . I didn't mean to startle you," he said.

"You own the gallery?"

"Yes. This is my place."

Allison could discern a mixed French American accent. He seemed bemused by something she could not fathom.

Allison began talking in French. "These boxes . . . they're quirky."

He responded in French. "They're optical illusions . . . but such fun, such fun."

"Yes. Initially, I had a fleeting thought that they might be holographic, but clearly they're not."

"Please continue looking. I didn't mean to interrupt you."

"Are there more animals?" she asked.

"Yes . . . and, well, no. You'll see."

The bemused expression had been fixed to his face the whole time, and he then motioned her to continue with an open hand pointing to the next cube.

She proceeded to it, but when she peered in, it contained not another animal but the same lion swallowing a sun. "It's the same."

She looked for an acknowledgment, and, after a short pause, he chuckled, which confused her as her remark did not seem that comical.

He recovered his composure. "Yes . . . and, well, no. Look again."

Peering in, and this time straining her eyes to their limit, something appeared that she had not seen before. What she had assumed was surface texture or maybe fur was not actually texture. Script emerged from the surface of the lion, which was barely legible.

Just able to make sense of it, she remarked, "It's a Middle Eastern language. I've seen script like that before. Is it from a book? Is it some kind of narrative?"

The owner walked over to the plinth. They both looked into the cube.

"Yes. It's *The Conference of the Birds*: a poetic narrative. Written on each lion is a page or extract maybe. So the artist tells me. And the green lion is an alchemical symbol. When a person on a higher spiritual plane allows the green lion to eat them, they become purified. They become spiritual gold. It's the metaphysical version of the transmutation of metals. Their soul is transmuted. And can you see the seven stars on the side of the lion? The artist told me that the stars are a reference to the seven valleys. The birds must go through them to reach the goal of their quest. The Simorgh is what they seek. It's like the Phoenix. It's the King of Birds."

She had a fleeting thought of the Seven Stars Café on the previous night and wondered if there was an odd and subtle crisscross connection.

"*The Conference of the Birds*. I've never heard of it," she said. She looked at the sculpture again. "Wow, it's amazing. It must have taken an eternity. The script . . . it's unbelievably tiny," she said.

"Yes, unbelievable and, yes, tiny. It's fun, isn't it?" He wrinkled his forehead and raised his eyebrows. "But of course, dear, everything took an eternity. It is before us . . . and behind us." He paused for a moment. "Everyone must traverse eternity," he said, then chuckled. And then his face went through the strangest transformation as it went from a smile to an expression of utter seriousness. She had seen all the wrinkles on his forehead smooth out, and she had noted his eyes, which were an unusually saturated blue. There was nothing in his expression now. It was vastly empty. An infinite horizon to walk through with no goal, no beginning, and no end. For just a moment she thought she heard him whisper, and a faint harmonic resonated above the whisper. But she was not sure if the whisper she had heard was her own dim thoughts or if perhaps his thoughts had melded with hers.

"It is before us and behind us, eternity."

She had continued to look at his mouth, and it had not moved. A fading reverberation of his words echoed through her mind, and somehow her thoughts carried that peculiar mixed accent of his, and they even seemed to exude a mental identity that was not hers.

Perplexed by the accent that permeated her thoughts, and uncomfortable with the silence that ensued, Allison was about to say something to move the conversation along, but, appearing in the periphery of her vision, a middle-aged woman left the street and entered the gallery. The owner must have heard the woman's footsteps behind him. He grinned and bowed to Allison as he backed away and spun around.

"Excuse me, my dear, have a look at the others, please, why don't you," he said over his shoulder as he walked off to greet the woman. Allison explored the remaining sculptures. All the lions had the same stance and green patina and were differentiated only by the script covering their bodies. She counted nine lions as she panned around.

Her hands were regaining feeling now after the cold wind of earlier. She looked at her watch and decided to move on and find some of the more alternative galleries in Soho. When she turned and looked for the gallery owner and the woman, they could not be seen. Both had disappeared. She felt strangely alone in the space, strangely exposed.

———

Later that day, after passing through several galleries dotted around Soho, Allison slowly made her way toward Midtown where she had arranged to meet Hooman at his work toward the end of the day. He was leaving work early today. But she ran out of time at Madison Square Park, so she took a taxi for the remaining distance and eventually got out at Bryant Park. Hooman's building was facing the park on 42nd Street. She walked through the park near the New York Public Library, and then she crossed 42nd Street until she walked through the rotating doors.

In the lobby she sat on a hard, minimalist chair and waited for him to finish work. She observed workers depart through the rotating doors. Studying the black granite flooring, she stared into the line of wear made by many years of shoes treading over the surface. Looking into the more polished sections, she noticed a dark reflection moving toward her. She lifted her head up and saw Hooman's face beaming at her.

"Hello there!" he said with brightness in his voice. "How was your day exploring the city?"

"Great, thanks. I had a good day. I really think I am going to love living here. For a while at least."

"It's good to hear that. I want to know your impressions of the city."

She got up, and they walked to the back of the lobby, where they descended the stairs to the basement parking garage. Hooman had borrowed Nava's car for the day. Once they were in the car, he drove onto 42nd Street and headed toward Downtown Manhattan via 5th Avenue.

"I thought we were going to New Jersey. Isn't that where you guys live?" she said after they had been driving for a few minutes.

"Yes, but I was talking to Nava today. We thought we would try getting some tickets to *The Lion King*. We haven't seen it but have always heard it's good, and we wanted to take you to a show."

"That's sweet, but you don't have to."

"Not your thing, eh? I told Nava you might prefer something arty. Off-Broadway, perhaps."

"Sometimes . . . but no, that's fine. I don't mind the glossy productions now and then. I meant I didn't want to trouble you guys, that's all."

"Don't worry about that. We like doing this. It gives us a chance to see things we wouldn't normally make time for. And besides, Nava and I can be your cultural guides while you are here with us."

"Well, that's fine, then. I think I might enjoy this. A bonanza of the obvious."

"It's fun, isn't it?" he said.

These words stretched out and resonated. They touched Allison gradually. "It's fun, isn't it" floated in her mind for a while more. She had heard this. The realization found her eventually. "Sorry. What did you just say?" she asked.

"I said it's fun, isn't it . . . going to these big Broadway productions."

"Oh, yes, yes, that's true." She sought to conceal her thoughts, but her dimly agitated body language filtered through her.

"What's up?"

"You just reminded me of that gallery owner. I told you about him when we were in the parking garage."

"Oh, right, the guy with the French accent."

"Yes. It's just that you said something that he said to me."

"Really. What was that?"

"You said: 'It's fun, isn't it.'"

"Oh, okay."

"But it doesn't really mean anything."

They did not talk much after this as Hooman was concentrating on navigating the rush-hour traffic. He turned onto Broadway. Allison looked up at the city buildings passing by in the beginning of the late afternoon sunlight. After twenty minutes, the car rounded a corner, and the World Trade Center came into view. Looking out the window, Allison looked at the looming towers as they reached into the sky. The upper floors disappeared into clouds, but eventually the blue sky beyond was clear when they came closer. She looked up through the gaps in the passing clouds.

"Look at that. Wow! A monument to capitalist democracy," she said.

Hooman crouched forward over the steering wheel. "Yeah, tall, aren't they? Looking up at them from their base is the best way to appreciate them properly. We come here for shopping now and then."

"Shopping?"

"In the basement, under the main towers."

"Oh, okay."

"This is where we're picking Nava up from. There's a last-minute ticket place in the lobby of the North Tower. We'll have to take you up there one day—to the top, I mean. If you liked the view on the bridge last night, there's a restaurant on the top floor you might like. The city is amazing from up there. It has a certain unreal quality from that perspective. It's like seeing the world in miniature colored dots and lines of light—an abstraction of our humanity."

"I'd like that."

"Ah! Here she is. That saves us looking for a parking spot."

Nava ran down the steps near the North Tower. She wobbled on her high heels as she came.

Waving them down from the sidewalk, she launched herself into the back seat. "Hey, sweetie, give us a hug." She leaned over the front seat, partially strangling Allison, then turned to Hooman. "Well, there were no tickets for the show tonight. Only separate seats, not three together. I'll have to try some other sources I know. What a waste. Damn."

"That's a pity. I was ready for a night out," said Hooman. He raised his forehead and continued. "Well, it's back to our place for dinner instead as we originally planned. Sorry, Allison."

"Hey, that's fine. There's plenty of time for shows. I've only been here two days now . . . there's no rush."

As they turned into a street heading back uptown, Allison looked over her shoulder. Staring at the towers, now framed by the car's rear window, she thought about their monumental style. They seemed, in a way she could not totally pin down, like two gigantic megaliths from an age long gone. The cloud front broke for a few minutes and revealed the upper floors fully.

Later that afternoon the car joined the traffic entering the Lincoln Tunnel just as the snow began to fall. Eventually, at the New Jersey end, the car drove out and passed into a small stretch of riverside suburbia.

The convergence and divergence of all aspects of America relative to her past life in Australia was still fresh in her eyes because she was still peering at New York through the lens of a cultural voyeur. On the way to Hooman and Nava's home, Allison had once more taken in the obscure detail that she presumed New Yorkers would not see as anything other than ordinary. She saw that the grubby tiles on the old tunnel walls contrasted sharply with the many clean and modern cars filing through the tunnel; it was like seeing fresh blood in old veins, she mused. New York as a world city flexed in growth, age, and continual adaptation.

They drove through New Jersey. Allison observed the riverfront with its white picket fences accompanied by simple wooden houses. Nearly all these houses were painted white. The pervading whiteness of the scene, augmented by the snowbound streets, was occasionally broken by American flags drifting around in the breeze. The reds and blues on many of these flags appeared washed out and faded from either the sun or the cycles of many seasons; roughly every fourth or fifth house had a flag.

As she continued to look out at the suburb, she saw Hooman in the periphery of her vision look over his shoulder for a moment.

"Have you noticed all the flags hanging off the fronts of the houses here?" he said.

"Yes, I have. I am looking at them now." She did not look over at him but continued to look out at the houses and the side streets, where she could see even more flags in the distance.

"Interesting, eh?" he said.

"Yes, they are interesting. I have never seen this many flags on a suburban street in Melbourne."

"All the flags here was one of the first things I noticed when I moved here. They're everywhere, but you get used to them eventually and then stop seeing them. They just sort of blend in and become just ordinary. If you know what I mean," Hooman said.

She finally looked over at Hooman, but he had looked back at the road and continued to drive. The car hit some ice on the road and lost traction for a few seconds; Allison felt the car slide sideways slightly before correcting itself. She continued to look at yet more flags as they passed by more houses.

Allison thought about a Jasper Johns painting of the American flag, which was painted using similar muted, washed-out tones; she had written an essay about the painting in an art history class that was a part of her photography certificate. At the time it seemed to her as if Johns had stripped the flag of some of its patriotism and recontextualized it as a purely artistic object.

The flags in these streets seemed that way to her now: a pattern of colors and shapes without an undercurrent of national identity, because she was still detached from American culture, an outsider, looking in with both fascination and curiosity.

Though beyond Allison's curiosity, American culture was not straightforward; there were many incompatible elements within the American Dream, either implicit or explicit, like any culture, even her own. Clearly, there were winners and losers as not everyone could attain the dream; hidden inside it was a false promise: equality. In fact, it was deeper than just winners and losers. For there to be winners, there had to be losers.

Allison thought about the long struggle that African Americans and American Indians had faced to find cultural and economic equality over hundreds of years; even now that equality had not been fully realized in these two communities.

Since the early 1980s, Australia seemed to be drawing nearer to American culture, more than at any time in the past. Allison saw a blurring of distinct cultural identity between the two nations. Today, as Australia's strong socialistic past gradually disappeared, aspects of American culture, particularly laissez-faire capitalism, seeped in to fill the gaps, revealing many incongruous elements within Australian culture.

She thought about the poverty and incarceration rates within First Nations peoples across Australia that was similar to the experiences of many African Americans in America. Not that Allison had seen this growing up in Melbourne in the seventies and eighties. Her eyes had only been opened to this after she had finished high school, when she started hanging out with a more socially aware crowd of people. A colloquialism in Australia that reflected its socialist ideals was the idea of "a fair go," which was the idea of fairness to all or equal opportunity when trying to achieve success within Australian culture, be that material or social, and it paralleled aspects of the American Dream. This value was being challenged now, and even globally the gap between the poor and the wealthy was slowly widening.

And when she had taken her photographs of homeless people in Melbourne for the end-of-year exhibition, she had spent a lot of time with these dispossessed and placeless people, even sleeping on the streets for many weeks with her newfound friends; they were birds with nowhere to rest or land, always hovering above an unequal earth, hoping someone would see their humanity and lift them up, so they could escape their poverty and find a home, either metaphorically or literally.

A desert metaphor illustrated the incongruities of national identity perfectly and encapsulated both her curiosity and her disappointments within American and Australian culture. She had been on her way to Hattah-Kulkyne National Park in northern Victoria on the same day that she had left Melbourne and had stopped to take a walk into scrub that had been burned by a forest fire. She found wild honey from a beehive hidden in the hollow of a blackened tree stump and had slit her tongue on a sharp leaf that she had used to scoop the honey out of the stump; in the peculiar taste of blood mixed with honey was her personal metaphor for nation.

Issues of equality across the world were not all negative in Allison's mind; there were many positive dialogues developing in many countries across the world that addressed issues of racial and economic equality. Although, there was still much to be done that might take many generations to fix before we could be satisfied that we had reached the pinnacle of our ideals of equality both within and across national boundaries in our emerging global community.

Eventually, they passed away from the white wooden houses and entered a part of New Jersey that was dotted with high-rise apartments overlooking the Hudson River and facing the Manhattan skyline. She looked back at the houses through the back window of the car and realized that this encounter with New Jersey suburbia was the first truly resonate experience of the precise reality of American culture that she had hoped to see.

———

Allison's decision to come to America was more than just a place to finish her master's degree, which she could have easily done in Melbourne, and she had said this to Paul not long before leaving Australia. "I want to get up close and personal . . . and, anyway, it's the minutiae I want to see. That precise reality that you can never know unless you go to a place. I want to be properly immersed in American culture."

Paul responded, "But life is the same everywhere, just about. At least in Western countries, I suppose. Why do you want to go there? It's nothing special."

However, it was not only that she needed to experience the special phenomena of the place. It was far more personal, even if she would not admit it to herself. She needed a new mirror: a larger and different cultural surface on which to project her meager image.

———

The snow dwindled as the car entered the underground parking garage at Hooman and Nava's apartment complex. From the parking garage ramp, Manhattan, across the river, was visible through portholes, and Allison watched the viewpoint lower and eventually disappear as the car corkscrewed deeper into the complex.

4

A BOOK OF BIRDS

And if, by the help of the Creator, he findeth on this journey a trace of the traceless Friend, and inhaleth the fragrance of the long-lost Joseph from the heavenly herald, he shall straightway step into THE VALLEY OF LOVE *and be consumed in the fire of love. In this city the heaven of rapture is upraised, and the world-illuming sun of yearning shineth, and the fire of love is set ablaze; and when the fire of love is ablaze, it burneth to ashes the harvest of reason.*[1]

— BAHÁ'U'LLÁH, *THE SEVEN VALLEYS*

In Hooman and Nava's apartment, Allison warmed her hands in front of a wall radiator that was mounted under the window. She studied the view of the Hudson River and beyond that the Manhattan skyline. The low sun was fading and peeked through the horizon as it cast its diagonal light. Clouds spread ephemeral shadows on the water as they moved. The warm light also illuminated the buildings close to Manhattan's waterfront, and these subtle gray-red tints changed from moment to moment. It reminded her a little of the muted hues in the desert back home. The desert expressed a certain severe beauty, which the city now mirrored, as both possessed attributes paradoxically full and empty.

Allison's thoughts were broken as she heard Nava and Hooman rummaging about the kitchen.

"Can I make you a coffee or herbal tea or something cold, perhaps?" Hooman's muffled voice came through the kitchen doorway.

"Yes, please. Have you got any chamomile?"

A few moments later Hooman leaned out of the doorway. He read the tag to her. "Chamomile mixed with spiced apple. Is that okay?"

"That's fine. Thanks."

With warmth back in her blood, she left the window and the radiator and looked around. The apartment was not what she had envisaged from the little she knew of Hooman. The size of the apartment was a peculiar conundrum. It was too small for a lawyer of the stature described by Nava. He seemed to her to be a somewhat conservative person, with restrained but not inarticulate tastes, and she concluded that the apartment must have been his place originally. The interior was fairly plain, with white walls and worn parquetry wood floors, and Nava would have moved in later, adding the hard-edged designer furniture, which Allison now observed with a smile.

On the opposite wall, facing the view of Manhattan, was an entire wall of books. The stark adjoining wall hosted only a single large and colorful abstract canvas, which Allison knew must be Nava's too, as it was over-designed and not art so much as wall decoration.

At the bookshelf she began to browse through the many titles. It seemed to Allison that every genre and category of book she could think of was represented. Hooman appeared with two cups of steaming herbal tea.

"Ah, thanks," she said. He passed her a cup. "I'm just looking at your books here. You have some interesting and rare titles."

"Thanks. Yes, I haven't read half of them. My collecting outstrips my ability to read them all."

"Could I borrow some of these sometime?"

"Of course you can. No problem! Whatever you like, go for it. You might like some of the philosophy, religion, and psychology books over there." He pointed to the lower shelves at the other end of the room. "I mean, you won't find anything to help you with your master's degree. There is nothing as intense or convoluted as a university textbook, but you're most welcome nonetheless."

She made her way to the lower shelves and crouched down. Her fingers moved across the spine of each book. Methodically she read each one. From time to time she paused to blow on her tea to cool it down before taking a tentative sip. Occasionally, she voiced a title aloud, "Plato, *The Republic*," then reverting to her mumbling, she continued along the shelf, "Jung, *Dreams* . . . The Buddha, *Lankava Sutra*, Rumi, hmm." The aroma of the spiced apple and chamomile tea and the smell of the old books transported her into the world of the printed word. She contemplated the breadth of knowledge that the bookshelf held. "This is like a small bookshop, really," she commented.

He laughed. "This is not everything, either. I have boxes full in the closet and under my bed," he said.

She smiled and took another sip of her chamomile tea. As her eyes refocused on the bookshelf, they picked out the words *The Conference of the Birds*. The print on the spine was cracked, and certain letters had faded away. She put her cup down and reached out for the book. Sliding her fingers over the cover, she read the title out twice and in a quizzical tone.

"Found something that would interest you?" he asked.

"Yes, strangely, but it's weird."

"Why?"

"This is the same text that was on the lions in those optical boxes today at the gallery in Soho. Strange, huh?"

"You didn't mention they had text on them."

"It didn't seem important then. I think it was Arabic script."

"Oh no, it has to be Persian, for sure. Attar, the guy who wrote the book, was Persian."

"Do you mind if I borrow this?"

"No, go for it. My favorite part is:

"Come you lost Atoms to your Centre draw,
And be the Eternal Mirror that you saw:
Rays that have wander'd into Darkness wide
Return, and back into your Sun subside" [2]

He gulped the last dregs of tea down and went over to the table for the book he had purchased on the previous night. "I'll just find a place for this in the architecture section. Do you want any more tea?"

"No thanks, I'm fine. I might start reading this."

Allison watched Hooman place the new architecture book on the shelf and then started reading through *The Conference of the Birds*. The fibrous and yellowed pages were frail as she turned them over.

"That book is a first edition of the second English translation. Shidan, a good friend of mine, bought it for my birthday a couple of years ago."

"Oh, are you sure you want to lend this to me?"

"Yeah, sure. And it needs to be read. I haven't picked it up for ages. Anyway, it's not worth that much."

She found it strange that on the same day that she had seen the text on the sculptures in Soho the book had made its way toward her. And it puzzled Allison why this could be so significant. The story she made out, as she skimmed through the scenes, was an archetypal theme of a group of birds on a journey together: a quest. The story was not particularly remarkable, she thought. She left the bookshelf and returned to the chair in front of the window to continue reading the book. As she read, her eyes took occasional snapshots of the city.

The sun had gone now as night glided into Allison's focus, and the horizon had an orange afterglow that faded into blue. As she ate her dinner, she occasionally looked up at the city and its lights. Allison questioned them about ghormeh sabzi, which was a traditional Persian dish.

"It's a mix of lamb, dried limes, and chopped greens," Hooman answered.

She mixed it with rice and yogurt on her plate before spooning the mixture into her mouth and muffling a response. "Wow, this is so tasty. Do you guys have it often?"

Nava burst out, "Are you kidding? This kind of cooking requires a woman at home with plenty of spare time and no career prospects. Feminists don't make ghormeh sabzi."

Allison laughed.

"We eat takeout a lot," Hooman added quietly.

"But you are privileged, though. Hooman did most of the preparation last night, after we got back from the café. He was up late."

"It was an excuse, having you around, to do something special," he said, smiling at Allison. "I was going to make kebabs, but I thought this would be better."

"Thanks, Hooman, I do feel privileged. It was nice of you to go to so much trouble." She leaned over and patted him on the arm. "Thanks, mate," she said with an exaggerated Australian accent.

Allison thought he seemed a little self-conscious with her attention. Half expecting some nominally self-deprecating line, she was surprised when he said nothing in reply; instead, he smiled and shrugged.

"You would make a good partner, you know. What do you think, Nava?"

"Uh huh, definitely. He's a better cook than I am. That is, if he makes an effort and goes out and finds someone."

Allison saw immediately where the topic was leading. She remembered a series of conversations about Hooman at Jasper Coffee in Melbourne many years before. It was in 1992, from memory. The three friends would occasionally go there after Jasper's lectures at the University of Melbourne. The owner of Jasper Coffee was Wells Trenfield, Jasper's father, and Wells had named the business after his son, Jasper. Allison could feel sympathy for Hooman welling up as she recalled a long conversation about Hooman knocking back several women over the years. Jasper had said to Nava, "Look, Nava, it is Hooman's life. Leave him in peace. It is better that he takes his time to find the right person, or no person at all, if he feels that that is his destiny."

Back in the present, while savoring Hooman's Persian lamb dish, Allison could sense that Hooman's eyes were upon her.

"What about you, Allison? Have you ever found anyone you wanted to spend this brief life with?" Hooman said.

"There were a few guys that I thought might be life partners, but they cleared off when things became difficult, or when I dashed their rather limited idea of a relationship. And I could never picture the future with just one person. The future seems too uncertain a thing to spend an entire life with just one person."

"The future is uncertain for us all, yes. But isn't that half the *fun* of it? Not knowing what will come next. Wouldn't you want to spend a life with someone and find out together what that future could be?"

The word "fun" in Hooman's words resonated in Allison's thoughts again and with the same tone that the gallery owner had used earlier in the day. "Fun" now carried another connotation, which somehow meant that the future was a comic cipher. Life could then be mysterious and beautiful but also ridiculously funny in the darkest possible fashion as it bled into eternity. This was her conclusion, and her thoughts flowed back to the conversation in the present again as Hooman waited for a response from her.

"I suppose, on the positive side, even though none of my relationships ever worked out in the long term, I figured out that love is not the feeling of being loved or being attracted to another person as much as it is mutual self-sacrifice. Relationships break down when one person doesn't want to sacrifice something of themselves anymore. I'm not saying I can commit to that sacrifice myself; I just recognize what is needed."

"That's an interesting idea," Hooman said.

Nava raised her voice. "Can you believe it? He is looking for someone to spend eternity with. He's always banging on about going through 'all the worlds of God.'" She rolled her eyes and shook her head. "Can you imagine what an advert in a singles column would sound like? 'Looking for someone who is willing to travel throughout infinite spiritual dimensions. Must have active imagination. Must be spiritual.'"

He scrunched up his face. "Well, Nava is making fun of me now, but that is essentially true. I won't deny it."

"My god! Who would ever answer that ad? Hooman. Really!" continued Nava.

"Some qualities of compassion and kindness would be good too, not superficially happy-go-lucky, but a person able to take the vicissitudes of life with grace. That would do."

"And that basically rules out a large chunk of perfectly reasonable girls. And, Hooman, you're not as spiritual as you believe you are."

Allison smiled as she put her chin in her hands and leaned on the table. She looked between Hooman and Nava.

"Nava, you're right. I am not exceptionally gifted in the spirituality department, but so what? I aspire to it. That's all anyone can expect! If a partner is more spiritual than me, then great."

Allison chuckled but perceived Hooman was being unfairly browbeaten. She tried to defend him a little. "Look, I think there is nothing basically wrong with that, Nava. If that is what he wants, then leave him be."

"Finally, support. Thank you. You see?" he appealed to Nava.

She sighed and shook her head. After a short silence, Nava began rubbing her temples. "He's ridiculous! I've been watching him for years as girls throw themselves at him like the surf onto rocks. He's completely unmoved."

Allison perceived that this conversation had expressed a fundamental part of Nava's being. "It's my duty, as a sister, to help find him a partner, but he's always so unwilling." That slice of conversation from 1992 at Jasper Coffee popped into Allison's head. At the time she thought Nava was being a bit meddlesome in the life of her brother but had not said anything to the contrary because it seemed like one of those intractable issues.

Allison took her last spoonful of the lamb dish and, in a diversionary tactic, pointed out the window. The clouds that had obscured the city during dinner had moved on. There were now only fragments floating in the night sky. "Look, you can see the city clearly now."

The others followed the direction of Allison's pointing hand.

"Yes . . . it's great . . . I knew you would like it. I never tire of it. Do you want to go onto the balcony for a better look? It won't last long. The clouds will be back soon," Hooman said.

"Yes, please." As they stood up, Allison glanced at Nava. "Are you coming too?"

Still dimly agitated with the unresolved conversation, Nava replied in quiet resignation. "No, it's too cold. I see it every night." Diverting her gaze, she began clearing the dishes.

"I'll just get our jackets and gloves," he said.

On the balcony a blanket of snow covered most surfaces.

"Thanks for the exit to the conversation in there." Hooman smiled.

"That's okay." Allison smiled back.

She looked down at her feet and then began to walk in slow and deliberately even steps, trying, as she did on her first night in New York, to make a perfect circle in the snow. Taking a glove off and crouching down, she patted the crunchy snow inside the circle. Scooping several handfuls from the center, she made a snowball. Looking up at him, she tried not to smile but felt her cheeks holding a perceptible grin.

Searching his face as she stood up, she discerned that he had preempted the shape of her thoughts. "You don't mind, then?" she asked.

"No, be my guest."

"This is my first ever snowball fight . . . well, not really, but I want to pretend it is. I've never seen this much snow before, in suburbia, in a city like this. In Australia you have to travel to the mountains to find this amount of snow."

Allison's face changed from deep reflection to mischievous fun. "Are you ready?"

He stood still. He was a calm totem with closed eyes as the snowball hit him in the chest. He opened his eyes and looked down. "Hmm. You're a good shot. That's dead center."

"You're not going to fight back?"

"Me? No."

"Go on."

He hesitated. "No, it's okay. Maybe another time."

"Okay . . . but you're being a party pooper, you know that?"

"Well . . . anyway, we came out for the view." He brushed himself down, smiled, and leaned on the railings.

"Yes, we did, but you have to promise to get me back another time; otherwise, I'll feel guilty." Allison joined him at the railings.

They gazed out over the river and beyond that to Manhattan.

"Okay, I promise. I'll get you back some other time," he said as he stared straight ahead.

The sounds of New Jersey traffic moving along the river edge rose up to meet them, and Manhattan's muted noises, drifting across the water, mingled with the traffic noise in a delicate interplay.

They listened to these sounds for a few minutes in silence, and Allison tried to disentangle the source of each sound.

After a while she said, "I'd love to get a shot of all this. I totally forgot to use my camera today. I was just so absorbed by everything . . . though I'd definitely need a tripod in this light. I have a good one back in Australia, but it was too bulky to bring here."

"I think Nava has a tripod for her work. She got it ages ago for interior shots, and I don't think she ever opened the box. It's brand new."

"It was just a vague wish. I'm going to buy a small one for myself soon, anyway. I could do it another time," Allison said.

"Nava wouldn't mind, but it's up to you."

She thought about it for a moment. "You think so?"

"Yeah. And we can go up to the roof to take some shots, if you like."

Energized by the randomness of going to the roof, she clapped her hands. "A mini adventure . . . wow! It might be fun!"

Less than fifteen minutes later, after searching for the tripod, Hooman and Allison were standing on the roof of the apartment complex. Hooman stood with his back to Allison as he looked out at Manhattan. His hands were in his pockets and his shoulders were slightly hunched as he braced himself against the cold.

Allison set up the tripod and wondered what he was thinking. She placed the camera on the top of the tripod, and it clicked into place.

After a while she asked, "Do you want to take some shots?"

He turned to face her. "Me? I don't know anything about photography. Nothing would turn out."

"Have a go. I'll show you what to do."

He walked over to her. When he came to the camera, he looked at the dials and numbers quizzically. He then held the cable release, and his face went blank.

She smiled, and leaning over the camera, she set the focus to infinity. "Right . . . ready to go. When I give you the go-ahead, you squeeze this cable lever and hold it until I say release. We can take a series of shots at different times and see which ones work out. Oh, but before we start, I should compose the shot first."

Holding his arm and steadying herself on the icy rooftop, she crouched down and looked through the viewfinder. Making minor adjustments to the angle of the lens, she then stood up and smiled at him. "That's good. Here, hold the cable again. I'll time it."

She looked down at her watch. "I can't see the dials on my watch." She swiveled around and tried to find an angle at which indirect city light would illuminate her watch face.

"Here, use mine . . . it has an internal light." He undid the wristband and passed her his watch.

In the gloom two things were obvious about this watch: its intense shininess and its expense. The watch was made by Cartier. It was a real Cartier, and this was the first time in her life that she had seen one up close.

Standing behind him, she watched the scene, smiling internally, as he continually stared at the city and then back at the cable with a blank look on his face. She counted down time, initially at a twenty-second interval, then an interval of thirty seconds.

Between each shot she observed him gingerly winding fresh film into the frame.

"This is easier than I thought," he said after another shot.

"Yes, it is." She smiled and shook her head once he had turned back to look at the city.

Even though she had only seen a limited glimpse of his personality in the few days she had known him, she had found him interesting and still did. Allison actually knew a fair amount about Hooman already through conversations with Nava in Melbourne all those years ago. And what Nava had said about him was now revealed. He had a mix of qualities she had not seen before in a single person. She mused over the fact that he was paradoxically liberal and conservative in the same instance. But he gave off mixed signals.

"Sixty seconds . . . okay, release," she said.

He released the cable lever and continued to look out over the Hudson at Manhattan. He had the typical appearance of a lawyer, with his suits and glistening silk ties and his Cartier watch. She looked at the watch face again and counted time. The watch seemed to symbolize how far away she was from the life that Hooman led. Normally, she would be slightly repelled by someone like him. One of the mixed signals he gave off was his choice not to live at a level to which he was clearly capable of financially, and there were other incongruous elements sitting underneath the sheen of his urbane existence, like his book collection, which gave her a measure of his intellect. His interests were clearly broad and deep, and this made him compelling to her in a manner that was mostly indefinable but that she knew would become clearer as time passed.

"Two minutes. Now." As she continued to press the button for the light on his watch, she finally concluded that she liked him, and he would be a friend: a good friend.

She surveyed the hazy air on the upper part of the Hudson River. The weather was changing rapidly. A mist and a bank of heavy snow clouds moved in from the Bronx. The clouds swallowed Washington Bridge as they crossed the river toward the apartment complex. At first, small snowflakes appeared. Then gradually a barrage of larger, feather-like flakes descended. The snow cut a diagonal swath through the blackness and further obscured the city, which appeared now only as a dull glow behind a coarse veil of fabric. They took a shot of the snow engulfing the city.

Hooman turned around. "Are we finished now?" he said.

"Yeah, that'll do. Anyway, we can't see much with the snow like this." She released the camera from the tripod and then packed it into its pouch along with the cable release.

"You know, this camera reminds me of Iran when I was a child," he commented.

"Really, why?"

"I knew I'd seen this camera before. I just realized. I think one of my uncles had this exact model, a Zenit. There were a few Soviet-built goods in the country at that time. The communists tried to infuse Iran with more than just their ideology."

"That is so interesting."

"What . . . about Soviet goods in Iran?"

"No . . . I mean, what I meant was, I'm connected to your life now, through this camera. I'm a part of your history, your childhood memory. Objects always have an interesting life as they pass through time and intersect with our lives," said Allison.

"You know, I can remember taking a picture of the extended family with my uncle's help. He held the camera, as it was too heavy for me. And I pressed the button. That was in 1972. You know, mop-tops, flared jeans, and miniskirts. We were in his pomegranate grove in Southern Iran. It was one of the family's yearly reunions, just outside of Esfahan. And I gorged myself on pomegranates at dinner later on that day." Hooman smiled. "It's a nice memory."

"Sounds bizarre . . . like an Iranian version of *The Brady Bunch*. I'm not sure I'm ready for that yet."

He laughed.

Once back inside the apartment, they brushed the snow off their coats and hung them in a closet near the door. Nava had recovered most of her good humor.

"So how was it? Did you get some good shots?" Nava asked with excitement in her voice.

"I don't know. We'll see. I'll show you the results when we see each other next, but Hooman was the main camera operator."

"Really? I would have liked to have seen that. His photography skills are as good as my cooking skills. He can barely take good happy snaps."

"Well, he did okay, I think."

"It wasn't so hard," he said.

Nava grinned. "Yeah, whatever."

She shot Allison a knowing glance, which she didn't attempt to hide from Hooman. She kissed the air in his direction and smiled.

"Hey, can I use your computer?" asked Allison. "I assume you guys have internet. I want to send an email to my brother and let him know I've landed."

"Yeah, my laptop is in the spare room. I'll show you, and then I'll make hot chocolate for us all, shall I?" he said.

After showing Allison the spare room, Hooman walked into the kitchen.

Nava spoke to him in Persian. "You look happy. So, what do you think?"

"Of Allison, you mean? From what I can tell, she is very perceptive, quite unconventional, in a way that is interesting."

"Cute, eh?" He knew immediately that Nava intended to fish ever so non-subtly. He smiled at her in his mind.

"Yes, nice. Don't speak in Persian, please. Speak English. You know I don't like it. Especially with guests around."

"She would make a good friend, I think," Nava continued in Persian. She smiled.

"Yes, but I guess I don't know her well enough yet. You can't presume, Nava," Hooman responded in English.

"Yes, but I know her, and she is worth getting to know, believe me."

Looking at her sideways, he smiled affirmatively, despite his vaguely cynical thoughts, because firstly he did not want to crush her enthusiasm, but also he sensed an assenting possibility. Nava was not a hugely competent judge of character, and she had said this many times before and had proven to be universally wrong. Now, by sheer chance, she might be right, and he thought about chance meetings and Allison coming through JFK after he had bought the new book with Terminal 5 on the cover. But then she had not flown into that terminal. Terminal 7 was the one that she had mentioned coming through, so it was probably nothing. He had a thought of the Seven Stars Café, and the number seven resonated in his mind.

Reverting to English, Nava asked, "What's up, Hooman? You've gone all quiet. What happened to the hot chocolate?"

Standing in front of three empty cups for some time, he saw what he should be doing and opened the cupboard in search of chocolate powder.

———

Allison decided to go back to her hotel that night and suppressed any attempts to insist she stay the night. And she refused a ride in Nava's car. She decided to catch the bus back to Manhattan. Hooman then offered to ride on the bus with her, but she said no to this also. They had just put their jackets and gloves on. He had just managed to wear her down to being escorted to the bus stop in front of the building when, in mid-conversation, she spun around and walked out of the apartment. He stood with half a word in his mouth and was befuddled for a moment by her abrupt departure. He noticed himself staring straight at the book she was going to borrow but had now left behind. It sat alone on the dining table.

Running down the corridor in a way that made him feel moderately indecorous, he managed to slip the book through the closing gap in the elevator doors. She was vigorously thrashing the button that closed the door.

"Thanks," she said and ripped the book from his hand. She laughed as she hit the button again one last time, but he was already halfway through the door.

"Hey, hey! Stop trying to leave without me."

They reached the first floor, and as they exited the building through the lobby doors, they walked into a rush of cold air. The snow on the path crunched under their shoes as they moved to the edge of the road. Hooman stopped and pointed at the bus stop, which was under a slightly orange streetlamp on the other side of the road.

He cautioned her about the black ice on the edge of the road. "It's very slippery. You can't always see it in this light. The salting of the road doesn't always cover it all."

She ignored his advice and crossed the road in a diagonal line.

"God . . . stubborn," he muttered quietly with muted frustration. A feeling of playful annoyance transformed itself into an uncharacteristic impulse. He watched himself, with calm detachment, as he leaned down and padded together a snowball. Just as she had crossed over to the other side of the road, it landed in the back of her head.

The shock of the blow and the ice on the road propelled her to stumble forward onto her knees. One of her hands sunk deep into icy slush in the gutter, and the book skidded along the road over the black ice. It stopped six feet away from her, just on the edge of the slush.

"Oh my god!"

He ran over to her, slipping as he went. When he reached her, she had pulled her hand out of the gutter and was sitting on her knees laughing. He stopped behind her and helped her to stand upright. She turned to him, smiling.

"Oh god! I'm really sorry. Are you okay?" And he brushed the snow from her hair.

But she laughed again. "You really keep your promises, don't you? I knew you would get me back eventually, but I never thought it would be tonight."

"I don't know what I was doing. Sorry."

"No. You're feistier than I thought, Hooman. It's a good thing."

She looked down at her wet knees and gloves. Turning her hands over, she smiled.

He took his gloves off and offered them to her. "I'm really sorry. You have these."

"Don't sweat it. Here . . ." She took her wet gloves off and passed them to him. They were the gloves he had lent her earlier in the night. "They're yours anyway. I'll buy some tomorrow. I saw a little hat and glove stall this morning on the corner of 72nd and Amsterdam Avenue."

He pushed his gloves at her again, but she pushed them away. Leaning up, she put both her hands on his shoulders and kissed him on the cheek. "I've gotta go now. The bus is here," she said.

He turned and saw it coming down the street toward the stop.

"Oh, I almost forgot," she said.

She took a few steps and picked up *The Conference of the Birds* from the road.

Stepping up through the bus door, she stopped on the first step and turned. She waved with a sweet smile. It penetrated him in a subtle way. She turned again and continued up the stairs as the door closed behind her.

As the bus moved off, she opened a window, shouting, "Hey! It's my turn next to get you back!"

He tried to think of something remotely interesting to say, but nothing arrived in that moment. He felt unsophisticated. It was a sensation almost forgotten from his teenage years that washed over him. Continuing to wave self-consciously, he watched the bus becoming smaller as it drove farther along the main road in suburban New Jersey, and he listened to the engine whining occasionally when the bus lost traction on the ice. Eventually the bus faded into the darkness.

5

THE HARLEM APARTMENT

Wherefore, O friend, renounce thy self, that thou mayest find the Peerless One; and soar beyond this mortal world, that thou mayest find thy nest in the abode of heaven. Be as naught, if thou wouldst kindle the fire of being and be fit for the pathway of love. . . . Wherefore must the veils of the satanic self be burned away in the fire of love, that the spirit may be cleansed and refined, and thus may apprehend the station of Him but for Whom the world would not have been created [1].[2]

— BAHÁ'U'LLÁH, *THE SEVEN VALLEYS*

Ten days passed, and it was Christmas Eve. Allison's birthday was on the 19th. It passed without her mentioning it to anyone. She did not want to make a fuss. She was twenty-six.

In broad, arching sweeps Allison cleaned the walls of her room with a large sponge. Steam from a bucket of warm water drifted toward the ceiling. A myriad of small water spheres were caught, released, and frozen again in a series of snapshot stills that her mind carved in imagined time. Dan, one of her new roommates, had lent her his CD player, and one of his compilation CDs was playing in the background.

She pressed her cheek flat against the wall. Her eyes searched for a well-placed shadow to provide a stronger contrast for the drifting steam. She shuffled on her knees, moving closer to the window. Her movement disturbed the dust on the floor. A swirl of dust angels joined the warm air rising from the bucket. Allison plunged the sponge into the bucket and continued to clean the wall.

Occasionally, she rested her arms and stared at the wall, which was now a clearer pitch of white.

———

The room had been described on a small scrap of paper in the window of a café close to the university.

Room available in an apartment in Harlem, near Morningside Park on West 116th Street. Share with other Columbia students. We are a friendly bunch of people, looking for a happy-go-lucky person to complete our group. Rent includes bills. $220 per week. Call Dan. Phone: 212 221 8894.

She knew that "happy-go-lucky" did not describe her, but few, if any, advertisements would ask for an "intense" or "serious-minded" person. She thought that it sounded like she would be sharing with lots of Nava types, and she thought that would work for her.

When she first saw the room, it was bare except for a single mattress on the floor. It was obvious that this had been a student apartment for some time. Most of the furniture was falling apart, an assorted accumulation of several disjoined styles. She said, "Yes, I'll take it," and moved in four days later.

Allison realized on the day after moving in that the other roommate, Maddy, whom she had not met during the interview, was even more serious than her. So, in the end, she knew that relative to Maddy she was actually quite happy-go-lucky.

———

While continuing to scrub the walls, the word "dust" emerged from her thoughts. The song "Into Dust" by Mazzy Star began to play on Dan's CD player. In her mind she began to repeat the word once more, but the word did not end in the normal way. It dissolved before the last two letters could be completed, and she could taste a faint but tangible sensation of dust in her mouth. As this strange sensation left, an associated childhood memory arose in its place.

———

She saw her mother and father in the front seat of the family car. The family was traveling through Northern Queensland on their way to Cairns. Allison was twelve years old at the time. It was 1984. The sun was streaming into the interior of the car, and there was absolute blue above them. Allison looked over the contours of Paul's face in the intense light. He was asleep in the back seat with his head resting in her lap. Sitting in the front seat, her mother had leaned over and prodded Paul from sleep. He got up. Their mother then directed the kids to look out the windows at a pineapple farm that they were passing. Allison looked at a huge fiberglass pineapple on the farm, which was an attraction for tourists. Her mother had then pointed out the color of the earth; it was a rich red, like blood, amongst the ordered rows of forming pineapples.

———

Allison was puzzled by the memory, and why it should be associated through taste with the word "dust." After a few moments of staring at the wall, the remaining part of that memory came to her.

———

She had dreamed of the farm while she was asleep on the previous night, and particularly the large fiberglass pineapple, so what she saw from the car was almost exactly what she had seen in her dream.

"Mum, I saw this farm in a dream. I saw this farm, Mum."

But her mother had not taken any notice. "Look kids, more farms. Bananas now," she said to the kids as they passed another farm.

———

Another memory came of a time many years later. She was nineteen then, and her mother's coffin was being lowered into the ground shortly after her death on December 9, 1992. The priest expressed the familiar words: "ashes to ashes, dust to dust." The color of the earth was a similar shade of red to that of the pineapple farm. She now understood the connection to "dust," which had come from the priest's words, and now she added the word "fruit" to the associations in her memory. In the cemetery the fruit of the human temple was laid in ordered rows in the red earth, and from those seeds something new would grow and form in a new world: a world unseen but tangible in our imagination.

The rain had fallen earlier in the day, and the mound of earth near the burial hole was sodden, so the earth had stained her hand as she threw it onto the coffin. After everyone else left, she stood next to Paul at the base of the hole. Neither she nor Paul had cried when everyone was around them, but now she allowed herself to weep. It began to rain again, and, from under the umbrella that Paul held, she stretched her hand out. The rain fell into her palm. The earth that had stained her hand was then wet enough for it to run and "bleed" red dust.

———

Allison had forgotten, until now, the dream in her childhood that had allowed her to see into the future and link the metaphor of fruit and death. Like the dust in her mouth, this was not the first time she had uttered a word in her mind and a physical sensation of its attributes had taken over her awareness. In the years before she had left for New York, the same kind of forceful memory had overtaken her mind. As much as she had tried to divert her thoughts from the implications of all her memories, an emotion, disturbing and unknown, rose up in her. The emotion was a fear of something hidden from her conscious mind but obvious in its subtle manipulation of her thoughts and feelings. The shape of her mind had an uncharacteristic pattern. This change in the structure of her mind had formed slowly over several years and was now clearer than ever. Something or someone was interfering with her mind. The word "dust" had come into her mind from nowhere, and she had not been thinking about dust or anything associated with that word. Why and how had it just arisen

67

with no obvious cause? Words and thoughts, disconnected from her conscious will, rose up and shook her mind's encapsulated identity. She allowed herself to think this far but then began to suppress any conclusion.

After a while she realized that she had been sitting on her knees, staring into space. The song "Into Dust" finished, and she leaned over and pressed the stop button on the CD player. She immersed the sponge in the water and watched the diminishing steam snaking around her arm. She observed it as it blew off course. The wind had picked up, and a gust of cold air was blowing from a slight gap in the window. She felt the cold air on her face, so she got up and walked over to the window to shut it. She looked at the snow gathered on cars on the street below and then at Morningside Park, which was at the end of the street. The snow covered the lawn area, the paths, and the hill on the far side of the park. She shut the window and returned to the bucket to finish cleaning the walls.

Two hours later, once the walls were mostly dried, Allison pinned up a few movie posters. She had been shopping during the week for a few secondhand items to fill the room and give it some character: posters, a large mirror, and a few old books. She had found a copy of Dante's *Divine Comedy*. Was it a comic cipher? she wondered.

The wooden frame on the mirror had been sanded back, and she had a small corner section to finish, so she moved it out of her room toward the fire escape to avoid getting dust in her room. The phone rang. She had just managed to slide the mirror halfway through the window onto the fire escape.

Nava almost shouted down the line. "Hey, you, how about we catch up tonight? How's the new apartment going?"

"Good. Good. I've been cleaning my room today, but we can't catch up tonight. I said I would go to a Christmas Eve party. My new room-mate is going. But actually, you could come too, I think. If you want to come, I'll ask Maddy. I don't think she'll mind."

"Totally! I'm there," Nava said.

"Great. What about Hooman? Do you think he'd like to come?"

"Yeah, sure. I think he's okay to come. He's a bit tired from his trip to Europe. He got back last night."

"What was he doing in Europe?"

"A conference or something. He mentioned delivering a paper on globalization or something like that. God knows."

"Sounds interesting. Oh! By the way, do you have anything black you can wear? Anything with overtones of Morticia Addams will do. And you better tell Hooman as well. He should be fine in a black suit. I don't suppose he has a black tie?"

"No, I don't think so. Anyway, this sounds interesting. Is it a goth party?"

"Yes. Maddy was a bit sparse on the details, but I'm assuming it's a goth gathering of some description. I went shopping a few days ago for some secondhand black clothes."

By the time Nava and Hooman arrived at her new apartment, Allison was dressed like a goth and was out on the fire escape sanding the last section of the mirror frame. The snow had fallen earlier in the day, and the surrounding streets had a light blanket of snow covering them.

Allison shouted down through the iron railings as they neared the apartment. "Wait there, guys. I'll be down in a sec. The party is close by, so we can walk from here." She pulled the mirror through the window and leaned it against the living room wall.

"Maddy, we can go now," she shouted.

At the party Maddy brushed over introductions quickly and in a monotone voice. "This is Allison," then she pointed at Hooman and Nava, "and her friends."

None of Maddy's friends responded, and they all wore expressions that were blank and unrevealing. Allison quickly realized that Maddy had made a mistake in inviting them. The party was a private gathering: for the initiated only. Without further elaboration, and without introducing her own friends, Maddy turned around and walked away. She was swallowed by the swell of people in the room. Her friends were unmoved by her abrupt disappearance.

Nava was the first to speak and directed her comment to the middle of a rough circle that had formed during the introductions. "Do you guys believe in death as the final end to life?"

"That depends on who you talk to," a woman responded.

"My brother believes in many after-life dimensions," Nava added.

"Really? Many?" asked the woman with interest.

"Yes, many worlds. Are you interested in what lies beyond this life?" Hooman inquired.

"You're wrong. There's nothing when you die: just extinction, man, oblivion, nothing else. I accept that, while others deny the truth," a man said. His face was empty of emotion.

"Really? Do you like the idea of extinction?" Hooman replied.

"Yeah," the man said.

Silence ensued for a few moments.

The woman spoke again. "Don't mind him. Goths have many different ideas about death. There's no one truth about it. But what do you mean by many worlds?"

"There are five infinite worlds, including this one, the mortal world. Although they are infinite, so dividing them into five is just one way to conceptualize them," said Hooman.

Nava pulled at Allison's shoulder. "Let's go to the bathroom. Let Hooman pick this one up. Anyway, we need to put some makeup on," she whispered.

Weaving through a mass of people dancing, they found their way eventually to what looked like the bathroom door.

"Wasn't that a little mean, leaving him in the middle of that conversation, alone?" asked Allison.

Nava smirked. "He'll be fine. You watch. He is way too polite to be in any danger. He has a habit of endearing himself to almost anyone. You'll get to know him in time. You'll see what I mean. Don't worry. He'll be fine."

"Why did you mention life after death? Isn't that a bit random?"

"Hooman talks about it quite a bit. He calls the afterlife the 'worlds of God.' And, anyway, goths are fairly obsessed with death. I mean, they are always dressed in black. Isn't that a symbol of death or something?"

"That's true, I suppose."

In the bathroom, the mirror, bright and large, captured a brief snapshot of two worlds. One was their world, and the other was all the goths in the bathroom. As Allison observed everyone in the mirror, she noticed that despite their efforts to blend in, it was clear, in the omission of certain precise details, that both she and Nava were unmistakable fakes. Hooman was even more out of sync. He had come dressed in a black suit and a shimmering red tie. Nava passed her eyeliner to Allison.

Allison leaned into the mirror and began to apply black outlines to her eyes. Occasionally, she snatched glimpses of Nava applying black lipstick. She wondered about death being no more than extinction, which was a popular perception in the West: a total extinction of the body, of the senses, and of consciousness at the moment of death. But clearly some people did believe in an afterlife. And what if we could choose, as if by some fantasy, between these two options? Those who wished for death as the complete and final end would attain it. They could pass into dust, extinction, and nothingness as they had emerged from it at birth, like her father had believed. While others, wanting another life, a life beyond, could follow that line into eternity.

She remembered something her father had once told her about immortality after she had relayed a conversation to him that she had had with one of her school friends. The girl was from a Christian family, and she had elaborated on the idea of an eternity beyond this life and the immortal soul transcending the body at the moment of death.

Her father said finally, "Allison, if you get buried next to an orange tree when you die, your body is recycled. You get sucked up through the roots, and someone eats you when they pick the fruit. That is the only immortality. It's a physical immortality of matter at the atomic level. There is no eternity beyond this. And a child is made from ancient, recycled matter, from the dust of stars, so there is no ultimate death or birth, old age or youth, just changing states in matter. That and the fact that others carry a memory of you, but even this fades in time. Sorry to say that, but it's the truth."

But Allison was not sure of that truth now, and would those people who chose the option of dust and extinction as the final end really be happy? Surely not, if their consciousness could move to another dimension of existence in some altered form. An afterlife seemed like a neat solution in a way, as opposed to living forever in this world. Physical immortality, if science found a way to extend life indefinitely, would not be viable just from an ecological point of view. Space would be at a premium after a few generations, so death seemed natural, and it was right that we die, she mused. For death to be banished, birth would need to go too. Life was a fine balance of dualities that were tied into the cyclical process of change and transformation in matter and being, and these dualities could never be separated, as they were interdependent. And if we chose a segment of the timeline and called it death or birth, then it was only linguistic artifice. And if there was nothing there when we died, we should not protest. We should just merge into nothingness without complaint. We could even be happy about it as we made way for future generations. As we slipped into the void, we could go in the knowledge that someone was emerging from it to take our place.

In that light, dying had an element of selflessness: civilizations came, disappeared, and rolled over like seasons, and individual lives in that scheme were only a delicate, evanescent, and beautiful second in time.

Nava interrupted Allison's thoughts as she put her arms around Allison's waist and leaned into her.

"How are you feeling, girl? You look good. I'm sure you're fine. You look fine to me."

"Yeah. Fine, I am. No jet lag now."

"No, I mean after the operation and everything. The cancer."

"Oh, that. It's clear so far. I had another checkup before I left Australia, and it's all okay, so the doctors told me. I mean the second operation, to remove a small tumor from my left breast, was only a few months back." Allison shrugged and started applying black lipstick.

"Oh, I didn't know about the second operation . . . you didn't have chemo, did you? After the first operation?"

"No. I thought I would try alternative therapies."

"So when are you going to have a reconstruction? Of your breast."

"I'm not."

"Really, why?"

"It's fine as it is. Anyway . . . I don't want it to be a waste of effort."

"My god, don't say that. You're not going to die or anything." Nava's face partially pressed into Allison's back, and her eyes peeked over Allison's shoulder. Although others in the bathroom seemed oblivious to their conversation, Nava lowered her voice. "Really, Allison, you have to do something about it," directing her eyes at Allison's chest. "It looks unbalanced . . . it needs a companion."

"A companion?"

They both laughed.

But Allison had wondered recently why it should be so problematic.

The remaining breast was not large, and it was not that noticeable with loose clothes on, though even expressing this sentiment to Nava would be inadvisable. The loose clothes hiding her lack of a breast could be interpreted as a ploy to look normal or even desirable to men.

"Seriously, Nava. My breast doesn't need a companion, and nor do I, if that is where this is leading . . ."

"I wasn't suggesting anything. I just—"

"Yes, you were! Do you think I don't know you well enough by now? Don't kid yourself. I don't care what other people think. And I'm not going to start wearing padding in my bra either. I want to cut you off on that score too, before you suggest it."

Staring into the mirror, they were silent for a while. Nava still had her hands around Allison's waist, and she felt Nava squeeze her. She then rested her chin on Allison's shoulder and smiled.

Nava's views were bolstered with a societal undertow and were fed by the meaningless struggle with fading youth that was so prevalent in Western culture. Allison was not going to give in to a limiting idea of herself. She wanted her body to reflect an honesty about herself. Of course, Nava would never understand this, but at least Nava was fairly transparent, which made her easier to deal with. She mused, as she had many times, over the magical otherness of their friendship because Nava would accept most things in their relationship at face value. It was Nava who made their friendship work, so Allison conceded a little.

"Well, I might think about an operation in the future sometime."

Nava stood up straight. She grinned. "Anyway! I have some good news to take your mind off your impending studies. I beat the waiting list. I got tickets for . . . wait for it . . . *The Lion King* . . . finally! A client of mine knew someone in *The Lion King* production team, and they got the tickets for me. Boy, that cost me a lot, I'm telling you. Blood and money. And I hope you are going to appreciate this and not come out with some downer comment at the end of the show, some cryptic one-liner."

Allison laughed and imagined all the maneuvering Nava would have gone through to get the tickets.

"Cool. Hooman will finally get his wish," Allison said.

"What's that?"

"A fun distraction from his work. He was genuinely disappointed when we couldn't go the other week."

"He's such an idiot. He works too hard. He just needs to slow down. I don't know why he works so hard. He doesn't need to. And he's way too serious about everything. You two are dangerously serious when you start talking. You're not good for each other in that way," added Nava.

The diversion of topic that Nava had attempted to change the mood had not reached its objective entirely. The line drawn around Allison's private thoughts on mortality widened now. She continued to think about death underneath the conversation about *The Lion King*. Death stretched out to embrace her own self, and not just civilization viewed from a safe philosophical distance. Allison's own figure, as a mental object, was clear and delimited now, thanks in part to Nava's comment about her cancer and subsequent disfigurement. Allison admitted her attachment to living now. She reflected on her father's orange-tree metaphor for physical life beyond the human grave with the body's decomposition. She wanted to taste every drop from this soggy orange called life: this house of recycled star dust with its perennial wheel of birth and death.

Averting any more questions or conclusions on death, and feeling perturbed, she turned to Nava. "Maybe we better go home now. Anyway, I don't think we're supposed to be here tonight. Maddy's friends never meant for us to come, and I think we're going to find it hard to fit in. Let's get Hooman and go back to my place."

"But Allison, we just got here! This is so typical of you."

"I don't care. We can have a party of three . . . back at the apartment."

———

Opting to make coffee while the others relaxed on the couch, Nava found the kitchen. The sound of her turning the water on came through to the living room.

"Hey, Allison, it's a bit grubby in here. You need to clean," she shouted.

"Yeah, I know. I'll get around to it soon."

Allison asked Hooman, "Hey, do you want to see my new room? I've been decorating it. Actually, I might get you to help me move my mirror."

"Sure. Is this it?" He pointed to the mirror leaning against the living room wall near the back window.

Once the mirror was back in place in her room, she sat next to it on the end of her mattress. She picked up a pile of photos and began to stick them to the edge of the mirror frame with adhesive putty. He immediately recognized the pictures as the ones they had shot on the roof of his New Jersey apartment block. He crouched down and studied how each exposure time had affected the depth and contrast of black and white.

"They turned out well, eh? I like them," he said.

"Yes . . . interesting, aren't they?"

"Why didn't you use your Leica? It's a better camera, isn't it?"

"The cheaper lens in the Zenit has a softening effect on the photos it produces. If I want sharper images, I use the Leica."

"Ahh . . . okay, that makes sense. These photos do have a soft, fuzzy appearance."

He then noticed the movie posters, and raising his eyebrows, he stood up and commented on one poster in particular.

"Hitchcock, *North by Northwest*. I've seen that . . . a long time ago." Then his eyes traced around the room until he saw a pile of rusty nails sitting on newspaper in one corner of the room. "What's that?"

He walked over to the pile, and Allison got up and followed him.

"I'll show you." She scooped up a handful of nails. "This is a mental note. It's like a Post-it note, but more concrete. I found them near the bins in the alley a few days ago. What do you think it means?"

"I have no idea."

"Guess."

"Well, they're rusting. So maybe that's about getting old: decay, perhaps. I don't know. Maybe it's about time too: Chronos, the god of time," he said and smiled.

"Good! You're right on topic but take it one step further. Elaborate. Here, hold out your hand."

She put the handful of nails back on the pile and took his hand. Turning his palm up, she wiped the powdered rust onto his hand and smiled. They gazed at the rust particles on his skin for a moment.

"Is it about decay . . . and merging into an origin? Perhaps back to the earth, where the iron came from originally," Hooman said.

She clapped her hands casually. "That's it. I might have said death and change for simplicity's sake, but that's pretty much it. Death is the soil in which the new flower is born. It's a symbol that exists at every level of life. In fact, death becomes the flower, so it never was death to begin with. It's transfigured into the deathless mask, the illusion of time. Actually, I was thinking about death at the party tonight, after that conversation with Maddy's friends, about death being only extinction."

"I see. So this pile here reminds you of certain ideas connected to death and change. Certain philosophical lines of reasoning," he said thoughtfully. "That's quite a lateral thing to do," and he continued to stare at the pile of nails.

She looked at his palm. "And you know your hand, covered in this red dust, reminds me of my own hand many years ago, at my mother's funeral. And I'm reminded of a painting by Bruegel, *The Triumph of Death*," she said.

"I've never heard of that particular work, although the name Bruegel is familiar."

"Bruegel was Dutch. He lived around the 1500s."

"What is the meaning of the painting?" Hooman asked.

"In the picture, every means of deferring death is explored but to no avail, and the armies of skeletons sweep through from a hellish landscape to take all from earthly existence. It's supposed to highlight the fragility and impermanence of this life. And I think it is a moral tale about being attached to this fleeting existence over and above an eternity beyond death."

"I can see you think in ways that don't occur to everyone. It's not simple or obvious to use physical objects like this for thought associations. I've already mentioned him, but you should meet Shidan. I think he would love to chat with you. I'll introduce you sometime."

"Okay, thanks." Allison removed the oversized black male shoes she had worn to the party and placed them in the other corner of the room.

"But why go to so much trouble? Why not just write these ideas on paper?" Hooman asked.

"I do sometimes. It's just that this is more tangible than words in a certain way. Anyway, words can be distant, don't you think? Reading words is no substitute for the direct experience that words describe. Would you prefer to read the word 'ocean' or swim in the real thing? It seems to me that words are like cardboard men in a cardboard world: a signpost of reality and a placeholder of real existence."

"Yes, I see what you mean. But sometimes there are worlds in words that are hidden from the senses. Words allow the mind to rise above reality and become more abstract, to recast reality in an imaginative light, which concrete physicality doesn't allow. This comes from semiotics and the——"

Allison interrupted Hooman. "By 'semiotics' you mean . . ."

"Semiotics is the study of signs and symbols and their use or interpretation."

"That's right. I remember now."

"Signs, symbols, and words can describe the invisible principles that shape the physical universe. And there is a mental framework of spirituality beyond the physical world that exists only in words." Hooman paused for a moment, then added reflectively, "In words, there are worlds that are strange and sublime. I think this to be true." He raised his eyebrows. "Don't you think so?"

She responded after a pause. "Yes . . . yes. You're right. And actually, what occurs to me now is that words can contain symbols, metaphors, and references to concrete attributes or associated memory with lateral networks of other words inside each other. And when imagination, perceptible realities, and words collide and meld into each other, something new and unique is born. Imagine that? Wouldn't that be fabulous? To transcend the senses and live through words in a purely intellectual sphere. You're right. Words do have a unique power in the mind to transcend the senses."

———

At the end of the night, Allison went into her room and picked out two photos of Manhattan obscured by snow. She put them in Hooman's hand.

"I remember you saying you took photos when you were a kid, in Iran. Do they still exist? I'd love to see them," she said.

"Yes, I still have a few, but most of them are in a box in Perth . . . at our parents' place. But my uncles and aunts took most of them."

"The other night I was trying to imagine the sixties and seventies in Iran, as you described it to me on the roof. I liked how your experience of your childhood departed from my preconceived ideas. It seems that Iran would have been an interesting place to be in at that time."

"It was. I was born in 1967 and left for Perth with my family in December 1975. This was two and a bit years before the Iranian revolution. I'll have to search for those photos. Nava, have you seen any of our old photos?"

"No, not recently. They're in a box somewhere," Nava replied disinterestedly.

"Don't worry about it. If you come across them, then that's cool, but don't go out of your way," Allison said.

"No, it's okay. I'll have a look for them. Anyway, we'll see you soon, and I'll let you know how I got on," said Hooman.

Hooman kissed Allison on both cheeks and hugged her. Nava just hugged her.

"Nava, you give such good hugs. Thank you," said Allison.

Nava and Hooman turned and moved through the door, then descended into the stairwell.

"Hey, Hooman, do you think people can see into the future?" Allison asked.

He stopped and looked back at her. "Yes, it's possible. Not that I have ever done it, but it can happen. Why do you ask?"

"I was thinking about it today. I've never asked anyone about it before. I just thought it would be something you might believe in."

"Do you believe it's possible too?" he asked.

"Yes. I do."

"I haven't ever looked into this topic much myself. I might try and read up on it in the meantime. I have a few books lying around somewhere that might shed some light on it."

She leaned over the balustrade and waved as they descended farther into the stairwell and disappeared. Momentary glimpses of Hooman's hand were visible as he spun around the rectangular spiral of the stairwell. Eventually, he vanished as they reached the lobby, and a few vague echoes of Nava and Hooman's indiscernible conversation merged with the street sounds. She watched the empty stairwell for a while before going back through the front door.

The apartment was too empty now, and her bare feet on the creaking wooden floors were the only sound. She picked up the empty coffee mugs and took them to the kitchen. As she watched herself wash the mugs in the sink, a part of her wished they had taken her home with them. Another part of her fought this feeling adamantly. Maddy would probably not appear again until late, and her other roommate, Dan, was out with his girlfriend. She was happy to have the place to herself, and she did not feel like socializing anymore that night.

After a quick shower, she sat cross-legged and naked in front of the mirror. Staring at the photos of Manhattan for a moment, she then ran her hand over the smooth texture of the wooden frame. Working backward through time, she arrived at the conversation with Nava at the party. She traced the line of the scar where her breast used to be. She noted its subtle undulations. Her hand had traveled diagonally from under her right arm toward the base of her remaining breast.

Although she may have said to Nava that she accepted her body as it was, she felt diminished by her body image: the grief of losing part of her physical being. She did not think her scar was unattractive. But others would, particularly men, and this relinquished barrier that protected her ego cut a way into her. Water welled in her eyes as her stark outline in the mirror softened, blurred, and abstracted into shifting, fluid shapes and forms, a result of her reflection passing through her tears. A price for being altered must be paid, and, as for death, she did hope for something after it, even if it was no more than a wishful dream. As she looked again at the reflection of her face in the mirror, a memory from many years before arrived in her mind.

———

She had been sitting alone in her Holden after having only just arrived at Hattah-Kulkyne National Park on December 27, 1992, when she was twenty years old. She stared at the desert dunes in the evening light and observed the many tufts of grass being pushed around by the wind. Her memories returned to an earlier time.

As a sixteen-year-old, she had come to this desert as part of a school excursion in 1989. Some heavy metal was playing on the radio in the school bus. She was alone in the bus, sitting in the driver's seat. She turned the dial, and there was some arts program on about some obscure Australian poet, and she remembered a line in one of the poems: "The beauty we behold in life is equal to the pain we relinquish."

———

In the present she dwelled on the memory of the phrase in the poem about relinquished pain.

6

THE ICE RINK AND THE CHRISTMAS TREE

And if, confirmed by the Creator, the lover escapeth the claws of the eagle of love, he will enter THE REALM OF KNOWLEDGE *and come out of doubt into certitude, and turn from the darkness of wayward desire to the guiding light of the fear of God. His inner eye will open and he will privily converse with his Beloved; he will unlock the gates of truth and supplication and shut the doors of idle fancy.*[1]

— BAHÁ'U'LLÁH, *THE SEVEN VALLEYS*

On a Saturday morning after New Year's Day 1999, Allison was sitting on the fire escape applying the last coat of clear varnish to her mirror frame. She had spent New Year's Eve in Times Square with Hooman and Nava. She was tired today and anticipated that going to see *The Lion King* would be difficult and not the entertainment that Nava had promised.

All her submerged insecurities were floating upward and were buoyant with an undercurrent of depression. She felt both a need for some company but also a need to be alone. These two conflicting needs oscillated back and forth in her mind. She could not say why she felt depressed exactly. But as she thought about it more, Paul entered her thoughts. She missed him. Her life in Australia was at a distance, and she concluded that there was an element of homesickness to her mood.

She put the brush down and picked up a cup of coffee. She took a sip. After a few minutes of looking at people milling down the street, she got up and moved the mirror to the window. She put a few sheets of newspaper on the floor in the living room and pulled the mirror through the window, then leaned it against the wall to dry.

Dan and Maddy had left the apartment earlier and were going about their lives in ways only vaguely imagined by Allison. She put her coffee on the side table and sat on the couch, trying to reread the last few pages of *The Conference of the Birds*.

Because of the poetic and condensed structure of the text, it had been hard to penetrate the meaning of the poem, which was why she had to keep rereading sections, but eventually what she was able to make out was that thirty birds, those left at the end of the journey—among them the pheasant, nightingale, parrot, owl, and partridge—had been challenged to take the "Road" toward the Simorgh (God), in the form of a Phoenix; however, at the beginning, each bird had an excuse not to make the journey due to some earthly attachment, which was pure anthropomorphism, as it was clear that the birds were meant to mirror human attachment to this world and all its earthly distractions.

Eventually, the birds are convinced to make the journey by the hoopoe bird and begin a series of tests as they fly through the various valleys, seven in all, until through self-negation and the annihilation of the lower self, in the last valley, they are transformed by suffering, symbolized as the fire and ashes of the Phoenix, and they finally meet the Simorgh only to realize that they had journeyed toward themselves as they merged into the Phoenix and that they had always been the Phoenix, even when they had regarded themselves as distinctly separate at the beginning of their journey.

Not only had they been transformed, but also the earth itself was now burned to ashes and had been transformed: the death of all things. The journey was the transfiguration of the soul and this world. The very things that had stood in the way of spiritual development were also the means of growth, thus the lines:

I was the Sin that from Myself rebell'd:
I the Remorse that tow'rd Myself compell'd: [2]

The poem was an allegory, charting human identity and our hidden spiritual potential, particularly if we identify as humanity both individually and collectively (the thirty birds). Each individual identity is needed to see the whole of the image of the Phoenix, and our potential within that identity is interdependent since we all represent a different aspect of the world. She had used Dan's computer and had visited www.bahai.org and had seen the phrase: "Unity in diversity." In the poem Attar expressed this idea as drops of rain that have come from the ocean that then fall and meld back into the same ocean: Universal Main ("Main" being archaic for "ocean"). So, he expressed humanity's journey as that of the journey of water.

She read the end of the poem one more time just so she was clear on its meaning.

For such a Prayer was his—"O God, do Thou
With all my Wealth in the other World endow
My Friends: and with my Wealth in this my Foes,
Till bankrupt in thy Riches I repose!"
Then, all the Pile completed of the Pelf
Of either World—at last throw on Thyself,
And with the torch of Self-negation fire;
And ever as the Flames rise high and higher,
With Cries of agonizing Glory still
All of that Self burn up that burn up will,
Leaving the Phoenix that no Fire can slay
To spring from its own Ashes kindled—nay,
Itself an inextinguishable Spark
Of Being, now beneath Earth-ashes dark,
Transcending these, at last Itself transcends
And with the One Eternal Essence blends.

. . .

Once more they ventured from the Dust to raise
Their Eyes—up to the Throne—into the Blaze,
And in the Centre of the Glory there
Beheld the Figure of—Themselves—as 'twere

Transfigured—looking to Themselves, beheld
The Figure on the Throne en-miracled,
Until their Eyes themselves and That between
Did hesitate which Sëer was, which Seen;
They That, That They: Another, yet the Same:
Dividual, yet One: from whom there came
A Voice of awful Answer, scarce discern'd
From which to Aspiration whose return'd
They scarcely knew; as when some Man apart
Answers aloud the Question in his Heart—
"The Sun of my Perfection is a Glass
Wherein from Seeing into Being pass
All who, reflecting as reflected see
Themselves in Me, and Me in Them: not Me,
But all of Me that a contracted Eye
Is comprehensive of Infinity:
Nor yet Themselves: no Selves, but of The All
Fractions, from which they split and whither fall.
As Water lifted from the Deep, again
Falls back in individual Drops of Rain
Then melts into the Universal Main.
All you have been, and seen, and done, and thought,
Not You but I, have seen and been and wrought:
I was the Sin that from Myself rebell'd:
I the Remorse that tow'rd Myself compell'd:
I was the Tajidar who led the Track:
I was the little Briar that pull'd you back:
Sin and Contrition—Retribution owed,
And cancell'd—Pilgrim, Pilgrimage, and Road,
Was but Myself toward Myself: and Your
Arrival but Myself at my own Door:
Who in your Fraction of Myself behold
Myself within the Mirror Myself hold
To see Myself in, and each part of Me
That sees himself, though drown'd, shall ever see.
Come you lost Atoms to your Centre draw,
And be the Eternal Mirror that you saw:

Rays that have wander'd into Darkness wide
Return, and back into your Sun subside."—

This was the Parliament of Birds: and this
The Story of the Host who went amiss,
And of the Few that better Upshot found;
Which being now recounted, Lo, the Ground
Of Speech fails underfoot: But this to tell—
Their Road is thine—Follow—and Fare thee well.[3]

The second to last stanza was the most interesting; it said that we are birds of fire and light, or immortal sun birds, and that we must merge back into the Sun and return to our source as pure light. Since she knew that Attar must have been inspired by Islam, she searched a digital version of the Qur'án and found a quote that might have been his inspiration for the allegorical theme underlying the poem.

Indeed we belong to Allah, and indeed to Him we will return.[4]

—Qur'án 2:156

But she knew that there was a difference between Sufi and Bahá'í notions of merging into God's essence. She had done some research and found a Bahá'í website full of scholarly articles that discussed the fact that the human soul could never merge into the essence of God in any absolute way as this would be a movement from state to state, whereas 'Abdu'l-Bahá had said that the soul could only transform or evolve within its own state through an increase of spiritual perfections: virtues and the Names of God. So, the Bahá'í idea was that the soul merged into its own higher potential, or that the human soul was like a mirror that only reflected the Sun, but this did not make it the Sun, only a perfect reflection.

So, because of this, it was clear from the Bahá'í model that humanity would always need an intermediate soul to make these transitions in perfection, such as a Manifestation of God or a prophet, symbolized in the poem as the hoopoe bird.

But this whole idea of God was problematic, and she still felt that it was humanity that had created God to satisfy what she felt was a void of meaning in this world. The existentialists had always said that it was a brave soul that realizes that there is no meaning to anything in this world other than what we ascribe to it, that we must face this emptiness or nothingness without fear, that we could never escape the subjectivities of the human mind, and ultimately that there was nothing hidden within or behind reality. Being was encapsulated and complete with only a hole in reality where God might have been in the past. This hole had been made by science and secular philosophy as Christian and Islamic ideas of God had been challenged over many centuries.

And God had never revealed his reality in any way that departed from the laws of physics, other than a few miracles.

The station of prophethood in the form of a human body was clearly the schema of God throughout history; the world was then a closed unit. We were always just left with our own image no matter how hard we tried, like Sisyphus always rolling the same boulder of meaning up the hill only for it to roll back down again, and we would have made no progress toward or into the essence of God. Apart from the development of science and technology in the last century, the only transformation was internal, within the human mind. So then it was true that we could never become God anyway.

She thought about the last stanza of the poem and the eternal mirror and thought about her own mirror in the apartment and the words "And be the Eternal Mirror that you saw." This clearly meant that we should reflect God within ourselves so that when we looked into each other, then all we should see is God, or rather our higher spiritual reflection, and as she had thought before we would become immortal firebirds reflecting the Glory of the Sun.

If there was a God, then she knew she would have to think deeply about the possibility, but she had inherited some fairly fixed and maybe limiting ideas from existentialism and postmodern philosophy.

Eventually, she lost concentration and stared aimlessly at the many varied shapes inside the faded wallpaper. She then listened to the faint hum of the city outside the apartment. Her head rested on the arm of the couch as she lay down, and the book rested on her chest beneath her crossed hands. She stared at the ceiling, then closed her eyes, and at that exact moment the phone rang. She got up, putting the book on the coffee table, and walked over to the receiver near the kitchen.

Hooman sounded happy to hear her voice. She could not bring herself to mention not wanting to go out, especially because Nava had gone to so much trouble to find the tickets.

"Hey! I had a great idea just now."

She responded to his enthusiasm and hid her mood. "Yes?"

"Well, I thought we could go ice skating in Central Park today. A few hours before we see the show. What do you think? It's near the bottom of the park, near 5th Avenue. Meet us there at five o'clock."

"Okay, that sounds good," she said with as much energy as she could summon, and it was a deception that succeeded. Before she hung up, she noticed that his voice was still chirpy. He had not discovered her real mood.

In the afternoon she caught a train downtown. She spent the time trying to cheer up and drag life-affirming thoughts reluctantly from her mind. In her distraction she nearly missed her stop. She got off at Columbus Circle Station, and making her way to street level, she walked through the bottom quarter of Central Park along Central Park Driveway. Surrounding her were snowbound lawns and stark, denuded trees lining the road, and after a short walk, she turned right down a path that would lead her to the ice-skating rink.

The winter clothes she had purchased in the last couple of weeks kept her body warm, but after a long walk, she was overheated. As she neared the edge of the rink, she took her gloves off and unzipped her puffer jacket. It took a few moments to locate the other two. They were already skating on the ice. Both saw her and came to a halt on the other side of the barrier.

Hooman leaned over the barrier and kissed Allison on the cheek. "You can get skates over there." He pointed to a building near the entrance to the rink.

"I'm sorry, guys, I'm just going to watch. I don't feel up to it. Sorry, Hooman, I know you really wanted me to skate, but I didn't sleep well, and I've changed my mind now. Is that okay? Plus, there's the fact that I'm a hopeless skater. I don't feel like crashing on the ice today."

"Of course, that's fine. There are seats near the entrance." He pointed to the main building again.

"She's depressed," Nava said to Hooman. "Typical."

"It's true, Nava, but I do want to be with you guys this afternoon. I just need to think and not exert myself. If I get too tired, I won't be able to concentrate on the show later on."

"That's fine. We won't be long. Take it easy," Hooman said.

"I'll watch you skate. That's enough fun for me."

Hooman and Nava merged back into the crowd of people circling around on the ice, and Allison walked to the seating area. She brushed away a section of snow with large, sweeping arcs and then sat down, watching the others with her chin in her hands.

After five minutes, Allison saw that Hooman had stopped a couple who were walking near the rink barrier. He was talking and shaking hands with them while Nava kept skating. A dark-skinned child was sitting on her White father's shoulders. The mother was also White, and Allison assumed the child had been adopted. After several minutes, the couple and their child walked down the path that she had come along earlier. Hooman waved at the couple as they walked away and began skating again.

She mulled over some of the ideas that she had thought about earlier in the day and recalled the last section of *The Conference of the Birds*. She eventually lost track of Hooman and Nava on the ice.

She found it interesting how the birds, in their search for the Simorgh, had found their image reflected at the end of the journey. The idea of transfiguration was interesting to her: We become what we are searching for. We came to the end of the road only to see that we were already that reality when we started on our journey but had not seen who we truly were, what our true destiny was.

She thought about the idea of God in Attar's poem. Maybe a part of her did believe in God as our higher potential or being, but not the God that most people believed in; the Simorgh was just a symbol of a deeper and more expansive humanity. Her friend Jasper had said many times that God was a reality beyond any known human reality. At the time she had never really pursued this idea to its completion, but it made sense to her now. Jasper said that we anthropomorphize our own reflection onto the face of God and then disbelieve in our own limited and distorted image of God and not God's true image, reality, or being.

There was one interesting thing that came from the poem that she felt deeply connected to: the idea of the Road, with a capital *R*. She had thought immediately about her road trip through Australia alone and in emotional isolation for much of the trip. It was clear that the desert, the defining feature of her trip, was a mirror of nothingness and being. That its emptiness was actually full of that nothingness and a perfect mirror for identity: that Eternal Mirror. The Road was pure. A Road that we are always walking along, always moving through, always seeking ourselves in.

And what was even more fascinating was that Attar and Sartre were pursuing two different kinds of nothingness and different kinds of being, both with the realization that the world was empty but with different end goals. For Attar the world was empty because of its superficiality and impermanence. For Sartre it was empty of absolute meaning, beyond our subjective constructions of God and reality.

In *The Conference of the Birds* the last valley was that of poverty and annihilation; from it came a nothingness that left all the worldly attributes behind. They were burned away as the birds entered the internal spiritual worlds of being: of being with God and without this earthly world.

Attar wanted the soul to seek God, hidden in creation, and then transcend the world as it is, whereas Sartre wanted to transcend the need for God and exist without transcendence from purely intellectual and human outcomes for meaning within being and from being without any other higher reference point. Maybe Sartre was sincere in attempting to reject outmoded systems of belief in God, superstitious and limited.

In the end Attar had said: "Their Road is thine—Follow—and Fare thee well."

This meant that her Road was a road that must lead to God within the limits of her own being, and maybe, as she had thought before, the birds had realized they had always been on this road their whole life but had not known it until the end of their journey. Follow that Road and fare thee well, she thought: this was interesting and profound.

Hooman shocked her out of her reverie soon afterward. "Hey, Allison, do you want some company now?" he shouted.

She got up and walked over to meet him at the barrier.

"I don't mind either way. But you should skate. That's why we're here."

"Oh, okay, that's fine. I'll leave you be."

"Hey, I saw you talking to some people just now."

"Oh, yeah, that was Paul Nightingale and his wife, Sophie. And Alison is their daughter. I met Paul at a law conference I attended in the Netherlands this week. The conference took place in the Hague, the home of international law and arbitration. I was delivering a paper on trends in globalization and world citizenship. He liked it. It was just a coincidence that he was passing by with his family. He lives nearby in the Upper West Side somewhere. He asked me to come and work for him, but I'm not sure I want to leave my current firm."

"Conference and bird," she said slowly.

"Sorry, what did you say?"

"Today I was reading that book you gave me. Remember? *The Conference of the Birds*. You went to a conference and you met Paul Nightingale. It's a bird name and it's from the book. The nightingale attempts to reject the journey toward the Simorgh, saying that its love for the rose is sufficient. The hoopoe bird, the guide bird, then tells the nightingale that its love for the rose is a superficial attachment to this world of dust. The rose's beauty is ephemeral. It dies and fades."

"Yes, I remember that part of the book, but why is that interesting?" asked Hooman.

"It doesn't matter, really. It's just that I like to match up words, to see patterns in names and places. As you mentioned after the party on Friday, there are worlds in words. But, you know, the most interesting thing is my brother, and his partner are called Paul and Sophie. And, of course, Paul Nightingale's daughter is Alison—she has my name. Do you see the symmetry of names?"

"That is an interesting coincidence. Strange, really, now that I think about it."

Nava interrupted them as she skated past. "Come on, Allison, don't be boring. Go get some skates and join us."

"Don't feel pressured by her. You stay here, take it easy, and I'll get going and leave you alone for a bit more."

Hooman began skating slowly as he waited for Nava to circle around and catch up to him. Hooman reached out and took Nava's hand as they continued to skate.

Allison went back to the seat. Brushing away more snow, she lay down. The sky was gray-white, with clouds catching the beginning of the evening light. She thought about the strange convergence of Hooman's life and her own. Her eyes closed, and a pleasant emptiness overtook her mind where only the cold breeze on her face was present. After a few minutes of relative emptiness in her mind, she felt the weight of someone sitting on the seat next to her head. When she opened her eyes, Hooman was there, leaning back and looking straight ahead.

"Sorry to come and disturb you. I know you probably want to be alone."

"Yes and no. I think I needed company today, despite myself. I miss my brother, Paul."

"You're close, I gather?"

"Quite close, even though we are very different people."

"The other day, you asked me about seeing the future. About precognition," said Hooman.

"Yes . . . it's because I had a dream about the future when I was a kid. We were on our way to Cairns for the Christmas vacations in December . . . 1984. I was twelve at the time. It has happened a few times in my life . . . these moments of lucid daydreams or visions maybe, I can't always tell, in which fragments of the future come to me."

"That's fascinating, and I've been reading up on this. There is a theory that the soul, as opposed to the body, sits outside of time and space in an eternal world that some call Malakut. This is the world of angels. It is also known as the world of images. So the soul doesn't exist in the physical world, and it is neither in nor outside the body. Its reality is only reflected in the mortal world of time and space like an image on a mirror. Actually, the whole physical world is only a metaphoric expression of Malakut. For every reality in the physical world, there exists a counterpart, or image, of it in the spiritual worlds. In eternity the past and future are visible and more tangible, whereas here in the physical world, for the most part, we experience only the present moment without knowing what lies in the future. And the past only exists as a memory. We are bound by the reality of linear time through the limits of the senses. So, because of the nature of eternity, it is possible to see future events in the dream world. Dreams are our link to these other worlds."

"Yes, I've read things like that in the past, informally though," added Allison. "A lot of that kind of writing is labeled as crackpots spouting pseudoscience. Modern readers don't take those writers too seriously."

"Yes, but for me it rings true. The idea of an eternity beyond time is the basis of my belief in the afterlife," said Hooman seriously.

"I guessed as much." Allison closed her eyes again and noticed the noise of the many conversations on the ice. The light around Hooman and her had faded a little. As she opened her eyes, Hooman was still staring ahead at what she guessed was either Nava or the other skaters on the ice. She got up and unzipped her puffer jacket. She then tucked her legs inside it.

"My knees are getting cold now."

He looked at her and smiled. "I see you have some good cold-weather clothes now."

"Yes." She put her gloves back on and stretched her fingers out. "I still have to get you back for that snowball you threw at me the other week."

He smiled. "Yes, that's true."

The other day at the party, you said there are five spiritual worlds."

"Yes, I did."

"I'm curious. What are they?" Allison turned her head and gave her full attention to Hooman.

Hooman responded in kind, swiveling slightly as he turned to face Allison. "Well, Nasut is the physical world and is symbolized by the color red. As I mentioned before, Malakut is the angelic world, or world of images, which is green. Jabarut is the world of command and eternal spiritual laws and is yellow. Lahut is the world of the creative essence, the Word, the attributes and names of God, which is white. And lastly there is Hahut, the world of the hidden essence, which is also white."

"Are these higher worlds accessible to us?" asked Allison.

"No, these worlds are way beyond the average person. It is only the world of Malakut that we can see with any certainty, and even this can only be expressed through metaphor or simile. In fact, each world is a veil to the next world, which is higher up, in the same way that the physical world, Nasut, veils the world of Malakut. It is like the child in the womb who can never picture the physical world outside the womb until it is born. The fetus also develops the five senses and arms and legs, which it will only use after it is born. So, in the physical world we must develop our spiritual qualities, such as compassion, truthfulness, kindness, and all the others, so that we can progress in the spiritual worlds now and after death."

"That's interesting. And it makes sense. You have to practice compassion to grow in compassion, and practice kindness to become better at being kind. I can see that. So, I suppose all the worlds are interlocked and interdependent. Like the foundation of the physical world where mineral, vegetable, animal, and human are all built on top of each other."

Hooman nodded and continued. "Hahut is the invisible and inaccessible foundation for all the worlds. In fact, the relationship between the essence and the attributes is like the TV signal and the TV set." Hooman started to move his hands to help with his explanation. "We can't see the signal with our senses, but we can infer its existence because of the images we see on the TV set, though ultimately this inference is just the unseen realities in the physical world. And although it completely surrounds us, no being knows the reality of Hahut. It exists beyond any comprehension and beyond either direct or indirect experience. It is an absolute mystery." His hands stopped moving, and he was quiet for a moment. "You know, you're an interesting person," he said with brightness in his voice.

"I am?"

"Yes. When we talk, I find myself thinking about things that I like to think about but that I don't normally. It's because I don't make the time and because I usually don't have anyone to talk to who is interested or at least open to talk about these kinds of ideas. You know what I mean?"

"Yes, I know what you mean. I find that I am very much alone in my thoughts too, and I'm happy to be that person for you," said Allison.

"That's good, then. We can be a mirror to each other, but don't tell Nava," Hooman replied.

Allison laughed and then became serious. "You know, speaking about interesting things, I wonder what you think about symmetry. Not just symmetry in names but other kinds of symmetry, because I think there must be many unique mixtures of it in life. Before I met you at

Bryant Park last week, I was wondering about the relationship of diverse and typically unrelated areas in life. How they connect laterally and symmetrically."

"Like what?" Hooman asked.

"Well, imagine that the shape of a coffee spill was mirrored by the formation of many people across town wearing red socks. I mean, I know it's highly unlikely that this would happen, but it was a thought experiment." Allison was warming to her topic and became more animated.

"So, you're saying if these things lined up, that would be a kind of lateral symmetry."

"Yes. I think these things, in a very toned-down way, might happen all the time, but we don't see them because we exist in a finite bubble of awareness, which is set around the limits of our senses, and we only see the person next to us in their bubble. But I guess if we could pull back and see every person from a distance, all the dots could merge into lines of interconnection in symmetry and asymmetry, uniting diversely separated aspects of physical reality and maybe even our minds. Like the repetition of the words 'It's fun, isn't it?' you said the other day and how it aligned with the gallery owner's own words in Soho. And then you said the word 'fun' later in that day, which also resonated in my mind. And we may even have the same thought patterns as other people without knowing it. And when these two kinds of symmetries merge into each other, you then have a new overarching thing, a super-symmetry, I suppose. Does that make sense?" Allison stopped to let Hooman respond.

"I get what you are saying, but what you call super-symmetry, I call a sign of God. And although God is beyond every physical and mental attribute, His signs are there, which again point to the unknowable essence. I am reminded of *The Seven Valleys*: 'He beholdeth in illusion the secret of reality, and readeth from the attributes the riddle of the Essence.'[5] And it seems to me that like *The Conference of the Birds*, all the birds' the diverse personalities merge together to form a symmetry. And the riddle of the essence might be from this symmetry—that the reality of the souls of humankind is one of the signs of God, a symmetry of diversity. Are you following me?" Hooman stopped to let Allison respond this time.

"I see. Yes, I think I do see what you mean. I am not sure if I agree, though. The words sound lovely. I like the words you use," Allison responded.

Hooman continued. "The soul, like the essence, is an unfathomable mystery beyond all comprehension. Its core will never be discovered. So you see, it is a sign of its Creator: a reflection of His Glory, of His Mystery."

"Don't get me wrong. That's fine. I just think the term 'God' these days is historical, and it might be obsolete. But what you say is interesting to me."

"There is a way to free the historical concept of God from the past so that it is relevant to today's modern world, but that would involve many conversations over a long time. About the unity of science and religion."

"Well, convince me if you think you can," Allison replied.

Nava had come off the ice and taken her ice skates back to the hire place.

She walked toward them. "Well, I got a guy's number, but I don't think I will call him," she said. "Although he was cute."

Hooman got up. "Excuse me for a moment. I'll just take my skates back."

———

They walked toward the car down snow-covered paths that ran parallel to East Drive. After fifteen minutes, they found the car, which was parked a little way down East 60th Street.

As they had walked, Allison had looked up at all the expensive apartment blocks surrounding Central Park.

This part of Manhattan was very different from the part of Harlem she lived in, and against Nava's advice she had even explored South Bronx for a day one week before. She had got the train from 125th Street Station on Line 6 and got off at Hunts Point Avenue Station and walked north through the Foxhurst neighborhood. She then went west into Forest Houses and then south into Melrose and Mott Haven. The area had a touch of urban decay, but Allison knew, from research on the internet, that in the seventies and eighties, the urban decay was far more extreme, with all the demolished and fire-damaged buildings, bricked-up windows in houses, and the general detritus scattered around some of the streets, which had made it almost post-apocalyptic. A few people stared at her in a strange way as she walked by, and one woman even came up to her and said she should not have her camera around her neck; it would be an invitation for someone to mug her. Allison then realized how stupid it must have looked to the locals. She put the camera in her backpack for the rest of the day and only took it out to take discreet photographs. Toward the end of the day, she circled around and returned to Hunts Point in the evening. The prostitution and gang activity were obvious to Allison as she made her way through the neighborhood. She had seen a drug deal going down in a side alley as she passed by on Hunts Point Avenue. A man had passed what was either crack or heroin wrapped in aluminum foil to another man.

Having walked from the ice rink to Hooman's car, Allison and Nava sat in the back seat. Allison leaned forward and put her hand on Hooman's shoulder as he was turning the ignition over.

"The other night, on New Year's Eve, Nava told me that your law firm does a lot of consulting work for the United Nations."

"Yes, it does."

"So what was your paper about? The one you delivered in the Hague."

She leaned back and put her seat belt on.

He moved the car out of the parking spot and drove down East 60th Street. He slowed behind a buildup of traffic.

"Well, basically it focuses on the need to develop better ways to regulate global companies and nations. To make an ethical interface that balances the interconnected needs of different sectors of the global community. But it's not enough to change societal institutions alone. There is a twofold process between the spiritual and intellectual transformation of the individual and institutions. Together they have a symbiotic relationship."

"Interesting idea," Allison said. Nava just stared out of the window.

"At the moment there are many different models of economic globalization, each benefiting different sectors of society, but I think we need to expand this idea of only economic integration and develop a model with a basis in fundamental human rights. It's as the preamble to the

Universal Declaration of Human Rights suggests. The fragment I like is: 'Whereas recognition of the inherent dignity and of the equal and inalienable rights of all members of the human family is the foundation of freedom, justice and peace in the world.'"[6]

"I have never read it," Allison said.

He leaned forward and looked up at the sky for a moment, then continued. "We haven't quite understood this very simple sentence and all its implications. Let's hope the future brings us closer to its true meaning. And to achieve this, a much deeper and richer level of global unity has to take place, which will only happen when most people on the planet have a fundamental identity entrenched in global citizenship, in the spiritual oneness of the human race."

"That might take some time to eventuate. In the West we need to leave behind us the models of capitalism that we currently subscribe to. At least I think we do," added Allison.

"The current system is based on competition, which is a structure that has self-interest at its heart."

"Yes, it has a Darwinian ethic to it, doesn't it? I suppose the survival of the fittest is supposed to lead to innovation and material success."

"But really that is an old-world model with severe limitations for the future. We need cooperative structures, and cooperation is more dynamic than competition. It is a selfless model. Imagine if corporations shared knowledge and innovations rather than keeping them secret and profiting from them," Hooman said reflectively.

"Well, that's a new kind of utopia that I haven't heard about before . . . good luck with that! But really, I'm happy you are pushing such a positive model. When I used to volunteer at Friends of the Earth, I read things that I didn't like about trends in globalization. There is a good reason for anti-globalization organizations to push against some of the current trends, particularly the nefarious influence of some of the large multinational companies. Although I must admit, some of the anti-glob-alization people go about dissent in a violent way. Not all, but some, which I don't agree with. When I was in London, I took part in the May Day protests. At the time it all got a bit out of hand," Allison admitted.

As they came to the intersection of East 60th Street and 5th Avenue, she looked over Central Park. The sun had disappeared from the horizon, and she looked into the dark clouds over the city. Snow began to fall as they drove down 5th Avenue. Eventually they turned onto West 49th Street and passed by Rockefeller Plaza. At its center Allison saw a large Christmas tree lit up against a dark night sky. The tree was still up from Christmas.

Nava jumped in her seat. "Let's stop and have a look . . . can we?"

Hooman pulled up near the plaza and let the girls out. He went to find parking close by.

At the base of the tree, Allison stared at the dark sky and the skyscrapers surrounding the square. Her eyes moved around the tree and passed over the large and shiny baubles. She enjoyed watching snowflakes fall and dissolve on the tree's many lights. Nava put her arm around Allison's waist. They looked up in silence for a few minutes. Allison thought about the different colors in the baubles and wondered about the color codes of the various spiritual worlds described by Hooman at the ice rink. Maybe the worlds were like the spectrum of color in light where the colors eventually bled back into white.

Hooman approached them and stopped behind Allison. "It's pretty," he said.

"Yes, it reminds me of my childhood. Our family would go on vacations in North Queensland. Although the Christmas tree we had when I was nine wasn't as grand as this one, since we were in an RV park at the time, I still thought it was marvelous. It was the best Christmas tree I had had in my life up to that point," Allison said. Nava wandered around to the other side of the tree. She looked up as she walked.

"I was thinking about what you said before at the rink," Hooman said.

"Yes."

"Paul Nightingale."

"What about him?"

"His last name reminds me of a small section of a tablet by Bahá'u'lláh, which I say semi-regularly. It's called the *Tablet of Ahmad.* The first part of it goes: 'Lo, the Nightingale of Paradise singeth upon the twigs of the Tree of Eternity, with holy and sweet melodies, proclaiming to the sincere ones the glad tidings of the nearness of God . . .'"[7]

"Nice words, but what do they mean?"

"Bahá'u'lláh is referring to himself as the nightingale. He is the intermediary between God and humanity. His voice is singing to humanity and drawing them into paradise and eternity. He is like the hoopoe bird, guiding the other birds toward the Simorgh."

"Interesting."

"The nightingale is a bird of the night. It sings in the night, and the night is a metaphor for this time in history. It's the dark time before the dawn of a new era."

"Even more interesting."

———

Hooman had driven them on from Rockefeller Plaza and pulled into a parking garage near Times Square. On 7th Avenue they walked toward the Minskoff Theater. They crossed two intersections as they passed through Times Square. Allison looked up at the many billboards advertising every conceivable product. The windows on the cars moving through 7th Avenue reflected the multicolored advertising lights that flashed and throbbed in the night. Her body, as she looked down at her hands, was like a subtle mirror. Her skin was saturated with the light around her, which changed from moment to moment. She looked at the mirrors of other people's bodies as they passed by and thought about the nature of reflection and its illusion. And from illusion came the secrets of true reality: the mirror in her apartment, the lion sculptures in the gallery, and the baubles on the Christmas tree at Rockefeller Plaza. All these were a symbol and a metaphor of the real reflection, which was the eternal mirror of time and eternity, and the soul reflecting its image into the body, as Hooman had said at the ice rink. There must be other worlds beyond this one, she thought, where there was no illusion and all reality was peeled back to its essence.

Elliot stood outside the theater, huddled against the wind. As they approached her, she was shouting into her cell phone to some unknown person. In front of the entrance, Nava distributed the tickets to everyone.

"This is going to be fabulous," she said.

They found their seats in the theater. Elliot sat with Hooman, and they chatted about work matters and the highlights of the law conference in Europe.

Allison watched them interacting during the performance of *The Lion King*, and they both seemed to like the show.

Preoccupied with her thoughts, she could not concentrate on the show. She saw only fragmentary glimpses of the story's narrative, and the whole thing was just a disconnected blur of color, sound, and movement.

Later on in the night, they had found a café adjacent to Times Square, and they began to conduct a postmortem of the show. Allison could barely contribute to the conversation. She had thought again about the large red, green, yellow, and silver-white baubles on the Christmas tree at Rockefeller Plaza. Though this time she did not think of the spiritual worlds but rather of the psychological worlds in which each spherical image held a distortion of her face and body. The baubles were like mental filters in which we view life, and in which everything is tinted with a specific color, leading to a diversity of identity through culture and society. This was a feature of postmodernism. That ideas we regarded as objective were always tinged with the subjectivities of our culture and the age into which we were born and developed within. But although some cultural diversity was subjective, there had to be universal aspects of our own reality that we all shared. There must be a universal metanarrative that we could all live by, one that could overcome some of the negative aspects of metanarratives associated with specific cultures, nations, and belief systems.

Allison's thoughts returned to the book she had read earlier in the day. She borrowed a pen from Hooman and then took out a subway ticket from her pocket. On the back of the ticket, she wrote: "Allison Bird, Paul Nightingale = law conference = *The Conference of the Birds*." She put the ticket back in her pocket and stared at Hooman as he chatted to Elliot. She passed the pen back to him when he stopped talking to Elliot and looked over at her for a moment. Her mind wandered into blankness as she stared at the advertising lights and people in Times Square moving past the café.

In the end she tried not to say anything disparaging about the show.

As Nava did not have enough tickets, Shidan could not join them initially, but he came to the café after the show.

Shidan came through the door and greeted everyone in turn. Allison was the last person to be addressed.

"My dear, you must be Allison. It's an absolute pleasure to meet you. Hooman thinks you are a rare mind. Is that true?"

"Well, he might be exaggerating, but anyway, it's great to meet you."

Shidan sat next to her, and they talked exclusively for half an hour. Allison could see Hooman was right about Shidan, but it was clear that Shidan was the rare mind and not her.

As they were walking back to the car, Nava engaged Elliot and Shidan in conversation. Hooman walked with Allison.

"How is the preparation for the master's going? Is it all working out?" he asked her.

"The course is fine. I'm enrolled and have started looking at books on the reading lists of some of the coursework units. I start classes in two weeks, on January 19."

"You didn't really enjoy the show, did you? You seemed subdued and, well, distant."

"Today wasn't a good day. I'm not myself, really." Allison paused for a moment. "Actually, I wonder if we can talk about something?" she said.

"Sure."

"This is probably not the best place"—she looked toward Shidan, Nava, and Elliot, who were walking a fair way ahead of them—"and I want this to be just between us."

"Why don't we have a coffee one night this week? Toward the end of the week, if that is okay. I'll be away until Friday."

"Okay. Great, where?"

"Let me think about it, and I'll call you."

"I look forward to the surprise."

"Oh, I forgot. I have some photos to show you." Hooman reached into his jacket pocket and passed her a small stack of photos. "They're from Iran. That's me and Nava in our backyard in Tehran in March 1975. That was nine months before we left for Australia." The photo showed Hooman and Nava standing on the roof of a small shed next to a fruit tree. Nava, legs spread apart, had an apricot in her mouth and was smiling as her arms reached for the sky. Hooman looked more subdued but still happy. "We used to pick apricots. From the roof, we got the best pickings."

"Cute." Allison flipped to the next photo, which was a picture of the whole family, including what she guessed were grandparents. They were standing in front of an orchard.

"Those are pomegranate trees," Hooman said. "Do you remember that I said I took a shot on my uncle's Zenit?"

"Yes."

"This is that shot. A family reunion near Esfahan."

"Ahh . . . so this is the Iranian version of *The Brady Bunch*?"

"Yep, this is my family." Then he pointed at the clothes they were wearing. "You see, the clothing is typical seventies style. See the flared jeans and that miniskirt. This was pre-revolution, 1972. Close to six years after this picture was taken, everything changed to what you know of Iran today—Chadors and generally more conservative clothing. Clearly, the country wasn't ready for the change it encountered in the seventies. It reverted back to a more conservative version of Islamic culture. And we got out well before the whole revolution saga. As you probably know from Nava, we spent the rest of our childhood growing up in Perth."

"It is such a strange contrast between then and now. It's hard to believe it is the same country," mused Allison. "And there seems to be a distortion in the equality of women that has resulted from the revolution. I imagine men dominate women's lives now."

"You're right about that. Women carried a large portion of the burden of that society's expectations and still do."

Allison continued to flip through the remaining photos, which were mainly group family shots. Her mind returned to Hooman and Nava in their backyard picking apricots, so she flipped back to that photo and this time really pressed the image into her memory. Running through her life was a theme of fruit, which was symbolized by the orange, the pineapple, the pomegranate, and the apricot. The theme expressed the continuity of life through the seed and the cycle of birth and death.

"Thank you for showing me these. I know you a little better now," she said.

———

After camping in Hattah-Kulkyne National Park for five days in late December 1992, Allison packed up her tent and prepared for the drive southeast to Moama, this year's location for ConFest, which was an alternative lifestyle festival held every year in the Australian bush. She had been to the festival in the previous year, traveling there with people she had met at Friends of the Earth. This year she had agreed to manage the stall for Friends of the Earth for a day as she had done the year before.

She got into the car and was about to drive off when she decided to take one last look at the desert. She leaned over and took her camera from the back seat. She got out of the car and walked to the edge of the camping area. She then walked over several dunes before she found one that afforded her a good view of the surrounding desert. She looked through the viewfinder at her feet. They were partially submerged in the sand. She took the shot, then put the camera in her lap as she sat down, contemplating the expanse around her. Her mind turned to the books that Jasper had lent her, and many of the philosophical ideas that they had talked about in the previous year.

She had spent the week flicking through various existentialist books, plus a few books by Carl Jung. She had managed to get halfway through *Being and Nothingness* by Jean-Paul Sartre, and she thought that the desert was a perfect place to contemplate relative nothingness. Ultimately, she was interested in the idea of an existence with or without a God, and whether the meaning framework that underpinned consciousness was based on a template created by God or was purely from evolutionary processes like natural selection, whereby the meaning surrounding or underpinning being was subjective and self-defined.

If being came slowly from evolutionary processes, then it must have been initially a way to navigate spatial environments and manipulate physical objects through the five senses, purely to function for survival and reproductive needs, and then it must have begun to evolve higher functions, which allowed intellectual abstraction without reference to concrete reality, using creative and logic functions in the brain. The ability to build collective meaning must have come with the slow development of shared languages. And a good example of the abstraction of the physical environment is a metaphor, which is a word or phrase applied to an object or action to which it is not literally applicable. A part of our higher brain functioning was built on metaphoric and symbolic logic that would have been the foundational concepts on which religion and creation myths had needed to evolve.

These were precursors for natural philosophy and then eventually science, which discovered the true nature of causal realities in the physical world. So, in the last few hundred years, consciousness had evolved to its highest level: empirical logic. And existentialism had attempted to fill the void of meaning that science had left behind, making God obsolete. But Jasper thought that two things might be possible. Either God never existed and was constructed by human imagination to explain existence, or God did exist, but we were never able to explain God's reality sufficiently, and science was just clearing away thousands of years of historical superstition to make way for a more expansive understanding of the existence of God. And the peak of evolution was clearly consciousness itself because without that, religion, philosophy, and science would have never come into being.

Jasper had explained to her that consciousness was built from invisible conceptual frameworks that could exist within and outside of language frameworks. We used these frameworks every day as we moved through spatial environments and interacted with physical objects, and as she looked out at the dunes, she began to analyze her thoughts. She looked at the next dune in front of her and saw a tree half-buried by the next dune. She knew it was a tree without thinking about it with words in her mind. She stood up and walked down the dune face toward the tree. In fact, if we needed to use words every time we performed a physical or even mental action, our life would be one unending narrative speech. She did not say in her mind, "I am standing up. I am walking down the dune. I am touching the tree. I am plucking a leaf from its branch." Her mind just worked on the periphery of language, and she thought in formless conceptual frameworks. But we needed language to build a shared meaning of reality because we could not use telepathy to communicate directly.

She put the leaf into her pocket and turned around. She walked back over the dunes to the main camping area and got into the car. She put the leaf on the dashboard and drove off down the dirt road that eventually joined the main highway. Looking in the rearview mirror, she saw the dust kicked up by the car.

"Good bye, Hattah-Kulkyne. I will miss you," she said and smiled.

7

THE MUSEUM

He breaketh the cage of the body and the hold of the passions, and communeth with the denizens of the immortal realm. He scaleth the ladders of inner truth and hasteneth to the heaven of inner meanings. He rideth in the ark of "We will surely show them Our signs in the world and within themselves", and saileth upon the sea of "until it become plain to them that it is the truth." [1,2]

— BAHÁ'U'LLÁH, *THE SEVEN VALLEYS*

Standing in front of his apartment window, Hooman's eyes panned around the Hudson River before moving from the Manhattan docks to the Midtown skyline. He always picked out the Empire State Building and the Chrysler Building. All the other skyscrapers remained indistinct as they always did. The different light conditions and the play of light at different times of day were worn into his memory. He could almost keep time based entirely on the light reflecting off the Midtown skyline rather than his wristwatch.

————

Hooman's daily work routine was to catch a ferry from the terminal near his apartment in West New York and walk from the Manhattan terminal to his Midtown office.

After walking to the ferry through the snowbound streets of West New York, New Jersey, he got on the boat and sat near the front. If it was not taken by anyone else, he always sat in the same seat. From this position he liked to contemplate the water, the skyline, and the sway of the boat. His thoughts turned to Allison. He thought about the conversations they had had in the short time she had been in New York. He thought about what he had said to her at the ice rink: that he could talk to her about ideas related to metaphysics and religion; these were the specifics of mirroring each other. And her openness to these topics probably stemmed from her studies in philosophy. With all his other friends, there were certain limits to what he could express to them. Something in him knew that they would become good friends, and he wondered if God had arranged it all. He also wondered if she had come into his life for a particular reason that was unclear to him now but would reveal itself in the future. Because of her interest in art, Hooman thought she might like to visit MoMA, The Museum of Modern Art. He had called her from Philadelphia on the previous day, and they had arranged to meet at MoMA in the evening after work in the basement café.

––––––

Hooman paid the taxi driver and opened the door. He stepped onto the sidewalk before looking up at the night sky for a moment and then reading the sign above the entrance, The Museum of Modern Art.

He walked through its entrance doors and continued until he came to an escalator that took him down to the basement café. As he descended, he saw one person sitting alone at a table; her posture and body shape had become familiar to him now. She wore the same black clothes from the goth party a couple of weeks before. The only incongruous elements were her long brown hair and oversized brown worker boots. The boots in particular stood in isolation as they contrasted against her black-and-white striped stockings.

As he approached the table, he saw that she had one finger submerged in a glass of water. Hunched down, she tilted her finger at different angles.

"Is your finger thirsty?"

Allison looked up. "Oh, hello." She removed her finger from the glass and smiled.

"I am wondering what you are up to."

"I've developed an interest in the nature of visual distortions and optical illusions. It's a recent thing. It's my new obsession. I think it started with the green lions at the gallery in Soho. Remember?"

"Oh right. Yeah, actually I noticed the other night."

"What night? Oh, last weekend."

"You know, you seemed fascinated with those baubles on the Christmas tree at Rockefeller Plaza. I noticed you touching the baubles and staring. I was wondering what you were thinking about at that moment, and now I know."

"Right. You noticed that."

He smiled. "Yes. What is it about distortions that you like so much?"

"Well, it's not that I like them. It's more what they mean beyond the obvious, from a psychological perspective and, maybe more than that, a metaphysical viewpoint. Anyway, it is about the possibility for an object to give the illusion and projection of reality. I'm thinking of those white cube sculptures in particular where the lens makes it appear as if the sculpture is sitting on top of the cube when it is actually sitting trapped inside the cube. Glass bends light in some interesting ways, don't you think?" Changing the topic, she continued. "Shall we go see some art?"

Rising to her feet, she linked her arm into his, and they walked toward the escalator. He listened to her boots clip-clop on the floor and smiled.

They walked onto the escalator.

———

After exploring several of the collections on the first and second floors for half an hour, they eventually came to minimalism. In one of the larger rooms, Allison and Hooman faced an expansive canvas. It stretched from the floor to the ceiling, and they stood completely engulfed by the view. The painting was composed of two equal squares with two large circles, one inside each square. Allison looked at the left side, which was a black square with a white circle at its center, and on the right was a white square with a black circle.

"So, what is this painting about? Does it mean anything? Besides being a backdrop for your clothes," he said.

She laughed.

"You're right. It does go with my goth clothing. But as for meaning, I think it represents the division of perfection from one into two, the beginning of duality, of opposites. And it does this with a combination of symmetry and asymmetry. The two squares and circles are symmetrical, but the difference between the shades of black and white are asymmetrical."

"I would see this as being the black ink of words and the white of paper. These two circles look like two rather large periods."

Facing him, she raised her hand in a vertical line from her chin to her forehead. "So, take my face for instance. I want to talk about beauty and bilateral symmetry. My face is symmetrical in one way, okay? Because my facial features are equal from ear to ear. So, we have perfect symmetry, right?"

"Not exactly."

"Huh! We don't?"

"No, you have more freckles on your left cheek. You're not in perfect symmetry."

She smiled and ignored his comment. "Right . . . so from the top of my face to the bottom, from my forehead to my chin, my face is asymmetrical. You see. Otherwise, I might have lips on my forehead and likewise a chin where my forehead should be. It may be considered ugly by some."

"Very ugly, indeed. I like your face as it is."

"So do I. But let me finish. So, unless the human face has both symmetries in balance, beauty is not there. It combines both dual symmetric and asymmetric elements at the same time, creating a oneness between the two. That is the face."

"That's interesting," said Hooman. "So art is considered beautiful when it has these elements in balance, but there is also fluidity between everything because of relativity and context. It's the same in literature too, really. That side I know more. I never studied visual aesthetics much. But this conversation is great."

"There are many elements in art, but I suppose even color, shape, texture, concept, and many others conform to this basic template of a combined symmetric and asymmetric aesthetic," said Allison. "Hey, can we sit down?" She smiled. "My legs are getting tired."

They sat on a bench at the back of the room and continued talking.

Hooman spoke first. "Forms are all one at their root, I suppose."

"Yes, Plato talks about it in his writings. They are the perfect forms. He thought that this material world is a world of shadows, feeble approximations of the real ideal perfections that are eternal and changeless. They apparently transcend temporal and spatial dimension. And ideas are forms, basic templates, on which all physical and ethical objects are based. They are the physical, intellectual, and moral forms. He called the highest perfect form 'The Good,' which is the root form on which all others are based. You could appreciate that idea, I expect. Have you read Plato?"

"Yes, I have, and you know in a way he meant God by using the word 'Good.' You just need to remove an *o*. Plato said 'The Good' was the absolute measure of justice. And the world of ideas was in essence the next world, I think, an invisible empyrean—the highest and most pure heaven. Like I said the other day, the whole of the physical world, Nasut, is a metaphor for the next world, Malakut, and all forms in the physical world have their counterparts in the world of Malakut. The templates for all reality are the five interlocking worlds of God, where the essence and attributes are expressed like Russian dolls. An attribute on one level is an essence on the next level down. Of course, the worlds of God are infinite and countless in their range, and dividing the worlds of God into five tiers is based on the older Sufi traditions."

"That's interesting," said Allison. "I always wondered why, near the end of *The Republic*, Plato is talking about morality and truth and then presents this apparently random story about Er—the soldier who visited the Elysian Fields and Hades, then awoke from death while the wood was burning on his pyre. Plato obviously meant to connect 'The Good' with the afterlife. I suppose he wanted to connect justice with deeds and rewards and punishments with the afterlife. But I tend to think that ideas come from the physical world first, as we see them in nature, and are then manipulated in the mind, then regurgitated back into the phys-ical world as tangible objects or abstract scientific discoveries."

"That's true up to a point," said Hooman, "but I think there are objective truths that exist independent of time and the external world.

There is much beyond what the senses perceive directly. The mind allows us to see the invisible principles that shape the universe. The universe is inside us, in our minds. Look at the other artworks or nature itself." He swept his arm across the room. "These are all just mirrors, and what you see in them is yourself, an objective self, because we both know you exist." He put his hand on her shoulder. "That's an indisputable fact, a truth, but there's also a subjective self, in the sense that you can't entirely transcend the limits set around your finite individual perception. You can't move beyond the personal filters through which you view the world and interpret it. These are prone to untruth, or perhaps fractional truths that approach greater objectivity over time. It's like the distortions in the glass of water you were observing before. The senses and mind can deceive us since we see distortions in the glass and not the true form of an object that is projected through it. It's the truth of the water and glass but not the truth of the object that is the source of the reflection. This is why interpreting art, and indeed reality can be so subjective, so personal. And if duality exists, it is in the mind; in reality, all things are one undifferentiated emanation of God's mind. This is what I believe."

"I know where you're going with this," Allison responded with caution in her voice. "I'm persuaded, but not for the same reasons as you. So, you would say, then, that there is an objective and absolute foundation in the human mind?"

"Yes, pretty much, that's where I think Plato was going with 'The Good,'" said Hooman. "But there are limits to what we can see of this. It is infinite, whereas we are finite. One can't embrace the other fully. After death, it's easier, so I read in certain books. Once we pass into the world of Malakut, the world of forms, the truth becomes clearer."

"I agree that there are some objective truths or approximations of objectivity. I can go that far with you," said Allison. "After all, if the mind is completely subjective and prone to untruth, how could it discover facts that it maintains are physically objective and have a foundation of truth, like science? But I don't see why you have to add God to the mix." She was quiet for a period. "Well . . . I don't know. Maybe there is a place for God in reality. I am still unconvinced though."

Hooman turned away and looked at some of the other works in the room.

"On the weekend I said I wanted to talk to you about something. Something quite personal, actually," she said.

"Right. Yes. I almost forgot. That's why we're here, isn't it?"

"But whatever I say, it has to be between the two of us, okay?"

"Sure, no problem."

"I couldn't think of anyone else who might be open to what I want to say, at least in New York anyway. And after our conversation just now, I think you might be interested in what I have to say."

"Okay then, I'm intrigued. What is it you want to talk about?"

After a considerable pause, Allison turned to Hooman. "You know, it's just occurred to me that it's quite apt and coincidental that we've been talking about the true perception of reality. Have you heard of any situation where normal perception breaks down?" she said.

"Well, that's a sign of madness, I suppose."

She laughed. "I thought you might go there. That's why I find this hard to talk about. In case someone might misinterpret me, which is why I stopped talking to my brother Paul about certain things in my life in recent years. He wouldn't understand me."

"Really, you seem fine to me."

"Thanks for the vote of confidence, but I do feel that I've been slowly submerging into . . . well, a strange landscape. Like sometimes, something might appear fine on the surface, yet a part of me knows something is wrong with what I am seeing mentally. Like a mirror being ever so slightly bent that it looks normal, but at a certain angle something looks wrong or distorted."

"I'm not really following you. But is that why you've been interested in visual distortions?"

"Yes. But there are no visual distortions in my perception. I'm not hallucinating. It's psychological distortions that I see. Although I do sometimes hear extra harmonics on the top of other sounds, like in peoples' voices especially."

"Hey, me too," added Hooman. "I heard some harmonic overlays in a dream I had last year, and there was a little resonance in your voice when we first met at the café in Greenwich Village."

"Really?" Allison was pleased but returned to her topic of conversation. "And I can trace this to about a year after my first operation to remove my breast. You might know through Nava that I had cancer.

Anyway, I started having vivid flashbacks of my life. But not like normal memories. They seemed somehow more real. And the thoughts that triggered these memories seemed disconnected from my conscious will. Like they were not from a clear line of causation or free will in my mind. Something is dissolving the traditional symmetrical structure of my mind, and a new symmetry is rising up that connects both my inner and outer worlds. It's like my face is changing its form and shape, and a new face is emerging, a new mental identity."

"Wow, are you sure about this?" asked Hooman.

"Well, yes and no. It's been coming over me so slowly and gradually that it took a long time for me to even suspect something was wrong in the first place. But now there are some really odd things going on." Allison paused as a woman passed through the room. "Three weeks ago, at that gallery in Soho. Something strange happened," she said.

"You mentioned seeing bronze sculptures. They sound interesting."

"The thing is that the script on the sculptures was from that book I borrowed from you."

"Yes . . . *The Conference of the Birds*."

"And also, those sculptures were lions, and this was on the same day you decided to take me to see *The Lion King*. There were also seven stars on the side of each lion. This is connected to the fact that we went to the Seven Stars Café on my first night in New York. I also heard the gallery owner repeat a phrase that you repeated later on in the day, 'It's fun, isn't it?'"

"Yes . . . I did say that. I remember," agreed Hooman. "You mentioned it in the car that day."

"I won't forget it. You both said exactly the same phrase. Do you see the symmetry in these events? And his voice—it had a faint harmonic to it. His thoughts entered my mind, melding with my own thoughts. And the blue of his eyes—they were so intense. It was like looking at the sky."

"I see." He paused. "And so are you saying these were a series of synchronized and symmetrical events?"

"It's like in the present moment, the past and the future are expressed in symbolic form, in relation to those green lion sculptures, but I'm not absolutely sure of the links between these events."

"I do believe some people can be intuitive, and synchronicity exists, but we can also read purpose and point into the accidents of life. It happens all the time. It could be just chance."

"Yes, I thought so too for a while. I am with you on this. I'm not the type of person who reads purpose into chance happenings at all, but this is the totally strange thing. I went back to the gallery in Soho several days before last Christmas. It was a few days before you came back from Europe. I wanted to ask the owner about something he mentioned to me, about the nature of eternity, but he didn't remember meeting me, not at all. In fact, he seemed like a completely different person. He was colder than I remembered, unemotional. The lions were there, but he thought the work was garbage. He was merely indulging the tastes of his wife, who liked the artist. I'm telling you, he was a completely different person. Externally he looked exactly the same, but his personality was just too different for it to be a coincidence. I was totally flummoxed."

"Well, I must admit that sounds a little strange. Are you sure he didn't remember you? I mean, it was the same man. Are you really sure?" asked Hooman.

"Yes, absolutely. I kept insisting to the man that we'd met. He told me to leave. Can you imagine that? How out of this world is that?"

"It is odd. No doubt. I can't understand it myself, but if that's just an isolated incident, then I wouldn't worry about it."

"Yes. Maybe. It could be just me." She studied his body language. "I can see you still don't believe me."

He hesitated. Before he could answer, she added, "Look, I know how implausible it sounds. Don't think that I think this is normal either."

"I do believe you. I can see you're disturbed by it."

"Look, if you have an opinion other than it's just my imagination, which I already think anyway, then I'd love to hear it. But I suppose I'm just glad I could share it with someone."

"That's no problem. Although I don't think I've been much help to you."

"No, you have been a help. I am just going to the bathroom. I'll be back soon."

"Okay," he said.

She stood up and walked away. She found the escalator and descended down to the next level, eventually finding the ladies symbol.

————

Hooman wandered around the room and looked at more minimalist paintings before walking into an adjacent room. He stopped in front of a large stainless-steel cube and then circled around it. He thought about what she had said about the shape of her mind changing, assuming a new symmetrical form. If she was right, what did it mean? It could be something or maybe nothing, and he did not know her well enough yet to know the difference. After five minutes in minimalism, he wandered back to the escalators and waited for her. He missed her arrival but felt a gentle *tap-tap* on his arm.

"Hello. I am back," she said.

He turned around and smiled at her. "I am glad." He assumed that she must have gone into one of the adjacent rooms to view one of the other collections.

They then rode the escalators up to the Abstract Expressionist collection. They walked into the main room and stopped in front of a Jasper Johns painting, which was the American flag piece that he was known for. He had seen the painting before during his last visit to the gallery.

"I have seen this painting before," she said.

"Yeah, me too."

"I wrote an essay about it at uni."

They were quiet for a while.

"I have an admission," he said, finally.

"Oh yes, what?"

"When you first arrived, you know, the day you flew into JFK."

"Yes."

"Well, I was on my way to the café that night, and I had a strong impulse to buy a book. Mind you, I get these impulses a lot, so there is nothing interesting about that, but this was different somehow."

"Right, I remember it. You had a book with Terminal 5 on the front."

"Yes, but at the time I didn't have that particular book in mind or any title for that matter. Actually, Elliot picked it out. So, what I'm saying is, it occurred to me as a little odd, a coincidence maybe, that you arrived at JFK on the same night that I bought a book with Terminal 5 on the cover. It's a tenuous thread I know, but, well, I thought it might be significant. I don't know. You did seem to have an inordinate interest in the terminal, more than average. That's why I thought there might be a connection. A subtle connection . . . between us."

"That resonates," agreed Allison. "It does seem synchronistic, yes. I didn't think about it at the time, but in retrospect, I see your point, yes."

Hooman wanted to comfort her. "These things have happened to me too. But usually, they are isolated events, but even then, I can't always be sure if anything is obviously connected, or if it's just my imagination over-interpreting reality," he said.

"So, how do you explain my experiences, then?"

"Well, I see that God is not a large part of your life or you are yet to be convinced, as you have said tonight, but I believe that most events in life have some link to life's true objective reality."

"I'm not sure that I'm a complete nonbeliever. I am open to the possibility. It's just that I haven't seen or heard anything strong enough yet. God is more like a pure principle to me of goodness, that humans have as a goal to be better people, but not a conscious entity, up there, you know, in heaven or wherever God is supposed to exist." She pointed to the ceiling.

"I have another theory," he said.

"What's that?"

"Well, you know we were talking about the worlds of God the other day and just now about the connection to Plato's forms. And the relationship between the world of images and forms, Malakut, and the physical world, Nasut?"

"Yes."

"Well, I believe that the worlds of God beyond this life flow into the physical world, imparting purpose and energy. It is like the air, which, although it's invisible, we know exists because of the movement of objects, like the grass in a meadow, which moves and bends in submission to invisible realities."

"So, you are saying I have some connection to the world beyond."

"Yes, that's exactly what I'm saying. Other ways this can happen is through dreams and prayers. The dead can speak through the living. Not directly, but in a subtle way. 'Abdu'l-Bahá, the son of Bahá'u'lláh, talks about this when he says:

"'Those who have ascended have different attributes from those who are still on earth, yet there is no real separation. In prayer there is a mingling of station, a mingling of condition. Pray for them as they pray for you! When you do not know it, and are in a receptive attitude, they are able to make suggestions to you.' [3]

"And with regard to internal mental symmetry, I am reminded of a *Hidden Word* by Bahá'u'lláh:

"'O SON OF THE THRONE!

Thy hearing is My hearing, hear thou therewith. Thy sight is My sight, do thou see therewith, that in thine inmost soul thou mayest testify unto My exalted sanctity, and I within Myself may bear witness unto an exalted station for thee.'" [4]

"That's interesting," Allison responded. "So God stands within us as the base of our perception of the world, like an onion skin of consciousness, as layers within layers. I am not sure that fits—he could be the core of the onion rather than the skin—but I suppose it is good to have some theory rather than none."

"Sometimes, God is the silent witness within us, watching the thoughts and images that flow through our mind; and, at other times, we are the silent witness, and God's thoughts and images flow through our mind," Hooman explained.

"So, you think God broadcasts thoughts into our minds? We think our thoughts come from our own minds, which are completely cut off from others, but we never guess the origin of our thoughts. That is what people with schizophrenia experience. They believe other people are placing thoughts into their minds."

"There is a strange relationship between madness and religious revelation," he said.

"Hey, can we go somewhere less public? My legs are really tired now. Maybe we can continue at another café or something?" Allison asked.

"Oh, I know a place downtown. It is better than a café. It even has a big couch you can lie on if you want."

8

THE SYMMETRIES OF A FACE

He in this realm is content with the divine decree, and seeth war as peace, and in death findeth the meaning of everlasting life. With both inward and outward eyes he witnesseth the mysteries of resurrection in the realms of creation and in the souls of men, and with a spiritual heart apprehendeth the wisdom of God in His endless manifestations. In the sea he findeth a drop, in a drop he beholdeth the secrets of the sea.[1]

— BAHÁ'U'LLÁH, *THE SEVEN VALLEYS*

Hooman and Allison got out of a taxi they had caught from MoMA to Tribeca. Allison looked up at a large warehouse and the night sky beyond that. They walked into the building. Allison liked its patina and general atmosphere but knew it was an object of desire for a cashed-up hipster and not her. They came to a cage elevator and walked into it. Hooman closed the door, and they ascended to the top floor. They walked into a stark, modern loft apartment. Without a word Allison looked around.

"Yeah, it's a bit over the top, I know," he said.

"Who owns this? It's huge and shiny."

Hooman smiled. "A friend. You haven't met her yet. This is Sara's place."

"What does she do for a living?"

"She's a stockbroker. . . and relatively successful by all accounts."

"It shows. Where is she?"

"Away on a business trip. I don't know exactly where, but at a guess she is probably attempting to invest in more property somewhere. Don't ask me why she does it. She could retire now if she wanted. I don't follow that part of her life much these days. Anyway, I'll make some coffee. Have a seat."

Allison watched Hooman move into the kitchen. He opened a cabinet. Pulling out two mugs, he placed them on a stainless-steel countertop.

She walked around the couch to an expansive set of windows. She placed her hands and face on the glass. The wind pushed against the weight of her body on the other side of the glass. Pulling back, she focused on the condensation. Her hands and face were set in relief. Her body moisture revealed a crude photographic emulsion that had formed on the glass. The flimsiest of historical documents, she thought.

Behind the evaporating image of herself, she saw a thicket of Manhattan night towers reaching up into the dark sky. All their lights shone in the night. Turning around, she stood in front of a long brilliant-white couch. It was almost too clean. Afraid to leave a smudge on it, she looked over her sleeves and backside to see if they were in any way grubby. On her shirt sleeve was a slight mark from the rusty nails in her room. She then looked up at Hooman.

"Listen, don't worry about it. I've spilled coffee on it a few times. It's dry-cleaned quite regularly," he said.

"Well, okay, if you say so." Her eyes closed for a moment as she spun around and dropped backward onto the couch, relaxing deeply into its soft cushions.

"You seem impressed with this place . . . or at least a little impressed. I wouldn't have thought it possible," Hooman said.

She opened her eyes and turned toward the kitchen. He filled a French press up with hot water.

"Really! Why?"

"Oh, I don't know. You don't seem, well, overly concerned with material comforts. From the little I know of you."

"We all have a beast of desire within us. I try to keep mine tamed, not always with the success I would like. But what about you? Don't you like this place?"

"It's nice enough, but I would feel a degree of guilt living in something like this."

"Really! Why? You work hard, don't you? You deserve this lifestyle too."

"Why do you say that?"

"I guess it seems reasonable. Everyone works to better themselves."

"But there must be limits." He took a glass from the cabinet and filled it with water. He held it up to the light. "Take this glass of water, and let's say I could afford to purchase it, and you could not afford to buy any of it. Do I deserve to drink it all? Knowing full well that you will be deprived, and let's exaggerate to say you will probably die of thirst. What would stop me from letting you die?"

"That's a bit simplistic, don't you think?"

"Yes, of course it is, but this is just a thought experiment between you and me. In certain other contexts, not so far removed, like the developing world, it's perfectly true. Take bottled water. It is sold in developing countries to people who can hardly afford to pay for it. Many large multinational companies are making huge profits at the expense of the poor. Like Nestlé, which has just opened a factory that manufactures bottled water in Pakistan, where many don't have access to clean drinking water, and as a consequence, waterborne diseases continue to affect many people in the country. According to the World Health Organization, access to clean drinking water should be a human right. In fact, there are three central human rights: justice, education, and health.

"Let's talk about justice. What is justice? Is it a natural right, which transcends social and economic distinctions? Or is it a right that is dependent on one's ability to buy it? If justice, or any other human right, becomes commodified, is it any longer a right? Justice is a principle at the same level as the body's need for water. Nothing in society would function without it. It's a *perfect form* at its most ideal."

"Actually, I agree with you, in principle," said Allison. "But where do you draw the line? If you're a millionaire, do you choose to live in the gutter from social guilt?"

"Where the line is drawn is a decision for each person. But for me, it's a way to develop my spiritual potential. It's like fasting, but instead of denying myself food, I choose to give up certain material comforts. Like a car for instance, I don't have one. I go on public transport, take taxis, or borrow Nava's car. Plus, there's the principle of sharing limited resources."

"I see. Yes, I understand that."

"I know in a city like this, the shrine of a capitalist god, choice becomes obscured, lost in a morass of materialism, but really there is no such thing as a choice without a consequence. Everything exerts an influence, without exception. And if you have to start somewhere, start with yourself. Of course, that's just my choice. You have to make up your own mind. I try not to make judgments of other people."

"Mmm, you're interesting."

"Do you have sugar?" Hooman slowly pushed the plunger down.

"Yes, one please. With milk. So how do you know Sara?"

"Sara is one of my failed attempts at a relationship. Sara was a girl-friend . . . for a short time. We were together for just under a year."

"I see. I relate to that. My boyfriends too were sparse and brief. When you add them together, they just barely came to the outline of a whole man."

"Anyway, so we're good friends now, after nearly five years. That's why I still have a key to this place. And she's going out with Shidan now. So that all worked out well."

"Did your relationship just fizzle out or was it more to do with the issues we've been discussing just now?" She paused for a moment to think how far she could push it without getting too personal. "Of guilt and wealth."

He looked up from stirring the coffee. "You're analyzing the ethics of my relationships."

"Am I?"

He looked into her eyes. "Okay then, I'll be honest with you about Sara. I think Sara would like to think everyone can be a millionaire, potentially, okay. Something with overtones of the American Dream: 'I pay homage to the Deva of wealth within me,' or 'I deserve to be successful.' Mantras like that, but even that would be too yoga for her, but something like that. Anyway, you get my point. But I know for me that's just not true. Someone has to be poor for another to be wealthy.

That's the way our society is structured, with distorted hierarchies. We can't all live in lofts like this. Inequality is an unintentional aspect of the American Dream, and although nobody is organizing inequality within government bodies as a necessary part of capitalism, many in our society are ignorant of the consequences and illusion of wealth and how it manifests itself on a global stage when we do not share. And let's say seven billion or so people on the planet consumed like the average wealthy Westerner. Would the planet cope with the strain?"

"No, it wouldn't. I know that."

"So, I have to take less for others to take an equal share. But the problem is someone else who doesn't need the part that I am giving up will take it. Not those who need it. So there has to be regulation, a conscious balance. That's why I got into international law. It's about a form of global justice, of systems that have to be developed over time to create that balance, and a renaissance of spiritual values at the level of the individual that will moderate our consumption and create a vibrant global community where everyone has the resources they need to fulfill their human potential."

Allison thought about the day she had first driven to Hooman's apartment along the Hudson River. She had thought about the incompatible elements within the American Dream. Hooman had highlighted these ideas tonight, about the winners and losers. And what was fascinating to her now was that he had outlined ways to correct this. He saw what she saw, and he cared about the poor.

"Justice again. The conversation is circling around it."

"I can see I am ranting now."

"No, this is a great rant. I'm seeing you clearer now . . ."

He smiled and continued. "Shakespeare said: 'It is the mind that makes the body rich.'"[2]

He brought the coffees over and passed her a mug.

"But you're wealthy. I mean, I presume you are. As a lawyer, you earn a fair deal, right?"

"Yes, that's true. It's a side effect of my job, but it's not the primary reason I got into law in the first place. Besides, I give much of it away to various causes."

They got comfortable with their coffees and settled into the couch, repositioning and arranging cushions to prop up their bodies. Hooman placed one large cushion in front of him. He held his mug between his hands and rested it on top of the cushion. She observed his irises contracting as he focused on her face.

"Am I getting too intense for you?" he said.

"Intense . . . you? I don't think you know me well enough yet. I'm usually the intense one. Well, now I'm intrigued. Did Sara ever find this kind of conversation a bit hard to digest?"

"We never spoke at this level. I never thought it would interest her really, but don't get the impression that I think less of Sara because we don't agree on the state of global poverty, or that she thinks my beliefs are cute but deluded."

"Cute but deluded. I'll remember that. Nice phrase. But what do you really feel about people who don't hold your particular ideals? Be truthful. Do you really want to associate with people who have harmful materialistic ideas?"

He laughed at her suggestion.

"I do see your point, really. But if you believe in justice for the poor, I want you to think about something. Do you have any friends who live near the poverty line? Do you know what kinds of conditions poorer people live in? And I don't mean in theory. I mean in practice. I walked around Harlem the other day. I've seen it there and in South Bronx, and I lived amongst the poor in Australia on and off over the years. There's a big contrast between Harlem, South Bronx, and the rest of Manhattan. And I saw the poverty in East London and Paris, too, when I lived in those places. If your answer is no, then aren't you living in a kind of walled paradise: a private pleasure garden? Even if it's a humble one compared to this." She spread one arm out to encompass Sara's loft apartment. "You should move to South Bronx or Harlem and live near me. Then you can say you've known the poor."

He was silent and, from what Allison could gauge, shocked by her suggestion.

———

The ceiling, a featureless plane, could be sleep-inducing most nights, but now it provided a meditative surface. Hooman's eyes traced the empty planes of white paint and in contrast the visual stimulus where the familiar cracks and paint peels formed. The day's events replayed in his mind. He pondered the various things that he and Allison had discussed that night. She was a beautiful person. He was drawn to the things she said and the way her mind worked. He also thought about that morning and was convinced now that she had come into his life for a specific purpose.

The door to his room opened. Nava walked into the bedroom and slumped on the bed. "You are late," she said.

He put his arms around her shoulders. They both looked at the ceiling together now. "Yeah. I saw a friend. Sorry, I should have called."

"Anyway, I thought you might be working late, so I ordered takeout again. It's in the fridge if you want some."

"How was your day?" he asked.

"Good. I convinced a client not to change a few design elements. They would have brought my whole design down." She closed her eyes and seemed to Hooman to drift away.

He did not pursue the detail of her day. Instead, he carefully removed his arm from around her shoulders and said quietly, "Great. Good for you."

As he closed his eyes, his mind drifted away. His thoughts returned to Allison. She was independent, and to a point that seemed needlessly excessive. Once more she would not allow him to escort her home. He felt the same frustration that had moved through him on the night she had crossed the black ice in front of his apartment block. He was tempted to do something out of character again, and his irritation mystified him. But then he realized that it was because she lived in an unsafe part of town and did not seem to acknowledge this, or, if she knew it to be true, she brushed it aside carelessly. And although New York, and Harlem in particular, was safer now than it had been, it was still unsafe in certain circumstances, but the main issue was that she had somehow permeated and penetrated his being. She had burrowed into the private recesses of his mind—areas that he had forgotten himself and assumed were beyond question or reproach—and she had been right about his walled paradise. He had protected himself from a first-hand experience of the poverty in New York, and the truth of this made him feel hollow. His final conclusion was that her observation, although strangely uncomfortable, was somehow liberating.

Now he was curious to know who this person was, because she could be distant as well as warm and open. Something was given, and something was held back. He did not fully understand her, and that was what he could see now. There was a lifetime's worth of history that he did not know about. She was a puzzle to construct: a personality that must have taken so many interesting twists and turns in this life.

Nava stirred beside him.

He opened his eyes.

"Hey, does Allison have any sisters?" Hooman whispered.

"No, just a brother. Paul, remember? I mentioned him the other day."

"Oh, yes." He recalled that Allison had referred to him tonight and the day at the ice rink. "What about her parents?"

"They did own a few restaurants, in Lygon Street, the Little Italy of Melbourne."

"Were Allison's parents Italian?"

"Her father was."

"But her surname, Bird. It's not Italian, is it?"

"Her father changed his surname to integrate better into Australian culture. Originally it was some Italian name, but Paul runs the restaurants now."

"Did her parents retire?"

"No, not exactly. Both parents are dead. There was a car accident when Allison was sixteen. Her father was killed, and her mother was in a coma for some years, in some care home somewhere. She died about six years ago. Allison used to visit her mum a lot for a while. But she would never talk about her mother when we were together at university. Actually, it was Paul who told me all this."

"Oh, I see. She mentioned her mother's funeral last week. I remember now that she said she is close to Paul."

"Very close. For a long time, they only had each other."

"Her interest in death makes sense now."

"What makes sense?"

"It's nothing."

While still maintaining a conversation with Nava, his mind drifted back to the end of the conversation with Allison in the loft.

In an abrupt turnabout Allison had said to him, "I agree with you totally."

They were in the cage elevator descending to the lobby. "Agree with what?" He had looked at her face for an indication of playfulness, but he could not read her, and she seemed quite serious.

"Everything."

"Everything? What do you mean by everything?"

"I thought about your ideas earlier on, like justice, wealth, and poverty. It's all good. The God and spirituality thing I will need to look into further before I pass judgment. But on the whole, I'm convinced now that you're right, mostly, most of it . . . anyway, it's all good."

"Really?"

"Totally. In fact, I'm going to test this all out in my master's. I finished reading *The Conference of the Birds*. I think there's something in it. And look, even if I can't explore it in my master's because most of it is set papers, I might do my own personal studies and try and nut everything out."

"You will?" He was uncomprehending of the abrupt turnaround and said, "When did you decide this?"

"Just now . . . listen, I was only playing around with you before when I questioned you on wealth. I just wanted to see how your mind works. I have always thought about these things."

He did not dare make a joke. He did not know if she was sincere or just playing around again.

In the street he was thinking of something in response, but by the time he had prepared something it was too late.

She had kissed him on the cheek. "Bye," she said and turned around. She walked toward the stairs to the subway. Just before the entrance she turned her head toward him. "By the way, that Cartier watch is ridiculous. You know that, right?"

"Yes, I know it's ridiculous. Sara gave it to me."

"Well, I am glad to hear you weren't the one who bought it."

"Yes, I know. I was——"

She smiled, then turned and disappeared into the stairwell at Chambers Street Subway Station.

Nava had fallen asleep again. He swung his legs slowly off the bed and gently raised himself to a sitting position. He did not want to disturb Nava. He washed his hands and face meditatively in the bathroom sink before adjourning to the living room for his daily prayers and meditation.

He opened his prayer book and began to read his daily obligatory prayer aloud:

"'O Thou Who art the Lord of all names and the Maker of the heavens! I beseech Thee by them Who are the Day-Springs of Thine invisible Essence, the Most Exalted, the All-Glorious, to make of my prayer a fire that will burn away the veils which have shut me out from Thy beauty, and a light that will lead me unto the ocean of Thy Presence . . ."' [3]

But the words he uttered were a wall rather than a gate, and there was no path leading to a world of transcendence beyond. Even if his words could be a gate, he doubted his ability to open it, and this gate was made of letters, mere abstract shapes, whose fine tracery coiled, looped, and touched. They created an impregnable barrier and a mesh of restricting detail. To find a way through the tangle of letters and words, he looked to the white of the page to see the meaning. He thought about the painting at MoMA, and the positive and negative space of words, which was the white of paper and the black ink of words.

How often had he vainly hoped to possess spiritual abilities beyond himself? To be on the other side of the gate looking back at his past self who might be peering into a garden. A different garden than the one Allison had mentioned but connected. He saw that now, but no amount of wishing would help because he was still that past self. And he had hoped that one day he would find a word or a phrase acting as a catalyst or even a single letter as a secret gate handle. Once triggered, the words would unravel, and the locking tracery would unroll until only a book of pristine white pages remained. The ink would fade in the illuminating light and leave pure understanding above the form of words that hovered and shimmered above the radiant, undiscovered, untrammeled beauty of the pages beneath them.

But for the moment he would have to content himself with the sound of words and the sensation of the surface sheen of paper. He observed the oily mark from his thumbs in the page corners where he had read over those familiar prayers through the years. The more familiar they were, the more impenetrable they had become. He needed a fresh way to perceive his life: a way of being and a new beginning. His stomach leaped within faintly, which seemed insignificant at first, but then an image entered into his mind. It was a precursor to an admission. The image he saw was Allison. He had noted the symmetries of her face in MoMA and the freckles on her skin. She was very pretty, which was a pleasant sensation, but one that now outgrew itself and turned to pain. Now he saw her. Now he knew her anew as a painful form and not just a pretty face but instead a beautiful one, and this was uncomfortable in its consequence. He was beginning to love her.

———

More than six years earlier, after a three-hour drive, Allison arrived at the front gate of ConFest on December 31, 1992, in Moama, New South Wales, Australia, where she would see out the old year and welcome in the new one. She paid the entrance fee and drove through. She headed away from the main camping area and tried to find a camping spot on the northern bank of the Murray River that was isolated from most of the other campers. After a while, she could not take the car any farther because of the thickness of the scrub. She got out and propped the wheels with bricks to stop the car from rolling. She then walked along the river and eventually found campers who'd had the same idea as her and had set up in a small clearing next to the river.

So she walked back to the car, got her tent, her smaller backpack, and her hiking pack and set up next to the other tents in the clearing. She then walked to the bank of the river and put a blanket on the ground. She sat down and continued reading *Being and Nothingness*.

After half an hour of reading, she heard peoples' voices coming toward her. She closed the book and looked back at the campsite. Eventually, she saw two girls walk into the clearing. They were barefoot, wearing slightly familiar tie-dye skirts and large, loose-fitting tie-dye shirts. One girl had long blonde dreadlocks. They walked up to Allison.

The girl with the dreadlocks said, "Hello. I'm Aurélie." She had a thick French accent.

Allison stood up and hugged Aurélie.

"And I'm Io, but most people call me I."

Allison then hugged Io.

"You don't mind if I camp next to you?"

"No, not at all . . . I remember you from last year," Io said.

"I'm sorry, I don't remember you," Allison said.

"That's okay. We were in the same meditation workshop, and I visited you at the Friends of the Earth stall."

"Ahh . . . okay." Allison then remembered where she had seen the tie-dye shirts before. The clothes were from a clothing stall next to one of the workshop tents. She assumed that was where Aurélie had bought hers too.

"What are you reading?" Io said.

"Oh, this is *Being and Nothingness* by Jean-Paul Sartre."

Allison held the book up.

"Wow. I have heard that that is difficult," Aurélie said.

"Yes, it is."

"I am surprised to see you reading that. I mean, that is way too much . . . for the average person. Even in French I have heard that it is very difficult," Aurélie said.

"Hmm . . . yes, I suppose it would be. I would never attempt to read it in the original French. But changing the subject, where are you guys from?" Allison asked.

"Oh, I'm from Nimbin. It's near Byron Bay," Io said.

"And I'm from Paris. But I am staying in Sydney at the moment. I mean, my boyfriend is there right now," Aurélie said.

Allison had studied French in school, so she began talking to Aurélie in French. Allison could tell by the look on her face that Aurélie was impressed by her mastery of French. She explained to her that she was going to study French next year at the University of Melbourne. Allison asked where Aurélie had been in Australia so far.

"Nowhere really. My boyfriend and I arrived in Sydney last week," Aurélie said in English.

"Hey, we're going for a swim. Do you want to join us?" Io said.

"No . . . I'll keep reading. But thanks anyway."

"Okay, cool."

Allison went back to her blanket and sat down. The girls stripped off their clothes and jumped into the river.

Allison had spent a few hours toward the end of New Year's Eve Day managing the Friends of the Earth stall at the festival with a few people she knew from the organization in Melbourne. Aurélie and Io came to meet her after her shift. Allison saw them in the distance walking toward the stall through the gum trees in the campsite. They were both topless and barefoot but wearing their tie-dye skirts.

"Hello," Aurélie said brightly as they came to the stall.

"How was your day?" Io asked.

"Good," Allison replied.

Allison turned toward Bess. "Are you okay to run the stall for the rest of the day?"

"Yeah, sure. You guys go and enjoy yourselves. Oh, the fashion show is about to start if you want to go," Bess said.

"Ahh. Okay, sounds good," Aurélie said. "Do you want to check that out?"

Just next to the Friends of the Earth stall, a tantric sex workshop was under way. The girls passed by the workshop and headed toward the fashion show.

The fashion show was not at all like other fashion shows in mainstream society. There were many amazing folk wearing extremely odd and colorful clothes. It was meant to be a fun event celebrating social and cultural diversity. They sat down with many other people and watched the show continue.

Aurélie took Allison's hand. "I have been wondering about the book you are reading."

"What about it?"

"Yesterday, you said to me that you think there is no true meaning in life. Sorry, I have forgotten the word you used in English . . ."

"I said there is no true *objective* meaning in life beyond what we construct in our imagination?"

"Yes, that is right. 'Objective.' It sounds similar in French, as you probably know."

"And that God is no more than a mental construct that satisfies our search for ultimate meaning in this life."

"Yes, exactly," agreed Aurélie.

"Well, that comment was just from the viewpoint of existentialism. God, who has been defined in the past as the object of meaning and devotion, was only conceived of within the limits of human understanding at various times in history, and in many cases we had no real understanding of what God might actually be. And even existentialism was a reaction against this limited conception of God."

"Ahh. Okay, that is so interesting. So, people who reject God are really only rejecting old ideas of God?" asked Aurélie.

"Yes and no. It is an open question. Even though some people misconstrue God and use him as a puppet for their own limited ideas of his so-called true reality, that doesn't actually mean there is a God. A friend of mine, Jasper, believes that God's transcendent self will never be grasped by the human imagination no matter how far it progresses, and that humanity nearly always anthropomorphizes God's reality through the immanence of God's reflection in the physical world. He believes we will never escape our finite, subjective, perception-orientated human selves because by our very nature we have certain inbuilt fundamental limitations in us. But regardless of that argument, I am still not convinced that God exists beyond human intellectual projection."

"Wow! Interesting."

The next person to parade in the show was an old man with a multi-colored patchwork suit. He danced down the avenue of people sitting on both sides of the show. Everyone laughed and clapped their hands. Two young girls got up and danced with him.

The day eventually faded into night, and the girls went for another swim in the darkness before joining a circle of people sitting around a campfire burning in a forty-four gallon drum. Everyone was waiting for the new year to arrive.

"Hey, how are you guys getting back home tomorrow?" Allison asked.

"We were going to hitchhike. And there are people from ConFest going to Sydney."

"Why don't you come with me? I am going past Byron Bay. That's near Nimbin, right? But I am going to go south first, via Wilsons Prom. And then I plan to go to Sydney via the coast road rather than going straight there by the Hume Highway. It will probably take four or five days or longer than the usual eight-hour drive."

"That would be great. I have never been to Wilsons Prom," Io said.

"Nor me," said Aurélie. "Can we pick up my boyfriend on the way? He is in Sydney. We were planning on traveling up the east coast."

"That's fine. Can we share the driving?"

"No problem," Aurélie said.

9

NEW FRIENDS

Gazing with the eye of absolute insight, the wayfarer in this valley seeth in God's creation neither contradiction nor incongruity, and at every moment exclaimeth, "No defect canst thou see in the creation of the God of mercy. Repeat the gaze: Seest thou a single flaw?" [1,2]

— BAHÁ'U'LLÁH, *THE SEVEN VALLEYS*

Allison was sitting on the steps of the Visitors Center at Columbia University. She had her back resting against one of the neoclassical columns at the entrance of the center. She had just finished a lecture and was eating sandwiches for lunch. It was March 12, 1999, and Allison had been attending philosophy lectures for seven weeks.

Winter had gradually faded into spring. Allison had observed the slow departure of snow from the square. The square was surrounded by an assortment of neoclassical buildings. Most of her lectures were held in the philosophy department, which also faced the main square, and from there she had often walked around the lawns or down the central avenue of the South Lawn on her way to the Butler Library, where she had often worked on her essays or conducted research; however, as spring came, she had spent more time in a small room at the back of Shidan's bookshop. The name of the shop was the Sun

Tongue, and she was as attracted to the name as she was to the space itself. Shidan had mentioned that the word "tongue" when combined with "sun" was supposed to evoke the idea that words were like spoken light.

The room overlooked a light well with a cherry tree planted at one end. The light well had been modified when Shidan first bought the building. He had removed two brick walls from the back of the room and replaced them with floor-to-ceiling glass. Shidan's desk faced the light well. Allison would often stare through the glass wall for brief moments and then continue tapping away on Shidan's laptop, which she had borrowed for her essay writing. Shidan encouraged her to study there, and, as the weather had become tolerable, he had bought a table and chair for the light well. She had then moved from his desk into the light well to study.

Allison finished her sandwich and stood up. She walked toward her bicycle, which was chained up on Broadway. Dan, her roommate, had lent her his bike. So she used it to go shopping for food each week. She eventually left the square and walked between Dodge Hall and the school of journalism. She came to the bike and unlocked it. She rode down Broadway toward an Italian deli that was a few blocks away. She was planning to cook an Italian dinner for her roommates and wanted the raw ingredients to make homemade ravioli.

Initially her study had gone well, but recently Allison was finding it hard to concentrate. Her conclusion was that somehow the philosophy course appealed to her intellect but not to her heart. She realized that society often talks about the heart and the intellect as if they are separate things. One ruled by love and the other by logic, but this was a false dichotomy. They were intimately interconnected, so from the two came the one overarching "logic of love." She supposed that as long as love was the dominating principle in the soul, then we could not go astray in our life, and then indeed the combination of the heart and intellect would be light upon light. And we could speak our way into the light of eternity with our sun tongues.

So, despite her misgivings about the course, she pushed on.

The bookshop's interior was not unlike the university library, with antique wooden shelving, but where the shop departed from the university was in the exterior. The shop was a 1960s redbrick building, and it stood in contrast to the many neoclassical buildings at the university, but both buildings smelled similar, like old books or old paper and dust.

Shidan hardly ever managed the front of the shop. He hired a girl called Nikki to look after it, and he spent several months each year traveling around the world looking for rare manuscripts. Often these rare books never made it to the shelves in the bookshop, as the bulk of these items were purchased by people who never frequented the shop. The shop was partially a visual facade for the business, but it was also a hub for people who liked to be among books and book people, and the shop was well known as a source for very obscure titles that could be found nowhere else in Manhattan.

As the months since their first meeting went by, Allison and Shidan spent more and more time with each other. They went to cafés and movies and sometimes Broadway shows. Hooman and Nava would join them occasionally, but often they were alone and enjoying each other's company.

Over that time Allison had noted that Shidan had a habit of never looking directly at people when they were talking. He looked off somewhere else, and it was as if the human face was a distraction to him. And although he never appeared to observe a person's body language while in conversation, she had noticed that he did observe people when they were not talking. Silently he watched and took a person in, and it appeared, superficially at least, that although he was here living his life, a large portion of him seemed to be gone. He was traveling somewhere else in the broad expanse of his mind, but whatever his surface persona told Allison, she concluded eventually that a good portion of him must be here in the present moment. This was borne out by the fact that while he might say very little much of the time, when he did say something, it was highly rational and keenly observed, and it shot to the center of an issue with accuracy and always a certain dry irony. She could see why Hooman liked him.

After a short ride, she came to Milano Market where she locked her bike and entered the deli. She knew immediately that they would have everything she needed as her eyes panned around the interior of the shop, and she began selecting the different ingredients.

———

In the apartment that evening, Allison began preparing the ravioli. She hadn't made it for a long time, but it seemed like yesterday that she would assist the chefs in the restaurants back in Melbourne. Dan and Maddy were out and not due back for several hours. From the kitchen window she could see Morningside Park. She looked at the green lawns and the hill; it blocked a view of Columbia University that was on the other side of the hill.

After making the dough, she began to roll it out with a rolling pin. As she rolled it, she became aware of the smell of the dough rising up from the kitchen countertop and had a flashback of the kitchen in one of the restaurants in Melbourne. She had always loved the commingling aromas of all the different ingredients in the restaurant kitchen. She thought about Shidan and smiled. She had invited Shidan and Sara to dinner that night and was looking forward to getting to know Sara a little better.

———

The next day was Saturday, and Allison was sitting in the light well writing an essay out in longhand. She had just finished a draft and was leaning back on a chair, looking up at the pink blossoms and the sky.

Shidan opened the glass door and leaned out. "You ready to go?"

"Sure." Allison was still leaning back, and she took one last look at the blossoms to imprint them into her memory. She leaned forward and packed up her papers.

"The Chevy is out front."

Shidan kept a sports BMW at his mother's garage in Brooklyn, which he hardly ever used. The Chevy was for Manhattan, and it was covered in scratches and dents from being thrown around in open parking on the streets and exposed to the extremes of the seasons. The model was a 1959 Impala with flat fins at the back of the car. Allison loved the shapes in the body of the car. It almost seemed like some strange insect from another world or maybe a version of the 1966 Batmobile, except for the fact that it was white rather than black.

"Can I drive?" she asked.

"Of course you can. I knew you would ask." Shidan smiled and offered his hand to help her stand. She stood up, and they walked from the light well into the office. She put her camera into her backpack. Shidan closed the glass door to the light well.

"Let's get going," she said.

They then walked through a door into the front of the shop where Nikki was standing behind the front desk. She waved. "Bye, guys. Have a nice afternoon."

"We won't be long. I'll be back in a few hours or so," Shidan said as he opened the front door to the bookshop.

On the street Allison went around the car and opened the driver's door. Shidan slipped into the passenger seat and passed the keys to her. "Here you go."

She started the car, and they merged into the traffic on East 59th Street behind a large truck. She immediately smelled the diesel exhaust fumes from the truck and began to close the driver's side window. Shidan began to close his window too.

———

Hooman found a parking space adjacent to the Guggenheim Museum. Because 5th Avenue was one-way at this section of the road, he had gone north for several blocks before turning around and coming down 5th Avenue. He had turned onto East 88th Street and had then backed the car into the parking space. As he opened the driver's side door, he looked up at the large spiral form of the museum. They had arranged to meet in front of the museum, so Hooman and Nava walked toward the entrance. As they arrived, they saw Allison and Shidan driving down 5th Avenue toward them. Allison pulled over and pointed at the museum. "Hey, why don't we have a quick look inside before we go to Central Park," she shouted at Hooman and Nava.

Shidan nodded.

"Okay, why not," Hooman said. He turned to Nava.

"It's been a while since I was here. I hope they've managed to rotate the collection," Nava said.

Allison and Shidan found a parking spot nearby, and the friends walked into the building. They were soon making their way up the interior of the spiral form. Halfway up, Nava stopped in front of a painting by Marc Chagall, *Paris through the Window*. She took Allison's arm, and they were soon talking about the various compositional aspects of the picture. Hooman leaned over the railing and looked down at people milling about in the hall below. Shidan joined him.

"How's your mother? Nava said she's unwell," Hooman asked Shidan.

"It's nothing too serious."

Allison left Nava and linked arms with Shidan. "Hooman was telling me the other day that you lived in Iran during both the Iranian and Cultural Revolutions," she said.

"Yes, I did. I spent some of my time in Iran and some in England. I came back to Iran in the same year that the Iranian Revolution started. Bad timing, I know. Why do you ask?"

"Curiosity, I guess. A couple of months back Hooman showed me a few photos of Iran, before the revolution, and it got me thinking about the scale of change in Iranian culture during that time. I'm surprised that in the two and a half months we have known each other, you have never mentioned it once."

"I don't like to talk about it. My memories are full of paradox . . . and pain," replied Shidan.

"We missed it. I was eight when we got out. That was late in 1975 . . . two and a bit years before everything went bad. Nava and I spent our childhood growing up in Australia," Hooman said.

Shidan added, "And because of that Hooman has a certain nostalgia for Iran that I don't share. As a Bahá'í, he can never go back, or at least it would be difficult to live there. So, not long after the revolution started, some of my parents' assets were confiscated, but Maman, my mother, managed to get out of Iran with most of her wealth intact. She was independently wealthy from her father's side of the family and had invested in a few properties in London. And my sister and I were educated in English boarding schools in the early seventies, but she came back to Tehran before me and got married. Almost five years after the Iranian and Cultural Revolutions started, late in 1983, we came to America, and I went to New York University to study English literature. But it was a sacrifice for my parents. My father, in particular, wanted us to have a cultural education that was broader than just Iran. I can see his farsightedness now. He was broad-minded. And I suppose in the end he was sacrificed by his own virtue."

Hooman looked at Allison. "Shidan's father and sister were killed."

"I've tried to rationalize the mentality of my own culture," Shidan offered, "but I can't. It's as if I was sane but orphaned to a madhouse. You just had to be there to understand how stupid humans can be."

"Tell me about your sister," Allison said.

"She was married to a Bahá'í, and the cost of that union was her life, as well as contributing to my father's death."

"Why did they kill him?" she said.

"Dad was a journalist and secular philosopher. He was known to be sympathetic to the plight of unfortunates in the community, not just Bahá'ís but other minorities too. He used to write about the obvious inconsistencies in the regime, nothing outrageous, just the truth. He was in favor of the secularization of Iran that had come under the rule of the shah. Although he didn't like that particular regime, with all its corruption, he still thought that religion shouldn't rule societal institutions. So he and many other intellectuals were gradually snuffed out over the years."

"So terrible. So bizarre," Allison said.

"The mind boggles, Allison. And I'm afraid I have to lay the blame squarely at the feet of religion. Especially all forms of fundamentalist Islam. Wipe it out. Stop the fanatical madness of it all. The brainwashing. That society needs a big purging to rid it of the ticks and fleas gorging on its back. It's an authoritarian madhouse."

Hooman looked at Shidan. "But religion has also been a source of good in the world, historically speaking, and it can be again. Also, remember that Islam, at one point in history, brought great cultural and social development to the Middle East. This also had a civilizing effect on other cultures in the world at that time, both intellectually and spiritually. It only decayed later in history."

"Well, I do make some concessions for the Bahá'í Faith and some moderate forms of religion," Shidan said.

"Virtues are what define a religion. If a religion doesn't possess the basic attribute of living humanely, then it can't claim the name of being a religion," Hooman offered.

"I agree," said Allison, joining the discussion. "It doesn't matter if people call themselves religious outwardly. If they are not compassionate people, then there is no religion there—only a shell with no light in it, just empty words. I think some people have forgotten the true form of their respective religions, as has always happened throughout history."

"Religion always passes through natural cycles of both growth and decay. It's relative, not absolute. And with a renewal, things will change. I believe there will be a renaissance of the spiritual in the future. It will begin to wipe away all forms of prejudice and hate," Hooman said.

Shidan grinned, then answered Hooman. "A renewal. Hmm, I don't know. Maybe." Shidan looked over at Allison. "Has Hooman won you over to his viewpoint?" he asked her.

"No, no. I think I see both sides. In some cases there seems to be a need for it, and in other cases certain aspects of religion could be gradually abandoned. It depends on needs and contexts in the modern world."

"Shidan actually knows quite a lot about religion, despite his dislike of some of it," Hooman said.

Shidan looked thoughtful as he looked across the spiral form. "If what you say is true, then I suppose as Bahá'í principles spread, many of the problems with Islam will fade in time," he said.

––––––

After half an hour of visiting various side rooms adjacent to the main spiral form, the group of friends left the Guggenheim for Central Park. As they were about to cross 5th Avenue, Allison suggested that after walking to the top of the park, the group could then make their way toward Harlem's Marcus Garvey Park.

"After Marcus Garvey, we can wander up to 125th Street for a coffee or something. And there is a recreation center at the park that I want to look at. I am wondering if there are any photography classes for local Harlem kids. If there isn't anything like that happening, I thought I could start something in the future. I don't know. What do you think, Shidan?"

"Sounds like a good idea." Then he added, "Hey, people, why don't I take my car on ahead, so then I can drive you all back to your car near the museum."

"Okay. So meet us at the recreation center," Allison said.

"Fine. See you all there, guys."

Shidan watched awhile as the group of friends crossed 5th Avenue. They then walked along a path that skirted the lake near the middle of the park. He watched them disappear, then walked back to his car.

All the talk about the Iranian and Cultural Revolutions and his early years in Iran had uncovered memories that he did not normally dwell on. As he approached the car, he sifted over the conversation in the museum, and an image of his sister's face came to his mind.

———

On a spring day in the mountains north of Tehran, the snow was melting. Bleak and clean rock sat up on one side of a narrow gravel path. The rocks glistened in the sun. The sprawling city below ate, with cancerous fingers, into the base of the mountains.

Mona had chased Shidan up the path. He had slipped a snowball down her back, and he remembered her trying to be angry but bursting into laughter as she caught him. Some of her vibrancy and radiance was in Allison. Some of Hooman's kindness was in Mona's husband, Peshman. Walking up the track slowly, Peshman had caught up with them. They all embraced, laughing.

———

Shidan opened the car door. He sat in the driver's seat, staring ahead for a moment. Before turning the key, he stopped himself. He was trying to suppress more memories of a time one year after their mountain outing.

———

The Iranian Revolutionary Guard had dragged Peshman by his feet through the front door of his house and into the street. Shidan, twenty at the time, was watching from a street corner with his hands full with a dish of food that his mother had asked him to deliver to his sister. He had thought that if he had walked on over that invisible line toward the house he might not walk back. He could not go forward even when Mona ran from the house screaming. She clung to Peshman's body. The

Revolutionary Guard tried to pry her away but then decided to drag them both off. Crowds of neighbors and passersby gathered, yelling abuses. "Prostitute!" It was a word used for Bahá'í women who were considered immodest for their lack of a veil. Though officially she was not a Bahá'í, which was why Shidan could not understand their need to take her away.

Mona had seen Shidan looking at her just before being bundled into the back of a nondescript van. A man was putting handcuffs on her wrists. As she stared at Shidan, her face was expressionless for a while. She had looked at him first, then at the plate of food in his hands, and then back to his face. At the last moment she smiled. Her smile was sweet, like the day in the mountains, and he never saw her or Peshman again.

The family was informed one month later that they had been executed. The authorities refused to give a specific reason for the execution—all they said was that the two had committed crimes against the state—nor would they say where the bodies were buried. Not long after that time his father was taken away too. He was never seen again.

Shidan adjusted the rearview mirror and stared at his face for a few moments. He began to weep. He finally turned the ignition over and drove toward Harlem with lines of water running down his face.

———

In Central Park Allison observed the blooms that she had seen budding only a month ago. She bent down and smelled the faint honey scent from a large swath of white daisies. There was an array of different flowers in the Conservatory Garden swaying in the slight wind that was passing through the park. She pointed out the layout of the flowers to Hooman: they were laid out in large circular shapes surrounding hedges and a central fountain. Although the cherry blossoms in the bookshop had no definable scent when compared to the various flowers in the Conservatory Garden, she still preferred the cherry blossoms in the light well.

Beyond the garden was a series of open lawns and the Harlem Meer, which they passed, and after a short walk, the group of friends left Central Park behind. They walked up Malcolm X Boulevard and then turned down West 121st Street.

Marcus Garvey Park was in the distance at the end of the street, and Hooman pointed to it. "I don't think I have ever been to this park," he remarked.

"I think you'll like it. It is smaller than Central Park but lovely in its own way," Allison responded.

As they neared the middle of the street, Allison saw a "for sale" sign in front of a burnt-out shell of a house: a brownstone. The facade reminded her of Dutch houses that she had seen on the internet many years before. Allison saw the scorch marks on the tops of the windows. Crossing the street, they stopped at the gate.

The house was boarded up and covered in graffiti that was obscured by vines. Moving through the gate and up the stairs, Hooman removed a plank of wood from the window frame. Allison joined Hooman, and they both saw through to the space where the back door should have been. The back of the house was a paradise of lush weeds and grass reaching for the sky. The interior of the house was a charcoal cavern, and most of it was burnt out.

Nava peeked into the empty interior. "This might make a good investment property, Hooman," she said.

"I don't know . . . it needs a lot of work," remarked Hooman.

Nava took out her cell phone and recorded the number of the real estate company on the "for sale" sign. "I'll call on Monday and find out how much they want for it."

The friends then walked on to Marcus Garvey Park and found Shidan waiting near the front of the recreation center.

Allison approached Shidan. "I'll just take a quick look at the notices inside, then we can either walk around the park or head to 125th Street for coffee," she said.

Allison walked down a short sidewalk until she came to the front entrance of the center, and as she neared it, she saw a young African American girl leaning against the glass front. The girl must have heard Allison and Shidan talking. Allison approached her. "Hello. Are you looking for classes too?" the girl said.

"Hi there," Allison replied. "I am looking for classes, but not to join. What are you looking for?"

"There's a computer class that I've just signed up for."

"What's your name?"

"Jessica."

"I'm Allison." She smiled and then asked, "Jessica, do you know of any photography classes in the center here for young kids?"

"No. There aren't any photography classes here."

"Are you waiting for someone?"

"My friend is inside." She pointed over her shoulder at the door.

"Okay." Allison studied the girl's face for a moment. She was beautiful in a way that Allison could not quantify. "Do you mind if I take a photo of you?" she said.

"Sure." Jessica was still leaning on the glass front. The others walked up the path and stopped behind Allison.

Allison took the camera out of her backpack and crouched down to Jessica's head height. She took the shot.

After a few moments, another young African American girl came out of the recreation center. She walked up to Jessica. "Who are these people?" she asked.

"I don't know," Jessica said.

"My name is Allison. What's your name?"

"Sarah."

"Are you signing up for the computer class too?"

"No, I was putting up a lost sign for my cat, Mojo."

10

THE PHILOSOPHY OF THE HEART

. . . the denizens of the city of immortality, who dwell in the celestial garden, see not even "neither first nor last": They fly from all that is first and repulse all that is last. For these have passed over the worlds of names and, swift as lightning, fled beyond the worlds of attributes. Thus is it said: "The perfection of belief in Divine Unity is to deny Him any attributes." [1] *And they have made their dwelling-place in the shadow of the Divine Essence.* [2]

— BAHÁ'U'LLÁH, *THE SEVEN VALLEYS*

On the last day before spring break, Allison was sitting on the steps in front of the Visitors Center near the philosophy building. She was waiting for a lecture to start and staring at the lawns in the main square as students passed through it. She had finished her last essay a few days before and had submitted it by email to her tutor a few hours before coming to the university.

A week had passed by in which she had not seen anyone. Shidan had spent the week traveling around Europe. He also spent a day in London at a Sotheby's auction. He planned to acquire a Gnostic manuscript on behalf of the Smithsonian Libraries. He had arrived back in New York on the previous night, and they had arranged to catch up in the evening and go to Vineapple Café near his apartment in

Brooklyn Heights. He was only in New York for one day before he was scheduled to fly on to Washington, DC, to pass the manuscript over to the Smithsonian. He would then fly from there to Russia to see a private collector in Moscow who was ready to sell some of his collection to Shidan. After many years of resisting Shidan's offers of large sums of money for several rare books in his collection, he was now ready to talk to Shidan.

Allison was lost in her thoughts and looking up at the sky. She could feel a slight breeze on her face. She smelled that faint smell of the pipe tobacco drifting up from her bag. She took the tobacco pouch out and put it to her nose. It had a beautiful, deep sweet smell. She looked at her watch and realized she was now late for the lecture. She descended the stairs and walked down the path to the philosophy building. She walked through the doors and along the corridor until she came to the door of the lecture hall. Trying to make an innocuous entrance, she took a seat in shadow at the back of the lecture hall.

The lecturer moved his arms about with some enthusiasm as he talked about the various streams of political and ethical philosophy. Allison found she could not follow the lecture. His words droned on as background noise. Her thoughts were focused on her continued discontentment with her master's. Hooman had recently given her a Bahá'í journal called *Lights of Irfan* with an article by Ian Kluge about the relationship between the Bahá'í Faith and postmodern philosophy.

It became clear in that moment that what she needed was the philosophy of religion and not secular philosophy, which made up a large part of her course, like the existentialists, the nihilist philosophers, and the other contemporary secular philosophers attached to postmodernism. She remembered her promise to Hooman that she would follow up on his belief system and faith in the existence of God within the framework of Bahá'í ethics. Was there a philosophy of the heart that transcended the intellect, she wondered, or did the intellect need to be informed by the heart?[3]

With postmodernism there was no universal human reality, only competing subjective viewpoints that were all man-made and had some kind of power agenda. This left no room for a transcendent realm beyond death and no God interacting with the human realm and guiding it toward its higher potential. God was entirely constructed by the human imagination and used as a puppet for those who might have an agenda of power.

The end result of this was that there was no higher truth to be discovered, no progressive unfoldment of objective reality: truth was made flat in all directions and relativized.

Postmodernism was an empty belief system that failed to ignite the heart with hope for the future of humankind, and Allison felt a deadness in her heart from it, an emptiness. She knew quite keenly that postmodernism would not take her to her higher humanity or potential and knew that she now needed to reject its underlying assumptions about the nature of truth and being.

And to say that all metanarratives were equal was to deny history its atrocities. There was a difference between the Nazi metanarrative and that of the Western democratic nations. The universal declaration of human rights was born from the conflict between these metanarratives in the hope that it would never be repeated, the Holocaust and the bombings of Hiroshima and Nagasaki in particular. Unfortunately, history had continually shown us that hatred and violence between ideologies still existed and that only the unifying and healing metanarrative of the Bahá'í Faith, with its focus on the oneness of humanity, could bring about lasting peace; Allison knew this in her bones. And she knew that far from improving humanity's fortunes, secular philosophy was undermining it.[4]

And there was the social and spiritual ethics within the Bahá'í framework too, which focused on the unity of all religions and the oneness of humanity, creating a new paradigm for human existence. Bahá'u'lláh had said: "That which the Lord hath ordained as the sovereign remedy and mightiest instrument for the healing of all the world is the union of all its peoples in one universal Cause, one common Faith."[5] This would transform the current materialistic and capitalistic principles now circulating in global culture and change the course of history.

Again, she tried to follow the lecture. As she did, she noted the distinct British accent of the lecturer, and it occurred to her that a short trip to London during the spring break would be a good idea to take her mind off her studies. She had lived in London in the previous year and liked the city for its historical ambiance.

The more she thought about London, the more appealing it seemed. She could even quit her studies completely and just travel around Europe with no fixed plan. With that thought she got up and left the lecture hall.

Shidan had arranged to meet her at Columbia University, and they would then go to the café in Brooklyn Heights. She waited for him on the corner of Amsterdam Avenue and West 116th Street. As she waited, she took out the pipe she had bought in Melbourne. Stuffing the pipe with tobacco, she took a light to it. As she drew a few puffs, she sent a text message to Shidan. She told him that she had left her class early, and he could pick her up sooner if he wanted.

———

The cell phone in Shidan's pocket vibrated. He read Allison's text message and got up from his desk. Before he left the room, he looked out into the light well for a moment and then at a camping bed that he had set up for her. When she was working late on essays and research, she could avoid a trip back to her Harlem apartment. He smiled and took another look at the light well. There was something about her, about her way of moving through life. She was a true traveler. An explorer. An adventurer. A seeker. Not like him. He traveled mostly for business, and maybe she was traveling somewhere where he could not follow. He felt close to her even now after such a short time knowing her; it was like they had been friends from childhood and had a deep familiarity.

He went to his desk and, putting his cotton gloves on, picked up the manuscript that he had recently purchased in London.

He left his office for the front room. As he left, he said goodbye to Nikki.

He was about to open the front door when he stopped and turned. "Hey, Nikki, why don't you go home early today?"

"Gee . . . thanks."

"I don't think many people will come this afternoon. Close up, take some money from the cash register and treat yourself to dinner."

"Okay. Thanks!"

Shidan opened the door and stepped out onto the street. The Chevy was parked at the front of the shop, and Shidan was soon navigating the afternoon traffic. He skirted Central Park and Morningside Park before turning onto Amsterdam Avenue, and after a short drive, he saw Allison sitting on the sidewalk smoking a pipe.

"Hey there!" Shidan said. He leaned over to open the door for her.

As she was about to get into the car, she saw the manuscript sitting on the passenger-side seat and stared at it for a few moments.

"Here. Put on these gloves. Pick it up, but don't touch the pages," he said.

She got in, struggled into the gloves, with the pipe clenched tightly in her mouth so ash would not fall, and placed the manuscript carefully in the back seat. She then removed the gloves and placed them on the dashboard.

"How was London?" she said once she was relaxed. She fingered her pipe as he drove off and merged into traffic.

"London was its usual self. I visited my old school: Westminster School. Some of my teachers are still there after all these years." He stared at the pipe. "I haven't seen that pipe before," he said.

"I got it in Melbourne just before coming to New York. Take a few puffs if you like." She handed him the pipe and lay back with her head on the seat back. She stared up at what he assumed was the sky framed by the car's sunroof. He sucked air through the pipe. The smoke rose up and wafted toward and out through the sunroof.

"Do you believe in coincidences?" she said, still staring at the smoke's patterns through the sunroof.

She closed her eyes, saying, "Everything, it seems to me, has a reason larger than just chance . . . I think. Even the smallest events can have a huge impact on the lives of others. Everything is interlinked. Fate, if that is the right word for it, seems to touch our lives in unseen ways. Our destiny is transfigured within the light in our minds," she said.

"What, you mean some kind of greater destiny?"

"Yes . . . that is exactly what I mean. A greater destiny. Thank you. That's a beautiful thought, Shidan."

He laughed. "You're a funny girl, but I love you just the same. And you should save those thoughts for Hooman tonight. He will agree with you, I think."

He passed the pipe back to her.

After a long silence, they left Manhattan and drove over the Brooklyn Bridge.

He occasionally looked over at her as she stared at the bay and continued to smoke her pipe. She was always breaking female stereotypes. He loved her for that, like smoking the pipe, which normally only an old man would do. Something about her did seem old or maybe beyond time. Then she turned to him.

"I am thinking I might quit my studies."

"Really? But you haven't even completed the semester."

"I know, but I don't think I will enjoy it. The structure of the course follows a line of secular academia. It hasn't been very fulfilling so far, and I don't expect it will get any better. I didn't mind it so much in my undergraduate degree, but I'm a different person now. I need to do my own personal research into matters of faith. I think philosophy should touch the human heart."

"What will you do instead?"

"I don't know. I was thinking of going back to London. I think I might go soon. In the next week or so, once I clear up the cancellation of the course. I might use London as a base to explore Europe maybe. I could even head back to Paris for a while. I just have a feeling that I need to move on. And I miss London for some strange reason. When it comes to travel, I always use my intuition even when I can't rationalize my decisions."

"Well . . . you will be missed, very much. You know that."

"Yes, I will miss you as well. But you can come over and visit me. I know that your work takes you to Europe often."

"Yes, it does and, yes, I'll see you there. So you don't think you'll come back to New York?"

"It depends on the type of visa I can get in the future. If I did decide to come back to New York, I don't think I would qualify for a work visa. And the good thing about London is I can stay as long as I want. I have an Italian passport as well as my Australian passport, so I am an EU citizen."

At the end of the bridge, he turned off the main arterial road into Brooklyn Heights and, after a few minutes, stopped in front of his apartment on Orange Street.

He put his gloves on and reached over, taking the manuscript from the back seat. "I'll be back in a sec. I just have to put this in the safe. . . . Hey, why don't you come up."

"Sure."

They got out of the car and walked into the lobby and up the staircase to his apartment.

He opened the door, and they walked into his apartment. "I've cleaned up since you were here last."

"Have you moved some of the books to the bookshop?"

"Yes. I have." He smiled and raised his eyebrows.

They walked into his spare room. It was less chaotic, but there were still teetering piles of books spread around the room. He walked over to the safe. "If you could read Greek, you might like this manuscript." He opened the safe door.

"Why?"

"Because this manuscript is a very old Gnostic manuscript that includes the Gospel of Mary. In recent years there has been a lot of study of early versions of the Bible and early Gospels and texts that did not make it into the Bible as we know it today. Also, historians have now increased the legitimacy of Mary Magdalene's role as one of the early disciples. Early Christians had downplayed her role purely because she was a woman, and yet ironically it was early Christian women that had spread the religion throughout Europe and the Middle East. But then I suppose that history is always shaped and distorted by those that have the greatest power to manipulate it rather than those who were the embodiments of its true narrative."

"Oh, that is interesting."

"Yep . . . okay, let's go to the café."

"Hey, Hooman told me the other day that Truman Capote lived around the corner from you. And that Harper Lee used to hang out there."

"Yes. I pass the house all the time."

As they were about to leave the spare room, Shidan stopped. He walked back to one of the piles and rifled through it. He came back to her and handed her a book. "If you are going to look into the Bahá'í Faith, then you should start with this. It's an introductory book. Then you can look at something deeper and more philosophical later on."

She read the cover, *The Bahá'í Faith: The Emerging Global Religion.* "Thanks."

———

Shidan parked the car on Pineapple Street. Allison got out and walked toward Vineapple Café. She looked up at the surrounding buildings, noticing the old apartment buildings that reminded her of her part of Harlem, only the buildings here were better maintained.

The facade of the café was small. She waited for Shidan at the entrance. She expected the space inside to be small and poky, but, as they stepped inside, the back of the café opened up into a bigger space.

The owner of the café greeted Shidan.

"Hi, Oliver," Shidan replied. He put his hand on Allison's shoulder. "This is my friend Allison."

"Hi, Allison. Welcome."

She waved and smiled.

"This is my daily spot for coffee. I come here every morning before work."

Allison and Shidan sat at a table in the back of the café. The décor was shiny and trendy, unlike the shabby chic of the Seven Stars Café. On one side of the café was an old redbrick wall. On the other side of the café was a clean white wall. The floor was wood, and the furnishings were a mix of stainless steel and various woods. Allison rubbed the wooden table to feel its texture. She liked the ambiance of the place even though it was not quite her fit. It looked similar to many other cafés in New York: an upmarket, more sophisticated version of Starbucks.

"Nice table," she said. "What wood is this?" She tapped it with her knuckles.

"Not sure," he said.

She looked out of a large white window at other redbrick buildings next to and behind the café.

After a few minutes, Allison saw Hooman coming toward them.

She got up and embraced him. "How are you? I've missed you this last week," she said.

"Well, I'm fine, thank you," he said and took a seat opposite Allison. "Nava sends her love," he added and smiled.

Shidan put his hand on Allison's shoulder and looked at Hooman. "You don't know the big news."

"What news?"

"Allison is leaving us for London."

"Oh my god . . . really. . . but why?"

"My studies aren't working out as I thought they would . . . and I think I need a change of scene."

"When will you leave? Will you ever come back to New York?" Hooman asked. Allison could see he was slightly shocked.

"I'll leave in the next week, I think, and I'm not sure when or if I will come back. And, of course, I will be looking into metaphysical and religious issues that were not explicitly in the philosophy course. When I studied philosophy for my undergraduate degree, I wasn't very aware of the difference between religion and philosophy, but I am now, and I think they are very distinct. Maybe philosophy is a natural extension of religion and needs to be informed by religion." She stopped for a moment. Then continuing, said, "I also think I need to travel."

A waitress came to their table, and they ordered food and coffee and continued talking.

"Are you going on a journey of meaning?" Hooman said.

"Yes, I am. I have questions that I want answered. I am seeking a peak experience from where I can see the reality of truth beyond the many veils of everyday perception. And I need a mentor."

"Maybe reality can be your mentor," Hooman said.

"Yes, maybe it can."

"Do you seek a truth that places God at the center of all reality, or are you just seeking an enhanced perception of material reality, with some kind of intellectual transcendence?" Shidan asked.

"I think I can combine both. From my reading of *The Conference of the Birds*, which is basically a mystical journey, one finds oneself on the path to God. And as for material reality, I think there is a need for it; otherwise, why would we need this world to learn the lessons of existence? But, Shidan, I thought you hated most forms of religion?"

"Not all forms. Just those that are superstitious and ignorant in the modern world. And although I don't follow any path myself, I hope you find what you need. I think Hooman can help you at various stages in your search."

"Yes, that would be helpful. Thank you. That is thoughtful, Shidan. Are you going to help me, Hooman?"

"Sure. No problem."

"We can exchange emails while I'm in London."

"Oh, I almost forgot, I have a Bahá'í prayer book for you." Hooman passed the book to Allison.

"Thank you. I'll use this, I promise."

She put the prayer book down on the table and picked up the other book. She flashed it at Hooman.

"Shidan just gave me this to start off my search."

"Oh, that's a good book. It will give you a general outline of the Faith's belief system."

Allison leaned over and hugged Shidan. She then stood up and went around the table to embrace Hooman. He seemed a little shy and embarrassed. She took her seat again and smiled at them both in silence for a while before turning to Shidan.

"Oh, Shidan, can I leave some of my stuff with you?"

"Sure. You can throw it in my spare room."

"You can have my mirror if you want it."

"Is it a magic mirror?"

"Yes," she said, smiling.

"Oh, good. I can see who the fairest of them all is."

"Well, if it is my mirror, then I suppose that makes me the Evil Queen," Allison said.

"No way. You're definitely Snow White," Shidan said.

"The only thing that is missing is the Seven Dwarfs," she said.

They all laughed.

11

RETURNING TO LONDON

. . . "Guide Thou us on the straight path," [1] *which is: "Show us the right way; that is, honour us with the love of Thine Essence, that we may be freed from occupation with ourselves and aught else save Thee, and may become wholly Thine; that we may know only Thee, and see only Thee, and think of none save Thee."* [2]

— BAHÁ'U'LLÁH, *THE SEVEN VALLEYS*

Ten days later Allison had managed to book a flight to London. On Sunday morning she caught a train from Heathrow Airport. As it neared central London, the train descended into the ground with a slight rise and then dip reminiscent of a fairground ride. Her body, backpack, and red hiking pack rose and fell slightly as they synchronized with the other passengers in the carriage. The view from the windows, which had framed a blue dawn, was lost in the blackness of the tunnel. This changed the tone of the fluorescent light, which was harsher without the soft effect of the dawn light. As the carriages rounded a bend, she heard an unpleasant sound of grinding and screaming coming from the steel tracks.

Pale faces stared off in all directions, except into each other's eyes.

Her head dropped lower as her eyes closed involuntarily. In a vague dream she saw an abstract sequence of disconnected faces and voices flashing by. Toward the end of the dream, the faces resolved into Hooman's face. Then she saw a tent inside the burned-out house in Harlem. She and Hooman were camping inside the house. Inside the tent Hooman and her were lying beside each other holding hands and laughing.

"The next station is Knightsbridge," said a pre-recorded voice.

The accent was soft and rounded and almost too perfect. This pulled her back to consciousness, along with the abrupt halt at the stop. She had passed by a few stops already, but her drowsy mind had skipped over them in what seemed like only a few moments.

Looking at the tired, yellowed tiles on the station wall, she read the word "Knightsbridge" on an old sign. She had now arrived in central London. The doors opened, and there it was: that same familiar smell of the London Underground, dust mixed with warm, stale air. She enjoyed it for a minute before the train, and its passengers moved on.

After a few more stops, she changed trains at Euston Station for the Northern line, which would put her on track to Camden Town. She knew of a hostel in Camden that she had used when she last came to London. Her mind soon closed down again, and she lost contact with time.

As the train approached Camden Town, she tried to stay awake, and leaving the train at the stop, she took the escalator up to the surface. She drifted down Camden High Street toward the hostel. Inside, she checked in and left her hiking pack in her room.

On the street again she continued up Camden High Street until she came to Camden Lock Market, where she had been many times in the past. In a familiar café she ordered a coffee and took a seat. She stared at the canal lock for several minutes and tried to keep her eyes open. Long canal boats passed by. They rose up in the lock and, once the water equalized, continued on their way. Once her coffee arrived she got up and went to the entrance, where she had seen several notices of apartment rentals and people looking for roommates. One notice caught her attention; it was an apartment in a converted church. Tearing off the tab with the contact number, she sat back in her chair and punched the numbers into her cell phone. As the phone rang, she took a sip of her coffee.

"Hello, Jade speaking."

"Hi, my name is Allison. I'm just wondering if the room you've advertised is still available?"

"Oh yes, it will be free next week."

"Can I come and have a look at it? Today, if possible."

"Sure. Come."

"I'm in Camden Lock Market at the moment, so I presume I'm nearby. Hang on one sec." She took a notepad out of her backpack. "What's the address?"

"It isn't far from the market, a ten- to fifteen-minute walk. If you follow the canal toward Regents Park, you'll come to Gloucester Avenue. Turn right, walk for a bit, and then go left down Fitzroy Road, then it's right into Chalcot Road. Walk until you get to Chalcot Square. The church overlooks the square at the far end. It's apartment seven, twenty-seven Chalcot Road. Come whenever you like. Call me again if you get lost."

Jade hung up. Allison finished her coffee and left the café. She proceeded to walk down the canal. The coffee began to kick in, and she felt less tired. After a short walk, she found the square, which housed the church, her destination, at the far end. The church was partly obscured by old plane trees at her end of the square. As she walked toward the church, she became aware of the dappled light penetrating through the large, verdant-green, star-like leaves of the plane trees, moving over her face in soft, crisscross patterns.

At the entrance she pushed the doorbell and climbed the stairs. Walking past several apartment doors, she came to the end of the corridor. Jade was waiting at the door. Allison walked into the apartment and immediately looked up at the large wooden roof beams and the thick adjoining stone walls.

"Hello, Jade." Allison extended her arm and shook Jade's hand. "This is a beautiful conversion."

"Yes. I really love being here," Jade said.

"Is anyone else looking at the place?"

"A few people have come through in the last couple of days. But nobody has shown any interest so far."

"I'm surprised. It is such a nice place. Can I see the room?"

"Oh sure, it's through this door." The room was small, and she guessed that its size was the reason no one had taken it. She liked the windows, typical for a church, which were constructed with stone arches, and the glass was a lattice of diamond-paned sections. The room overlooked the square, and she anticipated staring at the lawns, plane trees, and people passing by and finding herself lost in daydreams.

"So, if you want, it's yours."

"Don't you want to ask me a few questions about who I am?" Allison said.

"No, no. I get a good vibe from you."

"Okay, great then. I'll take it. It's mine," she said and smiled. She looked up at the roof beams again. She felt a deep satisfaction about the apartment wash over her. She walked slowly over to the wall facing the square and ran her hand over the textured stone surrounding the window. More old things, she mused. Allison liked old things. She rested her head gently on one of the stone arches before looking more intently at the square again as a young couple strolled through it holding hands.

Allison and Jade went upstairs to the living room come kitchen, where they sat talking for half an hour.

Allison eventually left the apartment and crossed the street. She walked into the center of the square and sat on a bench; leaning back, she looked up at the sky. After a few minutes, the clouds opened up, and the warmth of the sun penetrated the skin on her face. She closed her eyes. Almost as soon as she had closed her eyes her cell phone rang.

"Hey, how is London?" Shidan said. She smiled.

"Good . . . I just found a room in an apartment near Camden Town."

"So, I guess it's settled, then. You aren't coming back to New York."

"Not soon, no. I've pretty much made up my mind."

"Do you feel like a little trip?"

"A little trip. To where exactly?"

"Oh, I don't know, I'm thinking Turkey and then possibly Iran. I have a book in Istanbul that I want to buy. An old copy of the Qur'án."

"That sounds like more than a little trip."

"So, are you coming?"

"I'm a bit low on funds right now, and I need to find a job soon. I can't keep asking Paul to send me money."

"Don't worry about money. I can cover all the expenses. I'll book the tickets and post one to you. All you have to do is cover the train trip to the airport, then the rest is on me. What do you think? I need a traveling companion. Iran is very beautiful in spring. And there are many cherry trees to see along the way, I promise."

She thought for a moment. "Sure, why not, it sounds interesting. I was hoping to travel soon. When are we going?" she asked.

"In one month. In May. It'll take a couple of weeks to arrange the visas for Iran and Turkey. I'll email the details on how to apply for the visas, and I can pick you up from the airport in Istanbul. We can go from there by car. I'm thinking of buying an old four-wheel drive in Turkey, then selling it once we make it to Tehran. And I can escort you back to London on the trip back."

"Okay then. But there is no need to pick me up at the airport. I'll make my own way to the center of Istanbul."

"Will you? Are you sure? I can pick you up, no problem."

"When I figure out where to meet you, I'll let you know via email."

"Okay, wonderful. I'll email you in a few days."

"Bye. And thanks for thinking of me for this trip."

"It will be great to have you with me. Anyway, you'll hear from me soon, okay?"

"Okay then. Bye. And say hi to Hooman when you see him next. Tell him that he was in my dreams today."

"I'll tell him."

"Oh, by the way. Why didn't you ask Sara to come on this trip?"

"I did, but she was busy with work."

———

Eight days passed, and Allison moved into the apartment. While waiting for the apartment to become available, she had spent the time looking for casual work in cafés and restaurants. She needed the flexibility of taking time off so she could travel through Turkey and Iran in May. When she had lived in London before, she had worked in a café in central London near Leicester Square. She went back there to see if the café had any work for her, but they were not hiring. She went to a café in Camden, but nothing was available there either. Jade suggested she try Spitalfields Market in East London, so one morning she traveled into Covent Garden and went to an internet café to print out a few copies of her résumé.

Coming out of the underground at Liverpool Street Station, she made her way to the market. In the first couple of cafés, she had no success, but in a café restaurant called Canteen she found a job and started work the next day.

On the day after ConFest 1993, the girls got up early to begin the drive south toward Wilsons Promontory. Before they left, Io went through the camp and said goodbye to old friends and people she had met at this ConFest. Allison hugged Bess as a few others packed up the Friends of the Earth stall.

"I'll see you in Melbourne in a year," Bess said.

"I'll miss you," Allison said, smiling and walking back to the car.

As she walked, Allison looked around the campsite. Many large workshop tents were still up, but many smaller tents were being dismantled, and belongings were being packed into cars. Some volunteers were cleaning the site by picking up litter and other items.

Allison came to the car and got into the back seat. Aurélie was sitting in the front passenger seat. They waited for Io to come back to the car. Io had agreed to begin the first shift of driving, so Allison lay down in the back seat, propping her head on a pillow, and tried to finish *Being and Nothingness*.

Aurélie switched on the ignition, and Allison heard her shuffling through the mixtapes. Aurélie put a tape into the stereo, and Allison waited for a song to begin playing; it was "Scarborough Fair/Canticle" by Simon & Garfunkel.

After a few minutes, Allison saw Io bend down and remove the bricks from the tires—the car stayed where it was—and Io jumped into the driver's seat. She backed up and turned around. They drove slowly out of the festival grounds. They came to the gates and drove out.

As they passed by the main township of Moama, they were stopped by the police. They gave Allison three days to have the taillight fixed. She concealed the fact that the handbrake didn't work. After the police let them go, they passed over the border from New South Wales back into Victoria, passing through Echuca.

Instead of driving through Melbourne, which was a quicker route, they went via the Yarra Ranges toward Warburton. They passed through many small and obscure towns on the way, only stopping once for gas. The main reason for the trip along this route was the Mountain Ash forests and the mountain ranges that began in the town of Taggerty. Once they came to Marysville, they were surrounded by mountains on all sides. At this point Allison stopped reading and sat up. She began to absorb the mountainous surroundings.

After a three-hour drive, they came to Warburton. It was a small tourist town nestled between two steep hills on both sides. Allison had been here with her parents when she was nine years old. It had changed significantly since then, but they did not stop there.

Allison took over the driving just outside Warburton, and Io navigated. They found an obscure dirt road through a forest.

"Wow, this forest is cool. We have nothing like this in France."

"It is cool, isn't it? That's why I wanted to come this way."

Allison took out her Leica, and they stopped in a few places so she could take shots of the forest. They found some particularly ancient Mountain Ash trees. Allison left the car and walked into the forest. She came to the base of one particularly large Mountain Ash, and looking through the viewfinder, she took a photo looking up through the canopy at the sky above.

They eventually came out of the mountains into flat ground near Yarra Junction. And after thirty minutes, they passed back into the mountains as they headed toward Nayook.

Beyond Nayook they drove into mostly flat farmland for two and a half hours until they came to Wilsons Promontory National Park. The first thing that Allison saw was a wetland area leading up to the base of a series of large hills. There were long grasses and reeds with patches of dark water.

They drove into these hills, and on the other side of them, they came to the main camping ground, Tidal River. They stopped at the visitors center, where they found maps of the different hiking trails.

They bought some supplies from the store near the center, then drove to the beginning of a hiking trail that started from the parking lot near the peak of Mount Oberon.

———

The sun was beginning to set as they arrived at the Sealers Cove camping ground after a three-hour hike. The two girls set up the tents and began to prepare a meal, and Allison took a walk down the beach at Sealers Cove. She was the only person on the beach. At the end of the beach, she lay down and watched the stars emerge as night came into focus. After an hour, the two girls found her.

"We brought you dinner," Aurélie said. Io passed Allison a bowl with boiled potatoes and a plastic bag with a salad inside it.

She sat up. "Thanks and sorry. I was about to walk back."

"That's okay. We can join you instead," Io said.

The two girls lay next to Allison as she ate dinner, and they watched the night sky together for another hour before they all went back to their tents.

12

FINDING MONA

If thou be a man of communion and prayer, soar upon the wings of assistance from the holy ones, that thou mayest behold the mysteries of the Friend and attain the lights of the Beloved: "Verily, we are God's, and to Him shall we return." [1,2]

— BAHÁ'U'LLÁH, *THE SEVEN VALLEYS*

Early in the morning Allison's plane landed in Istanbul at Ataturk Airport. Once she was outside the airport building, she waved down a taxi. The taxi driver got out and began to help her with her luggage.

"There's not much. Do you speak English?" she said.

"Yes, I do. But not too good. Get in. I get luggage."

She passed him her hiking pack and got into the back seat with her backpack, removing her camera and sitting it on her lap.

She heard him slam the trunk shut. He got into the driver's seat and turned around. "Where you going? Old city?"

"Yes. Have you heard of the house of Bahá'u'lláh? Do you know of the Bahá'ís here in Istanbul?"

"No. Where that house?"

She opened her backpack and pulled out a notepad. She read the address. "Meymenet Street, in Atikali."

"I know that place."

"Can you take me through the more modern suburbs on the way?"

"Modern?"

"New suburbs. Not the old city."

"Sure, but why?"

"I want to see the Istanbul that most Turkish people know."

"Sure, but very boring. Is that right English? There is another word, but I have forgot."

"Yes. You mean 'dull'."

"Yes, dull. Very dull. I take you by coast road. Better view, the sea."

"Yeah, sure. Thanks."

They left the airport and drove along a road that hugged the contours of the bay. It eventually turned into an expressway. She looked out over the water and then up at the sun for a moment. There were ferries and boats crisscrossing each other as they made their way to various destinations in the bay. In the distance, on the far side of the harbor, were hills. The harbor was beautiful and like Melbourne's Port Phillip Bay, a large encircling bay but on a larger scale as parts of the bay were just a horizon of sea. After a while, she looked at the coastal suburb that rimmed the road. The buildings were mostly six- to seven-story concrete apartment blocks. Some were new and modern, but many were cheap sixties and seventies constructions.

After twenty minutes, the taxi driver turned onto an exit ramp that took them away from the coastal road and into a suburb.

He turned again into backstreets, and after a few minutes, he said, "Is this what you want?"

"Yes. Perfect," she said as she panned around the suburb with her eyes and then her camera.

"This is Incirli. I grew up here."

"Oh, cool."

They drove for ten minutes through all the narrow backstreets. These buildings were all three- to four-story concrete apartment blocks. Many were very roughly constructed, but some were more modern and cleaner. The facades of all these buildings were quite plain, and it reminded her a little of the newer and poorer parts of Paris.

"We go back a bit, but I think you like it. I show you something."

"Sure."

"It not new, but I think you like it."

Eventually, they came to an intersection between two streets, where they stopped.

"Look," he said. "What you think?"

She looked up at a slightly rotten and wonky wooden house, with sections of the roof fallen in on the second story. "Wow, that is so cool. Thank you for bringing me here. This is amazing. That is really old. Can you wait here for a bit? I might be a while."

"Take as long as you want," said the taxi driver. "Use cell phone when you want me. I go get a coffee. We passed café one block back." He gave her his number. Allison got out of the taxi with only her camera and backpack and waved to him as he drove off.

She walked up to the house. The street sign said Revnakli Sk. The first floor of the house was surrounded by a solid metal fence to stop people going in; the house was probably a death trap and obviously very old. There were simple carvings in the corners of the eaves. All the paint had peeled away a long time ago, and it looked weather beaten and water stained. The wooden cladding was mostly a coffee color but was faded to gray in places. When she looked closer at the window frames, she saw traces of faded white paint that had mostly peeled away. It was not a house for a rich person; that was clear. It had a certain humility about it.

She guessed it dated from the mid to late 1800s or maybe earlier; it was hard to tell. And there must have been whole suburbs with buildings like this that were pulled down to build the modern apartment blocks that now surrounded the wooden house; it was like a small, rotten but beautiful island in time, sitting in a sea of concrete boxes, the remnant of a generation that was completely gone, with only the ghosts of people that had passed through history. Maybe it was waiting to be restored, she thought. She hoped, at least. Next to this house, on the other side of the intersection, were a few more like it but smaller. She looked up at them for a long time.

She looked back at the larger house and looked for a way to get inside. She walked closer to the house. She had to pull the metal fence back a little and was able to squeeze through. After shuffling along between the house and the fence, she found the weather-worn wooden front door. She walked up the steps. She then held the round brass door-knob and turned it. The door clicked open, and she walked in. The interior was empty and in much better condition than the exterior, but it was still slightly wonky. The house had clearly seen a lot of life passing through it. Allison looked down at the floorboards, which were polished with age and mottled from many people walking over them for at least a hundred and forty or more years. There was more wear near the front door. She wondered when it had stopped being a useful house. How long had it been in this dilapidated and unlivable state? Who had lived and died here?

She crouched down and ran her hand over the worn floorboards to feel their smooth surface texture. She then studied their unique patina. She sat down and crossed her legs as she moved her eyes around the entire interior. She took a few photographs that needed the camera's inbuilt automatic flash. The fire of life had been flickering away over many years and had eventually gone out and moldered; the bodies that had passed through the house had rotted, like the house, in the earth and in the ground of memory. The puppets were gone, but the stage still remained, if only a little faded. And now even the memories were gone, as anyone who had ever known the people in this house had also died and passed through their own houses of relativity into the obscurity of an unknown history. And here Allison was now trying to "renovate" those lost lives in her memory: in Latin she knew the word as "renovato." But she then realized that she did not know who had lived here, and without the exact knowledge of who they were, she could not renovate their lives even in her memory; their deaths made that impossible. There was no renovation of the dead body. The house could be renovated but not the people. The only way that a renovation of people could be realized was if someone else moved into this house after it had been renovated: someone living. And she then knew that the births and deaths in humanity and nature were a form of the renovation: spring renovated winter in the same way that one generation renovated the preceding generation.

She thought about a poem she had written many years before called "The House of Relativity." We throw our hearts to the sky, but it does not answer. So we long for the renovation of the house of time. It is a strange, broken mystery longing to be reborn in the light chamber of our dreams.

She looked over at the staircase and up to the second floor, where she saw the sun peeking through the collapsed roof. She decided against exploring the second floor as she might fall through the floorboards or the staircase.

She thought about the end of the poem. For the mirror to create illusion, it must empty its own self to become nothingness; the house of relativity is the secret mirror for the unchanging self to seek itself. But this is never declared to the house of relativity. It knows not its own self, so it is forced to look up, not down, for the sky, away from the lakes of forever and their reflection of the sky. The dream tells the dreamers that they are awake. They had never slept, so there was no need to wake. The dreamers in the house of relativity told the mirror, "Don't seek reality, but illusion, because that points to reality." The mirror foundation of forever said through the nothingness of reflection, "Don't seek reality either. Construct your own self from my image of nothingness because I don't understand myself, nor will you ever understand your own self."

She closed her eyes for a few moments, then stood up. She kissed the air. "I love you, house of relativity: house of time, house of death, house of decay."

She walked back out the door and down the steps, then rang for the taxi driver. "I am ready now," she said to the driver. She shuffled along the metal fence and back onto the street.

She dawdled, feeling deep connections while looking at the house. The taxi arrived just as she was ready to move on. "Thank you. That was enlightening and beautiful."

"I know somehow you like that. Even though I don't know you so well."

The taxi driver did a U-turn, and they moved back through the suburb and onto the expressway. After ten minutes, they turned away from the coast and joined another expressway. There were still more apartment blocks with flat facades yet a little more modern and better built. Eventually they entered an area that had more ambiance and character, with cafés and shops, but it was still not the typical old part of the city that was either Byzantine or from the Ottoman Era and the mostly stone-built structures that Allison had expected to see from her research of Istanbul.

The taxi arrived and dropped her near the house of Bahá'u'lláh with her luggage. There were a few people on the street.

She thanked him and paid for the ride.

She crossed the street and walked up to the entrance where she had arranged to meet Shidan.

The house was a fairly plain two-story building with a flat facade, but only Bahá'ís could enter the building. So she stood near the entrance looking up at it. She wondered about Bahá'u'lláh's continual stages of banishment from Iran, through Iraq, to Turkey, and eventually to an Ottoman prison colony—in Akka, which is in today's Israel—where he was imprisoned until a time close to his death in 1892. Bahá'u'lláh was the prophet founder of the Bahá'í Faith, and Allison knew a little about his life from conversations with Hooman. At that time in 1863, Istanbul was known as Constantinople. Bahá'u'lláh had arrived in the city on August 16 of that year with his family and a group of Bahá'ís. The only other thing she knew about Bahá'u'lláh's family was about his daughter Bahíyyih Khánum. She was seventeen then and had rejected the idea of marriage, which was unusual for a woman at that time.

She walked up to the front of the house and brushed her hands over the facade and looked into the windows, but the drapes were drawn.

As she was staring up at the building, she felt a hand on her shoulder. She turned around. Shidan was smiling at her. They embraced and then turned back to the house.

"I never visited this house in the past . . . but there is a mosque, the Blue Mosque, nearby that I have seen. Bahá'u'lláh visited it during his stay here," he said.

Allison did not respond and kept staring up at the building. Eventually, she turned to him. "Shall we get going?" she said.

"Sure."

She crossed back over the road, stowed her camera in her backpack, put her hiking pack on her back, and picked up the backpack.

The car was near Bahá'u'lláh's house, and, after a short walk, they got into the four-wheel drive.

"When did you buy the car?"

"I got here yesterday so I could get it for the trip." Shidan turned on the ignition. "We need to travel to Ankara. So our options are that we can stay here for the day, then drive to Ankara tomorrow. It takes a half day to drive. Or we could explore here for an hour or two, then drive to Ankara."

"What would you prefer?"

"Well, I've been here a few times before, so there is not much here that I haven't already seen, so it's up to you. The only thing I need to do before we leave is get the manuscript I came for."

"How about we explore here for a few hours and then head off? I'm not sure why, but my preference is to see as much of Iran as we can. I am sure Turkey is wonderful, but Iran seems somehow more resonant culturally. I would like to see Tehran, where Hooman and Nava grew up. Do you know much about Hooman's childhood in Tehran?"

"No, not really. I know the suburb where they grew up. It is near the place where Bahá'u'lláh first received his revelation, but I don't know the street."

"Oh, it doesn't matter. It would be good to just pass by the general area."

"We can drive through it when we get to Tehran."

They drove off toward the old city proper. They started in the suburb of Eminonu; it definitely reminded her of the older parts of Paris, and the buildings had a lot of character but were a bit shabbier and dirtier than Paris, with a largely inconsistent mix of buildings from different periods. The older Medieval or Byzantine parts of Istanbul were mixed in with newer Victorian-like buildings; the city definitely had a European edge to it.

After an hour of walking around the maze of narrow streets in the old parts of Istanbul, they stopped at the book dealer. It was a small, narrow shop opposite the Grand Bazaar. They stepped into the book-shop, and a man approached them.

"I am going to attempt my very basic Turkish and see if this guy speaks Arabic," said Shidan.

"Okay."

They exchanged what Allison thought was a polite Turkish greeting and a short, stilted conversation.

Shidan turned to her. "Luckily he speaks a bit of Arabic."

Allison looked around while Shidan began talking in Arabic to the shop owner, and they disappeared into the back rooms. She could hear them talk in a way that seemed animated. Her eyes ran over the many old books on the shelves. After a quarter of an hour of what she assumed was haggling, he stepped back into the front room of the shop and held it up.

"Got it," he said, smiling.

"What is it?"

"An old copy of the Qur'án. I got it for a fair price too." He patted the cover and laughed in an exaggerated manner, like Dracula. She smiled and half-chuckled.

They stepped back into the street, crossed over, and entered the Grand Bazaar. This was something that Allison had never seen before. They walked down narrow avenues with an array of small shops selling every conceivable obscure item. Allison stopped in front of a spice shop with many small mounds of different spices displayed out the front of the shop; it was a fragrant and colorful mix of sensations. The bazaar was packed and humming with people and noise. Shidan crossed over to a clothing shop on the opposite side of the avenue.

He came back and passed her a black silk headscarf. "You may want to wear this when we get to Iran. Otherwise, we will attract unwanted attention from the authorities."

Allison took the scarf and looked up at the arches in the roof of the Grand Bazaar. The arches were decorated with Islamic geometric designs and faded yellow paint. Light flooded down through arched windows near the roof of the Bazaar building, and it had an ethereal quality. For a wild moment the light seemed to transport her somewhere blissful. This impression soon faded, but she still felt slightly euphoric, which was strange and new, and she didn't understand where this feeling had come from.

A short time after exploring the Grand Bazaar and its market stalls, they decided to head toward Ankara, so they walked back to the car that was parked a few blocks away.

They got in.

"You don't want to see any of the old mosques or museums? Or any of the old Turkish palaces?"

"No, they don't interest me."

"I agree. The palaces were never filled with the most interesting people in the world. The kings and courtiers of the Ottoman Empire were nasty pasties for the most part."

"Yes. I agree. I don't want to be reminded of their superficiality. I saw what I needed to see earlier today in the taxi."

"What was that?"

"The poorer suburbs."

"Hmm . . . why don't we drive past the Blue Mosque, and you can at least see the outside."

"Okay." She smiled.

They drove on, and after five minutes, they passed in front of the Blue Mosque and stopped to look at the outside. Allison had to concede that it was beautiful with its stacked domes and minarets. She thought about taking a photograph of it but decided that there were enough pictures of it in the world should she ever need to be reminded of it. They got out of the car. Shidan took Allison's hand, and they strolled around part of its perimeter before retracing their steps and getting back into the car. Shidan drove off toward the Bosporus Bridge via an expressway that passed near the Central Business District where all the modern high-rise buildings were standing, hiding "her" old wooden houses; she knew more houses like the one she had seen that day must exist. Small time capsules in a sea of concrete and stone. It seemed like modernity was eating away at the past and engulfing it: the present could taste the past as it destroyed it.

As they left the city along an arterial highway, Allison noticed the transition from the older part of the city to the new modern suburbs. After a while, these outer suburbs faded out, and they were in the countryside, moving through green hills along the edge of the bay. The highway was interspersed with small towns and villages.

Allison observed the day slowly fade into night. It took five hours before they reached Ankara. When they arrived, it was dark, and after half an hour of driving around, they found a hotel they liked.

———

On the morning of the next day, Shidan and Allison drove around Ankara. Since they had decided not to visit any mosques, palaces, or museums, they concentrated on domestic architecture. They drove through all the modern and newer suburbs, which were similar to Istanbul with many multi-story concrete apartment blocks all packed tightly together. Then they came to the old city of Ankara—and particularly the suburb Hamamonu with all its restored 1920 to 1930 houses.

Allison thought this city was an interesting place but not as interesting as Istanbul. She wondered why she felt that way for a moment. Was it because of the limited architectural diversity here in Ankara compared to Istanbul? No, that was not it, she thought. Then a thought came into her mind of the house of Bahá'u'lláh. The house was beautiful for a reason she could not justify given its rather plain appearance. Then she looked up at the sun, and it was ethereal again, like the day before. It seemed like she had never seen it before, and it was incredibly beautiful. And that was what this drab little world was like most of the time; it had a mundane veil beyond which was a deeper, more resonant reality if only one could penetrate that veil.

It was lunchtime, so they decided to have lunch at a café that was next to a crumbling Tudor-revival building. They sat outside on the street at a small red table with matching red chairs. Their Turkish coffees were in hand, and they watched the world drift by the café. He had the Qur'án that he had purchased on the previous day in his bag. He put on his white cotton gloves and pulled it out, placing it flat on the red table. He opened it and carefully turned to random pages, mumbling in Arabic. She could tell it was valuable just by the quality of the script. The book was obviously hand drawn, and the calligraphy curled and looped around the page. At the beginning of each chapter, the script was formed into a circular shape, and the sentences were running diagonally from right to left. She knew this because she watched Shidan follow the text with his index finger traveling above the page as he read. It was also an illuminated manuscript with many geometric patterns incorporated into the text that would be typical of Islamic traditions.

"Is that old?"

"Yes, but not really old."

"It's so beautifully made. Like the early Christian texts that are illuminated."

"Yes, but the really old and expensive copies of the Qur'án are much simpler and have not been illuminated. They were meant to be used often for purely pragmatic purposes; it was the text itself that was meant to be beautiful and not the way it was made or embellished."

"Are there any interesting things in the Qur'án?" she said.

"I suppose there are a few things of interest. I studied the Qur'án when I was growing up in Tehran. That was before I went to London in the seventies. We used to learn it by rote. There is a small quote around here that expresses the idea that this life is a passing joy." He turned one page and then the next. "Here it is. It is in Sura 40—The Believer: 'O my people! This present life is only a passing joy, but the life to come is the mansion that abideth.'"[3]

"Thank you. Interesting." She thought about the house of relativity back in Istanbul. Whoever had lived in and through that old wonky house had passed on to a mansion that abideth; that wonky house was a clear symbol for this life.

———

The next day they left Ankara early in the morning. They passed through many small towns in Central Anatolia. The terrain between these towns was quite bare, with primarily broad hills and flat grassland between the hills; these were punctuated with farms that were growing a variety of crops that were in the middle of their cycle now that it was late spring. If there were trees, they tended to grow along the rivers they passed by.

Allison had her feet on the dashboard for most of the time. She stared for hours at the road lines and the mostly flat horizon. She and Shidan did not speak much; they did not need to.

The sun beat down on her skin, and the air pushed her hair around her face. It was quite exhilarating at different points on this journey, and she felt an indefinable freedom of self. She felt this way whenever she traveled somewhere unfamiliar. Allison consciously turned her mind on to record some of the images of the surrounding countryside, becoming hyper-aware of her awareness. Most of the time Shidan had the radio on, and Allison listened to the incomprehensible Turkish pop music with those eighties-style synthesizers blaring away. She looked over at Shidan from time to time and smiled as he was bopping away to the music.

Toward the end of the day, they drove toward a small city on the outer edge of Central Anatolia called Sivas. Twenty minutes before they came to the town, the highway began to run along the Red River. Allison guessed the name of the river came from the dark red color of the silt in the water. Ten miles before coming into the town, they stopped at a gas station where the *benzinci*, the gas station attendant, filled up their tank.

When they entered the town, Allison surveyed all the concrete apartment blocks. If there was an old part of the town, it had been swallowed up by all these quasi-modern buildings. There were bigger hills around this town than most of the terrain they had passed through during that day.

"Oh, by the way, if you are interested, Bahá'u'lláh and his family passed through this town on their way to Istanbul."

"Sivas must have been very different at that time," she said.

"I believe they camped on the north side of the Red River."

She tried to imagine the town during the time of Bahá'u'lláh. They occasionally passed by old stone walls and buildings that were part of the town all those years before, and she liked the idea of passing through history this way and using her imagination as a tool to strip modernity of its reality in the present. After fifteen minutes of driving around Sivas, they found a small hotel and stayed the night.

———

On the second day they passed into Eastern Anatolia with its isolated and vast landscapes of mountainous terrain and occasional plateaus in between. They passed through many small towns and villages. At dusk, after a nine-hour drive, they came to another plateau between tall mountains in the distance on each side of the town. Dogubayazit was a rather tired little town off the tourist track, but Allison liked it. It lacked some of the polish of Istanbul and Ankara but had its own unique dusty ambiance. They found a tired-looking hotel to rest their tired bodies overnight.

That night Allison lay in bed and listened to the sounds of cars and motorcycles passing in front of the hotel. All the images of the last two days traveling flowed through her mind. She saw the road. Of all things that remained, and it reminded her of her travels through Australia.

The road endured in the landscape and always remained the same even when the landscape changed; she thought about the last line of *The Conference of the Birds*: "Their Road is thine—Follow—and Fare thee well."[4] But the road was an internal road, not an external road, although the external road led to the internal road. In a vision she saw herself in the desert, walking on a desert highway, but it was a transcendent highway leading to fire and light and the absolute annihilation of self and transfiguration of identity. She closed her eyes, and in a dream she was still walking that road alone. She would never find another person in that new world; it was just Allison and the road: the illimitable road.

———

Late in the morning on the next day, Dogubayazit was behind them. The town was framed in miniature in the car's side mirror. Allison looked at the town for a few moments. She remembered men on the previous day playing backgammon in the bustling teahouses on the main street of the town.

Everything about Turkey had been a series of cultural revelations, and this was her first foray into a culture with strong Islamic history and traditions. Nothing could have prepared her for what she saw, and she was now up close to the culture with a mixture of mild culture shock and wonder, despite her statement that she thought Iran was more resonant culturally.

She turned her head to see the grasslands pass by as their four-wheel drive crossed a wide plateau. She observed the various small farms with old run-down-looking tractors and rusty farm equipment. The road turned, and they moved into a valley between low hills to the south and the snow-capped Mount Ararat to the north. For a few moments her view of Ararat was dulled by a haze of dust kicked up by the car in front of them. They came off the paved road and passed slowly by a broken-down truck that was sitting in the middle of the road. "Is that the same Ararat that's in the Bible? Noah's Ark? That mountain?" she asked as she pointed at it.

He glanced at the mountain for a moment, then looked back at the road.

"Well, it depends on whom you talk to. There's not much science that backs up this location. And I doubt they will ever find a *real* boat. Some have claimed it's in the hills closer to the border, but anyway, who cares about a few decayed sticks of wood? It's the symbol that matters. Don't you think? And symbols last longer too. The symbol never dies really. Although I am not a believer, I remember Hooman saying that while a physical boat decays, the idea of an ark remains forever in a plethora of symbolic transmutations in the minds of people. The real ark, according to Hooman, is the salvation of abiding by the spiritual laws of a religion, which see you through this life and eternity. It's the basic covenant between God and humanity that you will find in all religions."

She thought about Plato's book *Laws*, relating to both societal and religious laws, and how it related to the ideas in the *Republic*. "And I suppose the boat symbolizes safety from the changeable conditions of the material world. It's a pity Hooman isn't here to see this history. Whether it's real or not," she said.

"I did ask him to come with us, but he didn't want to, and he was afraid for us, plus he couldn't take the time off work. And I suppose he's right. We are taking a bit of a risk entering Iran now. Especially me, with my father's history of dissent toward the current regime."

"You didn't tell me you called him."

"I didn't think you needed to know. You know that's how I work; it's *Mission Impossible* here, babe."

"Typical," she said. She smiled and looked south at the landscape. The land was empty, with short green grass in the valleys ascending up to bare rocky outcrops in the hills.

They reached the border crossing after twenty minutes. The crossing was a low pass between hills. After an hour, their papers were processed, and finally they drove over the border into Iran. Allison put her black headscarf on as they drove into a small border town called Bazargan. Shidan had read the sign to her.

Several other cars and trucks had crossed the border with them, and this convoy wound around the mountain roads on either side of their four-wheel drive.

After half an hour, they entered a large, flat plain with patches of desert and only a few farms scattered around. Allison picked up her

Leica and took shots of the desert as they passed through it; they stopped at a gas station halfway through the plain. Allison got out of the car to stretch her legs and smelled the gas as a gas station attendant filled the tank. There was something amazing about being here in Iran like this, in these obscure little towns, a world away from big cities. She watched several trucks and cars pass by the station. Shidan, who was also stretching his legs, paid the attendant before he and Allison got back into the car and drove off.

After twenty minutes, they left the desert and passed back into yet more green farmland situated along another river. They then came to another mountain range. They followed that river until, after driving two and half hours from the Iranian border, they came to Marand, a small city in the East Azerbaijan Province of Iran, but they did not stop there. They continued driving along a bypass on the outskirts of the city. They eventually stopped in Sufian for lunch, a half-hour drive past Marand, where they found a small teahouse next to a relatively small mosque on the outskirts of the town.

Sitting in front of the teahouse, Allison took a bite of her salad sandwich, which was made with flatbread. To the right of the town, she stared into the distance at bare mountains. Her eyes then panned around until she was looking at a flat expanse to the south.

Her thoughts rewound back to the few minutes she had spent standing in front of the house of Bahá'u'lláh in Istanbul.

"Did you like the house of Bahá'u'lláh?" she asked.

"Yes, I suppose so. Though it was a plain-looking building."

"Yes, I thought that too. But there was something about it that I can't define intellectually, and I wonder how these holy places release spiritual power into the world. When I told Hooman I was going to Istanbul, he suggested I visit the house. He told me about their power. It's a pity we couldn't go inside."

"True, I suppose." Shidan took a sip of his tea.

"I mean, it is essentially only an empty house whose history has faded into the past, but there is something beautiful about its emptiness, which is a gift to the present."

"I guess these places are symbols," he said.

"So, you don't think these places have any sort of power to uplift a person's soul?"

"I don't know. Maybe. You're asking the wrong person. Only Hooman would know the answer to that. But then, I suppose these places must have some power. If believers of religions are supposed to turn toward them during prayer, then they must have some significance. When I was young, my mother got me to turn toward Mecca when I prayed. She was religious, unlike my father. But I never felt anything. Nothing obvious. I mean, I did feel a few positive things when I prayed as a young boy. But when I was at school in England, I gave up praying. Secular culture in England opened my eyes. One of my teachers and my father, too, taught me about secular humanism and other philosophies that divorce ethics from religion and thus make the need for religion less compelling. My intellectual development changed my mind about religion and fed my cynicism, but I sometimes miss the innocence of my childhood and the positive things I felt I got from Islam at that earlier time. I wonder if I will ever recapture those things: innocence and ignorance."

"Ignorance is a good thing to lose," said Allison.

"Yes, of course. I was meaning the loss of innocence, really. Of recapturing the positivity of an innocent belief in God. But strangely, my ignorance of secular belief is what allowed my innocence to exist within the context of Islam, so in a way, that ignorance was kind of positive at that time in my life."

"Hooman said these places are an outer symbol of an inner condition. That we should turn toward God both externally and internally. Bahá'ís turn to Bahjí, which I think is in Israel. Where Bahá'u'lláh is buried. Is that correct?"

"Yes, they do face Bahjí. That is correct." He looked out at the plain to the south of the town and took another sip of his tea. After a while, he turned to her. "Send Hooman an email when you get back to London. He'll have some firm ideas on this topic," he said.

Allison then heard Shidan's phone *bing*. He took his phone from his pocket and read it.

"It's Sara. She's wondering how we are going."

"Please send her my love."

"I will."

Shidan began to text a reply to Sara.

After enjoying a long, languid afternoon tea, they left Sufian and drove into the plain they had seen from the teahouse. Allison looked at the mountains to the north of the plain for a moment, then back at the flat expanse. The flatness was a mix of grassland and patches of desert. She had her feet on the dashboard again and continued staring at the expanse as they drove through it. The sand reminded her of the Australian desert and in particular the Nullarbor Plain, which she had driven through many years before; the nuanced differences between the two deserts were clear in her mind: one was more yellow and the other, the Nullarbor, redder. They passed a cement factory and, not long after that, a large factory complex.

Driving for another thirty minutes, they arrived in Tabriz at two in the afternoon; it was the largest city since Ankara.

Tabriz was surrounded on both sides by mountain ranges in the distance, and closer to the town were a series of low hills with a red-ochre tint. The haze of pollution sunk into the basin between these hills, and it softened the afternoon light. Allison looked at the low hills, and again their color reminded her of the outback in Australia.

They drove into the outer suburbs. They were mostly the concrete apartment blocks that she had come to expect. They also passed a few industrial areas on the outskirts, but as they came closer to the old city, she started to see several older eighteenth- and nineteenth-century buildings. The beauty of these buildings stood in stark contrast to the majority of the poorly designed 1970s-style architecture. After driving around semi-randomly, they passed in front of the Ark, and Shidan stopped in front of the building and looked up at it. Shidan read an information sign on the side of the road and explained that it was a fourteenth-century fortification that had been repurposed many times throughout Persian history. Allison noticed Shidan looking in the other direction at a hotel opposite. He explained to her that it was called Ark Hotel, obviously taking its name from the old building sitting opposite it.

"This hotel will do. Kind of appropriate since we were talking about the other Ark this morning," he said.

"So, what's next?" she asked.

"I want to call Tehran today. I have a cousin there, Payman . . . I have to talk to him. Maybe we can go exploring on foot for a few hours and have some dinner somewhere."

She put her hand on his arm. "We're going to Tehran to find your sister and father, aren't we? That's the real reason for this trip. There is no other business in Tehran, is there?" she asked.

"Aren't you perceptive."

"Do you think we'll find their graves?"

"Graves? I think nameless plots or trenches at best, not graves. We'll have to see, won't we? We'll get as close as we can. Anyway, if we just go to Tehran, that would almost be enough. You know I haven't been back for close to twenty years. I'll show you the house where I grew up and some of the streets I used to play in."

"Good, I look forward to seeing these places."

They got out of the car and walked into the Ark Hotel with their luggage. They left their luggage in their rooms and came back to the lobby. The concierge at the hotel gave them a map of the old city with the sights and restaurants. While Shidan was talking to the concierge, she saw a tourist brochure of a village on a small table in the lobby. It was written in Persian, so she could not read it, but the photos of the village intrigued Allison.

"This looks really beautiful." She brought the brochure over to the counter and gave it to the concierge. "What is this place called, and how far is it from Tabriz?"

Shidan translated her question into Persian.

"It's called Kandovan, and it's an hour each way," the concierge said.

"Okay, cool. Can we go?"

"Of course. We can have dinner down there and come back before nightfall," said Shidan.

They left Tabriz and found a highway heading south. Shidan got lost because he didn't take the correct turnoff. After asking around, he finally got onto a smaller road going southeast. They drove through a landscape of low, grassy hills until after an hour they came into Kandovan.

"This is absolutely incredible!" Allison exclaimed as they drove into the village.

Shidan looked over at her and smiled.

"This reminds me so much of Coober Pedy in Australia where everyone lived underground in rock dugouts, but here it is above ground and in these conical stone structures . . . this is crazy beautiful!"

"Calm down. Calm down. You're going to have a heart attack."

Allison laughed.

"Oh man, what an amazing accident of chance."

They drove into the narrow streets. Part of the village was made of regular stone structures that were partially rendered with mud, but toward the back of the village were the conical stone houses. They reared up into the hill. People had burrowed into the stone and hollowed out houses with wooden doors and windows.

They came closer to the hills and parked. They got out of the car and walked into the streets. Allison now saw that the conical stone was filled with holes and looked like molten molasses with all its organic undulations. It was incredibly beautiful to Allison, and she started taking black-and-white photos with the Leica.

"These must be volcanic formations," she said, looking through the viewfinder.

"Yes, plus a bit of erosion."

They kept walking around the village and eventually found a teahouse. They walked through the door and sat at a small wooden table near a window. Allison looked around at the interior stone walls that had been carved out.

"Amazing," she said.

Someone came up and put tea on the table.

Shidan got his cell phone out.

"I am just going to call my uncle and get Payman's cell number."

"Okay."

Shidan started talking in Persian. Allison listened for several minutes before he hung up.

"My uncle is going to text me Payman's number, but he thinks we are mad poking around for Mona's and Dad's graves. He told me to be very careful who we talk to about them. The Iranian secret police have a lot of informers."

"Are we going to visit your family?"

"No. I suggested it, but my uncle said no. He said I was selfish for even calling him and suggesting it. He was very angry at me toward the end of the conversation."

"Why?"

"Because he thinks I am putting the family at risk by coming to Iran now. But Payman might meet us. I grew up with him. I mean, we used to hang out quite a bit when I was young. Before the revolution. After that, not so much."

"What side of the family are they on?"

"Dad's side. Mum's sister died of cancer years ago, and my grandparents are all dead now."

"Hey, why don't we stay here tonight? I mean, I know we have the hotel back in Tabriz to go to, but it would be so cool to stay here tonight."

"Okay, sure. We passed a hotel a few streets back."

"Was it carved into the stone?"

"Sure was."

"Okay, cool."

Shidan's cell phone beeped.

"Ahh . . . that'll be Payman's number."

———

In the morning Shidan and Allison drove back to Tabriz from Kandovan to pick up their luggage from the Ark Hotel. Shidan paid the bill and they left, loading the car with their luggage. Shidan drove north toward the center of the old city.

"Let's head in the general direction of the Grand Bazaar," he said. When they did eventually come to the Grand Bazaar, he pointed at it and drove past.

"We're not stopping here?" she said. She looked back at the bazaar as they passed by it.

"It's not the bazaar I want you to see. It's something else, a little farther along. Here, take this." He passed her a hand-drawn map of a few streets in Tabriz. "Hooman drew it for me."

Under the map was a quote from the Báb. Hooman had written it in cursive, and it was obvious that he had taken great care to make it as beautiful as he could:

I am the Primal Point from which have been generated all created things. I am the Countenance of God Whose splendour can never be obscured, the Light of God

Whose radiance can never fade. Whoso recognizeth Me, assurance and all good are in store for him . . .[5]

"In 1844 the first founder of the Bahá'í Faith, the Báb, attempted to wipe away hundreds of years of Islamic dogma. For which he paid . . . with his life. It was a similar story with my father and sister. And you know their story."

"Yes, I do."

"Truth is a heavy burden for the ignorant. It burns a path as it makes a way forward . . . into the future, an unrepentant future. Hooman described those early beginnings as the heroic age of the Bahá'í Era, where many thousands lost their lives for upholding principles that were supposedly contrary to Islam. In fact, these were the very fulfillment of Islam. That's the irony of it."

After a few minutes, he pulled over and parked the car next to a tear-shaped square. Traffic passed around it on each side, and the space was large, with trees on its rim surrounding an open lawn area.

"This is Shohada Square," he said.

In the middle of the lawn sat a large circular fountain.

Walking through several lanes of traffic, they came up to the lawn. Farther on they stopped at the fountain. He sat down on its rim, looking at a building on the opposite side of the square. He ran his hand over the water as Allison listened to the falling water near the center of the fountain.

"What do you think I can see here?" He then pointed at the building. "That is a bank. Melli Bank."

"I can't see anything special here. What is it?" She looked in the direction he was pointing.

"It's not what is here now, it's what *was* here . . . in 1850."

Shidan stood up and spread his arms out to encompass the bank plus two other buildings on either side of it.

"This was once a military barracks and square. It took up all that area there. And there on my left . . . where that government building is —it's a finance department now—the Báb was executed, here somewhere, in this general area, by firing squad. Killed by the Mullahs and governmental authorities of the time. Let's get a better look at it. We can't see everything from here."

They left the fountain and walked to the other road on the opposite side of the square. They stopped under trees on the edge of the square, and he stared at the bank for a while in silence.

"I am going by the instructions from Hooman. He knew about the location. By the way, my cousin Payman doesn't want to meet us. I called this morning before you got up. He's jumpy because we'll be digging up the past in Tehran. But he did provide a useful contact."

"Who?"

"A former guard who used to work in Evin Prison in Tehran, where Mona spent her last days. He may be able to direct us to where she was buried. As I said before, it will most likely be some unmarked piece of ground somewhere . . . when I was younger, I never knew why she was killed. It was a form of mystery to me. I knew it was because of religion, but I didn't understand the absolute mechanics of it, the subtext. It seemed illogical to my limited worldview at the time, and I always wanted to know what it was about. I wanted the chain of causation, and now I finally see it. It started here. From this spot, where the Báb was killed, came reverberations that went through the society of that time, and still, one hundred and fifty-something years later, the ripples continue to spread out and engulf both this community and the whole world.

"And more than this, according to Hooman, the future will vindicate the Báb. In the distant future, and focalized through the revelation of Bahá'u'lláh, a resonant hum will exist from the shock wave sent out from here, this very spot, as humble as it seems to you and me now. Can you see? My sister's death is linked in causation to this death, the Báb's death. And, indeed, these Manifestations of God are life and death itself."

"Shidan, how do you know all this?"

"Conversations with Hooman over the years. And when I grew up in Tehran my sister and Peshman told me much of this. I didn't really understand it all in those early days, but I was able to put it all together later on and align the fragments. I have thought about the Bahá'í Faith quite deeply over the years. I suppose my dislike of religion stems from Islam, because it has caused so much pain in my life. Mona and Dad were swallowed by Islam."

"Yes, that's true."

"It's funny, I was thinking about their lives recently, and I was reflecting on what you said in New York, before you left for London. About there being a greater destiny for us all. How our lives intersect. How all our choices change other people's destiny."

"Yes, our choices do intersect."

"And I think that although Mona's life was short with Peshman, it was richer than it might have been without him. Death is a funny thing. Who knows why some die early and others not; it's a great mystery." Shidan was quiet for a while. "Remember, I said the symbol of Noah's Ark was more important than the actual boat," he said.

"Yes."

"The symbolic boat is the Covenant, a vessel of the ever-renewing faith in God, which comes in every age, like the Buddha, Christ, and Muhammad, and all the others. And the boat takes many symbolic forms that appear to differ in history. In the Bahá'í context, it is called the Crimson Ark. Bahá'u'lláh refers to himself as the Holy Mariner and bids his ark to ride upon the Seas of Light and for us to find its mysteries if we join him. Hooman says it's a face of light over which pass a thousand masks and into which the weave of the duality of hell and paradise splice into an abiding and transcendent oneness. And as I said before, where we are standing is a part of that symbol, which stands above the mundane appearance of these buildings and people and this time." He pointed to the bank again. "You see, the thread of every life will find its way, eventually, into this weave. We choose to be a luminescent thread, or a black thread, or an in-between thread, with a shade near white. That is the grayness of our being; we are children of the half-light."

Allison smiled. "Shidan, you are sounding like a Bahá'í."

"Me? No, not at all, but it is the only religion that I make concessions for. And I think you might become a Bahá'í one day."

"You think so?"

"Yes, definitely."

"It is possible."

He turned around. "Well, time to go. We've got a six-hour drive ahead of us before we get to Tehran. And if we stop for a rest, it will take longer."

"Can I drive?"

"Of course you can. Why didn't you ask earlier?"
"I was enjoying being a passenger."
"Of course you were."
Shidan laughed and took her hand.
They walked back to the car.

————

In Tehran, on the following day, Shidan took Allison to Pamenar—the suburb where Hooman and Nava grew up. They drove through the narrow streets, and there were many very old buildings from the 1800s, and some were even older. He explained that originally when Tehran was small, this part of the city had large walls around it with several gates, and, as the older part of the city had expanded north, this then became southern Tehran. Not far from Pamenar they then went on a tour of Shidan's teenage years. His old home—a traditional Persian dwelling with a courtyard and fountain—was gone; it had been replaced by an apartment block. The place where he had stood as he watched his sister being dragged away by the Revolutionary Guard was the same. The plane trees had grown taller, but the houses had stayed as they were all those years before. His sister's house had been illegally confiscated by the government after her death and sold on to another family. They stood near the house.

"I wish I could have known her."

"She was wonderful. She would have loved you dearly. I know it without any doubt."

They stared at the street for several minutes before Shidan said, "We should go now." They walked away. Shidan turned several times to take a few last snapshots in his mind. The street disappeared as they took a corner.

In the car they sat for a few moments in silence. "We have to drive past Evin Prison. She and Peshman were kept there for a month before they disappeared," he said.

He called his cousin again, but Payman still did not want to meet them.

The prison was located at the base of the mountains in the north of the city. They took a main arterial road, and, after half an hour, they passed by the prison. It was nondescript with high walls and a light blue gate. They didn't stop. They just looked and drove on. The building itself was ugly, which mirrored his feelings about the place and what went on inside the prison now and all those years before, but Shidan felt a sense of completion as he continued to look over the details of the building. He then looked up at the Elburs Mountains beyond the prison and recalled the memory when Mona had chased him up the gravel path just below the snow line. What resonated in his mind now was his embrace with Mona and Peshman and their laughter. And the only things now left to find were his sister, Peshman, and his father and the places where all their laughter ceased to be.

———

At the Tehran Grand Hotel in the afternoon, Shidan and Allison parked on the opposite side of the street, and Shidan saw that a police car was parked near the front of the hotel. Instinctively, he felt a sharp stab of fear in his gut, and as Allison was about to get out of the car, he grabbed her arm.

"Stop," he said.

"What. What's wrong?" she asked as she looked over at him.

"The police. Look. Over there."

He pointed to the police car across the street.

They waited for half an hour for the police to come out of the hotel and leave, and just to be safe, they waited another half hour. Shidan and Allison then left the car and crossed the street. In the lobby they approached the concierge at the front desk. He told them that the police had confiscated both Shidan's Iranian and American passports. The police had not taken Allison's passport. As they asked more questions, the concierge kept insisting they leave. So, Shidan packed the car, and they left the hotel behind. Before they drove off, he scanned the streets near the hotel to see if the police were parked nearby, but he could not see anyone.

As they drove, he spoke. "Don't worry, we'll leave Iran by Afghanistan, and from there we can travel to Pakistan, or we could go farther south and enter Pakistan directly. I can apply for another American passport at the embassy in Islamabad or the consulates in either

Karachi or Lahore. There's no American embassy in Iran or Afghanistan at the moment. I could apply for a new passport at the Swiss embassy, but it takes four to six weeks to process it, and we can't afford to wait here that long. I'll call Sara and ask her to forward my paperwork to the US embassy in Pakistan."

"What about the borders? How will we get across?"

"You'll be fine. They won't make trouble for a tourist. At least that's my guess. I just hope we weren't followed. We had better park the car and catch a metro train around the city and see what happens. Someone may already be on our tail." Shidan was thoughtful, then added, "I think if they wanted to arrest me, they would have done it by now. But what I can't figure out is how they knew I was here. I wonder if customs officials talked to the police." Then he wondered if his cousin or uncle had called the police to show their cooperative nature to the authorities and of course to divert attention away from the unfortunate family connection Payman and Shidan's uncle had with Shidan's father. The stigma of those deemed a threat to the state during the revolution often tainted whole families.

They parked the car a short drive from the hotel at Mofateh Metro Station and descended into the subway system via the escalators. They caught a train south and headed back toward the old part of the city.

"It's a cleaner version of the New York subway," Allison said.

"True," he said, slightly distracted. He kept looking around them and scanning the carriage as he watched people get on and off at the various stations. He could not see that they had been followed. After several stops, they got off at Khayyam Station. On the surface again, they walked to the Grand Bazaar.

The first part of the bazaar that they passed into was the carpet section. They walked past carpet shops. He looked around at the multitude of colors in the carpets and then up at the brick arches in the ceiling. He remembered this part of the bazaar because Peshman had had a carpet shop here, and, as a child, Shidan would often sit drinking tea with him while they looked out at the stream of people passing by. They came to the shop. He pointed at it. "This was once Peshman's shop." He walked into it, and Allison followed him.

A man came toward them. "Can I help you," he said in Persian.

"No, we are just looking." Shidan went to the wall and ran his hand over a carpet that was hanging from it. The shop had that familiar smell of new carpets, which were invariably made from wool. He thought about the police and turned to Allison. "I think we'll be okay. If it's just the police, we should be fine. If it's the Revolutionary Guard, then that's another matter. Although it might be better if you leave today and catch the next available flight to London," he said in a low voice.

"Yes, that might be a good idea."

"Once the police return to the hotel and find us gone, then things will escalate."

"What about tonight? Where will you stay?"

"There is a small obscure hotel nearby. We passed it before coming into the bazaar. I won't be asked any questions there if I give them money, at least for the first couple of nights. I shouldn't have told Payman where we were staying either. I made a mistake." He turned to the entrance. "Let's go. I want to show you something. And there are some other parts of the bazaar that are quite beautiful." They walked toward the door, and he thanked the owner as they walked through it.

After walking for a while, the carpets disappeared, and an assortment of shops appeared that sold everything from spices to clothing and every other obscure thing. He looked up at the brick arches in the roof of the bazaar. Old tin roofs soon replaced the arches; the sky peeked through in several spots. The walkways occasionally split off at right angles, and he weaved through the various forks in the rows. He followed his childhood memories of the layout of the bazaar.

He stopped for a moment in front of a bookshop. He turned to her. "When you fly out tonight, go to Turkey, and then you can catch a flight on to London from there," he said.

"But I don't want to leave you here, Shidan."

"Don't worry about me. I'll be fine. There are people who I can pay to help me pass over the borders in relative obscurity. I'll get out, don't worry. And I'm thinking I want to stay a few days longer and see if I can find the location of Mona and Peshman's bodies. And my father too, but I don't want to put you in any danger for my sake, so I think that is the best plan. You leave, and we'll meet back in London. Okay?"

"All right, but I'm worried for you."

They continued to walk, and the brick arches soon reappeared, and they came out into a large open space, which was situated in the jewelry section of the bazaar. The colored mosaic patterns in the roof were exquisite, and Shidan watched Allison look up at it. It was like a mosque in some ways and was very old. The roof structure had complex geometrical shapes with many interlocking and converging arches. They became smaller and smaller as they reached the apex of the roof. At its center was a circular skylight with light flooding down into the bazaar. Allison took out her camera to take a shot of the shops and the roof.

"I said I wanted to show you something."

"Yes, what is it?"

"Let's keep walking. We are almost there."

After several minutes, they left the bazaar and came out into a large, enclosed square. He pointed to a large building on the other side of the square, beyond a small jewelry store and on the other side of a street that ran through one side of the square.

"It's a bank now," he said as they walked toward it, "but a hundred and thirty or so years ago, it was part of the southern section of Golestan Palace. Somewhere behind, or maybe under the bank, I am not sure of its exact location, is the place where Bahá'u'lláh first received his revelation from God. It was known as the 'black pit' back then. In Persian we say Síyáh-Chál. It was originally a water reservoir for one of the public baths, but they turned it into a dungeon for criminals. It was destroyed in 1868 and filled in. They built an open-air theatre over the site, then this in turn was destroyed in 1947, and there is now the bank that you see. You seemed to have a fascination for Bahá'u'lláh's house in Istanbul, so I thought you may like to see this location."

"Yes, I do have a fascination for anything connected to his life. Do you know more about Bahá'u'lláh's time there?"

"Yes, Peshman explained it to me many times. To reach the prison a person would walk through a dark passageway and then down three flights of stairs. There were no windows, so it was pitch-black. Nearly one hundred and fifty prisoners were crowded into this dark space. The floor was covered with dirt and filth. Apparently, the smell was foul beyond belief. Under these conditions Bahá'u'lláh and a number of Bábís were imprisoned by the king. Bahá'u'lláh's feet were put in shackles, and a heavy chain was placed around his neck, which left a scar that would remain with him for the rest of his life. Bahá'u'lláh and his companions, also in chains, all huddled together in one cell. They had been placed in two rows, each facing the other. Bahá'u'lláh taught them to repeat certain verses. Every night they chanted. 'God is sufficient unto me: He verily is the All-sufficing,' one row would chant, and the other would reply, 'In Him let the trusting trust.' Into the early hours of the morning, the chorus of their happy voices could be heard. The king heard the chanting. 'What is this sound?' he asked. 'It's the anthem the Bábís are intoning' was the reply. The king fell silent."

Shidan continued telling the story as they walked on. "Every day, the jailers would enter the cell and would call out the name of one of the Bábís, ordering him to arise and follow them to the gallows. They jumped to their feet and, in a state of uncontrollable delight, would approach Bahá'u'lláh and embrace him. He would then embrace each of his companions and with a heart filled with hope and joy meet death."

He stopped talking, and they came to a circular fountain near the center of the square. He sat down on the edge of the fountain. He scooped up a handful of cool water before letting it run back into the fountain.

Allison stood next to him. "But what about Bahá'u'lláh's revelation?"

"Oh that. Yeah. He had a dream. A spirit spoke to him. A maiden. One night in a dream he heard, on every side, exalted words that no one could bear to hear. He experienced the force of his mission. It flowed like a large torrent of water from his head to his chest, and every limb of his body was set afire. In a vision the Most Great Spirit appeared to him in the guise of a maiden calling with a wondrous voice above his head while suspended in the air before him. She pointed her finger at his head, imparting words, which rejoiced his soul.

"Speaking to his inner and outer being, she referred to him as the Best-Beloved of the worlds, the Beauty of God, and the power of God's sovereignty. He was assured that he would be made victorious by himself and by his pen, and by the aid of those whom God would raise up."[6]

"Wow. Amazing," Allison said.

"Yes, it is kind of fabulous in a way. Peshman couldn't tell the story without tears in his eyes. And Bahá'u'lláh did not inform anyone of what had occurred until many years later when he declared his mission in Baghdad in the garden of paradise. Or the Garden of Riḍván as it is commonly known amongst Bahá'ís."

Shidan stood up. "I should take you to the airport now."

They walked up to the street, passing in front of the bank and caught a taxi back to the four-wheel drive and then drove on to the airport. He escorted her to the check-in counters. "Hopefully, you can get a flight tonight. Let's swap cell phones. I need a clean line. Nobody here knows your number." She passed him her cell phone. "Here, take my phone and call me just before take-off so I know you're safe. Do the same in Turkey when you land. Call me," he said. "Okay, I will see you back in London, then."

Shidan embraced Allison, but when he tried to break away, she was still holding him tight.

"Shidan . . . I've changed my mind. I want to keep traveling with you."

"Are you absolutely sure? It won't be safe."

"I know that, but I want to visit your sister's and father's graves. Wherever they may be."

"Okay then, we'll travel together." He smiled. "You're so brave, babe," he said.

———

Five days had passed before Shidan had been able to meet the former prison guard from Evin Prison. He had suggested two possible locations where he thought Shidan's sister and Peshman might be buried.

The first location was a factory on the outskirts of Tehran, and the second, which was probably where his father was also buried, was an unmarked mass grave that had been used for political dissidents in the eighties. The grave was adjacent to the Bahá'í section of Tehran's Anousha Cemetery, and he had been to the location a few times in his life. There was no sign of the police, so he assumed they had given up looking, or they could not locate him. At the start of each day, they had moved to a new hotel. They had been asked for their passports, but he passed over cash, and the staff usually said nothing about him not having a passport.

On the morning of their last day in Tehran, he stood outside a textile factory in an industrial part of Tehran known as Zeravshan Industrial City. If the information he had bought was correct, Mona and Peshman, along with many others, might be buried under the foundations of the factory, which had been built over the site one year after their execution in 1984. The only thing he did not know was where exactly, and he knew he could not do any more on this trip or possibly for a long time to come. He might even have to wait for decades to pass before he could come back to Iran, let alone dig up this location for a sign of her body. The Iranian regime currently in power, since the beginning of the revolution, might last for a long time. There had been talk over the years, after the Iranian hostage crisis, that America might invade and topple the government at some point, and only then might he return, or if there was some unforeseen transformation in the culture over time. He thought that it might take many generations before a groundswell, at the grassroots of Iranian society, would remove the extreme influence of the religious system currently in place. He speculated that it would take between thirty and fifty years to change. And he realized that if America invaded, it might retard this slow transformation as the populous would unify against the invaders and support the current regime. He could see inklings of a nonviolent movement forming in Iran, which made him hopeful.

He walked back to the car on the opposite side of the street and sat there looking at the factory for a full half hour before driving off. As he did, he began to weep.

"The guard from Evin Prison might have been wrong about this location," he said as he looked at Allison. He had paid a considerable sum to the guard, and he wondered if he had lied.

She put her hand on his shoulder. "Let's go to the cemetery. There's an equal chance that they are there. I can drive if you want," she said.

"No, I'm okay," he said, as he looked briefly at the other factories that passed by as they drove off. "Life can be so bitter sometimes. God, I hate what this country has become."

Driving toward the cemetery, which was on the other extreme of Tehran, they took an expressway that hugged the city limits. They passed many farms and orchards. He observed a large swath of cornfields, and other crops dispersed by small pockets of outlying suburbia.

Eventually, they came to another expressway heading south. Soon the farms disappeared, and he looked up at a large hill close by the road and then south at the flat expanse of desert beyond the hill. Shidan sat in the slow lane and watched cars overtaking him periodically.

An hour and a half after leaving the factory, they arrived near Anousha Cemetery. He drove onto an underpass and headed back to the cemetery on the opposite side of the expressway, where he pulled over and turned into a street running beside the cemetery.

They parked and walked through a gate. As they passed into the cemetery, he looked around, and he was hit by the bleakness of it. They were standing adjacent to the Bahá'í part of the cemetery. He knew his way around because of visits he and his mother had made just after his sister's and father's executions around April 1983. At the time there had been rumors in the community that this was where many of the political dissidents had been buried in a mass grave. This plot of land was known as the "graves of the infidels," but he and his mother never found where they were buried. Only years later, when people had dug around this location for a sign of their relatives, was the exact location revealed. By then, late in 1983, Shidan had moved to New York with his mother, where they were granted humanitarian visas.

In addition to his first impression of bleakness, he now added the word "desolation." They walked past a few headstones, which were flat on the ground and not upright in the typical fashion. Some graves had brick rims and small slabs of rough concrete with names inscribed with a stick or finger, but mostly it was gravel and sand with weeds and many tufts of grass sprouting up through the dry ground. He knew that the authorities did not allow some families to put up headstones here and there was no definitive order to the graves. And although there were some rows, like the other parts of the cemetery, it looked random on the whole.

Shidan and Allison walked up to an old lady kneeling on the ground next to a grave with a rectangle of broken cinder blocks and one rough blob of concrete in its center. She was arranging flowers in a glass bottle that was stuck in the ground. The mass grave that he was so desperate to find was in no way obvious or visible, and so he asked the old lady if she knew anything about it.

"The ones executed from 1981 onwards are there somewhere," she said in Persian as she pointed at a piece of ground in the near distance. She added, "Those killed in the massacre of 1988 are over there, beyond that avenue of trees, near the wall to the Armenian part of the cemetery."

"Who are these flowers for?" he asked the old lady.

"My son. They killed him," she said.

"Why did they kill him?"

"He was a writer and a communist."

He was about to ask her more about her son but thought better of it, as he did not want to upset her by dredging up the past. He thanked her, and they walked over to the area she had initially pointed to.

"Well, they are either here or back at the factory. I guess this is as close as we will ever get, and I can't do more than this."

"Who is buried in this mass grave?" Allison asked.

"Intellectuals, political dissidents, free thinkers, and even atheists I have heard. Basically, anyone opposed to the regime at the beginning of the Cultural Revolution. I think that the general term they used for them was apostate. There were thousands killed, so they can't all be buried here. And although Mona wasn't killed in '81 or '88, she might be here somewhere." He looked up at the sun for a moment and then at the mountain range beyond the cemetery. The mountains were bleak too. They mirrored his feelings about this place.

They left the cemetery and continued to drive southeast down the expressway. This would eventually bring them to either Afghanistan or Pakistan, and a whole day's drive was ahead of them. They had just passed by what looked like a crumbling mud-brick fortress.

"So where to from here?" Allison asked.

"I suppose we can drive south and enter Pakistan directly, or we could go via Afghanistan. What do you want to do?"

"Well, if we have a choice, I would like to see a bit of Afghanistan."

"No problem. Done. But one thing we need is a guide to get us over the Afghan border . . . I suppose once we reach the Iranian border towns, I can ask around."

He looked over at Allison. She was looking at the scenery slide by as they passed more farms that were separated by large sections of empty desert on a flat plain. The expressway followed the contours of a mountain range to the north, and they slowly drifted east toward Afghanistan.

"I haven't mentioned it to you before, but there was another Mona like my sister, but younger, who was executed at around the same time in 1983. She was a Bahá'í too. Peshman knew her father, Yad'u'lláh Mahmudnizhad. Peshman owned a carpet business in Shiraz in addition to his shop in the bazaar. And when he was staying in Shiraz, he would often go for dinner at the Mahmudnizhad's house."

He went on to explain that Mona was one of several Bahá'ís, including women and teenage girls, who were imprisoned in the fall of 1982 by the Islamic Revolutionary authorities in Shiraz. One of the last stories that Shidan's father documented, before his own execution, was Mona's story. He had sent the report to the BBC in London.

———

The prisoners, including Mona, endured months of abuse, interrogation, and torture as the Islamic judges and their Revolutionary Guards attempted to force them to deny their religion. All refused, and ten of the women, including Mona, were secretly sentenced to death by hanging in June 1983. In a final effort to break their wills, the authorities hanged the women one by one as the others were forced to watch.

Mona asked to be the final victim executed so that she could pray for the strength of each one who was hanged before her. When her turn came, she kissed the rope and put the noose around her own neck.

She had been arrested with her father, who was hanged in March 1983, several months before her.

When the Mahmudnizhad family first moved to Shiraz, they considered it a dream come true. In Tabriz they had prayed fervently that they would be able to visit the House of the Báb, the most holy place for Bahá'ís in Iran, and were thrilled that they would be living in the same city. But even when they were finally living in Shiraz, however, Yad'u'lláh still did not feel that he had earned the right to visit the House of the Báb on his own. "I shall not visit the Blessed House of the Báb unless he calls me himself," he told his family.

One day Yad'u'lláh received a phone call and was asked to go to a certain address to repair a television set. The television, as it turned out, belonged to the mother of the caretaker of the Báb's house. After doing the work, Mr. Mahmudnizhad was ready to leave. "Don't you want to visit the Blessed House? There is nobody there, and I will let you in," the woman said.

So, in this unexpected way, Yad'u'lláh had his prayer answered. He had been summoned to the House of the Báb to provide a service for the caretaker's family. Later he told his family that it was the happiest day of his life. He walked around the yard several times and then up and down the stairs, kissing the edge of each step; finally, he entered the room where the Báb had first declared his mission, and bowed his forehead to the ground, immersed in spiritual ecstasy. Every time he talked about this visit with family or friends, his eyes would fill with tears.

Because of the rise to power of the Islamic clergy, the Islamic Revolution inaugurated a new period of severe repression of the Bahá'í Faith. The mullahs had branded the Bahá'ís as "unclean infidels" at the earliest beginnings of the religion in 1844 and had continued to incite popular prejudice against them under all regimes. Over twenty thousand Bahá'ís had been put to death, often after barbaric and public torture, throughout the nineteenth century and in sporadic pogroms as recently as 1955 and 1963, when Bahá'ís were murdered and Bahá'í centers destroyed by the combined forces of the clergy and the late shah's army.

As the crisis for the Bahá'ís worsened, Mona had many disturbing thoughts of the destiny that God might have in store for her father and for herself. She had a dream in which both she and her father were killed for their faith. After the dream, Mona added another virtue to those she already possessed—fearlessness. As the persecutions worsened, she talked and wrote to her friends about the need for courage in the face of their fundamentalist persecutors, showing no fear of death.

Mona's life changed on September 10, 1980, when she turned fifteen, the age of spiritual maturity in the Bahá'í teachings. Mona had already begun following in her father's footsteps as a Bahá'í teacher and wanted to teach young children, for whom she had a special love, and she began teaching Bahá'í children's classes, which included the study of the great religions, developing spiritual qualities, encouraging the children to put their talents and education to the service of humanity, and especially learning to appreciate the oneness and diversity of the human family.

The persecution of the Bahá'ís extended to every level of society.

While the Islamic authorities tended at first to single out only the more prominent members of the Faith for arrest and execution, cancellation of pensions, freezing of bank accounts, and dismissal from employment, they extended their repressions even to the school level by expelling numerous Bahá'í children, especially those attending high school and university.

Arrests and executions of Bahá'ís were taking place all over the country. In Shiraz the public prosecutor had initiated mass arrests in late October 1982.

Mona's arrest occurred at 7:30 p.m. on October 23, 1982. Mona was at home with her parents. Her father opened the door, and four armed Revolutionary Guards demanded entry.

In the prison all of the Bahá'í women were interrogated, and several were severely beaten as well. These beatings took place separately from the interrogations, in the basement of the prison. The Bahá'í women were tied to a specially designed table and then beaten on the soles of their feet with a rod or a piece of wire cable. A woman was given a few lashes, allowed to regain sensitivity, and whipped again and again until they passed out. When they regained consciousness, the beatings resumed.

They were then made to walk on their bleeding feet and often additionally tortured by being taunted with a glass of water.

Mona was in Seppah Prison for a total of thirty-eight days and was interrogated for roughly one week during that time. In November 1982 she and five other Bahá'í women were transferred to Adelabad Prison.

During the second stage of Mona's interrogation, she was awakened at four o'clock in the morning and transferred an hour later by car to the prison. The session lasted most of the day. She was asked the same questions that she had been asked over and over again at Seppah about her beliefs. "I told them that I believed in God and all his messengers who had revealed a Holy Book and that we consider them all to be Messengers of God."

One day, which coincided with a Bahá'í holy day, Mona wanted to say prayers alone instead of joining a small prayer session organized by the Bahá'í prisoners.

Mona had been spending increasing amounts of time alone. Often, when the others would gather together, Mona would find an empty cell to pray and meditate in by herself. This time, however, her mother insisted that Mona join them, so she acquiesced.

Later in the day Mona then took her aside. "Mother, I want to tell you something, please come with me." She led her mother down a corridor that was so narrow that they had to walk in single file. Mona stopped and turned around.

"Mother, do you know that they are going to execute me?" Her mother became very upset and refused to listen.

She was completely unaware of the spiritual state that Mona had reached. "No, dear, you'll be free, released from the prison. You will have a family and children. I want to see your children. Please don't think this way," her mother said.

Mona became upset. "I swear to God that I don't wish this for myself, and you shouldn't wish it for me. I know that they are going to kill me, and I want to tell you what I am going to do when that happens. If you don't let me tell you now, you will regret it in the future. Do you want to let me tell you or not?" Mona said.

Mona's mother was stunned. "Yes, tell me," her mother said.

Then Mona faced her. "You know, Mother, they're going to take us to our execution soon. We will have to go up and stand on something high where they will put a rope around our necks . . . then I'm going to kiss the noose and say a prayer," Mona said.

Mona then folded her arms across her chest, closed her eyes, and with a blissful look on her face said a short prayer. Then she opened her eyes. "I'll say that prayer for the happiness and prosperity of all humankind and bid farewell to this mortal world and go to God," she said. Then she looked at her mother, who was staring at her in a state of confusion and bewilderment.

"That was a nice story, Mona," was all her mother could say.

Mona's eyes filled with tears. "Mother, it was not a story. Why won't you believe me?" she said quietly.

During their last visit together, Mona's sister realized that Mona would soon be executed and that she was fully prepared. "You're going to be executed too!" her sister said.

"I know. I know," Mona replied calmly, and added, "Taraneh, I have a request for you. I want you to pray for us, so we go to our execution dancing."

By that point, Mona was crying and laughing at the same time, talking about her execution as a foregone conclusion even though she had not yet even been sentenced.

———

The hangings of the ten women took place on the eve of June 18, 1983, under cover of darkness, in a nearby polo field. The driver of the bus, who later met the grandmother of one of the young women, told her, "They were all happy and were singing many songs on the way. I could not believe that they knew they were going to be executed. I have never seen people so happy."

The families of the women learned of the hangings the next morning. Mona's mother and sister Taraneh finally succeeded, after great difficulty, in getting permission to see the bodies. Mrs. Mahmudnizhad, who had been their companion until the last few days, kissed each woman on the cheek. "I wish the whole world could see through my eyes how those dead bodies testify to the love of the Bahá'u'lláh," she said.

Mona's sister later recounted, "It was a bitter day, and for the last time, without having thick glass in between, I kissed the tranquil face of my dear sister and said goodbye to her. I was hoping that she would open her eyes and smile. But I know that now, forever, she is observing us with an everlasting smile, and if I cried it would only upset her. So, because of you and the love that you have for Bahá'u'lláh and for humanity, I laugh to let the people know why you sacrificed your life and why all those wonderful women gave their sweet lives in His path."

A young man who was able to see the ten bodies after their hanging wrote, "When I found myself in the morgue, I felt as if I would explode. I could not stop crying . . . when I entered, the first thing I saw was Mona's face, lying with her head resting on Mahshid's shoulder. Mahshid looked as if she were in a deep sleep.

"To Mona's right was Shirin. Her eyes were covered by a blindfold.

"I could not believe that I would never see them again. I paused for a moment on the threshold and promised them all that I would continue their work by serving humanity."

The hangings of the women shocked the entire city. One person wrote, "Shiraz smelled of blood, of love and devotion. . . . The families were all in astonishment and awe."[7]

———

Shidan finished the story, and Allison had tears in her eyes. "Wow. What a beautiful soul."

"I know. They were all beautiful souls, Allison. Each and every one. And although my sister was not officially a Bahá'í, I think in her heart she was one. She must have said as much to the authorities so that she could die with Peshman. I think she could not live without him."

———

About six years earlier, on the morning of the January 3, 1993, Allison, Aurélie, and Io packed up the tents and began the three-hour hike from Sealers Cove back to the parking lot near Mount Oberon. Before getting into the car, Allison took her camera out of her backpack and took her shoes off. She took a photo of her bare feet on the asphalt; this was a part of her visual diary. Allison wanted to call her brother, Paul, and let him know she was okay, so they drove down to Tidal River. The girls went to feed the birds while Allison went to a phone box near the visitors center. Before making the call, she took a photo of the coins she was about to use in the payphone. She lined them up on the tops of her feet so they were symmetrical.

She called him at the restaurant. "Hi, babe," she said.

"Oh, babe, it's good to hear from you. Where are you?"

"Wilsons Prom."

"Are you okay?"

"Yep. Got stopped yesterday by the police about a faulty taillight. They didn't know about my handbrake. Io had her foot on the brake while I got out and chatted with the police about the light. If they had found out about it, they would have pulled me off the road right there, and that would have been the end of my big adventure. I promised to get the light fixed in the next town. I didn't, as you would expect," she laughed.

"You have to get that fixed, babe. Particularly if you are traveling at night."

"I will. I will. Promise. Okay, I'll get going. I just wanted to let you know where I am. I am heading toward Sydney today. We'll stop in Eden overnight. I'll call in a week or so."

"Okay, cool. Love you, babe."

"Love you too, bye."

"Bye."

Allison returned to the car and waited for the girls to finish feeding the birds. After fifteen minutes, they came back and got into the car. Io pulled the bricks from the front wheels, and they drove off.

"I want to stop at Squeaky Beach before we leave Wilsons Prom."

"Sure," the girls said almost in unison.

They drove from Tidal River toward the beach, and after a short drive, they came to the parking lot near Squeaky Beach. The girls walked to the beach, and Allison immediately walked toward the large granite boulders embedded in the sand at one end of the beach.

"Hey, the sand actually squeaks," Aurélie said as she followed Allison to the boulders.

The boulders were sixteen to nineteen feet high at the highest point and covered in red moss. The hue reminded Allison of fall leaves. A small stream ran around the boulders into the sea. Allison stopped to take her shoes off and walked into the stream. She stopped in the middle of the stream and looked down at her feet on the sandy bottom, which were slightly distorted by the rush of water. The cool water was nice against her skin. After a few moments, she walked on and came to the boulders. The stream water was running around them and there was no way to climb them here, so Allison went to the back of the boulders and stepped out of the stream. Aurélie followed behind her, and Allison looked around to see Io in the distance, walking toward the other end the beach.

Once the two girls had climbed the boulders, they sat down and looked out at the sea for several minutes in silence.

"What part of Paris do you come from?" Allison said in French.

"Oh, I'm in the seventeenth arrondissement. My neighborhood is called Épinettes. Do you know Paris?"

"No, I have no idea where that is."

"Épinettes is near Montmartre. If you are ever in Paris, then you are welcome to stay with me and Gabriel."

"Thank you," she said and put her hand on Aurélie's shoulder.

Allison and Aurélie sat on the boulders for thirty minutes and continued talking about various things in French. After a time, Io came and joined them. They sat there for another half an hour, staring at the sea and listening to the waves roll in. Allison then closed her eyes and just listened to the sea.

After a long while, she opened her eyes. "Okay, we better go. I want to make Eden by the end of the day, and then tomorrow we can make Sydney," Allison said. Before they left, Allison took a shot of her feet on the granite surface.

The girls climbed down from the boulders and stepped into the stream where, on the other side, they brushed the sand off their feet and put their shoes back on. They walked back up the beach, squeaking as they went, and then up the sandy track to the parking lot.

13

THE NIGHTINGALE

After passing through the Valley of Knowledge, which is the last station of limitation, the wayfarer cometh to THE FIRST STATION OF UNITY and drinketh from the cup of oneness, and gazeth upon the manifestations of singleness.[1]

— BAHÁ'U'LLÁH, *THE SEVEN VALLEYS*

On the morning of the following day, the sun shone down on a small town near the border of Afghanistan called Torbat-e Jam. Shidan had managed to sell the car that morning. In the evening on the previous day, they had found a guide with a good reputation; the owner of the hotel they stayed in knew of him.

Sitting in a courtyard at the back of a teahouse close to the hotel, they waited for their guide to arrive. Near the back wall were several weeping cherry trees. Half of the petals had fallen to the ground. Allison was sitting under one of the trees. She leaned back in her chair and brushed the cherry blossoms with her hand. The occasional petal glided down from the branches and landed gently on her face. It reminded her of the light well in Shidan's bookshop. She looked around the courtyard. She liked its rough mud-brick walls. She then looked up again. "Beautiful, Shidan . . . the sky. It's so intense today."

"Yes, intense is the right word." He looked up at the sky for a moment.

"When is this guy coming?" she asked.

"He should be here now."

"Where is he coming from?"

"Kabul. But by chance he was in a small city on the other side of the border when I called him last night."

Another fifteen minutes passed, and then a tall man stepped into the courtyard and approached them. "Hello," he said in Persian, "my name is Vahid." Allison leaned forward and put her hand out. Vahid looked about the courtyard. There were a few other people in one corner. "Sorry, normally I would shake your hand in private, but in public it would draw unwanted attention from others. You never know who is watching," he said in English.

"Oh, okay, sorry."

Vahid sat down next to Shidan.

"So, what is the plan?" Shidan asked in English.

"Well, we can pass over the border today. Are you ready now? I have a few people waiting for us in a village close by. They will help carry your baggage. We have to go on foot part of the way."

"Our bags are in the hotel. It's nearby."

"Okay. Great, let's go. I'll call now and let them know we are coming." Shidan passed Vahid a large wad of money. "This should get things going," he said.

After leaving the hotel, they found a taxi and drove toward the border village of Jannat Abad. On the way Allison observed all the small farms on the plain with wheat and other crops. Occasionally there were wild meadows saturated with red poppies. They then passed into hills until they arrived in Jannat Abad. The locals that Vahid had said would help carry their baggage got into the taxi and were all jammed into the back seat.

Eventually, they arrived at an obscure part of the border. They left the road and walked toward the border fence. They hunched down and passed through a hole in the wire. They walked toward low hills through a meadow of grass and poppies. Allison put her hands out and felt the tips of the grass brush against her palms and the warmth of the sun beating down on the backs of her hands.

It took an hour to walk around the base of the mountains along winding, rocky tracks. They slowly ascended until they came level to a small mountain road that was perched up on a high plateau. Allison was breathless when they came to Vahid's four-wheel drive; the road was surrounded by a panorama of undulating hills nearby. As the helpers packed the baggage into the car, Allison looked around at the surrounding hills. The view was beautiful and bare, with little or no vegetation. Before he got into the driver's seat, Vahid went to the back of the car and opened the trunk. He came around the other side of the car and opened the back door for Allison. He gave her a blue burka. "It will be good if you can wear this; otherwise, the Taliban will stop us. I will tell them that you are my sister. Is that okay?"

"That's fine." She looked at the color of the burka in her hands, and the shade of blue reminded her a bit of the color of the front gate of Evin Prison in Tehran. The burka was a mobile world that masked female identity.

"Oh, and you had better hide your hands when we are stopped. Your skin is a bit light."

Vahid walked around to the driver's seat, and Shidan got into the front. The people who had carried their luggage returned down the rocky track. As Vahid drove off, Allison looked back at the panorama of empty hills through the dust kicked up by the car. A montage of all the emptiness across Turkey and Iran ran through her mind. Then all the deserts she had ever seen in Australia also passed through her mind. It was a swirling mass of incoherent thought, and she liked it. The desert, the desert, the desert and the waves of sand and tumbling grains of time. Endless spectral dunes moving into each other, a slow-moving sea of sand on the curve of her eye. Never to see the end of life. You. The forever face and mask of eternity as I walk on in this dead expanse, watching my fictional death on a spinning blue Earth, this motion world circling the solar barge. The sky will kiss our skin with its light. The sun will come down to meet us. We spin entwined. Worlds spin with us.

Our love will create all things. Nothing we see will ever die. Swirling brisk milk sweet fairy sugar floss, our milky light galaxy. Us riding the dunes on our ships of desire and innocence. The desert, the desert, the desert and the waves of sand and tumbling grains of time spinning, spinning, spinning beyond death.

It was a bumpy ride through more mountainous terrain with small, winding dirt roads that were almost too small for the four-wheel drive, and after an hour, they came down from the mountains and found a main highway. They drove into a flat valley surrounded by a sparse ripple of hills and passed by several pomegranate orchards.

"I remember Hooman said his family owned a pomegranate farm in Southern Iran. Actually, I saw a photo of it now that I think about it," Allison said. She had a sustained flashback of walking in Times Square with Hooman.

"Yes, that sounds vaguely familiar," Shidan said.

After an hour and a half, they came to Herat, which was a small city. Just before they entered the outskirts, they came to a Taliban checkpoint. Vahid passed over a small amount of cash, and they passed through the checkpoint with no questions.

"I'm sorry, Allison, but because I didn't have much time, I wasn't able to get the paperwork for you to look at some of the tourist sites here in Herat. As a tourist, you need government paperwork to get into these old buildings."

"That's okay. I can look at the outside of these buildings, but, anyway, these suburbs and all this domestic architecture are great. Shidan and I have already seen a lot of really beautiful old buildings in Turkey and Iran."

They drove through the suburbs of Herat. The dwellings were a combination of baked brick, mud-brick, and concrete houses. They came to a few roadside stalls and what seemed to be the main shopping area, where they stopped for lunch.

"We'll get some supplies for the rest of the trip," Vahid said. He got out of the driver's seat and came around to Allison's window. "Can I get you anything to eat? A kebab? Sorry, but there isn't much choice here."

"Yes, please. Get me whatever you like."

Shidan got out, and he walked around the car and through the stalls.

Vahid asked Allison to stay in the car. She watched Vahid and Shidan walk away from the car and disappear into crowds of people. She looked around and became aware of all the traffic and people criss-crossing each other. There were muddy cars, three-wheel motorcycle taxis, and the shimmer of heat surrounding them. She looked at the many mud-brick structures, and a large, fortified wall that surrounded what she knew must be the old part of the city. She looked into the distance and saw a three-story wood and mud-brick house leaning sideways and crumbling.

After leaving Herat, they drove along an unpaved road parallel to a river in one continuous valley for many hours. Mountains sat up on both sides of the valley. They stopped in a few spots, and Allison took her Leica out to take black-and-white shots. Initially, she looked into the viewfinder through the crocheted mesh of the burka, but Vahid eventually told her that she could take it off when no one else was on the road near them. The landscape was bare, unadorned in yellow and red dirt. There were occasional rocky outcrops leading up to mountains and, at different points along the road, strips of flat green vegetation in narrow floodplains near the river. Locals were growing crops and vegetables where the landscape allowed. There were also sheep and goats grazing near the edges of the river in various meadows. Between the fields there were occasional mud-brick houses.

Vahid stopped in various places along the road and called ahead. This part of Afghanistan was dangerous, and he explained that he needed to call people he knew along the route to see if the road was safe to proceed along. People were often shot and killed by bandits over seemingly paltry objects like watches and jewelry, since most people wouldn't carry much cash anyway.

Allison realized that life here was cheap and challenging for everyone.

They passed through several small villages during that day. There were muddy buses and old cars passing them in both directions. And Vahid was weaving around on the road to avoid potholes and cars going past at ridiculous speeds, given how bad the roads were.

They decided to stop for a break in a small floodplain. Vahid pulled over next to a meadow saturated in red poppies. Allison got out and walked through the long grass and flowers with her burka on. With her arms spread out and her palms facing the sky, she spun around a few times before sitting down. She reached out to pick one of the flowers from beneath her burka. It seemed strange that most women here would have to live out their existence in this way—looking at the world through a strip of elongated hexagonal mesh, living a life invisible in public—but she was glad that she was able to experience their reality if only for a short time. After ten minutes, Vahid called out to her, and she came back to the car to continue on.

At one point they saw a Western couple riding mountain bikes. As they passed by, Vahid laughed and said, "These guys are either stupid or brave. I have a pistol. Not that I have ever used it, but it is there if I need it."

"You have a pistol?" Allison said brightly.

"Yep. Nine millimeter."

"Can I have a look at it?"

"Sure." He leaned over and took it out of the glove box. He passed it to Allison over his shoulder. "Careful, it is loaded, and don't touch the safety catch or trigger."

"Okay, I'll be careful." She turned it over in her hands. It seemed strange that a person would live in a country where they even needed a gun like this on a regular basis. She passed it to Shidan. He put it back into the glove box. In that moment it felt kind of wrong to enjoy the scenery passing by when people here lived in such poverty and danger every day. Her reality suddenly broke into two as she was now able to weld "beauty" to "danger" and see her own world and that of the Afghan people as two separate perceptual filters that tinted everything that was regarded as beautiful in different ways. And she felt more comfortable now as she was less a tourist and more a detached observer in two parallel worlds. For the rest of day, she did not see as much beauty in the surrounding countryside; it was now a changed and altered beauty.

The highway eventually left the river and began winding around dusty hills and valleys. Late in the night, after fifteen hours of driving, they rejoined the river and came to the village of Chaghcharan. The village was located on the southern side of the Hari River. Vahid had arranged their accommodation with a local village family. They had been passing mud-brick houses all day from Herat onwards, but now Allison saw inside one of these houses for the first time. They were very different from the mud-brick houses she had seen in Australia over the years, which were mostly in hippie communes.

The next day was another long journey, but the landscape was breathtaking with its sparse peaks and more green valleys with narrow floodplains. Allison tried to resist that beauty, attempting to regain her inner dichotomy from the previous day, but it was hard to separate herself from her delight in the landscape. At yet another small village, she observed the inhabitants going about their life. Some were harvesting in the fields, and there were children playing soccer. Several women were washing clothes in a river.

"I can understand why people fall in love with this country . . ." Shidan said. Then added, "The mountains are bleak, but they're so beautiful."

"I can't help falling in love with its beauty too, but I am conflicted. Peoples' lives here are difficult. Can you really see it as beautiful without feeling conflicted, given what people have to endure here?"

"I suppose you're right," he said. "My bad."

"And the Taliban have made life even harder than it was before," Vahid said.

"Hmm . . ." Allison guessed that Shidan was ruminating on something connected with the landscape and reality for Afghan people.

"How long will it take to get to Kabul?" she asked Vahid.

"It will be another days' drive, maybe more. It depends on traffic conditions and how fast I can go. As you can see, the roads here are not great."

After another full day of driving, they came to Gardandeh, where they spent the night in another mud-brick house owned by a local family. The house was perched up on an incline and nestled amongst many other mud-brick houses overlooking a series of valleys near the village. They unpacked the car and then had dinner with the family. Allison was tired and went to bed early.

In the morning Allison rolled out of her bed. Through the windows she could see the valley below. The light peeked over the mountains, and the light in the valley below was hazy. In that moment she had a thought to say a prayer. Her prayer book was in her backpack. She went to it and fished around until the book came into the light. She passed her hand over the leather cover and saw that it had a nine-pointed star impressed on it. She remembered vaguely that Hooman had said the star was a symbol of perfection, and the number nine was the numerical value of the word "Bahá," which meant "glory" in Arabic.

Sitting cross-legged on a large Afghan carpet, she opened the book randomly to a page, where she started reading a prayer by Bahá'u'lláh:

From the sweet-scented streams of Thine eternity give me to drink, O my God, and of the fruits of the tree of Thy being enable me to taste, O my Hope! From the crystal springs of Thy love suffer me to quaff, O my Glory, and beneath the shadow of Thine everlasting providence let me abide, O my Light! Within the meadows of Thy nearness, before Thy presence, make me able to roam, O my Beloved, and at the right hand of the throne of Thy mercy, seat me, O my Desire! From the fragrant breezes of Thy joy let a breath pass over me, O my Goal, and into the heights of the paradise of Thy reality let me gain admission, O my Adored One! To the melodies of the dove of Thy oneness suffer me to hearken, O Resplendent One, and through the spirit of Thy power and Thy might quicken me, O my Provider! In the spirit of Thy love keep me steadfast, O my Succorer, and in the path of Thy good pleasure set firm my steps, O my Maker! Within the garden of Thine immortality, before Thy countenance, let me abide for ever, O Thou Who art merciful unto me, and upon the seat of Thy glory stablish me, O Thou Who art my Possessor! To the heaven of Thy loving-kindness lift me up, O my Quickener, and unto the Daystar of Thy guidance lead me, O Thou my Attractor! Before the revelations of Thine invisible spirit summon me to be present, O Thou Who art my Origin and my Highest Wish, and unto the essence of the fragrance of Thy beauty, which Thou wilt manifest, cause me to return, O Thou Who art my God!

Potent art Thou to do what pleasest Thee. Thou art, verily, the Most Exalted, the All-Glorious, the All-Highest.[2]

She felt immediately refreshed and a little more grounded. She tried to absorb the beauty of the text, and, in particular, she liked the line ". . . essence of the fragrance of Thy beauty." She closed the prayer book and placed it on the carpet. As she did this, she noted the rich design, shapes, and colors in it. The overall design was floral. She ran her hand over and in amongst the texture of the carpet. Our configured destiny was like the weaving in a carpet. We were free to make our own unique design, and that was the fragrance of beauty, so each soul would then have a pattern of identity that could never be repeated, and the complexity of the existence of a mass of souls and their interdependent and interwoven designs must be incredible, where all the souls were a collective "we" as well as a collective "I." She wondered if we could recognize a person's spiritual identity as quickly as we could see their facial identity, and the symmetries of the face were absolutely unique, so the spiritual identity must be the same: a pattern of being. Then she remembered what Shidan had said in Tabriz. That every thread makes its way into the weave and destiny of the Manifestations of God, and that we choose to be a luminescent thread or a black thread or an in-between thread, which was the essence of free will.

She heard soft taps on the door. "Come in." She turned to see Shidan coming through the door.

"Hi. Are you ready to go? We have another full day's drive ahead. We should reach Kabul this afternoon," Shidan said.

"Ready and refreshed," replied Allison with a smile.

Once the car was packed, they thanked the family for letting them stay the night and left Gardandeh behind them.

———

In the afternoon they drove into the outskirts of Kabul. The mountains were behind them now as they entered a flat plain. Near the road they passed farms with an array of different crops. Small pockets of outlying suburbia occasionally punctuated the farms. In the distance Allison could just make out a series of low hills with houses ascending up the hills on steep inclines. The houses were an assortment of what she guessed were mud-brick and some concrete that blended into the hills. As they were about to enter the suburbs proper, they came to another checkpoint. Vahid pulled over to the side of the road, and her view of the city was partially obscured by dust that was kicked up by the car in front, which had also pulled off the road into the checkpoint.

Vahid rolled his window down and greeted one of the guards. They spoke in Dari, which is known as Afghan Persian. She guessed that they were talking about her because the guard looked at her for a moment and then back at Vahid and asked more questions. She was covered with the blue burka and was about to ask Shidan what the guard was saying when she stopped herself. She realized that if she said anything in English the Taliban would detain them.

Vahid passed over a roll of cash. The guard took the money and hesitated for a moment. He looked at her again, then back at Vahid. He turned to one of the other guards, who was sitting on a chair nearby with a Kalashnikov between his legs. The other guard must have said something about letting them go because the guard turned to Vahid and said something in Dari. He finally waved them off.

As they drove off, she looked back at the checkpoint. "I wasn't sure we would make it through this time," she said.

"Most of the time, money is all they want. If I didn't give them money, they would ask more unwanted questions," Vahid said.

"I almost blew it, Shidan. I was going to say something in English. What did they say?" Shidan did not respond. He was looking out at the city passing by.

"They just asked where we came from and where we were heading. He asked who you were. I told him that you're my sister," Vahid said.

"What did the other guy say?" she said.

Then Shidan turned and answered. "The other guy said something about making some tea. That it was someone's turn to make it."

"People here are obsessed with tea," Vahid said.

"Shall we explore? Or we could find a hotel?" she said.

"There's no need. You can stay with me . . . and my sister, unless you really want to stay in a hotel. It's up to you."

"Yes . . . why not. We'll stay with you," she said with a bright voice.

As they drove into the Kabul suburbs, Allison surveyed the range of hills she had seen before. They surrounded a flat plain where the main part of the city was located. She observed all the diversity of architecture through the mesh of her burka. Some were concrete apartment blocks and what she guessed were multi-story governmental buildings, but many were run-down and crumbling mud-brick houses that were mostly domestic dwellings. The poverty of the place was clearly visible, but the city had a certain interesting character that she could not define yet. They drove for twenty minutes down a main highway. As they went, she kept looking at the life on the side of the road. This life was a mix of muddy motorcycles, children in grubby clothes playing soccer, and some people riding old bicycles. The street vendors stood out, and she noted a man pushing a wooden cart with fruit and vegetables on it. And above shop fronts were the many faded signs in Dari, which she looked up at for a moment, and then she became aware of the warm light on her face coming through the mesh of the burka. She closed her eyes and felt the jolt of the car after it hit a pothole.

This was another world compared to New York or London. Even Tehran was not this run-down, but as she had this thought, they passed a modern-looking, glass high-rise building that looked completely alien in its surroundings.

"In the West, we take the material aspects of our lives for granted," she said as she leaned forward. She put her hand on Shidan's shoulder.

Shidan turned to her. "We do, don't we? Without doubt, war and poverty have had their impact here," Shidan said, then he turned back to look at the buildings passing by.

"Afghanistan is a cursed country when it comes to war," Vahid said.

Vahid's house was located at the base of one of the hills that Allison had seen coming into Kabul. The house was a concrete compound with high walls on all sides and nestled amongst mud-brick structures, which rose up into the hill. A small avenue ran along one side of the building. Once they stopped in front of the gates, Vahid got out and opened them. They passed into the compound. "Well, this is it. This is where I live. How do you say it in English? It's not much, but it's home," Vahid said.

A woman came out to greet them. "Hello," she said in English before continuing to talk to Vahid in Dari. He closed the gates and turned to the others. "My sister, Nasim, wants to know if you have enjoyed your travels through Afghanistan so far."

"Tell her we have." Allison walked around the car and took the burka off as she walked. She shook Nasim's hand. Shidan followed Allison and also shook Nasim's hand. Vahid started to take the luggage inside. Allison looked over the detail of the house, which was a shabby-looking two-story building.

Inside, they entered the living room. Allison was surprised to find a group of girls sitting in a circle. They were drawing a still life arrangement placed in the center of the room. The girls ranged in age from what she guessed were nine to sixteen years of age. "Who are these girls?" she asked Nasim.

"They are my hidden school." Nasim had attempted English.

"Hidden?"

Vahid came back into the room. "What she means is this is a secret school. If the Taliban found out, they would put us in jail. Women are not allowed to go to school, and they are definitely not supposed to do any kind of art. We had our piano confiscated about a year ago. Can you believe it? They took it into the courtyard and burned it. I managed to save some of the keys." Vahid walked over to the fireplace and took a partially burnt piano key off the mantelpiece. He waved it around and smiled. "It's a souvenir of the stupidity of the Taliban."

Allison asked Vahid to say hello to the girls. Some of them responded in Dari and others in broken English. After ten minutes, the girls finished up, and Nasim packed the colored pencils away. The girls then slowly left the house for the courtyard and put on burkas as they walked. They left in small groups of two or three through a small doorway that opened onto the avenue beside the house. Vahid explained to Allison that they avoided going in one large group to make sure they did not invite suspicion from the Taliban.

Allison and Shidan decided to explore the streets before dinner. They stepped out onto the avenue along with the last group of girls. The light over the city was beginning to fade.

The avenue was narrow, with no concrete paving or asphalt. The ground was just mud that was hemmed in on both sides with mud-brick houses. As they walked up the steep incline, she observed the crowds of people walking by them. She stopped in front of one boy with the bluest eyes she had seen in the Middle East and thought that the color of his eyes must be rare in this country. He smiled at her, then reached out to touch the fabric of her burka. She lifted the burka up and used her hand to ruffle his hair. The boy then said something in Dari and walked on past them.

"What did he say?" she asked Shidan.

"He said, 'Bye, mother.'"

"What a strange thing to say."

"But he was cute. His eyes were intense," Shidan said.

"Yes, true. Very cute."

After a few minutes, they came to small shops selling birds. The shops were just rough wooden lean-tos. Allison looked down at the hem of her burka, which was muddy now. They stopped at one shop. Allison looked into a wooden cage at a rather plain-looking bird. It sang, and Allison thought this compensated for its plain appearance.

"What bird is this?" she asked the owner.

Shidan translated for her, and then the owner responded to Shidan. "It's a nightingale," Shidan said.

———

After dinner, Vahid took them to the roof. They drank tea and watched the sun continue to fade. Allison observed the gradual afterglow beyond the mountains in the distance. The city lights came on slowly. Allison turned to look up at the lights from houses on the hill behind them. Everyone was quiet for a while as they sipped their tea. Allison listened to the sounds of the traffic as a few noisy motorcycles passed by in front of the house.

After a few hours of talking, everyone went to bed. Allison asked if she could sleep on the roof. Sitting on a mattress, she looked up at the night sky for a moment. An exterior light was shining down. She opened her prayer book randomly. She could just make out the words as she prayed again for the second time that day. This was another prayer by Bahá'u'lláh:

> *Create in me a pure heart, O my God, and renew a tranquil conscience within me, O my Hope! Through the spirit of power confirm Thou me in Thy Cause, O my Best-Beloved, and by the light of Thy glory reveal unto me Thy path, O Thou the Goal of my desire! Through the power of Thy transcendent might lift me up unto the heaven of Thy holiness, O Source of my being, and by the breezes of Thine eternity gladden me, O Thou Who art my God! Let Thine everlasting melodies breathe tranquility on me, O my Companion, and let the riches of Thine ancient countenance deliver me from all except Thee, O my Master, and let the tidings of the revelation of Thine incorruptible Essence bring me joy, O Thou Who art the most manifest of the manifest and the most hidden of the hidden!* [3]

———

The dawn was dark when they left Kabul for Jalalabad. Initially, they passed through a wide plain and, after a short time, left the suburbs behind. In the distance were mountains. Allison stared at them as they moved through the plain. Once they came to the mountains, they entered deep gorges. After a few hours of driving, the road began to hug a river. Along different points in the road, the traffic slowed due to a trail of trucks and cars winding around the narrow roads. She observed a tired and rusty red bus in front of the car. Strapped to the roof were luggage and a bike. Amongst the luggage was a crowd of Afghan men. They were wearing distinctive white turbans and baggy pants. Some of the men were wearing those brown Chitrali caps.

By 2:00 p.m. they came into Jalalabad where the terrain had flattened out again. They opted not to stop but to keep driving through and try and make the Pakistan border by the end of the day. Vahid did not know any customs officials at the main border control on the Torkham border crossing so they headed north. They skirted along the Afghan side of the border and passed through the Hindu Kush along a river. The mountains were snow-capped and exceptionally steep in places. Even though she had never been there, she immediately thought of Switzerland. The road was narrow and bumpy, but she felt a certain exhilaration as they passed through the mountain range. They stopped at a few places along the road, and she got out to take photos on the Leica.

Several hours after dusk, they passed over the border. Vahid knew a border control official there, and he passed over some cash. They passed into Pakistan and came immediately to the village of Arandu, where they stayed overnight.

The next day at dawn, they headed north for an hour until they reached the main highway heading south to Islamabad. It took close to a day to get to Islamabad, and they arrived just after dark. They went to a small, cheap hotel that Vahid knew about that was located in central Islamabad.

On the morning of the following day, Vahid took them to the US embassy. The standard time to process passports was around two weeks, but for Shidan they said they could process his in four days because Sara had already sent them all the required paperwork.

They left the embassy and drove back toward the hotel. On the way Allison noted the layout of the city, which was a grid of interlocking squares, a bit like New York in that way, but her immediate impression was that the architecture in central Islamabad was bland. The city lacked the worn-out look that Kabul had that was so attractive to her. She mentioned this blandness to Vahid as they drove through it.

"Well, if you find this place boring, we should go south to Rawalpindi. I know a good hotel there, and, anyway, it's close to the airport," said Vahid. "You can catch a taxi back to the embassy in a few days when the passport is ready."

So they went to the hotel for their luggage and drove south for half an hour.

When they arrived in the old part of Rawalpindi, Allison felt comfortable again, as it had that shabby ambiance but with no mud-brick buildings like Kabul. The architecture was of a higgledy-piggledy style and primarily concrete and brick. The layout of the streets was more organic too.

They found a café near their new hotel that was adjacent to the Nankari Bazaar. They sat in chairs on the street, drinking coffee and watching all the street life pass by.

She rummaged through her backpack and took out the burka that Vahid had given her at the beginning of the trip. "Thanks. I don't think I will need this now," she said as she handed it back to him.

She was now wearing the headscarf that Shidan had bought in Turkey.

"Did you enjoy pretending to be my sister?" he said.

"I did," she said. She smiled and titled her head sideways.

"My sister told me that she really liked you, Allison."

"I liked her too. It is amazing what she is doing with her school."

Shidan took out his billfold and gave Vahid the last installment of money for the trip. "There is a bit extra for Nasim," he said and smiled. "Thank you, by the way. You've been a good guide and very entertaining."

Vahid got up. "Well, I should go. It was good to meet you both. And good luck with the rest of your trip back to London."

Shidan stood up and shook his hand. Allison waved goodbye as Vahid left the café and headed back to his car. A little way down the street, he stopped and turned around. He waved and smiled, then continued until he disappeared into a crowd of people coming out of the bazaar. Allison then stood up and ran after Vahid, trying to find him amongst the crowds of people. Eventually, she saw him walking away, and she then caught up to him and put her hand on his shoulder. He turned around.

"Sorry, Vahid. Can I give you a hug? Would that be okay?"

"Sure," he said, and smiled.

They embraced.

"Thank you for looking after us."

"No problem."

"Okay, I'll let you go now. Bye."

"Bye," he said, and turned away.

She watched him fade into the street and stood there for a full minute before returning to the café. Shidan was sitting in his seat, and she sat down next to him.

"Vahid is such a nice person."

"Yes, he is."

They were quiet for a while. Allison was watching the people pass by the café.

"Hey, you know, I had a strange dream last night," she said.

"What about?"

"I was getting married to Hooman. Isn't that bizarre? We were somewhere in a meadow. Everyone was holding hands in a circle. I knew intuitively that it was Upstate New York."

"Hmm . . . interesting."

"Yes, it was. But in the dream, I didn't seem to mind. I was happy. Isn't that strange? Me and Hooman. Together."

Shidan then turned to her. "I want to go to Rome. I was going to go there after I dropped you off in London, but if you want, you can come with me. I think we can get a flight via Dubai. I want to make some inquiries about a manuscript."

"Rome would be an interesting diversion. My father was born there. And I have family there. I went there once when I was living in Paris."

"Okay, great. It's settled, then."

Allison took another sip of her coffee and paid attention to the abiding taste of cinnamon and cardamon, which were typical ingredients in Pakistani coffee.

She then put the cup down on the table and watched everyone walking by the café.

On the afternoon of their last day in Rawalpindi, they were scheduled to fly to Rome. They had gone back to Islamabad in the morning and picked up Shidan's passport and were now wandering through the streets near their hotel. Allison had stopped in front of a spice shop and was looking up at a faded sign above the shop. She was standing next to a street vendor selling yellow and red apples. As Shidan picked up the fruit and smelled it, a very tired but colorful bus drove toward them. The bus nearly collided with her, and she jumped out of its path just in time. In that moment she felt her cell phone vibrating in her pocket. She saw Hooman's number come up.

"Hello. Perfect timing. I was just thinking about you," she said.

"Hey! How are you guys going? Actually, I should say, Where are you?"

"We're in Pakistan. We fly to Italy this afternoon. In four hours."

"Oh, okay, great. So how did you like Iran?"

"It was fabulous, amazing, and awesome . . . I visited the suburb where you and Nava grew up. We searched for your old apricot tree from the streets, but we didn't know where your old house was, so we eventually gave up looking."

"Oh, right, yeah. You knew about that from the photo I showed you in New York."

"But we had trouble in Tehran. Shidan's passport was confiscated by the police. We had a guide take us over the border into Afghanistan and then on to Pakistan."

"I had a feeling that you might encounter some trouble. But I am glad you are both okay now."

"Yeah, we're fine. . . . Hey! I want to ask you something. When I was in Kabul, I was reading a prayer from that prayer book you gave me."

"Did you like the prayer?"

"Yes, I did, but I want to ask you about the last line of the prayer. It said something that I couldn't quite fathom. I'm paraphrasing it, but it went something like this: 'God is the most manifest of the manifest and the most hidden of the hidden.' How can this be? It's a paradox, isn't it? I got stuck on the word 'manifest,' which I have never heard before in that context."

"Well, there are a few possible interpretations of that line. I know the prayer you are talking about, by the way. I say it quite often. Well, anyway, God's essence is hidden, but his creation, his attributes, are manifest. It's like a mirror in which God's image is manifest, which is a metaphor for creation. And imagine that God is represented as a person standing in front of the mirror. The mirror itself has no ability to understand the reality of the person standing before it. So the person is hidden from the mirror because the mirror has no senses to perceive the person. And the difference between the person and the mirror, in terms of superiority, is infinite. One is in three dimensions, and living, and the other is a two-dimensional representation. All movement in the mirror comes from the person. And the mirror, no matter how far it progresses, can never become the person. Imagine also that at the atomic level, each atom in the mirror is a single human consciousness, which reflects only a fragment of the whole image, and so it is only when minds are unified that humanity can be conscious of the whole image projected onto it. So, the person is the essence, and the mirror is the collection of attributes that manifest the image of the person."

"So, is that related to the concept of immanence and transcendence? The word 'manifest' stands in for immanence, and the word 'hidden' is transcendence?"

"Yes, completely."

Allison had a thought pop into her head in that moment. Nasim had used the wrong word to describe her secret school. She had called it her "hidden school" before Vahid had corrected her. The school was manifest to Nasim and Vahid but hidden from the Taliban. And she wondered if there might be a hidden school in creation too, in which God teaches us about our true nature.

"Okay, thanks. That makes sense to me now."

"Great. Glad I could help. So anyway, I'll get going now. I just wanted to check that you guys were okay. I'll email you when you get back to London."

"Oh, oh . . . I almost forgot. I got to visit the house of Bahá'u'lláh in Istanbul."

"That's cool. Did you like it?"

"Yes, for reasons I can't understand. But I wanted to ask you about the house or these holy places. About how they work . . . how they affect the soul."

"Well, these holy places are transfigured symbols, pointing to a higher plane both internally and externally, but if there were no inner condition to make the journey of transfiguration, then they would be no different from any other house, but to a mature or illumined soul, they are utterly transcendent."

"Thank you. That is really helpful. That throws some light on my feelings toward the house of Bahá'u'lláh. Okay. Well, I'll let you go."

"Okay, cool. Bye."

Allison put her cell into her pocket. "I guess we should head toward the airport now," she said to Shidan.

"Sure. Here . . . have an apple."

He threw an apple at her. She caught it and smiled.

———

In the taxi on the way to the airport, Allison pulled out five packets of photos from her backpack that she had had developed that day. They were all the black-and-white photos that she had taken from Turkey to Iran and through Afghanistan and Pakistan. She took photos out of the first packet and began to flick through them.

Shidan looked over at her. "Where was that photo taken?" he said, pointing at an interior photo of the crumbling roof structure inside the old house in the suburb of Incirli.

"I call that 'the house of relativity.' That was in Istanbul. I took it just before I arrived at the house of Bahá'u'lláh."

"Hmm . . . interesting. It is definitely old."

"Isn't it amazing?"

"You absolutely have tastes in architecture that move beyond the average."

"Thank you. I will take that as a compliment."

"I can see why you were never interested in the usual tourist destinations. You have been trying to avoid the architectural clichés that normally qualify for beautiful."

"That's right. Exactly."

She continued to move through the stack of photos and was able to relive the stillness of time. She liked that photos represented a more tangible, concrete version of memory, where we could revisit moments that had faded in our memories.

"Can I see that house again?" Shidan asked.

She went through the stack and pulled out several shots of the interior. As she passed them to him, she said, "The puppets have gone, but the stage still remains, if only a little faded."

"How very Shakespearean of you. 'The world's a stage' and all that."

She laughed.

———

After a nine-hour drive from Eden, the girls arrived in the outer suburbs of Sydney close to 3:00 p.m. on Monday, January 4, 1993. They had arranged to meet Gabriel at Martin Place Station in Sydney's Central Business District. He was going to catch the train from the Blue Mountains after a meditation retreat. Allison found a parking garage, and the girls walked to the station. They intended to walk around Sydney for the day, then drive north to Wisemans Ferry at the end of the day and stay the night with Cathy, a friend of Io's.

As they walked toward the station, Aurélie waved, and Gabriel waved back. When the girls came to Gabriel, Aurélie and Gabriel kissed and hugged and uttered a few phrases in French.

"How was the meditation retreat?" Aurélie said in English.

"Good, good," he said.

Gabriel then hugged both Io and Allison in turn. "It is nice to meet you both," he said. Allison expressed a few polite phrases in French, then she asked about his childhood. Did he grow up in Paris or was he born in another part of France?

Gabriel laughed. "Oh, impressive. Your French is good. And no, I didn't grow up in Paris. I was born in Lyon. I went to Paris to study at École normale supérieure. That is where I met Aurélie."

"Okay, cool," Allison said.

"Okay, so what is the plan for today?" he asked the girls.

"Allison wants to go to the Art Gallery of New South Wales," Aurélie said.

"Is that okay?" Allison asked Gabriel.

"Sure. No problem," he said.

So they turned around and walked down Martin Place toward the Domain, where the gallery was situated. Once they were in the gallery, Allison suggested to Aurélie and Gabriel that they look at the Australian Aboriginal section.

"Have you guys seen any Aboriginal art before?" Allison said.

"I have seen a few pieces in the Centre Pompidou in Paris," Gabriel said.

They eventually entered the Aboriginal section, and Allison explained some of the backgrounds of the artists she was familiar with. They talked about the Dreamtime and what that meant to different tribes.

After spending an hour in the gallery, they walked out and began to walk through the botanical gardens toward the Sydney Opera House. Allison had seen the harbor a few times before as a child, but it was nice to see Sydney Harbour through an adult lens. They walked around the Opera House, and Allison sat on a bench as the others continued to walk. She lay down on the bench and closed her eyes. She felt the warm light on her face and listened to the sounds of the city around her. She pondered the road trip that was still ahead of her and felt a subtle contentment wash over her. She looked forward to expanding the depth of her relationship with the land and exploring relative emotional isolation.

After fifteen minutes, the others came back, and Allison opened her eyes and sat up.

"What else would you like to do?" Allison said.

"Can we catch the ferries around the harbor? Io has been telling us how cool that is," Aurélie said.

"Sure. I have never caught the ferries myself."

They walked away from the Opera House toward Circular Quay and embarked on a ferry that was headed for the inner part of the harbor, a route that naturally took it under the Sydney Harbour Bridge. Allison looked at the panorama of the water and surrounding suburbs and cliffs for several minutes until the boat passed under the bridge. She then looked up in awe at the bridge with all its tendrils of steel supports. They stayed on the ferry for an hour and a half as they looked out at

Sydney passing by. They went to the end of the line at Parramatta Wharf and then turned around and came back down the Parramatta River to Circular Quay. They arrived at the Quay in the evening and then walked back to the car at Martin Place and drove on to Wisemans Ferry to stay with Cathy overnight.

14

PRAYERS AT THE GRAVES

In this station he pierceth the veils of plurality, fleeth the realms of the flesh, and ascendeth unto the heaven of unity. With the ear of God he heareth; with the eye of God he beholdeth the mysteries of divine creation. He steppeth into the inner sanctuary of the Friend and, as an intimate, shareth the pavilion of the Well-Beloved. He stretcheth forth the hand of truth from the sleeve of the Absolute and revealeth the mysteries of divine power.[1]

— BAHÁ'U'LLÁH, *THE SEVEN VALLEYS*

On a sunny fall day, Sunday, May 23, 1999, the sun streamed down on St. Kilda Pier. With a stab of pain in her left foot, Sophie lost focus on reading. She looked down at the fibrous pier planks warming her bare feet. She tucked several A4 pages under her arm and balanced on one foot. With her free hand she removed a wooden splinter, then dropped her flip-flops next to her feet and slipped into them.

She took the pages and flipped back and forth through a few printed emails. She tried to follow Allison's movements. Paul had printed out three emails from Allison. Two she had sent from London before traveling in the Middle East, and the other one was recent, from Italy.

His voice touched her thoughts through the breeze from the bay but soon dissipated into that breeze. She was distracted by his voice as she heard him, louder now, talking to a man fishing nearby. The air buffeted the three sheets of paper she was attempting to read. Their conversation faded as she held the top of the paper back with her thumb and forefinger to prevent the wind from moving through the paper again. She began to read the most recent email from Allison.

To: paul.bird43@yahoo.com.au
From: allisonbird1919@yahoo.com
Date: May 22, 1999
Subject: Hello from Rome

Hey Paul,

I'm in Rome with Shidan. We managed to get out of Iran and Afghanistan with a bit of maneuvering on Shidan's part. The police took his passport in Tehran. Anyway, today we've been sitting in a café adjacent to the main square in Trastevere, just sipping lattes and watching the Italians go by with their usual exuberance. We spent yesterday climbing all seven of the Seven Hills in Rome. I visited Dad's sisters and brother, plus all the cousins, today. They are all well. I'm going to catch a plane to London tomorrow. As I said in a few emails back, the master's is on hold. I'm not sure when, or if, I will resume it.

Yesterday, I saw a Caravaggio painting in a church near central Rome, *The Conversion on the Way to Damascus.* Hooman thinks that, like St. Paul, maybe God will reverse the fortunes of humanity in the future, a renaissance of spiritual values and a collective conversion of sorts. He calls it "entry by troops." Anyway, sorry to bore you with that. Paul, could you please print this email out and recite this quote at Mom's and Dad's graves, as well as the two prayers in the other emails I sent from London?

O SON OF THE SUPREME! I have made death a messenger of joy to thee. Wherefore dost thou grieve? I made the light to shed on thee its splendor. Why dost thou veil thyself therefrom? [2]

—Bahá'u'lláh, *The Hidden Words*

It would mean a lot to me if you could do this. I'll let you know how I'm going in London in my next email. I will most probably be back in London when you read this, as I fly out from Rome tomorrow. Nothing more to tell you. I love you.

Allison

Roused from thought, she felt Paul's hand touch her back lightly through the fabric of her dress.

"What's up, Sophie?" he said.

"Hello."

"Shall we go home?"

"Actually, I wanted to pick up some bread from Acland Street." She looked at the end of the pier in the distance. "Why don't we go and walk to the end for another half an hour? The weather is so nice . . . and then you can take the car. I'll go get bread and walk home on foot."

"Okay. That sounds like a plan," he said.

They walked on.

"God, what a lovely day," she said.

She took his hand and swung it back and forth between them.

"Yes, it's a freak day, isn't it?" he responded.

"It's strange that Allison has dropped her master's . . . to go and make coffees in London . . . and why leave New York? I thought she liked it there. I suppose she thinks she'll learn philosophy serving lattes rather than through university. And the fees you paid are wasted now."

"Yeah, I know. It's typical of her, but it's her money too, and it was only one semester. Plus, she does have a stake in the business. At least half."

"But she was never there to support you, Paul. Or hardly ever."

"She was in the early days . . . anyway, I am tired of lecturing her." Paul laughed. He put his hand on his head. "She lives by a different set of rules to us. It's an unconventional way, but it makes sense to her, so I don't care anymore."

"When will you visit your parents' graves?"

"I'll go tomorrow."

They reached the end of the pier. Leaning on the railings, they surveyed the curve of the bay and the smoggy center of Melbourne city off on the right. With the water shining in a golden-white sheen, the dirty smudge on the skyline seemed almost romantic rather than the polluted haze that it was. Waves lapped at the pier pylons. In the light-saturated water, a school of fish swayed back and forth with the waves. They stared in silence at the fish for several minutes. Sophie felt the breeze from the bay on her face as it pushed her hair around.

Paul placed his elbow on the railing with his chin in his hand. "Did I ever tell you about her travels around Australia?" he asked.

"Briefly. I can't remember the details. It was a while ago that you told me the story."

"She left on the day after her exhibition. In that week she had bought a car for the trip, a Holden HT 1969 to 1970, I think it was. You could see the road through the floor of the passenger's side seat. The handbrake was broken, and she had to use a couple of bricks to prop up the wheels so the car wouldn't roll. Anyway, you get the picture."

"Yeah. Not surprising though. It sounds like her."

"She had the money to buy a better car, but I think she liked the character of it. I had a phone call a couple of weeks or so later. She had been stopped by the police a day before that. They gave her a ticket and told her to get the car's taillight fixed. She didn't mention to the police that the handbrake was broken. She never got it fixed, at least not straight away. No, wait, I just remembered. She got it fixed in Nimbin. She slept in the back seat for a year as she traveled around Australia."

"A year! Living in a car. Amazing."

"I think she supplemented the back seat with a tent here and there. Anyway, she had some interesting adventures on the road."

A large oil tanker on the horizon made its way toward the Melbourne docks.

"But what amazes me is how different you both are," she said to him.

"Maybe we're just two sides to one personality. Everyone has a place in the world, Sophie, even if we can't always see it."

"Well, you're more tolerant than I would be, but I suppose that is why I love you."

———

After a day's drive north from Sydney, they arrived in Byron Bay on Tuesday, January 5, 1993. Io's commune was in the hinterland, not far from Nimbin, the counterculture capital of Australia. After an hour's drive into the hinterland, they passed through Nimbin and then headed toward Tuntable Creek where they turned off the main road onto a dirt road that cut through thick subtropical rainforest. They drove for several minutes until they entered the commune.

The house Io and her partner lived in was not a very humble structure like most of the other wooden and mud-brick houses in the commune. It was a large wood and glass structure made of intersecting polygon shapes. These were constructed with intersecting triangles, and it was not built in the common fashion of a geodesic dome. The structure was more organic, with a sprawling, rounded, and soft asymmetric form, like large droplets of water that had partially merged into each other.

Io's husband was an architect, and they had decided to drop out of society after being in well-paid jobs in Sydney for over two decades. Io had asked Allison to stay in their spare room.

The next morning, as Allison had looked up at the sky from her bed, she noted the intersecting glass triangles and wondered if the minds of people could form complex shapes and intersections like this and whether collective consciousness had forms beyond the limits of the senses.

Allison spent the day exploring the commune. There was extensive virgin forest with several tracks passing through it. There were also orchards and a large vegetable garden. Then there were the animals: sheep, goats, and chickens. There were also several bush turkeys wandering around the property.

At the end of the day, everyone usually gathered at Io's house for dinner. It had the largest dining area of all the houses on the commune, so it was the default place for dinner every night. The resident composer, Simion, was playing his latest piece on a classical guitar, and his partner, Shelly, had been the cook that evening and was bringing out several dishes. Everyone else was eating dinner and talking as they sat at a large table. Children were playing in the background.

"Where will you go next?" Gabriel said.

"North. I have no fixed plan. I'll leave tomorrow," Allison said.

"Please stay with us a bit longer," Io said.

"No, I have to move on."

"Please stay longer," Io said.

"Hmm . . . well, okay. I could stay longer, I suppose."

Simion finished his piece, and everyone clapped.

"Great," Io said.

"And you must come and stay with us in Paris," Aurélie said.

"Okay, I promise. I will go to Paris too."

Allison smiled and turned to Io. "Are there any mechanics nearby? I should probably get my handbrake fixed. And I could smell gas in the car yesterday."

"Yeah, I smelled that too."

"You must have a leak somewhere," Gabriel said.

―――――

Alone with the night, Allison had liked the meditation of watching rolling white road lines emerge out of the darkness into the beam of the headlights before disappearing under the car, and the sound of the heating fan rattling away. It competed with Joni Mitchell's album *Blue*.

She had left the commune on Friday, February 5, 1993, after a month in Io's spare room. She had spent the day in Nimbin waiting for her car to be fixed by a mechanic. She was now having issues with the clutch after having the handbrake fixed a month before. She was driving toward the Queensland border, heading for a small town called Murwillumbah. Once she was near the town, she planned to pull off the road and sleep in the back seat for the night. Then on the next morning, before dawn, she would climb Mount Warning and watch the sun rise over the valleys and hills surrounding the mountain, all forming part of the ancient caldera.

―――――

Allison broke from her past memories of her road trip in Australia. She was inside her London apartment now on May 23, 1999. She found herself cross-legged and staring out of her window at the plane trees in Chalcot Square. Shidan came through the door to her room.

"I'm going now. I'll head back to my hotel and get my bags," Shidan said.

"Do you want company? I'll come to the airport."

"No, it's okay. I'll make my own way."

"When will you come back to London?"

"I'm not sure. I'll let you know when I have a clear plan."

"Thanks for letting me tag along. Through Iran and all the rest."

"It was an absolute pleasure. That's the best fun I've had in years. And I am sorry. I put you in unnecessary danger. I should have foreseen that. Sorry."

"No. It was fun. I don't regret a moment of it."

Allison got up and embraced Shidan. "It was wonderful. Thank you. When you get back, send my love to Hooman. I'm sure he will love to hear more about our travels. And particularly all the places that are meaningful to Bahá'ís."

"I'll let him know about everything. You know, he talks about you a lot. I think he misses you."

"Really?"

"Yep . . . okay, I'd better go."

Shidan turned to go but stopped at the door. He turned back and faced her.

"Do you like Hooman?"

"Yes, of course I do. He's a very sweet person and——"

"Hooman likes you."

"Yes, he's a great person."

"No . . . let me rephrase that. He loves you."

"He what! Since when?" Her voice lowered. "Hooman said that?"

"No, Hooman hasn't said anything, really. I noted a few things in conversation, that's all. Nothing overt. Just wondering how you were going in London and why you left New York so suddenly."

"So what does that mean? He never mentions that in our emails. It's just friendly conversation, as always."

"I've been reading the subtext in Hooman's emotions. He's been careful to hide his feelings. But I know that he loves you, absolutely. It's up to you if you want to do anything about it. Maybe he thinks that you think you are both not matched. That you would not see him as the right person for you. It is true that you are both quite different, but I don't think that matters."

"Right, yeah, I suppose. I haven't thought about it to be honest."

"Well, you have something to think about now."

15

THE PAPER BIRD

O My brother! A pure heart is as a mirror; cleanse it with the burnish of love and severance from all save God, that the true sun may shine therein and the eternal morning dawn. Then wilt thou clearly see the meaning of "Earth and heaven cannot contain Me; what can alone contain Me is the heart of him that believeth in Me."[1] And thou wilt take up thy life in thy hand and with infinite longing cast it before thy newly found Beloved.[2]

— BAHÁ'U'LLÁH, *THE SEVEN VALLEYS*

Allison came out of a train station stairwell at Oxford Circus intersection. A number 23 bus, an old Routemaster, stopped near the stairwell, sitting behind a car. She looked up at the remnants of dusk for a moment, then at the red bus that reflected orange and gray clouds on its windows. She ran and jumpedhoo onto the rear platform as the bus moved with a green signal. Her fist tightened around a pole as both she and the bus swung into the intersection. The bus continued down Regent Street.

Nine weeks had passed by since she had returned from her travels in the Middle East. She was surprised to calculate that almost seven months had elapsed since she and Hooman had first met in New York. He was a beautiful person. She had to admit it. She turned these things over in her mind. She had arranged to meet Hooman at Piccadilly Circus this evening. He had business in the Netherlands and had a day free to meet her in London before he went back to New York.

A habit of catching alternating odd- and even-numbered buses had progressed over the months that she had been in London. Her memory rewound back to the last bus she had caught near Oxford Circus intersection, and this was an odd-numbered bus; it was not even as it should have been. She realized that she was now out of sequence.

She climbed the cramped stairs to the top deck. The back seat was the only empty seat on the bus, so she slid into it and shuffled toward the window. She observed a Friday night swell: a bustle of people and the noise of their conversations. She undid the buckle on a tattered and slightly grubby canvas bag and opened it. She stirred through its contents. Her bag was a dumping ground for every significant moment in her life: movie tickets folded and bound in a rubber band, many receipts with words and numbers scrawled on them, and plentiful Post-it notes upon which dreams and memories were drawn and theorized about.

A map, her symmetrical destiny map, came to the surface of all the random objects tumbling in her bag. Amongst other things she had drawn bus routes on the map. She had felt that all our destinies were interlinked in a web of intricate balance and synergy, which was an equilibrium between free will and the grace of God. Unfolding the map, a large piece of A3 paper, she pushed her pencil in a sharpener and twisted it a few times before scrawling a note on the Regent Street route: At this intersection catch two even-numbered buses in a row, then continue with the odd then even pattern. That was her resolution to the conundrum of not catching an even-numbered bus on this night. That would bring her back into sequence and balance, but at some stops there was not a choice between buses, so in such cases she would catch whatever number was available.

This map also recorded shop signs and street names that seemed significant. "Singlepoint" was in her destiny map. It was a cell phone shop on Oxford Street where she had purchased a new SIM card for her cell when she first arrived in London. She had written a quote from the *Hadith* under the shop name: "Knowledge is a single point, but the ignorant have multiplied it."[3] Shidan had emailed her this quote prior to her leaving for the Middle East. At the time the quote intrigued her. She took it to mean that the single point was one reflection in the Eternal Mirror, and ultimately it was God who was the single point of knowledge and, even further, the oneness of all being, and she had elaborated on the oneness of being in relation to the senses and had written:

> *All the senses converge at a single point: an axis of the soul. This is an association between the eye, tongue, ear, nose, and touch but also transcendent above them. Beyond the duality and division of the senses, the soul exists on a plane of oneness in a visual soundscape. The soul sees with ears and hears with eyes until nothing exists except pure form.*

The compulsion to record words and names and even numbers from seemingly random sources in her travels around London had come from her ideas about the symmetric convergence of names of people, places, and objects, like *The Conference of the Birds* incident late last year when Hooman had met Paul, Sophie, and Alison Nightingale at the ice rink in Central Park. She loved the symmetry of their names with her own brother and his girlfriend, Paul and Sophie, and herself. And then there was the idea that Bahá'u'lláh was the Nightingale of Paradise in the nighttime before the dawn of the new era. Allison now knew that both the plain appearance of the house of Bahá'u'lláh in Istanbul and the nightingale in Kabul were metaphors for the veils of the physical world that hid the true beauty of the Manifestations of God in this world. And linked to that was the present time that also hid humanity's true potential, which must be unfathomably radiant and beyond anything that anyone could ever understand or unravel today; flowers would bloom in the future from the seeds that had been planted earlier in history. Shoghi Effendi had called them "seeds of undreamt-of potentialities."[4] She had stumbled upon this quote when reading sections of *God Passes By* online in the previous week at an internet café near Camden Town. And she now wondered if different classes of names possessed different spiritual potentialities.

There were the names of everyday physical objects that we classed as relatively mundane. But Allison knew that underneath this apparent ordinary surface was a mystical order with obscure patterns and relationships that a certain strange logic could reveal. Above this mundane class of names were the names of human virtues, like truthfulness, compassion, generosity, detachment, and courage; these were only a few amongst many.

These virtues fell within the realm of spiritual reality and were underpinned by the Word of God for this age, which had been revealed by Bahá'u'lláh. His teachings and spiritual reality were the seeds, and a template laid down by God that would allow human spirituality and virtues to spread and flourish and eventually transform the generality of humankind over the course of history. The source and power that underpinned these potentialities came from God's spiritual attributes, his names, which gave form to the created worlds of God: the Ever-Forgiving, the Most Compassionate, the Most Powerful, the All-Glorious, the Fashioner, the Creator, the Almighty, the Omnipotent, and the Omnipresent.

Allison recalled her thought experiment about the life-story depository at Times Square all those months before. The two attributes of "Omnipotent" and "Omnipresent" were a significant part of the life-story depository, and maybe it wasn't just a thought experiment but a reality in the worlds to come: a transcendent type of social media with highly complex profiles of people and all their interlocking destinies. Aspects of her symmetrical destiny map were linked to her idea of a life-story depository, but she had found it challenging to find how her life intersected with others because she didn't possess any form of omnipresence. And even though our intertwined actions in this world were becoming clearer as technology had developed, Allison's need for information beyond her finite awareness was still out of her reach, which had been her conclusion when she had been sitting in the Starbucks coffee shop on her second day in New York. It was only by linking all our awarenesses together through technology and an emerging global consciousness that humanity could achieve a human form of Omnipotence and Omnipresence, thus mirroring, to a degree, God's names and spiritual attributes in this world.

Finally, she concluded that if she continued to collect names and their patterns for her symmetrical destiny map, she might be able to unravel the spiritual potentialities of this world and her place within it to a limited degree. In fact, in an email Hooman had sent her not long after she had returned from the Middle East, he had called this world (the created world) the "Kingdom of Names," which meant that every-thing in this world had a name and without which nothing could func-tion; this demonstrated the power of names and their potentialities within the structure of language and within reality itself.

She folded the map. It went back in her bag, down deep below the everyday items.

Regent Street's shop-window displays slid past. She looked up through the bus window to find the orange aspect of the sky was gone. The light gray had been supplanted with darker charcoal in the clouds and a dark blue backlight: a sky now unencumbered by dusk. It began to reflect the beginning of the night.

She stared at the reflection of the bus interior with its people and the colors of their clothes splashed around the top deck. The dark glass presented a crisp image, and an unfamiliar face stared back.

For the first time since some vaguely remembered time in Australia, she had made an effort to look appealing. Acknowledging this more-than-conscious effort made her nervous. She grimaced at herself. Her hair fell straight about her shoulders; she looked at the geometry of a fresh haircut. Her lips were a glistening red, which was sympathetic to the bus's own coat of red paint. On her eyelids she wore a green shade of eye shadow: it was makeup that she hardly ever wore or knew how to apply with much skill. Around her eyes she had applied black eyeliner with almost Egyptian contours. And she felt a certain indefinable ridicu-lousness surrounding this culture of female adornment.

On the previous day, after her haircut, she had trawled through several department stores. In Selfridges she had found a backless yellow dress that expressed overtones of the sixties.

Cut off at the knees on the left side, the dress tapered farther down on the right, and she was wearing brown sandals she had found on Carnaby Street. The leather straps from the sandals wound up her legs. Something about her clothing felt primal; it could almost accompany a modern love dance but in parallel to some collective African tradition.

While studying the alien face in the window, her mind drifted back to the preceding month. She surveyed the strands of her emotional transformation: the reasons for her bus ride toward Eros and Hooman. The catalyst of her transformation began with a stream of seemingly insignificant thoughts that were carried along on the currents of daily consciousness. These thoughts revolved around books; eventually they matured into something resembling love.

On a day off work from the café restaurant, Canteen, she was walking down Charing Cross Road. She stopped in front of a bookshop that sold rare books. A book in the window display caught her attention: *Medieval Philosophy in Islam and Christianity*. Hooman would like this, she had thought, so with that innocuous beginning she found a series of similar books on metaphysics and spirituality. After a short time, she had posted him several titles. She had to have them, and a strange imperative overtook her.

To: allisonbird1919@yahoo.com
From: hooman.hassidim@nightingaleshapiro.com
Date: June 19, 1999
Subject: Thanks for the books

Hey Allison,

Thanks for the latest book. *The Alchemy of Happiness* has some fascinating ideas, and of course it might have been a precursor, a foundation stone, for Rumi's work, whom I think might have been influenced by the author later on in history.

On the topic of alchemy, I thought you might like this quote from Bahá'u'lláh:

> *Is it within human power, O Hakim, to effect in the constituent elements of any of the minute and indivisible particles of matter so complete a transformation as to transmute it into purest gold? Perplexing and difficult as this may appear, the still greater task of converting satanic strength into heavenly power is one that We have been empowered to accomplish. The Force capable of such a transformation transcendeth the potency of the Elixir itself. The Word of God, alone, can claim the distinction of being endowed with the capacity required for so great and far-reaching a change.*[5]

I expect this quote might help you with your own spiritual investigations. The quote is referring to the spiritual gold, the virtues in our character that are refined by leaving behind earthly attachments. And it is the metal in alchemy associated with the sun. The green lion is associated with vitriol or acid that corrodes all metals except gold. So gold is symbolic of virtue, and vitriol is symbolic of the acid that removes all other worldly attachments. And, of course, I was thinking of those sculptures you found. The green lion is a symbol for the world of Malakut (the angelic world), which is green, swallowing the sun, which is a symbol for the world of Jabarut (The world of command), which is yellow. Remember we talked about the different color codes of the worlds. And there is this quote from Bahá'u'lláh, which seems to be connected to the world of Lahut and the five-world mystical system:

> *Know thou, moreover, that the Word of God—exalted be His glory—is higher and far superior to that which the senses can perceive, for it is sanctified from any property or substance. It transcendeth the limitations of known elements and is exalted above all the essential and recognized substances. It became manifest without any syllable or sound and is none but the Command of God which pervadeth all created things.*[6]

I think you may know that alchemy was eventually superseded by chemistry and other branches of science. Today it seems a little primitive, but I think some of the symbolism is still valid, and this reflects the alchemy of the soul rather than elements and metals. For example, that book on alchemy that you sent me, *The Birds of Transmutation*, charts the five stages of spiritual development through the five birds: crow, white swan, peacock, pelican, and Phoenix.

Nava says hello, but I'll write a longer email soon, when I have finished the current book you sent, and maybe we can chat further over the phone sometime? Nava and I miss having you around, at close hand, you know, to talk about various things. I don't suppose you feel the same as we do. When you were in New York, you always seemed to me to be quite self-sufficient in many ways, kind of detached emotionally, but always interested in and kind to us. Well, anyway, thanks for your thoughts and ideas. The more we communicate, the more I like your imagination.

Your spiritual brother,

Hoo

Hooman Hassidim
Public International Law,
Nightingale Shapiro,
656A Fifth Avenue, New York, NY 10103.
hooman.hassidim@nightingaleshapiro.com
www.nightingaleshapiro.com

Making a latte in the café where she worked one Sunday morning, she had the thought that Hooman was a significant aspect of her own personal alchemy of happiness. She thought about his virtues and the radiance of his heart. He was kind, thoughtful, and intelligent. These quiet thoughts called to her from the periphery of her mind: the same subtle imperatives that had motivated her need to buy him books, which had formed in the weeks before. And amongst these thoughts was a simple realization: I miss him. He had been right about physical presence because there was no substitute for it. She wanted to read all the nuances of his body language.

Many things, precious and unspoken, had surfaced between them when they were in New York. She had only imagined they were incompatible based on those early times when she had made some superficial and sketchy assessments of his character. And she realized that it was only his outward appearance that was different. Internally, they were quite similar.

"Go back to New York" was the thought that tugged at her. Was London an "odd" city and New York "even," she wondered? Had she lost the correct symmetry of their destiny?

She had been hit too by his observation that she might be too self-sufficient. His observation was barely veiled code that he wanted her to reveal more of her private self to him. After work, she sat in an internet café and wrote a reply.

To: hooman.hassidim@nightingaleshapiro.com
From: allisonbird1919@yahoo.com
Date: June 28, 1999
Subject: I keep a map

Hello Hoo,

I want to share with you something of my inner life. I have this thing that I call "symmetrical destiny." It's based on our earlier conversations on symmetry and asymmetry in names and actions. Remember that conversation in MoMA? Anyway, I keep a map where I try to achieve alternating symmetries across a range of things in my life. To see if patterns arise when I choose to take ordered paths over chance.

I see symmetry in everything. I realize this may seem a bit odd, but I thought you might like to know. I am thinking, more and more now, that there are some utterly deep secrets out there, beyond material causes, and I want to know the invisible skeleton on which creation is hung: its hidden patterns and pathways. I can't be content with the cliché of actions that qualify as normal or desired in this life. But I think you know this about me. We had many chats before I left New York, right? Thank you for those chats, by the way. I realized that I never thanked you, and you are a dear friend because you did not expect thanks. I wrote this poem a few weeks back and thought you might like it.

"Passage"

In the night,
her naked body plunged silently into a mirror of stars.
Their light a configured radiance.
Their love a matchless beauty.
In the opalescent day, when the ripples had found the water's edge,
he could not tell that she had been that way.

Love, from your sister in mind and imagination,

Allison

P.S. Thunderbirds are go!

The last segment in the arc of her emotional transformation came in the form of a square package from New York. It came three days after her last email to Hooman. A notice came to her apartment saying she had to go into the local post office near Camden, but when she went to the depot, she found that the package had been misdirected to Holburn instead.

Walking back from the Holburn Post Office, she went into the Seven Dials intersection and stopped in the middle of the intersection. She thought about the Seven Dials as seven types of time and the convergence of seven types of destiny. She chose Upper St Martins Lane and thought about Martin Place in Sydney as she walked down the lane. At another intersection she stopped and decided to open the package in a café near Covenant Garden. On her way she passed a restaurant she had not noticed before—Simurgh. The name lodged in her head because she recognized it as the Phoenix-like bird from *The Conference of the Birds*. The spelling was different from the book, but the reference was the same. Although she had not read the book since New York, she had been thinking of the different animals in alchemical symbolism that were in the books she had sent to Hooman. A midafternoon sun-shower began as the café came into view, and she ran to avoid the rain. The package weighed her down, but finally she ran through the café door.

Slightly damp, she sat at a table with a warm coffee in her hand and stared at the package for a while. She initially tried to guess the contents, but then, impatient, she began to shred the cardboard box until she pulled a white wooden cube from the packing foam. She could smell fresh paint and knew from this that the sculpture had been created recently. On its top was a large, curved lens, and immediately she understood what this was. Hooman must have gone to some trouble to track it down. The sculpture was like those from the exhibition she had seen almost seven months before in Soho. He had remembered her fascination for these objects; however, when she looked through the lens, she was surprised to find a white bird with its wings outstretched and not the green lion she had expected. The Persian text, in minute form and inscribed all over the bird's body, she assumed was from *The Conference of the Birds*. She wanted to see the script close-up, so she removed the lens and reached in to see if she could remove the bird. The bird was slotted into the base of the cube with a long pin, and it slid out as she pulled it gently. She held it up to the light and spun it around by rubbing the pin between her thumb and forefinger. She then put the bird on the table and spun the cube around. There was a quote on the side. She knew it could have only come from Hooman. He must have asked the artist to inscribe the quote onto the cube. It read, "The Phoenix of the realms above crieth out from the immortal Branch: The glory of all greatness belongeth to God, the Incomparable, the All-Compelling!"[7]

The Simurgh Restaurant came to mind immediately, and she knew it was no coincidence that she had passed by it, and even the fact that the package had been misdirected to Holburn so that she had the opportunity to pass by the restaurant was perfect. Without fate pushing her, she would have never seen it. She then realized that she had passed through the Seven Dials intersection and connected it immediately to the seven valleys in *The Conference of the Birds*. The seven valleys had been supplanted by the Seven Dials and seven types of time with seven roads leading through it, which equated to seven roads of destiny. She had passed down one road that led her past the Simurgh Restaurant. She could hear the Phoenix of the realms above calling her. She could hear it cry from the immortal Branch. The Phoenix was also one of the alchemical symbols of rebirth and renewal, and she had passed from the first symbolic animal, "the green lion," with seven stars on its body, eating the sun, to the Phoenix. Her destiny in that day was delicate and subtle.

Touched by his gesture, she wrote, expressing her thanks. When he replied, he passed over the fact in a cursory fashion, and she observed that he did not realize how much this gift had meant to her.

To: allisonbird1919@yahoo.com
From: hooman.hassidim@nightingaleshapiro.com
Date: July 2, 1999
Subject: Hello again

Hi again,

I knew you would like the bird. I found the artist after making some inquiries at the gallery. He wasn't making lions anymore, but I didn't think you would mind.

Oh, by the way, I may be in your area soon. I have to do some work in the Netherlands and have the option to stop over in London for a day. I'll arrive on a Friday night and leave sometime in the afternoon on

Saturday. Maybe we could catch up? Would that be okay? Would you like that?

I really hope that we can meet soon,

Hoo

Hooman Hassidim
Public International Law,
Nightingale Shapiro,
656A Fifth Avenue, New York, NY 10103.
hooman.hassidim@nightingaleshapiro.com
www.nightingaleshapiro.com

Allison sat at a computer in an internet café on Oxford Street, suggesting, with restraint, that they could catch up before he was due back in New York. "If it's not too much trouble" was her casual insert at the end of the email. After the email left she regretted the casual tone in her email because there was a degree of suppressed emotion in her and she wanted to be honest about this. She just did not like those excessively romantic sentiments and the typical clichéd remarks that people expressed when they liked someone.

In the afternoon, a few hours afterward, she came back to Oxford Street and saw his reply. She had been thinking of ways to make a second email a little more urgent, but now he was coming anyway so it did not matter. She was really happy he was coming to London to see her.

Staring past her reflection, she observed people on the sidewalk walking down Regent Street. The number 23 bus became bogged down with traffic near the Piccadilly Circus intersection. It moved, crawling bit by bit, toward her destination. Allison watched the slow-moving traffic ahead on the curve of the street as it disappeared into Piccadilly Circus. Being late, and impatient to meet Hooman, she moved down the stairway. She jumped off the bus while it moved slowly on and walked the rest of the distance on foot. Her hands were shaking slightly, and she felt a trickle of sweat roll from her armpit and down her right side. At Piccadilly Circus she searched the hundreds of people at the Eros statue on the opposite side of the intersection. Hooman's figure was indistinguishable amongst the crowd.

———

Feeling quite relaxed, he stared up at the oscillating and flashing advertising lights in Piccadilly Circus. The atmosphere was similar to Times Square but on a smaller scale. He was standing in a crowd of people near the Eros statue.

He had stopped in Amsterdam to see the house of Anne Frank, then went on to the Hague, where he had a meeting with another law firm and several meetings with policy committees linked with European Union governance mechanisms. In the Hague he had visited the Escher Museum before flying on to London. One drawing by Escher interested him and reminded him of recent conversations with Allison. Her intellectual efforts were Escher-like: the geometry of humanity and particularly consciousness. Hooman compared it to a type of bounded infinity through pattern, like the Mandelbrot Set with broad relationships within the symmetry of minds and pushing the edge of the impossible. Her thought experiments were related to time and space on one level but beyond it in another way. He wondered how symmetrical destiny could work. He found it all fascinating but partially incomprehensible. And then the thought occurred that only in Malakut after we die would we be able to see the proper symmetry that exists between souls. Then we might be able to see how our thoughts and identity align and flow into each other without the restriction and boundaries of the physical world.

Before he could contemplate her ideas any further, a pair of hands emerged from between his arms and wrapped around his chest. He did not attempt to turn around. He knew the shape of her hands.

"Are you happy to see me?" he said eventually.

"I am . . . I'm happy." He turned around. She added, "You look well."

She immediately took his hand and led him away from Eros and down Coventry Street. "We have to find a cab."

"Where are we going?" She pulled his arm with some force.

"I've organized tickets for a Bach concert at the Barbican. I remember you said once you liked Bach. Right? Oh, here's a cab coming. Wave it down, quick."

The cab stopped. She opened the back door, and he got in. She followed him.

In the cab she pulled down a folding seat and positioned herself directly opposite him. Her hands were tucked under her legs. She smiled. Hooman stared at the quiet figure before him. Nothing seemed appropriate or worth uttering. The sounds and lights of London outside the cab kept distracting him, but then, in a moment of clarity, he absorbed her appearance properly.

"You're beautiful," he said without his usual censure, and paused for a moment, then continued. "Your dress. I've never seen you wear something like this . . . the yellow—"

"It's intense, isn't it? I went shopping yesterday. And it's funny . . . the first time I dress formally, in a long while . . . and you are now dressed utterly casual." Allison smiled and added with a wavering voice, "But it doesn't matter, we have switched our usual symmetry. Normally you are the one dressed formally, and I am the one dressed casually."

She had made an effort to dress, he thought, and it was out of character for her.

"I almost forgot what you look like," he said as he looked into her face and noted her straight hair resting on her shoulders. The dappled light moved around her body. He added, "And you know, I thought the other day that I don't have a single photo of you. Nothing substantial. Nava has a few grainy shots of you guys when you two were studying in Melbourne. You somehow managed to stay out of all the group shots I took in New York. And the other day, I saw an interesting bunch of photos you sent Nava. I think they were of your travels around Australia: of the road and horizon, the desert, and the sky. It reminded me of Western Australia. We made some trips into the desert there when I was nine, just after we came from Iran. The color of the earth there was so different from Iran. In Australia the earth is so red, and in Iran it seems mostly yellow."

"Yeah, I made it to Western Australia toward the end of that trip in 1993. And that was an interesting time in my life. A year on the road . . . you know, we almost met in Western Australia."

"We did? Oh god, yes . . . I remember now. You were going to come up to Perth for Christmas, but Nava got an interview that year, and we called it all off. I remember now. God, that's right. It's strange how things unfold. I wonder how different our destiny would have been had we met that year."

"Actually, I have to say thanks for sending the sculpture. I was, well, surprised is the right word when it came. I know it was probably ridiculously expensive. No one has ever given me anything like it."

"Everyone has missed you." He paused and picked up her last words. "Oh, the white box, yeah, right. Don't worry about it. I'm happy you liked it. It's not a big deal."

"It is definitely a big deal for me, Hooman. Thank you. And you know the best part is I passed a restaurant called Simurgh just before I opened it. Can you see the symmetry?"

"That's interesting for sure. I don't seem to attract it like you do."

"Yes, you do, Hooman. It's there if you look for it. It's just behind you. Every time you turn, it moves behind you again. You have to catch God out, with all his playful tricks."

"I often thought God created chance as a shield to hide the signs in creation that point to his essence," Hooman said.

"Chance does have symmetry to it, absolutely, I agree . . . and within the bounds of relativity, randomness can be shown not to exist at all. We only need to penetrate it with determined effort and some creative imagination to find a complex and precise order beyond chance. And even if the universe is built on no more than chance, then who rolled the dice? And if this is too much to presume, then how did the dice roll themselves?"

"Yes . . . I suppose we call it chance because we don't know all the variables. It is chance to us, but to God it may not be."

They got out of the cab in front of the Barbican Centre entrance. Hooman looked up at the building that rose above them, standing in stark relief against the night sky.

"Wow. It's kind of ugly and beautiful in the same breath."

"Yeah. That's the right way to look at it. It's called brutalist architecture. It's a concrete version of a termite mound, using the square form."

"Brutalist?"

"Yeah, it's based on the principles of Le Corbusier."

They walked through the entrance, and as soon as they walked into the foyer, he looked up at the roof, and then his eyes panned around the interior. It was made from many intersecting concrete cubes.

They walked toward the concert hall entrance.

"The acoustics here are amazing," she said as they walked into the concert hall.

As they took their seats, he observed, when they were shuffling past people, the space where the toe on her right foot should be.

Allison saw his discreet stare. "I was nine. My family was staying in Cairns for the Christmas vacation. I jumped off a rock cliff at the beach. As I landed, my toe got wedged between rocks and a section of broken glass from a bottle that was wedged into the rock. It came clean off at the joint. I think it was the angle . . . and I twisted around as I fell. It was one of those odd accidents."

"I noticed it at that picnic in Central Park, in the spring, but I didn't want to intrude, so I didn't ask about it."

"Why would you think that you're intruding? We were close enough then that you could have asked those things. I've been making an effort to try and reveal my more personal thoughts to you."

"Yes, I know. I observed that more recently. Thank you. I've been very interested in your activities and life here in London."

"Good, I'm happy to hear that. Hey, can I keep your ticket?"

"Sure." He gave it to her.

She took a pencil out of her bag and wrote their names on the back of the two tickets, then read out the seating numbers, which were Q 18 and 19. She then took out a wad of tickets from her bag and added them to the collection after she had removed the rubber band. Once the rubber band was around them again, she then dropped them into her bag. The orchestra tuned their instruments.

He saw her in his imagination, falling off a cliff somewhere, on some beach in Australia. The blood flowed from her foot and washed away in rock pools until it found a way into the ocean. He wished he could have been there and somehow been threaded into her childhood memories. He was in Perth at that point in her life. He missed not being a friend at that earlier time. He was fifteen then and Allison was nine. That is what he wished now but he acknowledged the uselessness of having these impossible thoughts and wondered why we always desire things that can never be. The words for this sentiment came out automatically. "I wish I could have been a friend when you were a child." She smiled and turned back to enjoy the concert proceedings. The orchestra started with Bach's Piano Concerto in F Minor.

The music played for two hours. They exchanged only a few words. Toward the end his eyes were closed. He was trying to concentrate on the music and felt her hand touch his arm.

"I want to show you something after this," she said in a low voice.

He opened his eyes to speak.

"Don't ask. Just let me take you there. I promise you'll like it," she said.

————

On the platform at Moorgate Station, the wind pressure from the train pushed through the tunnel in advance; a warm, musty wind increased until the train shot out of the tunnel and then slowed rapidly to a stop. They got on. The carriage was relatively empty for that time of night. They sat opposite each other and began talking.

"Did you like the concert?" she said.

"I did. It was more than beautiful. Thank you."

"How was Amsterdam?"

"Wonderful. I've been there plenty of times before, though."

"Cool."

"I visited the house of Anne Frank for the first time."

"How was it?"

"Interesting . . . Anne's story is one where the human spirit triumphs over the darkness of humanity. And that is despite the fact that she eventually died at the hands of the Nazis."

"Yes, I agree. . . . And I have always wondered why we don't learn the lessons of history. You would have thought that after the genocide in Germany we would never repeat that, but only five years back we had the Rwandan genocide."

"Yes, I know. I did quite a bit of research into the Nuremberg trials in my undergraduate law degree. And nearly all the Nazi officials were completely unrepentant about the extermination of the Jews. And as you may know, the United Nations was created after World War II to prevent this very thing happening again. The Holocaust was a sad indictment of humanity's capacity for hatred."

He was quiet for a moment, then said, "Oh, did I tell you I've switched jobs."

"Yeah, I noticed your new work email. Are you working for Paul Nightingale now?"

"Yes, I am. And the great thing is I am cutting my hours back to focus on writing. I have some ideas—half-formed—but I am not totally sure what I want to write about yet. I mean I have a few vague themes."

"That doesn't matter. At least you have made the space in your life. The words will follow. When you've had a chance to think more about what you want to write, I want to know all your thoughts. I've been reading about law and its application in Plato's utopian city of Magnesia. It was a thought experiment for the most part, but I remember you saying that you thought a utopian Bahá'í society would come about in the future. Is that what you are going to write about?" she said.

"Yes. Pretty much, and the seed of that future society is already here in the form of the Bahá'í community. The broader utopia will become a reality eventually. It's the fruition of all past religions. The community has achieved, to a limited degree, aspects of its potential. And there is a link between the laws of Plato's Magnesia and the citizen's acquisition of virtue, which leads to a utopian reality. Bahá'u'lláh also wrote a book of laws, the Kitáb-i-Aqdas. The law is the secret path and the way to acquire virtue for the individual and the society. Spiritual law unlocks the *gates of the heart*."

"What about exploring some of the dystopia in current society?"

"Yes, I suppose that might be the first part of the book—about global poverty."

"Good, I want to know everything."

"I suppose that there are both positive and negative tendencies ascending and descending in world culture at the moment. It's hard to know what will carry over into the future and what will die away."

"Yes, true. In the West many of us live in a materialist utopia and at the same time in a spiritual dystopia. But these things will reverse in the future as the extremes of wealth and poverty and other negative human traits fade into history. Bahá'u'lláh once said:

> "'Soon will the present-day order be rolled up and a new one spread out in its stead.'" [8]

"How long do you think it will be before the utopia you are talking about will appear?" she asked.

"Oh, I think hundreds of years. A long time. It is hard to say when it will come, but I have no doubt that it will come. There has to be a critical mass within the Bahá'í community relative to the wider community until Bahá'u'lláh's teachings spread. And humanity needs to reach a higher potential as well."

"Mmm . . . interesting."

They were quiet for a few minutes, and Allison thought about the idea that all humanity lived in perceptual relativity when judging if the society they lived in was ideal or not. Materialism in some Western societies, such as America, had created a buffer against experiencing many negative realities either within their countries or in the developing world. On the surface, America and other countries seemed utopian, but they harbored a level of indifference to the suffering of others in relation to poverty. And this had made them dystopian with a materialistic veneer of utopia. She let these thoughts float through her mind. After a few minutes she became aware that she was drifting mentally, and Hooman was waiting for her to come back to reality.

Allison continued, "I mean, I know that the common meaning of 'utopia' is an unattainable future society with perfect ideals and governance that are either unattainable or impractical. The word 'utopia' has been tarnished with many negative associations from failed utopian visions from the past, which has cast it as an object of derision with often very dismissive reactions toward any ideal of future societies. Strangely, the Nazis were attempting to build what they thought was a utopian society, and we know how bad that turned out: one person's utopia is another person's dystopian nightmare, primarily because inequality and hatred were built into their utopia as well as the motive of power and control. There must be a universal utopian existence for all humanity based around the ideal of perfect equality. And hopefully, we can claw back the negative associations of the term, recontextualize its meaning in the present and the future, and realize utopia as a society of staggering beauty and selfless potentialities."

"Yes. I think you are right about that. I have always thought of utopia as being a more positive word. Both utopia and dystopia could be applied to current world culture, in addition to any future society. Although, I think the dystopian aspect will fade eventually," Hooman said.

There was silence again. Then Allison began an entirely new topic of conversation. "Do you know London well?" she said.

"Not really, no. I've visited London quite a few times, but I have tended to stick to central London, and I was always on business, so I never strayed much to take a good look at the place."

Good, because I want this to be a surprise. So I won't tell you any more about where we are going."

———

Fifteen minutes after arriving at Highgate Station, they were weaving in and out of dark streets in the surrounding suburb. Just in the last few minutes the houses had become statelier.

Crossing a highway, she pointed as they walked. "There . . . I've found it."

Allison led him into a forest along a narrow gravel path. The path ran initially alongside a dark lake. The house lights on the far side of the lake were reflected in the water, but the path soon vanished entirely in the darkness of trees.

Walking in close to pitch-blackness, he could not see the outline of her figure. He stopped. "Allison . . . I can't see you."

Her hand touched him on the shoulder. "I'm behind you. I just had to remind myself where to go. The path forks in a few places, and it was a while ago that I came here with my roommate, Jade."

Beginning to adjust to the low light, his eyes made out the line of the path and his dark feet moving on the path. After several minutes in darkness, they came around a corner. The landscape widened out, and they were in the open again. He stopped to absorb a meadow, and through long grass his eyes traced the curve of a broad hill.

She walked past him. "It's beautiful here and almost better at night than in the day," she said.

Her figure grew smaller as she walked up the hill. An overlay of something familiar played out in his mind, and it was related to the place, the long grass, her dress, and even her hair. These familiar impressions eventually assembled into a compelling order.

This was connected to the dream he had had on the first day they had met. She was the girl in the yellow dress crossing Bryant Park. He was dumbfounded. It was her. He looked at the ground and the grass. He had seen a fragment of their future, which manifested in this moment. He looked at her again as she walked over the crest of the hill, and just before she had disappeared from his sight, he took another impression of her hair. It had been longer in New York, but now he saw the shape of the cut, the reduced length, and the end squared off. She was that girl, and he wondered about her crossing through the traffic so effortlessly on 42nd Street with absolute synchronicity. This was her symmetrical destiny. This was how she lived her life. This was her movement through the world, and she was utterly beautiful to him. He started walking up the hill.

As he reached the top of the path, the horizon of London spread out below the heath. All the lights turned up at the sky obscured the stars. People were sitting in the grass watching the city. He found her near the path but farther along. She was sitting away from the main gathering of people.

He sat down next to her and looked out at the panorama below.

"I knew you'd like it," she said.

"It's fantastic. Where is this? It's huge." He looked left, across a dark valley of grass meadows and forest below. He gazed at lights from the houses farther in the distance on the far side of the valley.

"This is Hampstead Heath."

For several minutes they looked at the city in silence.

After the long silence, he said, "I had a dream about you. It was on the same day that we first met in New York."

"Really . . . that's interesting."

"Only I didn't know it was you until tonight. Although at the café, I did have a fleeting impression that I had heard your voice before. There were faint harmonics in your voice."

"Yes, I remember that. How do you know it was me, then?"

"Because of the yellow dress you are wearing."

"Fascinating."

"Yes, it is."

"I wonder what it means."

"I'm not fully sure yet what it means."

She got up. "Let's walk farther into the heath. Let's be alone together," she said.

———

After several minutes following the path along the rim of a hill, Allison eventually saw a series of dark hills and valleys lower down. The lights of London vanished as they descended along another narrower path that branched away from the main path. On a lower hill they left this new path and slowly waded through knee-high grass, approaching the edge of a forest.

Allison turned around to look at the view below them. She saw darkness. The suburban lights had gone. "Here, let's stop for a while."

The heath surrounded them completely now, like the matrix of a dark womb. They were enveloped within a private world of meadows with forest walls. Allison dropped her bag at her feet, then lay down in the grass. She felt the grass push against her mostly bare back. Hooman sat next to her. The stars were now less obscured by the city light.

"I wanted to talk to you about something . . . Shidan told me something in London."

He hesitated for a moment. "Shidan told me a few days ago, when I told him I was going to meet up with you in London. I know what you want to talk about," he said.

"Shidan told me how you feel about me."

"I'm sorry. I wish I had said something earlier. I was working up to it, but just couldn't find the right moment to mention it."

Smiling, she sat up. "Well, I suppose it doesn't really matter now." She hesitated once more, then said, "Because I think we both have similar feelings for each other."

"Really?" She could see he was stunned. He added, "We do?"

"Yes, I think so," she said in a low, even voice. She lay back and rested on her elbows and looked at the diffuse light in the meadow. "Our relationship will be an interesting experiment for me," she added thoughtfully.

"An experiment?"

"I don't think I've ever loved another person properly. Only fractured pieces that didn't quite make a whole."

She lay back down again and looked at the sky.

She then patted the grass next to her. "Come . . . lie next to me."

He lay next to her, and she reached out and took his hand.

The grass swayed gently about her face. She imagined that, like thin black blades clashing, the grass speared and perforated a thin sheet of blue-black fabric floating just above their faces; she saw the light of eons weeping through the myriad holes as the grass pricked the night sky.

"Look, all those suns . . . and all that time from the past. The loves of long ago have gone," she said.

———

Alison Nightingale had long contemplated the paper bird her father had given her in the previous year, but it was an empty contemplation as she only viewed its planes and folds—nothing symbolic. As she sat at her desk, she turned the object over and around between her thumb and forefinger. This was a white swan, she concluded. She knew there were words among the folds, but until now she'd had no curiosity for them. In one fold she noticed the words "paper and ink heart." The words appeared crisp in the light coming through her window. She was now motivated to unfold the bird back to a flat plane. Once the paper was flat on her desk, she saw that the words "paper and ink heart" formed part of a poem. Its meaning made only partial sense to her, but she liked the pure sound and rhythm of the words in her mind.

Death turns my right palm to the sky,
we smile, as he turns my left palm to the earth.

In my right hand, an empty nest—a world.

In my left, another world, from which a broken eggshell falls.
A paper bird has flown.
Its story written and gone.
The loves of long ago faded—unfolded in light and its paper and ink heart.

Creases remain, shapes, and white bone, the source of paper,
Until even this is ground under foot into white dust, on a word road,
Where everything returns to its first form, absolute and complete, into form-
less words on formless paper.

What then remains of Death?
He too has flown.
Seeking his own death.

She wondered who had written the poem. As she had this thought, she saw names on the paper near the bottom of the poem; they were only just visible. When she held the paper up against the morning light, they became clearer. She put the paper back on the desk and rubbed one of the names with the broad side of her pencil tip, and it was then that one of the names became fully legible.

She was another Allison except with a different spelling. Alison concluded that the other Allison had been practicing her signature on a sheet of paper above the sheet with the poem on it. The signature she had revealed was large, and the letters looped and curved on the page. Alison put the tip of her pencil into the groove of one of the letters and continued tracing over the whole of the other Allison's name to make it even clearer.

16

THE SYMMETRICAL DESTINY MAP

Wherefore the lovers of the countenance of the Beloved have said, "O Thou Whose Essence alone can lead to His Essence, and Who transcendeth all likeness to His creatures."[1] *How can utter nothingness spur its charger in the arena of eternity, or a fleeting shadow reach to the everlasting sun? The Friend addressed by the words "But for Thee" hath said, "We have failed to know Thee"; and the Beloved alluded to by the words "or even closer"*[2] *hath said, "nor attained Thy presence."*[3]

— BAHÁ'U'LLÁH, *THE SEVEN VALLEYS*

On the morning of the following day, Hooman and Allison had arranged to meet at Green Park Station on Piccadilly Road. Coming out of the stairwell, Allison saw Hooman with his back to her. He was standing on a gravel path near the edge of the park, looking toward Buckingham Palace through an avenue of plane trees. She noticed him wearing a slightly beaten retro leather jacket. She walked toward him and embraced him from behind as she had done on the previous night at the Eros statue.

"Good morning," he said. He turned around to face her. "How did you sleep?"

He passed her a coffee and waved a small paper bag at her.

"I slept well, thank you. What's in the bag?"

"Croissants."

"Oh good, I love croissants." She looked up at the sky through the branches and leaves of the plane trees. "It's a beautiful day . . . hey, great jacket, by the way," she said.

"Thanks. You like it?"

"Yes, it's the sort of thing I would normally wear."

"I know. That's why I got it. To remind me of you."

She noticed the diagonal weave of leather strips on the side and top pockets of the jacket. It reminded her of the diamond weave on her watch face. She looked at her watch for a moment but did not take the impression any further.

She then linked arms with Hooman. "Let's walk," she said.

"Okay, where to?"

"I don't know. Let's see where these paths take us."

They began to walk down the avenue of plane trees toward the palace. She took a few sips of her coffee.

"So, what are we going to do now, about our relationship?" he asked.

"I'm not sure."

"Do you want to come back to New York?"

"Well, I can fly back in the next few weeks."

"What will you do about a visa?"

"I'm not sure about that either. I don't have a career that fits the visa criteria. So I won't be able to get a work permit."

"Yes, I know. I was thinking about it this morning. You'll either end up back in Australia or here in London. That's why I was thinking I could come here. It would be easy for me to find work in London."

"I know . . . but the thing is . . . I don't want to stay here anymore. It's simple in a way. I love you . . . and your life is in New York. So I'll come back. And besides, I do miss Shidan and Nava."

"Okay then. That part is solved."

"And I can apply for a tourist visa. That will last for six months, and I can get an extension for another six months if I need it, and we'll see how things between us pan out in that time."

They eventually came to a fork in the path. She looked into the distance at St. James Park beyond Buckingham Palace. She then looked right, in the direction of Hyde Park.

"Let's head down this path."

And they began walking along another path toward Hyde Park. They walked in silence for a few minutes. He put his paper bag and coffee in one hand, and with his free hand he took her hand.

"You know you can stay with Shidan when you get back to New York, if you want. He has a spare bedroom in his apartment that is jammed with books. Once he clears that room out, I am sure he would be happy to have you. And I can help financially too, since you won't be able to work on the visa," he said.

"I would love to stay with Shidan. And Paul sends me money from time to time, some of the profits from the restaurant businesses. So between the two of you, I should be okay. Besides, I don't need much money to live on."

As they came to the end of Green Park, she observed a large inter-section and Hyde Park on the other side. They stopped and watched buses and cars pass by for a while. She took another sip of her coffee.

Eventually she pointed at a stairwell. "Over there. Let's continue to the other side of the road," she said.

They descended the stairs into an underground tunnel, a walkway leading to Hyde Park, which passed under the intersection. Halfway through the tunnel Allison noticed a young homeless girl sleeping in an arrangement of cardboard boxes. Her bare feet, protruding out the end of the boxes, were covered in grime and dirt. Her hair was disheveled. Allison stopped when she came to the girl and crouched down.

She placed her hand on the girl's shoulder. "Are you hungry?" The girl opened her eyes but did not say anything. Allison looked up at Hooman. "Can you please give me one of the croissants?" she said.

Hooman bent down. He opened the paper bag and passed one of the croissants to the girl.

The girl sat up. "Thanks," she said and began to eat.

Allison passed the girl her cup of coffee. "I hope you don't mind drinking from a used cup. I haven't had much of it."

"No, that's fine," the girl said, and she gulped the coffee down in a hurry.

Allison and Hooman stood up again. "Bye," Allison said.

"Thanks," the girl said.

They continued through the tunnel and came out of a stairwell into one corner of Hyde Park. They entered the park through one of the neoclassical arches.

"God, I hate the powerlessness I feel when I see that kind of poverty," Allison said.

After a while, they walked through a large circular garden with many flowers and shrubs of diverse colors. Allison stopped at a lavender bush and rubbed a flower between her thumb and forefinger. She put her hand to her nose and smelled the fragrance floating in the air, then put her forefinger under Hooman's nose. "Nice," he said.

Beyond the garden they came to the Serpentine Lake, where they continued walking until they came to a bench. She sat down. He passed her his coffee and then took out the remaining croissant. He broke it into pieces. Walking to the edge of the water, he began to throw pieces into the lake. A group of birds, ducks, and black water birds with orange beaks bobbed in the water and began to congregate around him. He also threw some of the croissant onto the path, where a crowd of pigeons began to gather.

"Hey, Hooman, come sit down."

He walked over to the bench and sat down. Some of the birds followed him, but they soon dissipated, as he had nothing left to feed them.

Allison faced him as she sipped the coffee and pulled her legs into her chest. She took one of his hands. "I have a good feeling about us," she said.

"Yeah, me too."

"Do you think Nava and the others will be okay with us? It might seem a bit random."

"Random? For Nava, I don't think so." Hooman smiled.

"I had a dream we were married, you know. We were in New York, Upstate somewhere. And there was this tall grass, a meadow, like last night, and everyone we knew was there in a great circle. What was amazing to me was that we weren't in the middle of it. We were an equal part of the circle. When I woke up, I had the distinct feeling that I was married to everyone in the circle. Strange, huh? This was a couple of months ago when I was in Pakistan. You know I like circles."

Allison jumped up from the seat and put her hands out.

"Come, let's go."

Hooman stood up and took her hands in his. "Okay. Where do you want to go?"

"I don't know. Let's just wander." She pointed at the Serpentine Bridge in the distance. "Let's cross over there and head to Speakers' Corner."

He waved at the birds. "Bye-bye."

They continued along the edge of the Serpentine toward the bridge.

After walking over the bridge and crossing the open lawn area, they came to Speakers' Corner. They stopped to listen to people with their various causes for a few minutes, then went on to Oxford Street, where they passed a variety of shops that Allison had not seen before. Eventually they came to Selfridges. They stopped in front of a window display. One of the mannequins was wearing the same dress that Allison had worn on the previous night.

She turned to Hooman. "What do you think your dream about my yellow dress means?"

"I'm not totally sure. I just think that you were meant to be in my life from the beginning."

"Yes, I think so too," she said, smiling.

"I wanted to ask you more about your symmetrical destiny map. What is it? What does it mean? I mean you mentioned it in an email, but I wanted to know more."

"Well, my yellow dress is a good example of the symmetry and asymmetry that I look for to add to my map. There is symmetry between your dream back in New York and my life in London, and the dress that as an object has its own distinct destiny."

"I know. How is it even possible that I should dream about this exact dress seven months before you bought it." Hooman shook his head. "Amazing."

"It is kind of amazing when you think about it. And the dress might have not even existed seven months ago; it might have only existed in a designer's head or not at all. Interesting, really, how life works and how everything converges, like interlocking eddies, swirling into and away from each other with precise ineffable relationships, and on the surface life seems ordinary and coincidental."

"Yes. I think you're right, absolutely. I have often thought about that, but I have never been able to penetrate that surface. Actually, I don't think many people are able to see beyond the ordinary."

"This dress went from pure mental abstraction to concrete reality. So, yesterday I saw the dress in this window display. Then I went inside and counted the number of dresses on the rack, which came to eighteen. So, including the one in the display, the number comes to nineteen.

"If I were to tag that dress for future reference, I would call it 'dress yellow nineteen.' Then if I took the seventh dress on the rack, I would tag it as 'yellow seven Allison.' And if I were omniscient, I could know the names of all the women that bought that dress and in what order from the first to the last. And then I might want to see if there was a symmetry in the lives of those women, either with regard to their names, places of birth, or the streets they live on, and there are many other kinds of symmetry, all of which are linked in various ways, like words, numbers, shapes, colors, and all manner of objects. And I would use symmetry and asymmetry to make choices in my life that would otherwise be left to chance. And then I would try to see an overarching pattern in all the choices I could make and all the realities I could experience in the world around me."

"Okay, I think I understand what you mean now. So you are making your destiny more conscious. I was thinking about it in the Hague when I was at the Escher Museum. About his use of interlocking geometry and patterns, which merge into each other. And I was thinking that consciousness must have its own geometry, a hidden geometry that may only be apparent after death. And that maybe your symmetrical destiny map might uncover some of that in this life if life were a mystical cipher."

"Absolutely."

"Amazing . . . just amazing."

She smiled and took his hand.

"Come . . . let's keep walking."

They walked on and left Selfridges behind.

"So, is it a pattern that you have written down? Like you said, 'a map'?"

"Yes and no. Some of it is written down on an A3 piece of paper. Some of it is in various notebooks. Some of it is on my wall as a concept map, and some of it is in my head."

After a while, they came to the intersection of Oxford Street and Regent Street. Allison stopped. "Okay, last night I caught the number 23 bus, an odd-numbered bus, but today, or in the future when I come to this stop, I need to catch two even-numbered buses to complete the right symmetrical pattern. Even being 'symmetrical' and odd being 'asymmetrical.' You understand?"

"Okay, I understand. You are intensifying free will."

"Hey, that is a great way to describe it. I'll remember that."

"So, shall we head to my hotel now? Do you want to come to the airport to see me off?"

"Absolutely."

They turned left onto Regent Street and walked up to a bus stop.

After a few minutes, the number 12 bus came toward them, and they jumped on the back of the bus and took seats next to a window.

The bus passed by the shops that Allison had seen on the night before, and she thought about the asymmetry of night and day and how the geometry of space in the solar system and the universe in general set up circular rhythms and patterns.

They passed through Piccadilly Circus, and the bus then turned onto Haymarket Street, where they got off. They walked down Orange Street toward St Martins Lane Hotel. Allison thought about Shidan's apartment in Brooklyn Heights. It was also on Orange Street. She then thought about passing through Martin Place in Sydney during her road trip in 1993.

They came to the hotel and walked through the lobby.

"Do you want to wait here? I'll go get my suitcase."

"Sure."

Allison watched Hooman walk toward the elevator, then looked around the lobby, which was a homage to minimalism. She saw a set of brushed stainless-steel seats with red velvet cushions. Sitting in front of the seats was a row of large gold-colored teeth that she guessed were supposed to be tables. She walked over to the seats and sat down.

She thought about his comment that consciousness might have a specific geometry that would only be apparent after death, and that maybe the brain was not a self-contained organ but was instead a receiver of consciousness, like a wireless modem that received invisible radio signals, but since the soul transcended space and time these signals must be different from and far beyond the reality of radio signals. Allison remembered the metaphor that Hooman had used all those months before, that the body was a mirror, onto which the soul reflected its reality.

So, the soul didn't exist in the physical world, and it was neither in, nor outside, the body. Actually, as Hooman had said at the ice rink in Central Park, the whole physical world was only a metaphoric expression of Malakut.

And the invisible geometry might transcend language, which was only a partial carrier of its geometry, and have its own distinct, divine programming language that also manifested its reality in the mind.

And that there might be symmetrical geometric markers in the world that stood for this mental geometry in the same way that a metaphor carried the meaning of a reality or action to which it was not literally applicable. She thought of the idea behind semiotics and the abstraction of the world through words that had developed from visual signs. There was an underlying structure in reality that could be uncovered with language in the same way that mathematics described the patterns and structure underlying the universe. She also wondered if there was a divine, mystical, and formless language.

She thought of architecture and the word "house" that represented a finite location that housed the body. And the body was the house of the soul and mind, a house within a house. If you looked at the word "house" stripped of its concrete reality, it stood for the identity of self and the projection of self within the physical world. And if there was a world beyond death, then what did the idea of "house" represent in a more abstract mental existence where there was a more expansive notion of body and house?

She thought about the fact that this hotel was a large house with a collection of transitory rooms and that one's identity in such a hotel was not defined as strongly as it would be in one's own house. We only passed through hotels, and so we did not allow our notion of love and self to be associated so strongly with them. So, if we were to think of a "home," it could be a purely mental and spiritual reality disassociated from the physical world. The two houses of love between her and Hooman were now beginning to merge into one house. He lived in her heart now, in her house in eternity, in a way that he had never been before.

And one of those symmetrical markers was her yellow dress. It represented their collective destiny in eternity. And the clothes were a mask or veil of the body that was removed in the house and associated with the intimacy of sex, of becoming naked before the other person whom we loved. She would be removing the masks and veils of the mind, becoming naked spiritually and merging her identity with his, stripping bare the mind in the houses of eternity and mapping her destiny beyond the world of naked bodies: the transitory houses of our minds that only death could free.

After fifteen minutes, Hooman walked toward her with his suitcase trailing behind him. He smiled and took her hand as she stood up. "I called a cab from my room. It should be out front."

They left the lobby and stepped onto St Martins Lane. They got into the cab, which drove off and headed toward the airport.

———

At Heathrow Airport Hooman gathered his passport and ticket from the check-in counter and thanked the lady serving him. Hooman turned toward Allison. "I'll call you every day, or every few days at a minimum, okay?" he said.

"I think I'm going to miss you."

"What do you mean by 'think'? You're going to miss me, okay? Love is not some detached intellectual pursuit. It's better if you throw away any rules you know. Start again. Start at zero." Then he laughed and embraced her. "I know I'll definitely miss you. And none of this brave self-sufficiency, please, okay? There is no need for it. We are beyond that now."

"I promise. No self-sufficiency." Water began to well up in her eyes.

Hooman started walking toward the security area. With one hand he pulled his suitcase along, and with the other he took Allison's hand.

They came to the security barriers, and Hooman turned and embraced her again and then kissed her on the cheek.

"I love you," he said, then turned and began to line up to get through security. Not until he was gone for some time did she allow herself to cry fully.

17

THE BOOK OF THE DEAD

Indeed, the references that have been made to the degrees of mystic knowledge pertain to the knowledge of the effulgences of that Sun of Truth as it becometh reflected in various mirrors. And the effulgence of that light is present within the hearts, yet it is hidden beneath the veils of selfish desires and earthly attachments, even as a candle within a lantern of iron, and only when the cover is lifted doth the light of the candle shine out.

In like manner, when thou dost strip the veils of illusion from the face of thine heart, the lights of Oneness will be made manifest. [1]

— BAHÁ'U'LLÁH, *THE SEVEN VALLEYS*

On her last day in London, Allison passed through Hyde Park. She was due to fly to New York on the next day. Late in the morning she came to the spot near the lake where they had sat on the bench under the plane trees a few weeks before. Now she lay under the tree next to the bench, looking up through the layers of leaves to an unfamiliar sky. For most of the time that she'd spent in London the sky was its usual gray and overcast self. All these abnormally sunny days were a strange bliss: the weather held some otherworldly magic over everyone. Because of that, Hyde Park was full of people. Some were walking and others sunbathing. She saw a woman close by sitting on a tartan blanket reading a book.

Hooman had sorted out flying his parents over to America to meet her. And she had found someone to take her room at the church.

It was hard to fathom the change that the events of the past few weeks would spell in her future with Hooman. All of it, no matter how she looked at it, was amazing somehow, even if she did not know what "amazing" or "friendship" or "love" was. All these old words had a new shimmer.

The next few years would require adaptation and change. A new place in her mind would have to open up to accept who she might become. Marriage? She questioned the reality of her dream of marriage in Upstate New York. And what exactly was this thing called marriage? She was not sure that she knew absolutely, but it would be interesting to discover its meaning with Hooman. She threaded her thoughts through their recent conversations. He was calling her most nights, and she tried to trace a design or purpose to all this. When they talked, there was a new urgency in their life together. Their collective reflection in the world was rapidly changing from friend to partner.

Her focus on the leaves above her resumed, and as it did, a leaf, at the peak of the canopy, came floating toward her. It landed on her stomach. Picking it up and sitting up, she examined the leaf, which was young and fresh. A symbol perhaps of their new identity together, and in the midst of this thought, her mind said to her quite unreasonably, "Get up . . . leave." Her inner voice was commanding and compelling, so up she went. Her body, almost without her full consent, had picked itself up, and her legs walked automatically toward Kensington Road.

A red Routemaster slowed as she found the stop and put her hand out to hail the bus. The number of the bus was even, as it should be for this route. She sat down next to a window and relaxed as she watched the grand Kensington houses pass by; the bus headed towards Knightsbridge. She passed Rutland Gate where the Bahá'í Centre was based. She had attended two devotional meetings there in the last month, and after the last meeting, she had wandered into the Bahá'í bookshop at the center. She bought the book *Abdu'l-Bahá in London*, which chronicled his travels in the city. 'Abdu'l-Bahá had stayed in London in 1911 and had walked around Hyde Park on one particular day. She had bought the book about him because she had been reciting prayers written by him in the nineteenth century and the early part of the twentieth century and was curious about his life.

At Knightsbridge Station she took the descending escalator. As she stepped off it, a train pulled into the platform. After several stops, she eventually came to Leicester Square, where she changed to the Northern line, which would put her on track to Camden Town Station. Eventually she came to Warren Street Station, where she looked up at an advertisement offering a Spanish vacation. She read the advertisement: "Go back to the real Spain."

But the words "go back" were all her mind registered. She looked at the words again. "Go back."

The words began to feel like a threat, and she felt rattled as she realized what it meant. Fearful and panicked, she got off the train and changed platforms. After three minutes, she took a train going back in the opposite direction.

On the train she sat next to a man reading a book on Italian modernist architecture. The page that was open was a photo of a high-rise apartment building, and it seemed interesting, but why? The image pressed into her memory. Even though a part of her wanted to look away, another part of her would not allow it.

The Tottenham Court Road stop arrived. Framed by the train window, a perfume advertisement beckoned her, but it was less threatening now and almost playful: "Here is the real fragrance."

But only the word "here" jumped out of the advertisement at her. Understanding now, she got up and left quickly; she felt less manipulated now, and she drifted up the escalators to the surface. She thought about the line in the prayer she had read in Afghanistan: "unto the essence of the fragrance of Thy beauty, which Thou wilt manifest, cause me to return."[2]

As she came out of the stairwell, she observed the Tottenham Court Road and Oxford Street intersection and a colorful blur of people: shoppers, tourists, and Londoners of all shapes and sizes. They were compelled by a multitude of unseen goals as they crisscrossed each other. Although she was acutely aware of this collective purpose, her own purpose seemed more in the dark than ever.

In a shop-front window the news played out silently on a multitude of TV sets. She watched, only half interested, until she became aware of a background picture in the news program. Behind the news presenter was the exact image of the building she had just seen, only seven minutes before, in the book on modernist architecture; a light plane in Italy had crashed into the side of the building in a freak accident.

At first this event seemed only an odd coincidence. Its significance only asserted itself when amateur footage of the plane began to play in full. This is connected, she thought.

The news item changed to a fun-run. The word "run" came out at her with purpose, and at that precise moment a man brushed past her. He was running and weaving in and out of the milling people at the intersection before he disappeared in the reflection of the shop-front window. She turned around, but he was gone. Facing a newsstand attendant, she read the newspaper headline board next to him. The headline shot out at her, from which she deduced that a cabinet member was about to be dropped from his position in the Labour Party. At the exact moment she read the word "dropped," the newsstand attendant dropped his cup of coffee. It slipped from his hand and landed on his boot. He swore and stepped back to survey the spill.

She could hardly take in the immediacy of these events and in such quick succession too. Both shocked and expecting more, she stood fixed as she waited for something further to happen. Three minutes passed, and nothing seemed obviously strange or out of place. Streams of people passed by in the normal way. Relaxing a little, and figuring that this strangeness was now over, she wandered aimlessly across the intersection. She was floating along on a weird high. She walked along New Oxford Street, then turned left and walked on a little way down Bloomsbury Street until she stopped and looked right. She walked into a side street without a fragment of a notion of her direction. Two minutes later, after a slow meander, she stopped at the black iron gates in front of the British Museum and looked up at the sky. A cloud passed in front of the sun for a moment. As she passed through the gates, the clouds moved on, and for one full minute she stood and felt the warmth of the day on her uplifted face. Relaxing a little more, she was ready for her next new experience. The light and shadows falling on the neoclassical facade at the entrance invited her into the museum.

She passed through the Ionic columns and into the Great Court: a large square space. In its center was a circular reading room, and looking up, she noticed the diamond lattice structure of glass in the roof, which was backlit with an intense blue sky; she observed that the sun was at the midpoint in its arc. A memory of the Frenchman in the gallery in Soho flashed through her mind. His eyes were the same blue hue. She remembered the diagonal weave on the pockets of Hooman's jacket. She looked down at her watch for a few moments; it had a diamond lattice pattern as well, but with a green backing color rather than the blue above her.

Wandering up the grand staircase, winding around the reading room, she found herself in the Egyptian funerary section near the top of the staircase.

The first caption she saw read: "Osiris—Judge of the Dead; God of the afterlife, Otherworld, or unseen place."

The weighing of the heart was explained.

Before a soul went onto the section of afterlife it deserved to inhabit, it was asked if it had acted in a good way while on earth; its heart or deeds were then weighed on the scales of Maat (truth). If these deeds were determined to be good and truthful, its evolution in the world beyond would be assured.[3]

She realized that this was the same as the life review, which was a universal feature of people's near-death experiences regardless of their religion or even if they had no religion at all.

She walked toward the elaborate coffins. The intricate designs on each coffin leaped out at her. On some lids she saw a human figure with outspread wings as the soul symbolically took flight and moved to a higher plane. The caption next to the coffin read: "The Egyptians believed that birds were able to travel between this world and the afterlife." This thought moved her in a subtle way.

She continued to read: "The hieroglyph for the personality (Ba: a part of the soul) is a bird with a human head, and it is believed that this is where the idea for wings on the human figures on many of these coffins came from."

And how long had this idea of an afterlife been around? Maybe it did not matter. It may just be one of those intractable realities that just existed regardless of a person's belief in them. Some truths were changeless from one culture to another but may have shifted so much through time that people might think these were different realities unique to their own culture when in fact they were the same truth in the guise of different names and forms. She thought further about these differences and remembered her reflection in the colored baubles on the Christmas tree at Rockefeller Plaza. The baubles were a new metaphor for all the different religions. All these were the same reflection yet perceived in difference through color. This created a plurality and multiplicity of truth in religious identity, which reflected the limitations and relativities of the age in which each was born.

She noticed that one square-shaped coffin had hieroglyphs on its side. The information caption explained that *The Book of the Dead* was often used on coffins to help the dead pass into the Otherworld. From one of the funerary texts, forming a part of *The Book of Gates*, she read a small snippet about the soul passing through a gate and uttering a password to the keeper of the gate.

As she walked on, another caption came into view. She wedged herself amongst a group of schoolchildren and a teacher who were reading the caption: "Egyptians believed that this life was only a brief prelude to the afterlife. It was considered to be like a small antechamber inside the Otherworld."[4]

The physical world, the world of Nasut, was totally encompassed by Malakut, the angelic realm, and it was ultimately an emanation of Malakut. Allison thought about the energy and spiritual animation of the kingdoms of the physical world: mineral, vegetable, animal, and human. She contemplated the worlds higher up; maybe they were layered in a similar way with a cascading emanation cast down through the hierarchy of worlds.

So maybe the afterlife was the real life and this life only a limited temporal reflection of it, which was cast in change and impermanence: a cyclical wheel of birth and death ever turning over a transient and ephemeral world of beauty and decay. The world beyond might be a world of endless and changeless beauty but hidden in this world behind distortions and earthly conditions. It must have been hidden intentionally too, by God, behind thousands of veils of light. She remembered the snippet from the Qur'án that Shidan had read to her in Turkey. The life to come was the mansion that abideth. Allison felt convinced now that the same afterlife existed for everyone; however, the different realities or worlds in the afterlife that a soul went to were relative to the good and bad actions it had undertaken in this life. The next caption confirmed what happened to a soul after the weighing of the heart ceremony:

> *After the heart is weighed and found worthy, it joins Osiris. Merging with him, the deceased soul is both God and eternity, therefore God is eternal, and His servant partakes of the attributes of the Deity and lives forever with him. From The Book of Gates, we learn that in the Dynastic Period a belief was prevalent that those who lived according to Maat, i.e., uprightness and integrity (Truth), would receive a good reward because they had done these things. The texts in these books state that the beatified live forever in the kingdom of Osiris and feed daily upon the heavenly wheat of righteousness that springs from the body of Osiris, which is eternal; he is righteousness itself, and they are righteous, and they live by eating the body of their God daily. . . . If, however, the soul is found to be unworthy, it is thrown into the lake of fire.* [5]

Allison could not shake off the similarity of this concept with that found in Christianity. The analogy of the righteous wheat of Osiris, which sprung from his body as truth, translated directly to Christ: "I am the living bread which came down from heaven: if any man eat of this bread, he shall live forever: and the bread that I will give is my flesh, which I will give for the life of the world."[6]

It made sense that the Otherworld was a world of justice, and deeds determined one's position in it and one's closeness to God.

Reading further, the text stated:

> *Life as a blessed soul was not wholly guaranteed. The deceased would have to nego-tiate its way through a series of seven or more gates in Tuat (the Otherworld) both to find the Kingdom of Osiris and move within it. Tuat was divided by a river on which the Boat of Millions of Years, or the Boat of Eternity, would pass as it carried the dead to each division, or place, in Tuat. Osiris was the Mariner guiding this boat; it was at his behest that the dead could journey with him. But before they could pass into each division they would have to pass a gate protected by a wall of fire. Each gate had its Watchman, in the form of a serpent, and its Herald. In The*

> *Book of Gates, the soul is directed to utter the name of the gate and, to its keeper,*
> *secret words of power. Prayers or incantations were also required to open each gate*
> *and pass into a different region of heaven. But of utmost importance are good deeds,*
> *as they determine the state of the heart and allow the soul to progress onwards.*[7]

Allison was reminded of the fact that *The Conference of the Birds* stated
that there were seven valleys for the birds to traverse, and that *The Book
of the Dead* put the number of gates at seven too. Hooman had also said
that through prayer there was a mingling of stations or states of being.
But what really caught her attention was the fact that Osiris and
Bahá'u'lláh referred to themselves as Mariners on the Boat of Eternity,
or the Crimson Ark as Shidan had said in Iran. They rode on the Seas
of Light. The deceased and the living traveled in the boat with them.

Looking into another glass case, a large wooden sarcophagus was
painted with a ladder; the deceased was mounting the ladder. These
gates, or regions in heaven, could also be interpreted as ladder rungs,
denoting division, hierarchy, and mode of travel between earth and
heaven. In the Old Testament the story of Jacob's Ladder described
Jacob seeing a ladder connecting earth and heaven. Again, all these
traditions were talking about the same reality.

Wandering near the exit door, she was about to leave when another
caption forcefully impressed itself on her: "Temu. The evening form of
Ra: the Great Hidden God."

> *Egyptian scripture states that at one time death did not exist. This was before the*
> *Great Hidden God Temu created all the other Gods, angels, and humans. Temu was*
> *considered to be the father of Osiris. And from a collection and compilation of*
> *certain very old hieroglyphs, we can deduce with tolerable certainty that the Egyptian*
> *religion was monotheistic; it descended into polytheism only later and after a long*
> *period of time. Temu is described in the following terms in an ancient prayer: one*
> *and alone, without a second. He existed in the beginning when nothing else was.*
> *Father of beginnings, eternal, infinite, and everlasting. Hidden one. No man*
> *knoweth his form or can search out his likeness; he is hidden to gods and men and is*
> *a mystery to his creatures; his name is a mystery and is hidden. He is truth; he*
> *created but was not created. He made his own form and body. He himself is exis-*
> *tence; he neither increaseth or diminisheth. When he speaketh, what resulteth there-*
> *from endureth forever.*[8]

The forceful and direct nature of the words hit her in an epiphany. It was what Hooman meant when he said that no one has known God. Not even the gods knew him fully; neither Osiris nor Christ nor any other Manifestation of God that had come through history knew him in his hidden form. Only the hidden essence could show the way to the hidden essence. All they could do was reflect the light of God, of Temu, and she recalled the few lines in the prayer she had said in Afghanistan. God was the most manifest of the manifest and the most hidden of the hidden. The unfathomable world of Hahut shimmered through time.

She left the room down a small staircase in awe and wonder. On the first floor the Grand Egyptian Hall enveloped her. The hall was a large open space in the museum flooded with natural light. Whole temples had been moved here from the Nile and reassembled. She walked past one of these temples, then between two rows of seated stone gods. As she walked between them, they stared ahead, facing each other off with expressions halfway between a benevolent smile and vacant emptiness. They were lost in some far-off horizon and gazing into eternity.

Entering the Great Court again, she looked up at the sky. In her distraction, she tripped over a three-wheeled child's stroller. She fell flat on her face. Turning over slowly, and propped by her elbows, she smiled at the woman and then her child.

"I'm sorry, I didn't see you there," Allison said.

"Are you okay? You hit the floor pretty hard."

"Yeah. I think I'm okay."

The child in the stroller was laughing with delight from all the commotion, and his voice seemed to her more resonant somehow. She then heard a faint bell-like sound riding on top of the laughter, and it began stretching out and then slowing down. The woman's smile also penetrated her. The blue of the sky above descended toward her. The sky was richer and deeper, and it embraced her body tightly in a way that was intangible.

These sensations manifested slowly at first but eventually began to intensify and wash over her mind and body. She lost her way in the woman's smile, the child's laughter, and the blue closing in; these impressions penetrated the core of her being. This has always been here, and this realization was sweet beyond reckoning. Why had she not understood this? Why?

The woman knelt down and leaned over her. "Are you sure you're fine? You seem a little dazed," the woman said.

"Yes. I'm fine," she said slowly. "It's so beautiful."

Allison saw through the diamond lattice in the roof to the sky and sun above them, and the air seemed alive with a beauty unknown to her as she breathed it in. She lay down, and the coolness in the ochre marble floor pushed its fingers into her back. Stretching out her arms at right angles to her body, she lay her palms on the floor as she continued to look straight through the glass roof. She was strung to a cross and revealing that beauty and transfiguration of eternity in the physical world.

The woman's hair waved slowly above her face; these strands were ropes from the sky descending toward her. They lifted her higher. The woman grinned at the odd behavior of this stranger on the floor. Allison watched the woman look up at the roof to find the source of her glassy stare.

"I don't understand. What do you see?" the woman asked.

"We can stay here forever."

"Stay where?"

"It never had a beginning or end."

Allison began to cry and then laugh in joyful ecstasy, and a strange wonderment overtook her. She thought about Mona. She had laughed and cried before her execution. The child's bell voice joined in her laughing, and she remembered the words of the gallery owner in Soho: "Everyone must traverse eternity."

People in the museum walked past them unconcerned. The three were trapped in an unseen bubble. Ra was above them, hemmed by blue, and the Boat of Millions of Years surrounded them all. And nothing could eclipse its splendor, but only a few could perceive its truth. The whole culture that had worshipped Ra was now gone. All had died and faded into history. Only the sun remained, stripped of Ra.

"Everyone is already dead," she said.

The words resonated sweetly in her mind after she had said them. That was clear, and she remembered what Christ had said: "Let the dead bury their dead."[9] Our soul was only born, in the proper sense, into Malakut when we recognized the station and reality of the Manifestation of God for the age in which we lived. Then and only then would we be truly alive as death faded into immortality and we became free from the boundary and confinement of the physical world. And there were two kinds of death and birth, which overlapped in our lives: the spiritual and the physical.

We chose to see God or not, and that was the essence of free will and our configured destiny. Her mind rewound to her thoughts on death at the goth party, which seemed like it had happened only moments ago. And it seemed strange that we couldn't see God when he was as manifest as the sun. He was Ra shining on gate and wall without a veil, and the intensity of his shining had hidden him, but God had come to the town of the blind. He was a lonely old man with no one to love him or recognize his beauty, and he was replete with disappointed hopes. All those loves of long ago had faded. For a moment she was lying in the grass and staring at the stars above Hampstead Heath. She thought of Hooman's love for her.

Allison looked at the woman's smile, and it was not a plastic smile like the one expressed by the female flight attendant on her first day in New York. Allison saw through the woman before her to a transcendent reality. And she was beautiful beyond comparison to any earthly reality: supramundane.

The woman was now perturbed by Allison's strange behavior and stood up. "Goodbye. I have to go," she said as she disappeared with the child through the columns at the entrance of the museum.

A moment later, and broken by the woman's departure, Allison came back to herself quickly. The invisible light, the light of being, she saw suddenly turned down in her mind like a dimmer light, and she got up, hardly able to feel the weight of her body, which was tingling.

"Boy . . . that was bizarre," she whispered, and she was herself again.

Allison walked back to the train station on the intersection of Tottenham Court Road and Oxford Street. On the train Allison looked at every face. The veil between the two worlds became permeable again for a few brief moments. She felt an echo of her experience in the museum. Some people looked away, uncomfortable with her stare, but she could not help it, and she had to look at their eyes. She was compelled to look for something or somebody else. She floated around London aimlessly for a few hours trying to focus her mind and stopped in her favorite café in Convent Garden for a while. The white bird sculpture that Hooman had given her came to her mind. She was that Phoenix rising from the ashes of this dull, dreary world. She was flying high above this world of cardboard and paper people. They were burning: a conflagration of innocence and ignorance.

Not until the end of the day did she finally return to reality completely.

In her apartment she pulled her red hiking pack from under the bed. Pulling clothes out of drawers, she packed them away. She then looked under furniture for stray items. There wasn't much to pack anyway, and the only object she cared about was the cube with its bird trapped inside. And we were all trapped in our own way, she thought. New York waited, and she was ready for it. On the wall next to her bed, she began to pull down a complex arrangement of Post-it notes; the arrangement was a concept map exploring her theory of symmetrical destiny. She piled them up to be stowed somewhere in her hiking pack and was about to pull the last few from the wall when the phone rang upstairs.

"The phone!" Jade shouted down the stairwell. "I think it's for you. The number coming up . . . it's not local," Jade said.

Allison ran up to the living room, expecting Hooman, but it was Nava whose bright voice greeted her.

"Hello."

"My god. Finally. I've been calling all week. Where have you been?" Nava said.

"It's great to hear your voice."

"Of course it is. I can't believe it! Is it true what Hooman is telling me? He was keeping it secret for a while. I had to drag it out of him. I can tell you, I was as mad as hell when he did finally tell me."

"Yes, it is. What do you think?"

"I think it's fantastic."

"You don't think we're unsuitable?"

"No way. But I got the absolute shock of my life. You have been off my radar. When did you realize you liked him? Or even loved him?"

"We were always friends. But that deepened, and I am not sure why, but my mind has been moving toward him for a while now. I wasn't really aware of it until I came back from my trip to the Middle East. I think I saw his love and kindness. Is Hooman there?"

"No, he's at work. Listen, I'll see you at the airport tomorrow. Okay, well, I've gotta go, we can talk about it all tomorrow. I want to hear everything tomorrow. And I mean everything. Unbelievable. Allison, I'm completely blown away. All right, I'm going . . . bloody hell, Allison." Nava hung up.

Placing the telephone receiver on its holder, she felt tired. Going back downstairs, she pulled the last few Post-it notes off the wall and lay on the bed to read them. "Friends are strange people," was the last scrap of paper that she read, which seemed all too appropriate. Jade had said this recently after a long conversation with an old friend. Not just friends were strange, she thought. Actually, everything was strange, but we justified it. She reviewed the events of the day, which were also strange. She had seen the advertisements on the London Underground that she had been compelled to follow, and that had led her inexorably to the child and the woman in the Great Court. With that last thought she closed her eyes for what she thought would be a few short minutes. She still had to finish packing, but her eyes would not open until the next day.

In a dream Allison found herself in a meadow of luminous and semi-translucent flowers and knee-high grass. In the sky were charcoal and silver clouds, and beyond the clouds was a resonant blue. But the colors and their relationships diverged away from those on Earth, being more akin to layers in a watercolor painting, bleeding into each other. In the distance was an expansive city of light, with forms like vertically orientated shards of crystal floating above the ground. There were also other strange organic shapes moving around and merging into each other like liquid translucence. She walked through the meadow toward the city with her heart overflowing with ecstasy and joy. Her palms brushed the tips of the grass. The feeling in her hands was exquisite, both painful and pleasurable. At the other end of the meadow, she saw a pinpoint of light appear. It morphed into a human form and walked toward her. As this person approached, she saw that it was a young woman. Her body was emitting a light so intense that it was hard to look at her. The meadow also intensified its light, and the light flowed in waves through the grass. Eventually the woman approached Allison and embraced her. The woman then stepped back, and the light from her body and the meadow subsided slightly. Allison was fascinated by the appearance of her body, which was like translucent, light-filled glass. It still had a low and rhythmic light that flashed and throbbed periodically like a strobe light. And the surface and interior of her body looked like many stacked and layered semi-transparent circuit boards with millions of pinpoints of differently colored lights moving around on each circuit. Her body was a miniature city with incredible internal complexity. There were also unifying geometrical patterns apparent on each circuit board, like a triangle, a square, and a circle, as well as abstract organic three-dimensional shapes.

The woman took Allison's hands and kissed her on the cheek. "My name is Mona. I am Shidan's sister. I'm here to tell you a little about the world to come: the world of images and forms," she said.

"This is so beautiful. This place. And you . . . I am utterly dumbfounded. I don't have words to describe this place," Allison said.

"Yes, this is an intermediate world. It stands between the physical world and the spiritual worlds above it. We call it the shadow, or duplicate, of Nasut. And these duplicates are layered like a cake and eventually meld into Malakut in the proper sense. It is hard to describe the real relationship between the two worlds because everything is Malakut, really. And what you see is my light body."

"My god, this is amazing. This is not a dream, is it? I feel like I am immersed in a higher world. Like I am fully awake in my dream."

"What you say is true. The first thing I want to express is that you have been slowly passing into the spiritual worlds for the last few years. Hooman already suggested that this process was in play when he spoke to you in MoMA. Your thoughts and mind have been slowly synchronized with souls already in the world to come. You have only been partially aware of this. For the most part it has happened in the background of your consciousness, behind what we call the countless veils of light. You may have noticed the structure of your mind is changing, and this will continue for the rest of your life. You have three and a half years left to live before you die and merge with us in the absolute sense. We are waiting with joyous expectation for you to join us.

"Also, there are different levels of consciousness that you need to know about. The first is the individual soul separate from other souls with thoughts and identity encapsulated. The other is the collective of souls where thoughts and identity can be shared, transferred, and synchronized. This is one form of symmetry between souls, of unity and oneness, in the absolute worlds. On this level the dewdrop of the soul is cast with longing into the eternal ocean, and who can say if the drop exists after this.

"So, if a soul merges into Malakut before it dies in the physical world, the nature of its free will changes, and its choices in life flow into the needs of other souls. It lives in perfect symmetry with God's will as expressed in the physical world, and the higher worlds are then reflected into the physical world. This is a reflection of your idea of a symmetrical destiny map."

She remembered a quote from the Qur'án that Hooman had sent her in an email: "Nothing can befall us but what God hath destined for us."[10]

Mona continued, "Every choice a person makes is linked to every other soul and can change their future destiny. One choice here changes the choices of another. This is where the identity and minds of souls are so fused into each other, and the integration is so complete, that were one choice out of place the whole geometric structure would fall. It is like the structure of harmony and melody in music where the notes and phrases are absolutely unified. When you were younger, you were in Io's house, and you thought about the unity of minds, forming complex shapes and intersections in the structure of consciousness. It is exactly as you had thought. But the structure is so complex and beautiful that no earthly shape can do it justice. It is exalted beyond what the senses can perceive."

"Wow, that is amazing. I am dumbfounded. This is beyond my wildest dreams."

"You should also know that souls here are grouped in various ways and exist on different levels. The first is by name, then by color, and then by three-dimensional shape, but these shapes and forms are exalted beyond earthly forms. People who read the Word of God only understand its significance relative to their world or spiritual state. The Word transcends earthly languages. Those lower languages lack the subtlety and beauty to describe these higher realms. There are many other groupings, but I won't go into that now. Souls advance not just as indi-

viduals, but also as groups, all linked symmetrically in a delicate interplay of interdependence. This reality is like the interdependent systems
that we see in nature, which are a web of balance and spiritual integration."

Mona smiled and continued, "For the sake of familiarity, I am in a
human form. But you should know that the soul can take on many
forms in thousands of different bodies with thousands of transmutations. In our language we call them skins, but for your sake I'll call them
bodies. One is the light body, which I exist in now in conjunction with
the glass-thread body. They can be used separately or combined and
overlaid one on the other. The main body we use much of the time is
the glass-thread body, with all the other souls represented as singular
threads, or circuits, showing their linear and lateral connections to other
souls. You can touch a thread and see the history of a soul. If you want,
you can contact them. It is the spiritual version of the internet on
Earth."

Mona moved her light-filled arm toward Allison. "Here, look at my
arm. I want to show you something. See, I have a light tattoo on my
arm; it is an extension of the thread body. Can you see the colors and
shapes of flowers scrolling about my arm? If I pass my hand over the
yellow color of the tattoo, you will see many yellow threads. These are
the yellow group, and amongst these is a single thread. That is the other
Mona's eternal timeline, Mona Mahmudnizhad. And there are many
other Monas, and we are all connected. You will also notice that the
tattoo is continually changing, expanding, and moving about my arm,
and there are various points of light moving along each circuit. This
reflects the dynamic process of movement and ascension in the spiritual
worlds."

Mona moved her arm back to her body. "And as for worlds like the
Earth, we call them 'environments.' But they transcend the earthly
worlds. And nothing decays like Earth. Time here is also very different
to Earth. Everything here is changeless and eternal; it only has the
appearance of change. In the physical reality we can only really imagine
these worlds through metaphor and poetic image. These worlds are so
unspeakably glorious that words cannot express their true reality. The
words 'eternity,' 'absolute beauty,' and 'transcendence' are completely
useless and lost on this plane."

Allison was speechless and in awe for a while. "Wow! I had no idea of this form of reality," she enthused and then asked, "So the virtues and intellectual qualities that we acquire on Earth will see us through eternity?"

"Yes, that is true. Good deeds done in the mortal world of Nasut, which are metaphoric symbols, have their counterparts in Malakut. Their true relevance is obscured by earthly conditions."

Mona paused briefly before continuing. "One other reality is the relativity of hell and paradise and the proximity of God. To a soul on a higher level of reality, the stages below are like hell. But these lower conditions are paradise to another soul. Everything is relative to a soul's own level. We should be self-effacing to those souls that are lower than our station, with no trace of superiority. To those souls above us, we should have no envy and be the essence of contentment with God's will in that moment until we receive the command to move higher. The most important thing is continual motion toward God and fulfilling our innate spiritual and intellectual capacity. We should always strive to progress toward God."

"So we should also be concerned with other souls' spiritual growth in our group and individually," Allison said.

"Their progress is our progress. We wait until the last person has gone before us into paradise before we progress into paradise ourselves. That is the essence of selflessness. And you never know whether the mind and heart of a soul in the depths of hell may hold the key to your own progress. You can only truly love a person if you are prepared to descend into hell for the sake of their progress, but the paradox is that you take the higher worlds with you wherever you travel so you don't see the lower worlds as hell; everything is dynamically interactive and transcendent."

Part of Mona's body seemed to open up, and more light flooded out in a stream. "Here is a quote by Bahá'u'lláh that I want you to contemplate:

"*'O My servants! Could ye apprehend with what wonders of My munificence and bounty I have willed to entrust your souls, ye would, of a truth, rid yourselves of attachment to all created things, and would gain a true knowledge of your own selves—a knowledge which is the same as the comprehension of Mine own Being.*

Ye would find yourselves independent of all else but Me, and would perceive, with your inner and outer eye, and as manifest as the revelation of My effulgent Name, the seas of My loving-kindness and bounty moving within you'[11]

"You are now a student in the hidden school beyond the veils of the mortal world." Mona then embraced her, and as she did, Allison saw that light was now coming from her own body. The dream ended in that moment. Her consciousness dissolved into the deeper rhythms of sleep.

—————

On the morning of the following day, the girls embarked on the Northern line train at Camden Town and headed to the Tottenham Court Road stop. They had slept in and were running late to get to Heathrow Airport in time for Allison's flight to New York. A few minutes after they had left Camden Town Station, Allison pulled a small notepad from her backpack and began to write down her dream. Her notes ran to several pages, and she was writing so fast that her handwriting looked like a scrawl of loops across the page. Jade commented that her handwriting did not even look like English.

The train arrived at their stop, and they disembarked. Allison was weighed down with her red hiking pack, but she still moved as fast as she could up the escalators. On the street they ran down Charing Cross Road toward a bookshop.

Foyles Bookshop had a large section on Egypt, and there were various funerary texts connected to or a part of *The Book of the Dead*, which was a loose collection of these texts, spells, and incantations, with no absolute final form. Finally, *The Book of Gates* caught her eye. Flipping the book over, the back read: "*The Book of Gates* refers to different regions in the Egyptian afterlife called either regions or gates." That was it. That was what she knew would provide answers. This was the book referenced in the information captions at the British Museum on the previous day. She remembered that a soul came to a gate and uttered a secret password to the gatekeeper of that particular gate to pass through. She wondered if these worlds had some form of password security or cryptography and whether only souls with the right mental and spiritual development could access certain higher worlds.

She spoke to one of the staff about Osiris, the god of the afterlife, and the woman recommended *Osiris & the Egyptian Resurrection*, which were two volumes by Sir Wallis Budge. He had translated *The Book of the Dead* and had linked it to the cult and myth of Osiris. She immediately saw the link to Christianity through the idea of resurrection and asked the woman about this connection, but the woman said that Egyptians did not believe in a physical resurrection. They believed in the resurrection of the soul as it moved into the next world after death, and the soul's ultimate destination being the Field of Reeds, paradise for Egyptians, where they could eat the wheat of righteousness. The woman then explained the main theme underlying *The Book of Gates*, saying that the dead were ferried along a river in the afterlife in the Boat of Ra, the "evening boat," which was controlled by the god of the afterlife, Osiris, and the dead were left in the region of that world relative to their degree of righteousness, which was based on their good and bad deeds in this life. She also said that the gates could also be interpreted as the secret portals of the Mansion of Osiris in the Field of Reeds.

———

Allison and Jade came running into the airport building breathless.

The woman at the check-in counter issued Allison her boarding pass. "Your plane leaves in nineteen minutes. You might miss it, but you can try."

At the security entrance Allison turned and hugged Jade. "Are you going to come and visit me in New York?" Allison said.

"I'm not sure. Let me think about it."

"Okay. It's been really great getting to know you. I love you."

Jade laughed. "You don't love me. We haven't known each other that long."

"It doesn't matter."

"Mmm, you've been all weird on me since yesterday. What's come over you?"

"Well, anyway, I think you're a wonderful person."

"Okay. Whatever you say. You're a strange bird." Jade laughed. "And you had better go."

"Yeah, okay, well, see you later." Allison choked up. All this crying was getting to her. Jade laughed again and patted her on the shoulder. Allison rushed off. When she reached the security barriers and the X-ray machines, she turned and saw Jade wave. The words "strange bird" stuck in her head as she walked through the security portal.

After a run toward the gate, she made the plane just in time; the aircraft door closed behind her. And the thought occurred that this metal bird was a strange bird too, and a memory of her first day in New York resurfaced. Invisible hands held the plane up. The knowledge of flight had been hidden, like Temu, for millions of years, yet always visible in the shape of bird's wings. And the shape and power of the plane had to conform rigidly to the laws of physics to allow flight, and the spiritual laws were the same. The closer we came to living by these laws, the more spiritual freedom we attained, and she remembered something 'Abdu'l-Bahá had said: "As ye have faith so shall your powers and blessings be."[12] As she took her seat, she thought about the different gates in the airport being linked to the gates in the afterlife. The original means of transport for Egyptians moving along the Nile was a boat, so it seemed plausible that they should describe the means of transport in the afterlife as a boat, but today the main form of transport for long distances was the airplane.

Her mind was still as she looked out at London. The plane took off. She looked down at the city as it appeared intermittently through the clouds. She then opened *Osiris & the Egyptian Resurrection*, and the first page she opened to was a description of the nine parts of the soul in the Egyptian schema of immortality, eight of which were resurrected after death.

Khat: The physical body.
Ka: The vital essence, or spirit of the body, which left the body after death.
Ba: The personality, or center of the soul. It could travel between earth and heaven.
Shuyet: The shadow self.
Akh (Khu, Ikhu): The transfigured intellect.
Sah: The spiritual body. Somehow related to the physical body.
Sechem: The life-force of the soul.
Ib: The heart, and the source of good and evil.

Ren: A person's name. Related to the soul and important for the evolution of the soul.

The Ba was of most interest to Allison, as it was the part of the soul that could cross between the worlds: between earth and heaven. She remembered the discussion that she had had with Hooman at MoMA, and that 'Abdu'l-Bahá had said that in prayer there was a mingling of station, a mingling of condition. The Ba could travel into those worlds before physical death. She then realized that the plane she was traveling in was owned by British Airways, which if you took only the first initials was BA, or Ba (for the Egyptian soul); this was another connection in the meaning and symmetry of letters for her symmetrical destiny map. And indeed, people inside planes were like the soul inside the body.

She closed the book and stowed her new book in the flap on the seat in front of her and leaned back.

She closed her eyes. She thought of New York and Hooman.

18

A CIRCLE OF FRIENDS

These statements are made in the sphere of that which is relative. Otherwise, those souls who with but one step have traversed the world of the relative and the conditioned, and dwelt in the court of independent sovereignty, and pitched their tent in the realms of absolute authority and command, have burned away these relativities with a single spark, and blotted out these words with a mere dewdrop.[1]

— BAHÁ'U'LLÁH, *THE SEVEN VALLEYS*

Warm light filtered through the leaves of the cherry tree. Allison was sitting on the chair in the light well, looking up at the sky above the bookshop. Her legs were crossed, and her feet were resting on the edge of the table. She had just finished reading a Bahá'í book called *Bahíyyih Khánum: The Greatest Holy Leaf*. The book was sitting in her lap, and her hands were resting on it. She was waiting for Nava to come and pick her up after doing a shift at the bookshop. They were planning to go to a nail salon in Manhattan.

Just under a year had elapsed, and the seasons had completed another cycle, coming again to summer. During that time Allison and Hooman's love had deepened. They had decided to marry before Allison's visa options ran out. She closed her eyes and became aware of the intensity of the warm light on her face and hands.

After coming back to New York, Allison had moved into the spare room in Shidan's apartment in Brooklyn Heights. Although Shidan had moved most of the books in the room back into his shop, there were still piles of books in the room that she had picked out to read during the year. She had also spent the year helping Nikki in Shidan's bookshop, the Sun Tongue. She would sometimes manage the front desk or keep track of the stock. Occasionally, she traveled with Shidan as he looked for manuscripts overseas and within America. On one of his most recent trips, she had accompanied him to Rome, where he had managed to convince the Vatican Library to sell him an early Christian manuscript on behalf of the Smithsonian Libraries. Allison felt privileged to be able to read some of these rare books, those written in English. As many of these early books were of a religious nature, she became acutely aware of the continuity of all religious traditions, which in Bahá'í terminology was called "progressive revelation." She did not know what the word "revelation" meant at the time, and when she looked up its dictionary meaning, she liked it: "the divine or supernatural disclosure to humans of something relating to human existence."[2] The word "progressive" referred to the continuous linear unfoldment of God's plan for humankind's spiritual development both collectively and individually through the different religions, which appeared at different times in history and were therefore relative to the time and conditions of the human society in which they appeared. She wondered what her own personal unfoldment was relative to this time. What was God's specific plan for her?

And because the Bahá'í Faith was the latest installment of this religious succession, she had spent a considerable amount of time deepening herself in matters of Bahá'í metaphysics. Hooman had begun inviting her to many of the New York and New Jersey Bahá'í community events. Most of Hooman's Bahá'í friends were in the New Jersey community, so she had begun to meet and spend time with them. Allison had also begun to attend the core Bahá'í activities that the community was running, like devotional meetings and study circles. Since she had been living in Brooklyn with Shidan throughout that year, she had begun to attend the Ruhi Institute courses running in that borough. She had almost finished the fourth book, *The Twin Manifestations*. Because of all her interactions with the community and her continued study of the Bahá'í writings, she was now able to form a well-balanced view of the Bahá'í Faith, its belief structure, and its two main goals of serving and unifying humanity, which would eventually lead to the founding of the Divine Civilization that Hooman had talked about so often.

She had begun to read various books by Bahá'u'lláh and 'Abdu'l-Bahá, and her love for these two towering spiritual figures deepened, and there was a subtle symmetry between her love for Hooman, Bahá'u'lláh, and 'Abdu'l-Bahá. The book that had had the most impact on her was a book by Bahá'u'lláh called the *Kitáb-i-Íqán* (The Book of Certitude). She had read it several times and had concluded that it could not have been written by a mere human being and must have come from God, and from this she concluded that Bahá'u'lláh was what he purported to be: a Manifestation of God.

And she felt a profound sorrow and joy for Bahá'u'lláh and 'Abdu'l-Bahá; she could see a tacit delicacy and strength as these two emotions melded together: a joyous melancholy. They had sacrificed themselves for the sake of humanity with an unparalleled detachment that she knew she could never achieve in her own life. And there was a profound silence and a resonating emptiness in her mind that had never existed before, which flowed from her daily prayers. Bahá'u'lláh's words in her mind were exquisite, beautiful, and full of poetic metaphor, and they evoked worlds on the edge of her imagination.

She had also felt a strong connection to Bahá'u'lláh's daughter, Bahíyyih Khánum, the story of whom lay in her lap. Allison had first heard of her from Hooman in the months before her travels to Istanbul and had thought about her when she was standing in front of Bahá'u'lláh's house. There was not much available on the internet about her life nor were there many comprehensive books on her life, but Hooman had a very large collection of Bahá'í books, and he had gone through them, bookmarking everything he knew about her life. After reading these books, Allison began to piece together a sketchy image of her life. Probably the most profound insight into her status and rank within the Bahá'í community were her own father's words, which were the first words in the book she had just finished reading. She decided to read these words again in an effort to commit them to memory, so she opened the book to the first section and read:

LET these exalted words be thy love-song on the tree of Bahá, O thou most holy and resplendent Leaf: "God, besides Whom is none other God, the Lord of this world and the next!" Verily, We have elevated thee to the rank of one of the most distinguished among thy sex, and granted thee, in My court, a station such as none other woman hath surpassed. Thus have We preferred thee and raised thee above the rest, as a sign of grace from Him Who is the Lord of the throne on high and earth below. We have created thine eyes to behold the light of My countenance, thine ears to hearken unto the melody of My words, thy body to pay homage before My throne. Do thou render thanks unto God, thy Lord, the Lord of all the world.

How high is the testimony of the Sadratu'l-Muntahá for its leaf; how exalted the witness of the Tree of Life unto its fruit! Through My remembrance of her a fragrance laden with the perfume of musk hath been diffused; well is it with him that hath inhaled it and exclaimed: "All praise be to Thee, O God, my Lord the most glorious!" How sweet thy presence before Me; how sweet to gaze upon thy face, to bestow upon thee My loving-kindness, to favour thee with My tender care, to make mention of thee in this, My Tablet—a Tablet which I have ordained as a token of My hidden and manifest grace unto thee.[3]

She rested the book in her lap and let these words resonate in her mind. Then she looked up at the cherry tree again. The Sadratu'l-Muntahá was Arabic for "the tree beyond which there is no passing," or the boundary of the seventh heaven beyond which creation could not pass; it was also a metaphor for the authority of the Manifestation of God, or the authority of the various prophets in all the religious traditions that had become manifest throughout human history. Allison reached up and plucked a leaf from the cherry tree. She smiled as she thought about Bahíyyih Khanum's rank as the Greatest Holy Leaf. She was a divine template for all women who would come after her. She represented the ideal of faithfulness and obedience to God. She put the leaf into the page she had just read and closed the book.

She closed her eyes again, and her mind drifted back to the previous week. One day Allison had been in the Sun Tongue stacking books, and for some strange reason, which seemed random at the time, she saw a grape quite clearly in her imagination. She then had a strong desire to eat some grapes. At that exact moment Shidan came through the front door of the shop and asked if anyone was hungry. He had a bag of grapes swinging in his hand. She realized that the thought of the grape was not random. It felt like the symmetry of the universe, or a small fragment of it, had, in that moment, flowed through her. Shidan passed her the grapes and smiled. She was astounded, and then Nikki got up and went to put some music on. The song was "Slave to the Rhythm" by Grace Jones. And so, as the music started, she popped a grape into her mouth, and it seemed to be of a richer nature and more succulent than usual. The taste was extremely enduring, and she could not define it as it was beyond any known experience. The grape was destroyed on her tongue. The lyrics in the song were true; indeed, the rhythm of time and place was inside her. Who had put the desire to buy grapes into Shidan's mind, and how had she seen a fragment of the future? In time and eternity God could see the future and past, and she had been immersed in eternity for a small but exquisite moment.

Then she thought about the words "sun tongue," and the name had an underlying power to transcend and enhance the senses. An image pushed through her mind. In her imagination her tongue was shining with light, and she had a single mint leaf sitting on the tip of her tongue. What was strange was that she could almost taste it on her physical tongue. This image then changed to a chili pepper. That, too, was in her mouth, almost burning, and it had a peculiar strawberry afterglow. She compared it to *Charlie and the Chocolate Factory* and saw a mental projection of the everlasting gobstopper mixed with "lickable" wallpaper. As these sensations ceased and her mouth returned to normality, she was flabbergasted and dumbfounded. Nobody would ever believe her, even remotely. Shidan and Nikki would think she was mad if she told them.

Allison had left the door to the rest of the bookshop slightly ajar and heard Nava shout as she came through the front door of the shop. Her voice increased in intensity as she came toward the light well. Allison stood up as Nava came into the light well. They hugged.

"Okay, are you ready to have your nails done?"

"Yeah, sure. It's been a while since I had my nails done. Do you think it is really necessary?"

"Oh, babe, you can't get married with your nails like they are now. You have to have them done, babe."

"Okay . . . I suppose so."

"I'm so excited. I am *so, so* excited." Nava jogged on the spot and smiled as she reached for the sky.

"Yeah, me too. I never actually thought I would ever marry anyone."

"So, remember that I'll come early in the morning tomorrow, and we'll get your hair done in Brooklyn."

"Okay, cool."

"Okay, let's go."

They left the light well and walked into the main part of the bookshop. As they walked out of the bookshop, Allison closed the door behind them and locked it.

———

Allison stood in front of a mirror in the corridor of Shidan's apartment. It was mid-morning on the day of her marriage to Hooman. She had decided not to wear the usual white wedding gowns favored by most couples, nor would Hooman wear a black suit; instead, she wore the yellow dress she had bought in London, and Hooman was in his green herringbone suit. The colors of their clothes were intentional, as they represented the green lion swallowing the yellow sun from alchemical symbolism.

The mirror was the one she had bought when she first came to New York, the magic mirror. Hooman stood behind her. He embraced her from behind.

"You look amazing," he said.

Allison became aware that she had been staring into space. Hooman was smiling at her. She picked up his last words. "Thank you," she said, then added, "You look very dapper. Handsome, too, I might add."

"God, I feel fantastic. I don't know what has come over me," he said.

"You look utterly amazing, Hooman."

"Do I? I am not that good-looking, you know, but you are. Beautiful, I mean. Utterly beautiful. I am very lucky to have you."

Shidan walked through the front door into the corridor. "Are you guys ready to go? The car is out the front."

"Sure," Hooman said.

She took one last look in the mirror and saw how Hooman saw her for the first time. Maybe I am beautiful, she thought. She had never really considered herself that way before.

In Hooman's words was a euphoric realization: all her life she had been a beautiful but ephemeral shadow, passing over the horizon of life, over its unending deserts and their dunes, a shifting form projected by the illimitable clouds moving above us, and from that source, an immeasurable sun, with all the rain rolling down the faces of those dunes, forever: the tears of creation come from all the loves of long ago, in forgotten memories and lives, half-formed selves trying to grasp at an unattainable future in this world; and in each water bead on the sand a curved and unending world with a reflection of the sky: our eye, with a tear unknown until now forming and falling through and onto that shadow.

In this moment, she saw her true identity, her true poverty, her pure desert road, diverging away from this fleeting and dissonant world, into a place where nothing dies, where nothing changes, and everything of impermanence fades, and nothing remains of regret or desire, where that fractured sky resolves into staggeringly beautiful shapes and heals the sky's wounds, thereby merging all our true desires, into that vast and unending road, vast and unending suns and their moons overhead, looking down on us—worlds, each with its own Sun. A sun of being, of sublimity, of absolute perfection, and of a light unknown, but born from that tear: truth, unimpeded by incomplete illusions, perceived in an unalterable world that transcends the relatively of our understanding of eternity: how could we ever truly know it.

Now she was complete, truly complete, reflecting her shimmering Self, a transcended shadow, and with Hooman as her mirror and consort through all the worlds of God. All those unspeakable worlds in which we will never be separated, even by death. How could the soul be touched by our desires for this world, or touched by death: never, in any world, much less this one. There is just us, she thought. Just us, just our humanity, and nothing else will remain of our reflection in this world except love itself.

———

Allison's eyes moved between the road ahead and the forest framed by her window. Hooman and she were sitting in the back seat. All the foliage passed by as a light-filled blur and cast shadows and shifting light patterns around the interior of Shidan's car. Hooman squeezed her hand, and she looked over at him, smiling.

The drive to Upstate New York took roughly an hour and a half, but Allison and Hooman had said virtually nothing to each other; she had felt an abiding sensation of love and nervousness rise up in her body. Allison remembered how this forest had looked in the fall of the previous year. The effect of dappled light was the same, but the intense red-brown and yellow leaves had departed as it was now summer. At the time she had driven around this part of Upstate New York in a semi-random way. She had insisted to Hooman that she wanted to find the location of their wedding ceremony alone, so she had borrowed Shidan's BMW, the same car in which they were now traveling. She had spent a weekend driving from town to town.

Shidan looked over his shoulder at Hooman. "Almost there. It should be around the next bend."

Allison remembered this bend too. As they came around the bend, Allison saw the meadow in the distance. It was obscured by a tall hedge, and the car soon slowed. The road veered away to the left and ran between the forest and the hedge, but Shidan turned right onto a dirt road. Eventually the hedge disappeared, and they stopped next to a large meadow.

When Allison had driven down the dirt road, the hedge had disappeared, and she knew this was the place. It was breathtaking and as close to her dream of a perfect marriage place as she could find. She had stopped the car and walked into the knee-high grass, feeling a strange ecstasy and happiness that she was alone and that God had guided her to this place.

Shidan stopped at the same spot that Allison had during fall, and she was aware of the symmetry in time. They all got out and walked into the meadow. What Allison saw immediately was that a path had been cut into the meadow. Shidan had come up here a few days before and had marked out a large circle where there were now tables and seating. He had used a string line and wooden stakes before using a weed eater and a lawn mower to cut out the shapes; they were a little like crop circles with connecting paths.

There was a slight rise before them and another forest edge on the other side of the meadow. They walked up the rise and came to the spot where the ceremony would be held. The circle had been measured to accommodate the exact number of guests. They stood on the edge of the circle cut into the meadow.

"Oh, wow, Shidan, you did a great job."

"Thanks. Is this what you wanted?"

"Yes, this is exactly what I wanted, only better."

He turned. "I'll go back to the car and get a few things. The caterers should be here soon."

Allison took Hooman's hand and walked into the center of the circle. She guessed that this was where she had stood in the fall, the circle within the circle. After a few moments she gently pressed his hand, then let go of it, and they left the circle. Wading through the grass, she stopped and lay down. He lay down next to her and then took her hand again. They looked up at the sun together.

"So, this is it, then," said Allison.

"Yep, this is it."

"What are we doing together?"

"As you have said before, we are fulfilling our configured destiny," he said.

They turned their heads toward each other and smiled through the veil of long grass.

———

All the wedding guests slowly moved from the assembly area, from the larger circle into the smaller circle on the higher part of the meadow. People began to stand on the outer rim of the circle, facing inwards. Most of the guests were Hooman's friends. The majority were from either the New Jersey or the New York Bahá'í community, and then there were a few of his friends from work and his parents. Most of Allison's friends from her Bahá'í study circle had come too.

"Okay, can everyone please stand an even distance from each other and then hold hands," Shidan said.

He walked around the circle and spaced people. He then walked back to his place next to Sara and became a part of the circle. Allison and Hooman were standing opposite him on the other side of the circle. Shidan smiled at her for a moment as he waited for everyone to be quiet.

"Welcome, everyone, to the wedding of Allison and Hooman. We are going to hear from Nava first, then Elliot and Paul will read some Bahá'í prayers, followed by Allison, who will read a quotation from the Bahá'í writings about the nature of love, and then Allison and Hooman will exchange vows," Shidan said. He put his hand on Nava's shoulder. She was standing next to him, and Allison saw her look across at Hooman. She had tears in her eyes and waited for a while to collect her thoughts.

Finally, she began, "I'm sorry, I am kind of lost for words. But I am *so so* happy for you both. And I am happy that my brother never heeded my advice about finding someone, so that Allison had time to find him."

There was a titter from the gathered circle.

"He waited for the right person. And you are now my sister, Allison, and I love you so much. So *very* much."

"Thank you, Nava. I love you too," Allison said, and smiled.

"Okay, well, we will begin with prayers and readings, and then Allison and Hooman will say the Bahá'í marriage vows."

Elliot and Paul read several Bahá'í prayers in alternating order. Allison was last and read a passage from 'Abdu'l-Bahá:

> *"'Know thou of a certainty that Love is the secret of God's holy Dispensation, the manifestation of the All-Merciful, the fountain of spiritual outpourings. Love is heaven's kindly light, the Holy Spirit's eternal breath that vivifieth the human soul. Love is the cause of God's revelation unto man, the vital bond inherent, in accordance with the divine creation, in the realities of things. Love is the one means that ensureth true felicity both in this world and the next. Love is the light that guideth in darkness, the living link that uniteth God with man, that assureth the progress of every illumined soul. Love is the most great law that ruleth this mighty and heavenly cycle, the unique power that bindeth together the diverse elements of this material world, the supreme magnetic force that directeth the movements of the spheres in the celestial realms. Love revealeth with unfailing and limitless power the mysteries latent in the universe. Love is the spirit of life unto the adorned body of mankind,*

the establisher of true civilization in this mortal world, and the shedder of imperishable glory upon every high-aiming race and nation.'" [4]

Once Allison had finished reading the passage, she turned to Hooman. She paused significantly, reflecting on the words she was about to utter, and then said: "We will all, verily, abide by the Will of God."[5]

Hooman repeated this phrase, and they embraced. This was the Bahá'í marriage vow. Everyone clapped, and the circle slowly broke up. The guests returned to the large circle at the bottom of the hill, and the caterers served lunch. Waiters walked through and around the gathering handing out fruit juice and water.

Allison and Hooman walked over to a small portable table and signed the marriage certificate.

After signing, Allison embraced Hooman again. "You have no idea. I am so happy in this moment," Allison said.

"I think I have some idea," he said, smiling.

Hooman intimated to Allison with his eyes that Nava was coming over to the table. Nava embraced Allison and lifted her off the ground for a moment.

"This is so wonderful!" As Nava said this, tears began to well up in her eyes. She brushed them away and smiled.

"It is, isn't it?" Allison said. She smiled and put her hand on Nava's back.

"Yes . . . wonderful and amazing," Nava said.

Hooman and Nava's parents came over to convey their best wishes. A few people lined up behind them and waited for their turn to embrace the couple. Among them were Paul and Sophie, who conveyed their happiness and then signed the marriage certificate as witnesses.

Paul added his signature, which looped around the page. "I never thought I would see you married. Never," he said to Allison.

"Nor me," added Sophie as she kissed Hooman's cheek.

The sun overhead orbited gradually down in its arc toward the horizon. It began to sink beneath that horizon and muted the colors in the meadow.

Everyone returned to their cars and headed back to Manhattan or to surrounding boroughs.

Nava drove Allison and Hooman back to New Jersey. Hooman put his arm around her shoulder. They kissed. Allison was in a state of unfathomable joy.

———

Walking through Shidan's apartment, Allison gathered all her things. She was trying to remember everything that she needed and made a mental list so that she didn't forget anything. She had already packed her luggage a few days before for a honeymoon in Australia but had thought of a few last-minute things to take. Once she had everything, she descended the stairs and threw everything into the back of Nava's car and then got into the back seat and sat next to Hooman. Hooman had already packed his suitcase and had placed it in Nava's trunk on the previous day.

Nava pulled away from the curb and drove off down Orange Street and began to make her way to JFK Airport. Allison had arranged a night at Jasper's shack, just north of Fraser Island (K'gari in the Butchulla Aboriginal language). From there they would go to Cairns, which Allison had visited continually throughout her childhood. Hooman had never visited Queensland, so this trip was something new for him.

———

As they entered the airport, she looked briefly at the modernist Terminal 5 as they passed by. She then leaned into Hooman and took his hand. She placed his hand on her lap.

"Hooman, I have something I want to share with you."

"Oh, yes. What's that?"

"I think that I want to become a Bahá'í, you know, officially. What do I have to do? I sign a card, don't I?"

"First off, I just have to say that is the best news I have heard, ever. I am truly happy for you. And officially, all you need to do is sign a Bahá'í registration card. You sign it with the understanding that you accept Bahá'u'lláh as the Manifestation of God for this age, and that you will follow the spiritual precepts he has set down in his various books and tablets, particularly the Kitáb-i-Aqdas."

"I think I can do that. Anyway, I think I've been a Bahá'í for a while now, you know, informally. I mean, I have been praying and reading the Bahá'í writings for a while now."

Hooman smiled. "That's so wonderful. Absolutely wonderful," he said.

"I think I finally know who Bahá'u'lláh is now. I didn't want to become a Bahá'í until I understood his station fully, and the implications of living a Bahá'í life."

———

After spending the morning of Saturday, February 6, 1993, on the peak of Mount Warning, Allison drove over the border of New South Wales into Queensland. Her travels north from Melbourne through New South Wales and into Queensland had slowly, but not perfectly, acclimatized her to the increasing humidity and heat. The first city she came to was the Gold Coast. She drove into its southernmost suburb, Coolangatta. She stopped at a pawnbroker and bought a secondhand boogie board and then drove on to Kirra Beach, where she jumped into the surf and rode her board into the shore several times. The sky was clear, and the waves were big and forming into tubes. There were many surfers in the water around her and others behind her who were closer to the headland, Point Danger.

After half an hour, she drove on through the Gold Coast toward Jasper's shack. She passed through Brisbane on the way and stopped at South Bank for a few hours, where she walked along the Brisbane River, looking at the boats and ferries passing by.

She eventually left Brisbane and drove north past Hervey Bay. She was lost for an hour, trying to find the sandy road that led to the shack. Once she found the right road, she drove into a tea tree clearing, where she parked and walked along a track that led to the beach. The shack was nestled between tea trees at the back and dunes at the front. The tea tree scrub lined the coast in both directions. Before she unpacked the car, she went to the dune facing the beach, looking at the ocean.

Bundaberg was near Jasper's place, and Allison intended to work on the farms near the town as a fruit picker. She stayed at the shack for two months and each day made the commute into Bundaberg and the surrounding farmland. Now that the wet season was ending and summer was fading into fall, the heat had become more tolerable on some days, and the nights, too, were beginning to cool down.

In the last week she was on a lunch break at an avocado farm. She was sitting amongst several other fruit pickers under an avocado tree, mostly backpackers from outside Australia, when a Danish couple she had seen a few days before approached her.

"Hello, we heard from other people that you are heading north in a week."

"Yes, I am."

"Could we get a ride?"

"Sure, no problem. I was looking for someone to drive my car from Townsville to Cairns. I want to travel up the coast on any boat going up that way."

"We would be happy to drive your car up to Cairns for you."

"Great."

"Do you want gas money?" the girl said.

"No, that's fine. I was going that way anyway."

"We'll pay for gas from Townsville to Cairns."

"Sure, okay. That sounds fine."

After eight days, she packed up the car and picked up the Danish couple in Bundaberg. After a day's drive, arriving at six in the evening, they came to Townsville.

The next day the couple drove on toward Cairns, and Allison caught a ferry out to Magnetic Island, where she asked around if anyone was sailing north. In Horseshoe Bay she found someone on the beach with a boat willing to take her to all the boats anchored in the bay, and after talking to various people, she found a particularly large yacht owned by an American couple. She attempted to negotiate a price for taking her north to Cairns, but the couple welcomed her aboard and said they were happy to give her a lift north, gratis.

19

THE SHACK

And they swim in the sea of the spirit, and soar in the holy atmosphere of light.
Then what existence have words, on such a plane, that "first" and "last", or other
than these, should be mentioned or described? In this realm, the first is the same as
the last, and the last is the same as the first.
  In thy soul, of love build thou a fire
  And burn all thoughts and words entire.[1,2]

— BAHÁ'U'LLÁH, *THE SEVEN VALLEYS*

The wind beat at tufts of grass clinging to the sand on the dune in front
of the shack. It was Monday, July 17, 2000. Allison watched them
vibrate and flow as they were buffeted by the will of the air. She could
see the dunes through a large hole in the kitchen wall. The shack's walls
mirrored the movement of grass with appropriate whistling sounds; the
wind pushed incessantly through its porous skin. She heard the sea but
could not see it. She saw only the blue, unclouded sky that was visible
through the kitchen window. Hooman was sitting at the kitchen countertop on a stool. She was sitting behind him next to a small table. She
pushed her toast and egg around her plate with her fork. It was a late
breakfast or brunch as indicated by the old manual wall clock faintly

chiming eleven times. They had slept in and were trying to adjust to the new time zone.

The shack had been cobbled together by a local fisherman many years before with whatever he had been able to collect from the beach and the local garbage dump. The walls were made from bits of driftwood, a few doors, and other scraps of wood. In a few places there were a few olive oil tins, which had been flattened out and tacked over holes in the walls. With only two rooms and a very low roof, the place was small and cramped, but Allison loved its humility.

An additional space had been built nearby: a single room with a full glass front wall. The room was a short walk from the main shack. Jasper called the space his "writing room," and it was in this space that he worked on his philosophy lectures and books during semester breaks. The writing room had a better view of the sea and the beach. From the shack, the view of the beach was blocked by the dunes, where only the sea, sky, and birds were visible.

"Hooman."

"Yes."

"Do you think that we'll ever really know what love is? In its essence?"

"Well, I suppose its common meaning is attraction or affection for a person. But that is a very basic idea of love. Some people love material objects and others humanity and still others God and his spiritual reality. I suppose that the important aspect of it is the object of love. That defines the depth and impact of love in our lives and the priority of the other objects we love, whether they are material or spiritual."

He paused and then continued, "Take the love between us. That is a symbol of divine love. It can be sublimated for something higher and more profound."

"Yes, I agree, and there must be aspects of that higher love that are hidden and mysterious."

"Here, have some more egg." Hooman leaned over and lifted the frying pan from the stove.

"No, thanks, I'm full."

She heard the cry of gulls for a moment, flying over the roof of the shack.

Hooman paused for a moment, then said, "I think, as you said when we first met, that love is a form of self-sacrifice. We give up a part of ourselves for something greater. And I suppose when you view it like that, it is not really a sacrifice in the ultimate sense, because you gain something else higher in its place. Christ says: 'Greater love hath no man than this, that a man lay down his life for his friends.'"[3]

She thought of Mona Mahmudnizhad in Iran, who had sacrificed her life for her love of Bahá'u'lláh and his teachings for humanity. She had placed the rope around her neck with utter joy. She was a sun-bird flying in illimitable space, and Allison thought that if Mona had renounced her belief in Bahá'u'lláh, it would have been like renouncing her own soul, and that was the depth of her faith.

Hooman continued, "And Saint Paul says, 'If I have the gift of prophecy and can fathom all mysteries and all knowledge, and if I have a faith that can move mountains, but do not have love, I am nothing.'[4] And according to 'Abdu'l-Bahá there are four kinds of love. Some are knowable, and some are not knowable, but really all are infinite, so we will never know every aspect of them."

"Really, what are they?" she asked.

"Love from God to human, from human to God, from God to God, and lastly from human to human."

"Interesting. So, the love from God to God transcends what we believe we know?"

"Yes, I think so. God seeks the beauty of his own image reflected in creation. And part of that image is humanity."

"Well, since we can't ever know God's essence, then I suppose that makes sense."

Hooman had brought with him a small book by Bahá'u'lláh. The book was called *The Hidden Words,* and it was sitting on the table near her. "Have a look in that book. I have put a bookmark on the page I like," he said, placing the last egg on his plate. He adjusted his balance on the stool and resumed his gaze at the sea.

She picked up the book and turned to the page he had mentioned and read the quote:

O SON OF MAN! Veiled in My immemorial being and in the ancient eternity of My essence, I knew My love for thee; therefore I created thee, have engraved on thee Mine image and revealed to thee My beauty.[5]

After a moment she added, "I suppose that is the form of love that passes from God to humanity." She thought that by adding an extra *l* to *The Hidden Words* it then became "the hidden worlds," and she realized that the whole of creation was one unending love story without boundaries or beginning. Love was the story within the story and the theme of our life as we passed through history, never to be seen again on this physical plane. Love was the only thing that remained in this changeable world.

She then observed him taking a small sip of coffee. He made a face, then put the cup down on the kitchen countertop.

"The coffee must be ancient," Hooman said as he picked up the coffee packet and turned it over.

She assumed he was looking for the use-by date. He then put the coffee packet down and stared through the window. Since she could not see his face, she imagined certain shapes of pleasure forming on Hooman's face, and she waited for him to say something about the sea, which he did. "Look at that water! Isn't that wonderful? Look at the white surf when the waves roll over."

She stood up and looked out the kitchen window.

Hooman smiled and filled the sink with water. She passed her plate to him, then continued to look out over the dunes to where the sea met the sky, and those same shapes of pleasure formed in her mind.

When the sun approached the midpoint in the sky, Hooman suggested they go and sit on the dune facing the beach and watch the sea from there. They left the shack and walked toward the beach. From that dune, Allison saw a thick section of plywood with burnt edges. She assumed that it had washed up on the beach on the previous night. She wanted to try it out as a sand toboggan, so she walked down the face of the dune to the beach and picked the section of plywood up from the wet sand. After walking back up the dune, she put the board down and sat on it.

She looked over at Hooman and smiled. "Wish me luck," she said.

"You don't need luck."

She rode down the dune and managed to stand up before tumbling at its base.

Breathless after several runs to the top of the dune, she finally slumped down next to him.

"Do you want to try it?" she said.

"That looks like a good sand toboggan."

"Do you want a go?"

"No, I'll try it later, maybe. Let's sit and look at the water for a while."

Sitting in silence, they watched the waves for several minutes as they rhythmically rolled over, spread out flat, and diminished. The water then receded back down the beach into oncoming waves. The wind pushed Allison's hair around her face. The warm light beat down on her skin. Her eyes squinted at the sun as she looked up at it.

"Watch the patterns of foam as each wave goes back into the sea. They look somewhat like cloud formations. You see?" he commented.

"Yes, I see . . . you know, I've been reading in some of the Bahá'í prayers recently a focus on the concept of eternity. And, in fact, it was mentioned in that slice of *The Hidden Words* I read before: '. . . in the ancient eternity of My essence, I knew My love for thee . . .'[6] In recent times I have been wondering what eternity is. I mean, I have some idea, but I was wondering if you know any more about it? Because its common meaning is unending time, timelessness, or endless life after death with the immortality of the soul, but it must transcend this basic meaning."

They watched the sea for a long time. Finally, Hooman looked over at her. "You're twenty-seven, right? So how long has the universe been around?" he said.

"Billions of years."

"So, you've had twenty-seven years to understand billions of years of life . . . and that's just the time we know about. I think existence, maybe not time, or this kind of time, but the essential unity of all existence, has always been. It never had a beginning. Think about that. Can you imagine something never having a beginning?" he asked.

"No, not really."

"Is that a long time?"

Allison was quiet for a moment. "How can it be a long time if it never had a beginning?" she asked.

"Exactly! Talking about time is useless when trying to measure eternity. Try to imagine a clock with a second hand, like the watch on your wrist, that has always been going around . . . around and around . . . always. And the clock was always there, without a beginning. It just was. It was never born nor was it created."

"I can't. I mean, I can try, but it seems impossible, because my thoughts have a beginning and an end, so how can I think of something without a beginning unless I didn't have a beginning too. Like unless I was always there, uncreated, seeing the clock without a beginning too."

"True, and Allison, what I've said is just a linguistic device to try and free your mind from the bias of time as we know it on Earth. And that is why understanding this life, the exact nature of time and eternity, the next world, the true nature of love, and a range of other things is beyond our understanding, because at some point, we can't measure things beyond our finite limits.

In this life, all we can expect is a fleeting and veiled glimpse of these transcendent realities. Eternity is a different order of existence compared to time and space. Anyway, you get my meaning."

"Yes, I do. Fascinating. That is the first time in my life that I have ever thought of something not having a beginning," she said.

He continued, "You know, I have been thinking about your ideas of symmetry and asymmetry recently and applying them to time and even non-time. I have been researching it on the internet for a few months now, how matter reflects time without actually aging in the absolute sense."

"Oh, that is so cool. You are such a smart cookie," she chuckled

"As you may know, time is relative to gravity. Time runs slower where gravity is stronger, so you see, as you travel away from the Earth, time runs fractionally faster in space, which proves the relativeness of the relationship between time and space, or that gravity warps space and time equally and there is no time separate from space; time is the duration of space and matter relative to distance—spatial depth—and velocity. And our understanding of time allows us to measure and predict change and motion in space, like the spin of the Earth, on your old watch there"—which he pointed to—"because there is symmetry between the spin of the Earth and your watch that allows you to navigate through spacetime."

Allison looked down at her watch for a moment, then back at his face.

"Further, time is symmetrical in even gravitational fields; the intervals between seconds, minutes, and hours are even wherever you go on Earth. And although time is asymmetrical relative to different planet's gravitational fields, where gravity bends time into different speeds, the difference, as I said before, is miniscule, so we may not notice this difference when gauging it with our senses. We would only know there was a difference in time if we were to compare clocks on Earth to those we might place on other planets.

"When thinking about this idea of time symmetry, I wondered about other worlds in eternity and if they might have nonlinear time with greater asymmetrical structures, like different times in different gravitational fields but even more flexible, with uneven time intervals, or the ability to speed up and slow down time in eternity in a way that is not possible on Earth—to stretch it or contract it. Since there is no gravity or space as we know it on Earth, then time or timelessness in eternity would be manifested by different and possibly unknowable realities within those other non-spacetime worlds. And I use the word 'time' in eternity purely as a conceptual construct, given that time does not exist there as we know it here, but I have to use some generalized idea of time since it is all I know. You see, even I can't escape the bias of time."

"Yeah, no, that's fine. I understand what you mean. You are grappling with ideas that are without much context in this world."

"Yes, and as I said before, I call this concept of time nonlinear time, lateral time, or timelessness—three aspects of the same thing—but it is not really time that is passing because nonlinear time is transcendent and unchanging in its base configuration relative to our universe. And this might relate somehow to the four worlds mentioned in *The Seven Valleys*. I have also wondered if we might be able to have objective time and subjective time, experienced by each soul, which might be continually syncing back into a main, objective timeline, collectively accepted as 'the main kind of time' that is shared by all and with all lateral branches of subjective time running parallel to that main timeline.

"This might mean that nonlinear time is far more perceptual and subjective than time on Earth. Like the wavelengths of light, time might be spectral in nature, or there might be different flavors of time or time-lessness where one person's second is different from another person's second, where one plus one is not two but something else, strange and beautiful. As an example, one person's second could be nine hours and another's nine years, and yet when they sync back into objective time, their second is the same, which is to say that both nine hours and nine years both passed by in a single second. So an asymmetric experience of time by two souls finds symmetry on the main timeline . . . are you following me?"

"Totally."

"Good, and as a soul progresses up, notions of time as we know it on Earth may dissolve gradually as it passes through stages in nonlinear time, adjusting slowly to relative timelessness, where the past or future become perfectly symmetrical with both a forward and back-ward arrow in timelessness, because time for us on Earth is asymmet-rical relative to the past and the future; this is due to the forward direction of time. The future is almost never the same as the past, relatively speaking, and the universe evolves rather than devolves; it moves from simpler to more complex states. And although there is a lot a cyclical symmetry, or gravitational symmetry, between the past and the future, like the seasons, time on Earth is mostly asymmetrical."

Allison looked down at her watch again and tried to imagine the second hand moving at different speeds, uneven asymmetrical intervals, or skipping over certain intervals or just stopping in absolute stillness, where all motion in space might stop too and then magically start again after a moment of undefined timeless stillness, and then moving back-ward; she imagined the whole universe moving in reverse.

She looked at the sea for a moment and then said, "As you walk into the future, you will realize you have been walking into the past. All roads are forward in every direction, even when they go backward; the past finds perfect symmetry in the future and the reverse."

"Yes. Wait here. I brought *The Seven Valleys* with me. There is a quote about this, and I want to quote it correctly." He stood up and walked back to the shack. After a few moments, he came back with *The Seven*

Valleys. He sat down and flicked through the pages until he found the passage he was searching for. He read:

> "'. . . the denizens of the city of immortality, who dwell in the celestial garden, see not even "neither first nor last": They fly from all that is first and repulse all that is last. For these have passed over the worlds of names and, swift as lightning, fled beyond the worlds of attributes'" [7]

"And maybe eternity begins only partially when a soul reaches the Valley of Unity, as the relativities of beginnings and endings fade and our perceptions of time and space change. On Earth our body is trapped by time, but our mind is not."

She was silent for a while. "The body confines the mind to time."

He smiled. "Yes. Anyway, it's all speculation on my part, but it's interesting, don't you think?"

"What you've said is amazing." She had found a new dimension to her experience in the British Museum—her perception of time had been different as she lay on the floor looking up at the sky through the glass ceiling in the museum; it had seemed to have stretched and slowed. And then there was her dream of Mona in the world to come, where Mona had said that time in eternity was different from Earth, maybe nonlinear and lateral time as Hooman had said.

"Do you think time and space are an illusion at some level? I mean, are we really surrounded by timelessness, or is our world built on an unchanging foundation?" asked Allison.

"I think time is objective but finite, but perception plays a big role in creating how we experience time and space, so only our intellect can see aspects of the true foundation of time, whereas our senses cannot. Beyond that foundation we are surrounded by non-spacetime, but we cannot see or access it directly; we can, for the most part, only infer its existence. Like it says in *The Seven Valleys*, there is no real beginning or end to anything. So, if we can understand how we perceive time and change, then we will be able to understand how aspects of it are mutually constructed illusion."

"Yes, I agree. I suppose our body cannot be freed from earthly objective time, but our imagination and intellect can be freed. Like you just said."

Hooman didn't respond to her last comment. He looked at the sea again.

She looked at the sea and thought about the cultural and social notions of time that were used in everyday language to refer to and navigate through our world: the age of a child, the age of an evolutionary time period, or the diverse geological ages of the Earth, and that the conceptual structures attached to time and aging had illusionary and limited reference points that were a surface reflection of spacetime; they were objective on one level but conceptually relative on another level.

So, what the senses saw was only the surface of time, given that all matter was constructed and deconstructed dynamically from moment to moment as matter and energy continually changed their states (without actually being created or destroyed, which reflected the law of the conservation of energy and mass), and all matter appeared, on the surface, to be aging at diverse rates (molecular and biological), but this was not an indication of true infinite non-time.

Hooman continued, "I have been researching one of the as yet unproved string theories called 'supersymmetry.' It is attempting to find spacetime symmetry between particles in the Standard Model and sets of symmetric twins called 'superpartners.'"

"Oh, that sounds really interesting."

Yep, certainly is . . . and from what I understand, atoms, subatomic particles, and strings—the constituent indivisible parts of subatomic particles—do not age or get old as we understand it in daily life. We infer the age of matter from the relative configurations and interactions between atoms—molecular bonds—which have only relative and finite beginnings and endings as they transition from state to state but remain completely unchanging in their base configurations: the numbers of electrons, neutrons, and protons per atom, and the different vibrational frequencies of the strings that make up subatomic particles, like quarks, leptons, or bosons. So, atoms and their constituent parts are eternal and ageless as they paradoxically pass through, and are, *time*, and appear to be changing on one level but are not changing on another level; being just tiny vibrating strings or membranes that haven't stopped vibrating since the Big Bang."

Allison looked down at her vintage watch again. It gave the illusion of being old, yet both her body and the watch were made of atoms, like

Hooman had said before, that had not aged for billions of years. She looked at the gold leaf that had worn away over many years. The gold atoms were the same age that they had been from the moment they had been created inside stars. They had a finite beginning but no absolute end (total nothingness) and were ageless; some notable exceptions being antimatter, that converts matter into energy, but even this energy is not destroyed in the process. So, her watch had then only the subjective patina of time. And her body had been in existence for twenty-seven years biologically, but at the level of atoms, subatomic particles, and strings, it had not aged even a single second. Strangely, her watch would most probably outlive her as her body, with its complex organic molecules, was more prone to aging and death than the watch. So, she realized that the secrets and illusions of time could be found within the molecular bonds between atoms, because while atoms remained unchanged in their base configuration (protons, neutrons and electrons) and with regard to their basic atomic attributes, particularly light and energy, the molecular bonds that bound them together were always changing, and thus they reflected time and change more readily. The human body was a good example. Most of it was made from atoms of hydrogen, carbon, nitrogen, and oxygen in addition to an array of other elements. From these were formed more complex organic molecular bonds: proteins, fats, glucose, DNA, and many others; the covalent bonds were the only ones she could remember from her high school science class. Upon death these bonds break down, and all the complex organic molecules return all their originating atomic and molecular parts.

Allison thought that maybe time was the mask of eternity, which meant that we are surrounded by unchanging, timeless non-duality, which creates the illusion of time and change; we needed that "illusion" for purely psychological reasons as we were born, reached middle age, then grew old and died. From this strange illusion came the spiritual development of the individual soul and the advancement of human civilizations throughout history. Consequently, the past had not disappeared; it had gone nowhere but had only changed its atomic and molecular configurations and had always existed in the present as had the future, which was not out there waiting to happen, but rather here in the present among us as atoms continually changing their molecular states and moving forward through time toward the "future present."

Allison was staring at the sea and turning over these ideas when Hooman passed her the book and pointed to a particular section of the text:

> *Infer, then, from this the differences among the worlds. Though the worlds of God be infinite, yet some refer to them as four: the world of time, which hath both a beginning and an end; the world of duration, which hath a beginning but whose end is not apparent; the world of primordial reality, whose beginning is not to be seen but which is known to have an end; and the world of eternity, of which neither the beginning nor the end is visible. Although there are many differing statements as to these points, to recount them in detail would result in weariness. Thus some have said that the world of primordial reality hath neither beginning nor end, and have equated the world of eternity with the invisible, inaccessible, and unknowable Essence. Others have called these the worlds of the Heavenly Court, of the Celestial Dominion, of the Divine Kingdom, and of Mortal Existence.* [8]

She closed the book and handed it back to Hooman. "Thank you. That was really beautiful, and it gives me a better sense of the relationships between the worlds with reference to time and eternity."

She was fascinated by the idea that humanity had been within the mind of God for a very long time, that is not actually time, and not just "eternity," but "ancient eternity." And that God's love was now manifest in this world after all that endless non-time, which meant that there must be something special about this particular era and this particular world. Now the mask of eternity was being removed to a degree to reveal a reality and an existence of vast unending splendor: a face of formless marshmallow light.

Allison returned to the present moment. She was unconsciously looking at the sun, and, strangely, it did not hurt her eyes. She could look into the splendor of the sun now and see it anew as a symbol of God's unequaled reality and a veil that hid his staggering beauty in the created worlds.

Hooman stood up and looked back at the shack. He turned to her. "Well, how about we go down to the beach? Do you want to walk? Or are you tired?" he said.

"No. I'd love to go for a walk."

"Great! Then let's go." She watched him walk over the dunes toward the shack. He placed *The Seven Valleys* on a small stool next to the door. He then picked up Allison's flip-flops, which were on the ground next to the stool.

He came back. "Here, put these on," he said as he threw the pair of tattered red flip-flops at her feet. He had a pair of gray flip-flops on his own feet.

Taking her shoes off, she poured the sand out, then walked back to the shack and placed them near the door. She walked back over the dunes toward him. He was waiting for her on the top of the last dune. She took his hand. They descended the dune together and approached the water. At the edge of the water, they left their flip-flops behind on the sand. She walked into the waves up to her knees and let the water soak into her dress.

She turned to him.

"It's beautiful. The water and the air," he said.

"Yes . . . it is."

The current pulled at her legs. She looked down at the swirling haze of sand-filled water rushing past her obscured feet.

"It's strong," he said.

"Yes, we can't swim here . . . it's dangerous with the undertow. But you can swim when we get to Cairns tomorrow."

"How long will it take to drive there?"

"A day, I figure, maybe more . . . it depends. Do you want to see anything on the way? We could go south for a day and see Fraser Island, which is similar to this but with a few nice inland lakes, or we could just go straight north without seeing much until we reach Cairns."

"Well, I don't know if there is anything to see. What do you want to do?"

"I think get up early and drive straight."

"Okay. Fine by me."

She stared down at her feet again. The water was clear now as the current had changed direction and momentarily reflected the ephemeral shadows of the rippling water cast on the sand. In the pit of her stomach, she felt a barely perceptible affirmation: the body's precognition. Then her conscious mind caught up with her body, and the word that came to the fore in an exuberant tone was "patience." Years of waiting for the right person had finally elapsed and unfolded into this moment. Only she did not know that she had been waiting until now. It seemed as if Hooman had been with her for her entire life. As she looked into his eyes, she saw her own reflection on the curve of his eye, and there was no past or future without him.

The day slipped into dusk as they walked farther up the coastline. And as dusk began to morph into darkness, in the last remnants of light, they went back to the shack for fishing gear. Allison caught several fish. The fish found their way into foil and glowing coals along with some potatoes.

———

An hour later the smell of the fish and potatoes floated in the air. Hooman got up. He walked toward the writing room. As he walked along the track, he heard her voice intone a prayer. He was about to return down the track and let her finish without interruption when something in him decided to stay and listen, so he left the path and sat down on the crest of a dune. His eyes searched the darkness for a glimmer of the horizon, but by now it had faded into night. As he listened to the sound of the ocean mingled with Allison's voice, his eyes adjusted to the low light. He found a dim edge of the sea and a beginning of the sky. The glow of the town south of the property was also visible on the horizon. He strained to hear the order of words in the prayer. In time, he caught the stream of words midway through:

O Thou Who art the sole Desire of them that have recognized Thee, and the Object of the adoration of the entire creation, not to suffer them, now that Thou hast attracted them by Thy most exalted Word, to be far removed from the Tabernacle which Thou hast reared up by Thy name, the All-Glorious . . .

Her words disappeared into the sound of several large waves crashing to the shore; he picked up the continuation at:

. . . assist Thy servant who hath turned towards Thee, and hath spoken forth Thy praise, and determined to help Thee. Fortify, then, his heart, O my God, in Thy love

and in Thy Faith. Better is this for him than all that hath been created on Thine earth, for the world and whatsoever is therein must perish, and what pertaineth unto Thee must endure as long as Thy most excellent names endure. By Thy Glory! Were the world to last as long as Thine own kingdom will last, to set their affections upon it would still be unseemly for such as have quaffed, from the hands of Thy mercy, the wine of Thy presence; how much more when they recognize its fleetingness and are persuaded of its transience. The chances that overtake it, and the changes to which all things pertaining unto it are continually subjected, attest its impermanence.

Whosoever hath recognized Thee will turn to none save Thee, and will seek from Thee naught else except Thyself. Thou art the sole Desire of the heart of him whose thoughts are fixed on Thee, and the highest Aspiration of whosoever is wholly devoted unto Thee.

No God is there beside Thee, the Almighty, the Help in Peril, the All-Glorious, the Most Powerful.[9]

The prayer ended there, and it seemed like the right place, as the intonation on the last word expressed its expected cadence.

The door to the writing room opened. Allison turned the light off, then stepped out. He got up and walked toward her.

"Sorry, I didn't want to intrude. I was waiting for you to finish. The fish and potatoes are ready, I think."

"Oh, good. Let's go see."

They walked back down the track to the fire.

———

At midnight they went to bed. The sound of the ocean crashing into the coast kept her awake for a while as she lay next to Hooman. The bed was parallel to the coastline, and, through a hole in the shack wall, she observed the dark sea. In her imagination she visualized stars that were mirrored on patches of wet sand and a thin layer of water that was receding back into the ocean.

Fragments of the various conversations they had had during the day replayed themselves in her mind. She thought about endless nonlinear time and, if there was such a thing, timeless symmetry.

Eventually, she drifted into sleep with the sound of the rough sea as a backdrop. In a dream the sea's violence receded as it spread out submissively on the flat sand beneath the dunes. The dunes cradled the shack and its occupants. Still asleep in her dream, she thought she had woken from it, but she was still caught in her dream.

She left the shack and walked down the dunes to the calm water. She waded into the waves. She dove and swam in the darkened sea and knew she would never come back to the shore. She had passed a significant barrier in her life that was inherently about love: the unfathomable and unsearchable kind; she was passing into the Great Ocean.

20

ON THE ROAD

The wayfarer, after traversing the high planes of this supernal journey, entereth into THE CITY OF CONTENTMENT. *In this valley he feeleth the breezes of divine contentment blowing from the plane of the spirit. He burneth away the veils of want, and with inward and outward eye perceiveth within and without all things the day of "God will satisfy everyone out of His abundance."[1] From sorrow he turneth to bliss, and from grief to joy, and from anguish and dejection to delight and rapture.[2]*

— BAHÁ'U'LLÁH, *THE SEVEN VALLEYS*

The next day the sun had not yet emerged over the horizon, and what light there was lit up the pre-dawn sky with a pale light. He took one last mental snapshot of the sea and sky over the dunes before walking up to the door. The padlock on the door of the shack clicked shut as Hooman locked it in place. He put the key under a rock near the door and followed Allison through the tea trees as she walked up the track toward the clearing where the cars were parked. Her suitcase trailed behind her. It kept bogging down in the sand, and she had to drag it with more force. He saw her bare feet plunging down into the dry, squeaky sand with each step. After a short walk through the tea tree scrub, they arrived at the clearing. Hooman began to pack the luggage into the hire car in which they had driven from Brisbane Airport.

"Hey, why don't we take my Holden up to Cairns?" she said.

"I've never seen such a sorry-looking mode of transport. It's completely rusted out," Hooman remarked.

"Hey, steady on. I drove this car around Australia. It's been a faithful companion all these years."

"I'm amazed that it's still going."

"It has a completely new engine now, or reconditioned, but basically new. I drove it up from Melbourne several years ago. Jasper uses it from time to time."

"I suppose you do have a sentimental attachment to this car."

"Let's drive it. We can pick up the hire car on the way back."

"Sure, why not." He laughed. "I hope we make it back. Where is the key?" he said.

"It should be in the glove box."

Hooman began to load the bags into the old car. When he got into the driver's seat, he noticed immediately a crystal cluster glued to the dashboard. The light coming through the shards flickered as he looked into the formation. On the passenger's side of the dashboard were a few origami birds, pure in the morning light. As Allison got into the passenger's side, Hooman saw that a section of plywood had been placed on the floor under her feet.

Allison obviously saw him staring at the plywood and said, "There's a large hole in the floor." She smiled. He then saw her looking at the paper birds on the dashboard.

"Hey, do you want to hear one of my poems?"

"Sure."

She reached out and took one of the origami birds and began to open it up until it unfolded into a flat piece of paper. She began to read the poem:

"The Waves and the Sky"

The waves are illiterate.
The sky is illiterate.
They know no pain.

That is our domain.

That we should feel pain when we are amongst such immeasurable beauty.
That the sky should not see its reflection.
That the waves feel no sun bearing down.

The waves and sky read no words, but they are the Word.
What need does the Word have but to be read by others?
All things are built with words.
All things are built into a house of words.
A shelter for the illiterate seeking the illiterate sky and waves.
For those that know not themselves.
Know not the sky or waves.

The sky is comforted by the ignorant looking up.
The sky feels joy that it will never be understood except by the blind.

Hooman was quiet for a while before saying, "Wow. So beautiful. Unfathomable too."

"Thank you."

Hooman started the engine and then backed up before driving down a narrow sandy road.

Fifteen minutes later they emerged from the coastal bushland onto an asphalt road that took them onto a larger road leading them north-ward toward Cairns.

After a short time on the highway, Hooman said, "Is the road illiterate too?"

———

Dark water reflected a soft, open sky. Gentle distortions in the water spread out from the boat as it maintained an uncertain equilibrium against the pull of the Earth.

It had taken a day to drive to Cairns. Now, on the following day, a few hours after midday, they stood on a dive boat.

"Look. It's so bright and clear. The reflection," Hooman said.

Allison continued to look down into almost still water.

He turned away from his reflection in the water and smiled at Allison.

Allison said, continuing her subterranean gaze, "Yes, it is. It's like a two-way mirror. If there was light in the ocean, shining up from the bottom, then the reflection would disappear, and the world above could see the world below: the world beyond the mirror of this world."

She looked up at Hooman and followed his gaze, which moved diagonally along the water until he was looking at the harbor and its boats, moorings, and the jetties.

"Then the upside-down world would disappear," he said.

She laughed softly. He was referring to the reflection of Cairns harbor, which intersected with the real world. They were like two symmetrical twins, one living on the surface of the water and the other above it. "Yes, it would," she replied.

As she stared vertically down into the mirror of blue and the sunshine reflecting in it, the engine started up and broke the reflections they saw into fractured and twisted pieces. The captain began to outline the day's itinerary to a large contingent of Japanese tourists gathered around him. They listened in dutiful silence. He uttered a greeting in Japanese with a thick Australian accent.

Hooman went to sit down at a table near the back of the boat.

She joined him.

The boat began to move toward the harbor channel. She looked at him. "A beautiful day," she said.

"Yes," he confirmed.

———

The boat reached the first stop after forty-five minutes. A female dive supervisor took the children snorkeling near the back of the boat while the adults strapped on dive tanks, masks, and flippers and dropped out of sight to the reef below. Allison and Hooman were the only adults not diving with tanks, and after the main group had gone, they sat on the back of the boat with their legs dangling in the water. He had his flippers and mask on. She put a flipper on her foot, then, resting her chin on her knee for a moment, looked out at the gentle waves around the boat.

"Hey, let's go," he said. She put the other flipper and mask on, and they slipped into the water.

The reef below was a colorful and otherworldly sight and a fully self-contained world with its alien visitors floating above it. She reached out and took his hand. She felt the texture of his skin and his slender fingers.

———

A few hours later the boat came back to the harbor. From there they drove up to the tablelands to a hill town—Kuranda. As they drifted through the town, Allison commented on the changes to Kuranda since her childhood vacations. She had noted over the years an increased commercialization of the place, especially the tourist money, which paradoxically kept the town alive but also killed it in subtle and obvious ways. Several times, as they went from shop to shop, she picked up what appeared to be local handcrafted items or stuffed koalas and turned them over to reveal a tag. It invariably said: "Made in China."

She turned to him. "Isn't it funny, the obvious irony of a so-called genuine Australian experience? That tourists come to Australia to immerse themselves in its unique identity only to buy a stuffed koala made in China. Wouldn't that be ironic? Or singing the 'Star-Spangled Banner' to a Chinese-made flag. It would be a strange new kind of global patriotism," she said.

Allison observed Hooman listening carefully to her and seeing how intense she was about the globalization of the Australian and American economies.

They finished exploring the main township.

"Let's go to the market. I have many sweet memories of it as a child. You always say you want to know more of my childhood," she said.

"Yes, I do."

———

As they began to walk into the market, Allison observed the tropical rainforest surrounding them. Nothing about the forest seemed to have changed since her childhood. They walked down a slight hill through the main avenue, which was mostly fruit and vegetable stalls. Other stalls were selling local handicrafts, old stamps, rare bottles, and many other more modern products that were not part of her memories. A blue Ulysses butterfly flew past them. It flew from the present into a past memory and melded with all her childhood memories of the market.

———

Allison dragged her father by the arm. They vanished from the sight of Mum and Paul into the rainforest to find one particular stall, which was situated at the very end of the market. This shopping expedition was on the pretense of getting bananas, but what she really wanted most was to see the stall owner's gray beard cascading down his bare chest. His beard invariably had twigs stuck in it.

On this day, four days before her twelfth birthday, they found the stall, and Allison asked for two pounds of bananas. She watched as a stray green tree ant found its way onto his beard. After being crushed, it released the oddest aroma. The old man had waved the crushed ant under her nose, and then with a huge laugh, and to her special delight, he popped the ant into his mouth.

"Yum, yum . . . do you want one too?" the old man asked her.

After being persuaded by her dad not to eat them, she looked around for more green ants. A few steps away from the stall, she crouched down near the base of a large strangler fig tree and watched weaving lines of green ants moving up into the canopy. The tree's leaves cut and layered descending light into shifting and abstract patterns on the ground.

———

Allison remembered that time vividly and realized there was a purity of motive in her actions as a child that she had lost as an adult. The images in her mind seemed like a life review from the Egyptian weighing of the heart ceremony. She thought that we did not die at some unknown point in the future; we were slowly dying and being born every day. So life was then one long, unending review until all the images and sensations that made up our life faded into the abstract luminescence of eternity, and we emerged like the Phoenix from the ashes of the cyclical sun. Dying each day as we slept and being reborn on each dawn as we awoke.

She was shocked out of this reverie. "What memories from your childhood are most resonant for you?" Hooman asked.

She explained that memory in the market, and they walked toward the stall of the old man, but he was no longer there. Nor were there any green ants walking up the strangler fig tree near the stall. She wondered what had happened to him. Was he still alive and living near or in Kuranda, or had he merged into eternity and diverged from this life to remain only in her memories?

"That year, my parents had decided to spend the school vacation period in an RV park on the fringes of central Cairns. Those vacations have a strong resonance now."

They walked over to the strangler fig tree, and Allison sat on one of the protruding roots. Hooman remained standing and asked about her family. She looked up at him. "My father arrived in Australia in his early twenties. Most of his family were still living in Rome, so there were no relatives on my father's side of the family to spend Christmas with. My mother came from a fourth generation of Australian farmers. Her parents were dead by then, but she had siblings who were spread out all over the country, so a traveling Christmas developed into a tradition. Evolving initially from a need to visit my mother's relatives in Cairns, it became something different after a few years—a trip for its own sake, as Mum's sister and her husband sold the farm and moved down south to Brisbane; they had owned a sugarcane farm near central Cairns."

Allison stood up, and they turned around and began to walk back up the hill. Allison stopped for a moment and looked up at the canopy. She then turned to Hooman and said, "I remember sitting on the edge of a pool in the RV park.

"It was Christmas Eve, and my legs were dangling in the water, and I had been staring at my feet for a while, then when I looked up, there was a boy on the other side of the pool. He was standing there looking at me with an intense, expressionless face. I smiled and waved. He waved back and said hello. I had not seen him in the RV park before, and afterward I learned that he had arrived that day after a long road trip from Perth in Western Australia. He sat on the edge of the pool and stared into the water. We didn't speak for a while, then gradually, we began to talk in a shy, stilted way. After a while, he slipped into the water and swam over to me. After a few minutes, I felt more relaxed, and our conversation became more natural. It was strange, but for the first time I had met a male version of myself. After that day, we were close friends for the remainder of the vacation. We pretty much went everywhere together."

They left Kuranda's market and came down from the tablelands. They went south, away from central Cairns suburbia, and drove through farmland on the outskirts of the town. They passed the cane farm that Allison's aunt had owned. She pointed at it as they drove by. "I used to walk through the cane fields on my own."

"Where are we going?" Hooman asked after a while.

"Behana Creek," she said. At the exact moment that she had answered him, she saw a bridge ahead with a battered sign—Behana Creek.

They passed over the bridge and turned right off the highway onto a narrow dirt road. They drove along the edge of a cane field that hugged the curves of the creek. Ahead of them were lush green hills that formed another edge where the cane fields stopped, and in the distance a forest arced toward the tablelands. The creek widened out considerably, and Allison stopped the car.

"We're here . . . I used to come here too when I was young. See that swing," she said, pointing to a strangler fig tree on the other bank. Behind the tree was another cane field. The water running past the tree was only a thin strip under the swing, no more than a foot deep and seven feet wide.

"I presume there was more water when you used the swing," he said.

"Oh, yes. In the wet season the water is much higher. At least up to my shoulder in height."

They got out of the car and walked over six yards of smooth river stones to the edge of the water. Her mind drifted into the past.

———

Allison had asked her parents if they could take her new friend to the creek. Her mother had asked the boy's parents, and they agreed. She remembered the family driving through the cane fields along the same highway that she and Hooman had just taken.

The three kids were sitting in the back seat. She was between Paul and the boy. The full light was on the boy's face, and her eyes moved around the contours of light and shade on his body. The wind coming from the open window pushed his hair around. She watched him for a few minutes as he looked out at the cane farms passing by. In the half hour that it had taken to drive from central Cairns, he had said very little. Occasionally, he looked at her and smiled, and she felt immediately how self-contained he was.

She wanted to reach out and take his hand but felt another part of her resisting this urge. They came to the bridge, and after crossing it, they turned onto the dirt road. At this time of year, the creek was swollen with deep, clear water coming from the tablelands above them. They all got out of the car, and her parents started to carry coolers with food and drink to the edge of the water.

She, Paul, and the boy immediately walked into the water and swam over to the swing on the other side of the creek. They sat on the tangled roots of the strangler fig as each took a turn on the swing. After ten minutes, she suggested to the boy that they swim upstream. She pointed to a sandy bank in the distance. They both plunged into the cool water and began to swim upstream. Allison was looking at the bottom of the creek as she swam. She could see small Barramundi fish swimming over the large river stones on the bottom of the creek. Paul was hanging upside down on the swing by his knees.

Hauling their bodies onto the sandy bank, the boy and Allison sat shivering. The swing was a pendulum in time, swinging back and forth over the water. They both watched Paul swing back and forth, back and forth, before somersaulting into the water. The boy shifted closer to her. He reached out and held her hand.

That instant she remembered now with the same sensation of yesteryear flooding her nervous system, and it was a turning point in loving another human being. Loving someone other than a family member and its relevance was enhanced, as it was at a time before any sexual awareness had appeared in her mind. There was an indefinable purity to the relationship. The accumulation of several relationships' worth of experience and a fair deal of sentimental projection had elevated that moment in hindsight; she tried to see that memory without the filters of an adult mind.

And she then remembered leaving her boyfriend behind, which was a new and unfamiliar sensation. They talked about sending letters. She sent several. He replied, but after three letters he stopped writing. When the family had arrived back in Melbourne, she thought of visiting him in Perth. She could take the train. She imagined herself taking in the vast, silent desert on the way. But this desire was never fulfilled.

———

Now, at the creek, she remembered the beginnings of love, and she strained to remember the boy's name. And it was clear, too, that Hooman was the beginning of love, but also the end of another kind of love—a love formed within innocence and never tested by the harsher realities of life. The boy had disappeared into Perth, and Hooman had emerged from that city, so there was a degree of circularity and symmetry in time.

———

The yacht left Magnetic Island on the morning of Friday, April 9, 1993. The American couple that Allison had met on the previous night had hired a crew to help sail their boat from Long Island, New York, through the Caribbean and into the Pacific via the Panama Canal. They had been island hopping for several months—staying at American Samoa, Fiji, Vanuatu, and New Caledonia, just to mention a few of the main islands they visited—before reaching the east Australian coast near the Whitsunday Islands.

On the first day, they sailed to Orpheus Island. Allison spent several hours at the front of the boat staring at the ocean and the cloudless sky, smelling the sea spray. She had taken many photos of the shoreline and the expanse of the empty ocean with the Leica camera. She also took shots of the boat, which represented a kind of wealth that she had never seen up close before. After a while, Jennifer came and sat next to Allison. Jenifer's husband spent the time steering the yacht while the crew adjusted the sails and the rigging. She closed the book she was reading and smiled.

"What is your book about?" Jennifer asked.

"Oh, it's about the collective unconscious."

Allison raised the book, and Jennifer read it aloud. "*The Archetypes and the Collective Unconscious* by Carl Jung. I have heard of Jung vaguely, but what are the collective unconscious and archetypes?"

"They are supposed to be the foundational symbols and concepts that make up individual consciousness. They are inherited from the collective unconscious, which is all the psychic experience over the course of human evolution."

"You have lost me already."

"Well, instead of the idea that the mind is a blank slate at birth, a *tabula rasa*, we inherit a psychic structure of ideas, which forms a foundation for individual consciousness. Jung calls them archetypes, or primal ideas."

"Can you give me an example of an archetype?"

"Some archetypal opposites are 'light versus darkness,' 'meaning versus absurdity,' or 'chaos versus order.' Or there are individual archetypes like 'the mother,' 'the hero,' or 'the trickster.' Even the 'self,' or our core ideas of self, are an archetype. Then there is 'the other,' which is either another 'self' or the collective of 'selves,' society or culture. But my problem is that Jung assumed the archetypes were inherited from generation to generation, both through nature and nurture and that a child's mind was predisposed to archetypes even before birth. Even Plato's universal forms were working on the assumption that consciousness was built on an invisible and transcendent psychic structure beyond, but connected to, the physical world. And if this is not true, according to contemporary science, then how do you encode the collective unconscious or even consciousness itself into the structure of a human's DNA? In other words, does spirit or consciousness arise from and descend back into matter, or is spirit inserted into matter? Does consciousness cease when the body dies— the idea being that consciousness is just a property of matter—or does it transcend matter and death?"

"Again, I have no idea what you are talking about."

"Sorry. I am probably boring you."

"Not at all. I am just not much of an intellectual."

Allison put the book down and smiled. "Does what makes a person an individual, different from others, die when the body dies, or does this personhood essence—some would call it 'the soul'—live on into eternity after a body's physical death."

"Oh, I see. I think I understand."

"What part of Long Island do you live in?" Allison said.

"Westhampton Beach. And we have another vacation house on the beach at Montauk, the very extreme end of Long Island."

"Is Westhampton Beach a part of the Hamptons?"

"Yes, it is."

"Ahh . . . cool. I think I know where that is, roughly. Is that near Jackson Pollock's studio?"

"Yes, it is. He lived in East Hampton. I've been to his studio."

"Cool."

"Where are you traveling to?" Jennifer asked.

"Nowhere in particular. I am just traveling. I have given myself roughly a year to get back to Melbourne."

"Sounds like a good plan. We are going ashore at Orpheus Island to walk around some of the nature trails. You are welcome to join us if you want."

"Thanks, but I might walk on my own."

After half an hour, they came to the southern part of Orpheus Island. Allison swam to the beach, while the others took a small boat to another bay adjacent to the beach Allison had headed to. Once she reached the beach, Allison walked along it alone for half an hour, then sat in the water waist deep. The water was pure and clear with a light blue hue. She eventually swam back to the yacht over a reef, looking at the fish and coral on the way.

On the second day, they stopped at the larger Hinchinbrook Island. Allison walked along some of the sandy trails and raised boardwalks, which took her through mangrove estuaries and wetland and then thick rainforest, which melded into a mountain range along one end of the island. Toward the end of the day, they sailed on to Dunk Island, where they stayed overnight in Coconut Bay.

On the third day, they sailed out to different coral reefs, which collectively made up the Great Barrier Reef. Jennifer and her husband snorkeled on the reefs, and Allison followed behind them. By the end of the day, they arrived in Cairns harbor and docked at the main pier. Allison thanked the couple and the crew for taking her to Cairns. She gave Jennifer a hug before she stepped off the boat onto the pier.

She walked to a pay phone inside the Pier Shopping Centre complex. She called the Danish couple who were staying at a hostel nearby. They had parked the car in a parking lot behind the Pier complex, and after a short walk, Allison got into the car and drove through the suburbs of Cairns toward Mossman. On her way she made one stop at the RV park that she had stayed at during her childhood. As far as she could tell, it had not changed much since then.

On the first night, she slept in the back of the car in the parking lot near Mossman Gorge.

In the morning she walked through the rainforest until she came to the Mossman River. At the gorge she stripped down to her bikini and floated in the cold, clear water amongst large granite boulders. She looked up at the canopy of the rainforest surrounding her. After swimming for an hour, she followed one of the trails for a few hours, then came back to the parking lot. She drove on to the Daintree River, where she caught a car ferry and then drove on to Diwan, looking for a bed and breakfast.

The road was only paved for a few miles, and once she hit the dirt road, the car became bogged at various points along the road. After some effort, she came to Diwan and asked around if there were any good places to stay. Someone at the local supermarket suggested a bed and breakfast buried deep in the rainforest.

After walking along a track for fifteen minutes, she found the place. It was built over a creek. Her bedroom and a timber deck sat on the edge of the water. She took a photo of her feet dangling over the side of the deck, partially submerged in the water.

When night came, she lay on her bed, looking up at the dark sky. A storm came in from the ocean, and she looked at the lightning for a while before falling asleep to the sound of water in the creek, heavy rain, and occasionally a clap of thunder. Storm sounds and lightning never frightened her; their patterns absorbed her.

21

A CHARCOAL HOUSE

O friend, till thou enter the garden of these inner meanings, thou shalt never taste of the imperishable wine of this valley. And shouldst thou taste of it, thou wilt turn away from all else and drink of the cup of contentment; thou wilt loose thyself from all things and bind thyself unto Him, and lay down thy life in His path and offer up thy soul for His sake. And this, even though in this realm there is no "all else" that thou needst forget: "God was alone; there was none else besides Him."[1] For on this plane the traveller witnesseth the beauty of the Friend in all things.[2]

— BAHÁ'U'LLÁH, *THE SEVEN VALLEYS*

The new house took fourteen months to renovate. It was the burnt-out brownstone that they had found in Harlem roughly two and a half years earlier. Allison lifted her shirt to expose her pregnant belly to the sunlight that streamed through the bay window. Elliot was alone with her, waiting for the others to return. Elliot had become a friend now of Allison and Hooman's rather than simply a convivial colleague of Hooman's. Allison was staring down at brown, red, and yellow leaves in the street below. The leaves drifted in circles, interlocking eddies, converging and diverging.

"The change of seasons here—they're so well defined. More than what I'm used to in Australia. You know where you are in the year," Allison said.

"That's true enough," Elliot answered.

"I've been walking around the park a lot over the past few months." She looked down the street at the park. "And I've recently got into the habit of dragging my feet through the leaves. A little ceremony for every day. Sometimes I just sit on the benches for a few hours looking at the trees, or I sleep. It's funny. The other day, I woke up on a bench, and two old men had arrived in my sleep. They were stretched out, dozing on the benches on either side of mine. They had all their worldly belongings in two shopping carts. In another context and time, they might have been travelers seeking wisdom. I don't know why I thought that, but really, they are placeless citizens, of a fallen society, a dream of mutual deception. That's America."

"So, are you a New Yorker yet?" Elliot said.

"I guess I like being a foreigner here. I like being the *other*. It's more real to me."

The memory of the two homeless men mixed with the smell of fresh paint. The stark, refracted light from the white interior of the house pushed through her mind. These fragments and impressions of the newly renovated house shimmered in her consciousness, but the house represented two disjointed worlds that were only separated with a few thin sheets of glass in the bay window; the house was a luxuriant pod transported from the wealthier parts of downtown and disguised with a Harlem exterior.

Elliot interrupted the detached contemplation in Allison's mind. "I notice your accent has changed though . . . in places. You say just the odd word here and there with a New York accent. You have a mixed Australian and American accent, like Hooman. Have you noticed?" Allison did not answer her. She was still lost inside her mind, in a sense of detachment that was akin to looking through her eyes as if they were windows from within a hollow head. The leaves outside were swirling slowly now. The wind's intensity had faded.

"So, you're not a New Yorker, then?" Elliot said.

Allison watched an African American child kicking the fall leaves in the gutter. He then crossed the street and walked up the front steps of a house diagonally opposite. An affinity between her and the boy bonded them instantly—his legs kicking leaves were her legs kicking leaves.

"Sorry, what did you say?"

"I said, you're not a New Yorker, then?"

"I guess I am. I mean, I live here, right? How does one qualify? I'm in transition, and a part of me has crossed into the American collective mind. It's a kind of social gravity, I suppose."

"Exactly, although I might have expressed it more simply." Elliot smiled.

"I'm losing my objectivity, though. It worries me. I watch TV, and things that I used to find odd, they don't seem outrageously different anymore."

Elliot laughed and shook her head. "God, you're funny. Why do you worry about things like that?"

"I don't know. It's like losing one's sight, don't you think? I'm becoming culturally blinded. Not only is the newness of everything fading here, but also the aura of cultural strangeness too. And I guess that point of blindness is where one becomes a citizen. Qualification is blindness: seeing in one way and not seeing in another way. Strange, eh? And I am part homeless too, a placeless citizen."

She watched Elliot swivel her head around and up, looking at the polished floorboards for a moment and then the stark walls. "I just can't believe this is the same place you guys first bought. And I see all Hooman's books are here now, and that white bird sculpture he bought when you were in London," Elliot said as she nodded once at the new purpose-built bookshelves that engulfed a whole wall on her left.

"Yes, I guess Hooman feels at home now. And it softens the sharp-ness of Nava's minimalistic approach."

But the place was still off-kilter to her, and it was only when she left the building for the street or park or any other place in Central Harlem that she felt at home, but not in the house itself. She had become de facto gentry by association with Hooman and Nava, and she guessed that this was the source of her discomfort about the place. She hadn't wanted to seem ungrateful to Nava and Hooman, so she had kept her thoughts to herself.

"Where is Hooman? And I thought Nava would be here today."

"He went to buy some baguettes for lunch. Nava won't be joining us after all. She's spending the weekend setting up her new office in Soho. And she lives downtown, really. She only sleeps here."

"New office?"

"You know she has her own business, right? It's been mainly solo over the years."

"Yes, I know."

"But now she's rebranding and expanding. A few other designers have joined her, and she has developed some links with a few big architectural firms.

The downstairs door clicked open, and Allison heard footsteps echo up the stairwell. "Hello . . . I have lunch for us."

After a few moments, he appeared in the doorway, then walked into the living room. "Hey, Elliot. Hi there!" He put the shopping bags on the kitchen island and then came toward the girls, dodging a tattered cardboard box and a spread of Allison's photographs on the floor. He kissed Allison, then leaning over, he hugged Elliot. "How are you?" he said.

"Fine, thanks." Elliot smiled.

"It's good to see you. I'm just going to unpack the shopping and take the toiletries upstairs. I also have a few things to print out . . . so I'll come down after and make you all some salad baguettes. Is that okay?"

Elliot responded, "Fine. No rush. If you have a copy of your latest writing efforts, I would like to read it over lunch. Just a skim read, and I'll give it back. Is it a book or an article?

Allison told me you are writing something."

"It's a book. I'll give you a copy to take home, and you can go through it at your leisure."

He waved and disappeared farther up the staircase. Allison listened for a few moments to his muffled footsteps in the rooms above.

The various periods in Allison's life were scattered across the floor in the form of photographs. Several boxes of personal items had been shipped recently from Australia. She had spent the morning exploring the ebb and flow of her past life. Many of the photos were of her road trip around Australia. She had started to order them into different piles, but half were still out of order.

"So, how is your photography project going?" Elliot said.

"Doing fine. Thanks for asking."

"What's happening? I mean, I know you've got a bunch of kids together, and you're taking photos, but what for exactly? What will you do with the photos they take?"

"I don't know if it's going to lead to anything particular. It's hard to tell so far, but for my own selfish reasons, I wanted to contribute, to do something positive and artistic in the community here. It might be an exploration of identity. And I have been thinking I might try and organize an exhibition for them eventually."

"Sounds good to me," Elliot said.

They were silent for a while as Allison watched a new BMW pull up in front of a house a few houses down on her side of the street. An African American couple with two children got out and went into the house. The house was one of several, including their own, that had been restored in the last year.

Elliot continued. "I know things are changing here in Harlem, with all the poverty and crime abating and all that, but it still freaks me out a little. After parking the car up the street, near Marcus Garvey Park, there was this gang hanging off the steps of a crumbling building. Their body language, well, it was intimidating, and—"

"When I walk past them, I try to say hello, to be friendly. Sometimes I stop and chat for a few minutes."

Elliot shook her head. "I don't know how you do that. I wanted to cross the street, but by the time I saw them, it was too late. I thought it would look suspicious if I crossed, and they might follow me or harass me. So I walked past and tried to look collected."

"Look, sometimes it's just a bunch of kids hanging out. Not every kid is in a gang, Elliot, and they aren't used to seeing too many Whites up here. It's still mainly an African American neighborhood. If you try to leave your preconceived ideas behind when you come here, you'll fare a lot better. Like the kids in my photography project. They were a little suspicious of my motives in the beginning, but now they try to protect me whenever we are out together. We went for a photo session several blocks north of 125th Street the other week, and they said to me, 'Oh Ms Bird, don't go down that street, it's not safe,' and 'You can't say things like that here, Ms Bird. People don't like it.' They were trying to educate me. Anyway, it's been a growth experience for them and me, I think. I'm obviously still naïve about many things here in Harlem. I'm learning about their world."

Elliot smiled and shook her head again. "Well, if it makes you happy, go for it, but I have to say it seems a bit crazy to me. What does Hooman say?"

"He wouldn't say anything discouraging. And it was my idea to move here, and he didn't object. Initially, Nava bought the property as an investment. So I guess he is fine. I know he worries about me sometimes when I do risky things. But hey! Didn't your grandparents come from the slums in the Lower East Side . . . in the 1920s, with all the grinding poverty of the time?"

"Yes, but it wasn't like Harlem is today," Elliot said.

"Why? How do you know that? There might have been a lot of similar problems for your grandparents."

Elliot's face looked thoughtful. "I'm not going to get into this conversation if you are going to lay traps for me. I'm not prejudiced. I understand the difficulties that African Americans face here in Harlem."

"Good. I am glad you understand that while you and I have options as Whites, many African Americans cannot escape the gravity of the poverty they face here and in many of the poorer African American neighborhoods in other American cities. We can leave this poverty at any time, at any moment, whereas they, for the most part, cannot. They continue to experience systemic racism, a lack of employment opportunities, and ultimately the ongoing gentrification of Harlem. And I just wanted to remind you of your background and to say, don't forget. And don't get bourgeoisie on me, that's all."

"Bourgeoisie! What do you call this house? You're a landowner here, Allison."

"Yes, but at least I'm reminded of the poverty every day when I step out on the street. Most people lock themselves away in cloistered communities, filtered from the extremes of economic and social diversity. They drift along in life without the least curiosity or care for the plight of the poor. The ignorance from Whites of the ongoing poverty that many African Americans must endure is almost worse than overt racism. They are still second-class citizens in many respects relative to employment and particularly with their incarceration rates in American jails; there is a relationship between poverty and crime. Had they had better opportunities like Whites, then there would not be these high incarceration rates. Often with the police, there is an assumption of guilt that African Americans have to endure."

Elliot smiled. The sound of Hooman's footsteps echoed down the stairwell. He came in with a smile on his face. "Right, okay, girls. Time for lunch. Sorry to keep you waiting. Oh, I forgot. I printed a copy for you. Wait a sec," he said. He turned and went back up to the top rooms. A few minutes later he came back with a hefty manuscript.

"Here," he said as he passed it to Elliot, "take your time. Any feedback would be welcome."

Elliot flicked over the title page, which said *Untitled*, and read the first few pages while Hooman walked back to the kitchen to start preparing lunch.

"I like these paragraphs. Very powerful, I think." Elliot read out loud:

"After 157 years of technological change and innovation, the world has become a global village. We can now see a melding of economic, cultural, and social diversity. But the financial benefits, in the main, are accessible only to a small percentage of individuals, companies, or nations who exploit the poverty in the rest of the world. The developing world subsidizes the lifestyle of wealthy nations; the rich stand on the shoulders of the poor. And consequently, wage slavery in the developing world is seen as an acceptable part of the free market system."

Elliot stopped there but continued to read to herself for a while.

Allison eventually interrupted her. "You see, Elliot, this is exactly the situation in Harlem but on a smaller scale. Hooman is looking at a global scale," Allison commented.

Elliot responded thoughtfully. "Yes . . . I suppose it is. Here. This next paragraph is good too," and she passed the manuscript over to Allison, who read it in her mind:

If we were to strip away the contradictory elements of human diversity that lead to disunity, then we would find a common paradigm of being human, which transcends language, place, and outward appearance. So within this pattern we will find a new concept of global citizenry emerging that addresses inequality and begins to underpin a notion of human rights that transcends nationhood. When this consciousness of oneness is fostered, then the current poverty subsidy, among other global inequities, begins to be seen for what it is: a by-product of a facile, decadent, and immature notion of humanity as being little more than a unit of consumption prey to world market forces and fed by consumer propaganda. Surely our humanity is broader and richer than this limited materialistic vision. And, in fact, a grander renaissance of spiritual values has already begun its inexorable rise and will in time overshadow the current global hedonism, which is already crumbling under its own unsustainable weight.

————

Lunch passed by. Elliot had read more of Hooman's manuscript as she ate, and they discussed the various ideas raised that pointed to global citizenship as a new paradigm of equality. Eventually, she made her excuses and headed back to her house in Queens. A few minutes after Elliot left, Hooman went upstairs to continue working on his manuscript for a couple of hours. Allison went back to the bay window. She stared at the leaves again. They were being pushed around the street by a slight breeze. And there was also a warm light that pushed through the bay window and into her body. After a while, the sun disappeared behind a bank of clouds, and she lay down and closed her eyes.

He shook her out of her sleep later in the day.

She sat up and said, "Let's go to the park. I need to drag my feet through the leaves. Like the boy across the street."

"It's a bit cold out, and the sun's gone now. Are you sure you want to go?"

"Yes. I've been cooped up today. I need to get out. Is that okay?"

"No problem. I'll go get your coat."

Descending the steps in front of the house, they were about to walk toward the park when the boy she had seen before lunch came out of the house on the opposite side of the street. When he reached the sidewalk, he looked up at Allison and Hooman.

She waved. "Hello." But he did not reply.

Stepping into the gutter, he stared back for a moment, then turned and walked away, dragging his feet through the red-brown fall leaves.

They walked on toward the park. "He must be shy. Have you seen him before?" Allison asked.

"No. But we haven't been here that long, so it's no surprise, I guess."

"I've never seen him before today, but I was thinking maybe I have seen him but didn't register it. He is so familiar somehow. I feel like I have already met him."

In the park they were about to walk past the recreation center when she stopped. "Hey! You walk on. I just want to see if any kids have shown an interest in my photography project."

Allison had left a register for names on the noticeboard in the center.

"Okay. I'll meet you near the steps," he said.

———

Hooman sat on a bench next to the base of the hill that inhabited the center of the park. The steps that led up the hill were only a short walk away from the bench. He felt a cold breeze on his face. He looked toward the top of the park at the swimming pool before looking at the amphitheater that was situated behind the recreation center.

With nothing pressing in his work schedule during the week, he found his mind quite free today. He was thinking of nothing and worried about nothing. Even the sketchy first draft of his book was not the burden it had been when he had first started. He had reread some of the sections that Elliot had read during lunch; the manuscript looked hopeful and coherent.

Looking around the park, which was relatively empty, he saw a few old men sitting on benches near the edge of the lawn area that was adjacent to the baseball pitch. He had noticed, when he drove past with Nava every day on his way to work, that they were almost always in the park. Some were retired and others destitute, and he had noted one man in particular who always sat on the same seat every day.

Beyond work, it was as if he had pushed back the mundane moments in his life, and all aspects of his day had found an integrated place. He smiled and recalled making lunch for the girls. The task was a humble pleasure rediscovered: cutting bread, arranging the cheese slices, lettuce, tomatoes. The baguettes were a palette of flavors with some significance he could not rationalize; for a moment, the arrangement of ingredients felt sacred.

At the table at lunch, Allison had broken off a piece of banana and handed it to him. He had noticed the crystalline structures, illumined in the warm light, where the banana cells had torn and stretched into architectural threads: housing, he had imagined, for some advanced future race.

He had passed it back to her. "Look. A city, on the top of the banana, a yellow metropolis."

He had liked chatting about nothing in particular to the shopkeeper where he had bought the baguettes. He liked waiting here on the park bench, thinking of nothing or whatever happened to drift into his head. The 15 months since they had married had dissolved a part of his ambition for the future. He was living in the moment more than he ever had, and it felt good.

Of course, they did speak about things of significance too: movies, books, culture, and religion. Their relationship had liberated the suppressed elements in his personality. Other potentials and attributes were being released to find a new foundation in his life, and he felt himself becoming more like her.

Then there was the deepening relationship with the Bahá'í community in Harlem and its goals to build and enhance social diversity and equality through education and to foster community-building activities in collaboration with the Harlem community. Hooman and Allison were both moving through the sequence of Ruhi Institute courses; they had got as far as book six, *Teaching the Cause*. Allison's understanding of the spiritual principles of the Faith was deepening now, and their conversations about spiritual and social reality were becoming more nuanced and complex as they talked about the oneness of God, religion, and humanity.

———

Hooman looked over at the path alongside the recreation center and saw Allison walking toward him. She was wrapped tightly in her coat. When she was closer to him, she said, "You were right about it being chilly. I'm feeling it now. But I don't care." She smiled.

"How did you go?"

"No luck, I'm afraid."

"Perhaps next week you'll get more interest."

"One of the volunteers says she'll push it a bit harder for me and suggest it to kids who come into the center."

"That's good."

Opening her coat, she wrapped it around him as he got up from the bench.

"You have to keep me warm, and the baby too," she said with exuberance.

He placed her hood over her head and wrapped it around her face, which formed a tunnel with fur edges. He laughed after blowing warm air into the fur tunnel.

"Is that warm enough now?" he said.

Her muffled voice escaped the hood. "Yes," and she laughed and broke away. She removed her hood. "Let's walk to the top of the hill. That'll warm us up."

He took her hand, and they began to walk toward the stone staircase.

After a minute, they came to the staircase and then walked up it. At the top of the hill, they emerged from the wooded area into an open plateau paved with stone. They sat down on a stone wall that faced the downtown area, and looking through the trees on the edge of the hill, they looked down on 5th Avenue. They could just see one edge of Central Park with all its fall leaves in brown tones. The rest of Marcus Garvey Park, and Harlem beyond, stretched out beneath the hill. The golden-brown hue of fall trees blended harmoniously with the cool muted grays and the warm reds of the buildings surrounding the park.

She eventually looked over at him.

"So . . . Mr. Hooman, what are we doing here?"

"I don't know. I followed you here. Do you have any doubts?"

"No, it's just going to be more difficult than I originally thought."

"What did you expect? This is a tough part of town. Only ten or so years ago, we couldn't even contemplate moving here. I found out from the shopkeeper today that one house on our street was a crack house during the late eighties, early nineties. So at least it's real. We're not living in that walled paradise you mentioned a few years ago."

"No. You're right. No walled paradise for us." She smiled. "Really, I am happy here when I think about it. Those kids in my group are both amazing and frustrating. I realized the other day, when we were out, that some of them were having trouble concentrating because they don't get breakfast on a regular basis. I mean I know they get breakfast at school on the weekdays but apparently not always on the weekends. We are living in the developing world, right here in the middle of Manhattan."

"I know. Isn't it amazing that amongst all this wealth in Manhattan, such poverty can exist in such close proximity?" He pointed toward the downtown area. "And Bahá'u'lláh says, 'If ye meet the abased or the down-trodden, turn not away disdainfully from them, for the King of Glory ever watcheth over them and surroundeth them with such tenderness as none can fathom except them that have suffered their wishes and desires to be merged in the Will of your Lord, the Gracious, the All-Wise.'"[3]

"I saw some photos recently on the internet from the 1960s. Some of the poverty in Harlem from then to now has reduced, but, relative to the rest of Manhattan, there is still disparity, and South Bronx in particular still has extreme poverty rates. And, you know, I'm not comfortable with our house."

"I know, I know," Hooman said apologetically. "I would have lived in something humbler, but Nava insisted on making the house a showcase of her talents."

"It might be a good idea to sell the apartment in New Jersey, buy a brownstone here, and offer it to local artists as a series of free art studios or maybe even writing studios."

"Yes, we could do that. That's a wonderful idea, Allison."

She stopped talking for a moment, then took his hand into her lap. "One of the boys came with bruises on his face the other day. I don't know where he got them. He wouldn't talk about it."

"You mentioned the other day that there is a general anger in them too, just below the surface."

"Yes, it surfaces when we talk about racial identity and other issues related to race. Though it's not all bad. They are great kids and really bright on the whole. I was talking to Elliot about it today. She freaks out a bit when she is here, like Nava, but I didn't want to tell her about my issues with the kids because I didn't want to confirm any stereotypes she might have about the place and the kids. Things here are not straightforward. The complexities of the race issues are hard to put into easy terms, and I don't think she is ready for that conversation yet. Although I saw a change in Elliot's face after she read a little of your manuscript."

"Listen, why don't you ask the kids what they want to do. Try taking a more consultative approach, more inclusive. Sit back and let them take more of a lead."

"Okay, that's a good idea. I'll try that."

They sat on the stone wall for a few minutes in relative silence. Hooman thought again about their new life together in Harlem. He felt her slender fingers as they held hands. He liked to look over at her and watch what she was doing. She was looking at the downtown area. He saw the cars turning onto 5th Avenue and moving toward Central Park and listened to the sounds of the traffic and the ambient hum of the city.

———

Half an hour later they walked back to the house. They chatted about lighter subjects. When they came to the street, she kicked the leaves in the gutter. They reached the door, and she looked over at the house where the boy lived. Its windows were empty, darkened, but the house beckoned to her.

Once they were inside their house, they walked up the staircase into the living room. Allison offered to sit down and take Hooman chronologically through her photographs. So they sat down, and she started to shuffle through the photographs that had not been ordered yet. Most of them were taken in Australia, but there were a few shots of Paris and London from years before. She continued putting them in different piles, and he started to look at each one.

"This pile is the east coast of Australia," she said, "and this pile is central Australia."

"The desert shots are interesting. You are such a good photographer."

"Thanks, babe."

"What's this?" He passed her a photo of a series of coins and notes laid out on sand.

"Oh, that was part of my visual diary. On my road trip around Australia."

He picked up another photo. "Where is this? It's beautiful."

"That's the Bungle Bungles."

She picked up a photo of Cathedral Gorge and passed it to him.

"Wow. That's gorgeous."

"It had rained several hours before that shot was taken, so the waterfall inside the gorge was flowing."

She started to find more shots of Paris, so she added them to the Paris pile. She thought about all the wonderful cafés near Montmartre and Épinettes, where she had lived for three months in a cramped apartment with Gabriel and Aurélie.

He pointed to one photo of Centre Pompidou. "I recognize that from one of my own trips to Paris," he said.

In the photograph Centre Pompidou was partially obscured by an avenue of plane trees. She explained that she had been sitting outside near the Centre at a restaurant, Le Cavalier Bleu, when she had taken the photo.

Then she saw one photo of the entrance of the Abbesses metro station with all its Art Nouveau design. She kissed the photo and passed it to him. "Isn't the design fabulous?"

———

After four days in the Daintree, in Tropical North Queensland, Australia, she drove south for an hour and a half toward Cairns, passing through many sugarcane farms on the way. She took a turnoff before Cairns to drive into the hills, eventually passing through Kuranda. She stopped in front of the Kuranda Market for a few minutes, recalling her childhood memories. Once she passed through Kuranda, she left the rainforest behind and drove through the Atherton Tablelands, which was a mixture of rolling green hills and patches of forest, used mainly for cattle and sheep. Occasionally, she passed farms growing different crops that she could not always identify, but eventually, she left the rolling hills as she stopped driving south through the tablelands and went west into the center of Queensland. The countryside gradually flattened out, alternating between red and yellow dirt and filled with grass and a widely spaced spread of small eucalypts. It was not quite desert, but the isolation of the place felt desert-like. As the distance between the small towns increased, the population of these towns decreased, and the amounts of cars on the road also dwindled. This was the beginning of her social isolation and a singular connection to the land, her own personal being in nothingness, though a different "being" and a different "nothingness" to the one Sartre had intended. The desert was an emptiness that was actually full, and rather than nothingness being a void of absolute meaning in this life, the desert was a mirror to Allison of the lack of human presence, which allowed her to see her identity with more intensity: it was just her, the road, the desert, and the sky, where she could leave the world behind and find herself on the road.

It took five days to drive to Kakadu. Each night she pulled off the highway into truck stops and slept in the back of the car. The highway was not always a double lane. In places it turned into a single lane, and she had to be careful not to hit cars coming in the other direction. It was easier at night because she could see the headlights of the cars and trucks coming in the distance.

On the second day she left Queensland and passed into the Northern Territory. The size of the eucalypts gradually decreased before disappearing completely and being replaced with small bushes. The size of grass tussocks also decreased, and their color changed from a rich green to a yellow-gray. This terrain remained flat for most of the time, until she got closer to Kakadu, where she started to see rocky outcrops and low red hills.

On the last day of the trip to Kakadu, Allison arrived at a camping ground at dusk. It was situated in the heart of the Kakadu National Park. Once she had pitched her tent, she got into her car and drove a short way away to Yellow Water Billabong. She found a parking lot next to the billabong and parked. The colors and the dusk light reflected on the dark water were exquisite.

She was tempted to swim in the water but knew there would most likely be crocodiles, so instead she imagined herself swimming in the clear, dark water, brushing aside the water lilies as she swam.

Allison had been traveling for close to four months now. As she had traveled, she liked the anticipation of another small Australian town in the middle of nowhere. At times she had even traveled without her map, just moving from town to town with no understanding of the greater geography around her; she liked the surprise of finding something beautiful and unexpected.

And traveling, or driving in a car, appeared to her to be a metaphor for personal development—moving away from herself with every mile and arriving at herself simultaneously, like two opposing archetypes— future self and past self, moving through future land and past land, brought into focus in the present moment.

She had tried to compare the markers of change, to find what moments were transformative. When she crossed a desert, was it the emptiness that moved her—the lack of human presence? As she had contemplated before, the desert was like a mirror of identity. And then she thought about cities, where it was the opposite—with the fullness of human life and its alien diversity, which were also mirrors of identity. Allison saw that through this complex juxtaposition of identity through the emptiness and fullness of humanity, she might be able to find herself. By contrasting one's personality against the backdrop of others' unique and diverse personalities, one's own unique identity became apparent, and from that came the development of self.

But although the places she visited were a mirror for identity in one way, they were also detached from the people who passed through them and effaced identity in another way. They hardly ever fully recorded the identity of a visitor; identity faded like tracks in the desert sand, and when the wind blew, no traces remained of the person who had passed through that desert. So external identity, based within place, was a phantom. Even a city—more prone to recording the lives of its inhabitants—changed and wiped identity away as it moved forward and ground and crushed bones into the earth under it. It glided over humans and went on into infinity, and graves sprung up like flowers. That bright light shone down on death, and all that could be said with surety of a person or place was its impermanence, and whatever unique identity one developed in this life eventually passed with them into death, never to be seen again in this world.

22

THE NOTEBOOK

In fire he seeth the face of the Beloved; in illusion he beholdeth the secret of reality; in the attributes he readeth the riddle of the Essence. For he hath burnt away all veils with a sigh, and cast aside all coverings with a glance. With piercing sight he gazeth upon the new creation . . .[1]

— BAHÁ'U'LLÁH, *THE SEVEN VALLEYS*

That invisible country—with its borders between Black and White America—shimmered in Allison's mind as she caught train 2 from the corner of 125th Street and Malcolm X Boulevard. It was Wednesday, and she and Hooman had arranged to meet up in Greenwich Village during his lunch break. There was an obscure book written during the time of the civil rights movement at the Jefferson Market Library that she wanted to borrow. They were going to meet near the library and walk to the Seven Stars Café from there. She wondered why he wanted to meet at the library because it was just as easy to walk directly to the café.

She stood on the platform, looking around at all of Harlem's citizens. She was about to undergo a familiar process: the crossing. Allison began to cross Harlem's racial boundary as she stepped onto the train.

At 125th Street the carriages consisted almost entirely of African

Americans and a few Latinos. At the top of Central Park and Malcolm X Boulevard, a few White Americans would get in the carriages, and a few African Americans would leave. At 72nd Street and Amsterdam, still more would exchange positions, so by the time the train pulled into 42nd Street and Times Square, the carriage was an equal proportion of African Americans to White. And in the stops past 42nd Street, the trend completely reversed to almost entirely White Americans and a few other diverse faces from New York's culturally broad populous.

Hooman had compared the process to traveling on the high-speed trains in Europe when one crossed over a few country borders in quick succession, but in Manhattan it was compressed into an even tighter scale.

During the year she had read a book on the history of segregation in America, from the pre- and post-Lincoln times up to the fifties and sixties, with segregation in the South and the broader inequalities that had led to the civil rights movement and contemporary segregation along residential lines. She had weighed the arguments. If economic and cultural diversity were brought to Harlem, it would lose some of its character and individuality as an African American neighborhood, but it would become more culturally integrated. And Harlem would change further, in that she had no doubt, but the direction might take the default path of commercial necessity from property developers, which would be driven by White middle-class aspirations, of which she was a self-conscious part. As the rents increased, more White people would probably thin the ranks of the African Americans. She felt that if main-stream America pushed for more education and social empowerment within Harlem, then some of the poverty would dissipate, and more African Americans would find more jobs within the middle class, which would in turn push against White gentrification.

Her life there was on the end of a historical circle, which was close to making another rotation. Leading up to 1890, Harlem had been a wealthy White neighborhood, before the inflated housing market had brought about a bust. A second bust in 1905 triggered an influx of poorer African Americans, which transformed it into a largely African American neighborhood, and, if White gentrification continued, the circle of history would close out and show how poverty had affected cultural separation along residential lines.

Allison's thoughts turned to her young photography group: she wanted to gauge their perceptions of Harlem's negative and positive history. Harlem had become a flourishing cultural and artistic community, from the times of the Harlem Renaissance, which spanned from 1920 to 1930, up to the present day with Harlem's Studio Museum. And many other cultural, political, and artistic organizations had encouraged the community to thrive. Did her students have an opinion about it? Was there a sophisticated aesthetic way she could incorporate their understanding of their life and identity in Harlem into the pictures they took? Would they grow in their perceptions of Harlem by seeing it as more than just a separate enclave of those abandoned by a passive, but no less insidious, racism in America?

Passive racism was the inactivity and indifference of mainstream America to alleviate the decades of poverty and the lack of educational and economic opportunities endured by the African American community. This passivity had more subtle forms in the way American identity was portrayed in the media, but in totality it affected power distribution within American society and the common will to affect change.

Racism would have to be addressed at the individual, community, and institutional level, and on both sides of the racial divide, to address pervasive systemic racism built into social, political, and economic structures. There was a synergy between these different aspects of society, that once engaged properly, and at every level, would lead to a richer and more balanced perception of identity and nation and continue to blur distinct racial identity and deepen the ongoing process of America becoming a nation of vibrant, mixed-race people.

And although history had eradicated much of the overt superiority felt by Whites, there was still a subconscious superiority prevalent in some parts of American society. Whites would need to reach out with genuine friendship and address the grievances of the past and present within the African American community, and the African American community, on their part, would need to forgive the past wrongs against them, which was asking a lot more of them than was being asked of White people. Nothing short of genuine love, extreme patience, and persistent effort on both sides would resolve these issues, so that prejudice from within both Black and White communities would not find a foothold, and racism could continue to dissipate into history.

Near her final stop at Christopher Street Station, a Black poet beggar walked into the carriage and recited a poem. As he walked past people, he held his hand out for a few coins. Allison caught the last few lines as he neared her end of the carriage: "a forgotten people in a forgotten land. Swing low sweet chariot. Swing low to catch your sweet brothers and sisters. Lift their faces to heaven high." These words cemented her resolve about Harlem and its future. She would try to contribute to an alternate future of cultural diversity, which transcended a purely African American neighborhood, but which maintained a good part of its current identity as a Black community. It seemed to her that Harlem could absorb other cultures and depart from the limiting future that was currently playing out.

At Christopher Street Station she got off the train and headed to the surface.

———

Near the top of Union Square, Hooman saw one of those expensive stationary shops. He had caught a taxi from Midtown, close to where his new firm was located, and was now en route to meet Allison for lunch.

He tapped on the glass. "You can drop me here," he said to the driver.

"Don't you want to go to the Village?"

"I changed my mind. Here's the fare and a bit extra."

He left the taxi and crossed the street.

In the shop he went straight to the diary and notebook section. A few weeks back, as he was driving to work with Nava, he had seen the exact notebook he wanted in a window display of another outlet. The notebook was large. It was made of good-quality paper and bound in a thick leather cover, which had a flap to protect the paper edges. A long leather strap bound it shut as it wound around the notebook several times. Performing his usual ritual, he put his face into the open book. He smelled the paper and leather aroma mixing and drifting off the pages.

Once he had bought the notebook, he stepped outside and hailed another taxi. He asked the driver to head to the corner of 6th Avenue and West 9th Street.

———

"What are you thinking?" he asked.

Smiling, she opened her eyes. "Oh, nothing much, just listening to the sounds around me and thinking about a different kind of Harlem."

Allison was leaning against the fence of the Jefferson Market Garden, which was right next to the Jefferson Market Library.

"Did you find your book?"

"Yes, I did." She patted her bag and smiled.

"What is it?"

"It's a novel written during the middle of the civil rights movement. It's called *An Unequal Sun*. It's about an interracial couple who marry in Detroit in 1962, and it highlights the courage and determination that it took to live across the racial boundaries of that era."

"Sounds interesting."

"Yes, I've heard good things about it."

He took her hand, and they turned toward 6th Avenue.

As they crossed the street, she noticed Hooman carrying a bag. "What's in the bag?"

"I'm not telling . . . for the moment." He laughed.

"Don't tease, what is it?"

"I'll show you when we get to the café."

Once they were on the other side of the street, Hooman turned left, and they walked past the entrance to 9th Street Station.

Allison looked back over her shoulder for a moment. "Where are we going? The café is in the opposite direction."

"I want to show you something that I think may interest you."

"Oh . . . okay, cool. Is this why you wanted to meet me at the library?"

"Yep," he said.

They walked up 6th Avenue and then turned right down West 10th Street. Hooman led her to the left side of the street, and after a minute, he stepped onto the sidewalk and looked up at a modern apartment block that was surrounded on either side by older nineteenth-century-era buildings.

"Yep, this is fifty-one."

"Who lives here?"

"It's not who lives here but who lived here. Past tense, babe."

He waited for a moment with a big smile. "I give you . . . Kahlil Gibran," he said eventually with an excited tone as he raised both arms up to the sky to encompass the building.

"Kahlil Gibran lived here?" she said with an air of unbelievability.

"Yep, totally did . . . totally."

"I have read *The Prophet* . . . years ago, but I did read it. I had no idea he lived in New York."

"Well, I think you can guess that he didn't live in this more modern building. His studio apartment was here until 1955, when it was demolished. It had been, in Gibran's time, a series of artists' studios. He wrote *The Prophet* while he was living here. And I will show you another interesting thing. Come, follow me."

He stepped onto the street and almost bounced along until he stepped onto the sidewalk on the opposite side of the street and walked past four houses before he stopped in front of one. She followed him across the street and stopped next to him as he looked up.

"Who lived here?" she said.

"An early Bahá'í. An artist and close friend of Gibran—Juliet Thompson."

"Okay. I have never heard of her before."

"No, I knew that, but she was very close to 'Abdu'l-Bahá. Come, I have one more thing to show you."

"Okay, very cool so far. So this street is at least a part of why Greenwich Village got its bohemian reputation."

"Yep, along with the Beat poets, the sixties counterculture, and many of the abstract expressionists who lived in the neighborhood."

"Yeah, I knew about that part of its history. Although these days, most artists have been priced out of the market."

They crossed the street and walked until they came to 5th Avenue. As they walked, she said, "So Kahlil Gibran had a connection to the Bahá'í Faith?"

"Yes, he did. Gibran met 'Abdu'l-Bahá during his time in New York, and Gibran was deeply moved by him."

Hooman eventually stopped in front of a large church on their left.

He looked up at it. "This is the Church of the Ascension . . . 'Abdu'l-Bahá gave a speech here in April 1912, and the subject matter is kind of appropriate for my book because he used a metaphor of humanity as being a bird with two wings. One wing being material civilization and the other, divine civilization. Ultimately, without these two wings, humanity cannot make any progress, as a bird with only one wing will obviously not be able to fly."

"Yeah, that is a good metaphor," Allison said, looking around at the features of the church. They lingered in front of the church for a while in silence before Hooman took her hand, and they turned around and walked south down 5th Avenue. They circled around and eventually came to the Seven Stars Café on West 8th Street; the café was close to 6th Avenue.

Inside the Seven Stars Café, they sat at a table and ordered food and coffee. The table was toward the back of the café and overlooked the courtyard. She looked out at the red brick walls surrounding the court-yard and the intense red fall leaves of the Boston ivy growing on these walls, before leaning back for a moment and looking up at the stars painted on the roof of the café.

There were obviously seven large stars painted on the roof but also many other smaller stars that were arranged in a regular pattern of rows around the seven larger stars, which was supposed to represent the roofs in the interiors of many Egyptian tombs. And typically, *The Book of the Dead* and other funerary texts were placed inside a sarcophagus, or they were painted on the walls surrounding a sarcophagus. The café had always had that odd eclecticism with all the mismatched furniture, and then there was the Egyptian theme on the roof that was odd too. And for a moment Allison had an image in her mind of the whole café being transported into the interior of an Egyptian tomb. She then looked over at the front of the cafe where she and Hooman had sat on her first night in New York. The old leather armchair was still there. Her life had come a long way from that night and was circling back on itself.

The café was full and humming with conversations. Allison listened to these conversations as Hooman placed the bag on the table. "I bought you something. Guess what it is."

"I have no idea, but I can smell leather."

"It's a notebook." He pulled it out of the bag and handed it to her.

She unwound the leather strap and opened it to the middle pages. "Oh. It's really nice, Hooman. The paper is so lovely and thick. Thanks. This is so thoughtful of you." She closed the notebook and placed it on the table.

"It's for your boxes full of Post-it notes, scraps of paper, and the many small notepads you have lying around the house."

"You think I should consolidate? Yes, I could. I had a thought to do it but hadn't gotten around to it yet."

"I figured since you have left the idea of finishing your master's degree behind, you may as well start pulling all your own personal research together in one place. It'll give you something to do until the baby arrives."

"Yes, I will. That's a good idea. Thank you." She leaned over the table and kissed him.

The coffees and food arrived, and the shape of his face changed. She knew his mind had shifted gears, and she waited for a change in the topic.

"I wanted to ask how you're going. About things that I know will go into this notebook." He placed his hand on the cover and continued. "You have been very quiet about your inner life this past year. I haven't asked, not because I don't care, but because I didn't want to intrude. I know you don't like to talk about it too much."

"Nothing has changed, really. I mean, I still have these strange experiences in both my inner and outer worlds, though what is different is I've learned to integrate these experiences. I am no longer perturbed, as I was before, and there is symmetry in my life now that has come from my symmetrical destiny map and my efforts to see patterns of meaning and connection in this world."

"Do you mind if I ask you more about it?"

She smiled and reached out to take his hand. "I suppose I have been elusive. I'm sorry. I was thinking of telling you eventually."

She stopped and gathered her thoughts and began to think about different metaphors to describe her recent experiences. Eventually, she thought of a poem she had written that month called "The Glass Womb" that explored the veils between this world and the next.

"If the veil that separates this world from the next is thin, then for me, it is somehow thinner now. I exist in a glass womb that is slowly turning from opaque to transparent. I see the world outside the womb, and beyond that womb, I see the pattern of existence emerge from the illusion of this world as I pass through different gates in reality," she said.

She stopped speaking for a while and looked at the courtyard, her eyes focusing on the intense red leaves of the Boston ivy.

After a long pause, she smiled and continued, "When I was in London, I discovered a book, a translation of Egyptian scripture called *The Book of Gates*. It is a funerary text associated with *The Book of the Dead*. The dead were meant to use *The Book of the Dead* to navigate the afterlife, called the Duat by Egyptians. All these books feature a god, long obscured by history, called Osiris. He was commonly known as the god of the afterlife, but I think he was an actual person in the flesh. It's speculative on my part, but I think he might have been a messenger or a prophet who lived many thousands of years ago. Egyptologist Wallis Budge maintained that the Egyptian religion was at one time monotheistic, with Osiris as the prophet who was eventually deified into a man-god, and that the religion only degraded into polytheism much later in history. Osiris was always connected with the spiritual resurrection of the soul and immortality after death. Thus, Budge's book was named *Osiris & the Egyptian Resurrection*. I think you've seen me reading *The Book of Gates* now and then. It talks about the afterlife being divided into a series of gates or regions. *The Book of the Dead* describes seven gates, and other funerary texts associated with that book, like *The Book of Gates*, have twelve gates, based on the twelve hours of the night as Ra passes through the Otherworld each night on the 'evening boat' after a day, or twelve hours, in the sky. He then merges with Osiris during the night, becoming Temu: the hidden God, and the dead who have died that day travel with them on the evening boat into the Otherworld."

"Gates? Okay, that's interesting. That reminds me of the Báb. As you know, he is known as 'the Gate,'" said Hooman.

"And do you remember the holy day we went to a few weeks ago? At the Bahá'í Center."

"Yes."

Allison continued, "You were talking to someone, and I was browsing through the bookstall with Shidan at my side. He found an Arabic book by Bahá'u'lláh called *Gems of Divine Mysteries*. Shidan translated parts of it for me when I was at the Sun Tongue not long after that. And the Universal House of Justice is bringing out an English version next year. Of course, this extends what Bahá'u'lláh revealed in *The Seven Valleys*, and the concept of valleys was first used in *The Conference of the Birds*. Even some of the names of the valleys are similar. I read *The Seven Valleys* properly just before we were married. And, as you know, we studied parts of it together when we were on our honeymoon. The birds must traverse the seven valleys before they come to meet the Simorgh."

"Yes, I know the connection between *The Seven Valleys* and *The Conference of the Birds*. *The Seven Valleys* outlines the seven levels or conditions of closeness or proximity to God. But I have never read *Gems of Divine Mysteries*. My Arabic is not great. Is it similar to *The Seven Valleys*?"

"Yes, it adds extra levels, bringing the total to nine cities or valleys. So, these gates in the Egyptian afterlife are similar to the concept of valleys or cities from Bahá'u'lláh's writings. The gates restrict souls from going to levels that they are not ready for."

"How will a soul know which level to go to, then?" asked Hooman.

"Basically, Osiris will know where a soul deserves to be relative to the degree of righteousness it has attained in this life. And this comes from the 'weighting of the heart' ceremony that comes after death. So anyway, like I said before, the dead travel with Osiris and Ra through the afterlife along a river in the night. Ra then enters the 'morning boat' during the day, also called the Boat of Millions of Years; this boat is used to travel between both worlds.

"Ra is the creator of all the gods, the father of creation. Like I said before, he is also known as Temu, the great hidden God, and the night-time form of Ra. And the link between *The Conference of the Birds* and Ra is the Egyptian idea of the Phoenix. The Egyptians called it the Bennu, the sun-bird, which is similar to the Simorgh. The Bennu's cry at the beginning of creation marked the beginning of time. It's kind of like the Egyptian version of the Big Bang, I suppose. But what these various texts associated with *The Book of the Dead*, used from 1550 BCE to 50

BCE, indicate to me is that ideas that relate to the evolution in the life of the soul in the worlds of God, in Egyptian culture at least, have been around for many thousands of years, in times long forgotten. The oldest depictions of Osiris go back as far as 2300 BCE. And there is clearly symmetry between most of the major religions with regard to ideas that relate to the existence of an afterlife; it's a very old idea. And I think in nearly all cultures it must go back tens of thousands of years, if not hundreds of thousands of years.

"And what is really interesting is the similarity between Osiris and Bahá'u'lláh. In a tablet by Bahá'u'lláh, the *Tablet of the Holy Mariner*, he refers to himself as the Mariner of the Ark in the mysteries of the Seas of Light.[2] And there are linked ideas between *The Seven Valleys* and the *Tablet of the Holy Mariner*." Allison paused for a moment in recounting her thoughts and ideas to Hooman.

It was just enough time for Hooman to get a word in. "That is very interesting. So the symbol of the boat is similar in both religions?"

"Yes, but what I couldn't work out last year was that in the first three to four gates in the afterlife there are the lakes of peace and lakes of fire —the lakes of peace are on the right bank of the river and the lakes of fire on the left bank. The fire lakes cease eventually. And although hell is seen as the lowest levels, the grades of self, even the more sanctified levels above this, have the lakes of fire, which strip away lower attributes. This is linked to the Christian concept of purgatory, the transitional phase before entering heaven in the proper sense. The catalyst for change is represented as fire; it is the cleansing fire. We are burning like the Bennu or Phoenix in cyclical deaths and births of spiritual resurrection. You have to look at the idea of transformation through change leading to changeless and placeless states. 'A lover is he who is chill in hell fire.'[3] Because both hell and heaven burn away both sin and virtue; sin is transfigured by virtue, and virtue in turn is metamorphosized into more expansive and breathtaking higher attributes. So, if you travel through fire or water in eternity, you will be safe if God is inside you."

"Yes, I'm with you. Amazing," he said.

"Interesting, eh? That blew me away when I realized this idea, and as you always say, on the whole, it is one reality, one God, one afterlife, and one Holy Mariner." Allison watched Hooman turn to look at the courtyard. She continued when he looked back at her. "Yes, well, I haven't been able to fit *The Book of Gates* completely to *The Seven Valleys*, but I think they are connected. It is only that *The Book of Gates* has probably been reinterpreted so many times throughout Egyptian history that its original purpose and purity have been lost, but essentially, given this limitation of time, both books talk about the same process and are written approximately three and a half thousand years apart or maybe more; it's hard to say. It might be older. And when you read it through the prism of the Bahá'í writings, its meaning becomes clearer. Although there are many possible ways to unlock the meaning of *The Seven Valleys*, I have come up with a few simple ideas of my own.

"As a soul ascends through the valleys, they go from self to selfless, from change to changeless, from time to timeless, and from lower self to higher self, in God. And as the soul moves up or through these valleys or gates, they enter the spiritual worlds beyond Nasut, the physical world. Remember we had that conversation in Queensland during our honeymoon about the objective and perceptual nature of time and eternity. These transitions are related to that. I think that in the Valley of Unity our perception of time and space fold away as we become aware of the two kinds of time in Earth and heaven."

"Fascinating theory."

"And at the point in *The Book of Gates* where the fire lakes cease, it says that at the higher levels, the 'wheat of truth' is given equally to all, the same portion, which is a reference to the oneness of being. I think this corresponds with the Valley of Unity, level four, described in *The Seven Valleys*. It's where the plurality of our vision, or duality, ceases, and the levels of the oneness of perception begin—it is the unchanging reality beyond the 'tree of the knowledge of good and evil' from the Bible. In the *Tablet of the Holy Mariner* Bahá'u'lláh says, 'They passed the grades of worldly limitations and reached that of the divine unity, the center of heavenly guidance. Glorified be my Lord, the All-Glorious!'[4] This is probably the beginning of the world of Malakut.

"And, of course, the seventh level is called the Valley of True Poverty and Absolute Nothingness. Absolute nothingness means that you have left all attributes behind you, even higher attributes of oneness found in the valleys below, until only the changeless remains. This is immortality and eternal life. And this is the world of Jabarut."

"That's fascinating. So assuming this is true, how do your own experiences fit into the scheme of things?" he asked.

"Well, normally, in *The Book of Gates*, it is assumed that the person has died before they go through to the Otherworld or Duat. So, what I am saying is what you told me when we first met. The afterlife starts here—the physical world is not just a preparatory phase for the next world. Remember, you once said the worlds are comingling. Right? And it is the 'Ba,' the part of the soul according to the Egyptians, that can make this transition in the Boat of Millions of Years. The worlds are in the heart—the heart makes the transition."

"Yes, I did say the worlds are comingling. But how this happens is obscure. The knowledge of it is hidden, except for a few rare and holy souls. I mean, I suppose it is a very subjective and personal experience anyway, so how would a person even know if another soul was immersed in these higher worlds."

"You don't have to die to move through the worlds of God, Hooman. Even Muhammad confirms this: 'A believer is alive in both worlds.'"[5]

"True, I suppose."

"I started praying and meditating quite regularly when I was in London."

"Yes, you said that. I remember."

"My destiny flows naturally from my daily prayers and meditation. So, the secret incantations or passwords in *The Book of Gates* that allow you to pass through the different gates are just prayers to strip away earthly attributes and move you into an unchanging world. And the other key is through action, serving humanity. As you have said so many times, people are important. People are a mirror of each other. That's why I wanted to come to Harlem. So you see, the worlds are hidden inside people, like I said, in the heart. After all, the soul is the only constant between both worlds. People are the building blocks, the architecture of the next world. And mysticism is not a private pursuit or some obscure esoteric practice but one that takes place in the context of community. It always has.

"And as you move up the planes of consciousness, the world of people move up the ladder with you in oneness. Except those on lower planes are not aware of this upward movement or that they are able to give away secrets that they are unable to comprehend themselves. All the worlds are interfused perfectly. Everyone sees their own reflection in the other, no matter what level they inhabit. And there is also *The Seven Valleys*, which states: "Earth and heaven cannot contain Me; what can alone contain Me is the heart of him that believeth in Me."[6] And I think that he who contains God in his heart is contained by God and lives in absolute safety from the material world and its impermanence.

"Here, let me draw the nine gates or valleys. I know you've read these books, so you will understand my base premise, I think. Can I use your pen?"

He reached into his jacket pocket. "Sure." He passed it to her.

Opening to the middle of the new notebook, she began to draw a rough diagram by drawing a line across the page, then writing the word "time" under the line and "timeless" on the top of the line. Allison added commentary to the movement of the pen on the page. "The early levels are the grades of self. They represent the selfish soul, or the rational soul, attached to the physical world. These are the conditions of hell, and these first grades need to be burned away.

"Once this has happened, the soul comes to the first valley of faith, which is called the Valley of Search. Its main purpose is the recognition of the Manifestation of God, who in this day and age is Bahá'u'lláh. There are then two more valleys that come under the world of relative perfections, that are Love and Knowledge, and the soul is still in the world of Nasut here. In Love there is pain and in Knowledge certitude. Also, this is the soul whose identity and thoughts are encapsulated and separate from other souls."

She wrote these first three valleys under the line with the word "time."

She continued, "Then eternity and Malakut begin in the proper sense as time folds away, and the next three valleys are the worlds of oneness, the absolute planes. These are Unity, Contentment, and Wonderment; the soul is tossed in wonder on the seas of the absolute. This level is now the collective of souls where thoughts and identity can be shared and synchronized between souls in both worlds. This is a oneness where it is not clear where one soul begins and another ends. This is the soul completely devoted to the service of others."

The next three valleys she wrote above the line with the word "time-less" written on it.

She continued, "Then in Jabarut the face of God rises up from eternity. This is the Valley of True Poverty and Absolute Nothingness and is the beginning of the consciousness of the Manifestation of God. This is entering the presence of the Manifestation or the birds meeting the Simorgh. Then beyond this is the Valley of Immortality and then a valley with no name and no description, which is the central pivot of eternity and probably Lahut. Bahá'u'lláh also described the worlds of God as 'the world of time, which hath both a beginning and an end; the world of duration, which hath a beginning but whose end is not apparent; the world of primordial reality, whose beginning is not to be seen but which is known to have an end; and the world of eternity, of which neither the beginning nor the end is visible.'[7]

"After the city of Immortality, in the highest level, nine, Bahá'u'lláh explains that this city revolves around the seat of eternity. The sun of the Unseen shines above the horizon of the Unseen. A sun that has its own heavens and its own moons. But this reality is staggeringly transcendent, given that only God and his Manifestations are aware of this city.

"And these higher planes of oneness are way beyond the average soul. Bahá'u'lláh says that only the 'elect of the righteous' travel in these higher valleys. It is purely my own understanding, but I think that most people of faith exist in the first three valleys. Some enter Unity before death, or after it, depending on what God has willed for them and relative to their innate spiritual capacity. And although I think it would be very rare, Bahá'u'lláh also said that a soul could complete all these journeys and discover every mystery in less than the twinkling of an eye. But the only really important thing, which comes under free will, is the decision to recognize the Manifestation of God for this age and follow his laws. This eventually leads to liberation and moving from the 'human spirit' to the 'spirit of Faith.'

"If we have a fused existence with the Manifestations of God, we can travel in these higher worlds. Of course, in saying that, a blending of spiritual reality takes into account that the station of a Manifestation is inherently and forever different from, and immeasurably exalted above, that of a human being. But it is doubtful that many, while on

Earth, will ever reach these exalted worlds. At least not in this time, but in the future, as the utopian vision that Bahá'u'lláh saw in his heart comes to fruition, many will probably enter these higher states or worlds. As to Hahut, which is the hidden essence, nobody knows what happens in that world. Even the Manifestations of God are lost in utter bewilderment and awe at that world. But as we realize the reality of Malakut and are lost in awe, we contemplate the higher worlds as a series of metaphoric symbols. And each metaphoric symbol of these infinite worlds is a reflection of the Supreme Manifestation's heart, which flows down from the heights of Lahut, as the first dawning point of the essence, into the other three worlds below it."

She noticed that Hooman had listened intently to her spoken words while at the same time looking at her written words. "Wow, that's amazing. I'm stunned." Hooman was silent for a while. He then asked, "So what valley are you in?"

"I'm probably in the Valley of Unity, or maybe I'm in the Valley of Knowledge. I waver between them. But I think that although our soul is mostly in one valley, a part of our soul is in the valleys above and below this, like a bell curve. It might be like you said back in Queensland that timelessness might have a spectral nature, then so too would consciousness be spectral and layered by waves or vibrational frequency from low to high. And as you said, there could also be a more perceptual aspect in the worlds of God after death, where objectivity is more flexible, or a world's objective nature could be changed dynamically by the perception of the soul that is perceiving that world: perceptual objectivity. And many souls would see different aspects of a world depending on their own unique perceptual limitations and strengths.

"But I wanted to explain another idea. I think there is a relationship between ascension in these higher worlds and the laws in the Kitáb-i-Aqdas, since Bahá'u'lláh explains that the 'law' is 'the secret of the Path,'[8] which, as you may know, comes from *The Seven Valleys*. It is through spiritual law that one rises up, and by deviating from that law that one descends. Remember, you were the one who told me this when we were in London together."

"Yes, I remember that. It is true that law is the secret of the Path."

"But the spiritual laws are also intertwined with the laws of physics. After all, it is mainly through the senses of vision and hearing that we grow our spiritual virtues; it is not by chance that there are seven colors in the spectrum of light and seven notes in the musical scale most commonly used in modern Western music, known as the heptatonic scale. The physical world, with light and sound, is an expression of the four forces of nature, which in turn merge into one universal law as described by 'Abdu'l-Bahá. I'm using 'Abdu'l-Bahá's concept of 'one universal law' creatively by incorporating it into my own framework of ideas about the spectrum of light and the structure of sound. Plato also had the idea that all forms in the physical world have universal forms or laws based in the other worlds, and these are based on one universal template—The Good."

"Wow! These ideas are so interesting. So I'm probably still burning up selfish attributes in the Valley of Love, and I suppose most people in this world are tested by spiritual trials that equate to pain and suffering. Consequently, if they manage to transcend these trials, then they move away from pain into the Valley of Knowledge."

"Yes, that is true. 'Wherefore must the veils of the satanic self be burned away at the fire of love.'"[9] Allison continued, "Did I ever tell you about the first time I saw the desert properly? I was in my teens. I was on a secondary school art trip at Hattah-Kulkyne National Park, in Northern Victoria in 1989. It was two weeks before Dad died."

"No. Go on," said Hooman.

What came to her mind, as she explained it to Hooman, was a time when she stood on the peak of a large sand dune looking out at the desert. She had found a large, strangely shaped seed that she had never seen before and was now searching for more. "I eventually collected nine large seed pods. My teacher had found me out in the desert and explained that these seeds could only be germinated by the seasonal wildfires that spread through the desert periodically. For the tree to be born, its seed must germinate in fire: the outer husk must be scorched so that the seed's growth is triggered. So you see, the connection to the burning of earthly attributes in the soul leads to spiritual development. These are the lakes of fire in *The Book of Gates*, and once a soul has burned away its lower attributes, it can move through the next gate. If you have faith and walk into the fire, you will not be harmed—these are the seeds of the Phoenix emerging from the ashes from which it and we are reborn."

"Yes, I can see the connection," he said.

She had taken a series of photos on the side of a dune where she'd lain the nine seed pods in rows of three by three to form a square. "After I had taken photos of the seeds, I took them back to the campfire and scorched them in the coals. The next day, the last day of the school trip, I trudged out into the desert and buried them where I had found them. I never knew if they grew after that, but I always wondered." Allison was now thinking about the nine parts of the Egyptian idea of the soul as being like the nine "seeds of fire."

Hooman was too, because he said, "So, we are like those seed pods, right? I mean, maybe we are the seeds of the Phoenix, or the children of the Phoenix, created inside the glass womb or the womb of time, and once we are born and are able to burn and destroy the glass womb, we are free to fly from this world to the sun of the Unseen."

"That is a beautiful way to describe it, Hooman."

"Maybe there is a poet in me after all."

They laughed.

———

After lunch they walked to Union Square and entered the open paved area at the bottom of the square. They walked past the subway entrance and toward the statue of George Washington. They slowly circled around the statue, looking at the memorial that had sprung up since 9/11. After a while, Hooman sat on the semicircular stone bench surrounding the figure of George Washington, and Allison sat next to him.

Hooman recalled seeing the candlelight vigils on the news in the previous month after the September 11 attacks. He had come down here in late September, and there were still candlelight vigils even then. Now, as he looked around the statue and the surrounding area, there were thousands of candles and bunches of flowers spread around, peace banners on the ground, and chalk messages on the base of the statue and on the ground around it. The area was disordered and crowded with all manner of objects that represented people's collective grief.

What he found most moving were the pictures of those who had lost their lives in the attack. They were pinned up on walls, bus stop shelters, and even mailboxes. These makeshift memorials had appeared every-where in Manhattan, but Union Square had become the main focus of the city's collective grief, and it seemed like the whole world was in the square.

"I'm going to head to the market. I'll leave you here to think. I'll see you in a bit."

"Okay, I won't be long."

She left the statue of George Washington, walking to a path nearby that passed through the wooded and lawned area of the square. He looked over his shoulder for a moment and watched her walk toward the Greenmarket, located at the top of the square.

He had been in his office on the day of the attack and did not see the first plane hit the north tower from where he was. But moving to another room on the other side of his building, he joined his colleagues, and from there he saw the second plane hit the south tower, and then later both towers collapsed. He was acutely aware of the shock of everyone in the room and heard his boss, Paul, and several others swear in utter shock for the first and last time. Those first few days, and to a lesser extent the following weeks after the towers had collapsed, had the most surreal aura of unbelievability. This event was a moment in history that underlined his belief in a global village that was still coming to terms with its common humanity. And he thought then there were two kinds of poverty—material poverty and the poverty of the ideals of our equality, which leads to hate.

He stood up and left the statue, walking into the wooded area in the center of the square. Other images in his mind from the news reports were the smaller, more intimate vigils in this part of the square, where small circles of light hovered in the night like light-islands floating on a still, dark ocean. Now in the day, a few weeks later, he noticed the red fall leaves scattered around the base of trees, the colors of the leaves contrasting with the vivid green lawns. Some trees had turned yellow and red, and a few were still partially green as they resisted the oncoming winter.

When he caught up with Allison, she had already purchased a few vegetables. She had put them in the bag containing her new notebook. The sun continued to warm their faces as they moved through the various stalls and meandered toward the top of the square.

His cell phone vibrated in his coat pocket. "Hello. Oh hi, what's up? We're in Union Square. I'm heading back to work soon. Allison is here with me. We got some vegetables for tonight's dinner. Okay, we'll wait for you up on the corner of Park Avenue South and 17th. Okay, see you soon." He flipped his cell shut. "That's Nava. She has been talking to Shidan about organizing a surprise birthday for Sara. She is dropping Shidan off at the Sun Tongue. She's going to pick you up on the way. Shidan wants you to stop by for a while and chat about something. I'll catch a taxi back to the office."

"Hmm . . . I wonder what he wants to talk about?"

———

Fifteen minutes later Allison and Hooman left the Greenmarket and walked between two stall owners' trucks that were parked on 17th Street. They crossed over and walked up to a Barnes and Noble store. Allison stopped for a moment to look at the window display. Hooman embraced her from behind. He looked into the window display over her shoulder.

"Anything interesting?" he said.

"No, nothing obvious," she replied.

She turned and took his hand, and they walked toward Park Avenue South. At the intersection they crossed over and waited for Nava in front of the W Hotel. They didn't have to wait long before Nava's car pulled up in front of the hotel.

Nava rolled the window down. "Okay, get in, Allison."

Hooman and Allison embraced. "See you this afternoon," Hooman said.

"I can give you a lift to work if you want," Nava said.

"No, that's okay. I'll get a taxi."

He watched Allison climb into the back seat. She kissed Shidan on the cheek.

"Allison, how wonderful to see you," Shidan said. Then he added, "There is something I want to talk to you about at the shop." Shidan nodded and waved at Hooman, who waved back at Shidan as Allison closed the door behind her.

"Okay, I'll see you tonight." Hooman leaned through the window and kissed Allison.

Nava pushed into the afternoon traffic and headed toward Midtown East.

Hooman watched Nava drive up Park Avenue South until she disappeared into traffic. He turned toward the road and looked for a taxi to take him back to work.

———

Allison was lying on the leather couch at the back of the bookshop. Nava had dropped them off and gone back to her office. Shidan was in the back office kitchen making coffee. Nikki left the bookshop to get some lunch for herself.

Allison heard the kettle come to the boil and eventually splutter.

"I have missed you, my dear. It really has been too long since we saw each other. But of course, I understand, you have been busy with the baby coming and the renovations to the house." He raised his voice over the noise of the kettle.

"And you know, recently, I've been so unproductive. I just sit at home contemplating nothing in particular. But you could always come and see me at the house, you know," she said.

"I am with you completely. Yes. I should come up more often. I am sorry. Anyway, recently I've been overseas, but I won't bore you with that, and you can't say you've been unproductive. Pregnancy is a pretty intensive job. And you will be a full-time mother soon."

Shidan emerged from the back office with a tray and placed it on the coffee table. He sank into the armchair. "Ahh . . . blessed peace," he said.

"I haven't done anything. Pregnancy is all on autopilot," she said.

Shidan closed his eyes and leaned his head back. He took a deep breath and exhaled.

She waited for him to open his eyes. "Well, what did you want to talk about, Shidan? Hooman said you wanted to chat with me about something. And you said as much in the car."

"Oh, nothing much."

From the couch her eyes drifted over the details of the ceiling and the lampshade near her head. She turned her head toward him. "So, what's on your mind?"

Instead of answering, he leaned over to push the plunger down. Eventually, he poured two coffees and placed one on her side of the coffee table, near her head. He then relaxed fully. "I've noticed some changes in you, and I wanted to talk them through," he said.

"Oh . . . okay."

"I noticed today, for instance, that you are wearing those typical pastel overalls from—"

"Some trendy boutique."

"Right. Whereas last year you would be wearing, say—"

"Grubby mechanic's overalls."

"Thank you, yes. Well, maybe that's pushing the example a little to the extreme, but yes, essentially. Don't tell me you have capitulated to Nava's and Hooman's mainstream tastes."

"No, not really. I went shopping with Nava recently. She bought these for me. It wasn't my choice. If I didn't wear them, she would get upset. We've been shopping a few times this year for clothes that fit my belly. Once the baby is born, I will wear my usual stuff."

"You weren't built for mediocrity, my dear. That's not part of your greater destiny." He looked at her and smiled.

Nikki came through the front door with a selection of sushi in a plastic container. Shidan turned his head toward Nikki. "What do you think, Nikki? Does Allison look better in her more authentic clothing? And you know that's why I really like you. You're original, uncompromising, so anti-establishment, and it is such a breath of fresh air. You are more divergent than most people."

"Yes, I agree with Shidan. I prefer your usual look," Nikki replied. A customer came into the shop and started to talk to Nikki.

Allison turned her head to stare at the ceiling again. "You know, with you sitting in that armchair and me on this couch of yours, I feel like I'm getting free analysis."

He laughed. "Analysis. From me? You're already perfect . . . besides, your character flaws are great. Why would I ever try to make you boring?"

"I'm not entirely comfortable either. All of a sudden, I've slipped into the upper middle class. When I married Hooman, I inherited a new lifestyle, and it feels tight around me. It's not me, really. I can start wearing my retro leather jacket again. I'll wear it over these overalls."

Shidan smiled and took a sip of his coffee.

"Well, I can look like my old self externally, but internally I cannot turn back. And you know, I know Hooman has influenced me on a certain level, but I have arrived at this on my own, through my own search and investigation. I've had certain experiences in the last few years that have confirmed to me the existence of God, and as you know, I am a Bahá'í these days, and your prediction that I would become a Bahá'í came true. Isn't that amazing?

"And when I look at the social problems in Harlem, I realize that the whole problem is that there is a spiritual malaise in our world, a maladaptation to our true nature."

He did not respond. He looked off into space. She continued, "On that subject, I want to invite you to a study group that I am tutoring. It's called the Ruhi Institute courses. The first book in the series is called *Reflections on the Life of the Spirit*. I want you to come and chant something in Arabic and join us if you like. I know you used to chant prayers as a child."

"Me! Allison, you know I am agnostic."

The customer left the shop, and Nikki walked over to them.

"Nikki you can come too if you want."

"Cool," Nikki said. She came over to the couch and sat next to Allison's feet. She began to eat the sushi. Allison sat up and began to drink her coffee.

"You didn't mind discussing spiritual topics when we were traveling in Iran and Afghanistan. And I know you have a great voice, so why not? If you are so confident in your agnostic beliefs, then a single chant can't shake your principles, surely."

"I'll do it for you, my dear, but I assure you it will be like reading the dullest recipe." He sat up straight, impersonating a TV chef. "Three cups of sugar. Now, darlings, if you overcook the asparagus, don't you worry, darlings. I'm here to save you . . . blah, blah, blah. You know the rest."

"Look, I don't want you to come if it's a drag. I just wanted some cultural and linguistic diversity. And you are deeper than you think, Shidan, when it comes to spiritual matters."

"No, I'll come, and I'll behave myself too. Besides, it will disturb Sara. I can say I'm going back to my religious roots and have a little fun with her for a few days."

"Why are you so mean to her? I don't understand."

"Who knows? I'm going to change the topic now."

"I know who you are, Shidan. Treat her like you treat me." He did not answer but grinned, and she continued, "You're a good person."

"That is nice of you to say, but it isn't so. And I couldn't think of anything more boring than being good."

"I mean it. You're wonderful. Why don't you let Sara see what I see in you? That could be our secret birthday present this year, and I could try harder to get on with her myself. I know she thinks I am a hopeless, lazy hippie."

"Hmm . . . we'll see, won't we? That might be a good present. And as for Sara, well, she is materialistic, as you know. That is the very limited prism through which she sees everything in life. But underneath all that, I think she is a good person." He took another sip of coffee. "I've been reading something that may interest you. It's a poem by Enceladus Laurent."

Getting up, he walked over to a pile of books near the couch. Once in his chair again, he opened a book. "Okay, here it is," and he read it out in a compelling voice, which, as he read, centered itself in the emotional heart of her being.

"Water and Pain"

These are the tears of pain.
This water rolls into the corner of my mouth.
Once received the voice speaks of sacrifice.
Of the obliterated self.
Of the realm of absolute pain.
A pain unknown to humanity.

Because pleasure is a falsehood in the house of words.
Our dominion includes suffering but is beyond it.
To take pleasure away and exchange this with pain is a gift.

So, it is with the detached heart that we are able to walk forward into this realm.
Being leads to receiving and receiving leads back into being.
Faith leads to seeing what fact cannot know about itself.
I am the debased tree whose fruit led to the truth of death, and the truths that no one person could bear to hear.

It's the pain that makes us empathetic not the pleasure.
From this compassion is born.
From this eye comes the water of life, which is the transparent blood tear.
From here we go into ourselves.
And the tear retracts from the corner of my mouth.
It retraces its path back up my face.
It merges back into the corner of my eye.
And I see you for the first time.
And I love you beyond anything I have known in the future or the past.
And I see your eye give birth to the second tear in eternity.

The tear beyond pain.

"That's absolutely beautiful, Shidan!"

———

Shidan went to a parking garage for the car. Allison lay down again. She drifted into sleep. With her home life of late, she had gotten used to an afternoon nap, and her body had fallen into that rhythm.

A landscape appeared around her dreaming self. Standing on the side of a low hill, she observed the tall grass moving in rhythmic waves. The height and form of the grass reminded her of Upstate New York, where she and Hooman had been married, and unlike other dreams—which were dark, vague, and scripted—this dream was well lit. As with waking life, she was more in command of her own decisions and actions and knew that she was dreaming—a lucid dream.

She looked down at her bare feet, which were crushing the lush grass. Walking around for a bit, she caught sight of a small flower and bent down to observe it. The shape of the flower was like nothing she had seen before. The flower was otherworldly, almost alien, and exceptionally beautiful. It reminded her of the dream she had had in London with Mona. Although the grass and flowers were not translucent in this dream, the panorama around her sparkled with a light of exceptional clarity.

Deciding to walk up the hill, she heard voices near the summit. At the top of the hill, she could determine that the voices were coming from the other side, and she went forward over the rise. She could make out Hooman as she came closer. He appeared to be older, with grayer hair than he had now, and he was talking to a younger man in his late teens. As she neared them, they stopped talking and watched her approach. The younger man walked over to her. He bent down on his knees and proceeded to tap her swollen belly. At first she felt his light tapping, but then as he continued, she felt a strong pain. Aware that this was a contraction, she realized that she was beginning to give birth and needed to wake up. The pain increased. Then she crouched down to look into his eyes, which were the most intense iridescent blue. The color reminded her of the shimmering wings of the Ulysses butterflies that she had seen in her childhood in Northern Queensland. She looked around his face, which was both intensely youthful and paradoxically worn old, but his eyes were unblemished by time.

"I'm inside you, and I love you. You will not see me grow up, but I will see you in the world to come," he said just before she woke up.

The words he spoke were surrounded and interwoven by a bell-like harmonic.

———

In front of the shop, Shidan pulled up and turned off the ignition. He looked up at the skyscrapers in Midtown for a moment, then got out of the car. Opening the door to the shop, he stopped short of walking in. He saw Nikki and Allison standing near the couch. Allison stood with her legs slightly apart and was surrounded by a pool of fluid. Her water had broken. He stood in the doorframe in shock. She was still staring at her legs and the fluid. She looked up at him finally. "My god, Shidan. The baby . . . it's coming early."

———

After spending four days at Kakadu, Allison decided to hike in the Bungle Bungles in the northwest tip of Western Australia, a region that was called the Kimberley. The roads in the Purnululu National Park, where the Bungle Bungles were located, were inaccessible to cars other than four-wheel drives. After a day's drive, she came to Kununurra, looking for anyone who might be driving south that she could hitch a ride with. She had a map of the area but was not sure where the paved roads ended, and the dirt roads began.

She drove through the town and saw a sign for Hidden Valley RV Park. She spent the night in the RV park, and on the next day she walked around asking if anyone was driving to the Bungle Bungles. Eventually, she came to an older couple who were packing up their tent and belongings and putting them into the back of a Toyota Land Cruiser.

"Excuse me, but are you guys going south toward the Bungle Bungles?"

"Yes, we are."

"Oh, cool. Can I hitch a ride?"

"Yeah, sure, but we aren't coming back this way. We are going on to Fitzroy Crossing after the Bungle Bungles."

"That's okay, I've got my car here. Can I follow you until the entrance to the park?"

"Yeah, that's fine. There's an RV park near Ord River. You can leave your car there, and we'll take you on from there. You'll need to take food and water into the park."

"Great, thank you. I'll go get my car."

Before leaving Kununurra, Allison stopped at a supermarket for supplies. She then followed the couple along the Great Northern Highway. The landscape was mainly flat. There were a few red low-lying hills appearing from time to time and small stunted eucalypts living amongst sporadic tufts of green and yellow grass.

After two hours, Allison saw a dark-gray cloud mass coming toward her. She was listening to U2's "With or Without You" on the car stereo when the clouds passed over the two cars. It began to rain heavily. Even with the windshield wipers set to the highest setting, it was hard to see the couple in front of her. Both cars slowed down, and after an hour, they came out on the other side of the rain and clouds, and the sky was clear again.

After another hour and a half, Allison saw the sign for Ord River; the couple pulled over at the entrance to the Bungle Bungles.

"Follow us. Your car should be fine until we reach the RV park," the man shouted. Allison turned into the entrance and followed them along a dirt road.

Once they came to the RV park, Allison parked and took her supplies, hiking pack, a smaller backpack, and tent out of her car and packed them into the back of the Land Cruiser before jumping into the backseat. The road to the visitors center was rough and corrugated, and the four-wheel drive swung from side to side at certain points in the road. After two hours, they came to the center and paid the camping fee. Beyond the visitors center, they could see the Bungle Bungle range on the horizon.

They then drove south for half an hour and came to the Walardi campsite, where Allison and the couple pitched their tents and ate lunch. After lunch they drove another half an hour to the Piccaninny parking lot. As they neared the parking lot, Allison saw the Domes.

"We are only going to Cathedral Gorge today, then we will go back to the camping ground after an hour or so."

"That's fine. I want to start with the Domes, then try other hiking trails. I'll hitch back to the campsite this evening."

"Okay, just don't leave it too late, or you'll get stuck out here."

"Yeah, don't worry. I'll be fine. Thanks for the lift here, by the way."

"You're welcome."

The couple parked the car, and Allison headed toward the Domes trail on foot. As she came closer, the trail passed through tall yellow grass that looked almost like a large yellow hedge. After a while, she passed into the Domes. The rock formations had been described by some as a series of fluid conical hats. In some cases the domes stood alone, but in the majority of cases, the domes melded into each other with a fluidity similar to water. She wondered about the Aboriginal Dreaming for this land because if you didn't know anything about erosion and geography, then the creation of these domes would seem quite magical and supernatural. This land did seem to have a distinct spirit.

The trail came to a dead end, so she walked back to the parking lot and hiked on toward Cathedral Gorge.

When she came to the gorge, the waterfall was flowing due to the heavy rain that had come down several hours before. The gorge was a cross between a massive open cave, a waterfall, and a creek with a wide sandy bank. There were not many people around, so Allison changed into her bikini and swam in the shallow water for a while. Floating on her back, she looked up through the cliffs surrounding the gorge to the sky above and felt the cold water cocoon her body. After half an hour in the water, she changed back into her clothes before moving on to the Piccaninny Creek trail.

Toward the end of the day, with the light fading, Allison came back to the parking lot and walked on toward the campsite. After fifteen minutes a car came along the road, and a young couple gave her a lift. When she got to the campsite, she noticed that the older couple had gone, and she assumed they had moved on to the northern campsite where she intended to go on the following day.

23

AN IMAGE OF IDENTITY

After journeying through the planes of pure contentment, the traveler cometh to THE VALLEY OF WONDERMENT *and is tossed upon the oceans of grandeur, and at every moment his wonder increaseth. Now he seeth the embodiment of wealth as poverty itself, and the essence of independence as sheer impotence. Now is he struck dumb with the beauty of the All-Glorious.*[1]

— BAHÁ'U'LLÁH, *THE SEVEN VALLEYS*

Snow fell heavily outside the Studio Museum on 125th Street. Allison watched it fall for a few moments before swiveling back around to look at the children in her photography group sitting quietly before her; they sat cross-legged on the floor. She had also found Jessica, the girl she had met roughly three years before. Jessica had responded to the notice that Allison had put up at the Pelham Fritz Recreation Center in Marcus Garvey Park. And then there was Aliah, a child of one of the local Bahá'í parents.

Jessica put her hand up. "Ms Bird, I don't understand what you want us to do."

"I'm sorry, guys. Am I confusing you?" Allison asked.

"You want us to decide our own project. So you mean we have to think of what we want to take pictures of?"

"Yes, Jessica, that's exactly what I mean."

"But how?"

"Try to decide, as a group, whose ideas seem the best to everyone, through consultation."

Jessica's face went blank before she responded. "But Ms Bird, I can't think of anything right now."

"Does anyone have any ideas?" Allison asked. The rest of the group responded with silence and blank faces.

Noah was asleep in his travel bassinet, and Allison was sitting cross-legged next to him. She leaned over to check he was warm enough. She moved his blanket higher around his neck. The snow outside was lit by the mid-afternoon light, which was a dark, rich blue framed by the windows. Again, Allison looked at the street below for a moment; it seemed like night had come early. Its soft, deep colors contrasted profoundly with the hard whiteness of the fluorescent light inside the room. A bulb flickered at the back of the room. She looked back at the group and pressed on despite their lack of enthusiasm. She wondered how to turn the meeting around.

"Okay. Everyone, I have some good news." She waited to see if her words had any effect. "My husband, Hooman, you remember him from last year, right? He is going to purchase some old secondhand 35mm cameras for you. So, when we meet back after winter, I can start to show you how real cameras work, instead of these disposables."

With this news some of the group seemed to pick up a bit. Jessica put her hand up again. "Ms Bird, will we learn how to do black-and-white shots too?"

"Yes . . . definitely. That was my plan. We will learn about different lens filters for black-and-white film, mostly yellow and red filters."

Encouraged by the changing body language, Allison decided to go back to the topic of the group trying to determine its own direction, but this time with some leading questions.

"Okay, I want to ask you all about Harlem, and then we'll see if we can find some ideas for the group to follow. Is that okay with you all?" Allison said. They all assented in a relaxed but attentive manner. "First of all, I want to ask you, who owns Harlem? What I mean by this is who does it belong to, as a place. Do you know what I'm asking?"

One of the boys, Johnny, asserted, "Us." His face contorted with aggression.

"Who is us?" she asked Johnny.

"Blacks, Ms Bird."

"What does everybody else think?" Allison asked. She looked around at their faces. Jessica added in a tone of curiosity. "What about the Latino people in East Harlem?"

"Yeah, what about them?" Aliah said.

"Oh, yeah. Them too," Johnny added.

"Do you guys know that almost everyone in America comes from somewhere else originally? Where does everyone here come from?"

Voices murmured. "Africa."

"Thanks, that's right. And did you guys know that Harlem is a Dutch word? Originally, New York was called New Amsterdam. And before the Dutch, the American Indians were the custodians of the land."

One of the other girls responded for the first time that afternoon. "Ms Bird, we know that, so what?"

"You guys don't have to call me Ms Bird. You can use my first name, if you like."

"What Ms Bird is saying is we, everyone, has a right to live here. Not just Blacks," Jessica said.

"Yes. Thanks, Jessica. For instance, Hooman and I come from many places. He was born in Iran and grew up in Australia, but now his home is here in America. My father was from Italy, but I grew up in Australia, and now I am here, living in Harlem, with you. And have you heard the phrase from the American Constitution that 'All men are created equal,' which was a reference to all the British colonies in America at that time? It is true that at that time, the original founders meant mainly White men and not women or African slaves. But its meaning did expand over time to include all races in America. And in the future most people in America will probably be of mixed race. There are some things we have in common that unify us as a nation, and others that celebrate our cultural diversity, which allows us to be different but still American. And I wanted to discuss the fact that racial equality was not just given to African Americans. It was hard won and hard fought for by African Americans and Whites and all the other races in America. And there was the civil rights movement, which ran from 1954 to 1967. Do you know about the movement?"

"Yeah, we studied that last year," Johnny said.

Allison picked up the novel *An Unequal Sun* from the floor. "I've just finished reading this. It's a beautiful story about an interracial couple striving for equality in Detroit in the early sixties. It highlights the characters' struggles and triumphs and the power of love in the face of ignorance and hatred. And it reminds me of how far we have come and what we still need to achieve."

Allison looked around the room at all their faces. The conversation seemed to be dying again, so she decided to finish off the session and resume her project idea at another time. "Okay, everyone, let's all think about your group project over winter. In the meantime you could all take pictures of people from different nationalities and races that live here. Try to find as many different people as you can. Ask them how they came to live in Harlem. Find out about their story, which is collectively our story."

Next to her was a cardboard box full of unused disposable cameras. She passed it to Jessica, who got up and took the box around.

"So, everyone, the box is coming. Take two cameras each, because we won't be meeting again for a few months, and we can look at the pictures you've taken in the spring. I'm sorry I can't see you for a while. It's just that I need to spend time with Noah now, until he is a little older."

Allison glanced at her watch. Then looking down at the road through the heavy snow, she saw Hooman sitting in Nava's SUV; the headlights were on. She picked up Noah in the travel bassinet and reached into her pocket for the keys to lock the room.

"Okay, everyone, let's go. Because it's snowing so much today, I'll get Hooman to drop you younger kids off at your homes. Jessica, you're the exception because you live farther away than the rest. Thank you for coming. It has been really great seeing you all today, and I hope you have a great time in the next few months."

The children left the room and descended the stairs until they came out onto 125th Street. The older children began their walk home, while Allison took the younger ones and Jessica with her as she walked through the snow to the car.

"Say hi to your mum," Allison said to Aliah as she walked away.

"Okay, I will," said Aliah. "Bye."

Aliah waved and looked back at Allison as she continued to walk away.

After two of the children were dropped off, Jessica was alone in the back seat. Hooman pulled up in front of a run-down-looking building on St. Nicholas Avenue, which was adjacent to St. Nicholas Park. The trees in the park had a thick layer of snow on their branches. He turned to Jessica. "I think this is your house," he said.

"Thanks, sir."

"That's all right. It was nice to see you again. I hope you're enjoying Allison's project. Or maybe it's your project."

"Yes, sir."

Allison smiled at Hooman and looked back at Jessica. "Do you think the others like it too?" she asked Jessica.

"Oh yes, Ms Bird. Don't mind them. They like it. Some of them are just a bit grumpy because they've been told by our art teacher that they have to do it."

"Oh! I didn't know that. I knew most of you were from the same school, but I didn't realize you were from the same art class."

"Yes, Ms Bird, some, not all. Well, I know for sure that Johnny has to attend. Art is the subject he is failing in, and Miss Gates says that if he does well with this, she might pass him. But I wanted to be in the group, and some of the others did too."

"I'm glad you're enjoying it," Allison said.

"Oh yes, Ms Bird, I like photography." Jessica turned to Hooman and smiled. Looking back at Allison, she smiled again in silence. After a few seconds, perplexed and in a reflective way, she said, "You know, Ms Bird, I was thinking."

"What about?"

"We all do come from somewhere else, don't we?"

"Yes, Jessica, I think so. But people forget after a few generations."

"And do you think one day we'll all be able to live together with White folk and Latino and everyone? I mean, here in Harlem."

"I think so. Yes, and not just here, but in the whole world. Eventually they will all learn to live together."

"Okay, Ms Bird."

Jessica opened the door and jumped onto the snow beside the car. Allison heard the snow crunching under Jessica's boots as she walked through the falling snow. Allison watched her as she and the sound eventually disappeared into the building.

Six minutes later Hooman backed the car into a spot near the house. The tires slipped on the icy road, but with a little effort the car fit snugly in with cars close on either side.

Allison turned to him. "Do you remember the other day I took Noah to a movie theater downtown?"

"Yes, I remember. You mentioned you saw a dark but very interesting movie. Was it *Donnie Darko*?"

"Yes, it was," replied Allison, "and I was struck by a reference in the movie to the Smurf way of life. Donnie Darko, the main protagonist, was talking to his friends and said, 'Smurfette was sent into the Smurf village as the evil spy of Gargamel, the nemesis of the Smurfs, but Smurfette was transformed by the overwhelming goodness of the Smurf way of life.' And so, I was thinking that Bahá'u'lláh had the same thought too. That he hoped the Bahá'í community would transform humanity with that same overwhelming goodness."

"Bahá'u'lláh transformed the hearts of many he met, both those that were already receptive to his teachings and those who opposed him. In fact, all the great prophets were transformative through their deeds and words. Take Paul, one of the disciples of Christ, who was originally opposed to the Christian community, which he persecuted, but the love of Christ and the other Christians transformed him," Hooman said.

"And so, I hope in my heart that one day humanity will be transformed by overwhelming goodness."

"Yes, me too."

Down the street Allison saw the young boy she had seen months before. He was holding the hand of a middle-aged woman, and they were walking toward them on the opposite side of the street. The two turned off the street and ascended the steps to their building.

"Hooman, can you take Noah? I want to meet this kid."

Jumping out of the car, she ran down the street waving her arm and shouting, "Hello, hello . . . excuse me."

She managed to grab their attention. The woman had opened the door but turned around.

"Hi there. Hi. Sorry to stop you." She ran up the steps, breathing heavily. "Hi, my name is Allison. I'm your neighbor. I live across the street." She pointed to her house.

The woman studied her face. "Oh yes, I've seen you around. You moved in last year."

"Sorry to stop you at the door—it's snowing and cold, I know—but I won't take a minute. I just wanted to introduce myself, and I also wanted to ask your son something."

"Oh! He's not my son. He's my grandson."

"Oh, I see," she said and crouched down to his level. "Hello, what's your name?"

The boy hesitated as if to say something but did not respond.

"He's a bit shy," the woman said.

Allison looked up at the grandmother. "What's his name?"

"His name is Jonny Bell."

"And how do you spell his name?"

The woman spelled out his name to Allison.

Allison addressed the boy again. "Jonny, I saw you in the fall, kicking the leaves, and, you know, I like to drag my feet through the leaves too, well, recently at least. I started doing it just before I saw you. So, you see, we're connected in that way."

He did not reply to this either, and Allison got up. "I won't keep you any longer. But I would like to talk to you again about a photography group that I'm running. I want to see if Jonny would like to join us. Are you free later on tonight or perhaps tomorrow?"

"Tomorrow is better. I am heading out again soon. I have church in the morning, but you can come over any time after lunch, if you like. I'll be home all afternoon."

"Great! I'll see you tomorrow, then."

Allison reached the bottom of the steps. "Is that your husband over there?" the woman said.

Allison followed the line of the woman's stare. "That's Hooman and our son, Noah."

"Darling. I like that name. Noah is a good biblical name."

"Yes, it is. It was Hooman's mother's choice."

"Well, it's nice to see that some folks still have respect for the wishes of their parents."

Hooman saw that they were looking his way and waved. The lady waved back with a smile and a nod, then turned to Allison. "Have a good night, dear, and I'll see you tomorrow."

The woman led Jonny into the house and closed the door.

Allison crossed the street. Hooman opened the door to the house as Allison approached the steps. "What was that about?" he said.

"Nothing really. I was just wondering if that boy was interested in joining the group. I'm going over tomorrow afternoon to talk to his grandmother."

"Your brother and Sophie are arriving tomorrow afternoon."

"Yes, of course. I hadn't forgotten. I can do both. It won't take long. What time are they landing again? Is it one?"

"Yes, one."

"Fine, no problem. There's plenty of time." Noah started to cry. "I'd better feed him. Let's go upstairs."

They walked up the stairs, and Allison went straight to the bay window. The window was a cold spot, now that winter was peaking, but she could not keep herself from sitting there because of the view down the street and the park beyond. Turning the heat up, she sat in the bay window, and propping Noah up on one of her arms, he began to feed as he latched onto her breast. She looked into the blue, overcast light outside the house. She noted the denuded trees and the snow that had collected on cars. Looking back at Noah for a moment, she opened her notebook with her free hand. By now this notebook had absorbed all her previous notes, obscure quotes from various sources, and drawings. She had also recorded fragments of overheard conversations from friends and strangers that she felt were somehow insightful or just curious, and the notebook was now close to two-thirds full.

Before writing a new page or rereading past entries, she was in the habit of opening at the first page of her notebook. She had begun it with a quote from *The Seven Valleys* that stood out among all others, and that gave her entire notebook its meaning.

. . . in each realm, to every letter a meaning is allotted which pertaineth to that realm. Indeed, the wayfarer findeth a secret in every name and a mystery in every letter.[2]

All the fragments of the map she had started in London had now been fully absorbed into the notebook, and there was now more clarity and a deeper, more integrated aspect to her map where she had recorded the interconnected meaning and symmetry in names and places.

Under this quote was her first ever entry, where she had tried to unravel the mysteries of letters, words, and names.

The word "World" sat center page with the letter *l* crossed out, which made it "Word." Below this was the phrase "There are worlds in words" that was paraphrasing what Hooman had said when they first met, "In words there are worlds that are strange and sublime . . ." Under this sentence was the letter *l*, which was representative of the world of Lahut. So, by adding *l* to "Word," it was transformed back into "World." She had explored this idea when she was in Queensland at the shack when she had added an extra *l* to *The Hidden Words* so that it became "the hidden worlds."

Allison had made another entry a few months after that, which explored the idea that humanity is the embodiment of letters and language relative to the Word of God, and the Manifestations of God are the source of the power of language (the Point or starting point of each letter) and the Names of God. For example, the word "Baha" was the representation of the Glory of God, but she knew that the letters *Ba* or even just the letter *B* was the representation of the Manifestation of God, and in this case it referred to the Báb, the source of that glory, in conjunction with Bahá'u'lláh.

Within Bahá'í history were a group of early Bábís known as the "Letters of the Living," and these people were the first eighteen followers of the Báb (the Báb being the nineteenth letter), the first Manifestation of God in the Bahá'í era, who was the forerunner to Bahá'u'lláh. Allison had found an article on the Bahá'í Encyclopedia website that explored the relationship between the Báb and the Letters of the Living. She had copied parts of the article into the notebook:

> The term "Letters of the Living" is both a title and a theological statement . . .
>
> The term "letter" is symbolic, as is the Báb's use of the term Nuqtih (Point) to refer to the Manifestation or Messenger of God, who is the embodiment of the Primal Will. . . . The term "Point" indicates that everything originates with the

Manifestation, even as each letter and word originates with the mark made as the pen first touches paper . . .[3]

From the point, the mark that is made as the pen touches paper, emanate the letters of the alphabet, which are the primary and basic units of written language. The whole body of knowledge is based on these units. The letters are all different, but they have a common root in the point, the first mark made by the pen; no matter how numerous, they have one background, one common source. The letter is the intermediary between the point, which is the genesis of all letters, and words and sentences, which are composed of letters. Thus the term "letters" (hurúf), when attributed to the first to believe in a Manifestation, acknowledges these souls as letters coming forth from the Point, just as the form of every letter begins with a point made on a page . . .

In line with the symbolism of sacred script, including letters and points as discussed above, the point under the Arabic letter b, or ba, the first letter in each of the two invocations cited, relates to the famous Tradition attributed to Ali, the cousin and son-in-law of Muhammad and the first Imam of the Shia: "All of the knowledge of all the holy books is in the Qur'an, and all of the knowledge of the Qur'an is in the Fátiha *[the first sura], and all of the knowledge of the* Fátiha *is in the* Basmala *[i.e., the invocation* Bismi'lláhi'r-Rahmáni'-Rahím*], and all of the knowledge of the* Basmala *is in the letter* ba, *and all of the knowledge in the* ba *is in the point [*nuqtih*] under the* ba, *and I am that point." [4]* The Báb *is the letter b itself. All knowledge is in the nineteen letters of the* Basmala *and derives from the Báb as a Manifestation of God in the station of the Primal Point. The term "point" also refers to the Tradition that knowledge is a single point that the ignorant have multiplied.* [5]

She then thought about the transformative influence of the Word of God in every age, and that we traverse eternity with words and language; it was not just mere communication but a means of internal intellectual and spiritual movement, and we were destined to travel through all the worlds of God with its influence and energy, eventually leaving this exquisite, beautiful, but ultimately limited house of recycled star dust behind us, where we would find a world in every letter, and a matrix of words and worlds intertwined: from letters come words and from words sentences, from sentences come paragraphs, and beyond that the story of eternity, in worlds where this story unfolds, of our transcendent potentialities on that undreamed-of and radiant horizon.

Hooman was sitting on the couch reading a book. "I'm just going to watch the news for a bit. Let me know if it's too loud for you to concentrate." He turned the television on.

"The sound is fine like that," she answered.

Flipping randomly to page seventy-two, she read: "The number and names of people I meet is an indication of interconnectedness and significance."

This idea was another form of the Kingdom of Names, and she thought about her dream in London when Mona had said that all souls were grouped by name, color, shape, and many other hierarchical and lateral categories where thoughts and identity could be synchronized within these groups; this led to a oneness of mind and spiritual body. This was like drawing a circle around many souls and calling them a collective "I," so that "we" became "I" and "I" became "we," where threads of destiny intersected, and then lives became inextricably bound into each other in a beautiful interplay.

She could understand the name groups, so she had recorded all the names of people she met with whom she had some spiritual connection, and she wondered also if all the people in the world with the same "name group" could somehow have their actions and thoughts synchronized without them knowing. Like her thought experiments of hidden asymmetrical conjunctions recorded in her imaginary life-story depository, where all our actions were synchronized; it may be that a thousand people with the same name hugged other people in the same moment, or a thousand children of the same name skipped in the same moment. There were endless categories of actions synchronized in this way that may continue in endless and continuous loops around the world.

She thought about name synchronization and read all the names of people whom she had met that had some connection to her.

Names and Symmetry

1. *Paul Bird = brother*
2. *Paul Sparrow = miner in Coober Pedy, Australia*
3. *Paul = taxi driver first night in New York*
4. *Paul Nightingale = Hooman's boss*
5. *Frank Paul = served me latte, Starbucks*

6. Paul Frank = American designer
7. St. Paul (Saul of Tarsus) = Apostle of Christ (The Conversion of Saint Paul by Caravaggio)

Mona Mahmudnizhad = Bahá'í girl from Shiraz, Iran
Mona Mavaddat = Shidan's sister

Sophie Johnston = Paul's girlfriend
Sophie Nightingale = Paul Nightingale's wife

Alison Nightingale = Paul Nightingale's daughter
Allison Bird = Me

Sara = Friend
Sarah = Jessica's friend

Jasper Johns = painter of the American Flag in MoMA
Jasper Trenfield = Friend from Melbourne

The entry continued: "I have no clue what the connection to Hooman's boss is. I suppose I was meant to read about the nightingale in *The Conference of the Birds* and in *The Tablet of Ahmad* by Bahá'u'lláh."

These notes were extensive and continued for many pages. It was clear to her that she had been communing with the souls in the next world in an indirect and direct way and trying to understand a higher symmetry through earthly names and places.

Beneath the names that she had linked to her symmetrical destiny map, there was a series of places and objects that were also symmetrical relative to her life.

Places, Objects, and Symmetry

St. Martins Place = London, UK
Martin Place = Sydney, Australia

Pineapple Street = Brooklyn Heights, New York
The Big Pineapple = Queensland, Australia

Orange Street = London, UK
Orange Street = Shidan's apartment in Brooklyn Heights, New York

Simurgh Restaurant = London, UK
The Simorgh = The Conference of the Birds

1. The Seven Stars Café = Greenwich Village, Manhattan, New York
2. The Seven Dials intersection = London, UK
3. The Seven Hills = Rome, Italy
4. The Seven Valleys = Book by Bahá'u'lláh
5. Snow White and the Seven Dwarfs = Movie
6. Seven colors = light
7. Seven-tones scale = Western heptatonic scale

Noah finished suckling on her sole breast and stared up at her. He smiled at her, it seemed, for the first time. For the first month he appeared to be smiling into space, but now he saw her.

Closing her notebook, her thoughts turned to Paul and Sophie, who had planned to come for the birth of Noah, but since he came early, they had delayed until both Noah and her were more settled, which would allow Allison to drag Noah around New York as they traveled around and visited different sites in the city. When they were last in New York, they had not seen much of the place. They had only seen the small towns in Upstate New York that were close to where the wedding was held. At the time Paul could not spare time away from the restaurants. Now that they would be here for eleven days, Allison wanted to show them around a bit. She wanted them to see some of the famous landmarks.

"What can we show Paul and Sophie while they are here?"

"I don't know. Whatever they want."

He was absorbed by the news about Afghanistan. He had just switched channels to the BBC on satellite TV; a current affairs report announced that 2,775 civilians had been killed in Afghanistan by US bombs. Hooman put the book he was reading down and concentrated on the report.

She remembered her travels in Afghanistan. "I wonder how Nasim and Vahid are going. We need to call them soon," she said.

"There's no need. Shidan emailed them a few nights ago. I forgot to tell you. They are fine, and Nasim thinks they are better off without the Taliban, despite the violence in the country from the American invasion. At least she can run her school without fear now."

"Ahh . . . okay then. That is true."

She looked out at the street again. The blue light was fading into night, which made the warm, golden light inside the house seem stronger and more resonant. The shadows in the street were deeper, and she looked up at the hazy light in the clouds lit by the setting sun. She looked back at Noah. He had fallen asleep. She smiled.

————

After spending four days at the Bungle Bungles, Allison drove back to the Northern Territory via Kununurra. At Timber Creek she began driving northeast until she hit the Stuart Highway, which took her directly south to Alice Springs. It took two days to reach Alice Springs. On the first night, she pulled over and slept in the back of the car, and on the second day, she pulled into Alice Springs toward the end of the day.

On the following day she drove a short way out of Alice Springs to the MacDonnell Ranges and spent the day hiking through parts of the ranges along the Larapinta Trail.

The formation of the geology was quite distinct from the Bungle Bungles although they were the same shade of intense red. The hills in the Bungle Bungles were soft and fluid, almost feminine, whereas the MacDonnell Ranges were sharp and angular, and the rocky outcrops had been pushed up into layered diagonals. The formation of the Bungle Bungles in contrast was made from flat layers, like a tower of pancakes. And the scale of hills in the MacDonnell Ranges was larger too.

After returning from Stanley Chasm, Allison drove back to Alice Springs and spent the night at an RV park.

The next day, she drove further south toward Coober Pedy in South Australia. The land for most of the journey was flat desert with small bushes and red dirt. It took a day to reach the town, and after driving around the town, she found Riba's Underground Camping & RV Park, where she stayed for a week as she tried to find work and a roommate in a local house.

She found a room with a family in one of the underground houses that locals called dugouts.

She eventually found a job in a café, but what she really wanted to do was try mining for opals, so she found a part-time job assisting one of the miners, Paul Sparrow. For the most part she ended up removing rock rubble with a wheelbarrow, but Paul eventually allowed her to have a go at drilling. It was hard work physically, and at the end of each day mining, she had sore hands and arm muscles but felt content with the job. It was interesting to identify as a miner, if only fractionally.

———

After a month of working with Paul, he took her out into the desert surrounding Kati Thanda–Lake Eyre. The lake only filled once every three to four years, and this year the lake was empty. Allison and Paul walked into the salt flats. She enjoyed the crunch of salt beneath her bare feet. The lake bed was vast, and the low hills on the other side of the lake were many hours' walk away. Paul explained that when it filled, the pelicans and other birds would arrive in their tens of thousands. She tried to imagine the vast, still lake in her mind, with a rich blue reflection of the sky. Allison asked if she could be alone on the lake, so Paul walked back to the car, and she walked further into the center of the lake. After half an hour of walking, she sat down with her Leica and took shots with black-and-white film and a red filter, which would increase the contrast of light and dark in the images. She lay down flat and took a shot of her torso, legs, and bare feet with the hills in the distance on the other side of the lake; the immense flatness of the lake bed was intriguing. She then stood up, and the last few photos she took before walking back to the car were of her bare feet on the salt surface.

Paul and Allison didn't say much on the trip back to Coober Pedy. As they came into Coober Pedy, Paul asked, "Why are you mining with me?"

"I'll tell you when I know."

"You're strange. You know that?"

"Yes, I know that."

"Strange, but nice."

"Oh . . . thank you. It's always nice to get compliments."

"Why do you always want to do things alone?"

"That's hard to say."

He smiled and looked back at the horizon.

24

MY BROTHER

Now is he struck dumb with the beauty of the All-Glorious; again is he wearied out with his own life. How many a mystic tree hath this whirlwind of bewilderment snatched by the roots, how many a soul hath it worn out and exhausted. For in this valley the traveller is flung into confusion, albeit, in the eyes of him who hath attained, such signs are esteemed and well beloved. At every moment, he beholdeth a wondrous world and a new creation, and goeth from astonishment to astonishment, and is lost in awe before the new handiwork of Him Who is the sovereign Lord of all.[1]

— BAHÁ'U'LLÁH, *THE SEVEN VALLEYS*

Terminal 5 at JFK Airport was deserted; it had fallen into disuse in the previous year, October 2001. Allison was sitting in the back seat of the car with Paul and Sophie. They had just picked them up from Terminal 4, and Allison had asked if Hooman could drive to Terminal 5 and stop in front of it for a few minutes. She pointed the building out to Paul and Sophie as they stopped near it. "Look, over there, isn't it great? It's a piece of American history . . . iconic modernism. All the other terminals seem utilitarian by comparison; they lack a higher aesthetic purpose, I feel."

Paul and Sophie stared at the building in silence.

Allison's eye movements were fluid as her gaze moved over the sculptural forms of the building, almost caressing it in her mind; the bird, with its concrete wings outstretched, was covered in a layer of snow—a home for metal birds. An observation that she had made on her first day in New York, just before her plane touched down on that winter day at JFK Airport just over three years before.

There had been three birds on that day: the metal bird, the paper bird, and herself, the human bird. She wondered what had happened to that airplane. Was it still in service somewhere? Did she have a shared destiny with those who had flown in it? And she never knew what had happened to the origami bird that she had given away at the airport to that old woman who had traveled with her in that metal bird; both the origami bird and the plane were symbols of humanity's collective destiny. This realization shimmered in her mind as it had on her first day in New York. She reached out and took Paul's hand into her lap.

"Welcome to America," Allison said and smiled.

"Thank you. Sophie and I are really looking forward to discovering New York with you, babe," he replied.

"And your first trip here doesn't count, since you only saw Upstate New York, for the most part," she said.

Paul and Sophie smiled.

"Yes, true. At the time we were a bit preoccupied with your marriage," Paul said.

"Allison will be a good guide. She knows more about its history than I do," Hooman said as he looked back at them from the driver's seat. "She could easily take you on a walking tour of Harlem and show you who lived where during the Harlem Renaissance. I only know a few of the writers, but she knows most of the key players in the various streams of art, music, and writing. The Apollo Theater is being restored at the moment, and it will be incredible to see it once it is finished."

Allison looked back at the terminal, and as she did, an epiphany washed over her mind. She realized that Terminal 5 was a Phoenix, or a symbol of it at least, where metal birds came home to find themselves at the end of their journey after flying over the six valleys and landing in the seventh valley of Poverty and Annihilation; in this valley, the Phoenix is annihilated and destroyed in fire, and through this it is stripped of its attachments to objects in the material world, its poverty but conversely its wealth.

In his own time Attar could have never imagined that a flying machine was even possible, and that in the future, parts of the symbolism in *The Conference of the Birds* would be fulfilled with the technological metaphor that had just arisen in Allison's mind, and that the travel and migration of human beings around the Earth, along with the unfoldment of a new spiritual civilization, would lead to the real beginnings of global citizenship and the gradual and organic stages in the unfoldment of the oneness of humanity—an idea that Hooman was so committed too—and through that, the complete transformation of humanity at every level. And at that time in history, the whole of humanity would enter into a collective synergistic state of knowing the Phoenix, both our own higher potential and our humanity. So, in the end, Allison knew that airplanes were not just a symbol but an essential piece of technology that changed and enhanced our destiny in place and time, allowing us to find points of cultural integration as they effectively shrunk the globe into that well-worn cliché of the global village, and with the birth of the internet in 1983, the world was becoming a digital village, particularly with the advent of social media and internet search engines, which Allison could now see emerging.

"It's a Phoenix, Hooman. Maybe an American Phoenix."

"Okay, wow. So it has moved on from being just a bird to being a Phoenix," he said jokingly.

"I remember seeing it on my first night in New York. Do you remember that night, Hooman?"

"I shall never forget it. It's burned into my memory. You were beautiful and *outrageously* eccentric, and thankfully nothing has changed."

Allison laughed. "Okay, we can go now."

Hooman drove off, eventually joining the expressway, and the airport was lost to sight as Allison looked back at it one last time.

After half an hour of watching suburbia slide by, they came to the Queensboro Bridge. The traffic was sparse, even for a Sunday, and the car sped across unhindered. Everyone looked out at the Manhattan skyline in silence. Allison gazed through the steel supports flashing by in a blur. She remembered her first night in New York with the skyline of towers glowing in the night—those empty rooms with lights on—and the faint light in the interior of the taxi as she crossed the bridge, with that cool snow falling onto her warm face through the open window, although the symmetry of night and day in the past and the present had been switched.

She now compared the aspects of her life that had changed in that time. The intangible allure had dissipated, and she recalled her impression that the inhabitants of the city lived out an existence in a bliss of clichés. She was now a more integrated part of those clichés, because, as she had mentioned to Elliot three months ago, some of her cultural objectivity had departed; she had relinquished part of her identity as an outsider. She was becoming an American in subtle ways beyond the changes in her accent. And her own life had moved from partially objective observer, from an Australian viewpoint, to subjective participant within the contemporary American zeitgeist. What she now knew was that New York was her home, not Melbourne; she had made that transition in identity, being a dual citizen: both American and Australian.

What occurred to her in this moment was that a city, like New York or Melbourne, was not so much an objective place but a subjective object, where a series of subjective mental processes, underscored by each unique person's viewpoint—connected with others—formed into millions of conjunctions in consciousness: networks, where peoples' overlapping subjectivities were shared and from which collective viewpoints began to become semi-objective, and people then identified themselves as New Yorkers or Americans or sometimes, like her, with several subjective cultural identities, and still others identified themselves as tourists.

She now thought of Paul and Sophie's point of view as Australians in New York, and she knew she could guide them around the city and enhance their experience in Manhattan by throwing light onto their Australian identity and comparing and contrasting their experiences in New York with Melbourne; they were all now crossing two bridges: one physical and the other cultural.

As they came off the bridge, Paul and Sophie asked questions about the city and its history and were especially interested in Times Square.

"We won't be passing Times Square on the way to the house, but if you want, we could all go down and look at it in the evening, which is the best time to see it anyway," Hooman commented.

He looked at Allison in the rearview mirror. "Hey, I heard about a movie that's showing right now: *Metropolis*. Apparently, it's very interesting. A colleague from work mentioned it to me," he said.

"Yes, I've heard about it too. It's a Japanese anime, borrowing some ideas from the 1927 Fritz Lang movie of the same name." She turned to Paul. "Remember I used to see reruns of the original *Metropolis* at the Valhalla Movie Theater in Westgarth, in Melbourne?" Allison said.

"Yes, I remember . . . vaguely," Paul said, slightly distracted as he looked up at the buildings passing by.

"Since we would all be down that way anyway, we could see it at the movie theater near the square, then explore afterward. Maybe Sara could babysit for us tonight?" Hooman said.

"Sure. Sophie, do you want to see a movie tonight?" Paul asked.

Sophie nodded. Her face was absent as she stared out at the city.

————

After leaving Hooman to show Paul and Sophie around the house, Allison crossed the street to meet up with Jonny and his grandmother.

Propping her back up with a cushion and sitting in the middle of a large couch, her impression was one of being interviewed for a job. Jonny's grandmother had been polite while showing her into the house; however, she sensed immediately that the older woman was observing her intently. From the top of the stairs, Jonny had been quietly watching the scene. He made eye contact, but no emotions were evident in his face. Once they had moved into the living room, he descended the stairs and sat on the lowest step, looking through a doorway.

"So, dear, from what you tell me, this might be a good way for him to interact with children his own age," the woman said.

"Yes, there are some very sweet kids in the group who I know would befriend him."

She was thinking particularly about Jessica and the other older, brasher Johnny from the group—Johnny with a different spelling. She asked herself about the connection and repetition of the names "Jonny" and "Johnny." This confirmed to her that what she was doing was right.

She had a thought to make a new entry in her notebook exploring the names Jon, John, Jonny, and Johnny. In addition, she thought of the singer Joni Mitchell, whose music she had always liked and whose first name was only a small phonetic inflection away from the name Jonny. All names blended into an abiding whole. All names condensed into letters. All letters were found inside the word "Baha," which was an Arabic word for glory, which she had explored in her notebook.

"How old are they again?" the woman said.

"Fourteen . . . roughly. Some are younger."

"But Jonny is very shy, and he's only eleven. Will he get on in a group of older children?"

"I don't see it being a problem."

"Well, let's say he joins and, if all goes well, then . . . I mean if there is any bullying, I will pull him out without a second thought. You understand? Unfortunately, Jonny gets bullied a lot at school."

"Of course, I understand. But I assure you, I will not let that happen."

His grandmother looked at him through the doorway. She did not have to say anything, and, after a few moments, he nodded his approval. She smiled and turned back to Allison. "Well, that's fine, then, but I want to ask you more about yourself. I don't know anything about you. I mean, you're not a complete stranger, but you understand why I need to know a bit more."

A reasonable request, Allison thought. She placed her hands in her lap. "What would you like to know?" she said.

"Well, dear, why are you doing this? Where did you say you came from?"

"Australia."

"Yes, right, so it's rare, dear, that anyone from outside our community would show an interest in our kids. Harlem especially. It's a tough place for folks here, let alone those from outside."

"When Hooman and I moved here, I wanted to do something constructive for the community. I wanted to contribute in some way. To serve the community."

"Well, that's very Christian of you. I approve, dear, I do. Very Christian."

"Can I ask, does Jonny's mother live here with you?"

"Oh, her. No, she's a . . . well, let's just say her life has drifted off the path, and her husband, if you can call him that, is in a correctional facility. Jonny lives with us now. My husband works in banking."

Allison had been watching the woman's face. The woman had grimaced slightly as she mentioned her daughter and lifted contrastingly into unconcealed delight as she mentioned her husband's job.

"What's your husband do, dear?" the woman asked.

"He's a lawyer. He specializes in public international law."

"Oh! Top profession that. Top profession, yes. And what about you?"

At this point in the conversation, Allison was comfortable, but now she struggled to find something to say. She did not know what she did or had done.

If she was truthful, it could be said that she had drifted, like the woman's daughter, wavering on and off the path. And it was interesting that, for the sake of social ease, she would try to put her life's efforts into one limited box. This notion was annoying, but she did want to look credible to this woman. Something drew her to Jonny. He must join the group. Some future potential, which could not be quantified yet, was unfolding and would manifest eventually in Jonny's personality. She was connected to his future somehow. And she dwelled on her need to kick the leaves in the fall. She felt sure this desire came from Jonny and had been passed to her through the other worlds.

She was drifting through her thoughts, then realized the woman was waiting for a reply on what she did for work.

"I'm a mother," was the hesitating reply that eventually came. It seemed to satisfy the woman, but almost immediately Allison felt dissatisfied with this idea. She had barely been with Noah for a few months, and she was calling herself a mother? This was a title she was as yet unqualified for, and further subtext formed around what she had done in her life. Depressingly little, it seemed.

Jonny's grandmother had been patiently waiting for elaboration on the topic of being a mother, but Allison slipped into a blank reverie despite her awareness of the woman's expectation. She was only brought back to the present when another question came.

"So, dear, do you go to church?" the woman asked.

"Sorry. Church. Oh, no, not me. Not yet, anyway."

"Well, you're welcome to join me on any Sunday," came the sunny reply.

"Oh, thank you, that's very kind. And although I am not a Christian in the formal sense, I do believe in Christ. His influence in this world has been considerable."

"Yes, *yes*." The woman placed an approving emphasis on the last yes.

"But I also believe that other religions are equally valid, like Islam, Hinduism, Buddhism, to name only a few."

"I . . . oh no. No, dear, that doesn't sound right to me. Jesus is our only Savior . . . I don't understand. How can you believe in Jesus and also in the false gods of other faiths?" The woman now wore a pained and uncomprehending expression.

Allison felt sympathetic but could not find a way to ease the woman's obvious confusion, so she decided to ignore the question and answer it indirectly. "Well, I associate myself with my husband's faith. And that is that we should not pride ourselves on loving our own country, but rather we should love the whole world. So we should treat each other with kindness and compassion and never look with superiority at a person's skin color, social standing, culture, sex, or even religion. Doesn't that sound like something Christ would want?"

The woman wavered nervously. "Yes . . . I suppose."

"We need beliefs in human kindness. In an age of moral relativity."

"Moral what, dear?" The woman did not ask Allison anything more about her or her husband's faith. She guessed that the woman's primary concern had been assuaged, and that Jonny's welfare in the group had been assured.

At the door the woman turned to Allison. "Harlem can afford to welcome a few new people to her ranks, and I wish you all the best with your photography group. I think Jonny will gain a lot by attending."

———

Snow fell heavily around them as they came out of the movie theater onto West 42nd Street. The snow had begun falling while they were inside. As they walked through Times Square, Allison observed the relative emptiness of the place. The time was now 9:40 p.m., and Paul and

Sophie wanted to explore, but Allison was tired, so Nava offered to take them around while Hooman and Allison sat in the Starbucks overlooking the square; the café was the same one that she had sat in on her second day in New York. For a moment they watched the other three wandering off toward the top of the square into a light and snow-laden blur. Hooman went to the counter and ordered two café lattes. He soon came back and passed her a coffee as he sat opposite her. They were also sitting in the same chairs that Allison had sat in on her second day in New York.

"Did you like the movie?" he said.

"Oh yes, it was interesting. Thanks for taking me. It was nice of you to suggest it. You are so attentive to my tastes in art, my aesthetic sensibilities."

"I thought you would like the diversion."

"Yes, I did . . . I hope Sara is all right looking after Noah."

"She'll be fine."

Allison looked out to see if she could still see Nava, Paul, and Sophie, but they had disappeared into the crisscross of people. She looked at all the advertising lights for a moment and their strange collective abstraction, flashing and throbbing in the dark sky.

"So, the movie . . . was it like the original *Metropolis*?" he said.

"In places, yes. But I think that they are very different movies. I think I read somewhere that the director, Fritz Lang, was inspired by a visit to New York when he first saw the Manhattan skyline, and *Metropolis* was born in that moment, kind of like my own experience when I saw Manhattan for the first time as I was coming over Queensboro Bridge on my first night in New York. But I think my reaction was different from Lang's reaction. I remember that his experience of the Manhattan skyline was an aesthetic one, whereas I thought of the veneer of civilization, but ultimately *Metropolis* is about that veneer and indifference toward the suffering of others outside of one's class; the movie is a critique of capitalism really, and it tries to blend in some communist ideology too. Interestingly, the Nazis tried to highjack it and use it as a subtle form of propaganda, but in a strange twist they ended up fulfilling a part of the story by subjugating the Jews into a racial underclass and eventually exterminating them in acts of unbelievable cruelty and evil."

"Yes, I know a lot about that through my studies of the Nuremberg trials. It is shocking, really shocking, what they did."

"Yes, absolutely."

"So, New York is the true metropolis, then?" continued Hooman.

"Yes, it is, I suppose. One of the main plot points in the original *Metropolis* is that the city is made up of two classes: the elite, also called the leaders, and the workers. So you can see that New York mirrors this reality in many ways, without being quite as polarized as the movie: Lang was casting the classes into either the bourgeoisie or the proletariat.

"And it is interesting that the character Freder is at leisure in a pleasure garden, where he meets a young woman named Maria, who has brought a group of the workers' children to see the privileged lifestyle led by the rich. Maria and the children are asked to leave, but Freder is attracted to Maria and searches for her in the workers' part of the city. But at the end of the movie, the story doesn't really present any viable solutions beyond the vague resolution that love will conquer all, and Freder being the 'mediator' between the two classes, with the 'heart' bringing the 'head'—elite—and 'hand'—workers—together, a metaphor of unity between classes, but I am sure the real solution is far more complex and more difficult. It is true that love is a part of the answer, but I would add the words 'justice' and 'equality' to the mix, and I am sure that the whole of humanity will be needed to make the change and not just a few influential people from the elite sector of society. It may be hundreds of years before we see any absolute resolution. And do we really want any classes in society? Are we aiming for something more complex where robots and machines are the primary sources of production and everyone is mostly middle class? Who knows? It is an open question. Maybe we won't know until we actually get there; either way we have to eliminate extreme poverty and wealth as a first step."

"Interesting."

"I was thinking today, as we crossed the Queensboro Bridge," continued Allison, who was in the mood to share her thoughts, "that a city is an odd phenomenon, a space of large and complex webs of consciousness, almost unfathomable and untraceable at times, with huge shared subjectivities and objectivities. Though, for the most part, when you look at people walking by, like here in the square"—she pointed out the window—"you only see the superficial detail of their lives and not the deep, invisible connections and motivations. Even if you stop someone and ask them about their life, you only see their persona and not their deep self."

"Yes. That can be true," he said and paused. "But that is a wonderful observation."

"I don't think I ever told you about my idea of a life-story depository. It was a thought experiment for the most part that would help uncover these invisible connections we have with each other; a book for each person or object that reveals the deeper aspects of our connected reality, our configured destiny."

"No, you have never mentioned it. Sounds interesting. Your notebook is a little like that idea, isn't it?"

Allison didn't answer. She took a sip of her coffee and looked out the window again. She was lost for a moment in the whiteness of snow. "And a part of these invisible connections comes in the form of many large corporations, very much like the elite in *Metropolis*, whose influences are global, but the benefits, in terms of large amounts of money, usually flow back here to the corporations without any real obligations being fulfilled, which is to support smaller and poorer nations or even just poorer people within and outside of America. It's exactly as you have said in your book, *On the Shoulders of the Poor*. We all do stand on the shoulders of the poor," she said.

Hooman had begun writing a rough outline of the book just after they had met in London but didn't begin the first draft until after they were married. It was far from finished. He had shared excerpts of it with Allison throughout the writing process. "Yes, money, pursued for its own sake, can allow dilution of responsibility. It is rooted in the cult of individualism—free enterprise and the pursuit of profit—and the lack of ethical standards expected of corporations, which should be pursued by governing institutions. This individualism is expressed in two ways. It applies to those who run these corporations and governing institutions and the individuals that consume the products made by these corporations. People who run these institutions and companies should ask, Who should benefit from the products produced? Should it be a specific nation or shareholders, or should it be the whole of humanity? There needs to be an equal distribution of wealth at every level of the production of a product. I've said it before. There is a fundamental relationship between the spiritual transformation of the individual and institutions. You need to change both to achieve positive ethical growth in global culture. And individualism is fed by our materialist desires—materialism—served by the media, where we seek fulfillment from branded products. I think that people believe that consumption is the source of their happiness. And it's strange that many products use words to evoke spiritual states that do not exist in the products themselves; this is the false promise of the material world."

"You mean like the perfume 'Eternity' or 'Everlast'?"

"Yes, exactly," he said.

Allison drifted off into another stream of thought. "Oh well, although I can't see these invisible threads, I do see the way spiritual laws affect our actions, and I see why international law is so paramount to you. Now that I know more about you, in these last few years, I see your need for a new global identity. I wish I had done more in the past to further that cause like you."

"But in Harlem you've done plenty with the kids, trying to teach them to see their own humanity: an equal humanity. And with Noah, you're a mother. That's a powerful position. And you have had an interesting life, very unconventional and in the best kind of way. You have changed me, at least. I probably wouldn't have moved to Harlem without your influence. And you bring out the best in me spiritually, like no one else does. I love you so much because of that."

"Maybe you're right. And I have been trying to discuss with the children what it really means to be American. To identify oneself with nation and culture can be a strange phantom, which I hope some of them may come to realize one day."

"When 'Abdu'l-Bahá was in America in 1912," continued Hooman, "he designated New York as the City of the Covenant, and I think that despite the racial discrimination of the time, he thought that the city had the capacity to become a great spiritual center that could reflect the unity of the entire human race. I guess this is based on the broad racial diversity found here, more than many other cities, and, after all, the United Nations is based here, right? In many ways New York is the capital of the world: the global metropolis."

Hooman then began to talk about a specific day when Juliet

Thompson, an artist and early Bahá'í, had met a group of children in one of the tenements. Hooman reminded Allison that they had stood in front of Juliet's house in Greenwich Village almost three months ago. "Juliet had arranged for the children to meet 'Abdu'l-Bahá. He greeted them, one by one, with smiles and laughter. The last one was an African American boy, and when 'Abdu'l-Bahá saw him, his face lit up with a smile, and he exclaimed: 'Here is a black rose!' Everyone present was impressed with a feeling of wonder, which increased when 'Abdu'l-Bahá, distributing a handful of chocolates to each child with a kind word, picked up a particularly dark chocolate and without a word, but with a humorously piercing glance that swept around the group, laid the chocolate against the black cheek. 'Abdu'l-Bahá's face was radiant . . . and that radiance seemed to fill the room. The children looked with real wonder at the African American boy as if they had never seen him before."[2]

Allison thought that Jonny was a black rose too. She took Hooman's hand. "I'm so glad we're together. I really am," Allison said in a low voice.

"So am I," he said and smiled, looking at her. "I knew we would be okay somehow."

Getting up, and without breaking contact with his hand, she slipped into his lap. They embraced for a long time, framed in the Starbucks café window.

"I wouldn't be myself without you," Allison said. "I see myself in you more and more. We are a mirror of each other. Like you always say."

"Do you remember that dream I had on the first night we met? This moment, I think, is the last part of that dream, the meadow in Times Square."

"I know who you are," she said, responding to her own observation that they were a mirror to each other.

"Wow," he said.

"What?"

"What you just said is what you had said in my dream. You said, 'I know who you are.'"

"Wow . . . and you know, I think you might be a version of Freder. In your walled paradise that I rescued you from. And I might be a version of Maria. *Metropolis* applies to our life in New York. And New York is, in some ways, an urban dystopia, like the movie. Although, as I said before, I doubt we can change or mediate the reality of the class structure of New York as it stands today. That is for the whole of humanity to achieve in the future. And I think that the Bahá'í community will have a large part to play in that resolution."

"Yes, that is true. Although I don't really know the plot of *Metropolis*."

"We'll watch the original soon, and you can find out for yourself. And the false Maria, or the 'Maschinenmensch,' literally 'machine-human' in German, is a symbol of both individualism and materialism combined; the artificial human being lacks compassion."

"Yes, maybe that is everyone's nemesis." Hooman added, "And by overcoming these two, we begin to eradicate poverty and extreme wealth."

Allison pointed at the square. "Can you see Hampstead Heath overlayed here in Times Square? Use your imagination to see it in your mind."

He looked out the window. "Yes, I think I can see it now. Wow, amazing. The only thing that is missing is your yellow dress," he said.

She stood up and spun around a few times. "Can you see me wearing the yellow dress? Can you see it?"

As he was about to answer, Nava thumped on the café window. Nava, Paul, and Sophie were covered in snow, and Nava was jumping up and down excitedly. Hooman and Allison could not hear Nava's words but read her arm movements. They gathered their coats, helping each other into them, and left Starbucks.

25

DECODING REALITY

After scaling the high summits of wonderment, the wayfarer cometh to THE
VALLEY OF TRUE POVERTY AND ABSOLUTE NOTHINGNESS. *This station is
that of dying to the self and living in God, of being poor in self and rich in the
Desired One. Poverty, as here referred to, signifieth being poor in that which
pertaineth to the world of creation and rich in what belongeth to the realms of God.
For when the true lover and devoted friend reacheth the presence of the Beloved, the
radiant beauty of the Loved One and the fire of the lover's heart will kindle a blaze
and burn away all veils and wrappings. Yea, all that he hath, from marrow to skin,
will be set aflame, so that nothing will remain save the Friend.*[1]

— BAHÁ'U'LLÁH, *THE SEVEN VALLEYS*

The Rose Center for Earth and Space was a large open area that
spanned several floors of the American Museum of Natural History.
These floors were incorporated into a massive glass cube built with
interlocking squares of glass. Allison, Paul, and Sophie had just walked
out of the Hall of Planet Earth and taken an escalator up to the second
level. As they ascended, they looked at the Hayden Planetarium, an
enormous white sphere located in the center of this large open area.
Allison swiveled her head and stared through the glass walls at the snow-
covered terrace in the exterior of the museum. Her eyes then moved

back to the interior and came to rest on the planetarium again; its shape represented the sun, and it seemed almost to float near the roof of the glass cube. The nine planets in the solar system were strung up around it.

Coming off the escalator, they walked up to the railing and looked down at the café on the first floor.

"Do you guys want to look in here?" Allison asked Paul and Sophie as she pointed toward the planetarium; on this level it was the Hayden Big Bang Theater. The planetarium proper was on the level above the theater, inside the sphere.

"Let's look in here." Paul nodded at the room. There was a gangway between the second floor and the theater, and they walked along it and entered the theater through a doorway.

Once inside, the lights dimmed automatically, and a projected video, depicting the formation of the universe, appeared on the floor of the theater. Noah woke up when a deep voice began narrating the show.

"The universe, as we see it today, began with what we now call the Big Bang. An explosion of immense violence . . ."

The narrator's voice trailed off in Allison's mind as she leaned down to pull Noah out of the three-wheeled stroller. While the others watched the projection, she fed him and did not concentrate fully on the narration or the video projection, but as she was feeding Noah, she thought about a Bahá'í and poet, Robert Hayden, US Poet Laureate from 1976 to 1978. Obviously, the theater was not named after Robert Hayden, but she liked the connection to and repetition of Hayden's last name with the theater. She had read about his life recently in the book *From the Auroral Darkness: The Life and Poetry of Robert Hayden* and had also read some of his poetry, as Hooman had Hayden's complete collection on the bookshelf at the house. Allison knew, after reading only a few of his poems, that he was immensely talented and nuanced as a poet, and this threw light onto her own poetry, which she wrote more for herself rather than for other readers.

Toward the end of the show, she walked over to Paul and whispered, "Dost thou reckon thyself only a puny form when within thee the universe is folded."[2]

"Where's that from?" he said.

"Imam 'Alí."

"Strange fellow, I presume."

"No more than you."

"Ha. Very funny."

After the show, they walked down to the café via a spiral gangway that wound around the planetarium, eventually descending to the first floor.

They sat talking. Paul bounced Noah on his knees. Allison was looking up at the representation of the solar system floating above them. She sipped her coffee.

Paul turned to Sophie. "What did you think?" he asked.

"About the show? Yeah, good. I liked the special effects. It makes it easier to imagine how it all formed."

"What about you, Allison. Did you like it?"

"I couldn't concentrate on it all, but what I did see was good."

Allison took a bite from a poppy seed bun. Several seeds stuck to her palm and fingers, and she continued to speak with her mouth partially full. She muffled, "You know, Paul, what amazes me is that the universe was, at one time, smaller than this seed: the first seed of time." She pointed to a seed on the tip of her forefinger.

She aimed and flicked the seed at her brother. "Don't you think that is amazing? Who needs miracles when you have everything created from nothing or at least relatively nothing. Who knows what came before the Big Bang. Maybe it all comes from the womb of the essence or the womb of Malakut? I have been thinking about string theory recently. I think the universe might be made from one infinite and infinitesimally small string, packed and folded together like an infinite pack of invisible spaghetti that vibrates and unfolds in seemingly empty space to reveal the elementary particles."

Paul ignored her comments and continued bouncing Noah on his knee. He then lifted him above his head. "What about you, Noah? Did you like the show?"

Sophie laughed. "He was too busy having a feed. When did he have a notion to care about the universe?" she said to Paul.

"Take no notice, Noah." Paul put Noah back on his knees. "Hey, sis, how is your life in New York?"

"What about it?"

"Are you happy? I presume you are. But you never mention your life here or much of anything recently. Although I can't say I'm surprised. You never have been very revealing about the things you get up to, at least in recent times. We have no idea what your life is like here."

"I'm sorry, guys. I was meaning to keep in contact, but when I got pregnant, things got more hectic. And there was the building of the house, which took up a large chunk of my time. I pretty much had to project manage the whole thing."

"That's okay. Paul's just giving you a hard time. We knew you had your hands full with your new life," Sophie said.

"But you're happy?" Paul reiterated.

"Well, yes, I am, but happiness is complex. The short answer is yes . . . and Sophie, it's not a new life. It's the same life it has always been."

Sophie did not answer. She looked at Paul.

"Oh guys, I just had a thought, sorry. Excuse me for a bit."

Reaching down under the stroller, Allison pulled out her leather notebook and pencil. Opening to a new page, she wrote a question to herself: "What is the complexity of happiness?" She then added, "The alchemy of happiness is the transmutation of virtue."

After reading it several times to imprint it into memory, she then flicked through the pages to find a quote she had written down some months ago: the words she had whispered to Paul in the theater, which were contained within another quote. The extract came from *The Seven Valleys*:

> *Likewise, reflect upon the perfection of man's creation, and that all these planes and states are folded up and hidden away within him. "Dost thou reckon thyself only a puny form, when within thee the universe is folded?" Then we must labor to destroy the animal condition, till the meaning of humanity shall come to light.*[3]

She knew this had a double meaning. The quote referred to the mysteries in the physical universe that had been partially revealed by quantum mechanics and string theory but also the worlds of God, which had a conceptual framework, a spiritual universe, that was folded up tightly within our hearts.

Paul placed Noah back in the stroller and dangled some toys in front of him. Noah reached out and tried to grab the toys.

Paul looked over at Allison.

"What are you writing?" he inquired.

"Oh, just random thoughts and ideas."

"I noticed you had the notebook yesterday as well."

"Yeah, I pretty much take it everywhere. Hooman bought it for me. He encourages me to put all my thoughts in here."

"So, is it like a diary?" Sophie asked.

Allison's instinctive reaction was to divert Paul and Sophie's attention away from the notebook by saying something vague and unrevealing; however, something in her decided to tell the whole truth about it. It couldn't hurt, she thought, as they would not remotely believe a word she said anyway.

"It is not a diary," Allison said.

"What is it, then?" Paul asked.

"It's my symmetrical destiny map . . . I use it to decode reality," Allison said finally.

Stopping herself from bursting into laughter, Sophie put her hand over her mouth for a moment as she calmed herself down. "You're not serious, are you? But knowing you, you probably are," she said.

"Of course I am," Allison said.

"Yes, you are serious. I should know that," Sophie said.

Paul was quiet.

Not able to contain herself any longer, Sophie chuckled. She then looked at Paul for some reply, but Paul did not reply, so Sophie continued. "Allison, in some ways you have changed while you've been in New York, but in another way, you are the same as you ever were."

Paul asked Allison in a slow and precise manner, "So, how exactly does a person decode reality?"

"I read the world. I mean, through signs and meanings. In the patterns of people's speech, in the repetition of names. I see connections. Nothing is exempt. Even the way someone smiles. It's hard to explain how it works exactly. People and objects tell me things about reality, even without them realizing it. Remember I told you in an email a few years back that Hooman's boss and wife were called Paul and Sophie? Remember? I said it was an interesting connection of names, a symmetry of names. And then there is their daughter, Alison; she has my name."

"Yeah, okay, I remember," said Paul. "But, Allison, I know what reality is. And what exactly are you finding out while you're decoding? The truth is that there's nothing to decode. Reality is just physical. There's nothing more to it than that. We make our own meaning. You talk as if there is something behind reality."

"Yes! There is something behind reality! And if I have to be more specific, people from the next world communicate through objects and names. As I said before, even the pattern or texture of my own thoughts holds a certain significance."

"Do you hear voices?"

"No, it's the voices of everyday life that hide the supramundane. Every person and object speaks of themselves in their own way and in their own language, each with a unique voice. It's like, say I see a street advert that advertises strawberry ice cream, and then I meet someone on the same day who says to me: 'Gee, I really love strawberry ice cream. Have you got any?' Then I know I was meant to meet that person, and I listen to what they say more carefully. I look for more clues or signs. I learn things that way, about the deeper nature of reality, things that have always been there but are passed over because we are not imaginative enough to look for the obvious truth of it. You see, you both could be telling me something deeply mystical right now without realizing it; riding on top of your voice might be another voice, of transcendence, of beauty, of sublimity.

"Each person only perceives reality on their own level but can communicate knowledge that they are unaware of themselves to a person on a higher level of reality. When a person goes up the ladder of reality, the world moves up with them, but those on lower rungs don't see what those on higher rungs do. Each person is blissfully unaware of the higher worlds. They only see what is on their level and below. But of course, over time, which isn't really time, people move up to higher levels and realize that they were lower down in the past, but eventually the levels disappear, and everything flattens out, and everyone is the same on the horizon of eternity until even this fades in the glow from the essence, and everything is destroyed in pure beauty. Then only the Glory of God remains, which is a single word from God: 'Be.'"

Sophie laughed. "Oh my god! Oh . . . my . . . god . . . that is crazy talk, Allison. Strawberry ice cream! What a bizarre little imagination you have. Ha ha. Paul, this kind of conversation would keep me entertained for hours," Sophie said.

"Sophie, please be quiet. Let her speak." Paul's tone was not unkind, but it wounded Sophie anyway, and her smile melted away.

"So, I have developed a theory. The ancient Egyptians worked out how to enter the afterlife while they were still alive, or I am surmising that based on their understanding of the structure of the afterlife. The soul, the nine-fold soul, with the exception of the body, travels through a series of gates along a river. But it's the same phenomenon as Jacob's Ladder in the Bible, or Muhammad going through the levels of heaven on the ladder that reached up from the Dome of the Rock. The Sufis called it the seven cities or valleys, but I calculate nine levels. It's all the same. Do you see?"

"Well, no, not really, but continue," Paul said.

"So, through prayer and meditation and through reading certain signs and mystical names and hidden knowledge, our soul progresses through these levels. Absolutely everything in the material world is a part of this scheme: words, symbols, songs, movies, objects, and nature itself. Any sense-perceived reality is a metaphorical cipher of the higher worlds; the meaning of everything in the higher worlds potentially exists in this world. Everything you need to progress is already here. You don't need to die to find these ciphers and move upwards. They exist in fragments, like a puzzle, and you need to put them together to see the oneness of reality." Allison paused for a moment and said, "Oh, I have a quote from Bahá'u'lláh that explains this." She flicked through her notebook. "Here it is," and she read, "'Herein the lowly earth is in no conflict with the high heavens.'[4]

"And ultimately, only prayer can unlock these ciphers."

"Oh, I see. So, through reading words and objects in the world, a person finds this hidden knowledge," Paul said.

"That's it! You have it. I call it the 'hidden school.'"

Sophie interjected. "Paul, you're not considering . . . I mean, you don't think this is true?"

"No, no. I just want to hear her out. That's all."

"Thanks, Paul. I know this is hard for you guys to digest, but this is who I am. You know that. I won't change, or at least not in the way that you expect. This is where I'm going. It's where we're all going, in fact.

Everyone dies. Everyone goes to these spiritual worlds. This hasn't changed since the beginning of human history. The Egyptians called it the Boat of Millions of Years. We are traveling in it now, but we just don't know it. It's here, it's eternity, it's all around us. It's hidden behind time. And even timelessness is just another veil for the essence to hide behind."

"Well, all I see is the planetarium right now and these worlds"—and he pointed to the planets suspended from the ceiling—"but I'll take your word for it."

"Hey! I guess I'm not surprised. I just wanted you guys to know where I'm at, that's all. You asked, so I told you the truth of it. Of course, I don't expect you to believe it. I just wanted to be honest."

"Hey, sis, that's great, and I support you in it. You do whatever you like. It's none of my business what you believe. And you know me. I can't go in for that kinda stuff, never have, but whatever gives you kicks, you go for it.

"And I have to say that with regard to spiritual and religious ideas, you have changed here in New York. It seems that you have moved on from the various streams of existentialism and postmodern philosophy, not that I really understand any of that either."

"Existentialism focuses on the 'individual' being and postmodern philosophy on the 'cultural' being and on the relativities of culture and ideology, rejecting modernism's metanarratives. But I think that Bahá'í-based philosophy will incorporate both ways of 'being' and find unity within diversity. The Bahá'í Faith will be the first real global metanarrative for the future; it will be able to encompass all cultural and religious relativity without destroying diversity completely. I mean, some ideologies will fade, and others will remain or evolve."

"Hmm . . . no comment." He smiled.

She wanted to say that the world Paul saw was a pattern of thinking and a projection of concepts. If he could change the patterns and assumptions about what was "real," he could see another world. An emotion of frustration formed in her mind but was then overtaken by a feeling of extreme contentment. It washed over her. It did not matter. Nothing mattered. Paul and Sophie would know one day. They would see and know it for themselves. If this was the last word she uttered on the subject, then it didn't matter.

413

She smiled at Paul and Sophie. "I love you guys. And thanks for coming to see Noah and me."

Allison put her notebook and pencil back into the storage basket under the stroller, then got up and went to hug Sophie.

When Paul's turn came, he laughed as she sat in his lap and embraced him. "You keep my life interesting, and I thank you for that. It's a cliché, but the world is a better place with you in it," he said.

They spent the remaining time in the museum exploring various other halls adjacent to the Rose Center for Earth and Space. Allison reflected on the myriad cultures that had come and gone; these cultures were never to be seen again except here, in a static form, behind glass display units, like the African peoples, the South American cultures, and the American Indians, in particular the Plains Indians. Time had reduced whole cultures to this and would do the same to her own culture eventually. In three thousand years, all the cares and concerns, fashions, opinions, and ideas behind what New York had stood for in this moment may be completely effaced. There may be buildings preserved, books, and documentaries, but essentially the culture may be so changed that it would become completely transformed. And the language may even be Arabic, Chinese, or a hybrid of English. Or maybe a new language would evolve, like the language that existed behind the veil of this world, which she knew existed, but she understood only a fragment of its glory.

After coming from the Hall of African Peoples and passing through Birds of the World, they all walked into the Hall of Mexico and Central America. They walked slowly around the glass display units. Sophie stopped and pointed out an ornate gold necklace in the Mayan section. Paul walked toward her and the artifact. It was a circular disc of gold, a pendant, with gold spheres and exquisite blue stones shaped into interlocking conical shapes, which made up most of the necklace.

Allison, who was next to Paul, read the caption and exclaimed, "Wow! This is an early calendar. An early timepiece."

The pendant was designed with Mayan glyphs, signs, and other complex markings that Allison assumed were a representation of months. Allison thought about the person who wore it all those thousands of years before. All the emotions that may have been invested in the object were gone, but the object was still here, unmoved and uncaring of any concern for its own apparent beauty. The necklace was empty of true reality, and its beauty was only projected through human consciousness as a subjective object, not innate, and even if it existed for several hundred thousand years into the future, it would still be empty, like everything else in the city. All that did exist were peoples' minds and personalities aspiring for objects that were physical and the states of being associated with these objects. She could strip away meaning until nothing existed but the perception of the oneness of being and of the intermingling of all souls at the center of existence where all the illusions peeled away, all mysteries evaporated, until nothing in the changeable world was left to strive for, and immortality hummed and flexed in changelessness.

In that moment her mind broke through a subtle barrier. A sensation of indefinable joy and radiance passed over her. She looked at Sophie reading the caption beside the necklace. Sophie was transfigured before her eyes and became a beautiful, unfathomable being.

Allison put her arm around Sophie. "Beautiful, isn't it?" Allison said as they both continued to stare at the shining gold necklace.

And now the gold was a mirror of Allison's soul as its emptiness was filled.

"Yes, it is. So delicate in one way . . . but it also has a certain primal strength. Now that I look at it more, you know, it is so beautiful, Allison, it really is."

These words penetrated Allison on many levels as tears formed in her eyes. Riding on top of Sophie's voice was another voice, and it was an accent playful, joyful, and unimaginably sweet. Allison could not tell if it was a soul from another world or Sophie's own higher potential, but ultimately it did not matter to Allison. The words were Sophie's, but the tone and depth were transformed. They spoke of a meaning beyond Sophie's perception and far removed from earthly reality: that timeless world. Only Allison could hear that astonishingly sweet voice calling from another plane. It was, she now knew, a placeless sun whose invisible light reflected that higher realm. Sophie's words intimated that life is teasingly beautiful and so endlessly wondrous. Allison stopped herself from laughing in ecstatic joy. It all seemed like an amazing joke.

After a few seconds, Sophie's voice assumed its normal proportions again, and the wave of joy in Allison's body evaporated. She found herself back on earth once more. Her hands shook as she realized she had experienced another strange session of transfiguration, only this time it had overtaken her in such a way that she did not notice it until afterward. This session was shorter than her experience at the British Museum but essentially the same.

Paul patted her on the shoulder. "Are you okay? You look a bit dazed."

"Huh, oh, no, I'm okay, I, uh . . . I don't feel well," Allison said.

"Oh, okay. We should get going, then."

"Yes, I think I need to sleep."

———

In Allison's sleep she walked over a vast, flat desert, and the sand was wet and cool on the soles of her feet. She was completely naked, but the breast that had been removed after her cancer was now there, and she was whole again. It seemed as if she was on a long stretch of beach, and the waves had only just receded back into the ocean. She could even hear what sounded like an ocean in the distance, with huge crashing waves, but nothing of it could be seen on the horizon. No matter what direction she walked, she found herself no closer to the large body of water that she knew was out there. She looked up at an intense, cloudless sky; all the colors were polarized with deep contrasts, similar to the effect that a red filter has on a camera using black-and-white film.

In the near distance she saw the only object in any direction; it was red. As she came closer, she recognized it to be an oversized pomegranate. Crouching down on the sand, she took the fruit and broke it open with her thumbs. Allison saw immediately that the seeds were unripe and had a white, translucent structure, like semi-cloudy white crystal. She stood up and broke off a handful of the seeds and began to blow on them. Glowing like embers, they responded to her breath and changed slowly to crimson with a glowing red light source inside. The sound of the ocean grew louder but remained out of sight.

Once the seeds seemed ripe, she put one on the tip of her tongue. It tasted somehow transcendent and nothing like pomegranate, like all the fruits she had ever tasted but all at the same time: banana, watermelon, and strawberry were some that seemed obvious. She then swallowed the translucent ruby. It slid down her throat, and then a great wall of water, rising up 600 feet, came toward her. She dropped the fruit, and spinning around, she tried to escape, but there was nowhere to go. The water came from all directions. In the periphery of her vision, she saw that the other seeds on the sand and those still in the fruit had transformed into blood and flowed away into the sand. The circle of the ocean, which was threatening to crush her, reached only 650 feet from her when the dream ended.

26

THE TOURISTS

Whoso hath attained this station is sanctified from all that pertaineth to the world. Wherefore, if those who have reached the ocean of His presence are found to possess none of the limited things of this perishable world, whether earthly riches or worldly opinions, it mattereth not. For that which is with His creatures is circumscribed by their own limitations, whereas that which is with God is sanctified therefrom . . . This station is that poverty of which it is said, "Poverty is My glory." [1,2]

— BAHÁ'U'LLÁH, *THE SEVEN VALLEYS*

Allison opened her eyes and stared out the windows at the overcast sky above the house on the other side of the street. Its pale light came through the bedroom windows.

She then rolled over to face Hooman. His eyes were closed. She was thinking about her dream and the strange transformation of her consciousness on the previous day. As was her way, she decided to mention only her dream. He knew she kept back aspects of her life, and he seemed to tolerate it, but Allison did feel guilty. Though on the upside, she had been sharing many of the entries in her notebook recently, and he was obviously happy that she was sharing more of her inner world. She had noted that he was careful not to intrude too deeply into that world and was exceptionally nonjudgmental, even when her experiences seemed slightly strange or odd; she loved him for that, being so open in that way.

Allison put her hand on his shoulder. "Hooman, are you awake?"

His eyes opened, and he rolled over to face her. "Good morning. How do you feel?" He put his hand on her cheek. "You were in bed very early last night."

"Yes, I was tired yesterday, but I feel refreshed today."

Fragmented images of her dream flashed through her thoughts. "Hooman, I had a really odd dream last night. It was vivid, like no other dream. Although its clarity reminds me of a dream I had in Shidan's bookshop just before I gave birth."

She rolled back and looked at the ceiling. "I was in a flat desert, which was really an empty ocean basin. I saw a pomegranate on the sand, which I broke open. But I had to blow on the seeds to make them ripe, and then the seeds transformed into blood after I ate one. What do you make of that? What does that mean?"

"I think it signifies some kind of change, perhaps some new potential. And the morphing of the seeds into blood, that might mean some kind of sacrifice, giving up something lower for something higher."

"And just as I ate the fruit, at that moment of sacrifice, the ocean closed in on me. I would have drowned and been torn to shreds, but the dream ended before the water reached me."

"The ocean. Well, actually, I was reading something on the ocean last night." Hooman reached over to the bedside table. On it was a book by Bahá'u'lláh called *The Gleanings.* He opened to a page with a bookmark and read:

> *"'The one true God is My witness! This most great, this fathomless and surging Ocean is near, astonishingly near, unto you. Behold it is closer to you than your life-vein! Swift as the twinkling of an eye ye can, if ye but wish it, reach and partake of this imperishable favor, this God-given grace, this incorruptible gift, this most potent and unspeakably glorious bounty.'"* [3]

"That's interesting. The ocean is a symbol of God's grace and bounty in the spiritual worlds," she said.

"And in this world too," Hooman said.

Allison jumped out of bed and rummaged around her previous

day's clothes, which were crumpled on the floor next to the bed. Her notebook was revealed underneath her coat.

Hooman got out of bed. "I'm going downstairs to make coffee. You stay here and relax; write up your dream. I'll bring up some coffee."

He put his bathrobe and slippers on and walked through the door.

As he was partway down the staircase, she shouted, "Thanks, babe. Can you check on Noah on the way down? Is he with Nava?"

"He slept in Paul and Sophie's room last night," he said, raising his voice. "Oh, babe . . . I have some good news," he said and came back through the doorway. "The apartment in New Jersey just sold."

"Oh, that's great news. What do you want to do with the money?"

"Do what you suggested. Buy a brownstone, or maybe two, in Harlem and offer free accommodations and a wage, but I would like to create writing studios for Harlem writers, rather than art studios as we had discussed. Anyway, we can talk about it later. Oh, and Sara and Shidan said they will give us a couple of million to sink into the project. Sara is going to set the project up so that it is completely self-sustaining financially."

"Oh wow! That is so, *so* cool."

"I'll go get coffee," he said and walked down the stairs.

The air was cold, and she wanted to see the morning and the snow from the previous night. Wrapping the blankets around herself, she dragged half of the bed over to the window and sat in a cocoon on a chair near the window. She opened her notebook to a clean page. The whiteness of the page jumped out at her, and its pale purity was more impressive in the cool light, but something inside her could not write. The dream was so fresh, and the imagery so vivid that it did not need to be recorded. She knew it would always be there in her memory, and her mind had a sharpness now, which she realized was a remnant of her experience in the museum on the previous day. Closing the notebook, she wound the leather strap around the book and then placed it and her pencil on the floor near the window. She then pulled the covers tightly around her and looked at the snow in the street below.

The day was superficially dreary, but nothing could dislodge the happiness she felt. It seemed as if the world had been recreated afresh while she slept, and here it was in the morning for her personal pleasure, and it was a day unique and rare, which had never existed in this way before. Sophie had been right about the fundamental changes in Allison's life, and her dream prefigured another change that started with this new day; she was now seeking the Ocean through the pomegranate.

After fifteen minutes, Hooman came through the door, balancing two coffees. She heard him coming up the stairs and turned to see him come through the door. He walked over to the windows and sat beside her on the seat. She dislodged the tight cocoon of blankets that enveloped her to usher Hooman in; she wrapped the blankets around his shoulder and torso so that they were now comfortably cocooned together. He passed her a coffee.

She put her nose to it. "Thanks . . . smells good. Is this coffee new?"

"Yep, found it in a deli near work the other day. I think it's an Italian brand."

She took a sip, and they both looked out at the street for a while without speaking. "I love the snow," she said eventually.

"Yes, I know you do."

"There is something about it. About its symbolic purity, and at the same time it speaks of death. It seems to have something in common with the desert. They exist at opposite ends of the spectrum, but in a way they are the same as each other. This is a white desert; the snow covers the unique identity of every object, and so it equalizes everything."

"Why death?" he said.

"Well, it's winter, which represents death. Everything dies back in preparation for spring."

"Oh right, renewal for spring. Or death. All the seasons are interlocked, I suppose."

After taking the last gulp of coffee, he carefully unwrapped himself and rewrapped her before standing up. "Well, I suppose I had better get ready for work. What are you doing today?"

"Oh, I don't know. It depends on what Paul and Sophie want to do."

He smiled and turned toward the bathroom door.

Allison watched him disappear and waited for the sound of the shower to turn on. Turning back to the window, she took another sip of her coffee, which was now lukewarm. She thought that maybe the snow was not pure after all, nor did it stand for death. Snow was just a by-product of winter, which was caused by the Earth tilting away from the sun. The Earth did not feel or think anything of winter or summer or any season, so symbolic purity in snow was only a human projection. Even objects, fashioned and created with human imagination, seemed empty at a certain level; a thought of the emptiness of the Mayan necklace in the museum returned to her.

At that moment she thought about the expanse of the flat and empty ocean basin in her dream. That empty expanse, she knew now, was both the physical world and her own soul. She could see that with clarity. It was an empty ocean waiting to be filled with water: a symbol for spirit and God's bounty. And something was going to happen to her, but she did not know what. All she could say was that her soul was developing and changing but into something new and unknown to her, as a child knows vaguely it will be an adult one day but cannot visualize its own future.

Across the street, Jonny stepped out of his house. He looked up and found Allison's gaze. With initial hesitation, he slowly raised his hand and waved. She waved back and watched him descend the steps and walk past her on his way to school. He eventually disappeared around the corner facing Marcus Garvey Park.

———

Eight days had passed. Allison had shown Paul and Sophie as much of Manhattan as she could. They saw a fair amount of Harlem: both Central and East Harlem and the Bronx.

Allison had borrowed Nava's car, and they had driven out to Long Island for a day. Although Allison felt a little repulsed by the idea, Sophie wanted to see the Hamptons and look at all the old and new money mansions there, so they drove around the area for a few hours, eventually ending up on Meadow Lane, also known as billionaire lane.

They then drove on and stopped at Jackson Pollock's studio for an hour, which was more Allison's style. As they were walking around the artist's house and studio, Allison explained that there was a Bahá'í artist named Mark Tobey who had been a part of the abstract expressionism movement and whose work had some similarities to Pollock's action painting technique. Allison saw that Paul and Sophie weren't very interested in the topic, but she continued to push on and explain aspects of abstract expressionism and its part in the development of modernism as a rejection of realism. This was despite the fact that the camera, a mechanical eye, reflected realism by its very nature and had allowed art movements to abandon the burden of reproducing reality faithfully, as high renaissance painters had pursued, and by doing so had allowed broader artistic means within the twentieth century through to current times, allowing us to question the whole idea of representation in art, leading to a considerable diversification of artistic style within postmodernism, the death of large artistic movements, and a broader democracy within art.

They eventually drove on to Montauk at the extreme end of Long Island. They parked and walked onto the beach. A snow flurry covered the sand in a thick layer of snow. The snow was soft, and Allison felt her feet push through it, and she looked back for a moment at her footsteps. There were no other footprints in the snow, and she liked that they were the only people on the beach. Sophie was pushing Noah's stroller.

Allison thought of Jennifer and her husband, who she had met in Townsville, Queensland, on their large cruising yacht, and she remembered that they had a house in this part of Long Island. Where, she did not know, as they had not stayed in contact, but she wondered as she looked at the houses sitting up on the edge of the beach.

Eventually, they stopped, and Allison took her shoes off and gave Sophie her car keys and cell. She walked down the beach and into the water up to her waist. She raised her arms to the sky and shouted the word Alláh-u-Abhá nine times, before saying softly to herself, "I love you, Ocean. I love you . . . Ocean. You . . . the *ineffable* Ocean."

She turned back toward the beach and waded through the water, eventually coming out, and was shivering as she walked up the beach to Paul and Sophie. They walked back to the car and turned the heat on. She took her jeans off and got into the passenger's side seat. She put her hands to the air vent while Paul changed the setting on the heater to blow hot air onto her legs.

"You're a crazy woman. You know that?" Paul said, smiling.

"Yes. I know that. That's okay, isn't it?"

"Of course it is, babe; I'm just giving you a hard time."

"Oh, cool." She smiled and began rubbing her legs.

The next day Allison also took them to Canal Street, and from there they went up to Soho. They then did a semicircle, and from Soho they went to the Bowery, East Village, Union Square, and then down to Greenwich Village. Sophie wanted to see Park Avenue, so they descended into the subway at West 4th Street and Washington Square and caught a train back uptown on the F line. In the evening they took in a Broadway show—*Cats* at Times Square.

Today, on their last day in the city, they were wandering through Central Park. The park was relatively empty, and only a few people crossed their path. Paul walked ahead of the other two, taking photos with his digital camera. Near the edge of a broad, winding pathway, Allison brushed away the snow and sat on a bench. She checked Noah, who was asleep in the stroller. Sophie walked to where Paul was taking photos and stood beside him. The expansive lawn areas were covered with a heavy layer of snow, and beyond that were denuded trees. In the distance, at the far end of the park, were the high-rise apartments and other buildings that surrounded one edge of the park and were more visible now that fall and winter had stripped out the leaves on all the trees.

On the path Allison watched a pigeon puff up his neck and strut behind a female in a practiced dance. She flew away, uninterested. Feeling pity for the pigeon, she wondered what he would do next. Instead of a pursuit, which she had expected, he fluffed up his feathers and sat down on the path; the bird was a fat, mango-shaped fruit of feather and bone braced against the cold air. The impression that came to her mind was that of resignation; even in the natural world, this exists, she thought. At the exact moment in which the thought occurred, the pigeon retracted his head into his body and closed his eyes.

Allison leaned down to take her notebook out of the storage basket beneath the stroller. On a clean page she wrote the word "resignation." After a few moments, she added the words "radiant acquiescence." She thought about Mona Mahmudnizhad in Iran and how she had given her life so freely. Mona had been completely resigned to her fate. Allison wondered if she could ever give up her own life so easily, and then she thought about Hooman's comment that the blood in her dream was symbolic of sacrifice, and she wondered what she would have to sacrifice.

Sophie came back and sat next to Allison.

She put her arm around Allison's waist. "How is the decoding of reality going?" Sophie smiled and put her hand on the open book. "And I am sorry about laughing at your efforts the other day."

"That's okay. I don't mind," Allison said and smiled.

"What are you writing down today?"

"Nothing much. I was just thinking about resigning to God's will, about absolute self-surrender."

Sophie stared at Paul, arching his back. He took a photo of the branches on a large tree and the sky beyond.

"You're doing well here . . . and Hooman is the sweetest guy. You've landed on your feet here in America, Allison. You really have, in every sense of the word."

"Yes, I am happy. It may even be for the first time in my life. It's like I've woken from a long sleep."

"What amazes me is your ability to drift along and find yourself in interesting circumstances. You've changed, Allison. I can see that now."

"Do you think? For the better?"

"Yes, definitely for the better. And Hooman is a stable character. He has a solid career and social circumstances. Now also with a child to care for, you can settle down and make a real life for yourself."

Allison mused over the idea of a "real life." She was not sure what "real" was. Or at least they both had very different ideas of what "real" meant.

Paul came back down the path to where they were sitting. "Okay, girls, we should get going. Our flight leaves in five hours. We have to go pack our suitcases."

The girls got up, and they retraced their steps down the path, walking toward 5th Avenue, which would allow them to skirt Central Park and eventually return to the house.

———

Allison stayed in Coober Pedy for three months before moving on to Adelaide. She hugged Paul, took one last panoramic look at the town, got into the car, and rolled the window down before starting the car.

"You were never really looking for opals, were you?" Paul said.

"No, just the experience of being a miner. I'm mining the human psyche for the mental equivalent of gems."

"You're amazing. I have learned some obscure things from you."

"And I've learned plenty from you too."

"I'm not sure about that, but it has been interesting getting to know you. People like you don't come through Coober Pedy very often. I can tell you that. There has never been anyone in Coober Pedy as exotic as you."

She smiled and waved. "Bye."

She drove off and looked at Paul in the rearview mirror for a while as his figure became smaller, eventually disappearing as she took a corner and found the highway.

The trip down to Adelaide took eight hours. The first part of the journey was the usual flat redness that she had become accustomed to in central Australia. After she passed through Port Augusta, she noticed on the map that the rate of small towns would increase, so she pulled off the highway and took the backroads through these small towns. When she arrived in Adelaide, she drove to Glenelg and parked next to the beach and looked at the ocean for a while before going to a Coles Supermarket, where she bought a baguette and cheese for dinner that night. She slept in the back seat overnight.

She intended to stay in Adelaide for nine weeks, so she looked for short-term accommodations in café windows and on university notice-boards. After a week of sleeping in her car, she found a cramped room in a student house near the University of Adelaide. By chance one of the students was studying philosophy as a minor, and so they had many long debates about postmodernism and the death of objective reality. After three weeks, she found a job in a restaurant washing dishes; she liked the repetitive emptiness of the job. As she had promised Paul, she went for medical tests to see if her cancer had returned. Eventually, the tests came back negative, and she called Paul after this to let him know she was all clear.

————

After several weeks exploring Adelaide, Allison found an old factory packed with artists' studios. Her reason for staying in Adelaide was the artistic life of the city, which she had heard about from a fellow photography student in Melbourne the previous year.

One of the studios in the factory was rented by a photographer. Allison paid her a modest fee to use her darkroom.

One weekend she was sitting at a table in the photographer's studio and shuffling through all the contact sheets that she had made after processing all the negatives that she had accumulated during her trip so far. She was now deciding which specific shots to blow up, shots that evoked an emotional resonance in her.

It was interesting to look back at seven months of travel, and because she had made a conscious decision to build a visual diary of the trip, she'd taken shots that she wouldn't usually take. The camera was recording psychological moments that were subjective and bound uniquely to her consciousness; the objects and people in the photographs were things which would only interest her, and the photos were more intertwined in her reality than photos she had taken in the past: rather than her looking out at the world through the lens, the world was now looking back at her.

As she had taken each shot, she'd had to resist trying to make each shot beautiful through the way it was framed or by recording something that was beautiful in and of itself. These photos were supposed to be visual notes and not art, like a scientist taking notes after an experiment.

There were shots of plastic bottles in the landscape or bottle tops. There were many shots of the notes and coins she used to pay for things. She had also stopped many times to record dead animals, either flattened into the asphalt or lying beside the road; even in death objects were beautiful. She had also shot her bare feet on diverse types of ground: asphalt, granite, sand, dirt, grass, and leaves. She now laid out all the contact sheets on the table to get a better sense of all the shots of her bare feet on the ground, and finally she came to the black-and-white shots of her bare feet on the salt flats of Kati Thanda–Lake Eyre; she decided to start with this series of photos. She then carefully examined the negatives until she was able to find the series taken on the lake and then got up and went back into the darkroom.

After exposing a large sheet of photographic paper with light from the enlarger, she processed the sheet in the various chemical baths before taking it out into the daylight in the studio. Sitting back at the table, she examined her torso, legs, and her bare feet, taken as she was lying on the empty lake bed. The immense flatness of the lake bed and the hills on the other side of the lake were beautiful in a way she couldn't quantify. The photo was the closest she had come to having an experience of the land in deep psychological isolation. She realized that the hills were a future that she had never walked toward; there were many possible futures, she thought, that we would never fulfill but that we might see at a distance and wonder about.

27

A YEAR IN AMERICA

*This is the station wherein the multiplicity of all things perisheth in the wayfarer;
and the divine Countenance, dawning above the horizon of eternity, riseth out of the
darkness; and the meaning of "All on the earth shall pass away, but the face of thy
Lord"[1] is made manifest.[2]*

— BAHÁ'U'LLÁH, *THE SEVEN VALLEYS*

Just under a year had cycled past, from winter to winter, and it was
December 2002. Hooman and Allison had bought two adjoining
brownstones facing Marcus Garvey Park. They had begun to renovate
the interior of both buildings in addition to restoring the facades. They
intended that the buildings would be used as a writing studio where
local Harlem writers would have free accommodations and support to
help them create works of fiction or nonfiction. They would be paid a
wage so that they didn't have to work and could therefore focus on their
writing full time. Hooman was interested in supporting up-and-coming
writers who were in the early stages of their careers. Both Allison and
Hooman had also agreed that the writing studio could be used to host
Bahá'í community-building activities in collaboration with the Harlem
community, using the arts to help underpin the Bahá'í community's
efforts at community building.

Allison stepped onto the sidewalk on 125th Street after shopping at the local grocery. She looked down at the slush of snow surrounding her and then up at the sun for a moment before looking sideways at the fruit on the stand in front of the shop. She took her backpack off and took out her camera to take a shot of the fruit. But before she could take the shot, she felt someone tugging at her arm.

"Ms Bird." She recognized Jessica's voice.

She looked around and saw Jonny and Jessica. She assumed that their parents were shopping somewhere nearby. Jonny pointed at her Leica. She passed the camera to him.

A local Latino Muslim, with his distinctive white headdress, had wandered down from East Harlem, and then two tanned, blonde backpackers randomly arrived in the foreground of Jonny's sight. Jonny stopped these people by standing in front of them. Wordlessly, he led them by the hand into a graffiti-filled doorway.

"This is a photography project. Do you mind if he takes a photo of you?" Allison said to the people.

"No problem," one of the girls responded.

The man smiled. "Sure, why not," he said.

Allison asked where the girls came from. "Denmark," they replied, almost in unison.

The Muslim man sat on an empty milk crate, and the two girls sat on their hiking packs. Pointing, Jonny directed Jessica to sit across the laps of the two Danish girls. Jessica sat hugging a six-pack of toilet rolls that Allison presumed her mother had given her to carry.

These people were examples of diversity that Allison had attempted to outline to Jonny and the other kids over the past twelve months when they had talked about the civil rights movement and American identity being diverse. She had tried to highlight a future vision of Harlem as an increasingly mixed-race community in addition to downtown and lower Manhattan being more than just a White majority. Allison had tried to explain some of the complexities of historical segregation. That today, in certain neighborhoods, either wittingly or unwittingly, the Black and White communities lived separated lives, avoiding mixture. Though this conversation had not worked out as she had hoped, as most of the children did not see a problem with living separate lives. So she took another route, which was to just concentrate on the richness and value of racial diversity as it existed in their everyday lives, and New York was a multicultural city by its nature; its history of immigration, going as far back as the mid-nineteenth century, proved this. The city was also one of the most linguistically diverse in America, and the demographic makeup was complex and nuanced. Some of the main cultural groups were African Americans, South Americans, Middle Eastern Americans, Americans of European ancestry, Asian Americans, and American Indians, and there were many mixed neighborhoods and suburbs that had created a harmonious cosmopolitan whole where the variety of cultures were well integrated. Allison realized that it was better to build the children's understanding on a positive model rather than refuting the failings of the past, although much of the cultural separation between Harlem and other neighborhoods was purely down to poverty, as she knew from her own research and Hooman's book, where African Americans just couldn't afford to live in other wealthier neighborhoods, some being predominately White mixed with other diverse races. There were, however, other boroughs in New York where African Americans earned as much as Whites, if not more, in some circumstances. And all the children in the group now knew this, and it seemed to Allison that she had done something positive for the community here to highlight the beauty of their cultural identity in a sea of other diverse and equally beautiful races in New York.

The moment passed, and Jonny gave the camera back to Allison. She thanked the two Danish girls and the man from East Harlem. Jonny's grandmother emerged from a supermarket and motioned for him to follow her.

Jessica waved as she walked away. "Ms Bird, I'll see you at the exhibition next month," she said.

"Okay. Say hi to your parents for me."

"I will. Bye."

Allison watched the two children fade into the people walking on the street as she put her camera back into her backpack.

Allison retraced her steps down 125th Street, turning down 5th Avenue and heading toward Marcus Garvey Park; she had not been there for a few weeks and looked forward to sitting in the sun. After walking through the left side of the park, she approached a bench adjacent to a path. Sitting down, she put her shopping bags on the seat. She then slipped out of her backpack and placed it next to the shopping bags. She looked out at the open lawn area covered in snow and the plain trees, whose leaves had been stripped out by fall and winter.

She enjoyed the sun hitting her face and the slight, cool breeze pushing her hair around. Sitting on benches next to her were three homeless people that she had seen before. She waved at them. They smiled and waved back.

Fishing through her backpack, she found her change purse. She took fifty dollars from it and got up and passed it to them. She sat back down.

"Do you guys have somewhere to stay? I have a spare room in my house."

"We're fine. Thanks for asking. We have a place in an abandoned house a few blocks north," said a woman.

"Okay. Are you sure?"

"Yeah, no. We're all pretty well set up there. And we prefer it to shelters and other places."

"Okay, cool." Allison smiled.

As she put her change purse back, she saw her notebook and took it out. She unwound the leather strap and opened the notebook to a new page. The pencil had been bound inside it and fell out onto her lap. She picked it up and wrote the word "bondage." It was a word she had been contemplating recently, and its meaning fell into two categories: the laws of physics, which we were bound to and slaves of, and the cultural mores that bound us to see life through a limited prism, which in turn governed our identity and behavior that in turn determined our understanding of reality. Consequently, we did not realize that we were bound to an understanding of reality that was flawed. It was like a play—as Shakespeare had said: the world was a stage—where we had a predetermined part, bound within a specific culture, worldview, or individual identity, but many of us were unaware that we were in a play to begin with and had no knowledge of the world beyond the fictional reality we were trapped in and bound by, and the underlying laws of the universe were the stage on which the story of our lives unfolded. When we died in the play and woke up from that dreamlike existence, only then would we find ourselves free from that world and that unseen bondage, but we could begin to free ourselves from that stage before we died if we changed our assumptions about what constituted reality, and we would see this world as transitory and release our higher potential and thereby step off the stage and become free from the play, seeing clearly who we could become beyond that dream and beyond that stage.

She remembered a story about Bahá'u'lláh, who as a child, had seen a puppet show of a king, his princes, and the intrigues of the royal court. After the show, the puppeteer had remarked to Bahá'u'lláh that all the puppets in the show had been put into a box. Allison wondered if the puppeteer's box was a reference to a coffin; our life was put away eventually, and the stage faded into death. She had a fleeting thought of Coffin Bay and Memory Cove in South Australia, where she had stopped briefly during her road trip around Australia. The coffin was the last house for the body in this world, and after death, we only took who we had become and our memories with us. She then thought about the old wonky house in Istanbul, the house of relativity; the puppets had gone there too, but the stage had remained, if only a little faded.

She flipped back to a previous entry in her notebook that was about the relationship between predetermination (a type of bondage) and precognition, and how our higher destiny can unfold as we make better choices in our lives. These ideas had been inspired by a movie that she had seen in June. The movie was called *Minority Report* and had been based on a short story by Phillip K. Dick about a future society where murder could be predicted by three people with the psychic ability to see the future, called precogs or precognitives in the movie. Those committing the crimes were arrested before the crime was committed. The fundamental paradox was that by stopping the future crime from happening, they were changing the future. A person could be charged for the future intention of a crime that never actually occurred, but that would have happened had it not been prevented.

She had written a note to herself: "For precognition to work, there must be a certain amount of predetermination in the world and a clear line of causation through the linear structure of spacetime, so the question raised by the movie is this: is all destiny predetermined or changeable and dynamic under free will? I believe it is both predetermined and dynamic, but I think God can determine our destinies in advance and may even know a range of alternate destinies, so through the laws of probability, at a very high level, God will know, through the attributes of omnipresence and omniscience, what our future choices will be." She thought about the symmetry of her yellow dress in Hooman's dream as an example of predetermination, where all the linked actions of several people had to take place for this precise destiny to manifest, and was not all destiny this precise and beautiful?

She thought that if God can know every single cause in the universe, from vibrating strings (from string theory) right up to the exact shell and path of every electron in every atom to the spin of planets, then in turn, all destiny could be determined in advance. If time and space were not predetermined, we could never use clocks to arrange being at future events, which proved that we could predict the future within certain boundaries. We knew that on Friday at 12:00 p.m. the sun would be at a specific arc in the sky. Of course, the cause of much of our destiny was the three-way synergy between thought, action, and the world we moved through. All three were like an interacting feedback loop where we learned the lessons of life and being from birth to death.

She had written a quote from Albert Einstein:

> *Everything is determined, the beginning as well as the end, by forces over which we have no control. It is determined for the insect, as well as for the star. Human beings, vegetables, or cosmic dust, we all dance to a mysterious tune, intoned in the distance by an invisible piper.*[3]

She wondered, If we could see our future, would we still be bound to fulfill it, or could we choose to betray it with an alternate future? She had seen this idea explored in the movie *Donnie Darko*. The protagonist, Donnie, knows from being immersed in a tangent universe (parallel universe) that if he lives in the primary universe, then his girlfriend, Gretchen, will die, so he betrays a possible future destiny in the primary universe by allowing a jet engine, falling onto his house, to kill him. Allison found the last scene fascinating as Donnie laughs at the possibility of his own impending death and his self-sacrifice for a person, Gretchen, whom he will never meet in the primary universe.

She knew that precognition was possible because she had seen her future once in her life: as a child, when she had dreamed of the pineapple farm. Allison was twelve years old at the time. It was 1984. She thought that if the exact time of our death was fixed, might we be able to take different paths until we reach the time of death, so then our destiny was fixed but also dynamic and organic. In addition to a fixed death, there might be other predetermined milestones in our lives that we are bound to fulfill, like birth, our names, the number and gender of our siblings, marriage, sickness, or growing old.

A few of Bahá'u'lláh's writings dealt with precognition and the relationship between the waking world, the dream state, and the infinite spiritual worlds beyond the material world. The dream state was like an interface between the different worlds, and the relationship was mysterious and probably impossible to understand in all of its significance in this world. The reason many people dismissed dreams as not real was because of the immediacy of our experience in the material world through the senses. The dream world, for most people, could seem a bit hazy and surreal by comparison, but the surreal nature of dreams might be a faithful reflection of the afterlife. It might be very different from this world in many ways that we could not determine until we died, which Hooman had said many times. The fact was that in the dream world all our senses were active inwardly while our outer senses were inactive, which proved that the soul was not entirely bound by the limits of the body. For example, how could we see light in our dreams without actually seeing light, and how could we hear sounds without hearing actual sound? And so Bahá'u'lláh had discussed this mysterious relationship. She read the quote from her notebook, which she had pasted onto the pages after printing it out:

> *As to thy question concerning the worlds of God. Know thou of a truth that the worlds of God are countless in their number, and infinite in their range. None can reckon or comprehend them except God, the All-Knowing, the All-Wise. Consider thy state when asleep. Verily, I say, this phenomenon is the most mysterious of the signs of God amongst men, were they to ponder it in their hearts. Behold how the thing which thou hast seen in thy dream is, after a considerable lapse of time, fully realized. Had the world in which thou didst find thyself in thy dream been identical with the world in which thou livest, it would have been necessary for the event occurring in that dream to have transpired in this world at the very moment of its occurrence. Were it so, you yourself would have borne witness unto it. This being not the case, however, it must necessarily follow that the world in which thou livest is different and apart from that which thou hast experienced in thy dream. This latter*

world hath neither beginning nor end. It would be true if thou wert to contend that this same world is, as decreed by the All-Glorious and Almighty God, within thy proper self and is wrapped up within thee. It would equally be true to maintain that thy spirit, having transcended the limitations of sleep and having stripped itself of all earthly attachment, hath, by the act of God, been made to traverse a realm which lieth hidden in the innermost reality of this world. Verily I say, the creation of God embraceth worlds besides this world, and creatures apart from these creatures. In each of these worlds He hath ordained things which none can search except Himself, the All-Searching, the All-Wise. Do thou meditate on that which We have revealed unto thee, that thou mayest discover the purpose of God, thy Lord, and the Lord of all worlds. In these words the mysteries of Divine Wisdom have been treasured.[4]

So, it was clear to her from that passage that there was a relationship between the different worlds of God, both through time and space and after this, in a timeless and changeless realm where the future and past may be more flexible and fluid. She remembered the conversation with Hooman about the different kinds of time: standard spacetime, eternal time (nonlinear time), and beyond this, a formless timelessness.

Though as interesting as precognition was, it was clear that we were not meant to see our future very often; otherwise, we would be dreaming of the future every night in our dreams. So her conclusion about precognition was that it did not matter whether we could see or not see our future. It was the power our choices had in life to positively transform individuals and, indeed, the whole human race collectively. There were critical moments in our lives where one choice changed our future destiny utterly and completely. These moments could appear to be superficially insignificant at the time, so our destiny was not fixed when we were making choices about which road to pursue, and at every juncture in time, we could choose from a range of choices from most ideal to least ideal and everything in between; we could also compensate for poor choices in the past. Not just our own choices changed us, but how our choices intersected with the lives of others also changed us, which was the dynamic way our life unfolded into symmetrical destiny. We might be able to change the advancement of the human race by simple acts of love aimed at spiritual unification, and these waves would spread out and encompass the future as we passed through history and left our own unique mark on it. From this she concluded that no action passed by without consequence or effect. And Bahá'u'lláh's life and teachings had done exactly this. He was like all the great messengers of the past: Buddha, Christ, Muhammad, and all the countless others. Their one purpose was to liberate us from the bondage of the material world and allow us to fly in the illimitable spaces in our hearts. For that was where God really resided—without boundaries, beginnings, or endings—because there was no past, present, or future without God. Bahá'u'lláh had said:

So powerful is the light of unity, that it can illuminate the whole earth.[5]

Then she thought that within the bounds of the physical world, we had something to strive for, and then we had free will to see God or not, so all the grades of spiritual development were filtered out, and the "true believer" was created as the motivating force behind the whole of creation. We could then strive toward the apex of consciousness, and the oneness of God reflected over all creation. We could then become a creative player in that schema and take part in the creation process. The destiny of the "true believer," then, must be unspeakably glorious.

She then thought about an entry she had made in her notebook the previous week that referenced *The Four Valleys*. It was a small but powerful book by Bahá'u'lláh. In the seventh valley, The Valley of True Poverty and Absolute Nothingness, it was said that there were four stages of the heart, which she felt were outlined in *The Four Valleys*. She turned back a few pages to find a quote about the fourth valley. It was another printout that she had pasted into her notebook:

If the mystic knowers be among them that have attained the beauty of the Beloved, this station is the throne of the inmost heart and the secret of divine guidance. This is the seat of the mystery "He doeth what He willeth, and ordaineth what He pleaseth." Should all that are in heaven and on earth attempt to unravel this exalted allusion and subtle mystery, from now until the Day whereon the Trumpet shall sound, yet would they fail to comprehend even a letter thereof, for this is the station of God's immutable decree and His foreordained mystery. Hence, when asked regarding this matter, He made reply: "It is a bottomless sea that none shall ever fathom." And when the question was repeated, He answered: "It is the blackest of nights through which none can find his way."[6]

. . .

This is the realm of pure awareness and utter self-effacement . . . For this is the realm of God and is sanctified above every allusion of His creatures . . .

. . .

The first is His statement "O My servant! Obey Me, that I may make thee like unto Myself. For I say 'Be,' and it is, and thou shalt say 'Be,' and it shall be." [7]

And she thought that this valley might be linked to the world of Jabarut, the world of command and the eternal laws, and that maybe we could experience this world in a fused union with the being of the Manifestation of God. But she knew that the station of a Manifestation was immeasurably exalted above that of a human being, and any fused union was relative to the limitations of human beings. Then we could be truly unbounded and released into an unlimited radiance of being, and this was when the lower self had been entirely subsumed by the higher self, of God standing within the self, shimmering with transcendence.

Allison closed her notebook and mused over these thoughts and wondered if one day she would be truly free. That was her hope. She stood up, put the backpack over her shoulders, and walked over to the homeless people.

"My name is Allison. Can I give you all a hug?"

"Sure," they said in turn.

She gave each one a hug.

As she was about to get her shopping bags and walk off, the woman said, "Hey, do you want to come and have dinner with us? We'll buy some nice food with that money you gave us."

Allison turned toward them. "Sorry, this might seem rude, but do you have electricity at your abandoned house?"

"No, but we have propane camping stoves, heaters, and a few propane lamps."

"Okay, cool. When?"

"Tonight at six p.m."

"Okay. Can I bring my husband and son?"

"Absolutely," the woman said.

"Awesome. What is your address?"

Allison took out her notebook and tore a strip of paper from the back of the notebook. She then gave the woman her pencil. She wrote the address down and handed the paper and pencil back to Allison.

Allison smiled and walked off. "Nice to meet you guys, and see you tonight, then."

"Bye, and thanks for the money."

"No problem. Bye."

"By the way, my name is Rose, and this is Micheal and Michael."

"Wonderful repetition of names. See you all tonight."

She turned, waved, and began to walk toward the renovated brownstones with her bags swinging at her side as she went down the path.

Once she came to the Harlem Writers Studio, she walked up the front steps, looking up at the scaffolding that was up to restore the facade. The door was open. She walked through and looked around at the interior. Parts had been partially restored, and other sections had been gutted; it still looked chaotic and unfinished.

They had tried to maintain some of the original character of the building but also added quite contemporary architectural features. They wanted to make the two properties into one building with accommodations for five writers, each with their own self-contained studio, and other creative spaces for community events that would be based around writing. Hooman wanted to build a relationship with the Harlem Writers Guild, which had been in existence since 1950. There would also be an underlying tenet that young writers from Harlem would be a part of the writing studio, and they would try to build relationships with local elementary and high schools to scout for and encourage talented young writers.

Allison wanted to hire Harlem locals to do the work, so the architect and builder, who were both named Robert, had been hired.

"Robert," she shouted out.

"Robert . . . are you here?"

But no one was in the building, so she turned around and left, walking down the steps, assuming that they had all had a lunch break somewhere.

———

By the time Allison left Adelaide, it was early October 1993. She was actually sad to be leaving, which surprised her. But another more detached part of her knew it was time to leave. She drove north, back toward Port Augusta, which she had passed through while coming in the opposite direction from Coober Pedy.

Eventually, she left the highway, moving from town to town through farmland until she reached a coastal town called Wallaroo, two hours out of Adelaide. The town was unremarkable, but it led her on to a dirt road that hugged the bay. Wheat farms and beaches embraced each other, and she speculated that the road was probably only meant for farmers. It was slow going, with parts of the road corrugated, but the isolated coastline was beautiful and laid bare for her memory. She found that from Tickera onwards there were no more coastal roads, so she rejoined the highway.

She stopped in Port Augusta for lunch. She sat in the town square eating sandwiches and got to talking to a crowd of Aboriginal Australians sitting near her. She wondered where to go next. She had seen a visitors center as she had driven into the town, so she went back to the center and asked about the other side of the Spencer Gulf. She had seen several national parks on her map but was unsure if they were worth the extra drive-time south. The woman at the center suggested she visit the southernmost tip of the Eyre Peninsula. Allison then had two options: Lincoln National Park or Coffin Bay National Park, so Allison headed south and arrived at Lincoln National Park in the afternoon. Parts of the park had paved roads, and other areas were for four-wheel drives. She spent the remaining part of the day hiking the easily accessible trails, and at dusk she got a lift in a four-wheel drive heading to Memory Cove, where she camped overnight.

In the morning she walked along the beach, looking out at the island chain in the bay. It was a little like Wilsons Promontory: white sand, some low dunes, granite outcrops, and dense bush. After walking along the beach for half an hour, she got a lift back to her car. She wanted to make it to the last town before the Nullarbor Plain before the end of the day and drive through the plain at dawn, just to see what the quality of the light would be like at that time of day. Before heading to Yalata, she stopped for an hour at Coffin Bay. She drove out to the cliffs and stared at the sea for a while; she decided against hiking there because it seemed quite similar to Lincoln National Park.

She made it to Yalata just after dusk and pulled into a truck stop to sleep.

In the morning Allison left Yalata before dawn. She planned to take three or four photographs at different times in the dawn light. The first photo was of a dark horizon with a thin strip of light. She used her tripod for the first time on the trip. After half an hour, the light started to reflect the red earth beside the road. The Nullarbor Plain was primarily flat grasslands. There was just sky, road, and empty space. The desert was enticing and covered by a thin mask of death. She had thought about the plants and animals that survived in this environment. Nature produced such strange and beautiful adaptations when life was surviving at the margins of existence. After an hour there, she had only taken two shots. She took the last shot while leaning on the trunk of the car and looking out at the expanse. She resisted the urge several times to walk into it and never return. She eventually packed up the camera and tripod and started her drive across the Nullarbor Plain.

After one hour, the highway began tracing the edge of the ocean.

And two hours after leaving Yalata, she came out on the other side of the Nullarbor Plain, driving into a small town called Eucla. She asked around at the RV park about Eucla National Park, which she could see marked on her map. There were no paved roads, only rough tracks. So she drove to the nearest accessible dirt road, which ended near the old telegraph station; it was being slowly swallowed by a low dune. She got out of the car and walked past the sandstone building over the low dunes that would take her to the beach. This first set of dunes was covered in grass tufts and had trees growing in it, but as she came to the shore, she could see larger dunes in the distance. She found tire tracks on the beach, and so she followed these for forty minutes until she came to the Bilbunya Dunes. The dunes were the biggest she had ever seen, and she imagined that this was how the Sahara felt, but with an ocean view. The sand was the purest white she could remember of other dunes she had visited. She left the beach and began to climb the first large dune. She guessed that some of the dunes ahead of her were at least three hundred feet high. She looked back at the ocean for a moment before descending over the other side of the dune. Once she was deep inside the dunes, she sat down and took out her cameras; the Zenit had color film, and the Leica had black and white. She changed the red filter to a yellow one to tone down the contrast in the black-and-white images, and she began to snap a panorama of overlapping images; it was something that she had seen David Hockney do in the eighties. She saw banks of clouds pass over the sand, so she shot these in different light conditions, watching the shadows of the clouds passing over the dunes. She felt a strange mix of fatigue and exhilaration.

After a few minutes, she packed the cameras away and put a beach towel over her head to block out the sun. She lay down, her back straddling the peak of the dune, and after fifteen minutes, she was asleep.

28

THE EXHIBITION

From this most august and exalted station, and from this most sublime and glorious plane, the seeker entereth the City of Immortality, therein to abide forever . . .

He will quaff from the cup of immortality, tread in its land, soar in its atmosphere, consort with them that are its embodiments, partake of the imperishable and incorruptible fruits of the tree of eternity, and be forever accounted, in the lofty heights of immortality, amongst the denizens of the everlasting realm. [1]

— BAHÁ'U'LLÁH, *GEMS OF DIVINE MYSTERIES*

Just under four weeks passed. Allison had made all the preparations for the exhibition. Jonny's photo was printed and framed but had not been added to all the photos taken by the other children in the group. Jane, the curator at the Studio Museum in Harlem, was going to hang the photo today, a few hours before the opening at 6:30 p.m., Saturday, January 4, 2003.

Allison stood in front of a disused building on 125th Street; the building was on the other side of the street, with its windows bricked up with cinder blocks. She leaned against the window of a jeweler's shop. The shutter in her camera clicked open and closed, and the impression of the building she had been observing burned onto the film. She often walked by it whenever she came up for weekly food shopping. The crumbling structure sat propped up on both sides, a soon-to-be toppled old man, between a supermarket and a new clothing chain store.

Lowering the camera to her side, she stared at the emasculated windows and the rotting cast-iron balconies to imprint an exposure to her memory. The dark shell would not stand idle for long. One of the franchise stores would move in soon enough and either knock it down or restore it.

Snow crunched under her boots as she turned around to face the jeweler's shop. Medallions and other jewelry displayed in the front window sparkled in the sun. She looked down at the translucent snow around her boots. The snow somehow reflected her feelings of happiness. Her thoughts turned to the wonderment of life, and these feelings were beyond what she could explain to herself rationally, given that life seemed, for the most part, just ordinary. She had left behind the tendency of the previous year to interpret physical reality as being empty. Life was now full.

On the day before and in what seemed like a random pronouncement—but of course, it fell in exactly with her own thoughts—she was not surprised when Hooman said, "Hey, you know, I think this is the happiest I've ever been."

"I know; I feel the same. It's like an aspect of our life is just a thin film on the surface of something else, something expansive and extraordinary. It will reveal itself. I feel it, at any moment. Something is going to change soon. Something is going to play out that changes everything."

Hooman walked into the periphery of her vision. She turned and watched him intently as he walked toward her, pushing Noah's stroller. They smiled.

"You caught me. Sorry, I was loafing about taking photos. I'll go in and get the ring now," she said. On the tips of her toes, she stretched to kiss Hooman.

"That's okay, there's no hurry," he said.

She ducked down to check on Noah, who was happy to see his mum but was distracted by the movement of people on the street. Allison could see his fascination with a woman sitting nearby. She was selling umbrellas and spun a multicolored umbrella on its tip.

Allison stood up. "I only have to pay for it. I'll be back in a sec."

She walked into the jeweler's shop.

A few minutes later they crossed the intersection of Malcolm X Boulevard and 125th Street. They walked a little further down 125th Street. As they entered the Studio Museum, Allison asked, "Do you like my new ring?" She held her hand up. Fake diamonds flashed on a round silver face; the stones were arranged in a series of concentric circles.

"Yes, it looks good," he said.

As they entered the large open gallery space, she took a fleeting glance at the photographs hung around the room. The arrangement had not changed from the previous few days. The exhibition title, near the entrance, was now complete. The font type carried at least half the meaning. The letters were a decorative 1800s typeface, which could have been straight off a poster advertising passage on one of those old southern riverboats plying the Mississippi:

SLAVERY TRANSFIGURED

Well known in Harlem art circles, Hayden Robert was known for his sociopolitical statements, sometimes controversial, and this exhibition continued that tradition. The majority of the photographs in the exhibition were of African Americans in the service industries downtown, flipping burgers, serving wheatgrass at trendy juice bars, and making lattes. The photographs were all black and white and shot with a medium-format camera.

There was also a series of photos of a White woman and an African American man injecting heroin in the ruins of an abandoned house. Allison was struck by the dirt and detritus in the images that were focalized and intensified by the vivid texture of surfaces and the quality of light and shadow in the shots, which only a medium-format camera could reveal. In the first shot the man was injecting the heroin into the woman's arm. The next shot was of the two embracing each other. The last shot was of the woman curled up in his lap, her face expressing a placid ecstasy and her mind traveling in that far-off land. These three images were exquisite. And this raw beauty was a strange counterpoint to the desperate poverty and pathos in the lives of these people. A part of her wanted to reach out and merge into their life. During the hanging, Allison had asked how these three photos related to the theme, and Hayden had said that the woman, Ruby, had to prostitute herself to pay for the heroin, and thus this was a form of slavery to drug addiction but also a reflection of drug dealers who were dealing in this form of slavery.

One photograph, which was nothing more than a young teen serving French fries and a burger, had the title "We believe in your potential." Allison had asked Hayden about the meaning of the title. He explained that many companies offered work experience for the betterment of students' education, experience that usually had no relevance to students' actual study needs other than being cheap fodder for the company's coffers. This work was a form of economic slavery within the parameters of the poverty found in Harlem and the South Bronx. So, slavery had not been abolished altogether. It had morphed into a new and subtle form. And the transfiguration in the exhibition title was supposed to be ironic, given that its meaning was based on two kinds of transfiguration: capitalist transfiguration, achieved through brand propaganda, and true spiritual transfiguration, which from Allison's point of view, could be achieved through studying sacred texts, prayer, and meditation, and through that, striving to live within the bounds of a deeper and more expansive humanity. The meaning of these two types of transfiguration oscillated in her mind in duality. "Transfiguration" was a word used within the context of something transforming into something higher and more beautiful. And capitalism was all about material beauty, beautiful and desirable products, but within that was spiritual emptiness, "being in nothingness" that could paradoxically be filled with its opposite, spirituality, in a very broad sense; an unintended meaning of Sartre's book *Being and Nothingness* was that it could be used to highlight our relationship with capitalism (our being in that nothingness), but Allison also thought that capitalism might be transfigured in the future when this kind of economic exploitation had been wiped out, and so then it might be truly transfigured from material beauty to spiritual beauty.

She thought about child labor in much of the developing world, where children could not go to school because they had to eke out a meager living just to help their families survive, and although Harlem and South Bronx were not quite this extreme, there were some comparisons relative to the wealth of the average middle-class American. And as she had expressed to Elliot almost one year ago, Allison could escape this poverty at any moment if she chose to. As a White person, she had more choices in this life than many African Americans did. She possessed more socioeconomic freedoms purely by virtue of her birth into a particular racial identity.

Allison stretched her neck over Hooman's shoulder to see if Jane, the curator, was anywhere close. "Hello." She raised her voice. "Hello, Jane," but no reply returned to her, and Allison heard only the echo in the room.

A modest-sized room off the main gallery space housed the work of the children in her photography group. They moved into the room to find the past year framed in each child's unique perception of the world they inhabited in Harlem.

Lying on the floor beneath Jonny's photograph was a hammer, a length of wire, and a small spread of plaster dust from the drill hole made to hang the frame. The plaster dust fanned out on the concrete floor with the consistency of hourglass sand.

Crouching down, she pulled her finger through the plaster dust and formed a heart shape in the dust. A dry sensation of muted pain shot through her finger and up into her arm. As she rubbed the plaster dust between her fingers, for a fleeting moment, her whole body exuded a distant but distinctive sensation of white dust. She saw a vision of her body constructed with this dust, and her skin felt tighter, as if it were stretched. She clenched her hand into a tight fist and anticipated her skin peeling away like overcooked chicken flesh, but this was not what her outer eye saw as her imagination was overlaid with her sight. This vision soon faded, and there remained only her clenched fist in front of her face, and she wondered if this was only her imagination or one of the bodies from the spiritual world.

Hooman had stood over her, quietly observing. "Are you having one of your visions?" he asked.

"Yes, I am." She stood up and released her fist. "But don't worry though. I'm okay. It's gone now." She looked down at the heart shape her finger had made in the plaster dust. "But it's strange. My imagination, or my mind, seems to take certain obscure qualities in physical objects into my body or my mind's body. Like just now, I saw another body of white dust, abstract but connected to the physical world." She thought about the spirit body, Sah, in the Egyptian framework for the soul.

Hooman did not say anything. He only raised his eyebrows and shrugged.

"Anyway," she pointed at the framed photo to divert the conversation, "this is Jonny's work. What do you think?"

Hooman stepped closer and studied the photo. "There's something special about him, don't you think?"

The photograph was the one of the people Jonny had somewhat artificially gathered together on 125th Street. The whole composition had a strange but beautiful aura and was something akin to a Vermeer painting. It captured the stillness of time in a unique way. Jonny had taken the shot without signaling the moment, so only Jessica was staring through the lens at the viewer. Her face was beautiful: a radiant poverty lived in innocence.

Hooman leaned in closer to examine the details.

Footsteps echoed around the larger part of the exhibition and eventually came toward them. Allison leaned sideways through the doorway to see Hayden walking toward her.

"Hey there. Hey, hey, how's life?" Hayden said in a singsong tone and smiled. He walked into the side room and looked for a moment at Hooman, who was still standing in front of Jonny's photograph. "Hey, hey. Great shot, man, eh?"

"Thanks again for letting us join you in this," Allison said and raised her arms with her palms facing the roof, moving her arms down to the horizontal position, which had the effect of encompassing the whole gallery.

"Hey, hey, no problem. Glad to have you guys on board with me. Yeah, for sure."

"And I know our theme doesn't fit in exactly with you—"

"Theme. No, that's not true! Identity, it's a big issue in Harlem. We are all coming to terms with some major changes. Yes, yes, identity, that's where it's at. And, in fact, what you are doing is more important. You start here with the next generation. The generation, hopefully, that'll change the way we do things. African Americans have been weighed down with some pretty limiting stereotypes, created within and outside the community, and this is just what we need. It is, I promise you. We've got to loosen up, baby, ya know. There is still a lot of bitterness from the racism of the past and present. We have to let go. All humanity are slaves to their identity. In one way or another. Ya know? Most of us were gifted a cultural identity that we never made but that we blindly follow without question. Why do we do that? We all do it. Even me. Anyway . . . babe. I'm getting way too philosophical on ya," said Hayden.

"No. What you say is wonderful," she said.

Hayden then turned to Hooman. "Hey, you don't mind if I hug your wife?"

Hooman smiled and put his hands in his pockets. "Sure . . . go ahead."

"You don't need to ask his permission. I am my own person. You need to ask me," said Allison. "And the answer is yes, you may."

"Of course! Come here, babe." Hayden stooped down and smothered her. He lifted her off the ground for a moment and laughed. "You're very huggable, babe." Once she was back on the ground, he added, "Okay, hey, babe, so, let's look at these other photographs. I want to know each kid and each shot. Absolutely, okay?"

Without letting her move from his side, he steered her around the room as she explained the background behind each photograph and the significant vignettes of the children's lives.

———

A taxi arrived in front of the gallery. In Shidan's rush to get inside for the opening, he thrust his foot into the slushy ice water in the gutter. On the sidewalk he swore at the general surroundings before walking into the building.

As Shidan entered the main gallery space, Hayden closed off his speech to the packed gallery and opened his arms, smiling as Allison slipped through the crowd and into his embrace.

"I love this person," Hayden said. Everyone in the room laughed as he finally released her and stepped into the crowd.

"Don't leave me here alone," Allison said.

"Oh, okay then, I'll come back."

Hayden took a place beside her, and she linked her arm into his as she began to speak.

Shidan made his way to the front of the crowd of people for a better vantage point. He noted the odd word in Allison's speech wavered. She was obviously nervous.

"Hello, everybody, err, I'm feeling a bit shy now, so forgive me as I attempt to blunder my way through what I want to express to you about this exhibition and about my time in Harlem with the kids. First off, I need to thank Hayden for allowing us to make this occasion a joint exhibition. And also, I'd like to express my thanks to some of the amazing people here in the room that I've come to know in the last year, especially the kids in the group and, of course, their parents. Harlem has been a beautiful place to live in." She smiled.

Shidan was standing directly opposite Allison and beside Elliot, who put her hand on his shoulder. He turned his head. Elliot smiled at him. Allison talked to the crowd for a few moments before interrupting herself. She then addressed Shidan directly. "Hello, Shidan. Welcome."

He looked straight into her eyes and smiled.

She continued. "Although there is a crossover between the work of the kids and Hayden's themes, transfiguration and slavery through identity, I won't speak directly to the traditional issues of slavery. Hayden has already touched on this in his introduction. The ironies of slavery transfigured and recast in a capitalist mold. Most of you are familiar with these issues. What I want to look at exists in a wider circle, more generalized maybe . . ." She paused and took a breath before saying, "You know, it's a strange thing, which I have never really understood, that the greatest and most beautiful aspect of the human race is its diversity. And yet this is also the hardest thing for the human race to come to terms with, its own diversity. How can that be? It's so very strange and so peculiar. On the one hand, we have a strong need to make everyone the same as us, to abolish diversity, and to make others conform to a single idea of humanity. Then, on the other hand, we strive for uniqueness, distinction, and diversity, which is a paradox. I'm not just thinking of physical diversity, which equates to external racial identity, but of internal racial culture that carries more subtle distinctions of conformity. That is, that Whites should act like Whites and only take an interest in their sub-culture, or that African Americans should only be concerned with their race exclusively. Striving then, in each community, to keep people in bands of pure category, separate, where they must not stray, where they are forbidden to refigure themselves in a way which suits their own natural or desired intellectual and spiritual potential. This conformity seems to hold true for all culture, religion, and personality, or any type of internal diversity. So above race is common humanity, which celebrates diversity but is not limited by it and does not make distinctions of superiority or favor one race over the other. It's a fine line we walk between the celebration of one's own race and the exclusion of others."

Shidan saw that she was looking down at the ring on her finger, a ring he had not seen before.

She tilted it back and forth in the light before continuing. "So you see, my concerns include race but also span out in a wider circle to encompass all of humanity, and that is what I wanted to explore in the photography project I started here: identity.

"But the children also took their own paths, as you will see. When I first started the group, I didn't have any specific plans, and as I got to know them, I realized there were deep-seated issues surrounding racial identity. And who knows, maybe one day, in a future without racial prejudice, we can celebrate difference. I hope that this gallery, which now champions the development of Black art, will be able to widen its circle to include the Hispanic community, which is just down the road in East Harlem, or any other minority race in Harlem. Maybe? Which is not to say that supporting the art production of only one race is a negative thing. I think this creates opportunities for Black artists who would otherwise not have a voice. I just think that the future global society will make sure that everyone has a voice in an equal community. Anyway, I want you all to look at the photos the kids have produced with all this in mind. And I want to thank the kids for trusting me, for letting me into their lives." Allison paused and looked at Shidan with a smile. "Well, that's it from me." She then looked up at Hayden, who beamed at her, and she said, "Thanks. . . . Oh, I almost forgot, as you may already know, Hooman, Shidan, Sara, and myself are opening the Harlem Writers Studio in three or four months. Please support it and tell people about it. Thanks."

People in the gallery clapped as Hayden leaned down and hugged her. Shidan looked around to study everyone's faces. A few seemed unimpressed by her words, but most were accepting.

Hayden released her and jumped up. "Isn't she wonderful? This place is now officially open." He waded through the crowd in a chatty and excited fashion.

Shidan approached Allison. "Well done, you," he said.

"I know that what I've just said won't have gone down well with everyone in here."

"There's truth to it, so who cares. It just highlights, as you said, that the love of one's race is a fine line to walk. Personally, I have about an equal proportion of love and repulsion for my race, which leaves me at point zero, and it's a good place to be. More objective, I think. And that is what you want too. Am I wrong?"

"Shidan, you really spoil me. You know very well that that's just what I want to hear. Don't play with my ego."

He laughed and patted her on the shoulder. "Congratulations, it's great to see this happen. I'm very happy for you, dear. Very happy."

Shidan watched Allison's gaze move until she looked over his shoulder. He turned to find the source of her stare.

"Hey, let's go see Hooman. I've neglected him a little tonight. Hayden has had me wrapped up for the last hour or so."

"Sure, I haven't seen him for a few weeks myself."

They pushed through and around people until they reached Hooman and Noah. Hooman was talking to his boss, Paul Nightingale. Paul's daughter, Alison, was standing beside him.

Hooman turned to Allison. "Paul and Alison have something for you. It's a paper bird," he said.

"Oh really?"

Alison held her hand out and looked up at Allison.

"This is something you gave to my mother, Rose, at JFK Airport about four years ago," Paul said.

Shidan watched Allison crouch down to Alison's head height. "Oh, thank you. I remember this bird now, but I never guessed that the lady I gave it to was your grandmother," Allison said and then turned to look up at Paul.

"It took us a while to realize that you made it. Alison found and traced your signature on the paper. You must have been practicing your signature on the page above the page with your poem," Paul said.

"Yes, I have always changed my signature over time. I always allow it to morph and change, which is what I was doing as I practiced a new version of my signature on the page above the poem. But I don't need this. I gave it away. You can keep this if you want," Allison said to Alison.

"Alison wants you to have it back," Paul said.

Allison looked at the young Alison intently. "You want to give it back to me?"

"Yes."

"Okay, then." Allison took the paper bird from Alison and placed it into her jacket pocket. She then kissed the younger Alison on the cheek before standing up.

After a short conversation, Hooman spun Noah's stroller around. Shidan followed Hooman and Allison into the side room to find Jessica trying to entice a reluctant Jonny to come into a crowd of her girlfriends.

Jessica yelled. "Oh, oh . . . Allison . . . come. Come here."

They walked toward the crowd of girls.

Allison crouched down. "It's good to call me Allison, not Ms Bird. What's up?" she said to Jessica.

"Ask Jonny to come over here. We want to take a photo."

"Why doesn't he want to come over? Usually he doesn't mind."

"I don't know. He's being stubborn."

Shidan looked at Jessica's girlfriends, who were all giggling as they motioned the boy to come over. Jonny's face held a mixed expression of mild terror, indignation, and disgust. He crossed his arms and shook his head.

"Okay, okay, that's enough, girls. I'll ask him over nicely, but if he doesn't come, then you will have to leave him be," Allison said.

Allison went over to him and whispered something into his ear and then walked over to Shidan and Hooman. Shidan asked what she had said.

"I said, if you come now, the pain will be over quickly. He's accustomed to that kind of logic."

"Poor kid," Shidan observed as the boy walked slowly over to the girls with his hands in his pockets. "Straight into the mouth of the beast," he said.

"Shidan," Allison shook her head, smiling, "it's not that bad."

"No, I think I agree with Shidan," Hooman added.

They all watched Jessica, who was much taller than Jonny, stand behind him. She placed her hand on his shoulder, which he removed. One of the girls stood out in front, ready to take the shot.

"Oh, wait. Oh . . . Allison, you come, too, and Hooman."

Taking the camera from the girl, Shidan offered to take the photo. The two adults sat cross-legged as all the children stood behind them.

"Where's Sara?" Allison asked Shidan as he looked through the camera's viewfinder.

"I don't know. She said she was coming."

"What about Nava, where is she?"

"Same, I don't know."

Allison turned to Hooman. "Have you heard anything?"

"Nope. No news."

As Hooman said that and Shidan was about to take the shot, Nava yelled, "No, no, wait for me." She ran and launched herself across their laps.

The shot was finally taken, and at the last moment, when it was too late for him to react, Shidan saw that Jessica had placed her arm around Jonny's neck in a semi-embrace. Nava then jumped to her feet, chatting away excitedly at the group. She complimented all the work while breathing in the buzz and energy in the gallery. "This is exciting. Wow," Nava said.

Hayden came into the room. He waded toward them through a small crowd of people. He was chatting to everyone like a hummingbird moving from flower to flower as he flipped from person to person in a crazy flurry of movement. Finally, he stood directly behind an obstacle in his path. Nava was so wrapped in her stream of self-answered conversation that she had not seen the others staring behind her.

Hooman introduced her. "Hayden, this is my sister, Nava."

She swung around immediately and spoke to his chest. Giggling, she looked up at him. "Err, sorry. Hello. You're tall."

Hayden let out a scream while waving his arms above his head. Nava stepped backward, bewildered, but Hayden swooped down before she could retreat any further and lifted her off her feet. He then swung her around several times before letting her free.

"Well, *hello*, Nava. Is that the name I heard?" he said. He laughed and added, "You're the perfect weight for spinning into the sky."

The other three looked at each other and smiled.

Nava did not react in her usual gregarious way. She stood still and looked up at Hayden with nothing to say.

"Hey, little girl, how about another swing?" Hayden said.

She put her arms up in protest and stepped back again. "No. no."

"Aww, come on. How about a hug, then?"

She giggled and looked over her shoulder at the others. "He's kind of funny," and she did not have time to say any more before being crushed in another embrace.

———

Shidan looked up at the dark sky for a moment as a crowd of people from the gallery walked down Malcolm X Boulevard toward a café that someone knew. Hayden was now permanently attached to Nava's side. Shidan was trying to decipher the rapid babble they were firing at each other. Hayden would occasionally stop and spin her around, after which there would be a lot of laughter.

Hooman was pushing Noah along in the stroller. They were walking behind the main group of people heading to the café.

"Does Hayden hug everyone he meets?" Shidan asked.

"He does, yes. Man, woman, or object . . . without discrimination."

They laughed and watched him run back to the main group. He dragged Allison forward and walked with his arms around both girls.

They were quiet for a while, then Shidan asked, "I wanted to ask about Allison. She seems happy, but that's just my impression. How is everything really? Beyond surface appearance."

"We are really happy right now. I don't have a single desire beyond our current life."

Shidan studied his friend's face to see if anything was held back because he knew Hooman even better than his own muddy aura. Shidan had always been able to see through other people with clarity and had always been afraid to turn this on himself. He likened it to a light, which shined out on others but never on itself. He found something faint in Hooman's face. "Hooman, I know you are holding something back. What is it?" Shidan said.

Hooman was quiet for a while, then said, "Did you ever speak to Allison about her inner life? About her thoughts and the notebook."

"I know she has a notebook, but her *inner* life, what do you mean?"

"Well, she keeps a lot to herself, so it's not easy to explain it fully. She tells me half, and I try to guess the rest, but we have this arrangement now. She will tell me stuff, and I won't make a judgment, good or bad. I just hear what she is thinking, and I try to be neutral."

"Hooman, I'm not any clearer. What are you on about? She never told me anything about her inner life. Not beyond our little philosophical chats down at the bookshop."

"When we first met, she told me about these experiences she was having that scared her. Of course, that's in the past now, and she tells me that she has somehow integrated these experiences, but there is something else that I can't see. I have this sadness recently, mixed with the happiness in our lives, so I'm confused."

"What experiences, Hooman?"

"It's her imagination. It's been developing, extending into some unfamiliar ground, more than the average person. Her mind, too, in general, seems to have a more tangible existence. And well, one example, which is unrelated to her imagination, but it fits in, is that she feels people's lives before she meets them. Like Jonny, the kid at the exhibition. I remember a few months before we met him. She had developed this uncharacteristic obsession with kicking the fall leaves. And then, when we did meet him, I watched as nearly every week he would be trailing through leaves in the gutter on his way to school. And not long after she had met him, this obsession faded in her. Sometimes it's a color or a song or a seemingly random bunch of words. She explained it to me last year, so that's how I know. But now, I can see it in her behavior more clearly, and I know what's going on. It's so weird, but that's how she meets and makes friends. She knows they're coming months before and identifies a person, when she does finally meet them, by characteristics in her personality that have arisen in that time. People become threaded into her. She once called it attribute surfing. It's like a collective mind, an imaginative form of psychokinetic phenomena. I've seen it three times this year. One was Jane, the curator at the gallery, and the other was the parents of a few kids in her photography group that joined halfway through the year." Hooman stopped to take a breath of the cold air. "She expressed it once, that all objects and thoughts are in play. They flow perfectly interlocked through people, without borders and limitations, but most people are blind to this collective symmetry of souls. That world, the next world, is fused into this world, and that is the kind of symmetry that she sees."

"Well, I see why that might be odd to you. But I'm not surprised. I've always known Allison is in her own sublime little world, and it's very different from yours and mine. I knew that when we first met. Her agenda in this life has never fit with the average in humanity. And she's beautiful for it too. You are very lucky to have her. You know that?"

"A bit of her has rubbed off on me, some of her intuition. That's how I know something is going to happen soon. I can feel it. Something new is passing through her. For the last year she's been held up in the study every morning from four until dawn, praying, meditating. When I get up, she is watching the sun rise from our bedroom window, and she's always happy, always smiling. Her calmness is unnerving. It's not what she was when we first met. I'm unsettled by it."

"Hooman. Nothing at all seems wrong with that picture, not for her, it isn't."

"I know, I see that. That is why I can't get around it."

"Why don't you just ask her?"

"I have, but I don't think she knows herself. Something is going to happen . . . I'm sure of it. Something is going to play out, and I am not sure I'll be happy about it when it arrives in our lives."

———

Sara walked through the door of the café and apologized for her lateness. She explained to Allison that she had seen the exhibition after everybody else had left. Jane, the curator, had shown her around.

"Come and sit next to me," Allison said.

When Sara sat down, Allison put her arm around her waist and continued to talk to Hayden.

"Allison! Allison, sorry to interrupt, but I just wanted to say that I was moved by the exhibition. I was really moved. I think I can understand why you and Hooman moved here. I could never do it myself, but I can see why you did this," Sara said.

Shidan had followed her words from the end of the table and raised his eyebrows. He approved of her late interest in Allison's life in Harlem and of becoming partially enlightened. In many ways Sara's life had never been entirely in touch with the larger group of friends, and it was her wealth that had been the barrier; she lived in a materialistic bubble. Shidan had never tried to consciously pop that bubble, but he was glad that Allison's life had finally had an effect on Sara. And there was the fact that she had contributed a large sum of money for the development of the Harlem Writers Studio.

"Allison, did you hear me?" Sara said, raising her voice.

Responding belatedly, Allison laughed. "Oh, good. You and Shidan can move onto our street, then. A new place just went up for sale, a few houses down from ours. The whole of Harlem is up for sale right now," she added casually.

Then Allison jumped up in a sudden jerking movement, which surprised Sara.

"Oh god. Hooman! Oh god!" Allison said.

"What? What is it?" Hooman responded.

"I forgot to tell you. I had the most amazing dream last night . . . do you remember last year, I think it was, that dream I had? I dreamed about being in that empty basin, an ocean bed."

"Yes, I remember."

"Do you remember how I was surrounded by the ocean at one point, but I woke up before it reached me?"

"Yes, I think so. Yes."

"I thought you said it was empty," Sara inserted.

"Something in the dream triggered the ocean to start closing in on her. Is that right? Oh, I remember now, you ate the pomegranate seed," Hooman answered and turned to Allison.

"Yes . . . and, well, this time, the ocean came closer, and I knew I was going to be destroyed by it, by the crushing weight of the water. I knew I would be torn to shreds, but I didn't care. I was happy. It was so bizarre, but I lifted my arms up to greet it. I was so happy, laughing uncontrollably, then crying in a kind of bliss. The sun was directly above me, in perfect alignment with my body. And my eyes . . . it was strange, but they were not hurt as I looked directly at its white center. Then I saw the ocean in the periphery of my vision close around me in a perfect circle, aligned with the sky and the sun; they were two perfectly concentric circles. I felt the spray on my face just before I was going to die, and I woke up. The sound of the water, it was terrible, powerful, and unlike anything I've ever heard. My whole body vibrated with it. But it was so beautiful, you have no idea. I woke up with a sensation of ecstasy in my chest so strong that I felt a need to vomit."

Looking around the table, Shidan could see everyone was thinking of something to say. Before anyone could answer, Allison added quickly, "And I want to go up to Lake Placid soon. I want to go walking in the mountains nearby, where we were in the summer."

"What, in winter? Walking? Skiing, I could understand," Sara exclaimed.

"Yes, it's cold, but there are no tourists or not so many. The trails are almost empty at this time of year. There's only the odd cross-country skier around and people like us, winter hikers. We'd have the place all to ourselves. Please, what do you think?"

Shidan answered immediately. "I'll come. When are we going?" He turned to Hooman and asked, "What about you?"

"Yep. I'm in. Sara?" Hooman looked at Sara, who sat opposite him. "Do you want to come?"

"Me, no. That's where I draw the line. I hate it when my knees are cold."

"Elliot, what about you?" Hooman asked.

"No, I can't make it. I'm a bit busy for the next few months, but you guys enjoy yourselves. I know you will."

"I can't come either," Nava said.

———

After leaving the dunes near Eucla, Allison drove down the coast road toward Esperance. She stayed there overnight, and on the next day continued toward Albany, but after a four-hour drive, she saw a sign for Bremer Bay. On a whim she decided to have a look at that part of the coast. When she got there, the main town seemed a bit dull and deserted, but she continued toward the coast, and once she reached the beaches, she knew immediately that she would stop here for a few months before heading back to Melbourne. At Blossoms Beach she stopped at a resort and asked the owner if there were any houses close by that she could rent on a short-term basis.

"You're in luck," the woman said. "There is an old timber vacation cabin on the other side of the dunes."

The woman pointed into the distance. "You can't see it from here because it is nestled into scrub, but it's over there. The owner usually only comes here during Christmas vacations."

"Oh, that sounds cool."

After fifteen minutes, Allison found the vacation house and negotiated a two-month stay with the real estate agent back in the main township.

———

Allison spent the full lease period, from October 8 to December 20, 1993, in Blossoms Beach, reading and looking at the ocean beyond the dunes. She walked over the dunes to the beach almost every day, and there were also many tracks to other beaches that she walked along regularly. Allison had planned to arrive in Perth three or four days before Christmas and spend time with Nava and Hooman. He was planning to fly to Perth just before Christmas to spend a few weeks with his parents, but then the plans changed, as Nava had managed to get a job interview in New York in early January 1994. So Nava and her parents would need to go to New York for Christmas instead. Nava then decided to drive down to Blossoms Beach and spend four days with Allison before she went to New York a few days before Christmas. Allison then extended her lease to take her up to Christmas Eve on the twenty-fourth, after which she would begin the long drive back to Melbourne.

Allison was sitting on the balcony when she heard soft taps on the front door. She jumped up with excitement and went to the door. She opened it and hugged Nava.

"Oh, babe, it is so good to see you," Allison said.

"I know. I know."

Nava walked through the door and looked around the interior of the house. "Wow, it is a bit of a dump," Nava said.

"Wooh! Steady on there. It's perfect."

"A perfect dump, maybe."

Allison laughed and took Nava's hand. "Come, let's sit outside."

They walked onto the balcony and sat down.

"Look at that. What a view, eh?"

"Yes, it is nice."

"It's a perfect backdrop for reading and contemplation. So what's happening with New York?"

"If I can get a job in Manhattan, I'll move in with Hooman."

"Hmm, okay. Sounds good. Is there a particular reason you are going?"

"I want to be with Hooman, I suppose, but New York is a bigger pond. If I want to make it as an interior designer, then that's the place to do it."

"True, I suppose."

Nava looked down at the deck at a pile of books next to the chair Allison was sitting in. "What are you reading?"

"Oh, all sorts of things. Mostly related to philosophy. And mostly postmodernity."

"Have you applied for university?"

"Yeah, I filled out the forms last year. Paul sent them to the admissions center in August. I'll hear back in January or February, I think. Jasper thinks I won't have a problem getting into the University of Melbourne."

"I'll cross my fingers for you, babe."

"Thanks," Allison said. "Hey, I want to show you the beach."

They talked more about New York as they walked over the dunes. Allison had never thought of America as a place she would like to visit, but now that Nava's life was clearly merging into that city, Allison felt a thread of interest tugging at her.

"You must come to America. You must come to New York."

Allison wasn't listening now. She nodded and smiled as Nava kept talking about trips she had made to the US after Hooman had finished his law degree.

They followed the sandy track to the beach. When they came to it, they sat down, looking at the ocean.

"Are you coming? Are you going to come?"

"Come where?"

"America."

"Oh . . . America. I don't know. Maybe."

29

THE LAKE MEETS THE SUN

From this station the wayfarer ascendeth unto a City that hath no name or description, and whereof one heareth neither sound nor mention. Therein flow the oceans of eternity, whilst this city itself revolveth round the seat of eternity. Therein the sun of the Unseen shineth resplendent above the horizon of the Unseen, a sun that hath its own heavens and its own moons, which partake of its light and which rise from and set upon the ocean of the Unseen. Nor can I ever hope to impart even a dewdrop of that which hath been decreed therein, as none is acquainted with its mysteries save God, its Creator and Fashioner, and His Manifestations.[1]

— BAHÁ'U'LLÁH, *GEMS OF DIVINE MYSTERIES*

Three weeks had passed since the night of the gallery opening. The car meandered along the Hudson River. The water was a twisting cut pushed into the landscape by the tilt of the land. Over the hours that passed, the stretch of water bloated and thinned as it appeared and disappeared through trees that the cold had stripped out over the winter months. There was a deep layer of snow around these trees, which was faintly luminescent in the sun. As they drove through Upstate New York, they passed a series of small towns. Allison observed the many rustic wooden houses and cottages that were typically painted white. For most of the journey Hooman had followed the river along smaller roads rather than taking the main highway. This was the same route they had taken in the summer. As her memory rewound to summer, Allison compared the effect the different seasons had on the surrounding countryside over that time. The structure and form of trees were clearer without the softening effect of the leaves and showed the river clearly now, whereas it had been hidden in summer.

Allison watched the scenery slide by in the silence of her mind. She huddled in the back seat of the car with her head resting sideways on her knees. The blur of light and shadow from the passing trees passed over her face. She also listened to Shidan and Hooman talk in the front seats, but often she turned back to her own vague thoughts, so their words only came to her in fragments. Noah was asleep and lying next to her in his car seat.

Once they passed through Glens Falls, they began an ascent into the Adirondack Mountains, and the Hudson River diverged away as they joined the main highway. The stripped-out trees disappeared and were replaced by the green and white of snow-covered pines.

After an hour and a half in the mountains, they arrived at Lake Placid and descended into a valley along a winding road. Allison looked through the pines and saw the beginnings of the small town.

Something was wrong, and her gut tightened in worry when she thought about it. Since the night of the gallery opening, she had been vomiting more and more. The dream about the pomegranate and the ocean closing in on her kept replaying night after night until its meaning became clear, after which the dream stopped and was then replaced by a week of calm, blank sleep.

While packing for the trip on the previous day, she lost her balance for a few moments and fell, crashing sideways, into the bookshelves in the living room. She knocked the white cube from the shelf, and she had heard the lens break as it hit the floorboards. The white bird slid across the floor. She had been losing her balance for some months now and had managed to keep it all concealed from Hooman. In the last few days, the vomiting had dissipated, but this did not comfort her, as she still felt nauseous.

Allison was dying. The meaning of her dream was clear now, and she felt a paradoxical and oscillating mix of anxious worry and tranquility. The time had finally come as Mona had predicted, and her three and a half years were now up. The blood that flowed from the pomegranate into the sand in her dream was her own blood; that was the sacrifice she would make: her own life.

She would have to tell Hooman eventually, but when was hard to decide. She wanted to tell him at the right time and delay the sadness she knew would wash over him.

In the valley a clear view of a frozen lake appeared. Houses were dotted around its rim. The only thing that really bothered her was she was going to miss everyone and in particular Hooman and Shidan, and she also wondered how Hooman would cope bringing up Noah without her. She also thought of Jonny. She knew that he would become a photographer, a good one; that was her contribution to his particular destiny, and that was her contribution to Harlem. In recent weeks she had spoken to Hayden. He had agreed to mentor Jonny in the future.

Allison looked over Noah's relaxed features, which were warmed by the evening sun. She knew that she would always be a part of Noah's life, if only at a distance. Hooman and Shidan smiled at each other and talked about something she had not followed.

She would also miss the opening of the Harlem Writers Studio in the spring. They had worked so hard to realize it, but she knew that Hooman would be there to guide it in the right direction. The opening of the studio would also coincide with the publication of his book, *On the Shoulders of the Poor*, and she would miss that also.

When her symptoms first appeared, she knew it was a brain tumor. She knew this because of research she had done in the year her breast cancer had first appeared and more recently just after her vomiting began. She had typed her symptoms into Google. To confirm her fears she had gone to the hospital for a CAT scan, and the result was positive. The doctor at the hospital had said she would not have long to live, and he could not give a specific timeframe. He went on to say that some people die between six months to a year, and others die after only a month or two. The tumor, a large, spindly mass, was essentially inoperable because of its location in the brain, and it must have been there for some time. Her diagnosis also explained the headaches she had had over the last six months.

In the flat of the valley, they passed by Lake Placid and then moved on to a more intimate town farther down the road—Saranac Lake. The car turned off the highway onto a street leading to a small cottage sitting on the edge of Lake Flower. The cottage was the same one they had rented in the summer.

The boys unpacked the car. Hooman needed to go back to Lake Placid to buy some hiking equipment before the shops closed. He needed a new pair of snowshoes for himself and some poles for Allison. He kissed Allison, then got into the car and drove off. Shidan gathered some of the luggage and walked to the cottage door, which he opened after finding the key under a statue of the Buddha.

Allison followed him and took Noah into the cottage. She stopped in the middle of the doorframe and put one hand out, clutching the frame, to prevent herself from toppling over. She checked to see that Shidan hadn't seen her and then moved to a long wooden table and sat down with Noah in her lap, his head resting against her chest. She decided in that moment to ask either of the boys to carry Noah in the future, just in case she fell to the ground and injured him in some way. Through the large windows overlooking the frozen lake, Allison observed the light fading over the blue-white ice. The outline of houses on the opposite side of the lake was beginning to fade, but their lights grew in the gloom like jewels tossed and scattered on a dark horizon.

While Allison looked out at the horizon, Shidan lit a fire in a small woodstove near the kitchen. She watched him do this in the reflection on the window.

"I've got something symbolic for you. From Greek myth," he said once the fire was burning unassisted.

"Sorry, what did you say?"

Allison listened to him rustle through a plastic bag and waited until she saw his arm reach out in front of her. He placed something red and round on the table. Her stomach tightened when she realized what it was. A pomegranate fruit sat isolated on the table. And she immediately had a flashback of her dream with the pomegranate sitting on the sand; the fruit was now another point of future symmetry, like her yellow dress—her dream had now intersected with reality.

"Where did you get it?" she asked.

"A Persian shop. In Queens. It is probably from California, I would expect. I was at the shop with my mother a few days ago."

Staring at the red fruit for a few moments, her mind went blank.

She was about to formulate a question. Why give it to her? Why now? But before she could, he said, "It's the fruit of the dead. Or is it the food of the dead . . . anyway, something like that."

Her stomach tightened once more as he continued in a jovial fashion.

"Don't worry. I don't think you are dying or anything. No, it's just that I was reading about Hades the other day, the Greek underworld, and, well, it aroused my curiosity. I hadn't had a pomegranate for a while, and I never connected them with the myth of Persephone. She was tricked into eating the fruit, and in turn she descended to the underworld. And it has so much interesting and rich symbolic association." He pointed to the lake. "She's in Hades as we speak, Persephone. The queen of the underworld, of the dead." He went back to the woodstove to check on its progress. "Anyway"—he raised his voice—"I don't know why, but I thought of you. I thought you might like it. It was the last one in the shop. I saved it for you."

Allison could not help herself as her arm reached over and picked it up almost without her full consent. She broke the skin with her thumbs into two equal halves and placed one half on the table, and from the other she broke off a handful of the ruby-like seeds. They crumbled into her palms, and she picked her way through them. Occasionally, she held one up to the light, and their faceted, red translucence was curious and otherworldly: a soft, fleshy gem.

Shidan came back from the stove and sat next to her. She smiled at him as she placed her hand on Noah's head. Her new ring flashed in the low light.

"Hey, I saw that at the gallery. Why are you sporting gangster wares all of a sudden?"

"Yeah. I know, it's not really me, but it fits with my tattoo."

"*Your tattoo*! Since when?" He looked up and down her body for some invisible sign of it.

"Do you want to see it? I got it a few months back." She passed Noah to Shidan and slipped her arm out of her winter jacket and proceeded to roll up her sweater sleeve.

Shidan moved his chair closer to get a better view of her exposed arm. "Okay, I see now. The six concentric circles on your shoulder match those on your ring. That makes sense now, but what about these other three bands of color on your forearm?" He pointed to them.

"Well, the three bands on my forearm represent the three limited and relativistic levels or valleys. They are 'Search,' 'Love,' and 'Knowledge.'" She then pointed to the six multicolored concentric circles on her shoulder. "These represent the absolute valleys. They are 'Unity,' 'Contentment,' 'Wonderment,' 'True Poverty and Absolute Nothingness,' 'Immortality,' and the final level that has no name or description. I got the idea for the circles and bands of color from a composer called Simion. I met him in a commune near Nimbin during a road trip I did many years ago. He had exactly the same tattoo."

"Fascinating," he said.

"Yes, it is interesting. And thanks, Shidan. It was nice of you to think of me. This fruit is a perfect topic of discussion. For winter especially, I suppose. The fruit of the dead."

"Yes, when it is winter, she descends into Hades. And when she comes back to Earth, it is spring." But Allison knew that she wouldn't be returning in spring. Her trip into the underworld was one way.

She ate the last few seeds in the half she had started before. In calm resignation she added, "Shidan. These are my tickets to the underworld. My penny under the tongue, for the ferryman. To cross the river Styx or the Hudson River, whichever comes first."

He laughed. "I knew we would have fun talking about this."

Allison's bag was at her feet, and she leaned down to open it. Rummaging around, she took out a sheet of paper and her notebook. On the bottom of the paper, she wrote something. She then flipped it over and continued to write something on the back of it. She then flipped through the notebook and stopped at a particular page before continuing to write on the sheet of paper.

"What's that?" Shidan asked.

"It's a paper bird. It has one of my poems on it. Alison Nightingale gave it to me in the gallery. She wanted me to have it back. I made it on the plane on my first day in New York."

"Oh yeah. I remember Alison giving it to you."

"Sorry, this might take a while."

"That's okay. What are you writing?"

"It's a note for Hooman." She smiled and watched him look out at the lake as she continued to write. She ran out of room on the paper bird, so she opened the back of the notebook and continued writing.

Eventually, she finished writing and began to fold it back to its original shape. Shidan watched in silence until it assumed the shape of a bird again. She then placed it on the table and moved it around with her index finger. She noticed the shadows the bird cast on the table. Allison took Shidan's hand and smiled at him for a moment, then looked out at the dark lake.

———

In the morning they drove back through Lake Placid and down Route 73. After a short drive, they came to Heart Lake. Hooman parked the car beside the lake and took the map of the trails off the dashboard. He passed it to Allison. She opened it and traced her finger along the walking trail leading to Lake Tear of the Clouds. They had walked to it in the summer, and Allison wanted to see it now in the winter all iced over.

"How long is the trail?" Shidan asked.

"It's a sixteen- to twenty-two-mile round trip, depending on what trails we take. I'd like to go via Avalanche Lake and take a different route this time," she said.

"Apparently, Lake Tear of the Clouds is the highest source of the Hudson River," Hooman said to Shidan.

Allison then thought of the Boat of Ra. The boat had plied up the Hudson River as she had slept in the cottage next to Hooman on the previous night. The Boat of Ra was also known as the Night Boat, with Osiris and Ra merged together as they passed through the gates on their way up the river during each night. On the night before she had recited *The Long Healing Prayer* and the *Tablet of Ahmad* after her long obligatory prayer. These prayers had released her into the boat. She was traveling in it and now almost at the river's source.

They got out of the car, and Allison stared at Heart Lake for a moment before taking Noah out of his car seat. She passed the baby carrier to Shidan. He strapped Noah to his back. She looked over at the lake once more as she put her backpack on and remembered the heart shape in the dust that she had made in the gallery and now connected that with Robert Hayden's first book of poetry, *Heart-Shape in the Dust*. Allison felt, subjectively, that the title was a reference to this world and what we left behind—the shape of love in each other's hearts in this, a world of dust. Hooman would have her own heart shape in his soul that would last until his own death and take him on and into and through those other worlds. The same applied to all those whom she had ever loved in this world, and she could make a way for everyone to follow her and complete her symmetrical destiny map in those other worlds. And she also knew that Noah's destiny was important. She remembered her dream at the Sun Tongue before she gave birth. In the dream she had looked around Noah's face, which was both intensely youthful and paradoxically worn old, but his eyes were unblemished by time.

He had said, "I'm inside you, and I love you. You will not see me grow up, but I will see you in the world to come." She would leave her heart shape in his heart also, although it would be a vicarious heart shape through Hooman.

Hooman came around from the back of the car with all the equipment, and they all got into the snowshoes.

They then headed toward the beginning of the trails on the edge of the parking lot.

———

Lake Tear of the Clouds was only about an acre across and sat in a valley between Gray Peak and Mount Marcy on one side and Mount Skylight on the other side. After hiking through trails along the twists and turns of the Opalescent River and eventually Feldspar Brook, they arrived at the edge of the lake. Since their last visit here, summer had faded into winter, and the water in the lake had slowly been transformed into ice: the mirror had turned opaque as the reflection had gradually faded before disappearing completely.

Allison's legs were unsteady. She had to sit down for a while to ensure she did not lose her balance and fall down; she knew this was from the tumor. During the long hike, she had had to stop and rest several times. Getting to the lake had been a struggle, and she knew that Hooman knew there was something wrong, but he had said nothing.

"Are you okay, babe?" Hooman said.

"Yeah, just a bit tired," she said and smiled up at him.

She looked up at the snow on the slope of Gray Peak, then at the lower hills surrounding the lake. Panning her eyes around behind her, she observed the snow on the pines near the edge of the lake and Mount Skylight in the distance beyond the trees. She knew there was a panorama of mountains beyond the valley that she could not see now. When they had come in the summer, they had seen them from the top of Mount Marcy.

After a few minutes, she got up, and they skirted the edge of the lake and eventually found a flat clearing where they sat down and prepared lunch. The weather did not degrade as they had expected from the forecast; instead, the sun came out as they ate sandwiches and drank thermos coffee. Motivated by the pleasant oscillation of cool air and warm light on her face, she put her coffee down and stood up. She looked up at the big patches of sky.

"I'm just going to walk across the ice."

"Do you want company?" Hooman asked.

She smiled and thought for a moment. "No . . . no, you stay here and keep Shidan entertained. You'll be able to see me. I'll just walk out to the middle and back again. Okay?"

"Okay, we'll watch you from here."

Allison stepped onto the ice on the edge of the lake. She decided to leave both her gloves behind, and they dropped to the ice around her feet as she walked toward the center of the lake. Then she heard a soft voice in her mind with a faint harmonic overlay, "Allison, it's Mona, Shidan's sister. And the other Mona, Mona Mahmudnizhad, is with me too; our identities and voices are synchronized. Your destiny is with us now. You will soon begin to fold and unfold into us. This will be a little strange for you and quite intense, but don't worry, we will try to make this transition as easy as we can."

"Thank you for guiding me to this moment."

"You're welcome. Keep walking, you're almost with us."

The clouds had cleared completely now, and she looked up at the sun for a moment. Its arc was at the same angle that it had been in her dream.

She stopped hearing the crunch of snow beneath her boots, and instead, the immense silence of the desert and an invisible ocean surrounded her. Shidan's gift of a pomegranate was the clue she had needed to prepare herself for eternity and to release herself into it with radiant acquiescence.

The sun continued to penetrate the cold skin on her face as she looked up at it again. For a reason she could not fathom, she thought about the paper bird in her pocket, and so she felt around until her fingers closed around it.

At what she judged was the center of the lake she stopped, and at that moment an intense pain exploded in her head. She staggered sideways, then backward, clutching her head. The paper bird fell to the ice.

She collapsed to the ground. For a few moments she looked up at the sky, then lay back and spread her arms out with her palms facedown in the same way that she had done at the British Museum. She felt the cold from the ice flooding into her palms. Time began to fold away. The pain in her head subsided slightly as a pleasant sensation of joy radiated out from her chest in rhythmic waves, and unlike her time at the American Museum of Natural History, this time the sensations in her body were so pleasant that they were almost painful in their intensity. She began crying and laughing in the same moment. She stopped laughing for a moment and took a big breath before sighing. Life was so funny, so laughable. Why would a person not want to die and live on this new horizon? The comic cipher was partially unraveled and released into her, a joke with a punchline that always ended in death. The puppet now needed to be put in its box.

She took another deep breath and looked over at Hooman and Shidan briefly before looking back at the sun; its light was exhilarating. Hooman was running toward her, but the distance may as well have been unreachable, as Allison was already leaving the small circle of time and space. She now lost feeling in one of her arms. The other arm and her toes tingled with pins and needles. The most peculiar sensation was that of gravity. It slowly began to invert until it reached a full right angle. It seemed as if she was slung to a wall, but that wall was the Earth itself. Slightly panicked, she tried to calm herself. She was not sure what was stopping her from falling down off the lake and tumbling down the face of the Earth and into the sky.

The blissful waves continued to increase in intensity, and the sun also seemed to change dimensions now. It started to dilate and move toward her, slowly at first, then with speed. And as it came, a wavering bell-like harmonic traveled with it. She laughed uncontrollably now. The sun, as a vast fiery furnace, was dissolving her and the Earth into cinders in its horizon of death, fire, and light. She saw all things, all potentiality, all loves, all trees and flowers blossom and fruit in moments before being crumbled into red-and-black glowing ashes. The pleasure was unbearable now.

The disc of the sun, now a flat wall of light, was about to impact on her in a planet-sized panorama, and she was still laughing as her voice began to mingle with the bell noise. "It can't be this beautiful . . . it's not possible," she shouted, then laughed. It was hard to hear her voice above the bell sound. "It's not possible," she said again. She tried to squeeze out thoughts within the intense pressure in her being. "Nobody would believe it." Her laughing turned to sobbing in her mind. As she had in her dream, she tried to lift her arms to meet the sun, only to realize she no longer had any arms or a body to do this. She wept a million tears into a million oceans. She felt an immense rush in her mind as she left her body properly and shot off at an incredible speed. She passed into a series of nine colored concentric circles that formed a light tunnel, similar to her tattoo. The sun hit her in a vast shock wave, and she tumbled over and over, drowning in an immeasurable light, a soft and enveloping mass of molten marshmallow light, and she continued to sob in this new clarity that surrounded her. "Nobody could understand this . . . nobody."

She heard the words "You are with us now."

"I see you now . . . and you are so beautiful. So unbelievably beautiful. And beyond all words I have to describe you," Allison said. "Beyond all words" were her last thoughts, repeated over and over in a loop that could contain her mind forever: Beyond all words, Beyond all words, Beyond all words, Beyond all words, Beyond all words, Beyond all words, Beyond all words, Beyond all words, Beyond all words . . .

She disappeared into a vast, unsearchable eternity, where all time was a forgotten memory and all space a bitter dream of strange half mysteries lost in those charcoal houses where it had been hard to relinquish illusion, houses where all things burn. And the rain comes, and the sea comes, and nothing remains—only the placeless sun, the home of transfigured birds.

———

Hooman had seen Allison clutching her head and falling to the ice. He suddenly became aware of the panorama of the surrounding mountains compressing and flexing around Allison's small figure. She was lying on the lake in a kind of beautiful but terrifying solitude and isolation; the distance between them was now infinite, and he knew by intuition that Allison was already dead.

"Shidan, look. Something's very wrong." Hooman said, pointing at Allison lying on the ice as he stood up.

"Oh god! . . . she's dead, Shidan. I know it . . . I know it, absolutely," Hooman said.

"You go. I'll get Noah," Shidan said as he picked up Noah, stood up, and began to strap him to his back.

Tears began to well in his eyes as Hooman stepped onto the lake and ran toward her.

He came to her body and slumped down beside her. He pulled her body onto his knees, resting her head in his arms. Tears shot down his cheeks, running into the corner of his mouth initially, and then as he looked down at her, his tears splashed onto her face. He looked over at Shidan, who was only now starting across the ice, having strapped Noah to his back. When Shidan arrived, Hooman said, "She's gone . . . and I should have known this was coming. I'm so stupid."

Hooman became aware of the taste of his own tears as they ran into the corner of his mouth. He looked up at the sky for a moment, exhaled a breath, then looked back at her face, noticing the warm light on her skin. She was so beautiful to him, even in death. He knew already that all his love for her would turn to pain—a journey without end in this world, and a story where the hero never returns.

Shidan slowly bent down on his knees beside Hooman. As he sat, he slumped sideways slightly. He closed his eyes, tilted his head to the right, and began to weep. After a few moments, he opened his eyes and said, "My god . . . this is what you meant when you said that something was going to play out in your lives?"

"Yes, Shidan. This must be what I felt was coming."

Hooman saw Shidan looking at the paper bird on the ice, lying near her knees. Shidan took his gloves off and reached out and picked it up.

"This is the bird that the younger Alison gave her in the gallery three weeks ago," Shidan said, holding it up to the light.

"Yes, it is. It's strange that she brought it here."

"I saw her write something on it last night. You can see words on the surface of the paper."

Shidan began to unfold the paper bird. He passed it to Hooman once it was flat. Hooman took his gloves off, took it, and looked at it. He immediately noticed all the folds and shapes in the paper and its geometric symmetry and asymmetry before becoming aware of the poem that had been hidden inside this geometry for many years, folded up, waiting, secret, and sublime, its meaning waiting to be understood by him in this moment. Each fold was an intersection of beauty as it crossed other folds—other lives, each life an individual fold, each life a linear timeline from beginning to end—a symbol of all the people connected to her, all the people she had loved in this world.

He knew even before he read it that the poem would be a profound reflection of Allison's faceted soul, as all her poems were; they all mirrored aspects of her rich internal world and that utterly unique worldview that she had always expressed and that had been the reason for his abiding love for her. Hooman closed his eyes for a few moments, gathering himself, before reading the poem with a soft voice. Tears continued to stream down his face.

Death turns my right palm to the sky,
we smile, as he turns my left palm to the earth.

In my right hand, an empty nest—a world.
In my left, another world, from which a broken eggshell falls.
A paper bird has flown.
Its story written and gone.
The loves of long ago faded—unfolded in light and its paper and ink heart.

Creases remain, shapes, and white bone, the source of paper,
Until even this is ground under foot into white dust, on a word road,
Where everything returns to its first form, absolute and complete, into form-
less words on formless paper.

What then remains of Death?
He too has flown.
Seeking his own death.

Allison Bird
All is Sun Bird

Hooman thought about the meaning of the poem. She was the paper bird that had now flown, her story written and gone and faded into eternity as her bones were ground into dust on the word road. He remembered her vision in the gallery of her body made of white dust, and he wondered if it was bone dust that she had seen her own body made from, on the "bone" road rather than the "word" road. The bone road was the way we must all follow, even Death.

He then thought about the destiny of the paper bird itself, a sign and symbol of her own journey; it had found its way back to her purely because she had practiced her signature on the page above the poem. Otherwise, the younger Alison would have never known that the bird had originally belonged to Allison; that simple action of writing her signature had echoed through the years—the configuration and power of names and the circularity of Allison's destiny through such a simple object.

"Look at the words under her signature. It's like a line in a poem, but contained in her name: 'All is Sun Bird.' I saw her add that last night. You can tell. The color of the pen is different from the rest of the poem; it's blue, whereas the poem and her signature are written in pencil," Shidan said.

"It's so strange, but her destiny was encapsulated in her name; it was always there, all the time, and I never saw it; I suppose we are all birds of the sun, like her. That is what she means by saying 'All is Sun Bird,' and it's also a reference to the purpose of creation, the 'true believer,' and our relationship with God; we all reflect the light of the sun in our mirror-like hearts and fly like birds into the sun to destroy all our earthly qualities, and from these ashes we are reborn into cycles of immortality."

"I will miss her," Shidan said. He put his hand over his face and began to weep intensely, and he bent forward slightly, putting his other hand on the ice.

"I know, Shidan. Everyone will miss her."

Hooman saw the light refracted on the ice as it came through the back of the paper. He could see words were written on the back, so he turned the paper over. She had scribbled a note to him, which took up the whole of the page in quite tight and small writing:

Hooman, my love, I know as I write this that my death is close to me now. And I write this with Shidan close by me. He was the one to give me the final clue, a pomegranate, the key to my death; remember my dream about the ocean and the pomegranate. Otherwise, I would have never written this note to you. I am sorry I didn't tell you this was coming. I meant to, eventually. I hope you will forgive me some day. Think of me in your prayers. Think of our wonderful life together and don't be sad. However short my life was with you, I am grateful. Ever since we met, I have been counting my blessings each day. Your love will sustain me in those other worlds, and I'll be waiting for you there in absolute symmetry—a symmetry with no earthly equivalent, the geometry of the heart.

If you look through my notebook, you will find the secret to unlocking my symmetrical destiny map. It is in the number of repeated names, their different spellings, the number and order of letters in their first and last names, and the number of each letter in the alphabet. Also, odd numbers are asymmetrical and even are symmetrical. When you stack names and sentences on top of each other, you see the horizontal, vertical, and diagonal intersections of each letter. It is kind of like a huge alphabetical version of a sudoku puzzle, where you insert the numbers and letters into a grid consisting of nine squares, subdivided into a further nine smaller squares, but as you will see, I haven't been limited by grids of nine. I have made larger square grids. This is how I have been decoding reality. I have been looking for instances where the same numbers or letters are repeated three times or more, either horizontally, vertically, or diagonally. This is a mathematical and letter-based symmetry.

You will notice that all the letters in the alphabet are either symmetrical or asymmetrical or a combination of both, like A, which is symmetrical on a vertical axis, versus B, which is asymmetrical on a vertical axis but is symmetrical on a horizontal axis. There are mysteries here in the geometry of language. It is not by chance that letters have the shapes that they do. Look into the history of the English language and the origin of each letter from other languages like Latin and Greek, and it goes back even further into other older ancient languages too. And all languages are the expression of one system of symbolism and metaphor.

I've run out of room here on the back of the poem. The rest of this note will be at the back of the notebook; I have bookmarked the page for you.

"Did she bring her notebook?" Hooman asked.

"Yes. It's in her backpack. I saw her pack it this morning. Why?"

"She has written me a note."

Hooman showed Shidan the back of the poem.

"I'll go get it." Shidan stood up and walked over to the edge of the lake.

Hooman watched him open the backpack and then watched him come back over the ice.

Shidan passed her notebook to Hooman, who took it and opened it at the back, where he found what he was looking for. He continued to read.

You will also see that the symmetrical destiny map is a series of ciphers hidden within the "Kingdom of Names," both mathematically and symbolically. You'll see all the grids of letters are an abstract riddle full of different meaning patterns. I have worked on these throughout the notebook. Bahá'u'lláh says: "He beholdeth in illusion the secret of reality, and readeth from the attributes the riddle of the Essence." [2]

And remember, ultimately, the True Phoenix is "the Word of God." That is where we see our true reflection at the end of the journey. Attar suggests that we be that Eternal mirror that we saw, which is to show others the "Word" in our own hearts and reflect it back to them. When everything is stripped away from the mirror of creation, all that remains is the "Word," shimmering above the physical world, staggeringly beautiful, and beyond all comparisons or understanding. And then we return into our sun as birds, where we subside into a placeless, transcendent Sun— the actual sun is only a symbol of this higher, invisible Sun, the Sun of Being. In the ninth valley this new Sun has its own heavens and its own moons, as you know —the Sun of the Unseen is a hidden Sun; here, our destiny is immeasurable and unspeakably glorious.

"Therein the sun of the Unseen shineth resplendent above the horizon of the Unseen, a sun that hath its own heavens and its own moons, which partake of its light and which rise from and set upon the ocean of the Unseen. Nor can I ever hope

to impart even a dewdrop of that which hath been decreed therein, as none is acquainted with its mysteries save God, its Creator and Fashioner, and His Manifestations." [3]

My love, you must also learn the language of the birds: the divine, mystical language. It's a language of symbolism.

Below this was a quote from the Qur'án:

And Solomon was David's heir. And he said: O mankind! Lo! we have been taught the language of birds, and have been given of all things. This surely is evident favor. [4]

—Qur'án 27:16

Lastly, I am sorry I won't be here for the opening of the Harlem Writers Studio and for the launch of your book. I know the book will be amazing and really build understanding about the extremes of wealth and poverty and the need for balance on the world stage and within our local communities. I hope that you can continue what we started in Harlem and serve the needs of that community. As we discussed a few times, I think you need to make the Harlem Writers Studio a focus for Bahá'í activities; use the space for arts and community-building projects.

Hooman knew he could carry on the work they had started together, but then he wondered, What language was she talking about? He passed the notebook to Shidan. "Look at that quote from the Qur'án."

"My god, Hooman. I know that quote from my childhood. I memorized it growing up."

"I wonder what kind of bird the paper bird is," Hooman said.

"I am not sure. I wasn't paying attention." Shidan put the notebook on the ice, picked up the sheet of paper, and began to fold the paper back into the form of a bird.

As Hooman watched Shidan attempt to reconstruct the bird, he immediately thought of their honeymoon at the shack in Queensland and all the paper birds on the dashboard of her old car. He had not been paying attention there also, like Shidan. He knew only that she had made a variety of different bird species.

"It's a swan," Shidan said finally, passing it back to him.

Hooman rolled it around in his palm, looking intensely at the refracted light and shadows on its surfaces. He noticed the translucent quality of the paper with light passing through it and all the words on its body. "Oh god . . ." Hooman said in an epiphany, "I'm the white swan in alchemy. That's me. I'm the swan. It symbolizes illumination from the inner light that comes from first contact with the divine world, which begins in this moment. She has become the Phoenix, and I am the swan. I must pass through all the remaining stages within the alchemical symbolism of the five birds to learn the language of the birds, to learn the language of the Phoenix, to become a Phoenix, like her. That is the sun tongue: the language of fire and light."

"God, Hooman. That is crazy beautiful. You're right. The name of the shop was connected to her as well: the Sun Tongue, or the Tongue of the Phoenix."

"Yes . . . I think so. Everything and everyone was connected to her in some way. I have begun in this last year to see the symmetry and asymmetry she has been talking about all these years."

"How do you know about the five birds in alchemy? Over the years, I have actually sold several alchemical manuscripts that the five birds were highlighted within, but there isn't much written about them. It is a very obscure aspect of alchemy."

"It was in one of the books she sent from London. At the time it didn't mean much to me, but I read it at about the same time that I sent her that bird sculpture. That book, *The Birds of Transmutation*, is where I got the idea to put that quote from Bahá'u'lláh on the side of the white cube—the one about the Phoenix of the realms above crying out from the immortal Branch and the glory of all greatness belonging to God."

Shidan didn't reply. He continued to weep, and his head dropped as he closed his eyes. Hooman thought about the Harlem community. He would continue serving the needs of that community, relying upon the "society-building power of the Faith."[5] The Bahá'ís in the Harlem community would also need to push forward and continue the process of social transformation through spiritual education by broadening their outreach to neighbors and families and by inviting their participation.

Hooman brushed the snowflakes from her hair. The snow was so beautiful in the sun. He saw tears that had run down her face. He wiped one line of tears away with his finger. He put his finger on the tip of his tongue. "I can taste the Ocean that destroyed her," he said. He then closed his eyes for a moment and tilted his face towards the sun.

"Hooman! It's me . . . it's Allison."

"Oh god!" he said in wonderment. "I can hear your voice in my mind." He opened his eyes, and he was looking directly at the sun, squinting.

"Hear who?" Shidan asked.

"Don't worry. Everything will be fine," said the transfigured voice of Allison. "I will always be with you now. Always. I'll talk to you tomorrow, my love. And remember what the Qur'án says:

Nothing can befall us but what God has destined." [6]

—Qur'án 9:51

NOTES

Preface

1. "Praise be to God Who hath made . . ." Bahá'u'lláh, *The Seven Valleys*, in *The Call of the Divine Beloved: Selected Mystical Works of Bahá'u'lláh* (Haifa, Israel: Bahá'í World Centre, 2018), 5.

A Word on Symmetry

1. ". . . in each realm, to every letter a . . ." Bahá'u'lláh, *The Seven Valleys*, in *The Call of the Divine Beloved: Selected Mystical Works of Bahá'u'lláh* (Haifa, Israel: Bahá'í World Centre, 2018), Preface.
2. "How strange that the Beloved is as . . ." Bahá'u'lláh, *The Seven Valleys*, in *The Call of the Divine Beloved: Selected Mystical Works of Bahá'u'lláh* (Haifa, Israel: Bahá'í World Centre, 2018), 15.

1. Coming to America

1. "By My life, O friend! Wert thou . . ." Bahá'u'lláh, *The Seven Valleys*, in *The Call of the Divine Beloved: Selected Mystical Works of Bahá'u'lláh* (Haifa, Israel: Bahá'í World Centre, 2018), 5.

2. The Girl with the Yellow Dress

1. A reference to the Islamic profession of faith: "No God is there but God, and Muḥammad is the Messenger of God."
2. "The true seeker hunteth naught but the . . ." Bahá'u'lláh, *The Seven Valleys*, in *The Call of the Divine Beloved: Selected Mystical Works of Bahá'u'lláh* (Haifa, Israel: Bahá'í World Centre, 2018), 6.

3. The Lion and the Sun

1. "On this journey the wayfarer dwelleth in . . ." Bahá'u'lláh, *The Seven Valleys*, in *The Call of the Divine Beloved: Selected Mystical Works of Bahá'u'lláh* (Haifa, Israel: Bahá'í World Centre, 2018), 6.

4. A Book of Birds

1. "And if, by the help of the . . ." Bahá'u'lláh, *The Seven Valleys*, in *The Call of the Divine Beloved: Selected Mystical Works of Bahá'u'lláh* (Haifa, Israel: Bahá'í World Centre, 2018), 6.
2. "Come you lost Atoms to your Centre . . ." Attar, Farid ud-Din, *Bird Parliament* (also known as *The Conference of the Birds*), in *Letters and Literary Remains of Edward FitzGerald*, ed. William Aldis Wright, trans. Edward FitzGerald (London and New York: Macmillan and Co, 1889), sacred-texts.com, lines 1426–29.

5. The Harlem Apartment

1. An allusion to the Ḥadíth in which God is said to address the Prophet Muhammad in these words: "But for Thee, I would not have created the spheres." A Ḥadíth is an action or utterance traditionally attributed to the Prophet Muhammad or to one of the holy Imams. This Ḥadíth recognizes the station of Bahá'u'lláh as the manifestation of God for this age.
2. "Wherefore, O friend, renounce thy self, that . . ." Bahá'u'lláh, *The Seven Valleys*, in *The Call of the Divine Beloved: Selected Mystical Works of Bahá'u'lláh* (Haifa, Israel: Bahá'í World Centre, 2018), 7.

6. The Ice Rink and the Christmas Tree

1. "And if, confirmed by the Creator, the . . ." Bahá'u'lláh, *The Seven Valleys*, in *The Call of the Divine Beloved: Selected Mystical Works of Bahá'u'lláh* (Haifa, Israel: Bahá'í World Centre, 2018), 7.
2. "I was the Sin that from Myself . . ." Attar, Farid ud-Din, *Bird Parliament* (also known as *The Conference of the Birds*), in *Letters and Literary Remains of Edward FitzGerald*, ed. William Aldis Wright, trans. Edward FitzGerald (London and New York: Macmillan and Co, 1889), sacred-texts.com, lines 1414–16.
3. "With all my Wealth in the other . . ." Attar, Farid ud-Din, *Bird Parliament* (also known as *The Conference of the Birds*), in *Letters and Literary Remains of Edward FitzGerald*, ed. William Aldis Wright, trans. Edward FitzGerald (London and New York: Macmillan and Co, 1889), sacred-texts.com, lines 1262–76 and 1387–435.
4. "Indeed we belong to Allah, and indeed . . ." The Prophet Muhammad, Qur'án 2:156.
5. "He beholdeth in illusion the secret of . . ." Bahá'u'lláh, *The Seven Valleys and the Four Valleys*, trans. Marzieh Gail, 3rd ed. (Wilmette: US Bahá'í Publishing Trust, 1986), 21.
6. "Whereas recognition of the inherent dignity and . . ." In the preamble of the Universal Declaration of Human Rights (New York: Draft Committee, United Nations, 1948), 1.
7. "Lo, the Nightingale of Paradise singeth upon . . ." Bahá'u'lláh, *Tablet of Ahmad*, in *Bahá'í Prayers* (Wilmette: US Bahá'í Publishing Trust, 1991), 209–13.

7. The Museum

1. "'We will surely show them Our signs . . .'" The Prophet Muhammad, Qur'án 41:53.
2. "He breaketh the cage of the body . . ." Bahá'u'lláh, *The Seven Valleys*, in *The Call of the Divine Beloved: Selected Mystical Works of Bahá'u'lláh* (Haifa, Israel: Bahá'í World Centre,

2018), 8.

3. "Those who have ascended have different attributes . . ." 'Abdu'l-Bahá, *'Abdu'l-Bahá in London* (London: UK Bahá'í Publishing Trust, 1982), 96.
4. "O SON OF THE THRONE! Thy hearing . . ." Bahá'u'lláh, *The Hidden Words* (Wilmette: US Bahá'í Publishing Trust, 1985), 14.

8. The Symmetries of a Face

1. "He in this realm is content with . . ." Bahá'u'lláh, *The Seven Valleys*, in *The Call of the Divine Beloved: Selected Mystical Works of Bahá'u'lláh* (Haifa, Israel: Bahá'í World Centre, 2018), 7.
2. "It is the mind that makes the . . ." William Shakespeare, *The Taming of the Shrew* (1590).
3. "O Thou Who art the Lord of . . ." Bahá'u'lláh, "The Long Obligatory Prayer," in *Bahá'í Prayers* (Wilmette: US Bahá'í Publishing Trust, 1991), 7.

9. New Friends

1. "'No defect canst thou see in the . . .'" The Prophet Muhammad, Qur'án 67:3.
2. "Gazing with the eye of absolute insight . . ." Bahá'u'lláh, *The Seven Valleys*, in *The Call of the Divine Beloved: Selected Mystical Works of Bahá'u'lláh* (Haifa, Israel: Bahá'í World Centre, 2018), 8.

10. The Philosophy of the Heart

1. "The perfection of belief in Divine Unity . . ." From a Ḥadíth.
2. ". . . the denizens of the city of immortality . . ." Bahá'u'lláh, *The Seven Valleys*, in *The Call of the Divine Beloved: Selected Mystical Works of Bahá'u'lláh* (Haifa, Israel: Bahá'í World Centre, 2018), 8.
3. "Was there a philosophy of the heart that transcended the intellect, she wondered, or did the intellect need to be informed by the heart?" The expression of these and following ideas by the author are a paraphrase of Ian Kluge's writings. The nine excerpts from Kluge's writing that have formed the basis for this paraphrase can be found in the following text at the following nine page references respectively:
   "However, unlike the Counter-Enlightenment and its . . .", "There are two matters of interest in . . .", "It [truth] is a word for the 'will-to-power' . . .", "In regards to reason, the Writings adopt . . .", "However, unlike the Counter-Enlightenment and its . . .", "For God has endowed us with faculties . . .", "There are two matters of interest in . . .", "In a similar vein, 'Abdu'l-Bahá informs us . . .", and "The Writings tells us that a 'reliable . . ." Ian Kluge, *Postmodernism and the Bahá'í Writings*, part 2, vol. 9 of *Lights of Irfán*, (Evanston, IL: Irfan Colloquia, 2008), 116–17, 118, 125–26, 115, 116, 118, 118, 118, 120.
4. In addition to note 3 above, there are other ideas in this chapter that are paraphrased from Ian Kluge, *Postmodernism and the Bahá'í Writings*, parts 1 and 2, vol. 9. The excerpts from Kluge's writings that have formed the basis for the paraphrases, listed below, can be found in the following titles and page references respectively:
   "What postmodernism primarily offers in return for . . .", "This position has at least six consequences . . .", "'Truth' is therefore not something there, that . . .", "To the charge that this reduces it . . .", "Therefore, he rejects the belief that God . . .", and "Kant's influence may also be felt in . . ." Ian Kluge, *Postmodernism and the Bahá'í*

Writings, part 1, vol. 9 of *Lights of Irfan*, (Evanston, IL: Irfan Colloquia, 2008), 65–66, 72, 71, 66, 66–67, 68–69.

"Nor can they accept his sweeping statement . . .", "In regards to the 'will-to-power' . . .", "The Bahá'í teachings about the reality of . . .", "It is also clear that the Bahá'í . . .", "This relativism inherent in Lyotard's philosophy is . . .", and "The unification of humankind requires that we . . ." Ian Kluge, *Postmodernism and the Bahá'í Writings*, part 2, vol. 9 of *Lights of Irfan*, (Evanston, IL: Irfan Colloquia, 2008), 124, 126, 127, 137, 137, 139.

5. "That which the Lord hath ordained as . . ." Bahá'u'lláh, *Gleanings From the Writings of Bahá'u'lláh* (Wilmette: US Bahá'í Publishing Trust, 1983), 255.

11. Returning to London

1. "'Guide Thou us on the straight path,'" The Prophet Muhammad, Qur'án 1:6.
2. . . . . "Guide Thou us on the straight path . . ." Bahá'u'lláh, *The Seven Valleys*, in *The Call of the Divine Beloved: Selected Mystical Works of Bahá'u'lláh* (Haifa, Israel: Bahá'í World Centre, 2018), 9.

12. Finding Mona

1. "'Verily, we are God's, and to Him . . .'" The Prophet Muhammad, Qur'án 2:156.
2. "If thou be a man of communion . . ." Bahá'u'lláh, *The Seven Valleys*, in *The Call of the Divine Beloved: Selected Mystical Works of Bahá'u'lláh* (Haifa, Israel: Bahá'í World Centre, 2018), 9.
3. "O my people! This present life is . . ." The Prophet Muhammad, Qur'án 40:39. Sura 40: The Believer.
4. "Their Road is thine—Follow—and Fare . . ." Attar, Farid ud-Din, *Bird Parliament* (also known as *The Conference of the Birds*), trans. Edward FitzGerald (sacred-texts.com, 1889), line 1435. First published in *Letters and Literary Remains of Edward FitzGerald*, ed. William Aldis Wright (London and New York: Macmillan and Co, 1889).
5. "I am the Primal Point from which . . ." The Bab, *Selections from The Writings of the Báb* (Haifa, Israel: Bahá'í World Centre by the Universal House of Justice, 1976), 12.
6. "He was assured that he would be made victorious by himself and by his pen, and by the aid of those whom God would raise up." This story of the beginning of Bahá'u'lláh's revelation came from the following: Ruhi Institute, *The Twin Manifestations*, Book 4, Section 11 (Columbia: The Ruhi Foundation, 1996).
7. "The prisoners, including Mona, endured months of abuse . . . The families were all in astonishment and awe." Bahá'í Canada Publications, *The Story of Mona: 1965–1983* (Toronto: The National Spiritual Assembly of the Bahá'ís of Canada, 1985). Reprinted with permission. The original story has been edited and reduced. For the full text see https://www.dramacircle.org/the-story-of-mona.

13. The Nightingale

1. "After passing through the Valley of Knowledge . . ." Bahá'u'lláh, *The Seven Valleys*, in *The Call of the Divine Beloved: Selected Mystical Works of Bahá'u'lláh* (Haifa, Israel: Bahá'í World Centre, 2018), 9.
2. "From the sweet-scented streams of Thine . . ." Bahá'u'lláh, *Prayers and Meditations* (Wilmette: US Bahá'í Publishing Trust, 1938), 258–59.

3. "Create in me a pure heart, O . . ." Bahá'u'lláh, *Prayers and Meditations* (Wilmette: US Bahá'í Publishing Trust, 1938), 248.

14. Prayers at the Graves

1. "In this station he pierceth the veils . . ." Bahá'u'lláh, *The Seven Valleys*, in *The Call of the Divine Beloved: Selected Mystical Works of Bahá'u'lláh* (Haifa, Israel: Bahá'í World Centre, 2018), 9.
2. "O SON OF THE SUPREME! I have . . ." Bahá'u'lláh, *The Hidden Words* (Wilmette: US Bahá'í Publishing Trust, 1985), 11.

15. The Paper Bird

1. "'Earth and heaven cannot contain Me; what . . .'" From a Ḥadíth.
2. "O My brother! A pure heart is . . ." Bahá'u'lláh, *The Seven Valleys*, in *The Call of the Divine Beloved: Selected Mystical Works of Bahá'u'lláh* (Haifa, Israel: Bahá'í World Centre, 2018), 10.
3. "Knowledge is a single point, but the . . ." From a Ḥadíth.
4. "seeds of undreamt-of potentialities." Shoghi Effendi, *God Passes By* (Wilmette: US Bahá'í Publishing Trust, 1979), 294.
5. "Is it within human power, O Hakim . . ." Bahá'u'lláh, *Gleanings From the Writings of Bahá'u'lláh* (Wilmette: US Bahá'í Publishing Trust, 1983), 200.
6. "Know thou, moreover, that the Word of . . ." Bahá'u'lláh, *Tablets of Bahá'u'lláh* (Wilmette: US Bahá'í Publishing Trust, 1988), 140–41.
7. "The Phoenix of the realms above crieth . . ." Bahá'u'lláh, *Gleanings From the Writings of Bahá'u'lláh* (Wilmette: US Bahá'í Publishing Trust, 1983), 35–36.
8. "Soon will the present-day order be rolled . . ." Bahá'u'lláh, *Gleanings From the Writings of Bahá'u'lláh* (Wilmette: US Bahá'í Publishing Trust, 1983), 2.

16. The Symmetrical Destiny Map

1. "'O Thou Whose Essence alone can lead . . .'" From a prayer of 'Alí.
2. "But for Thee" refers to a Ḥadíth. "We have failed to know Thee" alludes to a prayer attributed to Muḥammad that says, "We have not known Thee, O God, as Thou oughtest to be known." "Or even closer" alludes to Qur'án 53:9.
3. "Wherefore the lovers of the countenance of . . ." Bahá'u'lláh, *The Seven Valleys*, in *The Call of the Divine Beloved: Selected Mystical Works of Bahá'u'lláh.* (Haifa, Israel: Bahá'í World Centre, 2018), 10.

17. The Book of the Dead

1. "Indeed, the references that have been made . . ." Bahá'u'lláh, *The Seven Valleys*, in *The Call of the Divine Beloved: Selected Mystical Works of Bahá'u'lláh* (Haifa, Israel: Bahá'í World Centre, 2018), 10.
2. "unto the essence of the fragrance of . . ." Bahá'u'lláh, *Prayers and Meditations* (Wilmette: US Bahá'í Publishing Trust, 1938), 258–59.
3. "Osiris—Judge of the Dead; God of . . ." and "Before a soul went onto the section . . ." E. A. Wallis Budge, *Osiris & the Egyptian Resurrection*, 2 vols. (London: P. L. Warner and

New York: G. P. Putnam's Sons, 1911). This quote has been edited for better reading. Some sentences have been paraphrased from other sources within *Osiris & the Egyptian Resurrection*, and the full quote is therefore an amalgam of several different sources.

4. "Egyptians believed that this life was only . . ." E. A. Wallis Budge, *Osiris & the Egyptian Resurrection*, 2 vols. (London: P. L. Warner and New York: G. P. Putnam's Sons, 1911), 2:143. This quote has been edited for better reading.

5. "After the heart is weighed and found . . ." E. A. Wallis Budge, *Osiris & the Egyptian Resurrection*, 2 vols. (London: P. L. Warner and New York: G. P. Putnam's Sons, 1911), 2:116, 2:160. This quote has been edited for better reading. Some sentences have been paraphrased from other sources within *Osiris & the Egyptian Resurrection*, and the full quote is therefore an amalgam of several different sources.

6. "I am the living bread which came . . ." John 6:51, The Bible, King James Version, 1769.

7. "Life as a blessed soul was not . . ." E. A. Wallis Budge, *Osiris & the Egyptian Resurrection*, 2 vols. (London: P. L. Warner and New York: G. P. Putnam's Sons, 1911), 2:159. This quote has been edited for better reading. Some sentences have been paraphrased from other sources within *Osiris & the Egyptian Resurrection*, and the full quote is therefore an amalgam of several different sources.

8. "Egyptian scripture states that at one time . . ." E. A. Wallis Budge, *Osiris & the Egyptian Resurrection*, 2 vols. (London: P. L. Warner and New York: G. P. Putnam's Sons, 1911), 1:357. This quote has been edited for better reading.

9. "Let the dead bury their dead." Matthew 8:22, The Bible, King James Version, 1769.

10. "Nothing can befall us but what God . . ." The Prophet Muhammad, Qur'án 9:51.

11. "O My servants! Could ye apprehend with . . ." Bahá'u'lláh, *Gleanings From the Writings of Bahá'u'lláh* (Wilmette: US Bahá'í Publishing Trust, 1983), 236–37.

12. "As ye have faith so shall your . . ." 'Abdu'l-Bahá, in May Maxwell, *An Early Pilgrimage* (1917; repr., Oxford: George Ronald, 1953).

18. A Circle of Friends

1. "These statements are made in the sphere . . ." Bahá'u'lláh, *The Seven Valleys*, in *The Call of the Divine Beloved: Selected Mystical Works of Bahá'u'lláh* (Haifa, Israel: Bahá'í World Centre, 2018), 11.

2. "the divine or supernatural disclosure to humans . . ." Angus Stevenson, ed., *Oxford Dictionary of English* (Oxford, UK: Oxford University Press, 2001).

3. "LET these exalted words be thy love-song . . ." Bahá'u'lláh, *Bahíyyih Khánum: The Greatest Holy Leaf* (Haifa, Israel: Bahá'í World Centre, 1982), 1–3.

4. "Know thou of a certainty that Love . . ." 'Abdu'l-Bahá, *Selections From the Writings of 'Abdu'l-Bahá* (Haifa: Bahá'í World Centre, 1982), 27.

5. "We will all, verily, abide by the . . ." Bahá'u'lláh, The Kitáb-i-Aqdas (Haifa: Bahá'í World Center, The Universal House of Justice, 1992), 105.

19. The Shack

1. "In thy soul . . . entire," Rúmí. Rúmí was a thirteenth-century Persian poet.

2. "And they swim in the sea of . . ." Bahá'u'lláh, *The Seven Valleys*, in *The Call of the Divine Beloved: Selected Mystical Works of Bahá'u'lláh* (Haifa, Israel: Bahá'í World Centre, 2018), 12.

3. "Greater love hath no man than this . . ." John 15:13, The Bible, King James Version 1769.

4. "If I have the gift of prophecy . . ." 1 Corinthians 13:2, The Bible, American Standard Version, 1901.
5. "O SON OF MAN! Veiled in My . . ." Bahá'u'lláh, *The Hidden Words* (Wilmette: US Bahá'í Publishing Trust, 1985), 4.
6. ". . . in the ancient eternity of My essence . . ." Bahá'u'lláh, *The Hidden Words* (Wilmette: US Bahá'í Publishing Trust, 1985), 4.
7. ". . . the denizens of the city of immortality . . ." Bahá'u'lláh, *The Seven Valleys*, in *The Call of the Divine Beloved: Selected Mystical Works of Bahá'u'lláh* (Haifa, Israel: Bahá'í World Centre, 2018), 8.
8. "Infer, then, from this the differences among . . ." Bahá'u'lláh, *The Seven Valleys*, in *The Call of the Divine Beloved: Selected Mystical Works of Bahá'u'lláh* (Haifa, Israel: Bahá'í World Centre, 2018), 11.
9. ". . . O Thou Who art the sole Desire . . ." Bahá'u'lláh, *Prayers and Meditations* (Wilmette: U.S. Bahá'í Publishing Trust, 1938), 115–17.

20. On the Road

1. "'God will satisfy everyone out of His abundance.'" The Prophet Muhammad, Qur'án 4:130.
2. "The wayfarer, after traversing the high planes . . ." Bahá'u'lláh, *The Seven Valleys*, in *The Call of the Divine Beloved: Selected Mystical Works of Bahá'u'lláh* (Haifa, Israel: Bahá'í World Centre, 2018), 12.

21. A Charcoal House

1. "God was alone; there was none else besides Him." From a Ḥadíth.
2. "O friend, till thou enter the garden . . ." Bahá'u'lláh, *The Seven Valleys*, in *The Call of the Divine Beloved: Selected Mystical Works of Bahá'u'lláh* (Haifa, Israel: Bahá'í World Centre, 2018), 12.
3. "If ye meet the abased or the . . ." Bahá'u'lláh, *Gleanings From the Writings of Bahá'u'lláh* (Wilmette: U.S. Bahá'í Publishing Trust, 1983), 314.

22. The Notebook

1. "In fire he seeth the face of . . ." Bahá'u'lláh, *The Seven Valleys*, in *The Call of the Divine Beloved: Selected Mystical Works of Bahá'u'lláh* (Haifa, Israel: Bahá'í World Centre, 2018), 12.
2. ". . . he refers to himself as the Mariner . . ." Bahá'u'lláh, *Tablet of the Holy Mariner*, in *Bahá'í Prayers: A Selection of Prayers* (Wilmette: US Bahá'í Publishing Trust, 1941). This is a paraphrase and not a direct quote.
3. "A lover is he who is chill in hell fire," Bahá'u'lláh, *The Seven Valleys*, in *The Call of the Divine Beloved: Selected Mystical Works of Bahá'u'lláh* (Haifa, Israel: Bahá'í World Centre, 2018), 7. These words were originally written by Saná'í (ca. 1045–1131), who was Persia's first great mystic poet.
4. "They passed the grades of worldly limitations . . ." Bahá'u'lláh, *Tablet of the Holy Mariner*, in *Bahá'í Prayers: A Selection of Prayers* (Wilmette: US Bahá'í Publishing Trust, 1941), 79.
5. "A believer is alive in both worlds," The Prophet Muhammad, Ḥadíth.

6. "Earth and heaven cannot contain Me; what . . ." Bahá'u'lláh, *The Seven Valleys*, in *The Call of the Divine Beloved: Selected Mystical Works of Bahá'u'lláh* (Haifa, Israel: Bahá'í World Centre, 2018), 10. It is also from a Ḥadíth.
7. ". . . the world of time, which hath both . . ." Bahá'u'lláh, *The Seven Valleys*, in *The Call of the Divine Beloved: Selected Mystical Works of Bahá'u'lláh* (Haifa, Israel: Bahá'í World Centre, 2018), 11.
8. "law" . . . "the secret of the Path," Bahá'u'lláh, *The Seven Valleys*, in *The Call of the Divine Beloved: Selected Mystical Works of Bahá'u'lláh* (Haifa, Israel: Bahá'í World Centre, 2018), 15.
9. "Wherefore must the veils of the satanic . . ." Bahá'u'lláh, *The Seven Valleys*, in *The Call of the Divine Beloved: Selected Mystical Works of Bahá'u'lláh* (Haifa, Israel: Bahá'í World Centre, 2018), 7.

23. An Image of Identity

1. "After journeying through the planes of pure . . ." Bahá'u'lláh, *The Seven Valleys*, in *The Call of the Divine Beloved: Selected Mystical Works of Bahá'u'lláh* (Haifa, Israel: Bahá'í World Centre, 2018), 13.
2. ". . . in each realm, to every letter a . . ." Bahá'u'lláh, *The Seven Valleys*, in *The Call of the Divine Beloved: Selected Mystical Works of Bahá'u'lláh* (Haifa, Israel: Bahá'í World Centre, 2018), 16.
3. "*Nuqtih*" and "Manifestation or Messenger of God, who is the embodiment of the Primal Will . . . paper," Báb, *Persian Bayán*, 3:11.
4. Translation by Todd Lawson (unpublished).
5. "The term 'Letters of the Living' is . . ." National Spiritual Assembly of the Bahá'ís of the United States, "Letters of the Living (*Ḥurúf-i-Ḥayy*)," *Bahá'í Encyclopedia Project* (2009), https://www.bahai-encyclopedia-project.org/index.php?view=article&catid=56%3Aa-selection-of-articles&id=65%3Aletters-of-the-living&option=com_content&Itemid=74.

24. My Brother

1. Now is he struck dumb with the . . ." Bahá'u'lláh, *The Seven* Valleys, in *The Call of the Divine Beloved: Selected Mystical Works of Bahá'u'lláh* (Haifa, Israel: Bahá'í World Centre, 2018), 13.
2. "Juliet Thompson, an artist . . . The children looked with real wonder at the African American boy as if they had never seen him before." 'Abdu'l-Bahá and Eliane Lacroix-Hopson, *'Abdu'l-Bahá in New York: The City of the Covenant*, rev. ed. (New York: Naturegraph Publishers, March 1, 1999). This is incorporated into the narrative from a direct quote.

25. Decoding Reality

1. "After scaling the high summits of wonderment . . ." Bahá'u'lláh, *The Seven Valleys*, in *The Call of the Divine Beloved: Selected Mystical Works of Bahá'u'lláh* (Haifa, Israel: Bahá'í World Centre, 2018), 14.
2. "Dost thou reckon thyself only a puny . . ." Bahá'u'lláh, *The Seven Valleys and the Four Valleys*, trans. Marzieh Gail, 3rd ed. (Wilmette: US Bahá'í Publishing Trust, 1986), 23. This saying is attributed to 'Alí.

3. "Likewise, reflect upon the perfection of man's . . ." Bahá'u'lláh, *The Seven Valleys and the Four Valleys*, trans. Marzieh Gail, 3rd ed. (Wilmette: US Bahá'í Publishing Trust, 1986), 23. This quote includes the saying attributed to 'Alí in note 2 above.
4. "Herein the lowly earth is in no . . ." Bahá'u'lláh, *The Seven Valleys and the Four Valleys*, trans. Marzieh Gail, 3rd ed. (Wilmette: US Bahá'í Publishing Trust, 1986), 40.

26. The Tourists

1. "'Poverty is My glory." From a Ḥadíth.
2. "Whoso hath attained this station is sanctified . . ." Bahá'u'lláh, *The Seven Valleys*, in *The Call of the Divine Beloved: Selected Mystical Works of Bahá'u'lláh* (Haifa, Israel: Bahá'í World Centre, 2018), 14.
3. "The one true God is My witness! . . ." Bahá'u'lláh, *Gleanings From the Writings of Bahá'u'lláh* (Wilmette: US Bahá'í Publishing Trust, 1983), 326.

27. A Year in America

1. "'All on the earth shall pass away . . .'" The Prophet Muhammad, Qur'án 28:88.
2. "This is the station wherein the multiplicity . . ." Bahá'u'lláh, *The Seven Valleys*, in *The Call of the Divine Beloved: Selected Mystical Works of Bahá'u'lláh* (Haifa, Israel: Bahá'í World Centre, 2018), 14.
3. "Everything is determined, the beginning as well . . ." Albert Einstein, quoted in an interview by G. S. Viereck, October 26, 1929, *Glimpses of the Great*, (1929; repr., New York: The Macaulay Company, 1930).
4. "As to thy question concerning the worlds . . ." Bahá'u'lláh, *Gleanings From the Writings of Bahá'u'lláh* (Wilmette: US Bahá'í Publishing Trust, 1983), 151–153.
5. "So powerful is the light of unity . . ." Bahá'u'lláh, *Gleanings From the Writings of Bahá'u'lláh* (Wilmette: US Bahá'í Publishing Trust, 1983), 90.
6. "It is a bottomless sea that none shall ever fathom" and "It is the blackest of nights through which none can find his way." From a Ḥadíth.
7. "If the mystic knowers be among them . . ." Bahá'u'lláh, *The Four Valleys*, in *The Call of the Divine Beloved: Selected Mystical Works of Bahá'u'lláh* (Haifa, Israel: Bahá'í World Centre, 2018), 14, 28–30.

28. The Exhibition

1. "From this most august and exalted station . . ." Bahá'u'lláh. *Gems of Divine Mysteries* (Adelaide: Griffin Press, 2002), 19.

29. The Lake Meets the Sun

1. "From this station the wayfarer ascendeth unto . . ." Bahá'u'lláh, *Gems of Divine Mysteries* (Adelaide: Griffin Press, 2002), 21.
2. "He beholdeth in illusion the secret of . . ." Bahá'u'lláh, *The Seven Valleys and the Four Valleys*, trans. Marzieh Gail, 3rd ed. (Wilmette: US Bahá'í Publishing Trust, 1986), 21.
3. "Therein the sun of the Unseen shineth . . ." Bahá'u'lláh, *Gems of Divine Mysteries* (Adelaide: Griffin Press, 2002), 21.
4. "And Solomon was David's heir. And he . . ." The Prophet Muhammad, Qur'án 27:16.

5. "society-building power of the Faith." Shoghi Effendi, *The World Order of Bahá'u'lláh*, "Community of the Most Great Name" (Wilmette, IL: Bahá'í Publishing Trust, 1991), 195.
6. "Nothing can befall us but what God . . ." The Prophet Muhammad, Qur'án 9:51.

BIBLIOGRAPHY

'Abdu'l-Bahá. *'Abdu'l-Bahá in London*. London: UK Bahá'í Publishing Trust, 1982.

———. "As ye have faith so shall your . . ." In May Maxwell, *An Early Pilgrimage*. 1917. Reprint, Oxford: George Ronald, 1953.

———. *Selections from the Writings of 'Abdu'l-Bahá*. Translated by a committee at the Bahá'í World Centre and by Marzieh Gail. Haifa: Bahá'í World Centre, 1982.

Attar, Farid ud-Din. *Bird Parliament* (also known as *The Conference of the Birds*). In *Letters and Literary Remains of Edward FitzGerald*. Edited by William Aldis Wright. Translated by Edward FitzGerald. London and New York: Macmillan and Co, 1889. sacred-texts.com.

The Báb. *Selections from the Writings of the Báb*. Haifa, Israel: Bahá'í World Centre, Universal House of Justice, 1976.

Bahá'í Canada Publications. *The Story of Mona: 1965–1983*. Toronto: The National Spiritual Assembly of the Bahá'ís of Canada, 1985. Reprinted with permission. The original story has been edited and reduced.

Bahá'u'lláh. Bahá'í Prayers: A Selection of Prayers Revealed by Bahá'u'lláh, the Báb, and 'Abdu'l-Bahá. Wilmette: US Bahá'í Publishing Trust, 1991.

———. *Bahiyyih Khanum, The Greatest Holy Leaf*. Haifa, Israel: Bahá'í World Centre, 1982.

———. *Gems of Divine Mysteries*. Adelaide: Griffin Press, 2000.

———. *Gleanings from the Writings of Bahá'u'lláh*. Translated by Shoghi Effendi. Wilmette: US Bahá'í Publishing Trust, 1983.

———. *Gleanings from the Writings of Bahá'u'lláh*. Translated by Shoghi Effendi. Pocket-size Edition. Wilmette: US Bahá'í Publishing Trust, 1990.

———. *The Hidden Words*. Translated by Shoghi Effendi. Wilmette: US Bahá'í Publishing Trust Publishing Trust, 1985.

———. The Kitáb-i-Aqdas. Haifa, Israel: Bahá'í Publishing Trust World Centre, Universal House of Justice, 1992.

Bibliography

————. *Prayers and Meditations.* Translated by Shoghi Effendi. Wilmette: US Bahá'í Publishing Trust Publishing Trust, 1938.

————. *Tablet of Ahmad.* In *Bahá'í Prayers.* Wilmette: US Bahá'í Publishing Trust, 1991.

————. *Tablets of Bahá'u'lláh: Revealed after the Kitáb-i-Aqdas.* Pocket-size Edition. Wilmette: US Bahá'í Publishing Trust, 1988.

————. *Tablet of the Holy Mariner.* In *Bahá'í Prayers: A Selection of Prayers.* Wilmette: US Bahá'í Publishing Trust, 1941.

————. *The Seven Valleys.* In *The Call of the Divine Beloved: Selected Mystical Works of Bahá'u'lláh.* Haifa, Israel: Bahá'í World Centre, 2018.

————. *The Seven Valleys and the Four Valleys.* Translated by Marzieh Gail. 3rd ed. Wilmette: US Bahá'í Publishing Trust, 1986.

Bible, American Standard Version, 1901.

Bible, King James Version, 1769.

Budge, E. A. Wallis. *Osiris & the Egyptian Resurrection.* 2 vols. London: P. L. Warner and New York: G. P. Putnam's Sons, 1911.

Editors. "Letters of the Living (*Hurúf-i-Hayy*)." *Bahá'í Encyclopedia Project.* National Spiritual Assembly of the Bahá'ís of the United States, 2009. https://www.bahai-encyclopedia-project.org/index.php?view=article&catid=56%3Aa-selection-of-articles&id=65%3Aletters-of-the-living&option=com_content&Itemid=74

Effendi, Shoghi. *God Passes By.* Wilmette: US Bahá'í Publishing Trust, 1979.

Einstein, Albert. Quoted in an interview by G. S. Viereck, October 26, 1929. *Glimpses of the Great.* Reprint, New York: The Macaulay Company, 1930.

Eliane Lacroix-Hopson. *'Abdu'l-Bahá in New York: The City of the Covenant.* Revised, New York: Naturegraph Publishers, March 1, 1999.

Hadíths.

Kluge, Ian. *Postmodernism and the Bahá'í Writings.* In *Lights of Irfan.* 2 parts. Vol. 9. Evanston, IL: Irfan Colloquia, 2008.

Lepain, Jean-Marc. "The Tablet of All Food: The Hierarchy of the Spiritual Worlds and the Metaphoric Nature of Physical Reality." Translated by Peter Terry. Bristol: *Bahá'í Studies Review*, Volume 16. Intellect Ltd, 2010: 43–60.

Qur'án.

Ruhi Institute. *The Twin Manifestations*. Book 4. Section 11. Columbia: The Ruhi Foundation, 1996.

Savi, Julio. *Towards the Summit of Reality*. Oxford: George Ronald Publisher Ltd, 2008.

Shakespeare, William. *The Taming of the Shrew*, 1590.

"Universal Declaration of Human Rights." New York: Draft Committee, United Nations, 1948.

ACKNOWLEDGMENTS

A writer is always immersed in a world of people that they see every day who indirectly help them by becoming templates for their characters. So here I acknowledge humanity for being a reflection of an underlying spiritual reality that is contained within us all, a reality I have tried to explore in this novel.

Then there are the people who help you more directly. And so here is where I would like to acknowledge those people.

To start, I would like to thank my Waiheke High School English teacher Helen Aldridge, whose guidance started me off on my journey as a writer all those years ago. Also, Bronwen and Ramin Safai, who always offered their house as a base for my research trips in New York over many years. In fact, the destiny of this book is tied up in their lives, because if they had not moved to America, the idea for this book may never have occurred to me. It was at JFK Airport in the year 2000, when I was visiting them for a week's stopover on my way to London, that the seed for the first chapter of this book came to me.

A portion of the plot and the characterization of the main protagonist, Allison, were taken from the real-life experiences of Roya Movafegh Roya lived in Harlem for a time and generously allowed me to interview her and weave aspects of her life into the Harlem chapters, in particular, and the photography group she started with young children in Harlem. Another significant experience I drew from was the life of my brother, Simion Tishler, and his year driving around Australia. His personality is also woven into my main protagonist, Allison.

For those chapters that take place in Iran, I thank Fariborz Varjavandi. Also, a thank-you for the Iranian chapters must go to the National Spiritual Assembly of the Bahá'ís of Canada, who allowed me to use the life of Mona Mahmudnizhad in *The Story of Mona: 1965–1983.*

I would also like to thank all my beta readers: Amelia Tishler, Mari Webb, Kanella Charles, Nik Sala, Danny Yap, Mary-Lin McMahon, Stef Strahle, Polly Nash, Cleo Tishler, and all the friends from my writer's group in Brisbane, Novel Ideas. They gave me invaluable feedback over the years as I was attempting to craft those early drafts.

I must thank Demelza Sutherland and Cally Jackson for helping me with the first major structural edit of this book in 2009. Their suggestions changed many aspects of the book.

Also, I must express my thanks to Nik Sala for his friendship over the years and all his philosophical and metaphysical suggestions. His feedback was invaluable with my last major structural revision of the novel in 2013. And thanks also to Veronica Paterson, who has been a sounding board and was most supportive when I was trying to finish the manuscript just before publication.

I started writing this novel in London at my kitchen table, and there I remember talking to my friend Fabrizio Nanni many times about acting and the visual construction of movies, which helped me write in a visual way.

The Bahá'í book and article that informed this novel in a significant way were Julio Savi's *Towards the Summit of Reality* and "The Tablet of All Food: The Hierarchy of the Spiritual Worlds and the Metaphoric Nature of Physical Reality" by Jean-Marc Lepain, translated by Peter Terry.

For all my American terminology and for being my American beta reader, I thank Kat Hall for her invaluable help.

Thanks to my proofreader, Elizabeth Thorlton, who provided the last polish to the manuscript, and Michael Johnson who did the last proofread before publication.

My last thank-you goes to Ann Philpott, my editor, who helped bring life to my manuscript in a way that I could have never achieved alone.

APPENDIX 1: BRIEF OVERVIEW OF SPIRITUAL PRINCIPLES AND TEACHINGS OF THE BAHÁ'Í FAITH

Some of the fundamental teachings of the Bahá'í Faith are:

o The oneness of God
o The essential unity of religion
o The unity of mankind
o Equality of men and women
o Elimination of all forms of prejudice
o World peace
o Harmony of religion and science
o Independent investigation of truth
o The need for universal compulsory education
o The need for a universal auxiliary language
o Obedience to government and non-involvement in partisan politics
o Elimination of extremes of wealth and poverty.

The independent search after truth, unfettered by superstition or tradition; the oneness of the entire human race, the pivotal principle and fundamental doctrine of the Faith; the basic unity of all religions; the condemnation of all forms of prejudice, whether religious, racial, class or national; the harmony which must exist between religion and science; the equality of men and women, the two wings on which the bird of humankind is able to soar; the introduction of compulsory education; the adoption of a universal auxiliary language; the abolition of the extremes of wealth and poverty; the institution of a world tribunal for the adjudication of disputes between nations; the exaltation of work, performed in the spirit of service, to the rank of worship; the glorification of justice as the ruling principle in human society, and of religion as a bulwark for the protection of all peoples and nations; and the establishment of a permanent and universal peace as the supreme goal of all mankind—these stand out as the essential elements [which Bahá'u'lláh proclaimed].

—Shoghi Effendi, *God Passes By*, pp. 281–82.

To be a Bahá'í simply means to love all the world; to love humanity and try to serve it; to work for universal peace and universal brotherhood.

—'Abdu'l-Bahá, quoted by J. E. Esslemont in *Bahá'u'lláh and the New Era*, Wilmette: US Bahá'í Publishing Trust, 1980, p. 71.

—From the Bahai Association at Stanford University, Stanford, California, US, <https://web.stanford.edu/group/bahai/Teachings.html>, accessed 22 July 2020.

APPENDIX 2: AN INTRODUCTION TO THE BAHÁ'Í FAITH

by Shoghi Effendi

The Bahá'í Faith upholds the unity of God, recognizes the unity of His Prophets, and inculcates the principle of the oneness and wholeness of the entire human race. It proclaims the necessity and the inevitability of the unification of mankind, asserts that it is gradually approaching, and claims that nothing short of the transmuting spirit of God, working through His chosen Mouthpiece in this day, can ultimately succeed in bringing it about. It, moreover, enjoins upon its followers the primary duty of an unfettered search after truth, condemns all manner of prejudice and superstition, declares the purpose of religion to be the promotion of amity and concord, proclaims its essential harmony with science, and recognizes it as the foremost agency for the pacification and the orderly progress of human society.

It unequivocally maintains the principle of equal rights, opportunities and privileges for men and women; insists on compulsory education, on eliminating the extremes of poverty and wealth, and on abolishing the institution of the priesthood; prohibits slavery, asceticism, mendicancy and monasticism; prescribes monogamy; discourages divorce; emphasizes the necessity of strict obedience to one's government; exalts any work performed in the spirit of service to the level of worship; urges either the creation or the selection of an auxiliary international language; and delineates the outlines of those institutions that must establish and perpetuate the general peace of humankind . . .

The Bahá'í Faith revolves around three central Figures, the first of whom was a youth, a native of Shíráz, named Mírzá 'Alí Muhammad, known as the Báb (Gate), who in May 1844, at the age of twenty-five, advanced the claim of being the Herald Who, according to the sacred Scriptures of previous Dispensations, must needs announce and prepare the way for the advent of One greater than Himself, Whose mission would be, according to those same Scriptures, to inaugurate an era of righteousness and peace, an era that would be hailed as the consummation of all previous Dispensations, and initiate a new cycle in the religious history of mankind. Swift and severe persecution, launched by the organized forces of Church and State in His native land, precipitated successively His arrest, His exile to the mountains of Ádhirbáyján, His imprisonment in the fortresses of Máh-Kú and Chihríq, and His execution, in July 1850, by a firing squad in the public square of Tabríz . . .

Mírzá Husayn-'Alí, surnamed Bahá'u'lláh (the Glory of God), a native of Mazindarán, Whose advent the Báb [Herald and Forerunner of Bahá'u'lláh] had foretold . . . was imprisoned in Tihrán, was banished, in 1852, from His native land to Baghdád, and thence to Constantinople and Adrianople, and finally to the prison city of Akká, where He remained incarcerated for no less than twenty-four years, and in whose neighborhood He passed away in 1892. In the course of His banishment, and particularly in Adrianople and Akká, He formulated the laws and ordinances of His Dispensation, expounded, in over a hundred volumes, the principles of His Faith, proclaimed His Message to the kings and rulers of both the East and the West, both Christian and Muslim, addressed the Pope, the Caliph of Islam, the Chief Magistrates of the Republics of the American continent, the entire Christian sacerdotal order, the leaders of Shí'ih and Sunní Islam, and the high priests of the Zoroastrian religion. In these writings He proclaimed His Revelation, summoned those whom He addressed to heed His call and espouse His Faith, warned them of the consequences of their refusal, and denounced, in some cases, their arrogance and tyranny.

His eldest son, 'Abbás Effendi, known as 'Abdu'l-Bahá (the Servant of Bahá), appointed by Him as His lawful successor and the authorized interpreter of His teachings, Who since early childhood had been closely associated with His Father, and shared His exile and tribulations, remained a prisoner until 1908, when, as a result of the Young Turk Revolution, He was released from His confinement. Establishing His residence in Haifa, He embarked soon after on His three-year journey to Egypt, Europe and North America, in the course of which He expounded before vast audiences, the teachings of His Father and predicted the approach of that catastrophe that was soon to befall mankind. He returned to His home on the eve of the first World War, in the course of which He was exposed to constant danger, until the liberation of Palestine by the forces under the command of General Allenby, who extended the utmost consideration to Him and to the small band of His fellow-exiles in Akká and Haifa . . .

The passing of 'Abdu'l-Bahá [in 1921] marked the termination of the first and Heroic Age of the Bahá'í Faith and signalized the opening of the Formative Age destined to witness the gradual emergence of its Administrative Order, whose establishment had been foretold by the Báb, whose laws were revealed by Bahá'u'lláh, whose outlines were delineated by 'Abdu'l-Bahá in His Will and Testament, and whose foundations are now being laid by the national and local councils which are elected by the professed adherents of the Faith . . .

This Administrative Order, unlike the systems evolved after the death of the Founders of the various religions, is divine in origin, rests securely on the laws, the precepts, the ordinances and institutions which the Founder of the Faith has Himself specifically laid down and unequivocally established, and functions in strict accordance with the interpretations of the authorized Interpreters of its holy scriptures . . .

The Faith which this order serves, safeguards and promotes is, it should be noted in this connection, essentially supernatural, supranational, entirely non-political, non-partisan, and diametrically opposed to any policy or school of thought that seeks to exalt any particular race, class or nation. It is free from any form of ecclesiasticism, has neither priesthood nor rituals, and is supported exclusively by voluntary contributions made by its avowed adherents. Though loyal to their respective governments, though imbued with the love of their own country, and anxious to promote, at all times, its best interests, the followers of the Bahá'í Faith, nevertheless, viewing mankind as one entity, and profoundly attached to its vital interests, will not hesitate to subordinate every particular interest, be it personal, regional or national, to the over-riding interests of the generality of mankind, knowing full well that in a world of interdependent peoples and nations the advantage of the part is best to be reached by the advantage of the whole, and that no lasting result can be achieved by any of the component parts if the general interests of the entity itself are neglected . . .

—Selections quoted from *Remembrance of God: A Selection of Bahá'í Prayers and Holy Writings* (India: Bahá'í Publishing Trust, 1990). Reprinted with permission.

APPENDIX 3: SYMBOLISM

by Dimitri Tishler, Author

(Spoiler alert: this section reveals plot points.)

Birds

Clearly, birds are one of the main symbols in *A Placeless Sun*. One of the main reasons birds are used so often in literature is their ability to fly. Flight itself is also a commonly used symbol, and for me, as the author, I believe our longing for flight represents our longing for God as signified by the sky and the sun and us flying in, through, and toward that reality in symbolic air and light. As you may have noticed, my use of birds in the story is related thematically to *The Conference of the Birds* by Sufi poet Farid un-Din Attar and the idea that the birds fly through progressive valleys and stages in a process of gradual spiritual transformation.

Allison goes through the same transformation in "spiritual" flight as the birds do in *The Conference of the Birds* as they journey toward the Simorgh (the King of Birds), which is a reference to our own journey toward God in this life and beyond in the more exalted worlds beyond our understanding and imagination in that longed for, but essentially unknown, horizon. Bahá'u'lláh refers to that horizon when he says:

> *The world beyond is as different from this world as this world is different from that of the child while still in the womb of its mother. When the soul attaineth the Presence of God, it will assume the form that best befitteth its immortality and is worthy of its celestial habitation.*

—Bahá'u'lláh, *Gleanings From the Writings of Bahá'u'lláh*, Pocket-size Edition, p. 346.

If we are to make the journey into the worlds beyond, like birds, we can only fly with wings, so Allison and all of us must develop spiritual wings in this world so that we can fly in those other worlds; that is, our souls need a metamorphosis so that we can take on the necessary spiritual values and key virtues to help us navigate this world and the worlds beyond. Some key virtues are truthfulness, detachment, compassion, justice, kindness, forgiveness, friendliness, and generosity, to name but a few. Although it is by no means definitive or exhaustive, you will find fifty-two virtues listed in connection with The Virtues Project. For more information on The Virtues Project and the function of virtues in spiritual development, search on the internet.

Farid un-Din Attar's idea of valleys or stages is reflected in Bahá'u'lláh's mystical composition *The Seven Valleys* and also in *Gems of Divine Mysteries*, which is one of the reasons I referenced these mystical writings so heavily in *A Placeless Sun*. But, really, *The Seven Valleys* is deeper than just the metaphor of the human soul traveling in valleys or cities as if going on any normal journey toward a destination. *The Seven Valleys* reveals the utterly transcendent transformation of the soul, a metamorphosis, that is needed for its journey toward God. In *The Conference of the Birds*, there is a bird (the hoopoe bird) that guides all the other birds toward the Simorgh (God); this could be interpreted as one of the intermediary souls between God and humanity, including Krishna, Moses, Buddha, Muhammad, Christ, the Báb, and Bahá'u'lláh. In the Bahá'í Faith they are known as Manifestations of God.

Bahá'ís believe that Bahá'u'lláh's writings are a reflection of God's attributes in this world and are needed for this symbolic flight. These writings represent the whole foundation of the Bahá'í Faith as a religion. The opening quotation in the preface reveals the exalted journey that all humankind need to take to progress toward God so that, according to Bahá'u'lláh, we "all may reach that summit of realities where none shall contemplate anything but that he shall perceive God therein." (*The Seven Valleys*, in *The Call of the Divine Beloved: Selected Mystical Works of Bahá'u'lláh*, pp. 1–2.)

The first use of the symbol of the bird is in the opening scene, where you might have noticed the origami bird with the poem inside it, revealing Allison's flight toward her death at the end of the book. The idea of a bird made of paper is a reference to the relationship between words and paper—"words" here being God's attributes and "paper" being God's creation (the physical world and all human spiritual reality). So, if we take the idea of flight and birds combined with paper, we can see how God's Word, or "spiritually exalted language," can be transformative to the human heart, and as it is written for the most part on paper, this allows us to fly symbolically and metaphorically within ourselves.

In addition to the origami bird is the symbol of the airplane (a metal bird—symbolizing migration in birds and humanity, a modern bird linked to cultural globalization*) in which Allison is sitting in the opening scene. There is also her last name, Bird, that eventually resolves itself in the last chapter. Hooman realizes that within Allison's full name is the key to her spiritual destiny: All is Sun Bird. Light birds are attracted to the sun to the point of destroying themselves when they fly into it (physical and symbolic death), thus merging into the sun. As Bahá'u'lláh explains:

Know thou of a truth that the soul, after its separation from the body, will continue to progress until it attaineth the presence of God, in a state and condition which neither the revolution of ages and centuries, nor the changes and chances of this world, can alter . . .

—Bahá'u'lláh, *Gleanings From the Writings of Bahá'u'lláh*, Pocket-size Edition, p. 346.

*The goal of the Bahá'í Faith is to develop a harmonious global community. See Appendix 1: Brief Overview of Spiritual Principles and Teachings of the Bahá'í Faith.

Trees

I thought it would be good to explore the idea of trees as symbols here because they are closely linked to birds. Why? Because birds shelter and nest in trees. Birds consider trees their home, and there are many instances of this symbolism within the Bahá'í writings. So, if humans are birds, then trees are God, our home.

Take 'Abdu'l-Bahá (the Most Mighty Branch) and *Bahíyyih Khánum* (Greatest Holy Leaf). Both are significant early Bahá'ís whose names are connected to the symbolism of trees. The reason they have these names is because of the symbolism connected with their father, Bahá'u'lláh, who Bahá'ís believe is the Manifestation of God for this age. The name that is related to his station as a Manifestation of God is the Divine Lote-Tree, or, literally, "the furthermost Lote-Tree," translated by Shoghi Effendi as "the Tree beyond which there is no passing," which in Arabic is "Sadratu'l-Muntahá." (Bahá'u'lláh, The Kitáb-i-Aqdas, p. 254, Note 128.)

The following quote from the Báb explores the symbolism connected with the Divine Lote-Tree and light in more detail:

> *Incline thine ear unto the voice of thy Lord, the Lord of all mankind, calling from the Divine Lote-Tree.*
>
> *By My life! This is the truth, and all else naught but error. This is the Day wherein the divine Lote-Tree calleth aloud saying: O people! Behold ye My fruits and My leaves, incline then your ears unto My rustling. Beware lest the doubts of men debar you from the light of certitude.*
>
> *Say, this indeed is the Frequented Fane, the sweet-scented Leaf, the Tree of the divine Revelation, the surging Ocean, the Utterance which lay concealed, the Light above every other light . . . Indeed every light is generated by God through the power of His behest. He of a truth is the Light in the kingdom of heaven and earth and whatever is between them. Through the radiance of His light God imparteth illumination to your hearts and maketh*

firm your steps, that perchance ye may yield praise unto Him. Say, this of a certainty is the Garden of Repose, the Loftiest Point of adoration, the Tree beyond which there is no passing, the blessed Lote-Tree . . .

—The Báb, *Selections from the Writings of the Báb*, pp. 154–55.

Boats

Boats are clearly another symbol I have used throughout the novel. One of its main representations is the idea of faith in God and the safety of being within God's covenant. In other words, being inside the boat and floating on the ocean safely is a symbol of being safe in God's covenant; most are aware of Noah's ark and that those within the ark were protected by their faith from the flood. So a boat is a symbol of spiritual salvation through a community of believers being obedient to the covenant of God through the Word of God; language and, in particular, Sacred Writings are that boat. And this idea is picked up in Bahá'u'lláh's *Tablet of the Holy Mariner*, where Bahá'u'lláh refers to himself as the Mariner on the Seas of Light, and that

Haply the dwellers therein may attain the retreats of nearness in the ever-lasting realm [and] . . . May know the mysteries hidden in the Seas of light.

—Bahá'u'lláh, *Bahá'í Prayers*, p. 268.

I also explored the idea of boats from the viewpoint of Egyptian scriptures where the God of the afterlife, Osiris, is the Mariner on the Boat of Millions of Years (I think this is a representation of the whole universe as a collective boat) or the sun (sun boat) existing for many millions or even billions of years. So, the sun also represents Ra, the sun god, that travels through the sky in the day and then passes through the afterlife in the night with the dead souls aboard the Night Boat. Ra is transformed (or merged) into Osiris during the night and then transformed back into the sun on the next day and again travels through the sky. It is important to note here that the Egyptian religion was polytheistic toward the end of its development. But According to Wallis Budge, it changed into this state from a more monotheistic form earlier in history. The god Ra (and Temu, the great hidden God) was the closest thing to this monotheism relative to other monotheistic religions. So, the many different gods in the Egyptian pantheon, like Hinduism, represent the various names or attributes of God, or different aspects of one God.

In the *Book of Gates*, which is an Egyptian funerary text, we see the idea that the afterlife is made up of gates that only the virtuous can pass through and that a soul's level of spiritual development dictates how far and to which gate they can travel to along the river in the afterlife.

Here there is a link to that idea in *The Seven Valleys* and *Gems of Divine Mysteries* where the valleys go up in levels of transcendence or oneness when merging with God. As a caveat, the idea of going up to higher and higher levels within our soul is bound to the limitations of time and space but is used because of our familiarity with ideas of location and time. It is easier for us to understand these terms, but really all these spiritual realities within Bahá'u'lláh's writings exist far and above language, either as symbols or metaphors, whether they are expressed as valleys, levels, stages, cities, or ladder rungs.

Bahá'u'lláh also says in *Gems of Divine Mysteries* that the higher valleys are only for the "elect of the righteous." For most of us who are mere mortals, it is probably safer to exist on the lower levels of consciousness. Reading chapter 11, "The Cosmic Vision," of the Hindu *Bhagavad Gita*, will shed some light on this experience of utter destruction and merging with God at the highest levels. Here we see that Arjuna sees Krishna as the Cosmic Form of God but is completely terrified by what he sees. So it is with the sun: we exist at a safe distance where we feel its life-giving qualities, but we would not venture any closer, as we would be destroyed by both the sun's creative and destructive power.

Names and Words

The very idea of names and words, or language, is that they are, by their nature, symbolic and metaphorical signifiers. They stand in place of other realities as pure representation and are paradoxically limited in one way and transcendent in another. The immersive experience of swimming in an ocean is always going to be better than just reading the word "ocean" on a page. But then if the word "ocean" is used to signify

God's transcendent world beyond and within the human heart, then the experience of swimming in an ocean will pale into insignificance. The water in the ocean cannot signify anything beyond itself. Water speaks of its own nature without words, and we infer its deeper nature as a symbol through the projection of meaning, as we do with all language as a symbolic shorthand for all existence.

So, names and words affect our destiny, and there is a relationship between the names that Allison encounters in her world and her destiny within the novel: Allison Bird or "All is Sun Bird" in the last chapter. The word "son" from Allison's first name is pronounced phonetically in the same way as "sun." So here we see how the difference of one letter can affect the meaning of a word or a sentence. And here the letter *o* in "son" is a mystical veil since it hides the letter *u* that then reveals the word "sun." Similarly, in chapter 23, Allison is able to explore that mystical reality and the power of single letters by either inclusion or omission. In her notebook she removes the letter *l* in the word "World," which then becomes "Word." Here we can see the power of and relationship between the "Worlds of God" and the "Word of God," which are different realities in one way but are the same reality in another way. Hooman also explains to Allison that "There are worlds in words," and that words or language are able to create intellectual and spiritual realities that explore, reveal, and simultaneously transcend the limitations of the physical world; in effect, they reveal realities beyond the limitations of the human senses.

A quick survey of the current thinking in physics shows us that physicists are finding a far greater and more powerful reality underpinning the universe that only the intellect can see with extremely abstract mathematics and an intimate knowledge of the laws of physics. You may recall the quotes used in chapter 15 where Bahá'u'lláh says:

> *Know thou, moreover, that the Word of God—exalted be His glory—is higher and far superior to that which the senses can perceive, for it is sanctified from any property or substance. It transcendeth the limitations of known elements and is exalted above all the essential and recognized substances. It became manifest without any syllable or sound and is none but the Command of God which pervadeth all created things.*

—Bahá'u'lláh, *Tablets of Bahá'u'lláh*, p. 269.

In the dream sequence in London, Allison travels to the next world and meets Mona (Shidan's dead sister). Here Allison finds out a little of the mystery of how souls relate to each other in that world. (This is pure speculation on my part but is done more to explain the possibilities of human interaction in this world.) This shows that souls can be related in groups almost like letters (see Appendix 4: Symmetry of Names and Letters) or words or even different fonts; it shows that all of us are letters, and God writes us into existence and vouchsafes to us a collective destiny that we can only unlock collectively through interdependence: each person unified with others and reflecting God in different and diverse ways. The Bahá'í term that is often used to express this idea is "unity in diversity."

Allison tries to unravel the mystery of names and words in her symmetrical destiny map. In it she unlocks the mystery from the Qur'án and the cell phone shop in London called Singlepoint. Again, here, by putting white space between the words "single" and "point," we can change the meaning. Of course, in the context of the phrase from the Qu'rán, and from Allison's subjective point of view, the single point of knowledge is God.

Consequently, there is power in the names of people and places. Another example of the importance of names is the locations in the last chapter. I wanted spiritual resonance in the names of the locations, like Heart Lake and Lake Tear of the Clouds. These are symbols or reflections of Allison's soul and almost a return to God after a long journey. God's tears fall down from the sky and fill her heart like a divine receptacle or a receptive lake.

Sun

The name of this novel, *A Placeless Sun*, is another reference to God—a transcendent non-physical sun—and the human soul as reflective of this sun, which according to the Bahá'í writings is neither in nor outside the body, and beyond time or space. Therefore, it has no location and is therefore placeless. The idea of being placeless also signifies the intermediary suns, represented by the Manifestations of God, including Krishna, Moses, Buddha, Muhammad, Christ, the Báb, and Bahá'u'lláh. A metaphor often used in Bahá'í writings is that we are the mirrors of God's light and that God is the sun, or source of spiritual and physical light. Light is also another symbol I use throughout the novel, and it represents on one level our total reliance on God, since nothing in the universe could exist without light, and on another level the human soul itself being like a mirror that can reflect God's symbolic light as spiritual attributes.

Another meaning in the use of the word "placeless" is that this world is not our final home. We are, then, placeless here, and like birds, once the cage of the human body is destroyed at death, we can fly to that other world and no longer be placeless.

In the last chapter of the book, Allison makes that transition from earth into that other world and does it by being destroyed by the sun and ultimately by being merged into that light, a home for transfigured birds, becoming then a "sun bird." I intentionally only used the words "placeless" and "sun" at the end of the novel as a way to create circularity in the story from the opening chapter, when Allison gives her paper bird away to a stranger at the airport, to the bird making its way back to her and then being passed on to Hooman at the end of the story. The paper bird represents Allison's "paper heart" into which God has written words of destiny. The paper bird also has been on a journey of its own, almost being separate from Allison's own soul; this shows that her heart is not entirely her own but guides her and returns both to her and to the heart's Creator, which is also our destiny. The following quote asserts that the human heart belongs to God.

All that is in heaven and earth I have ordained for thee, except the human heart, which I have made the habitation of My beauty and glory; yet thou didst give My home and dwelling to another than Me; and whenever the manifestation of My holiness sought His own abode, a stranger found He there, and, homeless, hastened unto the sanctuary of the Beloved. Notwithstanding I have concealed thy secret and desired not thy shame.

—Bahá'u'lláh, *The Persian Hidden Words 27*

. . . the heart is the dwelling of eternal mysteries, make it not the home of fleeting fancies; waste not the treasure of thy precious life in employment with this swiftly passing world.

—Bahá'u'lláh, *The Seven Valleys*, p. 34.

APPENDIX 4: SYMMETRY OF NAMES AND LETTERS

by Dimitri Tishler, Author

. . . in each realm, to every letter a meaning is allotted which pertaineth to that realm. Indeed, the wayfarer findeth a secret in every name and a mystery in every letter.

—Bahá'u'lláh, *The Seven Valleys*, Preface

(Spoiler alert: this section reveals plot points.)

In the beginning of this book, I briefly touched upon the idea of symmetry and asymmetry in everyday visual phenomena like flowers, three-dimensional shapes, and the human face, and ultimately in language. I tried to dispel any confusion that the reader might have had when encountering the same names for many of the characters within the novel, like Paul, where the reader encounters that name several times over the course of the story. I will now expand on the use of symmetry in letters, words, and language and explain why I chose to develop the symmetry of names throughout the novel, and I will also reveal some of its spiritual and mystical significance.

Words and Names

As you may already know, language is an abstract shorthand, or a system of the representation of meaning for all physical, intellectual, and spiritual reality, and it is constructed with a system of either glyphs, hieroglyphs, or letters and words in different languages. In fact, if every object, mental or physical, didn't have a name, we could not function, either through speech, through thought, or in movement through spatial environments; this world is often called the Kingdom of Names within the context of the Bahá'í writings. And many of these names are representations of deeper realities and attributes that transcend forms and the sense limitations of this world.

Before I go deeper into letters and words, I will explore hieroglyphs, which are interesting for the following reason: since they are usually a visual representation of a physical object (or less abstract than letters), they have the potential for deep symbolism and visual symmetry. Take the hieroglyph for the "personality," known as "Ba":* it is a bird (probably a hawk) with a human head. See below:

*The "personality" is one of the nine parts of a human being according to the Egyptian religion. Eight of the parts survive death and the body, the Khet, is left behind.

The phoenix, or "Bennu," is also a bird, the heron. See below:

You will notice immediately that both hieroglyphs are both symmetrical and asymmetrical. Since they are both birds, they are symmetrical, and since they are different species of birds, they are asymmetrical. And if we look at the English language, both the "hawk" and "heron" have the same "meaning" symmetry ("bird") rather than "visual" symmetry, like the above hieroglyphs, although they do have first-letter symmetry with the letter *h*.

No one will ever know why or how these particular hieroglyphs were created with the visual representations that they have, in particular using the representations of birds in different hieroglyphs, but I can speculate that the bird represented freedom through flight, which is a theme I explore in this book—particularly at that time in history (some three thousand years ago) when the physical world still had an aura of magic to it. Egyptians may have not known how flight was achieved with birds, so it might have seemed like a special or magical ability gifted to them by one of the gods.

Names have symmetry that we experience all the time but give no real attention to. For example, we meet many people with exactly the same name as us, but we don't think there is necessarily any connection to them that would affect our collective future destiny. This might be true to a large extent in this world, but I think in the other worlds beyond death, our name has a great power and spiritual significance that I wanted to explore within the context of the fictional world inside this novel.

The ancient Egyptians believed there was a spiritual significance for the part of the soul they called the name: the Ren. The name was considered extremely important for the ultimate destiny of the soul in both this world and the afterlife realm. In fact, if a person's name ever stopped being used or spoken, it was a form of death. And Egyptians attempted to protect their name with a magical rope hieroglyph. This is because the Ren was considered to be a representation of other parts of their soul, like the heart (Ib), the personality (Ba), the vital essence (Ka), and the intellect (Akh).

In the West, many consider a name to be just a tag to identify someone, and therefore it has no real significance beyond that, but I believe it is deeper and more profound than that. In the past this might have been different, given that many Western names were derived from the Bible and therefore had spiritual resonance associated with early Christian saints or spiritually important people within the Bible. Within the Bahá'í Faith, names do have deep spiritual import. Some of the early Bahá'ís were given names that pointed to their spiritual attributes or station, like the Báb (the Gate), Bahá'u'lláh (the Glory of God), 'Abdu'l-Bahá (Servant of Glory and the Most Mighty Branch), and Bahíyyih Khánum (Greatest Holy Leaf).

If you remember the scene that took place in London, chapter 17, "The Book of the Dead," Allison met Shidan's dead sister, Mona, in a dream. Mona explains to Allison that souls are grouped in different ways that affect their individual and collective destiny and, in particular, all those with the same names are connected in a form of "name destiny." There were other group destinies too, such as "color destiny."

Mona said, "Here, look at my arm. I want to show you something. See, I have a light tattoo on my arm; it is an extension of the thread body. Can you see the colors and shapes of flowers scrolling about my arm? If I pass my hand over the yellow color of the tattoo, you will see many yellow threads. These are the yellow group, and amongst these is a single thread. That is the other Mona's eternal timeline, Mona Mahmudnizhad. And there are many other Monas, and we are all connected. You will also notice that the tattoo is continually changing, expanding, and moving about my arm, and there are various points of light moving along each circuit. This reflects the dynamic process of movement and ascension in the spiritual worlds."

And you will have noticed that later in the novel, Allison collects the names of people that she has met and ponders over them, wondering about both their symmetrical and asymmetrical possibilities and their collective destiny, or how their destiny had converged with her own. Since she has met many people with her brother's name, the name Paul has deep significance to her. Frank Paul and Paul Frank are interesting since they are perfectly symmetrical if you switch their first name with their last name. Most names do not have this ability, since most first-to-last name combinations are mostly asymmetrical.

1. Paul Bird = brother
2. Paul Sparrow = miner in Coober Pedy, Australia
3. Paul = taxi driver first night in New York
4. Paul Nightingale = Hooman's boss
5. Frank Paul = served me [Allison] latte, Starbucks
6. Paul Frank = American designer
7. St. Paul (Saul of Tarsus) = Apostle of Christ (*The Conversion of St. Paul* by Caravaggio)

Mona Mahmudnizhad = Bahá'í girl from Shiraz, Iran
Mona Mavaddat = Shidan's sister

Then there is the meaning inside names themselves. Clearly, I could not reveal this idea until the last chapter of the book, where the reader becomes aware that there is a hidden meaning inside Allison's name that relates to her destiny and shows that she and all of humanity are birds of fire and light, or the Phoenix—Bennu in Egyptian religious terminology. "All is Sun Bird" refers to the fact that we are all related to, and seeking, God (Ra, or the sun symbolically). We are therefore birds of light and fire (the Phoenix).

Allison Bird
All is Sun Bird

If we take the name of Keira Knightley, we can see that her name relates to the Egyptian religion and the fact that Ra, the sun god, transforms into Osiris every night and travels through the afterlife on the Boat of Millions of Years, or the Night Boat. Clearly, Keira Knightley's name is the key to Ra and Osiris.

Keira Knightley
Key Ra nightly

—The hieroglyphs and some text of the nine parts of the Egyptian soul are taken from Wikipedia, <https://creativecommons.org/licenses/by-sa/3.0/>, accessed September 15, 2020.

Letters

Lastly we need to look at the power of letters and their symmetry inside words. An example of this comes from this novel:

> *Before writing a new page or rereading past entries, she [Allison] was in the habit of opening at the first page of her notebook. She had begun it with a quote from* The Seven Valleys *that stood out among all others and that gave her entire notebook its meaning. . . .*
>
> *The word "World" sat center page with the letter l crossed out, which made it "Word." Below this was the phrase "There are worlds in words" that was paraphrasing what Hooman had said when they first met, "In words there are worlds that are strange and sublime . . ." Under this sentence was the letter l, which was representative of the world of Lahut. So, by adding l to "Word," it was transformed back into "World." She had explored this idea when she was in Queensland at the shack when she had added an extra l to* The Hidden Words *so that it became "the hidden worlds." . . .*
>
> *She then thought about the transformative influence of the Word of God in every age, and that we traverse eternity with words and language . . .*
>
> *. . . where we would find a world in every letter and a matrix of words and worlds intertwined: from letters come words and from words sentences, from sentences come paragraphs, and beyond that the story of eternity, in worlds where this story unfolds, of our transcendent potentialities on that undreamed-of and radiant horizon.*
>
> —Chapter 23, "An Image of Identity"

Some of you may have heard of the term "palindrome," which is the term for the symmetry of letters within names or words. Although I haven't intentionally used any palindromes within the novel, I thought it would be good to explore the term here. Some common palindromes within names and words are Otto, Anna, civic, kayak, level, madam, mom, noon, tenet, and wow. These words are the same either forward or backward and are like mirror words.

Letters of the Living

Within the early history of the Bahá'í Faith, there were a group of believers that followed and acknowledged the station of the Báb (the Manifestation of God that preceded Bahá'u'lláh). They were all called the Letters of the Living, and there were eighteen in total. Even now, some 178 years later, their actions still affect the Bahá'í community.

Regarding the station of Quddús, he should by no means be considered having had the station of a Prophet. His station was no doubt a very exalted one, and far above that of any of the Letters of the Living, including the first Letter, Mulla Husayn. Quddús reflected more than any of the disciples of the Bab the light of His teaching.

—Written on behalf of Shoghi Effendi to an individual believer, November 11, 1936.
"Letters of Living, Dawn-Breakers, Quddús, Terraces." Bahai-library.com. Retrieved March 2, 2014.

https://bahai-library.com/uhj_letters_quddus_dawnbreakers#3.

You will see in the quotation below that Quddus (The last Letter of the Living) is considered to be the Last Name of God.

It may be helpful to consider that in the Dispensation of the Bab, Quddús is referred to as the "Last Point," and the "Last Name of God," is identified, as pointed out in God Passes By, with one of the "Messengers charged with imposture" mentioned in the Qur'an, and is one of the "two witnesses" into whom "the spirit of life from God" must enter, as attested by 'Abdu'l-Baha in Some Answered Questions, yet, despite these sublime stations, he is not regarded as an independent Manifestation of God.

—Written on behalf of the Universal House of Justice to an individual
believer, August 24, 1975.
"Letters of Living, Dawn-Breakers, Quddús, Terraces." Bahai-
library.com. Retrieved March 2, 2014.
https://bahai-library.com/uhj_letters_quddus_dawnbreakers#3

I hope I have been able to shed light on the importance of the symmetry in language—names in particular—and its spiritual themes in this book. This is by no means an exhaustive exploration of this idea; no doubt, the reader will find more on this topic in other books that are deeper and more comprehensive. This small explanation was a way to dispel any confusion and explain why I broke one of the cardinal rules of fiction, that is, not to have characters with the same or similar names.

ABOUT THE AUTHOR

 Dimitri Tishler is a British-Australian writer. He was born in England in 1970. Although he was born in England and spent several years living in London, he grew up in Melbourne, Australia, and spent most of his life in that city. *A Placeless Sun: Toward Our Configured Destiny* is his debut novel and was a labor of spiritual and literary love. Previous to this book he had only written poetry and several short stories.

The idea for this book began at JFK Airport in 2000, and the first chapter of this book is quite autobiographical. A few years later, during a sleepless night in Rome, Italy, at a friend's house, the book emerged into his mind almost fully formed. After returning to London, he began writing in 2003, and after a nineteen-year odyssey, the book was finally completed in 2022.

He is currently a full-time writer and working on his second novel, *The Illiterate Sky*.

Dimitri Tishler is a follower of the Bahá'í Faith, which was his main inspiration for this book. There is a brief introduction to the Bahá'í Faith in appendix 2 of this book, and if the reader would like to find out more about this faith, then www.bahai.org would be a good place to start.

In addition to writing, he has studied music composition in England and has composed several works for classical guitar and other instruments that can be found on SoundCloud.com or Apple Music.

If the reader would like to contact the author, please search for his profile on www.facebook.com and send a private message. Any feedback or questions would be welcome.

f facebook.com/dimitri.tishler
⊙ instagram.com/theninthbird

Ingram Content Group UK Ltd.
Milton Keynes UK
UKHW010013010723
424392UK00011B/157/J

9 780646 879314